Charles James Lever

Charles O'Malley, the Irish Dragoon

Charles James Lever

Charles O'Malley, the Irish Dragoon

ISBN/EAN: 9783743330795

Manufactured in Europe, USA, Canada, Australia, Japa

Cover: Foto ©Andreas Hilbeck / pixelio.de

Manufactured and distributed by brebook publishing software
(www.brebook.com)

Charles James Lever

Charles O'Malley, the Irish Dragoon

PREFACE.

The success of Harry Lorrequer was the reason for writing Charles O'Malley. That I myself was in nowise prepared for the favor the public bestowed on my first attempt is easily enough understood. The ease with which I strung my stories together—and in reality the Confessions of Harry Lorrequer are little other than a note-book of absurd and laughable incidents—led me to believe that I could draw on this vein of composition without any limit whatever. I felt, or thought I felt, an inexhaustible store of fun and buoyancy within me, and I began to have a misty, half-confused impression that Englishmen generally labored under a sad-colored temperament, took depressing views of life, and were proportionately grateful to any one who would rally them, even passingly, out of their despondency, and give them a laugh without much trouble for going in search of it.

When I set to work to write Charles O'Malley, I was, as I have ever been, very low with fortune, and the success of a new venture was pretty much as eventful to me as the turn of the right color at *rouge et noir*. At the same time I had then an amount of spring in my temperament, and a power of enjoying life, which I can honestly say I never found surpassed. The world had for me all the interest of an admirable comedy, in which the part allotted myself, if not a high or a foreground one, was eminently suited to my taste, and brought me, besides, sufficiently often on the stage to enable me to follow all the fortunes of the piece. Brussels, where I was then living, was adorned at the period by a most agreeable English society. Some leaders of the fashionable world of London had come there to refit and recruit, both in body and estate. There were several pleasant and a great number of pretty people among them; and, so far as I could judge, the fashionable dramas of Belgrave Square and its vicinity were being performed in the Rue Royale and the Boulevard de Waterloo with very considerable success. There were dinners, balls, déjeuners and picnics in the Bois de Cambre, excursions to Waterloo, and select little parties to Bois-fort, a charming little resort in the forest, whose intense cockneyism became perfectly inoffensive as being in a foreign land, and remote from the invasion of home-bred vulgarity. I mention all these things to show the adjuncts by which I was aided, and the rattle of gayety by which I was, as it were, "accompanied," when I next tried my voice.

The soldier element tinctured strongly our society, and I will say most agreeably. Amongst those whom I remember best were several old Peninsulars. Lord Combermere was of this number, and another of our set was an officer who accompanied, if indeed he did not command, the first boat party who crossed the Douro. It is needless to say how I cultivated a society so full of all the storied details I was eager to obtain, and how generously disposed were they to give me all the information I needed. On topography especially were they valuable to me, and with such good result that I have been more than once complimented on the accuracy of my description of places which I have never seen, and whose features I have derived entirely from the narratives of my friends.

When, therefore, my publishers asked me could I write a story in the Lorrequer vein, in which active service and military adventure could figure more prominently than mere civilian life, and where the achievements of a British army might form the staple of the narrative — when this question was propounded me, I was ready to reply, not one, but fifty. Do not mistake me, and suppose that any overweening confidence in my literary powers would have emboldened me to make this reply; my whole strength lay in the fact that I could not recognize anything like literary effort in the matter. If the world would only condescend to read that which I wrote precisely as I was in the habit of talking, nothing could be easier for me than to occupy them. Not alone was it very easy to me, but it was intensely interesting and amusing to myself to be so engaged.

The success of Harry Lorrequer had been freely wafted across the German Ocean, but even in its mildest accents it was very intoxicating incense to me; and I set to work on my second book with a thrill of hope as regards the world's favor, which—and it is no small thing to say it—I can yet recall.

I can recall, too, and I am afraid more vividly still, some of the difficulties of my task when I endeavored to form anything like an accurate or precise idea of some campaigning incident, or some passage of arms, from the narratives of two distinct and separate " eye-witnesses." What mistrust I conceived for all eye-witnesses from my own brief experience of their testimonies! What an impulse did it lend me to study the nature and the temperament of the narrator, as indicative of the peculiar coloring he might lend his narrative ; and how it taught me to know the force of the French epigram that has declared how it was entirely the alternating popularity of Marshal Soult that decided whether he won or lost the battle of Toulouse.

While, however, I was sifting these evidences, and separating, as well as I might, the wheat from the chaff, I was in a measure training myself for what, without my then knowing it, was to become my career in life. This was not, therefore, altogether without a certain degree of labor, but so light and pleasant withal, so full of picturesque peeps at character and humorous views of human nature, that it would be the very rankest ingratitude of me if I did not own that I gained all my earlier experiences of the world in very pleasant company—highly enjoyable at the time, and with matter for charming souvenirs long after.

That certain traits of my acquaintances found themselves embodied in some of the characters of this story, I do not seek to deny. The principle of natural selection adapts itself to novels as to nature, and it would have demanded an effort above my strength to have disabused myself at the desk of all the impressions of the dinner-table, and to have forgotten features which interested or amused me.

One of the personages of my tale I drew, however, with very little aid from fancy. I would go so far as to say that I took him from the life, if my memory did not confront me with the lamentable inferiority of my picture to the great original it was meant to portray.

With the exception of the quality of courage, I never met a man who contained within himself so many of the traits of Falstaff as the individual who furnished me with Major Monsoon. But the Major—I must call him so, though that rank was far beneath his own—was a man of unquestionable bravery. His powers as a story-teller were to my way of thinking unrivalled ; the peculiar reflections on life which he would passingly introduce—the wise apothegms—were after a morality so essentially of his own invention, that he would indulge in the unsparing exhibition of himself in situations such as other men would never have confessed to, all blended up with a racy enjoyment of life, dashed occasionally with sorrow that our tenure of it was short of patriarchal. All these, accompanied by a face redolent of intense humor, and a voice whose modulations were managed with the skill of a consummate artist,—all these, I say, were above me to convey, nor, indeed, as I re-read any of the adventures in which he figures, am I other than ashamed at the weakness of my drawing and the poverty of my coloring.

That I had a better claim to personify him than is always the lot of a novelist—that I possessed, so to say, a vested interest in his life and adventures, I will relate a little incident in proof; and my accuracy, if necessary, can be attested by another actor in the scene who yet survives.

I was living a bachelor life at Brussels, my family being at Ostend for the bathing during the summer of 1840. The city was comparatively empty, all the so-called society being absent at the various spas or baths of Germany. One member of the British Legation, who remained at his post to represent the mission, and myself, making common cause of our desolation and ennui, spent much of our time together, and dined *tête-à-tête* every day.

It chanced that one evening, as we were hastening through the park on our way to dinner, we espied the Major—for as Major I must speak of him—lounging along with that half-careless, half-observant air we had both of us remarked as indicating a desire to be somebody's, anybody's guest, rather than surrender himself to the homeliness of domestic fare.

"There's that confounded old Monsoon," cried my diplomatic friend. "It's all up if he sees us, and I can't endure him."

Now, I must remark that my friend, though very far from insensible to the humoristic side of the Major's character, was not always in the vein to enjoy it, and when so indisposed, he could invest the object of his dislike with something little short of antipathy. "Promise me," said he, as Monsoon came towards us,—"promise me you'll not ask him to dinner." Before I could make any reply, the Major was shaking a hand of each of us, and rapturously expatiating over his good luck at meeting us. "Mrs. M.," said he, "has got a dreary party of old ladies to dine with her, and I have come out here to find some pleasant fellow to join me, and take a mutton chop together."

"We're behind our time, Major," said my friend; "sorry to leave you so abruptly, but must push on. Eh, Lorrequer?" added he, to evoke corroboration on my part.

"Harry says nothing of the kind," replied Monsoon; "he says, or he's going to say, 'Major, I have a nice bit of dinner waiting for me at home, enough for two, will feed three, or if there be a short-coming, nothing easier than to eke out the deficiency by another bottle of Moulton; come along with us, then, Monsoon, and we shall be all the merrier for your company.'"

Repeating his last words, "Come along, Monsoon," &c., I passed my arm within his, and away we went. For a moment my friend tried to get free and leave me, but I held him fast, and carried him along in spite of himself. He was, however, so chagrined and pro-voked, that till the moment we reached my door he never uttered a word, nor paid the slightest attention to Monsoon, who talked away in a vein that occasionally made gravity all but impossible.

Our dinner proceeded drearily enough. The diplomatist's stiff-ness never relaxed for a moment, and my own awkwardness damped all my attempts at conversation. Not so, however, Monsoon; he ate heartily, approved of everything, and pronounced my wine to be exquisite. He gave us a perfect discourse on sherry, and Spanish wines in general, told us the secret of the Amontillado flavor, and explained that process of browning by boiling down wine which some are so fond of in England. At last, seeing, perhaps, that the protection had little charm for us, with his accustomed tact, he diverged into anecdote. "I was once fortunate enough," said he, "to fall upon some of that choice sherry from the St. Lucas Luen-tas which is always reserved for royalty. It was a pale wine, deli-cious in the drinking, and leaving no more flavor in the mouth than a faint dryness, that seemed to say, 'another glass.' Shall I tell you how I came by it?" And scarcely pausing for a reply, he told the story of having robbed his own convoy, and stolen the wine he was in charge of for safe conveyance.

I wish I could give any, even the weakest, idea of how he narrated that incident, the struggle that he portrayed between duty and temptation, and the apologetic tone of voice in which he explained that the frame of mind that succeeds to any yielding to seductive influences is often in the main more profitable to a man than is the vain-glorious sense of having resisted a temptation. "Meekness is the mother of all the virtues," said he, "and there is no being meek without frailty." The story, told as he told it, was too much for tho diplomatist's gravity; he resisted all signs of attention as long as he was able, and at last fairly roared out with laughter.

As soon as I myself recovered from the effects of his drollery, I said, "Major, I have a proposition to make you: let me tell the story in print, and I'll give you five naps."

"Are you serious, Harry?" asked he. "Is this on honor?"

"On honor, assuredly," I replied.

"Let me have the money down, on the nail, and I'll give you leave to have me and my whole life, every adventure that ever befell me, aye, and, if you like, every moral reflection that my experiences have suggested."

"Done!" cried I; "I agree."

"Not so fast," cried the diplomatist; "we must make a protocol of this; the high contracting parties must know what they give and what they receive. I'll draw out the treaty."

He did so at full length, on a sheet of that solemn blue tinted paper so dedicated to dispatch purposes,—he duly set forth the concession and the consideration. We each signed the document, he witnessed and sealed it, and Monsoon pocketed my five napoleons, filling a bumper to any success the bargain might bring me, and of which I have never had any reason to express deep disappointment.

This document, along with my university degree, my commission in a militia regiment, and a vast amount of letters very interesting to me, were seized by the Austrian authorities on the way from Como to Florence in the August of 1847, being deemed part of a treasonable correspondence,—probably purposely allegorical in form, —and never restored to me. I fairly own that I'd give all the rest willingly to repossess myself of the Monsoon treaty, not a little for the sake of that quaint old autograph, faintly shaken by the quiet laugh with which he wrote it.

That I did not entirely fail in giving my Major some faint resemblance to the great original from whom I copied him, I may mention that he was speedily recognized in print by the Marquis of Londonderry, the well-known Sir Charles Stuart of the Peninsula campaign. "I know that fellow well," said he; "he once sent me a challenge, and I had to make him a very humble apology. The occasion was this: I had been out with a single aide-de-camp, to make a reconnaissance in front of Victor's division; and to avoid attracting any notice, we covered over our uniform with two common gray overcoats which reached to the feet, and effectually concealed our rank as officers. Scarcely, however, had we topped a hill which commanded the view of the French, than a shower of shells flew over and around us. Amazed to think how we could have been so quickly noticed, I looked around me, and discovered, quite close in my rear, your friend Monsoon with what he called his staff, a popinjay set of rascals, dressed out in green and gold, and with more plumes and feathers than the general staff ever boasted. Carried away by momentary passion at the failure of my reconnaissance, I burst out with some insolent allusion to the harlequin assembly which had drawn the French fire upon us. Monsoon saluted me respectfully, and retired without a word; but I had scarcely reached my quarters when a 'friend' of his waited on me with a message,—a very categorical message it was too,—'it must be a meeting or an ample apology.' I made the apology, a most full one, for the Major was right, and I had not a fraction of reason to sustain me in my conduct, and we have been the best of friends ever since."

I myself had heard the incident before this from Monsoon, but told amongst other adventures whose exact veracity I was rather disposed to question, and did not therefore accord it all the faith that was its due; and I admit that the accidental corroboration of this one event very often served to puzzle me afterwards, when I listened to stories in which the Major seemed a second Munchausen, but might, like in this of the duel, have been amongst the truest and most matter-of-fact of historians. May the reader be not less embarrassed than myself is my sincere, if not very courteous, prayer.

I have no doubt myself that often, in recounting some strange incident,—a personal experience it always was,—he was himself more amused by the credulity of the hearers, and the amount of interest he could excite in them, than were they by the story. He possessed the true narrative gusto, and there was a marvellous instinct in the way in which he would vary a tale to suit the tastes of an audience; while his moralizings were almost certain to take the tone of a humoristic quiz on the company.

Though fully aware that I was availing myself of the contract that delivered him into my hands, and dining with me two or three days a week, he never lapsed into any allusion to his appearance in print, and the story had been already some weeks published before he asked me to lend him "that last thing—he forgot the name of it—I was writing."

Of Frank Webber I have said, in a former notice, that he was one of my earliest friends, my chum in college, and in the very chambers where I have located Charles O'Malley, in Old Trinity. He was a man of the highest order of abilities, and with a memory that never forgot, but was ruined and run to seed by the idleness that came of a discursive, uncertain temperament. Capable of anything, he spent his youth in follies and eccentricities; every one of which, however, gave indications of a mind inexhaustible in resources, and abounding in devices and contrivances that none other but himself would have thought of. Poor fellow, he died young; and perhaps it is better it should have been so. Had he lived to a later day, he would most probably have been found a foremost leader of Fenianism, and from what I knew of him, I can say he would have been a more dangerous enemy to English rule than any of those dealers in the petty larceny of rebellion we have lately seen amongst us.

I have said that of Mickey Free I had not one, but one thousand, types. Indeed, I am not quite sure that in my last visit to Dublin I did not chance on a living specimen of the "Free" family, much readier in repartée, quicker with an *à propos*, and droller in illustration than my own Mickey. This fellow was "boots" at a great hotel in Sackville street; and I owe to him more amusement and some heartier laughs than it has been always my fortune to enjoy in a party of wits. His criticisms on my sketches of Irish character were about the shrewdest and the best I ever listened to; and that I am not bribed to this opinion by any flattery, I may remark that they were more often severe than complimentary, and that he hit every blunder of image, every mistake in figure, of my peasant characters, with an acuteness and correctness which made me very grateful to know that his daily occupations were limited to blacking boots, and not polishing off authors.

I believe I have now done with my confessions, except I should like to own that this story was the means of according me a more heartfelt glow of satisfaction, a more gratifying sense of pride, than anything I ever have or ever shall write, and in this wise. My brother, at that time the rector of an Irish parish, once forwarded to me a letter from a lady unknown to him, but who had heard he was the brother of "Harry Lorrequer," and who addressed him, not knowing where a letter might be directed to myself. The letter was the grateful expression of a mother, who said, "I am the widow of a field officer, and with an only son, for whom I obtained a presentation to Woolwich; but seeing in my boy's nature certain traits of nervousness and timidity, which induced me to hesitate on embarking him in the career of a soldier, I became very unhappy and uncertain which course to decide on.

"While in this state of uncertainty, I chanced to make him a birthday present of 'Charles O'Malley,' the reading of which seemed to act like a charm on his whole character, inspiring him with a passion for movement and adventure, and spiriting him to an eager desire for a military life. Seeing that this was no passing enthusiasm, but a decided and determined bent, I accepted the cadetship for him, and his career has been not alone distinguished as a student, but one which has marked him out for an almost hare-brained courage, and for a dash and heroism that gave high promise for his future.

"Thank your brother for me," wrote she, "a mother's thanks for the welfare of an only son, and say how I wish that my best wishes for him and his could recompense him for what I owe him."

I humbly hope that it may not be imputed to me as unpardonable vanity—the recording of this incident. It gave me an intense pleasure when I heard it; and now as I look back on it, it invests this story for myself with an interest which nothing else that I have written can afford me.

I have now but to repeat what I have declared in former editions, my sincere gratitude for the favor the public still continues to bestow on me—a favor which probably associates the memory of this book with whatever I have since done successfully, and compels me to remember that to the popularity of "Charles O'Malley". I am indebted for a great share of that kindliness in criticism, and that geniality in judgment, which for more than a quarter of a century my countrymen have graciously bestowed on their faithful friend and servant,

CHARLES LEVER.

TRIESTE, 1872.

CONTENTS, VOL. I.

CONTENTS.

CONTENTS, VOL. II.

CHARLES O'MALLEY,

The Irish Dragoon.

CHAPTER I.

DALY'S CLUB HOUSE.

THE rain was dashing in torrents against the window-panes, and the wind sweeping in heavy and fitful gusts along the dreary and deserted streets, as a party of three persons sat over their wine, in that stately old pile which once formed the resort of the Irish members, in College Green, Dublin, and went by the name of Daly's Club House. The clatter of falling tiles and chimney-pots, the jarring of the window-frames and howling of the storm without, seemed little to affect the spirits of those within, as they drew closer to a blazing fire, before which stood a small table covered with the remains of a dessert, and an abundant supply of bottles, whose characteristic length of neck indicated the rarest wines of France and Germany. While the portly magnum of claret—the wine *par excellence* of every Irish gentleman of the day—passed rapidly from hand to hand, the conversation did not languish, and many a deep and hearty laugh followed the stories which every now and then were told, as some reminiscence of early days was recalled, or some trait of a former companion remembered.

One of the party, however, was apparently engrossed by other thoughts than those of the mirth and merriment around; for, in the midst of all, he would turn suddenly from the others, and devote himself to a number of scattered sheets of paper, upon which he had written some lines, but whose crossed and blotted sentences attested how little success had waited upon his literary labors. This individual was a short, plethoric-looking, white-haired man of about fifty, with a deep, round voice, and a chuckling, smothering laugh, which, whenever he indulged, not only shook his own ample person, but generally created a petty earth-

2   (17)

quake on every side of him. For the present, I shall not stop to
particularize him more closely; but when I add that the person in
question was a well-known member of the Irish House of Commons, whose acute understanding and practical good sense were
veiled under an affected and well-dissembled habit of blundering,
that did far more for his party than the most violent and pointed
attacks of his more accurate associates, some of my readers may
anticipate me in pronouncing him to be Sir Harry Boyle. Upon
his left sat a figure the most unlike him possible; he was a tall,
thin, bony man, with a bolt-upright air, and a most saturnine expression; his eyes were covered by a deep green shade, which fell
far over his face, but failed to conceal a blue scar that, crossing his
cheek, ended in the angle of his mouth, and imparted to that
feature, when he spoke, an apparently abortive attempt to extend
towards his eyebrow; his upper lip was covered with a grizzly and
ill-trimmed moustache, which added much to the ferocity of his
look, while a thin and pointed beard on his chin gave an apparent
length to the whole face that completed its rueful character. His
dress was a single-breasted, tightly-buttoned frock, in one button-
hole of which a yellow ribbon was fastened, the decoration of a
foreign service, which conferred upon its wearer the title of Count;
and though Billy Considine, as he was familiarly called by his
friends, was a thorough Irishman in all his feelings and affections,
yet he had no objection to the designation he had gained in the
Austrian army. The Count was certainly no beauty, but, somehow,
very few men of his day had a fancy for telling him so; a deadlier
hand and a steadier eye never covered his man in the Phœnix; and
though he never had a seat in the House, he was always regarded
as one of the government party, who more than once had dampened
the ardor of an opposition member, by the very significant threat
of "setting Billy at him." The third figure of the group was a
large, powerfully-built, and handsome man, older than either of the
others, but not betraying in his voice or carriage any touch of time.
He was attired in the green coat and buff vest which formed the
livery of the club; and in his tall, ample forehead, clear, well-set
eye, and still handsome mouth, bore evidence that no great flattery
was necessary at the time which called Godfrey O'Malley the handsomest man in Ireland.

"Upon my conscience," said Sir Harry, throwing down his pen
with an air of ill-temper, "I can make nothing of it; I have got
into such an infernal habit of making bulls, that I can't write sense
when I want it."

"Come, come," said O'Malley, "try again, my dear fellow. If
you can't succeed, I'm sure Billy and I have no chance."

"What have you written? Let us see," said Considine, drawing the paper towards him, and holding it to the light. "Why, what the devil is all this? You have made him 'drop down dead after dinner of a lingering illness, brought on by the debate of yesterday.'"

"Oh, impossible!"

"Well, read it yourself—there it is; and, as if to make the thing less credible, you talk of his 'Bill for the Better Recovery of Small Debts.' I'm sure, O'Malley, your last moments were not employed in that manner."

"Come, now," said Sir Harry, "I'll set all to rights with a postscript. 'Any one who questions the above statement, is politely requested to call on Mr. Considine, 16 Kildare street, who will feel happy to afford him every satisfaction upon Mr. O'Malley's decease, or upon miscellaneous matters.'"

"Worse and worse," said O'Malley. "Killing another man will never persuade the world that I am dead."

"But we'll wake you, and have a glorious funeral."

"And if any man doubt the statement, I'll call him out," said the Count.

"Or, better still," said Sir Harry, "O'Malley has his action at law for defamation."

"I see I'll never get down to Galway at this rate," said O'Malley; "and as the new election takes place on Tuesday week, time presses. There are more writs flying after me this instant than for all the government boroughs."

"And there will be fewer returns, I fear," said Sir Harry.

"Who is the chief creditor?" asked the Count.

"Old Stapleton, the attorney in Fleet street, has most of the mortgages."

"Nothing to be done with him in this way?" said Considine, balancing the cork-screw like a hair trigger.

"No chance of it."

"May be," said Sir Harry, "he might come to terms if I were to call and say, You are anxious to close accounts, as your death has just taken place. You know what I mean."

"I fear so should he, were you to say so. No, no, Boyle, just try a plain, straightforward paragraph about my death. · We'll have it in Falkner's paper to-morrow; on Friday the funeral can take place, and, with the blessing o' God, I'll come to life on Saturday at Athlone, in time to canvass the market."

"I think it wouldn't be bad if your ghost were to appear to old Timins the tanner, in Naas, on your way down; you know he arrested you once before."

"I prefer a night's sleep," said O'Malley; "but come, finish the squib for the paper."

"Stay a little," said Sir Harry, musing; "it just strikes me that if ever the matter gets out, I may be in some confounded scrape. Who knows if it is not a breach of privilege to report the death of a member? And to tell you the truth, I dread the Sergeant and the Speaker's warrant with a very lively fear."

"Why, when did you make his acquaintance?" asked the Count.

"Is it possible you never heard of Boyle's committal?" said O'Malley; "you surely must have been abroad at the time; but it's not too late to tell it yet."

"Well, it's about two years since old Townsend brought in his Enlistment Bill, and the whole country was scoured for all our voters, who were scattered here and there, never anticipating another call of the House, and supposing that the session was just over. Among others, up came our friend Harry, here, and the night he arrived they made him a 'Monk of the Screw,' and very soon made him forget his senatorial dignities.

"On the evening after his reaching town, the bill was brought in, and at two in the morning the division took place. A vote was of too much consequence not to look after it closely, and a Castle messenger was in waiting in Exchequer street, who, when the debate was closing, put Harry, with three others, into a coach, and brought them down to the House. Unfortunately, however, they mistook their friends, voted against the bill, and, amid the loudest cheering of the opposition, the government party were defeated. The rage of the ministers knew no bounds, and looks of defiance and even threats were exchanged between the ministers and the deserters. Amid all this poor Harry fell fast asleep, and dreamed that he was once more in Exchequer street, presiding amongst the monks, and mixing another tumbler. At length he awoke and looked about him. The clerk was just at the instant reading out, in his usual routine manner, a clause of the new bill, and the remainder of the House was in dead silence. Harry again looked around on every side, wondering where was the hot water, and what had become of the whisky bottle, and above all, why the company were so extremely dull and ungenial. At length, with a half shake, he roused up a little, and giving a look of unequivocal contempt on every side, called out, 'Upon my soul, you're very pleasant companions—but I'll give you a chant to enliven you.' So saying, he cleared his throat with a couple of short coughs, and at once struck up, with the voice of a Stentor, the following verse of a popular ballad:—

"'And they nibbled away, both night and day,
Like mice in a round of Glo'ster;
Great rogues they were all, both great and small,
From Flood to Leslie Foster.
"'Great rogues all.'

"'Chorus, boys!'

"If he was not joined by the voices of his friends in the song, it was probably because such a roar of laughing never was heard since the walls were roofed over. The whole House rose in a mass, and my friend Harry was hurried over the benches by the Sergeant-at-Arms, and left for three weeks in Newgate to practice his melody."

"All true," said Sir Harry, "and worse luck to them for not liking music; but come now, will this do?—'It is our melancholy duty to announce the death of Godfrey O'Malley, Esq., late member for the county of Galway, which took place on Friday evening, at Daly's Club House. This esteemed gentleman's family, one of the oldest in Ireland, and among whom it was hereditary not to have any children——''

Here a burst of laughter from Considine and O'Malley interrupted the reader, who with the greatest difficulty could be persuaded that he was again bulling it.

"The devil fly away with it," said he; "I'll never succeed."

"Never mind," said O'Malley; "the first part will do admirably; and let us now turn our attention to other matters."

A fresh magnum was called for, and over its inspiring contents all the details of the funeral were planned. As the clock struck four, the party separated for the *night*, well satisfied with the result of their labors.

CHAPTER II.

THE ESCAPE.

WHEN the dissolution of Parliament was announced the following morning in Dublin, its interest in certain circles was manifestly increased by the fact that Godfrey O'Malley was at last open to arrest; for as in olden times certain gifted individuals possessed some happy immunity against death by fire or sword, so the worthy O'Malley seemed to enjoy a no less valuable privilege, and for many a year had passed among the myrmidons of the law as writ-proof. Now, however, the charm seemed to have yielded, and pretty much with the same feeling as a storming party may be supposed to experience on the day that a breach is reported as practicable, did the honest attorneys retained in the various suits against him rally round each other that morning in the Four Courts.

Bonds, mortgages, post-obits, promissory notes,—in fact, every imaginable species of invention for raising the O'Malley exchequer for the preceding thirty years,—were handed about on all sides, suggesting to the mind of an uninterested observer the notion that had the aforesaid O'Malley been an independent and absolute monarch, instead of merely being the member for Galway, the kingdom over whose destinies he had been called to preside would have suffered not a little from a depreciated currency and an extravagant issue of paper. Be that as it might, one thing was clear: the whole estates of the family could not possibly pay one-fourth of the debt, and the only question was one which occasionally arises at a scanty dinner on a mail-coach road—who was to be the lucky individual to carve the joint, where so many were sure to go off hungry.

It was now a trial of address between these various and highly-gifted gentlemen who should first pounce upon the victim, and when the skill of their caste is taken into consideration, who will doubt that every feasible expedient for securing him was resorted to? While writs were struck against him in Dublin, emissaries were despatched to the various surrounding counties to procure others in the event of his escape. *Ne exeats* were sworn, and water-bailiffs engaged to follow him on the high seas; and as the great Nassau balloon did not exist in those days, no imaginable mode of escape appeared possible, and bets were offered at long odds that within twenty-four hours the late member would be enjoying his *otium cum dignitate* in his Majesty's gaol of Newgate.

Expectation was at the highest—confidence hourly increasing—success all but certain—when, in the midst of all this high-bounding hope, the dreadful rumor spread that O'Malley was no more. One had seen it just five minutes before in the evening edition of Falkner's paper, another heard it in the courts, a third overheard the Chief Justice stating it to the Master of the Rolls, and, lastly, a breathless witness arrived from College Green with the news that Daly's Club House was shut up, and the shutters closed. To describe the consternation the intelligence caused on every side is impossible; nothing in history equals it, except, perhaps, the entrance of the French army into Moscow, deserted and forsaken by its former inhabitants. While terror and dismay, therefore, spread amid that wide and respectable body who formed O'Malley's creditors, the preparations for his funeral were going on with every rapidity; relays of horses were ordered at every stage of the journey, and it was announced that, in testimony of his worth, a large party of his friends were to accompany his remains to Portumna Abbey—a test much more indicative of resistance in the event of any attempt to arrest the body than of anything like reverence for their departed friend.

Such was the state of matters in Dublin, when a letter reached me one morning at O'Malley Castle, whose contents will at once explain the writer's intention, and also serve to introduce my unworthy self to my reader. It ran thus:—

"DEAR CHARLEY:—Your uncle Godfrey, whose debts (God pardon him) are more numerous than the hairs of his wig, was obliged to die here last night. We did the thing for him completely; and all doubts as to the reality of the event are silenced by the circumstantial detail of the newspaper 'that he was confined six weeks to his bed from a cold he caught, ten days ago, while on guard.' Repeat this, for it's better we had all the same story till he comes to life again, which, maybe, will not take place before Tuesday or Wednesday. At the same time, canvass the county for him, and say he'll be with his friends next week, and up in Woodford and the Scariff barony. Say he died a true Catholic; it will serve him on the hustings. Meet us in Athlone on Saturday, and bring your uncle's mare with you—he says he'd rather ride home; and tell Father M'Shane to have a bit of dinner ready about four o'clock, for the corpse can get nothing after he leaves Mountmellick. No more now, from yours, ever,

"HARRY BOYLE.

"Daly's, about eight in the evening.

"To CHARLES O'MALLEY, Esq.,
O'Malley Castle, Galway."

When this not over-clear document reached me, I was the sole inhabitant of O'Malley Castle, a very ruinous pile of incongruous masonry, that stood in a wild and dreary part of the county of Galway, bordering on the Shannon. On every side stretched the property of my uncle, or at least what had once been so; and, indeed, so numerous were its present claimants, that he would have been a subtle lawyer who could have pronounced upon the rightful owner. The demesne around the castle contained some well-grown and handsome timber, and, as the soil was undulating and fertile, presented many features of beauty; beyond it, all was sterile, bleak, and barren. Long tracts of brown heath-clad mountain, or not less unprofitable valleys of tall and waving fern, were all that the eye could discern, except where the broad Shannon, expanding into a tranquil and glassy lake, lay still and motionless beneath the dark mountains—a few islands, with some ruined churches and a round tower, alone breaking the dreary waste of water.

Here it was that I had passed my infancy and my youth, and here I now stood, at the age of seventeen, quite unconscious that the world contained aught fairer and brighter than that gloomy valley, with its rugged frame of mountains.

When a mere child, I was left an orphan to the care of my worthy uncle. My father, whose extravagance had well sustained the family reputation, had squandered a large and handsome property in contesting elections for his native county, and in keeping up that system of unlimited hospitality for which Ireland in general, and Galway more especially, was renowned. The result was, as might be expected, ruin and beggary. He died, leaving every one of his estates encumbered with heavy debts, and the only legacy he left to his brother was a boy of four years of age, entreating him, with his last breath, "Be anything you like to him, Godfrey, but a father, or at least such a one as I have proved."

Godfrey O'Malley, some short time previous, had lost his wife, and when this new trust was committed to him, he resolved never to remarry, but to rear me up as his own child, and the inheritor of his estates. How weighty and onerous an obligation this latter might prove, the reader can form some idea. The intention was, however, a kind one; and to do my uncle justice, he loved me with all the affection of a warm and open heart.

From my earliest years his whole anxiety was to fit me for the part of a country gentleman, as he regarded that character—viz., I rode boldly with fox-hounds; I was about the best shot within twenty miles of us; I could swim the Shannon at Holy Island; I drove four-in-hand better than the coachman himself; and from finding a hare to hooking a salmon, my equal could not be found from Kilaloe to Banagher. These were the staple of my endowments. Besides which, the parish priest had taught me a little Latin, a little French, and a little geometry, and a great deal of the life and opinions of St. Jago, who presided over a holy well in the neighborhood, and was held in very considerable repute.

When I add to this portraiture of my accomplishments that I was nearly six feet high, with more than a common share of activity and strength for my years, and no inconsiderable portion of good looks, I have finished my sketch, and stand before my reader.

It is now time I should return to Sir Harry's letter, which so completely bewildered me, that but for the assistance of Father Roach, I should have been totally unable to make out the writer's intentions. By his advice, I immediately set out for Athlone, where, when I arrived, I found my uncle addressing the mob from the top of the hearse, and recounting his miraculous escape as a new claim upon their gratitude.

"There was nothing else for it, boys; the Dublin people insisted on my being their member, and besieged the club-house. I refused—they threatened—I grew obstinate—they furious. 'I'll die first,' said I. 'Galway or nothing!'" "Hurrah!" from the mob. "O'Malley forever!" "And ye see, I kept my word, boys—I did die; I died that evening at a quarter-past eight. There, read it for yourselves; there's the paper; was waked and carried out, and here I am after all, ready to die in earnest for you—but never to desert you."

The cheers here were deafening, and my uncle was carried through the market, down to the mayor's house, who, being a friend of the opposite party, was complimented with three groans; then up the Mall to the chapel, beside which Father M'Shane resided. He was then suffered to touch the earth once more, when, having shaken hands with all his constituency within reach, he entered the house, to partake of the kindest welcome and best reception the good priest could afford him.

My uncle's progress homeward was a triumph; the real secret of his escape had somehow come out, and his popularity rose to a white heat. "An' it's little O'Malley cares for the law—bad luck to it; it's himself can laugh at judge and jury. Arrest him! Nabocklish—catch a weasel asleep," &c. Such were the encomiums that greeted him as he passed on towards home, while shouts of joy and blazing bonfires attested that his success was regarded as a national triumph.

The west has certainly its strong features of identity. Had my uncle possessed the claims of the immortal Howard,—had he united in his person all the attributes which confer a lasting and an ennobling fame upon humanity,—he might have passed on unnoticed and unobserved; but for the man that had duped a judge and escaped the sheriff, nothing was sufficiently flattering to mark their approbation. The success of the exploit was twofold; the news spread far and near, and the very story canvassed the county better than Billy Davern himself, the Athlone attorney.

This was the prospect now before us; and, however little my readers may sympathize with my taste, I must honestly avow that I looked forward to it with a most delighted feeling. O'Malley Castle was to be the centre of operations, and filled with my uncle's supporters; while I, a mere stripling, and usually treated as a boy, was to be entrusted with an important mission, and sent off to canvass a distant relation, with whom my uncle was not upon terms, and who might possibly be approachable by a younger branch of the family, with whom he had never any collision.

CHAPTER III.

MR. BLAKE.

NOTHING but the exigency of the case could ever have persuaded my uncle to stoop to the humiliation of canvassing the individual to whom I was now about to proceed as envoy extraordinary, with full powers to make any or every *amende*, provided only his interest and that of his followers should be thereby secured to the O'Malley cause. The evening before I set out was devoted to giving me all the necessary instructions how I was to proceed, and what difficulties I was to avoid.

"Say your uncle's in high feather with the government party," said Sir Harry, "and that he only votes against them as *a ruse de guerre*, as the French call it."

"Insist upon it that I am sure of the election without him, but that for family reasons he should not stand aloof from me; that people are talking of it in the country."

"And drop a hint," said Considine, "that O'Malley is greatly improved in his shooting."

"And don't get drunk too early in the evening, for Phil Blake has beautiful claret," said another.

"And be sure you don't make love to the red-headed girls," added a third; "he has four of them, each more sinfully ugly than the other."

"You'll be playing whist, too," said Boyle; "and never mind losing a few pounds. Mrs. B.—long life to her—has a playful way of turning the king."

"Charley will do it all well," said my uncle; "leave him alone. And now let us have in the supper."

It was only on the following morning, as the tandem came round to the door, that I began to feel the importance of my mission, and certain misgivings came over me as to my ability to fulfil it. Mr. Blake and his family, though estranged from my uncle for several years past, had been always most kind and good-natured to me; and although I could not with propriety have cultivated any close intimacy with them, I had every reason to suppose that they entertained towards me nothing but sentiments of good will. The head of the family was a Galway squire of the oldest and most genuine stock; a great sportsman, a negligent farmer, and most careless father. He looked upon a fox as an infinitely more precious part of the creation than a French governess, and thought that riding well with hounds was a far better gift than all the learning of a Porson. His daughters were after his own heart,—the best-tempered, least-educated, most high-spirited, gay, dashing, ugly girls in the country,—ready to ride over a four-foot paling without a saddle, and to dance the " Wind that shakes the barley," for four consecutive hours, against all the officers that their hard fate, and the Horse Guards, ever condemned to Galway.

The mamma was only remarkable for her liking for whist, and her invariable good fortune thereat—a circumstance the world were agreed in ascribing less to the blind goddess than her own natural endowments.

Lastly, the heir of the house was a stripling of about my own age, whose accomplishments were limited to selling spavined and broken-winded horses to the infantry officers, playing a safe game at billiards, and acting as jackal-general to his sisters at balls, providing them with a sufficiency of partners, and making a strong fight for a place at the supper-table for his mother. These fraternal and filial traits, more honored at home than abroad, had made Mr. Matthew Blake a rather well-known individual in the neighborhood where he lived.

Though Mr. Blake's property was ample, and, strange to say for his county, unencumbered, the whole air and appearance of his house and grounds betrayed anything rather than a sufficiency of means. The gate lodge was a miserable mud hovel, with a thatched and falling roof; the gate itself, a wooden contrivance, one half of which was boarded and the other railed; the avenue was covered with weeds, and deep with ruts, and the clumps of young plantation, which had been planted and fenced with care, were now open to the cattle, and either totally uprooted or denuded of their bark, and dying. The lawn, a handsome one of some forty acres, had been devoted to an exercise-ground for training horses, and was cut up by their feet beyond all semblance of its original destination; and the house itself, a large and venerable structure of above a century old, displayed every variety of contrivance, as well as the usual one of glass, to exclude the weather. The hall-door hung by a single hinge, and required three persons each morning and evening to open and shut it; the remainder of the day it lay pensively open; the steps which led to it were broken and falling, and the whole aspect of things without was ruinous in the extreme. Within, matters were somewhat better, for though the furniture was old, and none of it clean, yet an appearance of comfort was evident; and the large grate, blazing with its pile of red-hot turf, the deep-cushioned chairs, the old black mahogany dinner-table, and the soft carpet, albeit deep with dust, were not to be despised on a winter's evening, after a hard day's run with the " Blazers." Here it was, however, that Mr. Philip Blake had dispensed his hospitalities for above fifty years, and his father before him, and here, with a retinue of servants as *gauche* and ill-ordered as all about them, was he accustomed to invite all that the county possessed of rank and wealth, among which the officers quartered in his neighborhood were never neglected, the Misses Blake having as decided a taste for the army as any young ladies of the west of Ireland. And while the Galway squire, with his cords and tops, was detailing the last news from Ballinasloe in one corner, the dandy from St. James's street might be seen displaying more arts of seductive flattery in another than his most accurate *insouciance* would permit him to practise in the elegant saloons of London or Paris: and the same man who would have "cut his brother," for a solecism of dress or equipage, in Bond street, was now to be seen quietly domesticated, eating family dinners, rolling silk for the young ladies, going down the middle in a country dance, and even descending to the indignity of long whist, at "tenpenny" points, with only the miserable consolation that the company were not honest.

It was upon a clear frosty morning, when a bright blue sky and a sharp but bracing air seem to exercise upon the feelings a sense no less pleasurable than the balmiest breeze and warmest sun of summer, that I whipped my leader short round, and entered the precincts of "Gurt-na-Morra." As I proceeded along the avenue, I was struck by the slight traces of repairs here and there evident; a gate or two that formerly had been parallel to the horizon had been raised to the perpendicular; some ineffectual efforts at paint were also perceptible upon the palings; and, in short, everything seemed to have undergone a kind of attempt at improvement.

When I reached the door, instead of being surrounded, as of old, by a tribe of menials, frieze-coated, bare-headed, and bare-legged, my presence was announced by a tremendous ringing of bells, from the hands of an old functionary, in a very formidable livery, who peeped at me through the hall window, and whom, with the greatest difficulty, I recognized as my quondam acquaintance, the butler. His wig alone would have graced a king's counsel, and the high collar of his coat, and the stiff pillory of his cravat, denoted an eternal adieu to so humble a vocation as drawing a cork. Before I had time for any conjecture as to the altered circumstances about, the activity of my friend at the bell had surrounded me with "four others worse than himself," at least, they were exactly similarly attired; and, probably, from the novelty of their costume, and the restraints of so unusual a thing as dress, were as perfectly unable to assist themselves or others as the Court of Aldermen would be were they to rig out in plate armor of the fourteenth century. How much longer I might have gone on conjecturing the reasons for the masquerade around, I cannot say; but my servant, an Irish disciple of my uncle's, whispered in my ear, "It's a red-breeches day, Master Charles—they'll have the hoith of company in the house." From the phrase, it needed little explanation to inform me that it was one of those occasions on which Mr. Blake attired all the hangers-on of his house in livery, and that great preparations were in progress for a more than usually splendid reception.

In the next moment I was ushered into the breakfast-room, where a party of above a dozen persons were most gayly enjoying all the good cheer for which the house had a well-deserved repute. After the usual shaking of hands and hearty greetings were over, I was introduced in all form to Sir George Dashwood, a tall and singularly handsome man of about fifty, with an undress military frock and ribbon. His reception of me was somewhat strange, for, as they mentioned my relationship to Godfrey O'Malley, he smiled slightly, and whispered something to Mr. Blake, who replied, "Oh! no, no, not the least. A mere boy; and besides——" What he added I lost, for at that moment Nora Blake was presenting me to Miss Dashwood.

If the sweetest blue eyes that ever beamed beneath a forehead of snowy whiteness, over which dark brown and waving hair fell, less in curls than masses of locky richness, could only have known what wild work they were making of my poor heart, Miss Dashwood, I trust, would have looked at her teacup or her muffin rather than at me, as she actually did on that fatal morning. If I were to judge from her costume, she had only just arrived, and the morning air had left upon her cheek a bloom that contributed greatly to the effect of her lovely countenance. Although very young, her form had all the roundness of womanhood, while her gay and sprightly manner indicated all the *sans géne* which only very young girls possess, and which, when tempered with perfect good taste, and accompanied by beauty and no small share of talent, forms an irresistible power of attraction.

Beside her sat a tall, handsome man of about five-and-thirty, or perhaps forty years of age, with a most soldierly air, who, as I was presented to him, scarcely turned his head, and gave me a half-nod of very unequivocal coldness. There are moments in life in which the heart is, as it were, laid bare to any chance or casual impression with a wondrous sensibility of pleasure or its opposite. This to me was one of those; and as I turned from the lovely girl, who had received me with marked courtesy, to the cold air and repelling hauteur of the dark-browed captain, the blood rushed throbbing to my forehead; and as I walked to my place at the table, I eagerly sought his eye, to return him a look of defiance and disdain, proud and contemptuous as his own. Captain Hammersley, however, took no further notice of me, but continued to recount, for the amusement of those about him, several excellent stories of his military career, which, I confess, were heard with every test of delight by all save me. One thing galled me particularly,—and how easy is it, when you have begun by disliking a person, to supply food for your antipathy,—all his allusions to his military life were coupled with half-hinted and ill-concealed sneers at civilians of every kind, as though every man not a soldier were absolutely unfit for common intercourse with the world—still more for any favorable reception in ladies' society.

The young ladies of the family were a well-chosen auditory, for their admiration of the army extended from the Life Guards to the Veteran Battalion, the Sappers and Miners included; and as Miss Dashwood was the daughter of a soldier, she, of course, coincided in many if not all of his opinions. I turned towards my neighbor, a Clare gentleman, and tried to engage him in conversation, but he was breathlessly attending to the Captain. On my left sat Matthew Blake, whose eyes were firmly riveted upon the same person, and heard his marvels with an interest scarcely inferior to that of his sisters. Annoyed and in ill-temper, I ate my breakfast in silence, and resolved that the first moment I could obtain a hearing from Mr. Blake, I would open my negotiation, and take my leave at once of Gurt-na-Morra.

We all assembled in a large room, called, by courtesy, the library, when breakfast was over; and then it was that Mr. Blake, taking me aside, whispered, "Charley, it's right I should inform you that Sir George Dashwood there is the Commander of the Forces, and is come down here at this moment to——" What for, or how it should concern me, I was not to learn; for at that critical instant my informant's attention was called off by Captain Hammersley asking if the hounds were to hunt that day.

"My friend Charley here is the best authority upon that matter," said Mr. Blake, turning towards me.

"They are to try the priest's meadows," said I, with an air of some importance; "but, if your guests desire a day's sport, I'll send word over to Brackely to bring the dogs over here, and we are sure to find a fox in your cover."

"Oh, then, by all means," said the Captain, turning towards Mr. Blake, and addressing himself to him—"by all means; and Miss Dashwood, I'm sure, would like to see the hounds throw off."

Whatever chagrin the first part of his speech caused me, the latter sent my heart a-throbbing; and I hastened from the room to despatch a messenger to the huntsman to come over to Gurt-na-Morra, and also another to O'Malley Castle, to bring my best horse and my riding equipments as quickly as possible.

"Matthew, who is this Captain?" said I, as young Blake met me in the hall.

"Oh! he is the aide-de-camp of General Dashwood. A nice fellow, isn't he?"

"I don't know what you may think," said I, "but I take him for the most impertinent, impudent, supercilious——"

The rest of my civil speech was cut short by the appearance of the very individual in question, who, with his hands in his pockets and a cigar in his mouth, sauntered forth down the steps, taking no more notice of Matthew Blake and myself than the two fox-terriers that followed at his heels.

However anxious I might be to open negotiations on the subject of my mission, for the present the thing was impossible; for I found that Sir George Dashwood was closeted closely with Mr. Blake, and resolved to wait till evening, when chance might afford me the opportunity I desired.

As the ladies had retired to dress for the hunt, and as I felt no peculiar desire to ally myself with the unsocial Captain, I accompanied Matthew to the stable to look after the cattle, and make preparations for the coming sport.

"There's Captain Hammersley's mare," said Matthew, as he pointed to a highly-bred but powerful English hunter; "she came last night, for as he expected some sport, he sent his horses from Dublin on purpose. The others will be here to-day."

"What is his regiment?" said I, with an appearance of carelessness, but in reality feeling curious to know if the Captain was a cavalry or infantry officer.

"The —th Light Dragoons," said Matthew.

"You never saw him ride?" said I.

"But his groom there says he leads the way in his own country."

"And where may that be?"

"In Leicestershire, no less," said Matthew.

"Does he know Galway?"

"Never was in it before; it's only this minute he asked Moses Daly if the ox-fences were high here."

"Ox-fences! then he does not know what a wall is?"

"Devil a bit; but we'll teach him."

"That we will," said I, with as bitter a resolution to impart the instruction as ever schoolmaster did to whip Latin grammar into one of the great unbreeched.

"But I had better send the horses down to the Mill," said Matthew; "we'll draw that cover first."

So saying, he turned towards the stable, while I sauntered alone
towards the road by which I expected the huntsman. I had not
walked half a mile before I heard the yelping of the dogs, and a
little farther on I saw old Brackely coming along at a brisk trot,
cutting the hounds on each side, and calling after the stragglers.

." Did you see my horse on the road, Brackely?" said I.

"I did, Misther Charles, and, troth, I'm sorry to see him; sure
yerself knows better than to take out the Badger, the best steeple-
chaser in Ireland, in such a country as this; nothing but awkward
stone-fences, and not a foot of sure ground in the whole of it."

"I know it well, Brackely; but yet I have my own reasons for
it."

"Well, maybe you have; what cover will your honor try first?"

"They talk of the Mill," said I; "but I'd much rather try 'Morran-a-Gowl.' "

"Morran-a-Gowl! Do you want to break your neck entirely?"

"No, Brackely, not mine."

"Whose then, alannah?" ·

"An English captain's—the devil fly away with him; he's come
down here to-day, and from all I can see is a most impudent fellow;
so, Brackely——"

"I understand. Well, leave it to me, and though I don't like the
only deer-park wall on the hill, we'll try it this morning with the
blessing; I'll take him down by Woodford, over the ' Devil's Mouth,'
—it's eighteen feet wide this minute with the late rains—into the
four callows; then over the stone walls, down to Dangan; then take
a short cut up the hill, blow him a bit, and give him the park wall
at the top. You must come in then fresh, and give him the whole
run home over Sleibhmich; the Badger knows it all, and takes the
road always in a fly,—a mighty distressing thing for the horse that
follows, more particularly if he does not understand a stony country. Well, if he lives through this, give him the sunk fence and the
stone wall at Mr. Blake's clover-field, for the hounds will run into
the fox about there; and though we never ride that leap since Mr.
Malone broke his neck at it, last October, yet, upon an occasion like
this, and for the honor of Galway——"

"To be sure, Brackely, and here's a guinea for you, and now trot
on towards the house; they must not see us together, or they might
suspect something. But, Brackely," said I, calling out after him,
"if he rides at all fair, what's to be done?"

"Troth, then, myself doesn't know; there is nothing so bad west
of Athlone; have ye a great spite agin him?"

"I have," said I, fiercely.

"Could ye coax a fight out of him?"

"That's true," said I ; " and now ride on as fast as you can."

Brackely's last words imparted a lightness to my heart and my step, and I strode along a very different man from what I had left the house half an hour previously.

CHAPTER IV.

THE HUNT.

ALTHOUGH we had not the advantages of a "southerly wind and cloudy sky," the day, towards noon, became strongly overcast, and promised to afford us good scenting weather, and as we assembled at the meet, mutual congratulations were exchanged upon the improved appearance of the day. Young Blake had provided Miss Dashwood with a quiet and well-trained horse, and his sisters were all mounted, as usual, upon their own animals, giving to our turn-out quite a gay and lively aspect. I myself came to cover upon a hackney, having sent Badger with a groom, and longed ardently for the moment when, casting the skin of my greatcoat and overalls, I should appear before the world in my well-appointed "cords and tops." Captain Hammersley had not as yet made his appearance, and many conjectures were afloat as to whether "he might have missed the road or changed his mind," or, "forgot all about it," as Miss Dashwood hinted.

"Who, pray, pitched upon this cover?" said Caroline Blake, as she looked with a practised eye over the country on either side.

"There is no chance of a fox late in the day at the Mill," said the huntsman, inventing a lie for the occasion.

"Then of course you never intend us to see much of the sport, for after you break cover, you are entirely lost to us."

"I thought you always followed the hounds," said Miss Dashwood, timidly.

"Oh, to be sure we do, in any common country ; but here it is out of the question ; the fences are too large for any one, and, if I am not mistaken, these gentlemen will not ride far over this. There, look yonder, where the river is rushing down the hill—that stream, widening as it advances, crosses the cover nearly midway. Well, they must clear that ; and then you may see these walls of large loose stones, nearly five feet in height ; that is the usual course the fox takes, unless he heads towards the hills, and goes towards Dangan, and then there's an end of it ; for the deer-park wall is usually a pull-up to every one, except, perhaps, to our friend Charley yonder, who has tried his fortune against drowning more than once there."

"Look, here he comes," said Matthew Blake, "and looking splendidly too—a little too much in flesh, perhaps, if anything."

"Captain Hammersley!" said the four Misses Blake, in a breath; "where is he?"

"No, it's the Badger I'm speaking of," said Matthew, laughing, and pointing with his finger towards a corner of the field where my servant was leisurely throwing down a wall about two feet high to let him pass.

"Oh, how handsome!—what a charger for a dragoon!" said Miss Dashwood.

Any other mode of praising my steed would have been much more acceptable. The word dragoon was a thorn in my tenderest part, that rankled and lacerated at every stir. In a moment I was in the saddle, and scarcely seated, when at once all the *mauvais honte* of boyhood left me, and I felt every inch a man. I often look back to that moment of my life, and, comparing it with many similar ones, cannot help acknowledging how purely is the self-possession which so often wins success the result of some light and trivial association. My confidence in my horsemanship suggested moral courage of a very different kind, and I felt that Charles O'Malley curveting upon a thorough-bred and the same man ambling upon a shelty were two and very dissimilar individuals.

"No chance of the Captain," said Matthew, who had returned from a reconnaissance upon the road; "and after all it's a pity, for the day is getting quite favorable."

While the young ladies formed pickets to look out for the gallant *militaire*, I seized the opportunity of prosecuting my acquaintance with Miss Dashwood; and even in the few and passing observations that fell from her, learned how very different an order of being she was from all I had hitherto seen of country belles. A mixture of courtesy with *naïveté*—a wish to please, with a certain feminine gentleness, that always flatters a man, and still more a boy that fain would be one—gained momentarily more and more upon me, and put me also on my mettle to prove to my fair companion that I was not altogether a mere uncultivated and unthinking creature, like the remainder of those about me.

"Here he is, at last," said Helen Blake, as she cantered across a field, waving her handkerchief as a signal to the Captain, who was now seen approaching at a brisk trot.

As he came along, a small fence intervened; he pressed his horse a little, and, as he kissed hands to the fair Helen, cleared it in a bound, and was in an instant in the midst of us.

"He sits his horse like a man, Misther Charles," said the old huntsman; "troth, we must give him the worst bit of it."

Captain Hammersley was, despite all the critical acumen with which I canvassed him, the very *beau ideal* of a gentleman rider; indeed, although a very heavy man, his powerful English thorough-bred, showing not less bone than blood, took away all semblance of overweight; his saddle, well fitting and well placed; his large and broad-reined snaffle; his own costume of black coat, leathers and tops, was in perfect keeping, and even to his heavy-handled hunting-whip I could find nothing to cavil at. As he rode up, he paid his respects to the ladies in his usual free-and-easy manner, expressed some surprise, but no regret, at hearing that he was late, and never deigning any notice of Matthew or myself, took his place beside Miss Dashwood, with whom he conversed in a low and under tone.

"There they go," said Matthew, as five or six dogs, with their heads up, ran yelping along a furrow, then stopped, howled again, and once more set off together. In an instant all was commotion in the little valley below us. The huntsman, with his hand to his mouth, was calling off the stragglers, and the whipper-in following up the leading dogs with the rest of the pack. "They've found!—they're away!" said Matthew; and as he spoke, a great yell burst from the valley, and in an instant the whole pack were off at full speed. Rather more intent at that moment upon showing off my horsemanship than anything else, I dashed spurs into Badger's sides, and turned him towards a rasping ditch before me. Over we went, hurling down behind us a rotten bank of clay and small stones, showing how little safety there had been in topping instead of clearing it at a bound. Before I was well seated again, the Captain was beside me. "Now for it, then," said I; and away we went. What might be the nature of his feelings I cannot pretend to state, but my own were a strange *mélange* of wild, boyish enthusiasm, revenge, and recklessness. For my own neck I cared little—nothing; and as I led the way by half a length, I muttered to myself, "Let him follow me fairly this day, and I ask no more."

The dogs had got somewhat the start of us, and as they were in full cry, and going fast, we were a little behind. A thought therefore struck me that, by appearing to take a short cut upon the hounds, I should come down upon the river where its breadth was greatest, and thus, at one *coup*, might try my friend's mettle and his horse's performance at the same time. On we went, our speed increasing, till the roar of the river we were now approaching was plainly audible. I looked half around, and now perceived the Captain was standing in his stirrups, as if to obtain a view of what was before him; otherwise his countenance was calm and unmoved, and not a muscle betrayed that he was not cantering on a parade. I fixed myself firm in my seat, shook my horse a little together, and with a shout whose import every Galway hunter well knows, rushed him at the river. I saw the water dashing among the large stones, I heard its splash, I felt a bound like the *ricochet* of a shot, and we were over, but so narrowly, that the bank had yielded beneath his hind legs, and it needed a bold effort of the noble animal to regain his footing. Scarcely was he once more firm, when Hammersley flew by me, taking the lead, and sitting quietly in his saddle, as if racing. I know of little in all my after-life like the agony of that moment; for although I was far, very far, from wishing real ill to him, yet I would gladly have broken my leg or my arm if he could not have been able to follow me. And now, there he was, actually a length and a half in advance! Worse than all, Miss Dashwood must have witnessed the whole, and doubtless his leap over the river was better and bolder than mine. One consolation yet remained, and while I whispered it to myself, I felt comforted again. "His is an English mare—they understand these leaps, but what can he make of a Galway wall?" The question was soon to be solved. Before us, about three fields, were the hounds still in full cry; a large stone wall lay between, and to it we both directed our course together. "Ha!" thought I, "he is floored at last," as I perceived that the Captain held his horse rather more in hand, and suffered me to lead. "Now, then, for it!" So saying, I rode at the largest part I could find, well knowing that Badger's powers were here in their element. One spring, one plunge, and away we were, galloping along at the other side. Not so the Captain; his horse had refused the fence, and he was now taking a circuit of the field for another trial of it.

"Pounded, by Jove!" said I, as I turned round in my saddle to observe him. Once more she came at it, and once more baulked, rearing up at the same time, almost so as to fall backward.

My triumph was complete, and I again was about to follow the hounds, when, throwing a look back, I saw Hammersley clearing the wall in a most splendid manner, and taking a stretch of at least thirteen feet beyond it. Once more he was on my flanks, and the contest renewed. Whatever might be the sentiments of the riders (mine I confess to), between the horses it now became a tremendous struggle. The English mare, though evidently superior in stride and strength, was slightly overweighted, and had not, besides, that cat-like activity an Irish horse possesses; so that the advantages and disadvantages on either side were about equalized. For about half an hour now the pace was awful. We rode side by side, taking our leaps exactly at the same instant, and not four feet apart. The hounds were still considerably in advance, and were heading towards the Shannon, when suddenly the fox doubled, took the hill-side, and made for Dangan. "Now, then, comes the trial of strength," I said, half-aloud, as I threw my eye up a steep and rugged mountain, covered with wild furze and tall heath, around the crest of which ran, in a zig-zag direction, a broken and dilapidated wall, once the enclosure of a deer-park. This wall, which varied from four to six feet in height, was of solid masonry, and would in the most favorable ground have been a bold leap. Here, at the summit of a mountain, with not a yard of-footing, it was absolutely desperation.

By the time that we reached the foot of the hill, the fox, followed closely by the hounds, had passed through a breach in the wall, while Matthew Blake with the huntsmen and whipper-in, was riding along in search of a gap to lead the horses through. Before I put spurs to Badger, to face the hill, I turned one look towards Hammersley. There was a slight curl, half-smile, half-sneer, upon his lip, that actually maddened me, and had a precipice yawned beneath my feet, I should have dashed at it after that. The ascent was so steep that I was obliged to take the hill in a slanting direction, and even thus, the loose footing rendered it dangerous in the extreme.

At length I reached the crest, where the wall, more than five feet in height, stood frowning above and seeming to defy me. I turned my horse full round, so that his very chest almost touched the stones, and, with a bold cut of the whip and a loud halloo, the gallant animal rose, as if rearing, pawed for an instant to regain his balance, and then, with a frightful struggle, fell backwards, and rolled from top to bottom of the hill, carrying me along with him. The last object that crossed my sight, as I lay bruised and motionless, was the Captain, as he took the wall in a flying leap, and disappeared at the other side. After a few scrambling efforts to rise, Badger regained his legs and stood beside me; but such was the shock and concussion of my fall, that all the objects around seemed wavering and floating before me, while showers of bright sparks fell in myriads before my eyes. I tried to rise, but fell back helpless. Cold perspiration broke over my forehead, and I fainted. From that moment I can remember nothing, till I felt myself galloping along at full speed upon a level table-land, with the hounds about three fields in advance, Hammersley riding foremost, and taking all his leaps coolly as ever. As I swayed to either side upon my saddle, from weakness, I was lost to all thought or recollection, save a flickering memory of some plan of vengeance, which still urged me

forward. The chase had now lasted above an hour, and both hounds
and horses began to feel the pace at which they were going. As for
me, I rode mechanically; I neither knew nor cared for the dangers
before me. My eye rested on but one object; my whole being was
concentrated upon one vague and undefined sense of revenge. At
this instant the huntsman came alongside of me.

"Are you hurted, Misther Charles? Did you fall? Your cheek
is all blood, and your coat is torn in two; and, Mother o' God, his
boot is ground to powder; he does not hear me. Oh, pull up—pull
up, for the love of the Virgin; there's the clover-field, and the sunk
fence before you, and you'll be killed on the spot."

"Where?" cried I, with the cry of a madman; "where's the
clover-field?—where's the sunk fence? Ha! I see it—I see it
now."

So saying, I dashed the rowels into my horse's flanks, and in an
instant was beyond the reach of the poor fellow's remonstrances.
Another moment, I was beside the Captain. He turned round as I
came up; the same smile was upon his mouth. I could have struck
him. About three hundred yards before us lay the sunk fence; its
breadth was about twenty feet, and a wall of close brickwork formed
its face. Over this the hounds were now clambering; some succeeded in crossing, but by far the greater number fell back howling
into the ditch.

I turned towards Hammersley. He was standing high in his
stirrups, and, as he looked towards the yawning fence, down which
the dogs were tumbling in masses, I thought (perhaps it was but a
thought) that his cheek was paler. I looked again; he was pulling
at his horse; ha! it was true, then—he would not face it. I turned
round in my saddle, looked him full in the face, and, as I pointed
with my whip to the leap, called out in a voice hoarse with passion,
"Come on!" I saw no more. All objects were lost to me from
that moment. When next my senses cleared, I was standing amid
the dogs, where they had just killed. Badger stood blown and
trembling beside me, his head drooping, and his flanks gored with
spur marks. I looked about, but all consciousness of the past had
fled; the concussion of my fall had shaken my intellect, and I was
like one but half awake. One glimpse, short and fleeting, of what
was taking place, shot through my brain, as old Brackely whispered
to me, "By my soul, ye did for the Captain there." I turned a
vague look upon him, and my eyes fell upon the figure of a man
that lay stretched and bleeding upon a door before me. His pale
face was crossed with a purple stream of blood, that trickled from
a wound beside his eyebrow; his arms lay motionless and heavily at
either side. I knew him not. A loud report of a pistol aroused me

from my stupor; I looked back. I saw a crowd that broke suddenly asunder, and fled right and left. I heard a heavy crash upon the ground; I pointed with my finger, for I could not utter a word.

"It is the English mare, yer honor; she was a beauty this morning, but she's broke her shoulder-bone, and both her legs, and it was best to put her out of pain."

CHAPTER V.

THE DRAWING-ROOM.

ON the fourth day following the adventure detailed in the last chapter, I made my appearance in the drawing-room, my cheek well blanched by copious bleeding, and my step tottering and uncertain. On entering the room, I looked about in vain for some one who might give me an insight into the occurrences of the four preceding days, but no one was to be met with. The ladies, I learned, were out riding; Matthew was buying a new setter; Mr. Blake was canvassing; and Captain Hammersley was in bed. Where was Miss Dashwood?—in her room: and Sir George?—he was with Mr. Blake.

"What! canvassing too?"

"Troth, that same was possible," was the intelligent reply of the old butler, at which I could not help smiling. I sat down, therefore, in the easiest chair I could find, and, unfolding the county paper, resolved upon learning how matters were going on in the political world. But, somehow, whether the editor was not brilliant, or the fire was hot, or that my own dreams were pleasanter to indulge in than his fancies, I fell sound asleep.

How differently is the mind attuned to the active busy world of thought and action, when awakened from sleep by any sudden and rude summons to arise and be stirring, and when called into existence by the sweet and silvery notes of softest music, stealing over, the senses, and while they impart awakening thoughts of bliss and beauty, scarcely dissipating the dreary influence of slumber! Such was my first thought as, with closed lids, the thrilling chords of a harp broke upon my sleep, and aroused me to a feeling of unutterable pleasure. I turned gently round in my chair, and beheld Miss Dashwood. She was seated in a recess of an old-fashioned window; the pale yellow glow of a wintry sun at evening fell upon her beautiful hair, and tinged it with such a light as I have often since then seen in Rembrandt's pictures; her head leaned upon the harp, and, as she struck its chords at random, I saw that her mind was far away from all around her. As I looked, she suddenly started from her leaning attitude, and, parting back the curls from her brow, she preluded a few chords, and then sighed forth, rather than sung, that most beautiful of Moore's Melodies,—

"She is far from the land where her young hero sleeps."

Never before had such pathos, such deep utterance of feeling, met my astonished sense. I listened breathlessly as the tears fell one by one down my cheek; my bosom heaved and fell; and when she ceased, I hid my head between my hands and sobbed aloud. In an instant she was beside me, and placing her hand upon my shoulder, said,—

"Poor dear boy! I never suspected you of being there, or I should not have sung that mournful air."

I started and looked up, and from what I know not, but she suddenly crimsoned to her very forehead, while she added, in a less assured tone,—

"I hope, Mr. O'Malley, that you are much better, and I trust there is no imprudence in your being here."

"For the latter I shall not answer," said I, with a sickly smile; "but already I feel your music has done me service."

"Then let me sing more for you."

"If I am to have a choice, I should say, sit down, and let me hear you talk to me. My illness and the doctor together have made wild work of my poor brain; but, if you will talk to me——"

"Well, then, what shall it be about? Shall I tell you a fairy tale?"

"I need it not; I feel I am in one this instant."

"Well, then, what say you to a legend, for I am rich in my stores of them?"

"The O'Malleys have their chronicles, wild and barbarous enough, without the aid of Thor and Woden."

"Then, shall we chat of every-day matters? Should you like to hear how the election and the canvass go on?"

"Yes, of all things."

"Well, then, most favorably. Two baronies, with most unspeakable names, have declared for us, and confidence is rapidly increasing among our party. This I learned by chance yesterday; for papa never permits us to know anything of these matters—not even the names of the candidates."

"Well, that was the very point I was coming to, for the government were about to send down some one just as I left home, and I am most anxious to learn who it is."

"Then am I utterly valueless; for I really can't say what party the government espouses, and only know of our own."

"Quite enough for me that you wish it success," said I gallantly. "Perhaps you can tell me if my uncle has heard of my accident?"

"Oh yes; but somehow he has not been here himself, but sent a friend—a Mr. Considine, I think; a very strange person he seemed. He demanded to see papa, and, it seems, asked him if your misfortune had been a thing of his contrivance, and whether he was ready to explain his conduct about it; and, in fact, I believe he is mad."

"Heaven confound him!" I muttered between my teeth.

"And then he wished to have an interview with Captain Hammersley; however, he is too ill; but as the doctor hoped he might be down stairs in a week, Mr. Considine kindly hinted that he should wait."

"Oh, then, do tell me how the Captain is."

"Very much bruised, very much disfigured, they say," said she, half smiling; "but not so much hurt in body as in mind."

"As how, may I ask?" said I, with an appearance of innocence.

"I don't exactly understand it; but it would appear that there was something like rivalry among you gentlemen chasseurs on that luckless morning, and that while you paid the penalty of a broken head, he was destined to lose his horse and break his arm."

"I certainly am sorry—most sincerely sorry—for any share I might have had in the catastrophe; and my greatest regret, I confess, arises from the fact that I should cause *you* unhappiness."

"*Me*—pray explain?"

"Why, as Captain Hammersley——"

"Mr. O'Malley, you are too young now to make me suspect you have an intention to offend; but I caution you, never repeat this."

I saw that I had transgressed, but how, I most honestly confess, I could not guess; for though I certainly was the senior of my fair companion in years, I was most lamentably her junior in tact and discretion.

The gray dusk of evening had long fallen as we continued to chat together beside the blazing wood embers; she evidently amusing herself with the original notions of an untutored, unlettered boy, and I drinking deep those draughts of love that nerved my heart through many a breach and battle-field.

Our colloquy was at length interrupted by the entrance of Sir George, who shook me most cordially by the hand, and made the kindest inquiries about my health.

"They tell me you are to be a lawyer, Mr. O'Malley," said he, "and, if so, I must advise you to take better care of your head-piece."

"A lawyer, papa; oh dear me! I should never have thought of his being anything so stupid."

"Why, silly girl, what would you have a man be?"

"A dragoon, to be sure, papa," said the fond girl, as she pressed her arm around his manly figure, and looked up in his face with an expression of mingled pride and affection.

That word sealed my destiny.

CHAPTER VI.

THE DINNER.

WHEN I retired to my room to dress for dinner, I found my servant waiting with a note from my uncle, to which he informed me the messenger expected an answer.

I broke the seal and read:

"DEAR CHARLEY:—Do not lose a moment in securing old Blake —if you have not already done so—as information has just reached me that the government party has promised a coronetcy to young Matthew if he can bring over his father. And these are the people I have been voting with—a few private cases excepted—for thirty odd years!

"I am very sorry for your accident. Considine informs me that it will need *explanation* at a later period. He has been in Athlone since Tuesday, in hopes to catch the new candidate on his way down, and get him into a little private quarrel before the day; if he succeed, it will save the county much expense, and conduce greatly to the peace and happiness of all parties. But 'these things,' as Father Roach says, 'are in the hands of Providence.' You must also persuade old Blake to write a few lines to Simon Mallock about the Coolnamuck mortgage. We can give him no satisfaction at present, at least such as he looks for; and don't be philandering any longer where you are, when your health permits a change of quarters.

"Your affectionate uncle,
"GODFREY O'MALLEY.

"P.S.—I have just heard from Considine; he was out this morning, and shot a fellow in the knee, but finds that after all he was not the candidate, but a tourist that was writing a book about Connemara.

"P.S. No. 2.—Bear the mortgage in mind, for old Mallock is a spiteful fellow, and has a grudge against me since I horsewhipped his son in Banagher. Oh, the world, the world!—G. O'M."

Until I read this very clear epistle to the end, I had no very precise conception how completely I had forgotten all my uncle's interests, and neglected all his injunctions. Already five days had elapsed, and I had not as much as mooted the question to Mr. Blake, and probably all this time my uncle was calculating on the thing as concluded; but, with one hole in my head and some half-dozen in my heart, my memory was none of the best.

Snatching up the letter, therefore, I resolved to lose no more time, and proceeded at once to Mr. Blake's room, expecting that I should, as the event proved, find him engaged in the very laborious duty of making his toilet.

"Come in, Charley," said he, as I tapped gently at the door; "it's only Charley, my darling; Mrs. B. won't mind you."

"Not the least in life," responded Mrs. B., disposing at the same time a pair of her husband's corduroys, tippet fashion, across her ample shoulders, which before were displayed in the plenitude and breadth of coloring we find in a Rubens. "Sit down, Charley, and tell us what's the matter."

As until this moment I was in perfect ignorance of the Adam and Eve-like simplicity in which the private economy of Mr. Blake's household was conducted, I would have gladly retired from what I found to be a mutual territory of dressing-room, had not Mr. Blake's injunctions been issued somewhat like an order to remain.

"It's only a letter, sir," said I, stuttering, "from my uncle, about the election. He says that, as his majority is now certain, he should feel better pleased in going to the poll with all the family, you know, sir, along with him. He wishes me just to sound your intentions— to make out how you feel disposed towards him; and—and, faith, as I am but a poor diplomatist, I thought the best way was to come straight to the point and tell you so."

"I perceive," said Mr. Blake, giving his chin at the moment an awful gash with the razor,—"I perceive; go on."

"Well, sir, I have little more to say; my uncle knows what influence you have in Scariff, and expects you'll do what you can there."

"Anything more?" said Mr. Blake, with a very dry and quizzical expression I didn't half like—"anything more?"

"Oh, yes, you are to write a line to old Mallock."

"I understand; about Coolnamuck, isn't it?"

"Exactly; I believe that's all."

"Well now, Charley, you may go down stairs, and we'll talk it over after dinner."

"Yes, Charley, dear, go down, for I'm going to draw on my stockings," said the fair Mrs. Blake, with a look of very modest consciousness.

When I had left the room, I couldn't help muttering a "Thank God!" for the success of a mission I more than once feared for, and hastened to despatch a note to my uncle, assuring him of the Blake interest, and adding that, for propriety sake, I should defer my departure for a day or two longer.

This done, with a heart lightened of its load, and in high spirits at my cleverness, I descended to the drawing-room. Here a very large party were already assembled, and at every opening of the door a new relay of Blakes, Burkes, and Bodkins was introduced. In the absence of the host, Sir George Dashwood was " making the agreeable" to the guests, and shook hands with every new arrival with all the warmth and cordiality of old friendship. While thus he inquired for various absent individuals, and asked most affectionately for sundry aunts and uncles not forthcoming, a slight incident occurred, which, by its ludicrous turn, served to shorten the long half-hour before dinner. An individual of the party, a Mr. Blake, had, from certain peculiarities of face, obtained in his boyhood the sobriquet of "Shave-the-wind." This hatchet-like conformation had grown with his growth, and perpetuated upon him a nickname, by which alone was he ever spoken of among his friends and acquaintances; the only difference being that, as he came to man's estate, brevity, that soul of wit, had curtailed the epithet to mere "Shave." Now, Sir George had been hearing frequent reference made to him always by this name, heard him ever so addressed, and perceived him to reply to it; so that, when he was himself asked by some one what sport he had found that day among the woodcocks, he answered at once, with a bow of very grateful acknowledgment, " Excellent, indeed, but entirely owing to where I was placed in the copse; had it not been for Mr. Shave there——"

I need not say that the remainder of his speech, being heard on all sides, caused one universal shout of laughter, in which, to do him justice, the excellent Shave himself heartily joined. Scarcely were the sounds of mirth lulled into an apparent calm, when the door opened, and the hostess appeared. Mrs. Blake advanced in all the plenitude of her charms, arrayed in crimson satin, sorely injured in its freshness by a patch of grease upon the front, about the same size and shape as the continent of Europe in Arrowsmith's Atlas; a swansdown tippet covered her shoulders ! massive bracelets ornamented her wrists; while from her ears descended two Irish diamond ear-rings, rivalling in magnitude and value the glass pendants of a lustre. Her reception of her guests made ample amends, in warmth and cordiality, for any deficiency of elegance; and as she disposed her ample proportions upon the sofa, and looked around upon the company, she appeared the very impersonation of hospitality.

After several openings and shuttings of the drawing-room door, accompanied by the appearance of old Simon the butler, who counted the party at least five times before he was certain that the score was correct, dinner was at length announced. Now came a moment of difficulty, and one which, as testing Mr. Blake's tact, he would gladly have seen devolve upon some other shoulders; for he well knew that the marshalling a room full of mandarins, blue, green, and yellow, was "cakes and gingerbread" to ushering a Galway party in to dinner.

First, then, was Mr. Miles Bodkin, whose grandfather would have been a lord if Cromwell had not hanged him one fine morning. Then Mrs. Mosey Blake's first husband was promised the title of Kilmacud if it was ever restored, whereas Mrs. French of Knocktumnor's mother was then at law for a title; and, lastly, Mrs. Joe Burke was fourth cousin to Lord Clanricarde, as is or will be every Burke from this to the day of judgment. Now, luckily for her prospects, the lord was alive; and Mr. Blake, remembering a very sage adage about "dead lions," &c., solved the difficulty at once by gracefully tucking the lady under his arm and leading the way. The others soon followed, the priest of Portumna and my unworthy self bringing up the rear.

When, many a year afterwards, the hard ground of a mountain bivouac, with its pitiful portion of pickled cork-tree, yclept messbeef, and that pyroligneous aquafortis they call corn-brandy, have been my hard fare, I often looked back to that day's dinner with a most heart-yearning sensation: a turbot as big as the Waterloo shield—a sirloin that seemed cut from the sides of a rhinoceros—a sauce-boat that contained an oyster-bed. There was a turkey which singly would have formed the main army of a French dinner, doing mere outpost duty, flanked by a picket of ham and a detached squadron of chickens, carefully ambushed in a forest of greens; potatoes, not disguised *à la maître d'hôtel* and tortured to resemble bad macaroni, but piled like shot in an ordnance-yard, were posted at different quarters; while massive decanters of port and sherry stood proudly up like standard-bearers amid the goodly array. This was none of your austere "great dinners," where a cold and chilling plateau of artificial nonsense cuts off one-half of the table from intercourse with the other—when whispered sentences constitute the conversation, and all the friendly recognition of wine-drinking, which renews acquaintance and cements an intimacy, is replaced by the ceremonious filling of your glass by a lacquey—where smiles go current in lieu of kind speeches, and epigram and smartness form the substitute for the broad jest and merry story. Far from it. Here the company ate, drank, talked, laughed, did all but sing, and certainly enjoyed themselves heartily. As for me, I was little more than a listener, and such was the crash of plates, the jingle of glasses, and the clatter of voices, that fragments only of what was passing around reached me, giving to the conversation of the party a character occasionally somewhat incongruous. Thus such sentences as the following ran foul of each other every instant:

"No better land in Galway"—"where could you find such facilities"—"for shooting Mr. Jones on his way home"—"the truth, the whole truth, and nothing but the truth"—"kiss"—"Miss Blake, she's the girl with the foot and ankle"—"Daly has never had wool on his sheep"—"how could he"—"what does he pay for the mountain"—"four and tenpence a yard"—"not a penny less"—"all the cabbage-stalks and potato-skins"—"with some bog stuff through it" —"that's the thing to"—"make soup, with a red herring in it instead of salt"—"and when he proposed for my niece, ma'am, says he"—"mix a strong tumbler, and I'll make a shake-down for you on the floor"—"and may the Lord have mercy on your soul"—"and now, down the middle and up again"—"Captain Magan, my dear, he is the man"—"to shave a pig properly"—"it's not money I'm looking for, says he, the girl of my heart"—"if she had not a windgall and two spavins"—"I'd have given her the rites of the Church, of coorse," said Father Roach, bringing up the rear of this ill-assorted jargon.

Such were the scattered links of conversation I was condemned to listen to, till a general rise on the part of the ladies left us alone to discuss our wine, and enter in good earnest upon the more serious duties of the evening.

Scarcely was the door closed when one of the company, seizing the bell-rope, said, "With your leave, Blake, we'll have the 'dew' now."

"Good claret—no better," said another; "but it sits mighty cold on the stomach."

"There's nothing like the groceries, after all—eh, Sir George?" said an old Galway squire to the English general, who acceded to the fact, which he understood in a very different sense.

"Oh, punch, you are my darlin'," hummed another, as a large

square half-gallon decanter of whisky was placed on the table, the various decanters of wine being now ignominiously sent down to the end of the board, without any evidence of regret on any face save Sir George Dashwood's, who mixed his tumbler with a very rebellious conscience.

Whatever were the noise and clamor of the company before, they were nothing to what now ensued. As one party was discussing the approaching contest, another was planning a steeple-chase; while two individuals, unhappily removed from each other the entire length of the table, were what is called " challenging each other's effects" in a very remarkable manner, the process so styled being an exchange of property, when each party, setting an imaginary value upon sòme article, barters it for another, the amount of boot. paid and received being determined by a third person, who is the umpire. Thus a gold breastpin was swopped, as the phrase is, against a horse; then a pair of boots, a Kerry bull, &c.—every imaginable species of property coming into the market. Sometimes, as matters of very dubious value turned up, great laughter was the result. In this very national pastime, a Mr. Miles Bodkin, a noted fire-eater of the west, was a great proficient, and, it is said, once so completely succeeded in despoiling an uninitiated hand, that after winning in succession his horse, gig, harness, &c., he proceeded *seriatim* to his watch, ring, clothes, and portmanteau, and actually concluded by winning all he possessed, and kindly lent him a card-cloth to cover him on his way to the hotel. His success on the present occasion was considerable, and his spirits proportionate. The decanter had thrice been replenished, and the flushed faces and thickened utterances of the guests evinced that from the cold properties of the claret there was but little to dread. As for Mr. Bodkin, his manner was incapable of any higher flight, when under the influence of whisky, than what it evinced on common occasions; and as he sat at the end of the table, fronting Mr. Blake, he assumed all the dignity of the ruler of the feast, with an energy no one seemed disposed to question. In answer to some observations of Sir George, he was led into something like an oration upon the peculiar excellencies of his native country, which ended in a declaration that there was nothing like Galway.

" Why don't you give us a song, Miles ? and maybe the general would learn more from it than all your speech-making."

" To be sure," cried out several voices together; " to be sure. Let us hear ' The Man for Galway !' "

Sir George having joined most warmly in the request, Mr. Bodkin filled up his glass to the brim, bespoke a chorus to his chant, and, clearing his voice with a deep hem, began the following ditty, to the air which Moore has since rendered immortal, by the beautiful song, "Wreathe the Bowl," &c. And-although .the words are well known in the west, for the information of less favored regions, I here transcribe

"THE MAN FOR GALWAY.

" To drink a toast,
  A proctor roast,
    Or bailiff as the case is,
  To kiss your wife,
  Or take your life
    At ten or fifteen paces;
  To keep game cocks—to hunt the fox,
    To drink in punch the Solway,
  With debts galore, but fun far more;
    Oh, that's 'the man for Galway.'
                    "Chorus—With debts, &c.

"The King of Oude
  Is mighty proud,
    And so were onst the *Caysars*—(Cæsars)
  But ould Giles Eyre
  Would make them stare,
    Av he had them with the Blazers.
  To the devil I fling ould Runjeet Sing,
    He's only a prince in a small way,
  And knows nothing at all of a six-foot wall;
    Oh, he'd never 'do for Galway.'
                    "Chorus—With debts, &c.

"Ye think the Blakes
  Are no 'great shakes;'
    They're all his blood relations,
  And the Bodkins sneeze
  At the grim Chinese,
    For they came from the *Phenaycians.*
  So fill the brim, and here's to him
    Who'd drink in punch the Solway;
  With debts galore, but fun far more;
    Oh! that's 'the man for Galway.'
                    "Chorus—With debts," &c.

I much fear that the reception of this very classic ode would not be as favorable in general companies as it was on the occasion I first heard it, for certainly the applause was almost deafening; and even Sir George, the defects of whose English education left some of the allusions out of his reach, was highly amused and laughed heartily.

The conversation once more reverted to the election, and although I was too far from those who seemed best informed on the matter to hear much, I could catch enough to discover that the feeling was a confident one. This was gratifying to me, as I had some scruple about my so long neglecting my uncle's cause.

" We have Scariff to a man," said Bodkin.

"And Mosey's tenantry," said another. " I swear, though there's not a freehold registered on the estate, that they'll vote, every mother's son of them, or devil a stone of the Court-house they'll leave standing on another."

"And may the Lord look to the returning officer!" said a third, throwing up his eyes.

" Mosey's tenantry are droll boys, and, like their landlord—more by token—they never pay any rent."

" "And what for shouldn't they vote?" said a dry-looking little old fellow in a red waistcoat. " When I was the dead agent——"

" The dead agent!" interrupted Sir George, with a start.

" Just so," said the old fellow, pulling down his spectacles from his forehead, and casting a half-angry look at Sir George, for what he had suspected to be a doubt of his veracity.

" The General does not know, maybe, what that is," said some one.

" It is the dead agent," said Mr. Blake, " who always provides substitutes for any voters that may have died since the last election. A very important fact in statistics may thus be gathered from the poll-books of this county, which proves it to be the healthiest part of Europe—a freeholder has not died in it for the last fifty years."

" The 'Kiltopher boys' won't come this time—they say there's no use trying to vote when so many were transported last assizes for perjury."

" They're poor-spirited creatures," said another.

" Not they—they are as decent boys as any we have—they're willing to wreck the town for fifty shillings' worth of spirits; besides, if they don't vote for the county they will for the borough."

This declaration seemed to restore these interesting individuals to favor, and now all attention was turned towards Bodkin, who was detailing the plan of a grand attack upon the polling-booths, to be headed by himself. By this time all the prudence and guardedness of the party had given way—whisky was in the ascendant, and every bold stroke of election policy, every cunning artifice, every ingenious device, was detailed and applauded in a manner which proved that self-respect was not the inevitable gift of " mountain dew."

The mirth and fun grew momentarily more boisterous, and Miles Bodkin, who had twice before been prevented proposing some toast by a telegraphic signal from the other end of the table, now swore that nothing should prevent him any longer, and rising with a smoking tumbler in his hand, delivered himself as follows:

4

"No, no, Phil Blake, ye needn't be winkin' at me that way—it's little I care for the spawn of the ould serpent." [Here great cheers greeted the speaker, in which, without well knowing why, I heartily joined.] "I'm going to give a toast, boys—a real good toast—none of your sentimental things about wall-flowers, or the vernal equinox, or that kind of thing, but a sensible, patriotic, manly, intrepid toast—a toast you must drink in the most universal, laborious, and awful manner—do ye see now? [Loud cheers.] "If any man of you here present doesn't drain this toast to the bottom—(here the speaker looked fixedly at me, as did the rest of the company)—then, by the great gun of Athlone, I'll make him eat the decanter, glass stopper and all, for the good of his digestion—d'ye see now?"

The cheering at this mild determination prevented my hearing what followed; but the peroration consisted in a very glowing eulogy upon some person unknown, and a speedy return to him as member for Galway. Amid all the noise and tumult at this critical moment, nearly every eye at the table was turned upon me; and as I concluded that they had been drinking my uncle's health, I thundered away at the mahogany with all my energy. At length, the hip, hipping over, and comparative quiet restored, I rose from my seat to return thanks. But, strange enough, Sir George Dashwood did so likewise; and there we both stood amid an uproar that might well have shaken the courage of more practised orators; while from every side came cries of "Hear, hear"—"Go on, Sir George"—"Speak out, General"—"Sit down, Charley"—"Confound the boy"—"Knock the legs from under him," &c. Not understanding why Sir George should interfere with what I regarded as my peculiar duty, I resolved not to give way, and avowed this determination in no very equivocal terms. "In that case," said the General, "I am to suppose that the young gentleman moves an amendment to your proposition; and, as the etiquette is in his favor, I yield." Here he resumed his place, amid a most terrific scene of noise and tumult, while several humane proposals as to my treatment were made around me, and a kind suggestion thrown out to break my neck, by a near neighbor. Mr. Blake at length prevailed upon the party to hear what I had to say—for he was certain I should not detain them above a minute. The commotion having in some measure subsided, I began : "Gentlemen—as the adopted son of the worthy man whose health you have just drunk——" Heaven knows how I should have continued—but here my eloquence was met by such a roar of laughing as I never before listened to; from one end of the board to the other it was one continued shout, and went on, too, as if all the spare lungs of the party had been kept in reserve for the occasion. I turned from one to the other—I tried to smile, and seemed to participate in the joke, but failed; I frowned—I looked savagely about where I could see enough to turn my wrath thitherward; and, as it chanced, not in vain; for Mr. Miles Bodkin, with an intuitive perception of my wishes, most suddenly ceased his mirth, and assuming a look of frowning defiance that had done him good service upon many former occasions, rose and said:

"Well, sir, I hope you're proud of yourself—you've made a nice beginning of it, and a pretty story you'll have for your uncle. But if you'd like to break the news by a letter, the General will have great pleasure in franking it for you; for, by the rock of Cashel, we'll carry him in against all the O'Malleys that ever cheated the sheriff."

Scarcely were the words uttered, when I seized my wine-glass, and hurled it with all my force at his head. So sudden was the act, and so true the aim, that Mr. Bodkin measured his length upon the floor ere his friends could appreciate his late eloquent effusion. The scene now became terrific; for though the redoubted Miles was *hors de combat*, his friends made a tremendous rush at, and would infallibly have succeeded in capturing me, had not Blake and four or five others interposed. Amid a desperate struggle, which lasted for some minutes, I was torn from the spot, carried bodily up stairs, and pitched headlong into my own room, where, having doubly locked the door on the outside, they left me to my own cool and not over-agreeable reflections.

———

CHAPTER VII.

THE FLIGHT FROM GURT-NA-MORRA.

IT was by one of those sudden and inexplicable revulsions which occasionally restore to sense and intellect the maniac of years' standing, that I was no sooner left alone in my chamber than I became perfectly sober. The fumes of the wine—and I had drunk deeply—were dissipated at once; my head, which but a moment before was half wild with excitement, was now cool, calm, and collected; and, stranger than all, I, who had only an hour since entered the dining-room with all the unsuspecting freshness of boyhood, became, by a mighty bound, a man—a man in all my feelings and responsibility, a man who, repelling an insult by an outrage, had resolved to stake his life upon the chance. In an instant a new era in life had opened before me; the light-headed gayety which fearlessness and youth impart was replaced by one absorbing thought—

one all-engrossing, all-pervading impression, that if I did not follow
up my quarrel with Bodkin, I was dishonored and disgraced: my
little knowledge of such matters not being sufficient to assure me
that I was now the aggressor, and that any further steps in the affair
should come from his side.

So thoroughly did my own griefs occupy me, that I had no
thought for the disappointment my poor uncle was destined to meet
with in hearing that the Blake interest was lost to him, and the
former breach between the families irreparably widened by the
events of the evening. Escape was my first thought; but how to
accomplish it? The door, a solid one of Irish oak, doubly locked
and bolted, defied all my efforts to break it open; the window was
at least five-and-twenty feet from the ground, and not a tree near to
swing into. I shouted, I called aloud, I opened the sash, and tried
if any one outside were within hearing; but in vain. Weary and
exhausted, I sat down upon my bed and ruminated over my fortunes. Vengeance—quick, entire, decisive vengeance—I thirsted
and panted for; and every moment I lived under the insult inflicted
on me, seemed an age of torturing and maddening agony. I rose
with a leap; a thought had just occurred to me. I drew the bed
towards the window, and fastening the sheet to one of the posts with
a firm knot, I twisted it into a rope, and let myself down to within
about twelve feet of the ground, when I let go my hold, and dropped
upon the grass beneath, safe and uninjured. A thin misty rain was
falling, and I now perceived for the first time that in my haste I had
forgotten my hat; this thought, however, gave me little uneasiness,
and I took my way towards the stable, resolving, if I could, to
saddle my horse, and get off before any intimation of my escape
reached the family.

When I gained the yard all was quiet and deserted; the servants
were doubtless enjoying themselves below stairs; and I met no one
in the way. I entered the stable, threw the saddle upon Badger, and
before five minutes from my descent from the window, was galloping towards O'Malley Castle at a pace that defied pursuit, had any
one thought of it.

It was about five o'clock on a dark wintry morning as I led my
horse through the well-known defile of out-houses and stables which
formed the long line of offices to my uncle's house. As yet no one
was stirring; and as I wished to have my arrival a secret from the
family, after providing for the wants of my gallant gray, I lifted the
latch of the kitchen door—no other fastening being ever thought
necessary, even at night—and gently groped my way towards the
stairs. All was perfectly still, and the silence now recalled me to
reflection as to what course I should pursue. It was all-important

that my uncle should know nothing of my quarrel, otherwise he would inevitably make it his own, and, by treating me like a boy in the matter, give the whole affair the turn I most dreaded. Then, as to Sir Harry Boyle, he would most certainly turn the whole thing into ridicule, make a good story, perhaps a song out of it, and laugh at my notions of demanding satisfaction. Considine, I knew, was my man; but then he was at Athlone—at least so my uncle's letter mentioned; perhaps he might have returned; if not, to Athlone I should set off at once. So resolving, I stole noiselessly·up stairs, and reached the door of the Count's chamber. I opened it gently, and entered; and though my step was almost imperceptible to myself, it was quite sufficient to alarm the watchful occupant of the room, who, springing up in his bed, demanded gruffly "Who's there?"

"Charles, sir," said I, shutting the door carefully, and approaching his bedside. "Charles O'Malley, sir. I'm come to have a bit of your advice; and as the affair won't keep, I have been obliged to disturb you."

"Never mind, Charley," said the Count; "sit down; there's a chair somewhere near the bed—have you found it? There; well now, what is it? What news of Blake?"

"Very bad; no worse. But it is not exactly *that* I came about; I've got into a scrape, sir."

"Run off with one of the daughters?" said Considine. "By jingo, I knew what those artful devils would be after."

"Not so bad as that," said I, laughing. "It's just a row, a kind of squabble; something that must come——"

"Ay, ay," said the Count, brightening up; "say you so, Charley? Begad, the young ones will beat us all out of the field. Who is it with—not old Blake himself—how was it? Tell me all."

I immediately detailed the whole events of the preceding chapter, as well as his frequent interruptions would permit, and concluded by asking what further step was now to be taken, as I was resolved the matter should be concluded before it came to my uncle's ears.

"There you are all right—quite correct, my boy. But there are many points I should have wished otherwise in the conduct of the affair hitherto."

Conceiving he was displeased at my petulance and boldness, I was about to commence a kind of defence, when he added,—

"Because, you see," said he, assuming an oracular tone of voice, "throwing a wine-glass, with or without wine, in a man's face, is merely, as you may observe, a mark of denial and displeasure at some observation he may have made, not in anywise intended to injure him, further than in the wound to his honor at being so insulted, for which, of course, he must subsequently call you out. Whereas, Charley, in the present case, the view I take is different; the expression of Mr. Bodkin as regards your uncle was insulting to a degree—gratuitously offensive, and warranting a blow. Therefore, my boy, you should, under such circumstances, have preferred aiming at him with a decanter—a cut-glass decanter, well aimed and low, I have seen do effective service. However, as you remark it was your first thing of the kind, I am pleased with you—very much pleased with you. Now, then, for the next step." So saying, he arose from his bed, and striking a light with a tinder-box, proceeded to dress himself as leisurely as if for a dinner party, talking all the while.

"I will just take Godfrey's tax-cart and the roan mare on to Meelish; put them up at the little inn—it is not above a mile from Bodkin's—and I'll go over and settle the thing for you. You must stay quiet until I come back, and not leave the house on any account. I've got a case of old. broad barrels there that will answer you beautifully; if you were anything of a shot, I'd give you my own cross handles, but they'd only spoil your shooting."

"I can hit a wine-glass in the stem at fifteen paces," said I, rather nettled at the disparaging tone in which he spoke of my performance.

"I don't care sixpence for that: the wine-glass had no pistol in his hand. Take the old German, then; see now, hold your pistol thus: no finger on the guard, there, these two on the trigger. They are not hair-triggers; drop the muzzle a bit; bend your elbow a trifle more; sight your man outside your arm—outside, mind, and take him in the hip, and, if anywhere higher, no matter."

By this time the Count had completed his toilette, and, taking the small mahogany box which contained his "peace-makers" under his arm, led the way towards the stables. When we reached the yard, the only person stirring there was a kind of half-witted boy, who, being about the house, was employed to run messages for the servants, walk a stranger's horse, or to do any of the many petty services that regular domestics contrive always to devolve upon some adopted subordinate. He was seated upon a stone step, formerly used for mounting, and though the day was scarcely breaking, and the weather severe and piercing, the poor fellow was singing an Irish song, in a low monotonous tone, as he chafed a curb chain between his hands with some sand. As we came near he started up, and, as he pulled off his cap to salute us, gave a sharp and piercing glance at the Count, then at me; then once more upon my companion, from whom his eyes were turned to the brass-bound box beneath his arm. Then, as if seized with a sudden impulse, he started on his feet, and set off towards the house with the speed of a greyhound, not, however, before Considine's practised eye had anticipated his plan ; for, throwing down the pistol-case, he dashed after him, and in an instant had seized him by the collar.

"It won't do, Patsey," said the Count; "you can't double on me."

"Oh, Count, darlin', Mister Considine, avick, don't do it, don't now," said the poor fellow, falling on his knees, and blubbering like an infant.

" Hold your tongue, you villain, or I'll cut it out of your head," said Considine.

"And so I will; but don't do it—don't, for the love of——"

" Don't do what, you whimpering scoundrel ? What does he think I'll do ?"

" Don't I know very well what you're after, what you're always after, too? oh, wirra, wirra !" Here he wrung his hands and· swayed himself backward and forward, a true picture of Irish grief.

" I'll stop this blubbering," said Considine, opening the box, and taking out a pistol, which he cocked leisurely, and pointed at the poor fellow's head; "another syllable now, and I'll scatter your brains upon that pavement."

"And do, and divil thank you ; sure, it's your trade."

The coolness of the reply threw us both off our guard so completely, that we burst out into a hearty fit of laughing.

" Come, come," said the Count, at last, " this will never do; if he goes on this way, we'll have the whole house about us. Come, then, harness the roan mare, and here's half-a-crown for you."

" I wouldn't touch the best piece in your purse," said the poor boy ; " sure it's blood-money, no less."

The words were scarcely uttered when Considine seized him by the collar with one hand, and by the wrist with the other, and carried him over the yard to the stable, where, kicking open the door, he threw him on a heap of stones, adding, " If you stir now, I'll break every bone in your body"—a threat that seemed certainly considerably increased in its terrors from the rough gripe he had already experienced, for the lad rolled himself up like a ball, and sobbed as if his heart were breaking.

Very few minutes sufficed us now to harness the mare in the tax-cart, and when all was ready, Considine seized the whip, and locking the stable-door upon Patsey, was about to get up, when a sudden thought struck him. "Charley," said he, "that fellow will find some means to give the alarm; we must take him with us." So saying, he opened the door, and taking the poor fellow by the collar, flung him at my feet in the tax-cart.

We had already lost some time, and the roan mare was put to her fastest speed to make up for it. Our pace became, accordingly, a sharp one; and as the road was bad, and the tax-cart no "patent inaudible," neither of us spoke. To me this was a great relief. The events of the last few days had given them the semblance of years, and all the reflection I could muster was little enough to make anything out of the chaotic mass—love, mischief, and misfortune—in which, I had been involved since my leaving O'Malley Castle.

"Here we are, Charley," said Considine, drawing up short at the door of a little country ale-house, or in Irish parlance, *shebeen*, which stood at the meeting of four bleak roads, in a wild and barren mountain tract beside the Shannon. "Here we are, my boy! jump out and let us be stirring."

"Here, Patsey, my man," said the Count, unravelling the prostrate and doubly-knotted figure at our feet; "lend a hand, Patsey." Much to my astonishment, he obeyed the summons with alacrity, and proceeded to unharness the mare with the greatest despatch. My attention was, however, soon turned from him to my own more immediate concerns, and I followed my companion into the house.

"Joe," said the Count to the host, "is Mr. Bodkin up at the house this morning?"

"He's just passed this way, sir, with Mr. Malowney of Tillnamuck, in the gig, on their way from Mr. Blake's. They stopped here to order horses to go over to O'Malley Castle, and the gossoon is gone to look for a pair."

"All right," said Considine; and added, in a whisper, "we've done it well, Charley, to be beforehand, or the governor would have found it all out, and taken the affair into his own hands. Now, all you have to do is, to stay quietly here till I come back, which will not be above an hour at farthest. Joe, send me the pony—keep an eye on Patsey, that he doesn't play us a trick—the short way to Mr. Bodkin's is through Scariff—ay, I know it well, good-bye, Charley— by the Lord, we'll pepper him."

These were the last words of the worthy Count as he closed the door behind him, and left me to my own not very agreeable reflections. Independently of my youth and perfect ignorance of the world, which left me unable to form any correct judgment on my conduct, I knew that I had taken a great deal of wine, and was highly excited when my unhappy collision with Mr. Bodkin occurred. Whether, then, I had been betrayed into anything which could fairly have provoked his insulting retort or not, I could not remember; and now my most afflicting thought was, what opinion might be entertained of me by those at Mr. Blake's table; and, above all, what Miss Dashwood herself would think, and what narrative of the occurrence would reach her. The great effort of my last few days had been to stand well in her estimation, to appear something better in feeling, something higher in principle, than the rude and unpolished squirearchy about me, and now here was the end of it! What would she, what could she, think, but that I was the same punch-drinking, rowing, quarrelling bumpkin as those whom I had so lately been carefully endeavoring to separate myself from? How I hated myself for the excess to which passion had betrayed me, and how I detested my opponent as the cause of all my present misery. "How very differently," thought I, "her friend the Captain would have conducted himself. His quiet and gentlemanly manner would have done fully as much to wipe out an insult on his honor as I could do, and, after all, would neither have disturbed the harmony of a dinner-table nor made himself," as I shuddered to think I had, "a subject of rebuke, if not of ridicule." These harassing, torturing reflections continued to press on me, and I paced the room with my hands clasped and the perspiration upon my brow. "One thing is certain,—I can never see her again," thought I; "this disgraceful business must, in some shape or other, become known to her, and all I have been saying these last three days rise up in judgment against this one act, and stamp me an impostor; I that decried—nay, derided—our false notion of honor. Would that Considine would come! What can keep him now?" I walked to the door. A boy belonging to the house was walking the roan before the door. "What had, then, become of Pat?" I inquired; but no one could tell. He had disappeared shortly after our arrival, and had not been seen afterwards. My own thoughts were, however, too engrossing to permit me to think more of this circumstance, and I turned again to enter the house, when I saw Considine advancing up the road at the full speed of his pony.

"Out with the mare, Charley—be alive, my boy—all's settled." So saying, he sprang from the pony, and proceeded to harness the roan with the greatest haste, informing me in broken sentences, as he went on, of all the arrangements.

"We are to cross the bridge of Portumna. They won the ground, and it seems Bodkin likes the spot; he shot Peyton there three years ago. Worse luck now, Charley, you know: by all the rule of chance, he can't expect the same thing twice—never four by honors in two deals—didn't say that, though—a sweet meadow, I know it well; small hillocks, like molehills, all over it—caught him at breakfast; I don't think he expected the message to come from us, but said that it was a very polite attention, and so it was, you know."

So he continued to ramble on as we once more took our seats in the tax-cart, and set out for the ground.

"What are you thinking of, Charley?" said the Count, as I kept silent for some minutes.

"I'm thinking, sir, if I were to kill him, what I must do after."

"Right, my boy; nothing like that, but I'll settle all for you. Upon my conscience, if it wasn't for the chance of his getting into another quarrel and spoiling the election, I'd go back for Godfrey; he'd like to see you break ground so prettily. And you say you're no shot?"

"Never could do anything with the pistol to speak of, sir," said I, remembering his rebuke of the morning.

"I don't mind that: you've a good eye; never take it off. him after you're on the ground—follow him everywhere. Poor Callaghan, that's gone, shot his man always that way. He had a way of looking, without winking, that was very fatal at a short distance— a very good thing to learn, Charley, when you have a little spare time."

Half an hour's sharp driving brought us to the river's side, where a boat had been provided by Considine to ferry us over. It was now about eight o'clock, and a heavy, gloomy morning. Much rain had fallen over night, and the dark and lowering atmosphere seemed charged with more. The mountains looked twice their real size, and all the shadows were increased to an enormous extent. A very killing kind of light it was, as the Count remarked.

CHAPTER VIII.

THE DUEL.

THE boatmen having pulled in towards the shore, we saw, a few hundred yards off, a group of persons standing, whom we soon recognized as our opponents. "Charley," said the Count, grasping my arm tightly, as I stood up to spring on the land— "Charley, although you are only a boy, as I may say, I have no fear for your courage; but, still, more than that is needful here. This Bodkin is a noted duellist, and will try to shake your nerve. Now, mind that you take everything that happens quite with an air of indifference; don't let him think that he has any advantage over you, and you'll see how the tables will be turned in your favor."

"Trust to me, Count," said I; "I'll not disgrace you."

He pressed my hand tightly, and I thought that I discerned something like a slight twitch about the corners of his grim mouth, as if some sudden and painful thought had shot across his mind; but in a moment he was calm and stern-looking as ever.

"Twenty minutes late, Mr. Considine," said a short, red-faced little man, with a military frock and foraging cap, as he held out his watch in evidence.

"I can only say, Captain Malowney, that we lost no time since we parted; we had some difficuly in finding a boat; but, in any case, we are here *now*, and that, I opine, is the important part of the matter."

"Quite right—very just indeed. Will you present me to your young friend—very proud to make your acquaintance, sir; your uncle and I met more than once in this kind of way. I was out with him in '92—was it? no, I think it was '93—when he shot Harry Burgoyne, who, by the bye, was called the crack shot of our mess; but, begad, your uncle knocked his pistol hand to shivers, saying in his dry way, 'He must try the left hand this morning.' Count, a little this side, if you please."

While Considine and the Captain walked a few paces apart from where I stood, I had leisure to observe my antagonist, who stood among a group of his friends, talking and laughing away in great spirits. As the tone they spoke in was none of the lowest, I could catch much of their conversation at the distance I was from them. They were discussing the last occasion that Bodkin had visited this spot, and talking of the fatal event which happened then.

" Poor devil," said Bodkin, "it wasn't his fault; but you see some of the —th had been showing white feathers before that, and he was obliged to go out. In fact, the Colonel himself said, 'Fight or leave the corps.' Well, out he came. It was a cold morning in February, with a frost the night before going off in a thin rain. Well, it seems he had the consumption or something of that sort, with a great cough and spitting of blood, and this weather made him worse, and he was very weak when he came to the ground. Now, the moment I got a glimpse of him, I said to myself, 'He's pluck enough, but as nervous as a lady;' for his eyes wandered all about, and his mouth was constantly twitching. 'Take off your greatcoat, Ned,' said one of his people, when they were going to put him up; 'take it off, man.' He seemed to hesitate for an instant, when Michael Blake remarked, 'Arrah, let him alone; it's his mother makes him wear it for the cold he has.' They all began to laugh at this, but I kept my eye upon him. And I saw that his cheek grew quite livid, and a kind of gray color, and his eyes filled up. 'I have you now,' said I to myself, and I shot him through the lungs."

"And this poor fellow," thought I, "was the only son of a widowed mother." I walked from the spot to avoid hearing further.

and felt, as I did so, something like a spirit of vengeance rising within me for the fate of one so untimely cut off.

"Here we are, all ready," said Malowney, springing over a small fence into the adjoining field—"take your ground, gentlemen."

Considine took my arm and walked forward. "Charley," said he, "I am to give the signal; I'll drop my glove when you are to fire, but don't look at me at all. I'll manage to catch Bodkin's eye, and do you watch him steadily, and fire when he does."

"I think that the ground we are leaving behind us is rather better," said some one.

"So it is," said Bodkin; "but it might be troublesome to carry the young gentleman down that way—here all is fair and easy."

The next instant we were placed, and I well remember the first thought that struck me was, that there could be no chance of either of us escaping.

"Now, then," said the Count, "I'll walk twelve paces, turn, and drop this glove, at which signal you fire, and *together*, mind. The man who reserves his shot, falls by my hand." This very summary denunciation seemed to meet general approbation, and the Count strutted forth. Notwithstanding the advice of my friend, I could not help turning my eyes from Bodkin to watch the retiring figure of the Count. At length he stopped—a second or two elapsed—he wheeled rapidly round, and let fall the glove. My eye glanced toward my opponent, I raised my pistol and fired. My hat turned half round on my head, and Bodkin fell motionless to the earth. I saw the people around me rush forward; I caught two or three glances thrown at me with an expression of revengeful passion; I felt some one grasp me round the waist, and hurry me from the spot, and it was at least ten minutes after, as we were skimming the surface of the broad Shannon, before I could well collect my scattered faculties to remember all that was passing, as Considine, pointing to the two bullet holes in my hat, remarked, "Sharp practice, Charley; it was the overcharge saved you."

"Is he killed, sir?" I asked.

"Not quite, I believe, but as good; you took him just above the hip."

"Can he recover?" said I, with a voice tremulous from agitation, which I vainly endeavored to conceal from my companion.

"Not if the doctor can help it," said Considine; "for the fool keeps poking about for the ball. But now let's think of the next step; you'll have to leave this, and at once, too."

Little more passed between us. As we rowed towards the shore, Considine was following up his reflections, and I had mine, alas! too many and too bitter to escape from.

As we neared the land, a strange spectacle caught our eye. For a considerable distance along the coast crowds of country people were assembled, who, forming in groups, and breaking into parties of two and three, were evidently watching with great anxiety what was taking place at the opposite side. Now, the distance was at least a mile, and therefore any part of the transaction which had been enacting there must have been quite beyond their view. While I was wondering at this, Considine cried out suddenly, "Too infamous, by Jove! we're murdered men."

"What do you mean?" said I.

"Don't you see that?" said he, pointing to something black which floated from a pole at the opposite side of the river.

"Yes; what is it?"

"It's his coat they've put upon an oar to show the people he's killed—that's all. Every man here's his tenant, and look—there! —they're not giving us much doubt as to their intention." Here a tremendous yell burst forth from the mass of people along the shore, which, rising to a terrific cry, sunk gradually down to a low wailing, then rose and fell again several times as the Irish death-cry filled the air and rose to heaven, as if imploring vengeance on a murderer.

The appalling influence of the *keen*, as it is called, had been familiar to me from my infancy, but it needed the awful situation I was placed in to consummate its horrors. It was at once my accusation and my doom. I knew well—none better—the vengeful character of the Irish peasant of the west, and that my death was certain I had no doubt. The very crime that sat upon my heart quailed its courage and unnerved my arm. As the boatmen looked from us towards the shore, and again at our faces, they, as if instinctively, lay upon their oars, and waited for our decision as to what course to pursue.

"Rig the spritsail, my boys," said Considine, "and let her head lie up the river, and be alive, for I see they're hauling a boat below the little reef there, and will be after us in no time."

The poor fellows, who, although strangers to us, sympathized in what they perceived to be our imminent danger, stepped the light spar which acted as mast, and shook out their scanty rag of canvas in a minute. Considine, meanwhile, went aft, and steadying her head with an oar, held the small craft up to the wind till she lay completely over, and, as she rushed through the water, ran dipping her gunwale through the white foam.

"Where can we make without tacking, boys?" inquired the Count.

"If it blows on as fresh, sir, we'll run you ashore within half a mile of the castle."

"Put an oar to leeward," said Considine, "and keep her up more to the wind, and I promise you, my lads, you will not go home fresh and fasting, if you land us where you say."

"Here they come," said the other boatman, as he pointed back with his finger towards a large yawl which shot suddenly from the shore, with six sturdy fellows pulling at the oars, while three or four others were endeavoring to get up the rigging, which appeared tangled and confused at the bottom of the boat; the white splash of water, which fell each moment beside her, showed that the process of bailing was still continued.

"Ah, then, may I never—av it isn't the ould *Dolphin* they have launched for the cruise," said one of our fellows.

"What's the *Dolphin*, then?"

"An ould boat of the Lord's (Lord Clanricarde's) that didn't see water, except when it rained, these four years, and is sun-cracked from stem to stern."

"She can sail, however," said Considine, who watched with a painful anxiety the rapidity of her course through the water.

"Nabocklish, she was a smuggler's jolly-boat, and well used to it. Look how they're pulling. God pardon them; but they're in no blessed humor this morning."

"Lay out upon your oars, boys; the wind's failing us," cried the Count, as the sail flapped lazily against the mast.

"It's no use, your honor," said the elder; "we'll be only breaking our hearts to no purpose; they're sure to catch us."

"Do as I bid you, at all events. What's that ahead of us there?"

"The Oat Rock, sir. A vessel with grain struck there, and went down with all aboard, four years last winter. There's no channel between it and the shore—all sunk rocks, every inch of it. There's the breeze"—the canvas fell over as he spoke, and the little craft lay down to it till the foaming water bubbled over her lee bow— "keep her head up, sir; higher—higher still;" but Considine little heeded the direction, steering straight for the narrow channel the man alluded to. "Tear and ages, but you're going right for the cloch na quirka!"

"Arrah, an' the devil a taste I'll be drowned for your devarsion," said the other, springing up.

"Sit down there and be still," roared Considine, as he drew a pistol from the case at his feet, "if you don't want some leaden ballast to keep you so. Here, Charley, take this, and if that fellow stirs hand or foot—you understand me."

The two men sat sulkily in the bottom of the boat, which now was actually flying through the water. Considine's object was a clear one; he saw that in sailing we were greatly over-matched, and that our only chance lay in reaching the narrow and dangerous channel between the Oat Rock and the shore, by which we should distance the pursuit, the long reef of rocks that ran out beyond requiring a wide berth to escape from. Nothing but the danger behind us could warrant so rash a daring. The whole channel was dotted with patches of white and breaking foam—the sure evidence of the mischief beneath—while here and there a dash of spurting spray flew up from the dark water, where some cleft rock lay hid below the flood. Escape seemed impossible; but who would not have preferred even so slender a chance with so frightful an alternative behind him! As if to add terror to the scene, Considine had scarcely turned the boat ahead of the channel when a tremendous blackness spread over all around; the thunder pealed forth, and, amid the crashing of the hail and the bright glare of lightning, a squall struck us, and laid us nearly keel uppermost for several minutes. I well remember we rushed through the dark and blackening water, our little craft more than half filled, the oars floating off to leeward, and we ourselves kneeling on the bottom planks for safety. Roll after roll of loud thunder broke, as it were, just above our heads, while, in the swift dashing rain that seemed to hiss around us, every object was hidden, and even the other boat was lost to our view. The two poor fellows! I shall never forget their expression. One, a devout Catholic, had placed a little leaden image of a saint before him in the bow, and implored its intercession with a torturing agony of suspense that wrung my very heart; the other, apparently less alive to such consolations as his Church afforded, remained with his hands clasped, his mouth compressed, his brows knit, and his dark eyes bent upon me with the fierce hatred of a deadly enemy; his eyes were sunken and bloodshot, and all told of some dreadful conflict within; the wild ferocity of his look fascinated my gaze, and amid all the terrors of the scene I could not look from him. As I gazed, a second and more awful squall struck the boat, the mast bent over, and with a loud report like a pistol-shot, smashed at the thwart, and fell over, trailing the sail along the milky sea behind us. Meanwhile, the water rushed clean over us, and the boat seemed settling. At this dreadful moment the sailor's eye was bent upon me, his lips parted, and he muttered, as if to himself, "This it is to go to sea with a murderer." O God! the agony of that moment—the heartfelt and accusing conscience that I was judged and doomed—that the brand of Cain was upon my brow—that my fellow-men had ceased forever to regard me as a brother—that I was an outcast and a wanderer forever. I bent forward till my forehead fell upon my knees, and I wept. Meanwhile, the boat flew through the water, and Considine, who alone among us seemed not to lose his presence of mind, cut away the mast, and sent it overboard. The storm now began to abate, and as the black mass of cloud broke from around us, we beheld the other boat, also dismasted, far behind us, while all on board of her were employed in bailing out the water with which she seemed almost sinking. The curtain of mist which had hidden us from each other no sooner broke than they ceased their labors for a moment, and looking towards us, burst forth into a yell so wild, so savage, and so dreadful, my very heart quailed as its cadence fell upon my ear.

"Safe, my boy," said Considine, clapping me on the shoulder, as he steered the boat forth from its narrow path of danger, and once more reached the broad Shannon—"safe, Charley, though we had a brush for it." In a minute more we reached the land, and drawing our gallant little craft on shore, set out for O'Malley Castle.

CHAPTER IX.

THE RETURN.

O'MALLEY Castle lay about four miles from the spot we landed at, and thither accordingly we bent our steps without loss of time. We had not, however, proceeded far, when, before us on the road, we perceived a mixed assemblage of horse and foot, hurrying along at a tremendous rate. The mob, which consisted of some hundred country people, were armed with sticks, scythes, and pitchforks, and although not preserving any very military aspect in their order of march, were still a force quite formidable enough to make us call a halt, and deliberate upon what we were to do.

"They've outflanked us, Charley," said Considine; "however, all is not yet lost. But see, they've got sight of us—here they come."

At these words the vast mass before us came pouring along, splashing the mud on every side, and huzzaing like so many Indians. In the front ran a bare-legged boy, waving his cap to encourage the rest, who followed him about fifty yards behind.

"Leave that fellow for me," said the Count, coolly examining the lock of his pistol; "I'll pick him out, and load again in time for his friends' arrival. Charley, is that a gentleman I see far back in the crowd? Yes, to be sure it is. He is on a large horse—now he's pressing forward, so let—no—oh—ay—it's Godfrey O'Malley him-

self, and these are our own people." Scarcely were the words out
when a tremendous cheer arose from the multitude, who, recognizing
us at the same instant, sprung from their horses and ran forward to
welcome us. Among the foremost was the scarecrow leader, whom
I at once recognized to be poor Patsey, who, escaping in the morning, had returned at full speed to O'Malley Castle, and raised the
whole country to my rescue. Before I could address one word to
my faithful followers, I was in my uncle's arms.

"Safe, my boy, quite safe?"

"Quite safe, sir."

"No scratch anywhere?"

"Nothing but a hat the worse, sir," said I, showing the two bullet
holes in my headpiece.

His lip quivered as he turned and whispered something into Considine's ear which I heard not; but the Count's reply was, "Devil a
bit,—as cool as you see him this minute."

"And Bodkin, what of him?"

"This day's work's his last," said Considine; "the ball entered
here; but come along, Godfrey; Charley's new at this kind of thing,
and we had better discuss matters in the house."

Half an hour's brisk trot—for we were soon supplied with horses
—brought us back to the Castle, much to the disappointment of our
cortége, who had been promised a *scrimmage*, and went back in very
ill humor at the breach of contract.

The breakfast-room, as we entered, was filled with my uncle's
supporters, all busily engaged over poll-books and booth-tallies, in
preparation for the eventful day of battle. These, however, were
immediately thrown aside to hasten round me, and inquire all the
details of my duel. Considine, happily for me, however, assumed
all the dignity of an historian, and recounted the events of the
morning so much to my honor and glory, that I, who only a little
before felt crushed and bowed down by the misery of my late duel,
began, amid the warm congratulations and eulogiums about me, to
think I was no small hero, and, in fact, something very much resembling "the man for Galway." To this feeling a circumstance
that followed assisted in contributing. While we were eagerly discussing the various results likely to arise from the meeting, a horse
galloped rapidly to the door, and a loud voice called out, "I can't
get off, but tell him to come here." We rushed out and beheld
Captain Malowney, Mr. Bodkin's second, covered with mud from
head to foot, and his horse reeking with foam and sweat. "I am
hurrying on to Athlone for another doctor; but I've called to tell
you that the wound is not supposed to be mortal—he may recover
yet." Without waiting for another word, he dashed spurs into his

5

nag and rattled down the avenue at full gallop. Mr. Bodkin's dear-est friend on earth could not have received the intelligence with more delight, and I now began to listen to the congratulations of my friends with a more tranquil spirit. My uncle, too, seemed much relieved by the information, and heard with great good tem-per my narrative of the few days at Gurt-na-Morra. "So, then," said he, as I concluded, " my opponent is at least a gentleman ; that is a comfort."

"Sir George Dashwood," said I, "from all I have seen, is a re-markably nice person, and I am certain you will meet with only the fair and legitimate opposition of an opposing candidate in him—no mean or unmanly subterfuge."

"All right, Charley. Well, now, your affair of this morning must keep you quiet here for a few days, come what will; by Monday next, when the election takes place, Bodkin's fate will be pretty clear, one way or the other, and if matters go well, you can come into town ; otherwise, I have arranged with Considine to take you over to the Continent for a year or so; but we'll discuss all this in the evening. Now, I must start on a canvass. Boyle expects to meet you at dinner to-day ; he is coming from Athlone on purpose. Now, good-bye !"

When my uncle had gone I sank into a chair, and fell into a musing fit over all the changes a few hours had wrought in me. From a mere boy, whose most serious employment was stocking the house with game, or inspecting the kennel, I had sprung at once into man's estate, was complimented for my coolness, praised for my prowess, lauded for my discretion, by those who were my seniors by nearly half a century! talked to in a tone of confidential inti-macy by my uncle, and, in a word, treated in all respects as an equal —and such was all the work of a few hours. But so it is; the eras in life are separated by a narrow boundary :—some trifling accident, some casual rencontre impels us across the Rubicon, and we pass from infancy to youth—from youth to manhood—from manhood to age—less by the slow and imperceptible step of time than by some one decisive act or passion, which, occurring at a critical moment, elicits a long latent feeling, and impresses our existence with a color that tinges it for many a long year. As for me, I had cut the tie which bound me to the careless gayety of boyhood with a rude gash. In three short days I had fallen deeply, desperately in love, and had wounded, if not killed, an antagonist in a duel. As I medi-tated on these things, I was aroused by the noise of horses' feet in the yard beneath. I opened the window, and beheld no less a person than Captain Hammersley. He was handing a card to a servant, which he was accompanying by a verbal message. The impression of something like hostility on the part of the Captain had never left my mind, and I hastened down stairs just in time to catch him as he turned from the door.

"Ah, Mr. O'Malley!" said he, in a most courteous tone; "they told me you were not at home."

I apologized for the blunder, and begged of him to alight and come in.

"I thank you very much; but, in fact, my hours are now numbered here. I have just received an order to join my regiment; we have been ordered for service, and Sir George has most kindly permitted my giving up my staff appointment. I could not, however, leave the country without shaking hands with you. I owe you a lesson in horsemanship, and I'm only sorry that we are not to have another day together."

"Then you are going out to the Peninsula?" said I.

"Why, we hope so; the Commander-in-Chief, they say, is in great want of cavalry, and we scarcely less in want of something to do. I'm sorry you are not coming with us."

"Would to Heaven I were!" said I, with an earnestness that almost made my brain start.

"Then, why not?"

"Unfortunately, I am peculiarly situated. My worthy uncle, who is all to me in this world, would be quite alone if I were to leave him; and although he has never said so, I know he dreads the possibility of my suggesting such a thing to him, so that between his fears and mine, the matter is never broached by either party, nor do I think ever can be."

"Devilish hard—but I believe you are right; something, however, may turn up yet to alter his mind, and, if so, and if you do take to dragooning, don't forget George Hammersley will be always most delighted to meet you; and so good-bye, O'Malley, good-bye."

He turned his horse's head and was already some paces off, when he returned to my side, and, in a lower tone of voice, said,—

"I ought to mention to you that there has been much discussion on your affair at Blake's table, and only one opinion on the matter among all parties—that you acted perfectly right. Sir George Dashwood—no mean judge of such things—quite approves of your conduct, and I believe wishes you to know as much; and now, once more good-bye."

CHAPTER X.

THE ELECTION.

THE important morning at length arrived, and as I looked from my bedroom window at daybreak, the crowd of carriages of all sorts and shapes, decorated with banners and placards; the incessant bustle; the hurrying hither and thither; the cheering as each new detachment of voters came up, mounted on jaunting-cars, or on horses whose whole caparison consisted in a straw rope for a bridle, and a saddle of the same frail material—all informed me that the election day was come. I lost no further time, but proceeded to dress with all possible despatch. When I appeared in the breakfast-room, it was already filled with some seventy or eighty persons of all ranks and ages, mingled confusedly together, and enjoying the hospitable fare of my uncle's house, while they discussed all the details and prospects of the election. In the hall, the library, the large drawing-room, too, similar parties were also assembled, and, as new comers arrived, the servants were busy in preparing tables before the door and up the large terrace that ran the entire length of the building. Nothing could be more amusing than the incongruous mixture of the guests, who, with every variety of eatable that chance or inclination provided, were thus thrown into close contact, having only this in common—the success of the cause they were engaged in. Here was the old Galway squire, with an ancestry that reached to Noah, sitting side by side with the poor cottier, whose whole earthly possession was what, in Irish phrase, is called a "potato garden," meaning the exactly smallest possible patch of ground out of which a very India-rubber conscience could presume to vote. Here sat the old simple-minded, farmer-like man, in close conversation with a little white-foreheaded, keen-eyed personage, in a black coat and eye-glass—a flash attorney from Dublin, learned in flaws of the registry, and deep in the subtleties of election law. There was an Athlone horse-dealer, whose habitual daily practices in imposing the halt, the lame, and the blind upon the unsuspecting for beasts of blood and mettle, well qualified him for the trickery of a county contest. Then there were scores of squireen gentry, easily recognized on common occasions by a green coat, brass buttons, dirty cords, and dirtier top-boots, a lashwhip, and a half-bred fox-hound; but now, fresh-washed for the day, they presented something of the appearance of a swell mob, adjusted to the meridian of Galway. A mass of frieze-coated, brown-faced, bullet-headed peasantry filled up the large spaces, dotted here and there with a sleek, roguish-eyed priest, or some low electioneering agent, detailing, for the amusement of the company, some of those cunning practices of former times, which, if known to the proper-authorities, would in all likelihood cause the talented narrator to be improving the soil of Sydney, or fishing on the banks of the Swan River; while at the head and foot of each table sat some personal friend of my uncle, whose ready tongue, and still readier pistol, made him a personage of some consequence, not more to his own people than to the enemy. While of such material were the company, the fare before them was no less varied. Here some rubicund squire was deep in amalgamating the contents of a venison pasty with some of Sneyd's oldest claret; his neighbor, less ambitious, and less erudite in such matters, was devouring rashers of bacon, with liberal potations of potteen; some pale-cheeked scion of the law, with all the dust of the Four Courts in his throat, was sipping his humble beverage of black tea beside four sturdy cattle-dealers from Ballinasloe, who were discussing hot whisky punch and *spolcaion* (boiled beef) at the very primitive hour of eight in the morning. Amid the clank of decanters, the clash of knives·and plates, the jingling of glasses, the laughter and voices of the guests were audibly increasing, and the various modes of "running a buck" (*Anglicè*, substituting a vote), or hunting a badger, were talked over on all sides, while the price of a *veal* (a calf) or a voter was disputed with all the energy of debate.

Refusing many an offered place, I went through the different rooms in search of Considine, to whom circumstances of late had somehow greatly attached me.

"Here, Charley," cried a voice I was very familiar with—"here's a place I've been keeping for you."

"Ah, Sir Harry, how do you do? Any of that grouse-pie to spare?"

"Abundance, my boy; but I'm afraid I can't say as much for the liquor; I have been shouting for claret this half-hour in vain; do get us some nutriment down here, and the Lord will reward you. What a pity it is," he added, in a lower tone, to his neighbor—"what a pity a quart bottle won't hold a quart; but I'll bring it before the house one of these days." That he kept his word in this respect, a motion on the books of the Honorable House will bear me witness.

"Is this it?" said he, turning towards a farmer-like old man, who had put some question to him across the table; "is it the apple-pie you'll have?"

"Many thanks to your honor—I'd like it, av it was wholesome."

"And why shouldn't it be wholesome?" said Sir Harry.

"Troth, then, myself does not know; but my father, I heerd tell, died of an apple-plexy, and I'm afeerd of it."

I at length found Considine, and learned that, as a very good account of Bodkin had arrived, there was no reason why I should not proceed to the hustings; but I was secretly charged not to take any prominent part in the day's proceedings. My uncle I only saw for an instant; he begged me to be careful, avoid all scrapes, and not to quit Considine. It was past ten o'clock when our formidable procession got under way, and headed towards the town of Galway. The road was for miles crowded with our followers; banners flying and music playing, we presented something of the spectacle of a very ragged army on its march. At every cross-road a mountain-path reinforcement awaited us, and, as we wended along, our numbers were momentarily increasing; here and there along the line, some energetic and not over-sober adherent was regaling his auditory with a speech in laudation of the O'Malleys since the days of Moses, and more than one priest was heard threatening the terrors of his Church in aid of a cause to whose success he was pledged and bound. I rode beside the Count, who, surrounded by a group of choice spirits, recounted the various happy inventions by which he had on divers occasions substituted a personal quarrel for a contest. Boyle also contributed his share of election anecdote, and one incident he related which I remember amused me much at the time.

"Do you remember Billy Calvert, that came down to contest Kilkenny?" inquired Sir Harry.

"What! ever forget him!" said Considine, "with his well-powdered wig, and his hessians. There never was his equal for lace ruffles and rings."

"You never heard, maybe, how he lost the election?"

"He resigned, I believe, or something of that sort."

"No, no," said another; "he never came forward at all; there's some secret in it, for Tom Butler was elected without a contest."

"Jack, I'll tell you how it happened. I was on my way up from Cork, having finished my own business, and just carried the day, not without a push for it. When we reached—Lady Mary was with me—when we reached Kilkenny, the night before the election, I was not ten minutes in town till Butler heard of it, and sent off express to see me; I was at my dinner when the messenger came, and promised to go over when I'd done; but, faith, Tom didn't wait, but came rushing up stairs himself, and dashed into the room in the greatest hurry.

"'Harry,' says he, 'I'm done for; the corporation of free smiths, that were always above bribery, having voted for myself and my father before, for four pounds ten a man, won't come forward under six guineas and whisky. Calvert has the money; they know it.

The devil a farthing we have; and we've been paying for all our fellows that can't read in Hennesy's notes, and you know the bank's broke these three weeks.'

"On he went, giving me a most disastrous picture of his cause, and concluded by asking if I could suggest anything under the circumstances.

"'You couldn't get a decent mob and clear the poll?'

"'I am afraid not,' said he, despondingly.

"'Then I don't see what's to be done, if you can't pick a fight with himself. Will he go out?'

"'Lord knows; they say he's so afraid of that, that it has prevented him coming down till the very day. But he is arrived now; he came in the evening, and is stopping at Walsh's in Patrick street.'

"'Then I'll see what can be done,' said I.

"'Is that Calvert the little man that blushes when the Lady-Lieutenant speaks to him?' said Lady Mary.

"'The very man.'

"'Would it be of any use to you if he could not come on the hustings to-morrow?' said she again.

"''Twould gain us the day; half the voters don't believe he's here at all, and his chief agent cheated all the people on the last election, and if Calvert didn't appear, he wouldn't have ten votes to register. But why do you ask?'

"'Why, that, if you like, I'll bet you a pair of diamond earrings he shan't show.'

"'Done,' said Butler; 'and I promise a necklace into the bargain, if you win; but I'm afraid you're only quizzing me.'

"'Here's my hand on it,' said she; 'and now let's talk of something else.'

"As Lady Mary never asked my assistance, and as I knew she was very well able to perform whatever she undertook, you may be sure I gave myself very little trouble about the whole affair, and when they came, I went off to breakfast with Tom's committee, not knowing anything that was to be done.

"Calvert had given orders that he was to be called at eight o'clock, and so a few minutes before that time a gentle knock came to the door.

"'Come in,' said he, thinking it was the waiter, and covering himself up in the clothes,—for he was the most bashful creature ever was seen,—'come in.'

"The door opened, and what was his horror to find that a lady entered the room in her dressing-gown, her hair on her shoulders, very much tossed and dishevelled! The moment she came in she closed the door, and locked it, and then sat leisurely down upon a chair.

"Billy's teeth chattered, and his limbs trembled, for this was an adventure of a very novel kind for him. At last he took courage to speak.

"'I am afraid, madam,' said he, 'that you are under some unhappy mistake, and that you suppose this chamber is——'

"'Mr. Calvert's,' said the lady, with a solemn voice, 'is it not?'

"'Yes, madam, I am that person.'

"'Thank God,' said the lady, with a very impressive tone; 'here I am safe.'

"Billy grew very much puzzled at these words; but hoping that, by his silence, the lady would proceed to some explanation, he said no more. She, however, seemed to think that nothing further was necessary, and sat still and motionless, with her hands before her and her eyes fixed on Billy.

"'You seem to forget me, sir?' said she, with a faint smile.

"'I do, indeed, madam; the half-light, the novelty of your costume, and the strangeness of the circumstance altogether, must plead for me—if I appear rude enough.'

"'I am Lady Mary Boyle,' said she.

"'I do remember you, madam; but may I ask——?'

"'Yes, yes, I know what you would ask; you would say, why are you here? how comes it that you have so far outstepped the propriety of which your whole life is an example, that alone, at such a time, you appear in the chamber of a man whose character for gallantry——?'

"'Oh, indeed—indeed, my lady, nothing of the kind.'

"'Ah, alas! poor defenceless women learn too late how constantly associated is the retiring modesty which decries with the pleasing powers which ensure success——'

"Here she sobbed, Billy blushed, and the clock struck nine.

"'May I then beg, madam——'

"'Yes, yes, you shall hear it all; but my poor scattered faculties will not be the clearer by your hurrying me. You know, perhaps,' continued she, 'that my maiden name was Rogers?' He of the blankets bowed, and she resumed. 'It is now eighteen years since that a young, unsuspecting, fond creature, reared in all the care and fondness of doting parents, tempted her first step in life, and trusted her fate to another's keeping. I am that unhappy person; the other, that monster in human guise that smiled but to betray, that won but to ruin and destroy, is he whom you know as Sir Harry Boyle.'

"Here she sobbed for some minutes, wiped her eyes, and resumed her narrative. Beginning at the period of her marriage, she detailed a number of circumstances, which poor Calvert, in all his anxiety to come *au fond* at matters, could never perceive bore upon the question in any way; but as she recounted them all with great force and precision, entreating him to bear in mind certain circumstances to which she should recur by-and-by, his attention was kept on the stretch, and it was only when the clock struck ten that he was fully aware how his morning was passing, and what surmises his absence might originate.

"'May I interrupt you for a moment, dear madam? Was it nine or ten o'clock which struck last?'

"'How should I know?' said she, frantically. 'What are hours and minutes to her who has passed long years of misery?'

"'Very true—very true,' replied he timidly, and rather fearing for the intellects of his fair companion.

"She continued.

"The narrative, however, so far from becoming clearer, grew gradually more confused and intricate, and as frequent references were made by the lady to some previous statement, Calvert was more than once rebuked for forgetfulness and inattention, where, in reality, nothing less than shorthand could have borne him through.

"'Was it in '93 I said Sir Harry left me at Tuam?'

"'Upon my life, madam, I am afraid to aver; but it strikes me——'

"'Gracious powers! and this is he whom I fondly trusted to make the depository of my woes—cruel, cruel man.' Here she sobbed considerably for several minutes, and spoke not.

"A loud cheer of 'Butler for ever!' from the mob without now burst upon their hearing, and recalled poor Calvert at once to the thought that the hours were speeding fast, and no prospect of the everlasting tale coming to an end.

"'I am deeply, most deeply grieved, my dear madam,' said the little man, sitting up in a pyramid of blankets, 'but hours, minutes, are most precious to me this morning. I am about to be proposed as member for Kilkenny.'

"At these words the lady straightened her figure out, threw her arms at either side, and burst into a fit of laughter, which poor Calvert knew at once to be hysterics. Here was a pretty situation. The bell-rope lay against the opposite wall, and even if it did not, would he be exactly warranted in pulling it?

"'May the devil and all his angels take Sir Harry Boyle and his whole connection to the fifth generation,' was his sincere prayer, as he sat, like a Chinese juggler, under his canopy.

"At length the violence of the paroxysm seemed to subside, the sobs became less frequent, the kicking less forcible, and the lady's eyes closed, and she appeared to have fallen asleep.

"'Now is the moment,' said Billy; 'if I could only get as far as my dressing-gown.' So saying, he worked himself down noiselessly to the foot of his bed, looked fixedly at the fallen lids of the sleeping lady, and essayed one leg from the blankets. 'Now or never,' said he, pushing aside the curtain, and preparing for a spring. One more look he cast at his companion, and then leaped forth; but just as he lit upon the floor, she again roused herself, screaming with horror. Billy fell upon the bed, and, rolling himself in the bedclothes, vowed never to rise again till she was out of the visible horizon.

"'What is all this? what do you mean, sir?' said the lady, reddening with indignation.

"'Nothing, upon my soul, madam; it was only my dressing-gown!'

"'Your dressing-gown!' said she, with an emphasis worthy of Siddons; 'a likely story for Sir Harry to believe, sir. Fie, fie, sir.'

"This last allusion seemed a settler, for the luckless Calvert heaved a profound sigh, and sunk down as if all hope had left him. 'Butler for ever!' roared the mob; 'Calvert for ever!' cried a boy's voice from without. 'Three groans for the runaway!' answered this announcement; and a very tender inquiry of, 'Where is he?' was raised by some hundred mouths.

"'Madam,' said the almost frantic listener—'madam, I must get up; I must dress. I beg of you to permit me.'

"'I have nothing to refuse, sir. Alas! disdain has long been my only portion. Get up, if you will.'

"'But,' said the astonished man, who was well-nigh deranged at the coolness of this reply—'but how am I to do so if you sit there?'

"'Sorry for any inconvenience I may cause you; but, in the crowded state of the hotel, I hope you see the impropriety of my walking about the passages in this costume?'

"'And, great God! madam, why did you come out in it?'

"A cheer from the mob prevented her reply being audible. One o'clock tolled out from the great bell of the cathedral.

"'There's one o'clock, as I live.'

"'I heard it,' said the lady.

"'The shouts are increasing. What is that I hear? *Butler is in.* Gracious mercy, is the election over?'

"The lady stepped to the window, drew aside the curtain, and said, 'Indeed it would appear so. The mob are cheering Mr. Butler.' [A deafening shout burst from the street.] 'Perhaps you'd like to see the fun, so I'll not detain you any longer. So, good-bye, Mr. Calvert; and as your breakfast will be cold, in all likelihood, come down to No. 4, for Sir Harry is a late man, and will be glad to see you.'"

CHAPTER XI.

AN ADVENTURE.

WHILE thus we lightened our way with chatting, the increasing concourse of people, and the greater throng of carriages that filled the road, announced that we had nearly reached our destination.

"Considine," said my uncle, riding up to where we were, "I have just got a few lines from Davern. It seems Bodkin's people are afraid to come in; they know what they must expect, and if so, more than half of that barony is lost to our opponent."

"Then he has no chance whatever."

"He never had, in my opinion," said Sir Harry.

"We'll see soon," said my uncle, cheerfully, and rode to the post.

The remainder of the way was occupied in discussing the various possibilities of the election, into which I was rejoiced to find that defeat never entered.

In the goodly days I speak of, a county contest was a very different thing indeed from the tame and insipid farce that now passes under that name; where a briefless barrister, bullied by both sides, sits as assessor—a few drunken voters—a radical O'Connellite grocer—a demagogue priest—a deputy grand purple something from the Trinity College lodge, with some half-dozen followers, shouting, "To the devil with Peel!" or "Down with Deus!" form the whole *corps de ballet.* No, no; in the times I refer to, the voters were some thousands in number, and the adverse parties took the field, far less dependent for success upon previous pledge or promise made them than upon the actual stratagem of the day. Each went forth, like a general to battle, surrounded by a numerous and well-chosen staff; one party of friends, acting as commissariat, attended to the victualing of the voters,—that they obtained a due, or rather undue, allowance of liquor, and came properly drunk to the poll; others, again, broke into skirmishing parties, and, scattered over the country, cut off the enemy's supplies, breaking down their post-chaises, upsetting their jaunting-cars, stealing their poll-books, and kidnapping their agents. Then there were secret service people, bribing the enemy and enticing them to desert; and lastly, there was a species of sapper-and-miner force, who invented false documents, denied the identity of the opposite party's people, and, when hard pushed, provided persons who took bribes from the enemy, and gave evidence afterwards on a petition. Amid all these encounters of wit and ingenuity, the personal friends of the candidate formed a species of rifle brigade, picking out the enemy's officers, and doing sore damage to their tactics by shooting a proposer, or wounding a seconder—a considerable portion of every leading agent's fee being intended as compensation for the duels he might, could, would, should, or ought to fight during the election. Such, in brief, was a contest in the olden time; and when it is taken into consideration that it usually lasted a fortnight or three weeks, that a considerable military force was always engaged (for our Irish law permits this), and which, when nothing pressing was doing, was regularly assailed by both parties,—that far more dependence was placed in a bludgeon than a pistol,—and that the man who registered a vote without a cracked pate was regarded as a kind of natural phenomenon, some faint idea may be formed how much such a scene must have contributed to the peace of the county, and the happiness and welfare of all concerned in it.

As we rode along, a loud cheer from a road that ran parallel to the one we were pursuing attracted our attention, and we perceived that a cortége of the opposite party was hastening on to the hustings. I could distinguish the Blake girls on horseback among a crowd of officers in undress, and saw something like a bonnet in the carriage-and-four which headed the procession, and which I judged to be that of Sir George Dashwood. My heart beat strongly as I strained my eyes to see if Miss Dashwood was there; but I could not discern her, and it was with a sense of relief that I reflected on the possibility of our not meeting under circumstances wherein our feelings and interests were so completely opposed. While I was engaged in making this survey, I had accidentally dropped behind my companions; my eyes were firmly fixed upon that carriage, and in the faint hope that it contained the object of all my wishes, I forgot everything else. At length the cortége entered the town, and, passing beneath a heavy stone gateway, was lost to my view. I was still lost in reverie, when an under-agent of my uncle's rode up.

"Oh! Master Charles," said he, "what's to be done? They've forgotten Mr. Holmes at Woodford, and we haven't a carriage, chaise, or even a car left to send for him."

"Have you told Mr. Considine?" inquired I.

"And sure you know yourself how little Mr. Considine thinks of a lawyer. It's small comfort he'd give me if I went to tell him. If it was a case of pistols or a bullet mould, he'd ride back the whole way himself for them."

"Try Sir Harry Boyle, then."

"He's making a speech this minute before the Court-house."

This had sufficed to show me how far behind my companions I had been loitering, when a cheer from the distant road again turned my eyes in that direction; it was the Dashwood carriage returning after leaving Sir George at the hustings. The head of the britska, before thrown open, was now closed, and I could not make out if any one were inside.

"Devil a doubt of it," said the agent, in answer to some question of a farmer who rode beside him; "will you stand to me?"

"Troth, to be sure I will."

"Here goes, then," said he, gathering up his reins and turning his horse towards the fence at the roadside; "follow me now, boys."

The order was well obeyed, for when he had cleared the ditch, a dozen stout country fellows, well mounted, were beside him. Away they went at a hunting pace, taking every leap before them, and heading towards the road before us.

Without thinking further of the matter, I was laughing at the droll effect the line of frieze coats presented as they rode side by side, over the stone walls, when an observation near me aroused my attention.

"Ah, then, av they know anything of Tim Finucane, they'll give it up peaceably; it's little he'd think of taking the coach from under the judge himself."

"What are they about, boys?" said I.

"Goin' to take the chaise-and-four forninst ye, yer honor," said the man.

I waited not to hear more, but darting spurs into my horse's sides, cleared the fence in one bound. My horse, a strong-knit half-bred, was as fast as a racer for a short distance; so that when the agent and his party had come up with the carriage, I was only a few hundred yards behind. I shouted out with all my might, but they either heard not or heeded not, for scarcely was the first man over the fence into the road, when the postilion on the leader was felled to the ground, and his place supplied by his slayer; the boy on the wheeler shared the same fate, and in an instant, so well managed was the attack, the carriage was in possession of the assailants. Four stout fellows had climbed into the box and the rumble, and six others were climbing to the interior, regardless of the aid of steps. By this time the Dashwood party had got the alarm, and returned in full force—not, however, before the other had laid whip to the horses, and set out in full gallop; and now commenced the most terrific race I ever witnessed.

The four carriage-horses, which were the property of Sir George, were English thorough-breds of great value, and, totally unaccustomed to the treatment they experienced, dashed forward at a pace that threatened annihilation to the carriage at every bound. The pursuers, though well mounted, were speedily distanced, but followed at a pace that in the end was certain to overtake the carriage. As for myself, I rode on beside the road, at the full speed of my horse, shouting, cursing, imploring, execrating, and beseeching at turns, but all in vain; the yells and shouts of the pursuers and pursued drowned all other sounds, except when the thundering crash of the horses' feet rose above all. The road, like most western Irish roads until the present century, lay straight as an arrow for miles, regardless of every opposing barrier, and in the instance in question crossed a mountain at its very highest point. Towards this pinnacle the pace had been tremendous; but, owing to the higher breeding of the cattle, the carriage party had still the advance, and when they reached the top, they proclaimed the victory by a cheer of triumph and derision. The carriage disappeared beneath the crest of the mountain, and the pursuers halted, as if disposed to relinquish the chase.

"Come on, boys. Never give up," cried I, springing over into the road, and heading the party to which by every right I was opposed.

It was no time for deliberation, and they followed me with a hearty cheer that convinced me I was unknown. The next instant we were on the mountain top, and beheld the carriage half way down beneath us, still galloping at full stretch.

"We have them now," said a voice behind me; "they'll never turn Lurra Bridge, if we only press on."

The speaker was right. The road at the mountain foot turned at a perfect right angle, and then crossed a lofty one-arched bridge, over a mountain torrent that ran deep and boisterously beneath. On we went, gaining at every stride, for the fellows who rode postilion well knew what was before them, and slackened their pace to secure a safe turning. A yell of victory arose from the pursuers, but was answered by the others with a cheer of defiance. The space was now scarcely two hundred yards between us, when the head of the britska was flung down, and a figure that I at once recognized as the redoubted Tim Finucane, one of the boldest and most reckless fellows in the county, was seen standing on the seat, holding— gracious heavens! it was true—holding in his arms the apparently lifeless figure of Miss Dashwood.

" Hold in !" shouted the ruffian, with a voice that rose high above all the other sounds. " Hold in ! or, by the Eternal, I'll throw her, body and bones, into the Lurra Gash !" for such was the torrent called that boiled and foamed a few yards before us.

He had by this time got firmly planted on the hind seat, and held the drooping form on one arm, with all the ease of a giant's grasp.

" For the love of God !" said I, " pull up. I know him well—he'll do it to a certainty if you press on."

"And we know you too," said a ruffianly fellow, with a dark whisker meeting beneath his chin, " and have some scores to settle ère we part——"

But I heard no more. With one tremendous effort I dashed my horse forward. The carriage turned an angle of the road—for an instant was out of sight—another moment I was behind it.

" Stop !" I shouted, with a last effort, but in vain. The horses, maddened and infuriated, sprang forward, and, heedless of all efforts to turn them, the leaders sprang over the low parapet of the bridge, and hanging for a second by the traces, fell with a crash into the swollen torrent beneath. By this time I was beside the carriage. Finucane had now clambered to the box, and, regardless of the death and ruin around, bent upon his murderous object, he lifted the light and girlish form above his head, bent backwards, as if to give greater impulse to his effort, when, twining my lash around my wrist, I levelled my heavy and loaded hunting whip at his head; the weighted ball of lead struck him exactly beneath his hat, he staggered, his hands relaxed, and he fell lifeless to the ground. The same instant I was felled to the earth by a blow from behind, and saw no more.

CHAPTER XII.

MICKEY FREE.

NEARLY three weeks followed the event I have just narrated ere I again was restored to consciousness. The blow by which I was felled—from what hand coming it was never afterwards discovered—had brought on concussion of the brain, and for several days my life was despaired of. As by slow steps I advanced towards recovery, I learned from Considine that Miss Dashwood, whose life was saved by my interference, had testified her gratitude in the warmest manner, and that Sir George had, up to the period of his leaving the country, never omitted a single day to ride over and inquire for me.

"You know, of course," said the Count, supposing such news was the most likely to interest me— "you know we beat them?"

"No, pray tell me all. They've not let me hear anything hitherto!"

"One day finished the whole affair. We polled man for man till past two o'clock, when our fellows lost all patience, and beat their tallies out of the town. The police came up, but they beat the police; then they got soldiers, but begad they were too strong for them too. Sir George witnessed it all, and knowing, besides, how little chance he had of success, deemed it best to give in; so that a little before five o'clock he resigned. I must say no man could behave better. He came across the hustings and shook hands with Godfrey; and, as the news of the scrimmage with his daughter had just arrived, said that he was sorry his prospect of success had not been greater, that, in resigning, he might testify how deeply he felt the debt the O'Malleys had laid him under."

"And my uncle, how did he receive his advances?"

"Like his own honest self; grasped his hand firmly; and upon my soul I think he was half sorry that he gained the day. Do you know, he took a mighty fancy to that blue-eyed daughter of the old General's. Faith, Charley, if he was some twenty years younger, I would not say but—— Come, come, I didn't mean to hurt your feelings; but I have been staying here too long. I'll send up Mickey to sit with you. Mind and don't be talking too much to him."

So saying, the worthy Count left the room, fully impressed that, in hinting at the possibility of my uncle's marrying again, he had said something to ruffle my temper.

For the next two or three weeks my life was one of the most tiresome monotony. Strict injunctions had been given by the doctors to avoid exciting me; and, consequently, every one that came in walked on tiptoe, spoke in whispers, and left me in five minutes. Reading was absolutely forbidden; and, with a sombre half-light to sit in, and chicken broth to support nature, I dragged out as dreary an existence as any gentleman west of Athlone.

Whenever my uncle or Considine was not in the room, my companion was my own servant, Michael, or, as he was better known, "Mickey Free." Now, had Mickey been left to his own free and unrestricted devices, the time would not have hung so heavily; for, among Mike's manifold gifts, he was possessed of a very great flow of gossiping conversation; he knew all that was doing in the county, and never was barren in his information wherever his imagination could come into play. Mickey was the best hurler in the barony, no mean performer on the violin, could dance the national bolero of "Tatter Jack Walsh" in a way that charmed more than one soft heart beneath a red woolsey bodice, and had, withal, the peculiar free-and-easy devil-may-care kind of off-hand Irish way that never deserted him in the midst of his wiliest and most subtle moments, giving to a very deep and cunning fellow all the apparent frankness and openness of a country lad.

He had attached himself to me as a kind of sporting companion; and, growing daily more and more useful, had been gradually admitted to the honors of the kitchen and the prerogatives of cast clothes, without ever having been actually engaged as a servant; and while thus no warrant officer, as, in fact, he discharged all his duties well and punctually, was rated among the ship's company, though no one could say at what precise period he changed his caterpillar existence and became the gay butterfly, with cords and tops, a striped vest, and a most knowing jerry hat, who stalked about the stable yard and bullied the helpers. Such was Mike. He had made his fortune, such as it was, and had a most becoming pride in the fact that he made himself indispensable to an establishment which before he entered it never knew the want of him. As for me, he was everything to me. Mike informed me what horse was strong, why the chestnut mare couldn't go out, and why the black horse could. He knew the arrival of a new covey of partridges quicker than the *Morning Post* does of a noble family from the Continent, and could tell their whereabouts twice as accurately; but his talents took a wider range than field sports afford, and he was the faithful chronicler of every wake, station, wedding, or christening for miles round; and as I took no small pleasure in those very national pastimes, the information was of great value to me. To conclude this brief sketch, Mike was a devout Catholic, in the same sense that he was enthusiastic about anything; that is, he believed and obeyed exactly as far as suited his own peculiar notions of comfort and happiness. Beyond *that*, his skepticism stepped in and saved him from inconvenience; and though he might have been somewhat puzzled to reduce his faith to a rubric, still it answered his purpose, and that was all he wanted. Such, in short, was my valet, Mickey Free, who, had not heavy injunctions been laid on him as to silence and discretion, would well have lightened my weary hours.

"Ah! then, Misther Charles," said he, with a half-suppressed yawn at the long period of probation his tongue had been undergoing in silence—"ah! then, but you were mighty near it."

"Near what?" said I.

"Faith, then, myself doesn't well know. Some say it's purgathory; but it's hard to tell."

6

"I thought you were too good a Catholic, Mickey, to show any doubts on the matter?"

"Maybe I am—maybe I ain't," was the cautious reply.

"Wouldn't Father Roach explain any of your difficulties for you, if you went over to him?"

"Faix, it's little I'd mind his explainings."

"And why not?"

"Easy enough. If you ax ould Miles there, without, what does he be doing with all the powther and shot, wouldn't he tell you he's shooting the rooks, and the magpies, and some other varmint? but myself knows he sells it to Widow Casey, at two-and-fourpence a pound; so belikes Father Roach may be shooting away at the poor souls in purgathory, that all this time are enjoying the hoith of fine living in heaven, ye understand."

"And you think that's the way of it, Mickey?"

"Troth, it's likely. Anyhow, I know it's not the place they make it out."

"Why, how do you mean?"

"Well, then, I'll tell you, Misther Charles; but you must not be saying anything about it afther; for I don't like to talk about these kind of things."

Having pledged myself to the requisite silence and secrecy, Mickey began:

"Maybe you heard tell of the way my father—rest his soul, wherever he is—came to his end. Well, I needn't mind particulars, but, in short, he was murdered in Ballinasloe one night, when he was batin' the whole town with a blackthorn stick he had, more by token, a piece of scythe was stuck at the end of it; a nate weapon, and one he was mighty partial to; but these murdering thieves, the cattle dealers, that never cared for divarsion of any kind, fell on him and broke his skull.

"Well, we had a very agreeable wake, and plenty of the best of everything, and to spare, and I thought it was all over; but somehow, though I paid Father Roach fifteen shillings, and made him mighty drunk, he always gave me a black look whenever I met him, and when I took off my hat, he'd turn away his head displeased like.

"'Murder and ages,' says I, 'what's this for?' but as I've a light heart, I bore up, and didn't think more about it. One day, however, I was coming home from Athlone market, by myself on the road, when Father Roach overtook me. 'Devil a one o' me 'ill take any notice of you now,' says I, 'and we'll see what'll come out of it.' So the priest rid up, and looked me straight in the face.

"'Mickey,' says he—'Mickey.'

"'Father,' says I.

"'Is it that way you salute your clargy,' says he, 'with your caubeen on your head?'

"'Faix,' says I, 'it's little ye mind whether it's an or aff, for you never take the trouble to say, "By your leave," or "Damn your soul," or any other politeness, when we meet.'

"'You're an ungrateful creature,' says he; 'and if you only knew you'd be trembling in your skin before me, this minute.'

"'Devil a tremble,' says I, 'after walking six miles this way."

"'You're an obstinate, hard-hearted sinner,' says he, 'and it's no use in telling you.'

"'Telling me what?' says I, for I was getting curious to make out what he meant.

"'Mickey,' says he, changing his voice, and putting his head down close to me—'Mickey, I saw your father last night.'

"'The saints be merciful to us!' says I; 'did ye?'

"'I did,' says he.

"'Tear an ages,' says I; 'did he tell you what he did with the new corduroys he bought in the fair?'

"'Oh! then you are a could-hearted creature,' says he, 'and I'll not lose time with you.' With that he was going to ride away, when I took hold of the bridle.

"'Father, darling,' says I, 'God pardon me, but them breeches is goin' between me an' my night's rest; but tell me about my father?'

"'Oh! then he's in a melancholy state!'

"'Whereabouts is he?' says I.

"'In purgathory,' says he; 'but he won't be there long.'

"'Well,' says I, 'that's a comfort, anyhow.'

"'I'm glad you think so,' says he; 'but there's more of the other opinion.'

"'What's that?' says I.

"'That hell's worse.'

"'Oh! melia-murther,' says I; 'is that it?'

"'Ay, that's it.'

"Well, I was so terrified and frightened, I said nothing for some time, but trotted along beside the priest's horse.

"'Father,' says I, 'how long will it be before they send him where you know?'

"'It will not be long now,' says he, 'for they're tired entirely with him; they've no peace night or day,' says he. 'Mickey, your father is a mighty hard man.'

"'True for you, Father Roach,' says I to myself; 'av he had only the ould stick with the scythe in it, I wish them joy of his company.'

"'Mickey,' says he, 'I see you're grieved, and I don't wonder; sure it's a great disgrace to a decent family.'

" 'Troth, it is,' says I, ' but my father always liked low company. Could nothing be done for him now, Father Roach?' says I, looking up in the priest's face.

" ' I'm greatly afraid, Mickey ; he was a bad man—a very bad man.'

" ' And ye think he'll go there?' says I.

" ' Indeed, Mickey, I have my fears.'

" ' Upon my conscience,' says I, ' I believe you're right; he was always a restless crayture.'

" ' But it doesn't depind on him,' says the priest, crossly.

" ' And, then, who then?' says I.

" ' Upon yourself, Mickey Free,' says he ; ' God pardon you for it, too.'

" ' Upon me?' says I.

" ' Troth, no less,' says he.; ' how many masses was said for your father's soul?—how many aves?—how many paters?—answer me.'

" ' Devil a one of me knows !—maybe twenty.'

" ' Twenty, twenty—no, nor one.'

" ' And why not?' says I ; ' what for wouldn't ye be helping a poor crayture out of trouble, when it wouldn't cost you more nor a handful of prayers?'

" ' Mickey, I see,' says he, in a solemn tone, ' you're worse nor a haythen : but ye couldn't be other ; ye never come to yer duties.'

" ' Well, father,' says I, looking very penitent, ' how many masses would get him out?'

" ' Now you talk like a sensible man,' says he. ' Now, Mickey, I've hopes for you. Let me see'—here he went countin' upon his fingers, and numberin' to himself for five minutes—' Mickey,' says he, ' I've a batch coming out on Tuesday week, and if you were to make great exertions, perhaps your father could come with them ; that is, av they have made no objections.'

" ' And what for would they?' says I ; ' he was always the hoith of company, and av singing's allowed in them parts——'

" ' God forgive you, Mickey, but yer in a benighted state,' says he, sighing.

" ' Well,' says I, ' how'll we get him out on Tuesday week? for that's bringing things to a focus.'

" ' Two masses in the morning, fastin',' says Father Roach, half aloud, ' is two, and two in the afternoon is four, and two at vespers is six,' says he; ' six masses a day for nine days is close by sixty masses—say sixty,' says he; ' and they'll cost you—mind, Mickey, and don't be telling it again, for it's only to yourself I'd make them so cheap—a matter of three pounds.'

"'Three pounds!' says I; 'be-gorra ye might as well ax me to give you the rock of Cashel.'

"' I'm sorry for ye, Mickey,' says he, gatherin' up the reins to ride off—'I'm sorry for ye; and the time will come when the neglect of your poor father will be a sore stroke agin yourself.'

"'Wait a bit, your riverence,' says I—'wait a bit. Would forty shillings get him out?'

"'Av course it wouldn't,' says he.

"'Maybe,' says I, coaxing—'maybe, av you said that his son was a poor boy that lived by his indhustry, and the times was bad——'

"'Not the least use,' says he.

"'Arrah, but it's hard-hearted they are,' says I. 'Well, see now, I'll give you the money, but I can't afford it all at onst; but I'll pay five shillings a week—will that do?'

"'I'll do my endayvors,' says Father Roach; 'and I'll speak to them to treat him peaceably in the meantime.'

"'Long life to yer riverence, and do. Well, here now, here's five hogs to begin with; and, musha, but I never thought I'd be spending my loose change that way.'

" Father Roach put the six tinpinnies in the pocket of his black leather breeches, said something in Latin, bid me good morning, and rode off.

"Well, to make my story short, I worked late and early to pay the five shillings a week, and I did do it for three weeks regular; then I brought four and fourpence—then it came down to one and tenpence half penny—then ninepence—and, at last, I had nothing at all to bring.

"'Mickey Free,' says the priest, 'ye must stir yourself; your father is mighty displeased at the way you've been doing of late; and av ye kept yer word, he'd be near out by this time.'

"'Troth,' says I, 'it's a very expensive place.'

"'By coorse it is,' says he; 'sure all the quality of the land's there. But, Mickey, my man, with a little exertion, your father's business is easily done. What are you jingling in your pocket there?'

"'It's ten shillings, your riverence, I have to buy seed potatoes.'

"'Hand it here, my son. Isn't it better your father would be enjoying himself in Paradise than if ye were to have all the potatoes in Ireland?'

"'And how do ye know,' says I, ' he's so near out?'

"' How do I know—how do I know, is it?—didn't I see him?'

"'See him! Tear an' ages! was you down there again?'

"'I was,' says he; 'I was down there for three-quarters of an hour yesterday evening, getting out Luke Kennedy's mother. Decent people the Kennedys—never spared expense.'

" 'And ye seen my father?' says I.

" ' I did,' says he; ' he had an ould flannel waistcoat on, and a pipe sticking out of the pocket av it.'

" ' That's him,' says I. ' Had he a hairy cap?'

" ' I didn't mind the cap,' says he; ' but av coorse he wouldn't have it on his head in that place.'

" ' Thrue for you,' says I. ' Did he speak to you?'

" ' He did,' says Father Roach; ' he spoke very hard about the way he was treated down there, that they was always jibin' and jeerin' him about *drink*, and fightin', and the course he led up here, and that it was a queer thing, for the matter of ten shillings, he was to be kept there so long.'

" ' Well,' says I, taking out the ten shillings and counting it with one hand, ' we must do our best, anyhow; and ye think this'll get him out surely?'

" ' I know it will,' says he ; ' for when Luke's mother was leaving the place, and yer father saw the door open, he made a rush at it, and, be-gorra, before it was shut he got his head and one shoulder outside of it, so that, ye see, a thrifle more'll do it.'

" ' Faix, and yer riverence,' says I, ' you've lightened my heart this morning.' And I put my money back again into my pocket.

" ' Why, what do you mean?' says he, growing very red, for he was angry.

" ' Just this,' says I, ' that I've saved my money; for av it was my father you seen, and he'd got his head and one shoulder outside the door, oh, then, by the powers!' says I, ' the devil a gaol or gaoler from hell to Connaught 'ud hould him; so, Father Roach, I wish you the top of the morning.' And I went away laughing; and from that day to this I never heard more of purgathory; and ye see, Master Charles, I think I was right."

Scarcely had Mike concluded when my door was suddenly burst open, and Sir Harry Boyle, without assuming any of his usual precautions respecting silence and quiet, rushed into the room, a broad grin upon his honest features, and his eyes twinkling in a way that evidently showed me something had occurred to amuse him.

" By Jove, Charley, I musn't keep it from you, it's too good a thing not to tell you; do you remember that very essenced young gentleman who accompanied Sir George Dashwood from Dublin, as a kind of electioneering friend?"

" Do you mean Mr. Prettyman?"

" The very man; he was, you are aware, an under-secretary in some government department. Well, it seems that he had come

down among us poor savages as much from motives of learned research and scientific inquiry, as though we had been South Sea
Islanders; report had gifted us humble Galwayans with some very
peculiar traits, and this gifted individual resolved to record them.
Whether the election week might have sufficed his appetite for
wonders I know not, but he was peaceably taking his departure from
the west on Saturday last, when Phil Macnamara met him, and
pressed him to dine that day with a few friends at his house. You
know Phil; so that when I tell you Sam Burke, of Greenmount, and
Roger Doolan were of the party, I need not say that the English
traveller was not left to his own unassisted imagination for his facts;
such anecdotes of our habits and customs as they crammed him with,
it would appear, never were heard before—nothing was too hot or
too heavy for the luckless Cockney, who, when not sipping his
claret, was faithfully recording in his tablet the mems. for a very
brilliant and very original work on Ireland.

"'Fine ccuntry—splendid country—glorious people—gifted—
brave—intelligent—but not happy—alas! Mr. Macnamara, not
happy. But we don't know you, gentlemen—we don't, indeed, at
the other side of the Channel; our notions regarding you are far,
very far from just.'

"'I hope and trust,' said old Burke, 'you'll help them to a better
understanding ere long.'

"'Such, my dear sir, will be the proudest task of my life. The
facts I have heard here this evening have made so profound an impression upon me, that I burn for the moment when I can make
them known to the world at large. To think—just to think, that a
portion of this beautiful island should be steeped in poverty—that
the people not only live upon mere potatoes, but are absolutely
obliged to wear the skins for raiment, as Mr. Doolan has just mentioned to me.'

"'Which accounts for our cultivation of lumpers,' added Mr.
Doolan; 'they being the largest species of the root, and best adapted
for wearing apparel.'

"'I should deem myself culpable, indeed I should, did I not
inform my countrymen upon the real condition of this great country.'

"'Why, after your great opportunities for judging,' said Phil,
'you ought to speak out. You've seen us in a way, I may fairly
affirm, few Englishmen have, and heard more.'

"'That's it—that's the very thing, Mr. Macnamara. I've looked
at you more closely, I've watched you more narrowly, I have witnessed what the French call your *vie intime.*'

"'Begad you have,' said old Burke, with a grin, 'and profited by
it to the utmost.'

"'I've been a spectator of your election contests—I've partaken of your hospitality—I've witnesssd your popular and natural sports—I've been present at your weddings, your fairs, your wakes; but no, I was forgetting, I never saw a wake.'

"'Never saw a wake?' repeated each of the company in turn, as though the gentleman was uttering a sentiment of very dubious veracity.

"'Never,' said Mr. Prettyman, rather abashed at this proof of his incapacity to instruct his English friends upon *all* matters of Irish interest.

"'Well, then,' said Macnamara, 'with a blessing, we'll show you one. Lord forbid that we shouldn't do the honors of our poor country to an intelligent foreigner when he's good enough to come amongst us.'

"'Peter,' said he, turning to the servant behind him, 'who's dead hereabouts?'

"'Sorra one, yer honor. Since the scrimmage at Portumna the place is peaceable.'

"'Who died lately in the neighborhood?'

"'The widow Macbride, yer honor.'

"'Couldn't they take her up again, Peter? My friend here never saw a wake.'

"'I'm afeerd not, for it was the boys roasted her, and she wouldn't be a decent corpse for to show a stranger,' said Peter, in a whisper.

"Mr. Prettyman shuddered at these peaceful indications of the neighborhood, and said nothing.

"'Well, then, Peter, tell Jemmy Divine to take the old musket in my bedroom, and go over to the Clunagh bog—he can't go wrong—there's twelve families there that never pay a halfpenny rent, and *when it's done,* let him give notice to the neighborhood, and we'll have a rousing wake.'

"'You don't mean, Mr. Macnamara—you don't mean to say——' stammered out the Cockney, with a face like a ghost.

"'I only mean to say,' said Phil, laughing, 'that you're keeping the decanter very long at your right hand.'

"Burke contrived to interpose before the Englishman could ask any explanation of what he had just heard—and for some minutes he could only wait in impatient anxiety—when a loud report of a gun close beside the house attracted the attention of the guests; the next moment old Peter entered, his face radiant with smiles.

"'Well, what's that?' said Macnamara.

"''Twas Jimmy, yer honor. As the evening was rainy, he said

he'd take one of the neighbors, and he hadn't to go far, for Andy Moore was going home, and he brought him down at once.'

"'Did he shoot him?' said Mr. Prettyman, while cold perspiration broke over his forehead. 'Did he murder the man?'

"'Sorra murder,' said Peter, disdainfully; 'but why wouldn't he shoot him when the master bid him?'

"I needn't tell you more, Charley; but in ten minutes after, feigning some excuse to leave the room, the terrified Cockney took flight, and offering twenty guineas for a horse to convey him to Athlone, he left Galway, fully convinced 'that they don't yet know us on the other side of the Channel.'"

CHAPTER XIII.

THE JOURNEY.

THE election concluded, the turmoil and excitement of the contest over, all was fast resuming its accustomed routine around us, when one morning my uncle informed me that I was at length to leave my native county, and enter upon the great world as a student of Trinity College, Dublin. Although long since in expectation of this eventful change, it was with no slight feeling of emotion that I contemplated the step, which, removing me at once from all my early friends and associations, was to surround me with new companions and new influences, and place before me very different objects of ambition from those I had hitherto been regarding.

My destiny had been long ago decided; the army had had its share of the family, who brought little more back with them from the wars than a short allowance of members and shattered constitutions; the navy had proved, on more than one occasion, that the fate of the O'Malleys did not incline to hanging; so that, in Irish estimation, but one alternative remained, and that was the bar. Besides, as my uncle remarked, with great truth and foresight, "Charley will be tolerably independent of the public, at all events; for, even if they never send him a brief, there's law enough in the family to last *his* time"—a rather novel reason, by the bye, for making a man a lawyer, and which induced Sir Harry, with his usual clearness, to observe to me,—

"Upon my conscience, boy, you are in luck. If there had been a Bible in the house, I firmly believe he'd have made you a parson."

Considine alone, of all my uncle's advisers, did not concur in this determination respecting me. He set forth, with an eloquence that certainly converted *me*, that my head was better calculated for bearing hard knocks than unravelling knotty points ; that a shako would become it infinitely better than a wig ; and declared, roundly, that a boy who began so well, and had such very pretty notions about shooting, was positively thrown away in the Four Courts. My uncle, however, was firm, and, as old Sir Harry supported him, the day was decided against us, Considine murmuring, as he left the room, something that did not seem quite a brilliant anticipation of the success awaiting me in my legal career. As for myself, though only a silent spectator of the debate, all my wishes were with the Count. From my earliest boyhood a military life had been my strongest desire ; the roll of the drum, and the shrill pipe that played through the little village, with its ragged troop of recruits following, had charms for me I cannot describe ; and had a choice been allowed me, I would infinitely rather have been a sergeant in the dragoons than one of his Majesty's learned in the law. If, then, such had been the cherished feeling of many a year, how much more strongly were my aspirations heightened by the events of the last few days. The tone of superiority I had witnessed in Hammersley, whose conduct to me at parting had placed him high in my esteem—the quiet contempt of civilians, implied in a thousand sly ways—the exalted estimate of his own profession, at once wounded my pride and stimulated my ambition ; and, lastly, more than all, the avowed preference that Lucy Dashwood evinced for a military life, were stronger allies than my own conviction needed to make me long for the army. So completely did the thought possess me, that I felt if I were not a soldier, I cared not what became of me. Life had no other object of ambition for me than military renown, no other success for which I cared to struggle, or would value when obtained. *"Aut Cæsar, aut nullus,"* thought I ; and when my uncle determined I should be a lawyer, I neither murmured nor objected, but hugged myself in the prophecy of Considine, that hinted pretty broadly, "the devil a stupider fellow ever opened a brief ; but he'd have made a slashing light dragoon."

The preliminaries were not long in arranging. It was settled that I should be immediately despatched to Dublin, to the care of Doctor Mooney, then a junior fellow in the University, who would take me into his especial charge, while Sir Harry was to furnish me with a letter to his old friend Dr. Barret, whose advice and assistance he estimated at a very high price. Provided with such documents, I was informed that the gates of knowledge were more than half ajar for me, without an effort upon my part. One only portion of all the arrangements I heard with anything like pleasure ; it was decided that my man Mickey was to accompany me to Dublin, and remain with me during my stay.

It was upon a clear, sharp morning in January, of the year 18—, that I took my place upon the box-seat of the old Galway mail, and set out on my journey. My heart was depressed and my spirits were miserably low. I had all that feeling of sadness which leave-taking inspires, and no sustaining prospect to cheer me in the distance. For the first time in my life, I had seen a tear glisten in my poor uncle's eye, and heard his voice falter as he said, "Farewell!" Notwithstanding the difference of age, we had been perfectly companions together; and as I thought now over all the thousand kindnesses and affectionate instances of his love I had received, my heart gave way, and the tears coursed slowly down my cheeks. I turned to give one last look at the tall chimneys and the old woods, my earliest friends; but a turn of the road had shut out the prospect, and thus I took my leave of Galway.

My friend Mickey, who sat behind with the guard, participated but little in my feelings of regret. The potatoes in the metropolis could scarcely be as wet as the lumpers in Scariff; he had heard that whisky was not dearer, and looked forward to the other delights of the capital with a longing heart. Meanwhile, resolved that no portion of his career should be lost, he was lightening the road by anecdote and song, and held an audience of four people, a very crusty-looking old guard included, in roars of laughter. Mike had contrived, with his usual *savoir faire*, to make himself very agreeable to an extremely pretty-looking country girl, around whose waist he had most lovingly passed his arm, under pretence of keeping her from falling, and to whom, in the midst of all his attentions to the party at large, he devoted himself considerably, pressing his suit with all the aid of his native minstrelsy.

"Hould me tight, Miss Matilda, dear."

"My name's Mary Brady, av ye plase."

"Ay, and I do plase.

> "Oh, Mary Brady, you are my darlin',
> You are my looking-glass, from night till mornin';
> I'd rayther have ye without one farthen,
> Nor Shusey Gallagher and her house and garden.

May I never av I wouldn't, then; and ye needn't be laughing."

"Is his honor at home?"

This speech was addressed to a gaping country fellow, that leaned on his spade to see the coach pass.

"Is his honor at home? I've something for him from Mr. Davern."

Mickey well knew that few western gentlemen were without constant intercourse with the Athlone attorney. The poor countryman accordingly hastened through the fence, and pursued the coach with all speed for above a mile, Mike pretending all the time to be in the greatest anxiety for his overtaking them; until at last, as he stopped in despair, a hearty roar of laughter told him that, in Mickey's parlance, he was " sould."

" Taste it, my dear; devil a harm it'll do ye; it never paid the king sixpence."

Here he filled a little horn vessel from a black bottle he carried, accompanying the action with a song, the air to which, if any of my readers feel disposed to sing it, I may observe bore a resemblance to the well-known " A Fig for St. Denis of France "

"POTTEEN, GOOD LUCK TO YE, DEAR.

"Av I was a monarch in state,
    Like Romulus or Julius Caysar,
With the best of fine victuals to ate,
    And drink like great Nebuchadnezzar,
A rasher of bacon I'd have,
    And potatoes the finest was seen, sir;
And for drink, it's no claret I'd crave,
    But a keg of ould Mullens' potteen, sir,
        With the smell of the smoke on it still.

"They talk of the Romans of ould,
    Whom they say in their own times was frisky;
But trust me, to keep out the could,
    The Romans at home here like whisky.
Sure it warms both the head and the heart,
    It's the soul of all readin' and writin';
It teaches both science and art,
    And disposes for love or for fightin'.
        Oh, potteen, good luck to ye, dear."

This very classic production, and the black bottle which accompanied it, completely established the singer's pre-eminence in the company; and I heard sundry sounds resembling drinking, with frequent good wishes to the provider of the feast—" Long life to ye, Mr. Free," " Your health and inclinations, Mr. Free," &c.—to which Mr. Free responded by drinking those of the company, " av they were vartuous." The amicable relations thus happily established promised a very lasting reign, and would doubtless have enjoyed such, had not a slight incident occurred, which for a brief season interrupted them. At the village where we stopped to breakfast, three very venerable figures presented themselves for places in the inside of the coach. They were habited in black coats, breeches, and gaiters, wore hats of a very ecclesiastic breadth in their brim, and had altogether the peculiar air and bearing which distinguishes their calling, being no less than three Roman Catholic prelates, on their way to Dublin to attend a convocation. While Mickey and his friends, with the ready tact which every low Irishman possesses, immediately perceived who and what these worshipful individuals were, another traveller, who had just assumed his place on the outside, participated but little in the feelings of reverence so manifestly displayed, but gave a sneer of a very ominous kind as the skirt of the last black coat disappeared within the coach. This latter individual was a short, thick-set, bandy-legged man, of about fifty, with an enormous nose, which, whatever its habitual coloring, on the morning in question was of a brilliant purple. He wore a blue coat, with bright buttons, upon which some letters were inscribed, and around his neck was fastened a ribbon of the same color, to which a medal was attached. This he displayed with something of ostentation, whenever an opportunity occurred, and seemed altogether a person who possessed a most satisfactory impression of his own importance. In fact, had not this feeling been participated in by others, Mr. Billy Crow would never have been deputed by No. 13,476 to carry their warrant down to the west country, and establish the nucleus of an Orange Lodge in the town of Foxleigh: such being in brief the reason why he, a well-known manufacturer of "leather continuations" in Dublin, had ventured upon the perilous journey from which he was now returning. Billy was going on his way to town rejoicing, for he had had most brilliant success. The brethren had feasted and fêted him; he had made several splendid orations, with the usual number of prophecies about the speedy downfall of Romanism; the inevitable return of Protestant ascendency; the pleasing prospect that, with increased effort and improved organization, they should soon be able to have everything their own way, and clear the Green Isle of the horrible vermin St. Patrick forgot when banishing the others; and that if Daniel O'Connell (whom might the Lord confound!) could only be hanged, and Sir Harcourt Lees be made Primate of all Ireland, there were still some hopes of peace and prosperity to the country.

Mr. Crow had no sooner assumed his place upon the coach than he saw that he was in the camp of the enemy. Happily for all parties, indeed, in Ireland, political differences have so completely stamped the externals of each party, that he must be a man of small penetration who cannot, in the first five minutes he is thrown among strangers, calculate with considerable certainty whether it will be more conducive to his happiness to sing "Croppies Lie Down," or "The Battle of Ross." As for Billy Crow (long life to him!), you might as well attempt to pass a turkey upon M. Audubon for a giraffe, as endeavor to impose a papist upon him for a true follower of King William. He could have given you more generic distinctions to guide you in the decision than ever did Cuvier to designate an antediluvian mammoth; so that no sooner had he seated himself upon the coach, than he buttoned up his greatcoat, stuck his hands firmly in his side-pockets, pursed up his lips, and looked altogether like a man who, feeling himself out of his element, resolves to "bide his time" in patience, until chance may throw him among more congenial associates. Mickey Free, who was himself no mean proficient in reading a character, at one glance saw his man, and began hammering his brains to see if he could not overreach him. The small portmanteau which contained Billy's wardrobe bore the conspicuous announcement of his name; and as Mickey could read, this was one important step already gained.

He accordingly took the first opportunity of seating himself beside him, and opened the conversation by some very polite observation upon the other's wearing apparel, which is always in the west considered a piece of very courteous attention. By degrees the dialogue prospered, and Mickey began to make some very important revelations about himself and his master, intimating that the "state of the country" was such that a man of his way of thinking had no peace or quiet in it.

"That's him there, forninst ye," said Mickey, "and a better Protestant never hated mass. Ye understand?"

"What!" said Billy, unbuttoning the collar of his coat, to get a fairer view at his companion; "why, I thought you were——"

Here he made some resemblance of the usual manner of blessing one's self.

"Me! devil a more nor yourself, Mr. Crow."

"Why, do you know me, too?"

"Troth, more knows you than you think."

Billy looked very much puzzled at all this. At last he said,—

"And ye tell me that your master there's the right sort?"

"Thrue blue," said Mike, with a wink; "and so is his uncles."

"And where are they when they are at home?"

"In Galway, no less; but they're here now."

"Where?"

"Here."

At these words he gave a knock of his heel to the coach, as if to intimate their whereabouts.

"You don't mean in the coach, do ye?"

"To be sure I do; and, troth, you can't know much of the west, av ye don't know the three Mr. Trenches, of Tallybash. Them's they."

" You don't say so ?"

" Faix, but I do."

" May I never drink the 12th of July if I didn't think they were priests."

" Priests !" said Mickey, in a roar of laughter—"priests !"

" Just priests."

" Be-gorra, though, ye had better keep that to yourself, for they're not the men to have that same said to them."

" Of course, I wouldn't offend them," said Mr. Crow; " faith, it's not me would cast reflections upon such real out-and-outers as they are. And where are they going now ?"

" To Dublin straight; there's to be a grand lodge next week; but sure Mr. Crow knows better than me."

Billy after this became silent. A moody reverie seemed to steal over him, and he was evidently displeased with himself for his want of tact in not discovering the three Mr. Trenches, of Tally-bash, though he only caught sight of their backs.

Mickey Free interrupted not the frame of mind in which he saw conviction was slowly working its way, but, by gently humming in an under-tone the loyal melody of "Croppies Lie Down," fanned the flame he had so dexterously kindled. At length they reached the small town of Kinnegad. While the coach changed horses, Mr. Crow lost not a moment in descending from the top, and, rushing into the little inn, disappeared for a few moments. When he again issued forth, he carried a smoking tumbler of whisky punch, which he continued to stir with a spoon. As he approached the coach door, he tapped gently with his knuckles, upon which the reverend prelate of Maronia, or Mesopotamia, I forget which, inquired what he wanted.

" I ask your pardon, gentlemen," said Billy, " but I thought I'd make bold to ask you to take something warm this cold day."

" Many thanks, my good friend; but we never do," said a bland voice from within.

" I understand," said Billy, with a sly wink; " but there are circumstances now and then—and one might for the honor of the cause, you know. Just put it to your lips, wont you ?"

" Excuse me," said a very rosy-cheeked little prelate, " but nothing stronger than water ——"

" Botheration," thought Billy, as he regarded the speaker's nose. "But I thought," said he, aloud, " that you would not refuse this."

Here he made a peculiar manifestation in the air, which, whatever respect and reverence it might carry to the honest brethren of 13,476, seemed only to increase the wonder and astonishment of the bishops.

"What does he mean?" said one.

"Is he mad?" said another.

"Tear and ages!" said Mr. Crow, getting quite impatient at the slowness of his friend's perception,—"tear and ages, I'm one of yourselves."

"One of us," said the three in chorus—"one of us?"

"Ay, to be sure"—here he took a long pull at the punch—"to be sure I am; here's 'No surrender,' your souls! whoop"—a loud yell accompanying the toast as he drank it.

"Do you mean to insult us?" said Father P——. "Guard, take the fellow."

"Are we to be outraged in this manner?" chorused the priests.

"'July the 1st, in Oldbridge town,'" sang Billy, "and here it is, 'The glorious, pious, and immortal memory of the great and good——'"

"Guard! Where is the guard?"

"'And good King William, that saved us from Popery——'"

"Coachman!—guard!" screamed Father ——.

"'Brass money——'"

"Policeman! policeman!" shouted the priests.

"'Brass money and wooden shoes;' devil may care who hears me," said Billy, who, supposing that the three Mr. Trenches were skulking the avowal of their principles, resolved to assert the pre-eminence of the great cause single-handed and alone.

"'Here's the Pope in the pillory, and the devil pelting him with priests.'"

At these words a kick from behind apprised the loyal champion that a very ragged auditory, who for some time past had not well understood the gist of his eloquence, had at length comprehended enough to be angry. *Ce n'est que le premier pas qui coûte,* certainly in an Irish row. "The merest urchin may light the train; one handful of mud often ignites a shindy that ends in a most bloody battle." And here, no sooner did the *vis a tergo* impel Billy forward, when a severe rap of a closed fist in the eye drove him back, and in one instant he became the centre to a periphery of kicks, cuffs, pullings, and haulings, that left the poor Deputy-Grand not only orange, but blue.

He fought manfully, but numbers carried the day; and when the coach drove off, which it did at last without him, the last thing visible to the outsides was the figure of Mr. Crow, whose hat, minus the crown, had been driven over his head down upon his neck, where it remained like a dress cravat, buffeting a mob of ragged vagabonds, who had so completely metamorphosed the unfortunate man with mud and bruises, that a committee of the grand lodge might actually have been unable to identify him.

As for Mickey and his friends behind, their mirth knew no bounds; and, except the respectable insides, there was not an individual about the coach who ceased to think of and laugh at the incident till we arrived in Dublin, and drew up at the Hibernian, in Dawson street.

CHAPTER XIV.

DUBLIN.

NO sooner had I arrived in Dublin, than my first care was to present myself to Dr. Mooney, by whom I was received in the most cordial manner. In fact, in my utter ignorance of such persons, I had imagined a college fellow to be a character necessarily severe and unbending; and as the only two very great people I had ever seen in my life were the Archbishop of Tuam, and the Chief Baron, when on circuit, I pictured to myself that a University fellow was in all probability a cross between the two, and feared him accordingly.

The Doctor read over my uncle's letter attentively, invited me to partake of his breakfast, and then entered upon something like an account of the life before me, for which Sir Harry Boyle had, however, in some degree prepared me.

"Your uncle, I find, wishes you to live in college; perhaps it is better, too; so that I must look out for chambers for you. Let me see : it will be rather difficult just now to find them." Here he fell for some moments into a musing fit, and merely muttered a few broken sentences, as, "To be sure, if other chambers could be had— but then—and, after all, perhaps, as he is young—besides, Frank will certainly be expelled before long, and then he will have them all to himself. I say, O'Malley, I believe I must quarter you for the present with rather a wild companion ; but as your uncle says you're a prudent fellow"—here he smiled very much, as if my uncle had not said any such thing—"why, you must only take the better care of yourself, until we can make some better arrangement. My pupil, Frank Webber, is at this moment in want of a ' chum,' as the phrase is, his last three having only been domesticated with him for as many weeks ; so that, until we find you a more quiet resting-place, you may take up your abode with him."

During breakfast, the Doctor proceeded to inform me that my destined companion was a young man of excellent family and good fortune, who, with very considerable talent and acquirements, preferred a life of rackety and careless dissipation to prospects of great

7

success in public life, which his connection and family might have secured for him; that he had been originally entered at Oxford, which he was obliged to leave; then tried Cambridge, from which he escaped expulsion by being rusticated, that is, having incurred a sentence of temporary banishment; and, lastly, with what he himself believed to be a total reformation, to stumble on to a degree in the "silent sister."

"This is his third year," said the doctor, "and he is only a freshman, having lost every examination, with abilities enough to sweep the University of its prizes. But come over now, and I'll present you to him."

I followed him down stairs, across the court, to an angle of the old square, where, up the first floor left, to use the college direction, stood the name of Mr. Webber, a large No. 2 being conspicuously painted in the middle of the door, and not over it, as is usually the custom. As we reached the spot, the observations of my companion were lost to me in the tremendous noise and uproar that resounded from within. It seemed as if a number of people were fighting, pretty much as a banditti in a melodrama do, with considerable more of confusion than requisite; a fiddle and a French horn also lent their assistance to shouts and cries, which, to say the best, were not exactly the aids to study I expected in such a place.

Three times was the bell pulled, with a vigor that threatened its downfall, when, at last, as the jingle of it rose above all other noises, suddenly all became hushed and still. A momentary pause succeeded, and the door was opened by a very respectable-looking servant, who, recognizing the Doctor, at once introduced us into the apartment where Mr. Webber was sitting.

In a large and very handsomely-furnished room, where Brussels carpeting and softly-cushioned sofas contrasted strangely with the meagre and comfortless chambers of the Doctor, sat a young man at a small breakfast-table beside the fire. He was attired in a silk dressing-gown and black velvet slippers, and supported his forehead upon a hand of most lady-like whiteness, whose fingers were absolutely covered with rings of great beauty and price. His long silky brown hair fell in rich profusion upon the back of his neck and over his arm, and the whole air and attitude was one which a painter might have copied. So intent was he upon the volumes before him, that he never raised his head at our approach, but continued to read aloud, totally unaware of our presence.

"Dr. Mooney, sir," said the servant.

"*Ton dapamey bominos, prosephe, crione Agamemnon,*" repeated the student, in an ecstasy, and not paying the slightest attention to the announcement.

"Dr. Mooney, sir," repeated the servant in a louder tone, while the Doctor looked around on every side for an explanation of the late uproar, with a face of the most puzzled astonishment.

"*Be dakiown para thina dolekoskion enkos,*" said Mr. Webber, finishing a cup of coffee at a draught.

"Well, Webber, hard at work, I see," said the Doctor.

"Ah, Doctor, I beg pardon! Have you been long here?" said the most soft and insinuating voice, while the speaker passed his taper fingers across his brow, as if to dissipate the traces of deep thought and study.

While the Doctor presented me to my future companion, I could perceive, in the restless and searching look he threw around, that the fracas he had so lately heard was still an unexplained and *vexata questio* in his mind.

"May I offer you a cup of coffee, Mr. O'Malley?" said the youth, with an air of almost timid bashfulness. "The Doctor, I know, breakfasts at a very early hour."

"I say, Webber," said the Doctor, who could no longer restrain his curiosity, "what an awful row I heard here as I came up to the door. I thought Bedlam was broke loose. What could it have been?"

"Ah, you heard it too, sir," said Mr. Webber, smiling most benignly.

"Hear it? to be sure I did. O'Malley and I could not hear ourselves talking with the uproar."

"Yes, indeed, it is very provoking; but, then, what's to be done? One can't complain under the circumstances."

"Why, what do you mean?" said Mooney, anxiously.

"Nothing, sir,—nothing. I'd much rather you'd not ask me; for, after all, I'll change my chambers."

"But why? Explain this at once. I insist upon it."

"Can I depend upon the discretion of your young friend?" said Mr. Webber, gravely.

"Perfectly," said the Doctor, now wound up to the greatest anxiety to learn a secret.

"And you'll promise not to mention the thing except among your friends?"

"I do," said the doctor.

"Well, then," said he, in a low and confident whisper, "it's the Dean."

"The Dean!" said Mooney, with a start. "The Dean! Why, how can it be the Dean?"

"Too true," said Mr. Webber, making a sign of drinking; "too true, Doctor. And then, the moment he is so, he begins smashing the furniture.　Never was anything heard like it.　As for me, as I am now become a reading man, I must go elsewhere."

Now, it so chanced that the worthy Dean, who, albeit a man of the most abstemious habits, possessed a nose which, in color and development, was a most unfortunate witness to call to character, and as Mooney heard Webber narrate circumstantially the frightful excesses of the great functionary, I saw that something like conviction was stealing over him.

"You'll of course never speak of this except to your most intimate ·friends," said Webber.

"Of course not," said the Doctor, as he shook his hand warmly, and prepared to leave the room.　"O'Malley, I leave you here," said he; "Webber and you can talk over your arrangements."

Webber followed the Doctor to the door, whispered something in his ear, to which the other replied, "Very well, I will write; but if your father sends the money, I must insist——"　The rest was lost in protestations and professions of the most fervent kind, amid which the door was shut, and Mr. Webber returned to the room.

Short as was the interspace from the door without to the room within, it was still ample enough to effect a very thorough and remarkable change in the whole external appearance of Mr. Frank Webber; for scarcely had the oaken panel shut out the Doctor, when he appeared no longer the shy, timid, and silvery-toned gentleman of five minutes before, but dashing boldly forward, he seized a key-bugle that lay hid beneath a sofa-cushion, and blew a tremendous blast.

"Come forth, ye demons of the lower world," said he, drawing a cloth from a large table, and discovering the figures of three young men, coiled up beneath.　"Come forth, and fear not, most timorous freshmen that ye are," said he, unlocking a pantry, and liberating two others.　"Gentlemen, let me introduce to your acquaintance Mr. O'Malley.　My chum, gentlemen.　Mr. O'Malley, this is Henry Nesbitt, who has been in college since the days of old Perpendicular, and numbers more cautions than any man who ever had his name on the books.　Here is my particular friend, Cecil Cavendish, the only man who could ever devil kidneys.　Captain Power, Mr. O'Malley—a dashing dragoon, as you see; aide-de-camp to his Excellency the Lord Lieutenant, and love-maker general to Merrion Square West.　These," said he, pointing to the late denizens of the pantry, "are jibs, whose names are neither known to the proctor nor the police-office; but, with due regard to their education and morals, we don't despair."

"By no means," said Power; "but come, let us resume our game."　At these words he took a folio atlas of maps from a small table, and displayed beneath a pack of cards, dealt as if for whist. The two gentlemen to whom I was introduced by name returned to their places; the unknown two put on their boxing-gloves, and all resumed the hilarity which Dr. Mooney's advent had so suddenly interrupted.

"Where's Moore?" said Webber, as he once more seated himself at his breakfast.

"Making a spatch-cock, sir," said the servant.

At the same instant, a little, dapper, jovial-looking personage appeared with the dish in question.

"Mr. O'Malley, Mr. Moore, the gentleman who, by repeated re-monstrances to the board, has succeeded in getting eatable food for the inhabitants of this penitentiary, and has the honored reputation of reforming the commons of college."

"Anything to Godfrey O'Malley, may I ask, sir?" said Moore.

"His nephew," I replied.

"Which of you winged the gentleman the other day for not pass-ing the decanter, or something of that sort?"

"If you mean the affair with Mr. Bodkin, it was I."

"Glorious, that; begad, I thought you were one of us. I say, Power, it was he pinked Bodkin."

"Ah, indeed," said Power, not turning his head from his game; "a pretty shot, I heard—two by honors—and hit him fairly—the odd trick. Hammersley mentioned the thing to me."

"Oh! is he in town?" said I.

"No; he sailed for Portsmouth yesterday. He is to join the 11th —game—I say, Webber, you've lost the rubber."

"Double or quit, and a dinner at Dunleary," said Webber. "We must show O'Malley—confound the Mister—something of the place."

"Agreed."

The whist was resumed; the boxers, now refreshed by a leg of the spatch-cock, returned to their gloves, Mr. Moore took up his violin, Mr. Webber his French horn, and I was left the only unem-ployed man in the company.

"I say, Power, you'd better bring the drag over here for us; we can all go down together."

"I must inform you," said Cavendish, "that, thanks to your phil-anthropic efforts of last night, the passage from Grafton street to Stephen's Green is impracticable." A tremendous roar of laughter followed this announcement; and, though at the time the cause was unknown to me, I may as well mention it here, as I subsequently learned it from my companions.

Among the many peculiar tastes which distinguished Mr. Francis Webber, was an extraordinary fancy for street-begging; he had over and over won large sums upon his success in that difficult walk; and so perfect were his disguises, both of dress, voice, and manner, that he actually at one time succeeded in obtaining charity from his very opponent in the wager. He wrote ballads with the greatest facility, and sang them with infinite pathos and humor; and the old woman at the corner of College Green was certain of an audience when the severity of the night would leave all other minstrelsy deserted. As these feats of *jonglerie* usually terminated in a row, it was a most amusing part of the transaction to see the singer's part taken by the mob against the college men, who, growing impatient to carry him off to supper somewhere, would invariably be obliged to have a fight for the booty.

Now, it chanced that, a few evenings before, Mr. Webber was returning, with a pocket well lined with copper, from a musical *réunion* he had held at the corner of York street, when the idea struck him to stop at the end of Grafton street, where a huge stone grating at that time exhibited—perhaps it exhibits still—the descent to one of the great main sewers of the city.

The light was shining brightly from a pastrycook's shop, and showed the large bars of stone beneath which the muddy water was rushing rapidly down, and plashing in the torrent that ran boisterously several feet beneath.

To stop in the street of any crowded city is, under any circumstances, an invitation for others to do likewise, which is rarely unaccepted; but when, in addition to this, you stand fixedly in one spot, and regard with stern intensity any object near you, the chances are ten to one that you have several companions in your curiosity before a minute expires.

Now, Webber, who had at first stood still, without any peculiar thought in view, no sooner perceived that he was joined by others, than the idea of making something out of it immediately occurred to him.

"What is it, agra?" inquired an old woman, very much in his own style of dress, pulling at the hood of his cloak.

"And can't you see for yourself, darling?" replied he, sharply, as he knelt down, and looked most intensely at the sewer.

"Are ye long there, avick?" inquired he of an imaginary individual below, and then waiting as if for a reply, said, "Two hours! Blessed Virgin! he's two hours in the drain!"

By this time the crowd had reached entirely across the street, and the crushing and squeezing to get near the important spot was awful.

"Where did he come from?" "Who is he?" "How did he get there?" were questions on every side, and various surmises were afloat, till Webber, rising from his knees, said, in a mysterious whisper to those nearest him, "He's made his escape to-night out o' Newgate by the big drain, and lost his way; he was looking for the Liffey, and took the wrong turn."

To an Irish mob, what appeal could equal this? A culprit at any time has his claims upon their sympathy; but let him be caught in the very act of cheating the authorities and evading the law, and his popularity knows no bounds. Webber knew this well, and, as the mob thickened around him, sustained an imaginary conversation that Savage Landor might have envied, imparting now and then such hints concerning the runaway as raised their interest to the highest pitch, and fifty different versions were related on all sides—of the crime he was guilty of, the sentence that was passed on him, and the day he was to suffer.

"Do you see the light, dear?" said Webber, as some ingeniously benevolent individual had lowered down a candle with a string— "do ye see the light? Oh! he's fainted, the creature." A cry of horror from the crowd burst forth at these words, followed by a universal shout of "Break open the street."

Pickaxes, shovels, spades, and crowbars seemed absolutely the walking accompaniments of the crowd, so suddenly did they appear upon the field of action, and the work of exhumation was begun with a vigor that speedily covered nearly half the street with mud and paving-stones. Parties relieved each other at the task, and ere half an hour a hole capable of containing a mail coach was yawning in one of the most frequented thoroughfares of Dublin. Meanwhile, as no appearance of the culprit could be had, dreadful conjectures as to his fate began to gain ground. By this time the authorities had received intimation of what was going forward, and attempted to disperse the crowd; but Webber, who still continued to conduct the prosecution, called on them to resist the police, and save the poor creature. And now began a most terrific fray. The stones, forming a ready weapon, were hurled at the unprepared constables, who, on their side, fought manfully, but against superior numbers; so that, at last, it was only by the aid of a military force the mob could be dispersed, and a riot, which had assumed a very serious character, got under. Meanwhile, Webber had reached his chambers, changed his costume, and was relating over the supper-table the narrative of his philanthropy to a very admiring circle of his friends.

Such was my chum, Frank Webber; and as this was the first anecdote I had heard of him, I relate it here that my readers may be in possession of the grounds upon which my opinion of that celebrated character was founded while yet our acquaintance was in its infancy.

CHAPTER XV.

CAPTAIN POWER.

WITHIN a few weeks after my arrival in town, I had become a matriculated student of the University, and the possessor of chambers within its walls, in conjunction with the sage and prudent gentleman I have introduced to my readers in the last chapter. Had my intentions on entering college been of the most studious and regular kind, the companion into whose society I was then immediately thrown would have quickly dissipated them. He voted morning chapels a bore, Greek lectures a humbug, examinations a farce, and pronounced the statute-book, with its attendant train of fines and punishment, an "unclean thing." With all my country habits and predilections fresh upon me, that I was an easily won disciple to his code need not be wondered at, and, indeed, ere many days had passed over, my thorough indifference to all college rules and regulations had given me a high place in the esteem of Webber and his friends. As for myself, I was most agreeably surprised to find that what I had looked forward to as a very melancholy banishment, was likely to prove a most agreeable sojourn. Under Webber's directions, there was no hour of the day that hung heavily upon our hands. We rose about eleven, and breakfasted; after which succeeded fencing, sparring, billiards, or tennis in the park; about three, got on horseback, and either cantered in the Phœnix or about the squares till visiting time; after which made our calls, and then dressed for dinner, which we never thought of taking at commons, but had it from Morrison's, we both being reported sick in the dean's list, and thereby exempt from the routine fare of the fellows' table. In the evening our occupations became still more pressing. There were balls, suppers, whist parties, rows at the theatre, shindies in the street, devilled drumsticks at Hayes's, select oyster parties at the Carlingford; in fact, in every known method of remaining up all night, and appearing both pale and penitent the following morning.

Webber had a large acquaintance in Dublin, and soon made me known to them all. Among others, the officers of the —th Light Dragoons, in which regiment Power was captain, were his particular friends, and we had frequent invitations to dine at their mess. There it was first that military life presented itself to me in its most attractive possible form, and heightened the passion I already so strongly conceived for the army. Power, above all others, took my fancy. He was a gay, dashing-looking, handsome fellow of about eight-and-twenty, who had already seen some service, having joined while his regiment was in Portugal; was in heart and soul a soldier, and had that species of pride and enthusiasm in all that regarded a military career that form no small part of the charm in the character of a young officer.

I sat near him the second day we dined at the mess, and was much pleased at many slight attentions in his manner towards me.

"I called on you to-day, Mr. O'Malley," said he, "in company with a friend, who is most anxious to see you."

"Indeed," said I; "I did not hear of it."

"We left no cards either of us, as we were determined to make you out on another day; my companion has most urgent reasons for seeing you. I see you are puzzled," said he, "and although I promised to keep his secret, I must blab: it was Sir George Dashwood who was with me; he told us of your most romantic adventure in the west, and, faith, there is no doubt you saved the lady's life."

"Was she worth the trouble of it?" said the old major, whose conjugal experiences imparted a very crusty tone to the question.

"I think," said I, "I need only tell her name to convince you of it."

"Here's a bumper to her," said Power, filling his glass; "and every true man will follow my example."

When the hip, hipping which followed the toast was over, I found myself enjoying no small share of the attention of the party as the deliverer of Lucy Dashwood.

"Sir George is cudgelling his brain to show his gratitude to you," said Power.

"What a pity, for the sake of his peace of mind, that you are not in the army," said another; "it's so easy to show a man a delicate regard by a quick promotion."

"A devil of a pity for his own sake, too," said Power, again; "they're going to make a lawyer of as strapping a fellow as ever carried a sabretasche."

"A lawyer!" cried out half a dozen together, pretty much with the same tone and emphasis as though he had said a twopenny postman—"the devil they are."

"Cut the service at once—you'll get no promotion in it," said the colonel. "A fellow with a black eye like you would look much better at the head of a squadron than a string of witnesses. Trust me, you'd shine more in conducting a picket than a prosecution."

"But if I can't?" said I.

"Then take my plan," said Power, "and make it cut *you*."

"Yours?" said two or three in a breath—"yours?"

"Ay, mine; did you never know that I was bred to the bar?

Come, come, if it was only for O'Malley's use and benefit—as we say in the parchments—I must tell you the story."

The claret was pushed briskly round, chairs drawn up to fill any vacant spaces, and Power began his story.

"As I am not over long-winded, don't be scared at my beginning my history somewhat far back. I began life that most unlucky of all earthly contrivances for supplying casualties in case anything may befall the heir of the house—a species of domestic jury-mast, only lugged out in a gale of wind—a younger son. My brother Tom, a thick-skulled, pudding-headed dog, that had no taste for anything save his dinner, took it into his wise head one morning that he would go into the army, and, although I had been originally destined for a soldier, no sooner was his choice made, than all regard for my taste and inclination was forgotten; and as the family interest was only enough for one, it was decided that I should be put in what is called a 'learned profession,' and let push my fortune. 'Take your choice, Dick,' said my father, with a most benign smile—'take your choice, boy. Will you be a lawyer, a parson, or a doctor?'

"Had he said, 'Will you be put in the stocks, the pillory, or publicly whipped?' I could not have looked more blank than at the question.

"As a decent Protestant, he should have grudged me to the Church; as a philanthropist, he might have scrupled at making me a physician; but as he had lost deeply by law-suits, there looked something very like a lurking malice in sending me to the bar. Now, so far I concurred with him, for having no gift for enduring either sermons or senna, I thought I'd make a bad administrator of either, and as I was ever regarded in the family as rather of a shrewd and quick turn, with a very natural taste for roguery, I began to believe he was right, and that nature intended me for the circuit.

"From the hour my vocation was pronounced, it had been happy for the family that they could have got rid of me. A certain ambition to rise in my profession laid hold on me, and I meditated all day and night how I was to get on. Every trick, every subtle invention to cheat the enemy that I could read of, I treasured up carefully, being fully impressed with the notion that roguery meant law, and equity was only another name for odd and even.

"My days were spent haranguing special juries of housemaids and laundresses, cross-examining the cook, charging the under butler, and passing sentence of death upon the pantry boy, who, I may add, was invariably hanged when the court rose.

"If the mutton were overdone, or the turkey burned, I drew up an indictment against old Margaret, and against the kitchen-maid as accomplice; and the family hungered while I harangued; and, in fact, into such disrepute did I bring the legal profession, by the score of annoyance of which I made it the vehicle, that my father got a kind of holy horror of law courts, judges, and crown solicitors, and absented himself from the assizes the same year, for which, being a high sheriff, he paid a penalty of £500.

"The next day I was sent off in disgrace to Dublin, to begin my career in college, and eat the usual quartos and folios of beef and mutton which qualify a man for the woolsack.

"Years rolled over, in which, after an ineffectual effort to get through college,—the only examination I ever got being a jubilee for the king's birthday,—I was at length called to the Irish bar, and saluted by my friends as Counsellor Power. The whole thing was so like a joke to me, that it kept me in laughter for three terms, and, in fact, it was the best thing that could happen to me, for I had nothing else to do. The hall of the Four Courts was a very pleasant lounge, plenty of agreeable fellows that never earned sixpence, or were likely to do so. Then the circuits were so many country excursions, that supplied fun of one kind or other, but no profit. As for me, I was what was called a good junior. I knew how to look after the waiters, to inspect the decanting of the wine, and the airing of the claret, and was always attentive to the father of the circuit, the crossest old villain that ever was a king's counsel. These eminent qualities, and my being able to sing a song in honor of our own bar, were recommendations enough to make me a favorite, and I was one.

"Now, the reputation I obtained was pleasant enough at first, but I began to wonder that I never got a brief. Somehow, if it rained civil bills or declarations, devil a one would fall upon my head, and it seemed as if the only object I had in life was to accompany the circuit, a kind of deputy-assistant commissary-general, never expected to come into action. To be sure, I was not alone in misfortune; there were several promising youths, who cut great figures in Trinity, in the same predicament, the only difference being that they attributed to jealousy what I expected was forgetfulness, for I don't think a single attorney in Dublin knew one of us.

"Two years passed over, and then I walked the hall with a bag filled with newspapers, to look like briefs, and was regularly called by two or three criers from one court to the other. It never took; even when I used to seduce a country friend to visit the courts, and get him into an animated conversation in a corner between two pillars, devil a one would believe him to be a client, and I was fairly nonplussed.

"'How is a man ever to distinguish himself in such a walk as this?' was my eternal question to myself every morning as I put on my wig. 'My face is as well known here as Lord Manners'; every one says, "How are you, Dick?" "How goes it, Power?" but except Holmes, that said one morning, as he passed me, "Eh, always busy?" no one alludes to the possibility of my having anything to do.'

"'If I could only get a footing,' thought I, 'Lord, how I'd astonish them! As the song says,—

> "Perhaps a recruit
> Might chance to shoot
> Great General Bonaparté."

So,' said I to myself, 'I'll make these halls ring for it some day or other, if the occasion ever present itself.' But, faith, it seemed as if some cunning solicitor overheard me, and told his associates, for they avoided me like a leprosy. The home circuit I had adopted for some time past, for the very palpable reason that, being near town, it was least costly, and it had all the advantages of any other for me, in getting me nothing to do. Well, one morning we were in Philipstown; I was lying awake in bed, thinking how long it would be before I'd sum up resolution to cut the bar, where certainly my prospects were not the most cheering, when some one tapped gently at my door.

"'Come in,' said I.

"The waiter opened gently, and held out his hand with a large roll of paper, tied round with a piece of red tape.

"'Counsellor,' said he, 'handsel.'

"'What do you mean?' said I, jumping out of bed; 'what is it, you villain?'

"'A brief.'

"'A brief: so I see; but it's for Counsellor Kinshella, below stairs.' That was the first name written on it.

"'Bethershin,' said he; 'Mr. M'Grath bid me to give it to you, carefully.'

"By this time I had opened the envelope, and read my own name at full length as junior counsel in the important case of Monaghan v. M'Shean, to be tried in the Record Court at Ballinasloe. 'That will do,' said I, flinging it on the bed with a careless air, as if it were a very every-day matter with me.

"'But, counsellor, darlin', give us a thrifle to dhrink your health with your first cause, and the Lord send you plenty of them.'

"'My first,' said I, with a smile of most ineffable compassion at his simplicity: 'I'm worn out with them; do you know, Peter, I was thinking seriously of leaving the bar, when you came into the room? Upon my conscience, it's in earnest I am.'

"Peter believed me, I think, for I saw him give a very peculiar look as he pocketed his half-crown and left the room.

"The door was scarcely closed when I gave way to the free transport of my ecstasy; there it lay at last, the long looked-for, long wished-for object of all my happiness, and though I well knew that a junior counsel has about as much to do in the conducting of a case as a rusty handspike has in a naval engagement, yet I suffered not such' thoughts to mar the current of my happiness. There was my name in conjunction with the two mighty leaders on the circuit, and though they each pocketed a hundred, I doubt very much if they received their briefs with one half the satisfaction. My joy at length subdued a little. I opened the roll of paper, and began carefully to peruse about fifty pages of narrative regarding a watercourse that once had turned a mill; but, from some reasons doubtless known to itself or its friends, would do so no longer, and thus set two respectable neighbors at loggerheads, and involved them in a record that had been now heard three several times.

"Quite forgetting the subordinate part I was destined to fill, I opened the case in the most flowery oration, in which I descanted upon the benefits accruing to mankind from water-communication since the days of Noah; remarked upon the antiquity of mills, and especially of millers, and consumed half an hour in a preamble of generalities that I hoped would make a very considerable impression upon the court. Just at the critical moment when I was about to enter more particularly into the case, three or four of the great unbriefed came rattling into my room, and broke in upon the oration.

"'I say, Power,' said one 'come and have an hour's skating on the canal; the courts are filled, and we sha'n't be missed.'

"'Skate, my dear friend,' said I, in a most dolorous tone; 'out of the question; see, I am chained to a devilish knotty case with Kinshella and Mills.'

"'Confound your humbugging!' said another; 'that may do very well in Dublin for the attorneys, but not with us.'

"'I don't well understand you,' I replied; 'there is the brief. Hennesy expects me to report upon it this evening, and so I am hurried.'

"Here a very chorus of laughing broke forth, in which, after several vain efforts to resist, I was forced to join, and kept it up with the others.

"When our mirth was over, my friends scrutinized the red tape-tied packet, and pronounced it a real brief, with a degree of surprise that certainly augured little for their familiarity with such objects of natural history.

"When they had left the room, I leisurely examined the all-important document, spreading it out before me upon the table, and surveying it as a newly-anointed sovereign might be supposed to contemplate a map of his dominions.

"'At last,' said I to myself—'at last, and here is the footstep to the woolsack.' For more than an hour I sat motionless, my eyes fixed upon the outspread paper, lost in a very maze of reverie. The ambition which disappointments had crushed, and delay had chilled, came suddenly back, and all my day-dreams of legal success, my cherished aspirations after silk-gowns, and patents of precedence, rushed once more upon me, and I resolved to do or die. Alas! a very little reflection showed me that the latter was perfectly practicable, but that, as a junior counsel, five minutes of very commonplace recitation was all my province, and with the main business of the day I had about as much to do as the call-boy of a playhouse has with the success of a tragedy.

"'My lord, this is an action brought by Timothy Higgin,' &c., and down I go, no more to be remembered and thought of than if I had never existed. How different it would be were I the leader! Zounds, how I would worry the witnesses, browbeat the evidence, cajole the jury, and soften the judges! If the Lord were in his mercy to remove old Mills and Kinshella before Tuesday, who knows but my fortune might be made? This supposition once started, set me speculating upon all the possible chances that might cut off two king's counsel in three days, and left me fairly convinced that my own elevation was certain were they only removed from my path.

"For two whole days the thought never left my mind; and on the evening of the second day I sat moodily over my pint of port, in the Clonbrock Arms, with my friend, Timothy Casey, Captain in the North Cork Militia, for my companion.

"'Fred,' said Tim, 'take off your wine, man. When does this confounded trial come on?'

"'To-morrow,' said I, with a deep groan.

"'Well, well, and if it does, what matter?" he said; 'you'll do well enough, never be afraid.'

"'Alas!' said I, 'you don't understand the cause of my depression.' I here entered upon an account of my sorrows, which lasted for above an hour, and only concluded just as a tremendous noise in the street without announced an arrival. For several minutes, such was the excitement in the house, such running hither and thither, such confusion and such hubbub, that we could not make out who had arrived.

"At last a door opened quite near us, and we saw the waiter assisting a very portly-looking gentleman off with his greatcoat, assuring him the while that, if he would only walk into the coffee-room for ten minutes, the fire in his apartment should be got ready. The stranger accordingly entered and seated himself at the fireplace, having never noticed that Casey and myself—the only persons there—were in the room.

"'I say, Phil, who is he?' inquired Casey of the waiter.

"'Counsellor Mills, Captain,' said the waiter, and left the room.

"'That's your friend,' said Casey.

"'I see,' said I; 'and I wish with all my heart he was at home with his pretty wife in Leeson street.'

"'Is she good-looking?' inquired Tim.

"'Devil a better,' said I; 'and he's as jealous as Old Nick.'

"'Hem,' said Tim; 'mind your cue, and I'll give him a start.' Here he suddenly changed his whispering tone for one in a louder key, and resumed: 'I say, Power, it will make some work for you lawyers. But who can she be? that's the question.' Here he took a much crumpled letter from his pocket, and pretended to read: '"A great sensation was created in the neighborhood of Merrion square yesterday, by the sudden disappearance from her house of the handsome Mrs.——" Confound it—what's the name?—what a hand he writes! Hill, or Miles, or something like that—"the lady of an eminent barrister, now on circuit. The gay Lothario is, they say, the Hon. George ——"' I was so thunderstruck at the rashness of the stroke, I could say nothing, while the old gentleman started as if he had sat down on a pin. Casey, meanwhile, went on.

"'Hell and fury!' said the king's counsel, rushing over; 'what is it you're saying?'

"'You appear warm, old gentleman,' said Casey, putting up the letter, and rising from the table.

"'Show me that letter—show me that infernal letter, sir, this instant!'

"'Show you my letter,' said Casey; 'cool, that, anyhow. You are certainly a good one.'

"'Do you know me, sir? answer me that,' said the lawyer, bursting with passion.

"'Not at present,' said Tim, quietly; 'but I hope to do so in the morning, in explanation of your language and conduct.' A tremendous ringing of the bell here summoned the waiter to the room.

"'Who is that ——?' inquired the lawyer. The epithet he judged it safe to leave unsaid, as he pointed to Casey.

"'Captain Casey, sir; the commanding officer here.'

"'Just so,' said Casey; 'and very much at your service, any hour after five in the morning.'

"'Then you refuse, sir, to explain the paragraph I have just heard you read?'

"'Well done, old gentleman; so you have been listening to a private conversation I held with my friend here. In that case we had better retire to our room.' So saying, he ordered the waiter to send a fresh bottle and glasses to No. 14, and, taking my arm, very politely wished Mr. Mills good night, and left the coffee-room.

"Before we had reached the top of the stairs, the house was once more in commotion. The new arrival had ordered out fresh horses, and was hurrying every one in his impatience to get away. In ten minutes the chaise rolled off from the door, and Casey, putting his head out of the window, wished him a pleasant journey; while turning to me, he said,—

"'There's one of them out of the way for you, if we are even obliged to fight the other.'

"The port was soon despatched, and with it went all the scruples of conscience I had at first felt for the cruel *ruse* we had just practised. Scarcely was the other bottle called for, when we heard the landlord calling out in a stentorian voice,—

"'Two horses, for Goran Bridge, to meet Counsellor Kinshella.'

"'That's the other fellow?' said Casey.

"'It is,' said I.

"'Then we must be stirring,' said he. 'Waiter, chaise and pair in five minutes—d'ye hear? Power, my boy, I don't want you; stay here and study your brief. It's little trouble Counsellor Kinshella will give you in the morning."

"All he would tell me of his plan was, that he didn't mean any serious bodily harm to the counsellor, but that certainly he was not likely to be heard of for twenty-four hours.

"'Meanwhile, Power, go in and win, my boy,' said he; 'such another walk over may never occur.'

"I must not make my story longer. The next morning, the great record of Monaghan *v.* M'Shean was called on, and as the senior counsel were not present, the attorney wished a postponement. I, however, was firm; told the court I was quite prepared, and with such an air of assurance that I actually puzzled the attorney. The case was accordingly opened by me in a very brilliant speech, and the witnesses called; but such was my unlucky ignorance of the whole matter, that I actually broke down the testimony of our own, and fought like a Trojan for the credit and character of the perjurers against us! The judge rubbed his eyes—the jury looked amazed—and the whole bar laughed outright. However, on I went, blundering, floundering, and foundering at every step, and at half-past four, amid the greatest and most uproarious mirth of the whole court, heard the jury deliver a verdict against us just as old Kinshella rushed into the court, covered with mud and spattered with clay. He had been sent for twenty miles to make a will for Mr. Daly of Daly's Mount, who was supposed to be at the point of death, but who, on his arrival, threatened to shoot him for causing an alarm to his family by such an imputation.

"The rest is soon told. They moved for a new trial, and I moved out of the profession. I cut the bar, for it cut me. I joined the gallant 14th as a volunteer, and here I am without a single regret, I must confess, that I didn't succeed in the great record of Monaghan *v.* M'Shean."

Once more the claret went briskly round, and while we canvassed Power's story, many an anecdote of military life was told, as every instant increased the charm of that career I longed for.

"Another cooper, Major," said Power.

"With all my heart," said the rosy little officer, as he touched the bell behind him; "and now let's have a song."

"Yes, Power," said three or four together, "let us have 'The Irish Dragoon,' if it's only to convert your friend O'Malley there."

"Here goes, then," said Dick, taking off a bumper as he began the following chant to the air of "Love is the soul of a gay Irishman:"

"THE IRISH DRAGOON.

"Oh love is the soul of an Irish Dragoon,
    In battle, in bivouac, or in saloon—
        From the tip of his spur to his bright sabretasche.
    With his soldierly gait and his bearing so high,
    His gay laughing look, and his light speaking eye,
    He frowns at his rivals, he ogles his wench,
    He springs in his saddle and *chasses* the French—
        With his jingling spur and his bright sabretasche.

"His spirits are high, and he little knows care,
    Whether sipping his claret or charging a square—
        With his jingling spur and his bright sabretasche.
    As ready to sing or to skirmish he's found,
    To take off his wine, or to take up his ground;
    When the bugle may call him, how little he fears,
    To charge forth in column, and beat the Mounseers—
        With his jingling spur and his bright sabretasche.

"When the battle is over, he gayly rides back
    To cheer every soul in the night bivouac—
        With his jingling spur and his bright sabretasche.
    Oh! there you may see him in full glory crown'd,
    As he sits 'mid his friends on the hardly-won ground,
    And hear with what feeling the toast he will give,
    As he drinks to the land where all Irishmen live—
        With his jingling spur and his bright sabretasche."

It was late when we broke up; but among all the recollections of that pleasant evening, none clung to me so forcibly, none sunk so deeply in my heart, as the gay and careless tone of Power's manly voice; and as I fell asleep towards morning, the words of "The Irish Dragoon" were floating through my mind, and followed me in my dreams.

CHAPTER XVI.

THE VICE-PROVOST.

I HAD now been for some weeks a resident within the walls of the University, and yet had never presented my letter of introduction to Dr. Barret. Somehow my thoughts and occupations had left me little leisure to reflect upon my college course, and I had not felt the necessity, suggested by my friend Sir Harry, of having a supporter in the very learned and gifted individual to whom I was accredited. How long I might have continued in this state of indifference, it is hard to say, when chance brought about my acquaintance with the Doctor.

Were I not inditing a true history in this narrative of my life, to the events and characters of which so many are living witnesses, I should certainly fear to attempt anything like a description of this very remarkable man, so liable would any sketch, however faint and imperfect, be to the accusation of caricature, when all was so singular and so eccentric.

Dr. Barret was, at the time I speak of, close upon seventy years of age, scarcely five feet in height, and even that diminutive stature lessened by a stoop. His face was thin, pointed, and russet-colored; his nose so aquiline as nearly to meet his projecting chin, and his small gray eyes, red and bleary, peered beneath his well-worn cap, with a glance of mingled fear and suspicion. His dress was a suit of the rustiest black, threadbare, and patched in several places, while a pair of large brown leather slippers, far too big for his feet, imparted a sliding motion to his walk, that added an air of indescribable meanness to his appearance; a gown that had been worn for twenty years, browned and coated with the learned dust of the *Fagel*, covered his rusty habiliments, and completed the equipments of a figure that it was somewhat difficult for the young student to recognize as the Vice-Provost of the University. Such was he in externals. Within, a greater or more profound scholar never graced the walls of the college; a distinguished Grecian, learned in all the refinements of a hundred dialects; a deep Orientalist, cunning in all the varieties of Eastern languages, and able to reason with a Moonshee or chat with a Persian ambassador. With a mind that never ceased acquiring, he possessed a memory ridiculous for its retentiveness even of trifles; no character in history, no event in chronology, was unknown to him, and he was referred to by his cotemporaries for information in doubtful and disputed cases, as men consult a lexicon or dictionary. With an intellect thus stored with deep and far-sought knowledge, in the affairs of the world he was a child. Without the walls of the college, for above forty years he had not ventured half as many times, and knew absolutely nothing of the busy, active world that fussed and fumed so near him; his farthest excursion was to the Bank of Ireland, to which he made occasional visits to fund the ample income of his office, and add to the wealth which already had acquired for him a well-merited repute of being the richest man in college.

His little intercourse with the world had left him, in all his habits and manners, in every respect exactly as when he entered the college, nearly half a century before; and as he had literally risen from the ranks in the University, all the peculiarities of voice, accent, and pronunciation which distinguished him as a youth adhered to him in old age. This was singular enough, and formed a very ludicrous contrast with the learned and deep-read tone of his conversation; but another peculiarity, still more striking, belonged to him. When he became a fellow, he was obliged, by the rules of the college, to take holy orders as a *sine quâ non* to his holding his fellowship. This he did as he would have assumed a red hood or a blue one, as bachelor of laws or doctor of medicine, and thought no more of it; but frequently, in his moments of passionate excitement, the venerable character with which he was invested was quite forgotten, and he would utter some sudden and terrific oath, more productive of mirth to his auditors than was seemly, and for which, once spoken, the poor Doctor felt the greatest shame and contrition. These oaths were no less singular than forcible, and many a trick was practised, and many a plan devised, that the learned Vice-Provost might be entrapped into his favorite exclamation of "May the devil admire me!" which no place or presence could restrain.

My servant Mike, who had not been long in making himself acquainted with all the originals about him, was the cause of my first meeting the Doctor, before whom I received a summons to appear, on the very serious charge of treating with disrespect the heads of the college.

The circumstances were shortly these:—Mike had, among the other gossip of the place, heard frequent tales of the immense wealth and great parsimony of the Doctor, of his anxiety to amass money on all occasions, and the avidity with which even the smallest trifle was added to his gains. He accordingly resolved to amuse himself at the expense of this trait, and proceeded thus:—Boring a hole in a halfpenny, he attached a long string to it, and having dropped it on the Doctor's step, stationed himself on the opposite side of the court, concealed from view by the angle of the commons wall. He waited patiently for the chapel bell, at the first toll of which the door opened, and the Doctor issued forth. Scarcely was his foot upon the step, when he saw the piece of money, and as quickly stooped to seize it; but just as his finger had nearly touched it, it evaded his grasp, and slowly retreated. He tried again, but with the like success. At last, thinking he miscalculated the distance, he knelt leisurely down, and put forth his hand; but lo! it again escaped him; on which, slowly rising from his posture, he shambled on towards the chapel, where meeting the senior lecturer at the door, he cried out, "H— to my soul, Wall, but I saw the halfpenny walk away!"

For the sake of the grave character whom he addressed, I need not recount how such a speech was received; suffice it to say, that Mike had been seen by a college porter, who reported him as my servant.

I was in the very act of relating the anecdote to a large party at breakfast in my rooms, when a summons arrived requiring my immediate attendance at the Board, then sitting in solemn conclave at the examination-hall.

I accordingly assumed my academic costume as speedily as possible, and, escorted by that most august functionary, Mr. M'Alister, presented myself before the seniors.

The members of the Board, with the Provost at their head, were seated at a long oak table, covered with books, papers, &c., and from the silence they maintained, as I walked up the hall, I argued that a very solemn scene was before me.

"Mr. O'Malley," said the Dean, reading my name from a paper he held in his hand, "you have been summoned here at the desire of the Vice-Provost, whose questions you will reply to."

I bowed. A silence of a few minutes followed, when, at length, the learned Doctor, hitching up his nether garments with both hands, put his old and bleary eyes close to my face, while he croaked out, with an accent that no hackney-coachman could have exceeded in vulgarity,

"Eh, O'Malley; you're *quartus,* I believe; a'n't you?"

"I believe not. I think I am the only person of that name now on the books."

"That's thrue : but there were three O'Malleys before you. Godfrey O'Malley, that construed *Calve Neroni* to Nero the Calvinist—ha! ha! ha!—was cautioned in 1788."

"My uncle, I believe, sir."

"More than likely, from what I hear of you—*Ex uno*, &c. I see your name every day on the punishment roll. Late hours, never at chapel, seldom at morning lecture. Here ye are, sixteen shillings, wearing a red coat."

"Never knew any harm in that, Doctor."

"Ay, but d'ye see me, now? 'Grave raiment,' says the statute. And then, ye keep numerous beasts of prey, dangerous in their habits, and unseemly to behold."

"A bull-terrier, sir, and two game-cocks, are, I assure you, the only animals in my household."

"Well, I'll fine you for it."

"I believe, Doctor," said the Dean, interrupting, in an under tone, "that you cannot impose a penalty in this matter."

"Ay, but I can. 'Singing-birds,' says the statute, 'are forbidden within the walls.'

"And then, ye dazzled my eyes at commons with a bit of looking-glass, on Friday. I saw you. May the devil—ahem!—— As I was saying, that's casting *reflections* on the heads of the college; and your servant it was, *Michaelis Liber*, Mickey Free—may the flames of—ahem!—an insolent varlet! called me a sweep."

"You, Doctor; impossible!" said I, with pretended horror.

"Ay, but d'ye see me, now? It's thrue, for I looked about me at the time, and there wasn't another sweep in the place but myself. Hell to—I mean—God forgive me for swearing! but I'll fine you a pound for this."

As I saw the Doctor was getting on at such a pace, I resolved, notwithstanding the august presence of the Board, to try the efficacy of Sir Harry's letter of introduction, which I had taken in my pocket, in the event of its being wanted.

"I beg your pardon, sir, if the time be an unsuitable one; but may I take the opportunity of presenting this letter to you?"

"Ha! I know the hand—Boyle's. *Boyle secundus.* Hem, ha, ay! 'My young friend; and assist him by your advice.' To be sure! Oh! of course. Eh, tell me, young man, did Boyle say nothing to you about the copy of Erasmus, bound in vellum, that I sold him in Trinity term, 1782?"

"I rather think not, sir," said I, doubtfully.

"Well, then he might. He owes me two-and-fourpence of the balance."

"Oh! I beg pardon, sir; I now remember he desired me to repay you that 'sum; but he had just sealed the letter when he recollected it."

"Better late than never," said the Doctor, smiling graciously. "Where's the money? Ay! half-a-crown. I haven't twopence—never mind. Go away, young man; the case is dismissed. *Vehementer miror quare huc venisti.* You're more fit for anything than a college life. Keep good hours; mind the terms; and dismiss *Michaelis Liber.* Ha, ha, ha! May the devil! hem! that is, do——" So saying, the little Doctor's hand pushed me from the hall, his mind evidently relieved of all the griefs from which he had been suffering by the recovery of his long lost two-and-fourpence.

Such was my first and last interview with the Vice-Provost, and it made an impression upon me that all the intervening years have neither dimmed nor erased.

CHAPTER XVII.

TRINITY COLLEGE—A LECTURE.

I HAD not been many weeks a resident of Old Trinity ere the flattering reputation my chum, Mr. Francis Webber, had acquired extended also to myself, and by universal consent we were acknowledged the most riotous, ill-conducted, disorderly men on the books of the University. Were the lamps of the squares extinguished, and the college left in total darkness, we were summoned before the Dean; was the Vice-Provost serenaded with a chorus of trombones and French horns, to our taste in music was the attention ascribed; did a sudden alarm of fire disturb the congregation at morning chapel, Messrs. Webber and O'Malley were brought before the Board; and I must do them the justice to say that the most trifling circumstantial evidence was ever sufficient to bring a conviction. Reading men avoided the building where we resided as they would have done the plague. Our doors, like those of a certain classic precinct commemorated by a Latin writer, lay open night and day; while moustached dragoons, knowingly dressed four-in-hand men, fox-hunters in pink issuing forth to the Dubber, or returning splashed from a run with the Kildare hounds, were everlastingly seen passing and repassing. Within, the noise and confusion resembled rather the mess-room of a regiment towards eleven at night than the chambers of a college student; while, with the double object of affecting to be in ill health, and to avoid the reflections that daylight occasionally inspires, the shutters were never opened, but lamps and candles kept always burning. Such was No. 2, Old Square, in the goodly days I write of. All the terrors of fines and punishments fell scathless on the head of my worthy chum. In fact, like a well-known political character, whose pleasure and amusement it has been for some years past to drive through acts of Parliament and deride the powers of the law, so did Mr. Webber tread his way, serpenting through the statute-book, ever gazing, but rarely trespassing, upon some forbidden ground, which might involve the great punishment of expulsion. So expert, too, had he become in his special pleadings, so dexterous in the law of the University, that it was no easy matter to bring crime home to him; and even when this was done, his pleas of mitigation rarely failed of success.

There was a sweetness of demeanor, a mild, subdued tone about him, that constantly puzzled the worthy heads of the college how the accusations ever brought against him could be founded on truth; that the pale, delicate-looking student, whose harsh, hacking cough terrified the hearers, could be the boisterous performer upon a key-bugle, or the terrific assailant of watchmen, was something too absurd for belief; and when Mr. Webber, with his hand upon his heart, and in his most dulcet accents, assured them that the hours he was not engaged in reading for the medal were passed in the soothing society of a few select and intimate friends of literary tastes and refined minds, who knowing the delicacy of his health—.here he would cough—were kind enough to sit with him for an hour or so in the evening, the delusion was. perfect; and the story of the Dean's riotous habits having got abroad, the charge was usually suppressed.

Like most idle men, Webber never had a moment to spare. Except read, there was nothing he did not do; training a hack for a race in the Phœnix—arranging a rowing-match—getting up a mock duel between two white-feather acquaintances, were his almost daily avocations. Besides that, he was at the head of many organized societies, instituted for various benevolent purposes. One was called "The Association for Discountenancing Watchmen;" another "The Board of Works," whose object was principally devoted to the embellishment of the University, in which, to do them justice, their labors were unceasing, and what with the assistance of some black paint, a ladder, and a few pounds of gunpowder, they certainly contrived to effect many important changes. Upon an examination morning, some hundred luckless "jibs" might be seen perambulating the courts, in the vain effort to discover their tutors' chambers, the names having undergone an alteration that left all trace of their original proprietors unattainable; Doctor Francis

Mooney having become Doctor Full Moon—Doctor Hare being, by the change of two letters, Doctor Ape—Romney Robinson, Romulus and Remus, &c.   While, upon occasions like these, there could be but little doubt of Master Frank's intentions, upon many others, so subtle were his inventions, so well-contrived his plots, it became a matter of considerable difficulty to say whether the mishap which befell some luckless acquaintance were the result of design or mere accident; and not unfrequently well-disposed individuals were found condoling with "Poor Frank!" upon his ignorance of some college rule or etiquette, his breach of which had been long and deliberately planned.   Of this latter description was a circumstance which occurred about this time, and which some who may throw an eye over these pages will perhaps remember.

The Dean having heard (and, indeed, the preparations were not intended to secure secrecy) that Webber destined to entertain a party of his friends at dinner on a certain day, sent a most peremptory order for his appearance at commons, his name being erased from the sick list, and a pretty strong hint conveyed to him that any evasion upon his part would be certainly followed by an inquiry into the real reasons for his absence.   What was to be done? That was the very day he had destined for his dinner.   To be sure, the majority of his guests were college men, who would understand the difficulty at once; but still there were some others, officers of the 14th, with whom he was constantly dining, and whom he could not so easily put off.   The affair was difficult; but still, Webber was the man for a difficulty—in fact, he rather liked one.   A very brief consideration accordingly sufficed, and he sat down and wrote to his friends at the Royal Barracks thus :—

"DEAR POWER :—I have a better plan for Tuesday than that I had proposed.   Lunch here at three—(we'll call it dinner)—in the hall with the great guns.   I can't say much for the grub, but the company—glorious!   After that we'll start for Lucan in the drag— take our coffee, strawberries, &c., and return to No. 2 for supper at ten.   Advertise your fellows of this change, and believe me,

"Most unchangeably yours,

"FRANK WEBBER.

"Saturday."

Accordingly, as three o'clock struck, six dashing-looking light dragoons were seen slowly sauntering up the middle of the dining-hall, escorted by Webber, who, in full academic costume, was leisurely ciceroning his friends, and expatiating upon the excellencies of the very remarkable portraits which graced the walls.

The porters looked on with some surprise at the singular hour selected for sight-seeing, but what was their astonishment to find that the party, having arrived at the end of the hall, instead of turning back again, very composedly unbuckled their belts, and, having disposed of their sabres in a corner, took their places at the fellows' table, and sat down amid the collective wisdom of Greek Lecturers and Regius Professors, as though they had been mere mortals like themselves.

Scarcely was the long Latin grace concluded, when Webber, leaning forward, enjoined his friends, in a very audible whisper, that if they intended to dine, no time was to be lost.

" "We have but little ceremony here, gentlemen, and all we ask is a fair start," said he, as he drew over the soup, and proceeded to help himself.

The advice was not thrown away, for each man, with an alacrity a campaign usually teaches, made himself master of some neighboring dish—a very quick interchange of good things speedily following the appropriation. It was in vain that the Senior Lecturer looked aghast—that the Professor of Astronomy frowned—the whole table, indeed, were thunderstruck, even to the poor Vice-Provost himself, who, albeit given to the comforts of the table, could not lift a morsel to his mouth, but muttered between his teeth, "May the devil admire me, but they're dragoons." The first shock of surprise over, the porters informed them that except fellows of the University or fellow-commoners, none were admitted to the table. Webber, however, assured them that it was a mistake, there being nothing in the statute to exclude the 14th Light Dragoons, as he was prepared to prove. Meanwhile dinner proceeded, Power and his party performing with great self-satisfaction upon the sirloins and saddles about them, regretting only, from time to time, that there was a most unaccountable absence of wine, and suggesting the propriety of napkins whenever they should dine there again. Whatever chagrin these unexpected guests caused among their entertainers of the upper table, in the lower part of the hall the laughter was loud and unceasing, and long before the hour concluded, the fellows took their departure, leaving to Master Frank Webber the task of doing the honors alone and unassisted. When summoned before the Board for the offence on the following morning, Webber excused himself by throwing the blame upon his friends, with whom, he said, nothing short of a personal quarrel—a thing for a reading man not to be thought of—could have prevented intruding in the manner related. Nothing less than *his* tact could have saved him on this occasion, and at last he carried the day; while, by an act of the Board, the 14th Light Dragoons were pronounced the most insolent corps in the service.

An adventure of his, however, got wind about this time, and served to enlighten many persons as to his real character, who had hitherto been most lenient in their expressions about him. Our worthy tutor, with a zeal for our welfare far more praiseworthy than successful, was in the habit of summoning to his chambers on certain mornings of the week his various pupils, whom he lectured in the books for the approaching examinations. Now, as these seances were held at six o'clock in winter as well as summer, in a cold, fireless chamber,—the lecturer lying snug amid his blankets, while we stood shivering around the walls,—the ardor of learning must, indeed, have proved strong that prompted a regular attendance. As to Frank, he would as soon have thought of attending chapel as of presenting himself on such an occasion. Not so with me. I had not yet grown hackneyed enough to fly in the face of authority, and I frequently left the whist-table, or broke off in a song, to hurry over to the Doctor's chambers, and spout Homer and Hesiod. I suffered on in patience, till at last the bore became so insupportable, that I told my sorrows to my friend, who listened to me out, and promised me succor.

It so chanced that upon some evening in each week Dr. Mooney was in the habit of visiting some friends who resided a short distance from town, and spending the night at their house. He, of course, did not lecture the following morning—a paper placard announcing no lecture being affixed to the door on such occasions. Frank waited patiently till he perceived the Doctor affixing this announcement upon his door one evening; and no sooner had he left the college than he withdrew the paper and departed.

On the next morning he rose early, and, concealing himself on the staircase, waited the arrival of the venerable damsel who acted as servant to the Doctor. No sooner had she opened the door and groped her way into the sitting-room, than Frank crept forward, and, stealing gently into the bed-room, sprang into the bed, and wrapped himself up in the blankets. The great bell boomed forth at six o'clock, and soon after the sounds of feet were heard upon the stairs. One by one they came along, and gradually the room was filled with cold and shivering wretches, more than half asleep, and trying to arouse themselves into an approach to attention.

"Who's there?" said Frank, mimicking the Doctor's voice, as he yawned three or four times in succession, and turned in the bed.

"Collisson, O'Malley, Nesbitt," &c., said a number of voices, anxious to have all the merit such a penance could confer.

"Where's Webber?"

"Absent, sir," chorused the whole party.

"Sorry for it," said the mock doctor. "Webber is a man of first-rate capacity, and were he only to apply, I am not certain to what eminence his abilities might raise him. Come, Collisson. Any three angles of a triangle are equal to—are equal to—what are they equal to?" Here he yawned as though he would dislocate his jaw.

"Any three angles of a triangle are equal to two right angles," said Collisson, in the usual sing-song tone of a freshman.

As he proceeded to prove the proposition, his monotonous tone seemed to have lulled the Doctor into a doze, for in a few minutes a deep, long-drawn snore announced from the closed curtains that he listened no longer. After a little time, however, a short snort from the sleeper awoke him suddenly, and he called out,—

"Go on ; I'm waiting. Do you think I can arouse at this hour of the morning for nothing but to listen to your bungling? Can no one give me a free translation of the passage ?"

This digression from mathematics to classics did not surprise the hearers, though it somewhat confused them, no one being precisely aware what the line in question might be.

"Try it, Nesbitt—you, O'Malley—silent all. Really, this is too bad !" An indistinct muttering here from the crowd was followed by an announcement from the Doctor that "the speaker was an ass, and his head a turnip ! Not one of you capable of translating a chorus from Euripides—' Ou, ou, papai, papai,' &c., which, after all, means no more than—' Oh, whilleleu, murder, why did you die ?' &c. What are you laughing at, gentlemen? May I ask, does it become a set of ignorant, ill-informed savages—yes, savages, I repeat the word—to behave in this manner? Webber is the only man I have with common intellect—the only man among you capable of distinguishing himself. But as for you—I'll bring you before the Board—I'll write to your friends—I'll stop your college indulgences—I'll confine you to the walls—I'll be d—, eh——"

This lapse confused him. He stammered, stuttered, endeavored to recover himself; but by this time we had approached the bed, just at the moment when Master Frank, well knowing what he might expect if detected, had bolted from the blankets and rushed from the room. In an instant we were in pursuit; but he regained his chambers, and double-locked the door before we could overtake him, leaving us to ponder over the insolent tirade we had so patiently submitted to.

That morning the affair got wind all over college. As for us, we were scarcely so much laughed at as the Doctor, the world wisely remembering, if such were the nature of our morning's orisons, we might nearly as profitably have remained snug in our quarters.

Such was our life in Old Trinity; and strange enough it is that one should feel tempted to the confession; but I really must acknowledge these were, after all, happy times, and I look back upon them with mingled pleasure and sadness. The noble lord who so pathetically lamented that the devil was not so strong in him as he used to be forty years before, has an echo in my regrets that the student is not as young in me as when those scenes were enacting of which I write.

CHAPTER XVIII.

THE INVITATION—THE WAGER.

I WAS sitting at breakfast with Webber, a few mornings after the mess dinner I have spoken of, when Power came in hastily.

"Ha, the very man!" said he. "I say, O'Malley, here's an invitation for you from Sir George, to dine on Friday. He desired me to say a thousand civil things about his not having made you out, regrets that he was not at home when you called yesterday, and all that. By Jove, I know nothing like the favor you stand in; and, as for Miss Dashwood, faith! the fair Lucy blushed, and tore her glove in most approved style, when the old General began his laudation of you."

"Pooh, nonsense," said I; "that silly affair in the west."

"Oh, very probably; there's reason the less for your looking so excessively conscious. But I must tell you, in all fairness, that you have no chance; nothing short of a dragoon will go down."

"Be assured," said I, somewhat nettled, "my pretensions do not aspire to the fair Miss Dashwood."

"*Tant mieux et tant pis, mon cher.* I wish to Heaven mine did; and, by St. Patrick, if I only played the knight-errant half as gallantly as yourself, I would not relinquish my claims to the Secretary at War himself."

"What the devil brought the old General down to your wild regions?" inquired Webber.

"To contest the county."

"A bright thought, truly. When a man was looking for a seat, why not try a place where the law is occasionally heard of?"

"I am sure I can give you no information on that head; nor have I ever heard how Sir George came to learn that such a place as Galway existed."

"I believe I can enlighten you," said Power. "Lady Dashwood —rest her soul!—came west of the Shannon; she had a large property somewhere in Mayo, and owned some hundred acres of swamp, with some thousand starving tenantry thereupon, that people dignified as an estate in Connaught. This first suggested to him the notion of setting up for the county, probably supposing that the people who never paid in rent might like to do so in gratitude. How he was undeceived, O'Malley there can inform us. Indeed, I believe the worthy General, who was confoundedly hard up when he married, expected to have got a great fortune, and little anticipated the three Chancery suits he succeeded to, nor the fourteen rent-charges to his wife's relatives that made up the bulk of the dower. It was an unlucky hit for him when he fell in with the old 'maid' at Bath; and had she lived, he must have gone to the colonies. But the Lord took her one day, and Major Dashwood was himself again. The Duke of York, the story goes, saw him at Hounslow during a review—was much struck with his air and appearance—made some inquiries—found him to be of excellent family and irreproachable conduct—made him an aide-de-camp—and, in fact, made his fortune. I do not believe that, while doing so kind, he could by possibility have done a more popular, thing. Every man in the army rejoiced at his good fortune; so that, after all, though he has had some hard rubs, he has come well through, the only vestige of his unfortunate matrimonial connection being a correspondence kept up by a maiden sister of his late wife's with him. She insists upon claiming the ties of kindred upon about twenty family eras during the year, when she regularly writes a most loving and ill-spelled epistle, containing the latest information from Mayo, with all particulars of the Macan family, of which she is a worthy member. To her constant hints of the acceptable nature of certain small remittances, the poor General is never inattentive; but to the pleasing prospect of a visit in the flesh from Miss Judy Macan, the good man is dead. In fact, nothing short of being broke by a general court-martial could at all complete his sensations of horror at such a stroke of fortune; and I am not certain, if choice were allowed him, that he would not prefer the latter."

"Then he has never yet seen her?" said Webber.

"Never," replied Power; "and he hopes to leave Ireland without that blessing, the prospect of which, however remote and unlikely, has, I know well, more than once terrified him since his arrival."

"I say, Power, and has your worthy General sent me a card for his ball?"

"Not through me, Master Frank."

"Well, now, I call that devilish shabby, do you know. He asks

O'Malley there from *my* chambers, and never notices the other man, the superior in the firm. Eh, O'Malley, what say you?"

" Why, I didn't know you were acquainted."

"And who said we were? It was his fault, though, entirely, that we were not. I am, as I ever have been, the most easy fellow in the world on that score—never give myself airs to military people—endure anything, everything—and you see the result—hard, ain't it?"

" But, Webber, Sir George must really be excused in this matter. He has a daughter, a most attractive, lovely daughter, just at that budding, unsuspecting age when the heart is most susceptible of impressions; and where, let me ask, could she run such a risk as in the chance of a casual meeting with the redoubted lady killer, Master Frank Webber? If he has not sought you out, then here be his apology."

"A very strong case, certainly," said Frank; "but, still, had he confided his critical position to my honor and secrecy, he might have depended on me; now, having taken the other line——"

" Well, what then?"

" Why, he must abide the consequences. I'll make fierce love to Louisa; isn't that the name?"

" Lucy, so please you."

" Well, be it so—to Lucy—talk the little girl into a most deplorable attachment for me."

" But how, may I ask, and when?"

" I'll begin at the ball, man."

" Why, I thought you said you were not going?"

" There you mistake seriously. I merely said that I had not been invited."

" Then, of course," said I, " Webber, you can't think of going, in any case, on *my* account."

"My very dear friend, I go entirely upon my own. I not only shall go, but I intend to have most particular notice and attention paid me. I shall be prime favorite with Sir George—kiss Lucy——"

" Come, come, this is too strong."

" What do you bet I don't? There, now, I'll give you a pony a piece, I do. Do you say, done?"

" That you kiss Miss Dashwood, and are not kicked down stairs for your pains; are those the terms of the wager?" inquired Power.

" With all my heart. That I kiss Miss Dashwood, and am not kicked down stairs for my pains."

" Then I say, done."

"And with you too, O'Malley?"

"I thank you," said I, coldly; "I'm not disposed to make such a return for Sir George Dashwood's hospitality as to make an insult to his family the subject of a bet."

"Why, man, what are you dreaming of? Miss Dashwood will not refuse my chaste salute. Come, Power, I'll give you the other pony."

"Agreed!" said he. "At the same time, understand me distinctly —that I hold myself perfectly eligible to winning the wager by my own interference; for, if you do kiss her, by Jove! I'll perform the remainder of the compact."

"So I understand the agreement," said Webber, arranging his curls before the looking-glass. "Well, now, who's for Howth? the drag will be here in half an hour."

"Not I," said Power; "I must return to the barracks."

"Nor I," said I, "for I shall take this opportunity of leaving my card at Sir George Dashwood's."

"I have won my fifty, however," said Power, as we walked out in the courts.

"I am not quite certain——"

"Why, the devil, he would not risk a broken neck for that sum; besides, if he did, he loses the bet."

"He's a devilish keen fellow."

"Let him be. In any case I am determined to be on my guard here."

So chatting, we strolled along to the Royal Hospital, when, having dropped my pasteboard, I returned to the college.

CHAPTER XIX.

THE BALL.

I HAVE often dressed for a storming party with less of trepidation than I felt on the evening of Sir George Dashwood's ball. Since the eventful day of the election I had never seen Miss Dashwood; therefore, as to what precise position I might occupy in her favor was a matter of great doubt in my mind, and great import to my happiness. That I myself loved her was a matter of which all the badinage of my friends regarding her made me painfully conscious; but that, in our relative positions, such an attachment was all but hopeless, I could not disguise from myself. Young as I was, I well knew to what a heritage of debt, lawsuit, and difficulty I was born to succeed. In my own resources and means of advancement I had no confidence whatever, had even the profession to which I was destined been more of my choice. I daily felt that it demanded greater exertions, if not far greater abilities, than I could command to make success at all likely; and then, even if such a result were in store, years, at least, must elapse before it could happen, and where would she then be, and where should I?—where the ardent affection I now felt and gloried in—perhaps all the more for its desperate hopelessness—when the sanguine and buoyant spirit to combat with difficulties which youth suggests, and which later manhood refuses, should have passed away? And even if all these survived the toil and labor of anxious days and painful nights, what of her? Alas! I now reflected that, although only of my own age, her manner to me had taken all that tone of superiority and patronage which an elder assumes towards one younger, and which, in the spirit of protection it proceeds upon, essentially bars up every inlet to a dearer or warmer feeling—at least, when the lady plays the former part. "What, then, is to be done?" thought I. "Forget her?—but, how? How shall I renounce all my plans, and unweave the web of life I have been spreading around me for many a day, without that one golden thread that lent it more than half its brilliancy and all its attraction? But then, the alternative is even worse, if I encourage expectations and nurture hopes never to be realized. Well, we meet to-night, after a long and eventful absence; let my future fate be ruled by the results of this meeting. If Lucy Dashwood does care for me—if I can detect in her manner enough to show me that my affection may meet a return, the whole effort of my life shall be to make her mine; if not—if my own feelings be all that I have to depend upon to extort a reciprocal affection—then shall I take my last look of her, and with it the first and brightest dream of happiness my life has hitherto presented."

*   *   *   *   *   *   *   *

It need not be wondered at if the brilliant *coup d'œil* of the ball-room, as I entered, struck me with astonishment, accustomed as I had hitherto been to nothing more magnificent than an evening party of squires and their squiresses, or the annual garrison ball at the barracks. The glare of wax-lights, the well-furnished saloons, the glitter of uniforms, and the blaze of plumed and jewelled dames, with the clang of military music, was a species of enchanted atmosphere which, breathed for the first time, rarely fails to intoxicate. Never before had I seen so much beauty: lovely faces, dressed in all the seductive flattery of smiles, were on every side, and, as I walked from room to room, I felt how much more fatal to a man's peace and heart's ease the whispered words and silent glances of those fair damsels, than all the loud gayety and boisterous freedom of

our country belles, who sought to take the heart by storm and escalade.

As yet I had seen neither Sir George nor his daughter; and while
I looked on every side for Lucy Dashwood, it was with a beating and
anxious heart that I longed to see how she would bear comparison
with the blaze of beauty around.

Just at this moment a very gorgeously-dressed hussar stepped
from a doorway beside me, as if to make a passage for some one,
and the next moment she appeared leaning upon the arm of another lady. One look was all that I had time for, when she recognized me.

"Ah, Mr. O'Malley—how happy—has Sir George—has my father
seen you?"

"I have only arrived this moment; I trust he is quite well?"

"Oh, yes, thank you——"

"I beg your pardon with all humility, Miss Dashwood," said the
hussar, in a tone of the most knightly courtesy, "but they are waiting for us."

"But, Captain Fortescue, you must excuse me one moment more.
Mr. Lechmere, will you do me the kindness to find out Sir George?
Mr. O'Malley—Mr. Lechmere." Here she said something in French
to her companion, but so rapidly that I could not detect what it
was, but merely heard the reply—"*Pas mal!*"—which, as the lady
continued to canvass me most deliberately through her eye-glass, I
supposed referred to me. "And now, Captain Fortescue——" And
with a look of most courteous kindness to me, she disappeared in
the crowd.

The gentleman to whose guidance I was entrusted was one of the
aides-de-camp, and was not long in finding Sir George. No sooner
had the good old General heard my name, than he held out both
his hands and shook mine most heartily.

"At last, O'Malley—at last I am able to thank you for the greatest service man ever rendered me. He saved Lucy, my lord—rescued her under circumstances where anything short of his courage
and determination must have cost her her life."

"Ah! very pretty indeed," said the stiff old gentleman addressed,
as he bowed a most superbly-powdered scalp before me; "most
happy to make your acquaintance."

"Who is he?" added he in nearly as loud a tone to Sir George.

"Mr. O'Malley, of O'Malley Castle."

"True, I forgot. Why is he not in uniform?"

"Because, unfortunately, my lord, we don't own him; he's not in
the army."

"Ha! ha! thought he was."

9

"You dance, O'Malley, I suppose? I'm sure you'd rather be over there than hearing all my protestations of gratitude, sincere and heartfelt as they really are.

"Lechmere, introduce my friend Mr. O'Malley. Get him a partner."

I had not followed my new acquaintance many steps, when Power came up to me. "I say, Charley," cried he, "I have been tormented to death by half the ladies in the room to present you to them, and have been in quest of you this half hour. Your brilliant exploit in savage land has made you a regular *preux chevalier;* and if you don't trade on that adventure to your most lasting profit, you deserve to be—a lawyer. Come along here! Lady Muckleman, the adjutant-general's lady and chief, has four Scotch daughters you are to dance with; then I am to introduce you in all form to the Dean of Something's niece; she is a good-looking girl, and has two livings in a safe county. Then there's the town-major's wife; and in fact I have several engagements from this to supper-time."

"A thousand thanks for all your kindness in prospective, but I think perhaps it were right I should ask Miss Dashwood to dance, if only as a matter of form—you understand?"

"And if Miss Dashwood should say, 'With pleasure, sir,' only as a matter of form—you understand?'" said a silvery voice beside me. I turned, and saw Lucy Dashwood, who, having overheard my very free-and-easy suggestion, replied to me in this manner.

I here blundered out my excuses. What I said, and what I did not say, I do not now remember; but, certainly, it was her turn now to blush, and her arm trembled within mine as I led her to the top of the room. In the little opportunity which our quadrille presented for conversation, I could not help remarking that, after the surprise of her first meeting with me, Miss Dashwood's manner became gradually more and more reserved, and that there was an evident struggle between her wish to appear grateful for what had occurred and a sense of the necessity of not incurring a greater degree of intimacy. Such was my impression, at least, and such the conclusion which I drew from a certain quiet tone in her manner, that went much further to wound my feelings and mar my happiness than any other line of conduct towards me could possibly have effected.

Our quadrille over, I was about to conduct her to a seat, when Sir George came hurriedly up, his face greatly flushed, and betraying every semblance of high excitement.

"Dear papa, has anything occurred? Pray what is it?" inquired she.

He smiled faintly, and replied, "Nothing very serious, my dear.

that I should alarm you in this way; but, certainly, a more disagreeable *contretemps* could scarcely occur."

"Do tell me; what can it be?"

"Read this," said he, presenting a very dirty-looking note, which bore the mark of a red wafer most infernally plain upon its outside.

Miss Dashwood unfolded the billet, and, after a moment's silence, instead of participating, as he expected, in her father's feelings of distress, burst out a-laughing, while she said, "Why, really, papa, I do not see why this should put you out much, after all. Aunt may be somewhat of a character, as her note evinces, but after a few days ——"

"Nonsense, child; there's nothing in this world I have such a dread of as that confounded woman—and to come at such a time."

"When does she speak of paying her visit?"

"I knew you had not read the note," said Sir George, hastily; "she's coming here to-night—is on her way this instant, perhaps. What is to be done? If she forces her way in here, I shall go deranged outright. O'Malley, my boy, read this note, and you will not feel surprised if I appear in the humor you see me."

I took the billet from the hands of Miss Dashwood, and read as follows :—

"DEAR BROTHER :—When this reaches your hand, I'll not be far off. I'm on my way up to town, to be under Dr. Dease for the ould complaint. Cowley mistakes my case entirely; he says it's nothing but religion and wind. Father Magrath, who understands a good deal about females, thinks otherwise; but God knows who's right. Expect me to tea, and, with love to Lucy, believe me yours, in haste,

"JUDITH MACAN.

"Let the sheets be well aired in my room; and if you have a spare bed, perhaps we could prevail upon Father Magrath to stop too."

I scarcely could contain my laughter till I got to the end of this very free-and-easy epistle, when at last I burst forth in a hearty fit, in which I was joined by Miss Dashwood.

From the account Power had given me in the morning, I had no difficulty in guessing that the writer was the maiden sister of the late Lady Dashwood, and for whose relationship Sir George had ever testified the greatest dread, even at the distance of two hundred miles, and for whom, in any nearer intimacy, he was in nowise prepared.

"I say, Lucy," said he, "there's only one thing to be done. If this horrid woman does arrive, let her be shown to her room, and for the few days of her stay in town, we'll neither see nor be seen by any one."

Without waiting for a reply, Sir George was turning away to give the necessary instructions, when the door of the drawing-room was thrown open, and the servant announced, in his loudest voice, "Miss Macan." Never shall I forget the poor General's look of horror as the words reached him; for as yet he was too far off to catch even a glimpse of its fair owner. As for me, I was already so much interested in seeing what she was like, that I made my way through the crowd towards the door. It is no common occurrence that can distract the various occupations of a crowded ball-room, where, amid the crash of music and the din of conversation, goes on the soft, low voice of insinuating flattery, or the light flirtation of a first acquaintance; every clique, every coterie, every little group of three or four, has its own separate and private interests, forming a little world of its own, and caring for and heeding nothing that goes on around; and even when some striking charac-ter or illustrious personage makes his *entrée*, the attention he attracts is so momentary, that the buzz of conversation is scarcely, if at all, interrupted, and the business of pleasure continues to flow on. Not so now, however. No sooner had the servant pronounced the magical name of Miss Macan, than all seemed to stand still. The spell thus exercised over the luckless General seemed to have extended to his company, for it was with difficulty that any one could continue his train of conversation, while every eye was directed towards the door. About two steps in advance of the servant, who still stood door in hand, was a tall, elderly lady, dressed in an antique brocade silk, with enormous flowers gaudily embroidered upon it. Her hair was powdered, and turned back, in the fashion of fifty years before, while her high-pointed and heeled shoes completed a costume that had not been seen for nearly a century. Her short, skinny arms were bare and partly covered by a falling flower of old point lace, while on her hands she wore black silk mittens; a pair of green spectacles scarcely dimmed the lustre of a most piercing pair of eyes, to whose effect a very palpable touch of rouge on the cheeks certainly added brilliancy. There stood this most singular apparition, holding before her a fan about the size of a modern tea-tray, while at each repetition of her name by the servant she courtesied deeply, bestowing the while upon the gay crowd before her a very curious look of maidenly modesty at her solitary and unprotected position.

As no one had ever heard of the fair Judith save one or two of

Sir George's most intimate friends, the greater part of the company were disposed to regard Miss Macan as some one who had mistaken the character of the invitation, and had come in a fancy dress. But this delusion was but momentary, as Sir George, armed with the courage of despair, forced his way through the crowd, and taking her hand affectionately, bade her welcome to Dublin. The fair Judy at this threw her arms about his neck, and saluted him with a hearty smack, that was heard all over the room.

"Where's Lucy, brother? Let me embrace my little darling," said the lady, in an accent that told more of Miss Macan than a three-volume biography could have done. "There she is, I'm sure; kiss me, my honey."

This office Miss Dashwood performed with an effort at courtesy really admirable; then, taking her aunt's arm, she led her to a sofa.

It needed all the poor General's tact to get over the sensation of this most *mal à propos* addition to his party; but by degrees the various groups renewed their occupations, although many a smile, and more than one sarcastic glance at the sofa, betrayed that the maiden aunt had not escaped criticism.

Power, whose propensity for fun very considerably outstripped his sense of decorum to his commanding officer, had already made his way towards Miss Dashwood, and succeeded in obtaining a formal introduction to Miss Macan.

"I hope you will do me the favor to dance the next set with me, Miss Macan?"

"Really, Captain, it's very polite of you, but you must excuse me. I was never anything great in quadrilles; but if a reel or a jig——"

"Oh, dear aunt, don't think of it, I beg of you."

"Or even Sir Roger de Coverley," resumed Miss Macan.

"I assure you, quite equally impossible."

"Then I'm certain you waltz," said Power.

"What do you take me for, young man? I hope I know better. I wish Father Magrath heard you ask me that question, and for all your laced jacket——"

"Dearest aunt, Captain Power didn't mean to offend you; I'm certain he ——"

"Well, why did he dare to—*sob, sob*—did he see anything light about me, that he—*sob, sob, sob*—oh dear! oh dear! is it for this I came up from my little peaceful place in the west?—*sob, sob, sob*— General, George, dear; Lucy, my love, I'm taken bad. Oh dear! oh dear! is there any whisky negus?"

Whatever sympathy Miss Macan's sufferings might have excited in the crowd about her before, this last question totally routed it, and a hearty fit of laughter broke forth from more than one of the bystanders.

At length, however, she was comforted, and her pacification completely effected by Sir George setting her down to a whist-table. From this moment I lost sight of her for above two hours. Meanwhile, I had little opportunity of following up my intimacy with Miss Dashwood, and as I rather suspected that, on more than one occasion, she seemed to avoid our meeting, I took especial care, on my part, to spare her the annoyance.

For one instant only had I any opportunity of addressing her, and then there was such an evident embarrassment in her manner, that I readily perceived how she felt circumstanced—that the sense of gratitude to one whose further advances she might have feared rendered her constrained and awkward. "Too true," said I; "she avoids me. My being here is only a source of discomfort and pain to her; therefore, I'll take my leave, and, whatever it may cost me, never to return." With this intention, resolving to wish Sir George a very good night, I sought him out for some minutes. At length I saw him in a corner, conversing with the old nobleman to whom he had presented me early in the evening.

"True, upon my honor, Sir George," said he; "I saw it myself, and she did it just as dexterously as the oldest blackleg in Paris."

"Why, you don't mean to say that she cheated?"

"Yes, but I do, though—turned the ace every time. Lady Herbert said to me, 'Very extraordinary it is—four by honors again.' So I looked, and then I perceived it—a very old trick it is; but she did it beautifully. What's her name?"

"Some western name; I forget it," said the poor General, ready to die with shame.

"Clever old woman—very!" said the old lord, taking a pinch of snuff; "but revokes too often."

Supper was announced at this critical moment, and before I had further thought of my determination to escape, I felt myself hurried along in the crowd towards the staircase. The party immediately in front of me were Power and Miss Macan, who now appeared reconciled, and certainly testified most openly their mutual feelings of good will.

"I say, Charley," whispered Power, as I came along, "it is capital fun—never met anything equal to her; but the poor General will never live through it, and I'm certain of ten days' arrest for this night's proceeding."

"Any news of Webber?" I inquired.

"Oh yes, I fancy I can tell something of him; for I heard of some one presenting himself, and being refused the *entrée*, so that Master Frank has lost his money. Sit near us, I pray you, at supper. We must take care of the dear aunt for the niece's sake, eh?"

Not seeing the force of this reasoning, I soon separated myself from them, and secured a corner at a side table. Every supper, on such an occasion as this, is the same scene of soiled white muslin, faded flowers, flushed faces, torn gloves, blushes, blanc-mange, cold chicken, jelly, sponge cakes, spooney young gentlemen doing the attentive, and watchful mammas calculating what precise degree of propinquity in the crush is safe or seasonable for their daughters to the moustached and unmarrying lovers beside them. There are always the same set of gratified elders, like the benchers in King's Inn, marched up to the head of the table, to eat, drink, and be happy—removed from the more profane looks and soft speeches of the younger part of the creation. Then there are the *oi polloi* of outcasts, younger sons of younger brothers, tutors, governesses, portionless cousins, and curates, all formed in a phalanx round the side tables, whose primitive habits and simple tastes are evinced by their all eating off the same plate and drinking from nearly the same wine-glass,—too happy if some better-off acquaintance at the long table invites them to " wine," though the ceremony on their part is limited to the pantomime of drinking. To this miserable *tiers état* I belonged, and bore my fate with unconcern; for, alas! my spirits were depressed and my heart heavy. Lucy's treatment of me was every moment before me, contrasted with her gay and courteous demeanor to all save myself, and I longed for the moment to get away.

Never had I seen her looking so beautiful; her brilliant eyes were lit with pleasure, and her smile was enchantment itself. What would I not have given for one moment's explanation, as I took my leave forever!—one brief avowal of my love, my unalterable, devoted love; for which I sought not nor expected return, but merely that I might not be forgotten.

Such were my thoughts, when a dialogue quite near me aroused me from my reverie. I was not long in detecting the speakers, who, with their backs turned to us, were seated at the great table, discussing a very liberal allowance of pigeon pie, a flask of champagne standing between them.

" Don't, now! don't, I tell ye; it's little ye know Galway, or ye wouldn't think to make up to me, squeezing my foot."

" Upon my soul, you're an angel, a regular angel. I never saw a woman suit my fancy before."

" Oh, behave now. Father Magrath says——"

" Who's he?"

" The priest ; no less."

" Oh ! confound him."

" Confound Father Magrath, young man ?"

" Well, then, Judy, don't be angry ; I only meant that a dragoon knows rather more of these matters than a priest."

" Well, then, I'm not so sure of that. But anyhow, I'd have you to remember it ain't a Widow Malone you have beside you."

" Never heard of the lady," said Power.

" Sure, it's a song—poor creature—it's a song they made about her in the North Cork, when they were quartered down in our county."

" I wish to Heaven you'd sing it."

" What will you give me, then, if I do ?"

" Anything—everything—my heart, my life."

" I wouldn't give a trauneen for all of them. Give me that old green ring on your finger, then."

" It's yours," said Power, placing it gracefully upon Miss Macan's finger, " and now for your promise."

" Maybe my brother might not like it."

" He'd be delighted," said Power ; " he dotes on music."

" Does he, now ?"

" On my honor, he does."

" Well, mind you get up a good chorus. for the song has one, and here it is."

" Miss Macan's song !" said Power. tapping the table with his knife.

" Miss Macan's song !" was re-echoed on all sides ; and before the luckless General could interfere, she had begun. How to explain the air I know not, for I never heard its name ; but at the end of each verse a species of echo followed the last word, that rendered it irresistibly ridiculous.

"THE WIDOW MALONE.

" Did ye hear of the Widow Malone,
Ohone\
Who lived in the town of Athlone
Alone ?
Oh ! she melted the hearts
Of the swains in them parts,
So lovely the Widow Malone,
Ohone!
So lovely the Widow Malone.

" Of lovers she had a full score,
Or more\
And fortunes they all had galore,
In store ;

From the minister down
To the clerk of the crown,
All were courting the Widow Malone,
    Ohone!
All were courting the Widow Malone.

"But so modest was Mrs. Malone,
    'Twas known
No one ever could see her alone,
    Ohone!
Let them ogle and sigh,
They could ne'er catch her eye,
So bashful the Widow Malone,
    Ohone!
So bashful the Widow Malone.

"Till one Mr. O'Brien from Clare,
    How quare!
It's little for blushin' they care
    Down there;
Put his arm round her waist,
Gave ten kisses at laste,
'Oh,' says he, 'you're my Molly Malone,
    My own;
'Oh,' says he, 'you're my Molly Malone.'

"And the widow they all thought so shy,
    My eye!
Ne'er thought of a simper or sigh,
    For why?
But 'Lucius,' says she,
'Since you've made now so free,
You may marry your Mary Malone,
    Ohone!
You may marry your Mary Malone.'

"There's a moral contained in my song,
    Not wrong,
And one comfort it's not very long,
    But strong;
If for widows you die,
Larn to *kiss*, *not* to *sigh*,
For they're all like sweet Mistress Malone,
    Ohone!
Oh! they're very like Mistress Malone."

Never did song create such a sensation as Miss Macan's; and certainly her desires as to the chorus were followed to the letter, for "The Widow Malone, ohone!" resounded from one end of the table to the other, amid one universal shout of laughter. None could resist the ludicrous effect of her melody; and even poor Sir George, sinking under the disgrace of his relationship, which she had contrived to make public by frequent allusions to her "dear brother the General," yielded at last, and joined in the mirth around him.

"I insist upon a copy of 'The Widow,' Miss Macan," said Power.

"To be sure; give me a call to-morrow—let me see—about two.

Father Magrath won't be at home," said she, with a coquettish look.

"Where, pray, may I pay my respects?"

"No. 22 South Anne street—very respectable lodgings. I'll write the address in your pocket-book."

Power produced a card and pencil, while Miss Macan wrote a few lines, saying, as she handed it,—

"There, now, don't read it here before the people; they'll think it mighty indelicate in me to make an appointment."

Power pocketed the card, and the next minute Miss Macan's carriage was announced.

Sir George Dashwood, who little flattered himself that his fair guest had any intention of departure, became now most considerately attentive—reminded her of the necessity of muffling against the night air—hoped she would escape cold—and wished her a most cordial good night, with a promise of seeing her early the following day.

Notwithstanding Power's ambition to engross the attention of the lady, Sir George himself saw her to her carriage, and only returned to the room as a group was collecting around the gallant Captain, to whom he was relating some capital traits of his late conquest—for such he dreamed she was.

"Doubt it who will," said he, "she has invited me to call on her to-morrow—written her address on my card—told me the hour she is certain of being alone. See here!" At these words he pulled forth the card, and handed it to Lechmere.

Scarcely were the eyes of the other thrown upon the writing, when he said, "So, this isn't it, Power."

"To be sure it is, man," said Power. "Anne street is devilish seedy—but that's the quarter."

"Why, confound it, man," said the other, "there's not a word of that here."

"Read it out," said Power. "Proclaim aloud my victory."

Thus urged, Lechmere read:—

"DEAR P.,—Please pay to my credit—and soon, mark ye—the two ponies lost this evening. I have done myself the pleasure of enjoying your ball, kissed the lady, quizzed the papa, and walked into the cunning Fred Power.   Yours,

                              "FRANK WEBBER.

"'The Widow Malone, ohone!' is at your service."

Had a thunderbolt fallen at his feet, his astonishment could not have equalled the result of this revelation. He stamped, swore, raved, laughed, and almost went deranged. The joke was soon spread through the room, and from Sir George to poor Lucy, now covered with blushes at her part in the transaction, all was laughter and astonishment.

"Who is he? that is the question," said Sir George, who, with all the ridicule of the affair hanging over him, felt no common relief at the discovery of the imposition.

"A friend of O'Malley's," said Power, delighted, in his defeat, to involve another with himself.

"Indeed!" said the General, regarding me with a look of a very mingled cast.

"Quite true, sir," said I, replying to the accusation that his manner implied; "but equally so, that I neither knew of his plot nor recognized him when here."

"I am perfectly sure of it, my boy," said the General; "and, after all, it was an excellent joke—carried a little too far, it's true; eh, Lucy?"

But Lucy either heard not or affected not to hear; and, after some little further assurance that he felt not the least annoyed, the General turned to converse with some other friends, while I, burning with indignation against Webber, took a cold farewell of Miss Dashwood, and retired.

CHAPTER XX.

THE LAST NIGHT IN TRINITY.

HOW I might have met Master Webber after his impersonation of Miss Macan, I cannot possibly figure to myself. Fortunately, indeed, for all parties, he left town early the next morning, and it was some weeks ere he returned. In the meanwhile, I became a daily visitor at the General's, dined there usually three or four times a week, rode out with Lucy constantly, and accompanied her every evening either to the theatre or into society. Sir George, possibly from my youth, seemed to pay little attention to an intimacy which he perceived every hour growing closer, and frequently gave his daughter into my charge in our morning excursions on horseback. As for me, my happiness was all but perfect. I loved, and already began to hope that I was not regarded with indifference; for although Lucy's manner never absolutely evinced any decided preference towards me, yet many slight and casual circumstances served to show me that my attentions to her were neither unnoticed nor uncared for. Among the many gay and dashing companions of our rides, I remarked that, however anxious for such a distinction, none ever seemed to make any way in her good graces; and I had already gone far in my self-deception that I was destined for good fortune, when a circumstance which occurred one morning at length served to open my eyes to the truth, and blast, by one fatal breath, the whole harvest of my hopes.

We were about to set out one morning on a long ride, when Sir George's presence was required by the arrival of an officer who had been sent from the Horse Guards on official business. After half an hour's delay, Colonel Cameron, the officer in question, was introduced, and entered into conversation with our party. He had only landed in England from the Peninsula a few days before, and had abundant information of the stirring events enacting there. At the conclusion of an anecdote—I forget what—he turned suddenly round to Miss Dashwood, who was standing beside me, and said, in a low voice,—

"And, now, Miss Dashwood, I am reminded of a commission I promised a very old brother officer to perform. Can I have one moment's conversation with you in the window?"

As he spoke, I perceived that he crumpled beneath his glove something like a letter.

"To me?" said Lucy, with a look of surprise that sadly puzzled me whether to ascribe it to coquetry or innocence—"to me?"

"To you," said the Colonel, bowing; "and I am sadly deceived by my friend Hammersley——"

"Captain Hammersley?" said she, blushing deeply as she spoke.

I heard no more. She turned towards the window with the Colonel, and all I saw was, that he handed her a letter, which, having hastily broken open, and thrown her eyes over, she grew at first deadly pale, then red, and, while her eyes filled with tears, I heard her say, "How like him!—how truly generous this is!" I listened for no more—my brain was whirling round and my senses reeling. I turned and left the room. In another moment I was on my horse, galloping from the spot, despair, in all its blackness, in my heart— and, in my broken-hearted misery, wishing for death.

I was miles away from Dublin ere I remembered well what had occurred, and even then, not over-clearly. The fact that Lucy Dashwood, whom I imagined to be my own in heart, loved another, was all that I really knew. That one thought was all that my mind was capable of, and in it my misery, my wretchedness, were centred.

Of all the grief my life has known, I have had no moments like the long hours of that dreary night. My sorrow, in turn, took every shape and assumed every guise. Now I remembered how the

Dashwoods had courted my intimacy and encouraged my visits; how Lucy herself had evinced, in a thousand ways, that she felt a preference for me. I called to mind the many unequivocal proofs I had given her that my feeling, at least, was no common one; and yet, how had she sported with my affections and jested with my happiness! That she loved Hammersley I had now a palpable proof; that this affection must have been mutual, and prosecuted at the very moment I was not only professing my own love for her, but actually receiving all but an avowal of its return—oh! it was too, too base; and in my deepest heart I cursed my folly, and vowed never to see her more.

It was late on the next day ere I retraced my steps towards town, my heart sad and heavy, careless what became of me for the future, and pondering whether I should not at once give up my college career and return to my uncle. When I reached my chambers, all was silent and comfortless. Webber had not returned; my servant was from home; and I felt myself more than ever wretched in the solitude of what had been so oft the scene of noisy and festive gayety. I sat some hours in a half-musing state, every sad, depressing thought that blighted hopes can conjure up rising in turn before me. A loud knocking at the door at length aroused me. I got up and opened it. No one was there. I looked around, as well as the coming gloom of evening would permit, but saw nothing. I listened, and heard at some distance off my friend Power's manly voice, as he sang,—

"Oh love is the soul of an Irish dragoon!"

I hallooed out, "Power!"

"Eh, O'Malley, is that you?" inquired he. "Why, then, it seems it required some deliberation whether you opened your door or not. Why, man, you can have no great gift of prophecy, or you wouldn't have kept me so long there."

"And have you been so?"

"Only twenty minutes, for as I saw the key in the lock, I had determined to succeed, if noise would do it."

"How strange! I never heard it."

"Glorious sleeper you must be. But come, my dear fellow, you don't appear altogether awake yet."

"I have not been quite well these few days."

"Oh, indeed! The Dashwoods thought there must have been something of that kind the matter, by your brisk retreat. They sent me after you yesterday; but wherever you went, Heaven knows! I never could come up with you, so that your great good news has been keeping twenty-four hours longer than need be."

"I am not aware what you allude to."

"Well, you are not over-likely to be the wiser when you hear it, if you can assume no more intelligent look than that. Why, man, there's great luck in store for you."

"As how, pray? Come, Power, out with it, though I can't pledge myself to feel half as grateful for my good fortune as I should do. What is it?"

"You know Cameron?"

"I have seen him," said I, reddening.

"Well, Old Camy, as we used to call him, has brought over, among his other news, your gazette."

"My gazette! what do you mean?"

"Confound your uncommon stupidity this evening. I mean, man, that you are one of us—gazetted to the 14th Light—the best fellows for love, war, and whisky that ever sported a sabretasche. 'Oh love is the soul of an Irish dragoon!' By Jove! I am as delighted to have rescued you from the black harness of the King's Bench as though you had been a prisoner there. Know, then, friend Charley, that on Wednesday we proceed to Fermoy, join some score of gallant fellows—all food for powder—and, with the aid of a rotten transport and the stormy winds that blow, will be bronzing our beautiful faces in Portugal before the month's out. But come, now, let's see about supper. Some of ours are coming over here at eleven, and I promised them a devilled bone. And as it's your last night among these classic precincts, let us have a shindy of it."

While I despatched Mike to Morrison's to provide supper, I heard from Power that Sir George Dashwood had interested himself so strongly for me, that I had obtained my cornetcy in the 14th; that, fearful lest any disappointment might arise, he had never mentioned the matter to me, but that he had previously obtained my uncle's promise to concur in the arrangement if his negotiation succeeded. It had done so, and now the long sought-for object of many days was within my grasp. But, alas! the circumstance which lent it all its fascinations was a vanished dream; and what but two days before had rendered my happiness perfect, I listened to listlessly and almost without interest. Indeed, my first impulse, on finding that I owed my promotion to Sir George, was to return a positive refusal of the cornetcy; but then I remembered how deeply such conduct would hurt my poor uncle, to whom I never could give an adequate explanation. So I heard Power in silence to the end, thanked him sincerely for his own good-natured kindness in the matter, which already, by the interest he had taken in me, went far to heal the wounds that my own solitary musings were deepening in my heart. At eighteen, fortunately, consolations are attainable that become more difficult at eight-and-twenty, and impossible at eight-and-thirty.

While Power continued to dilate upon the delights of a soldier's life,—a theme which many a boyish dream had long since made hallowed to my thoughts,—I gradually felt my enthusiasm rising, and a certain throbbing at my heart betrayed to me that, sad and dispirited as I felt, there was still within that buoyant spirit which youth possesses as its privilege, and which answers to the call of enterprise as the war-horse to the trumpet. That a career worthy of manhood, great, glorious, and inspiriting, opened before me, coming so soon after the late downfall of my hopes, was in itself a source of such true pleasure, that ere long I listened to my friend, and heard his narrative with breathless interest. A lingering sense of pique, too, had its share in all this. I longed to come forward in some manly and dashing part, where my youth might not be ever remembered against me, and when, having brought myself to the test, I might no longer be looked upon and treated as a boy.

We were joined at length by the other officers of the 14th, and, to the number of twelve, sat down to supper.

It was to be my last night in Old Trinity, and we resolved that the farewell should be a solemn one. Mansfield, one of the wildest young fellows in the regiment, had vowed that the leave-taking should be commemorated by some very decisive and open expression of our feelings, and had already made some progress in arrangements for blowing up the great bell, which had more than once obtruded upon our morning convivialities; but he was overruled by his more discreet associates, and we at length assumed our places at table, in the midst of which stood a hecatomb of all my college equipments, cap, gown, bands, &c. A funeral pile of classics was arrayed upon the hearth, surmounted by my "Book on the Cellar," and a punishment-roll waved its length, like a banner, over the doomed heroes of Greece and Rome.

It is seldom that any very determined attempt to be gay *par excellence* has a perfect success, but certainly upon this evening ours had. Songs, good stories, speeches, toasts, bright visions of the campaign before us, the wild excitement which such a meeting cannot be free from, gradually, as the wine passed from hand to hand, seized upon all, and about four in the morning, such was the uproar we caused, and so terrific the noise of our proceedings, that the accumulated force of porters, sent one by one to demand admission, was now a formidable body at the door; and Mike at last came in to assure us that the Bursar, the most dread official of all collegians, was without, and insisted, with a threat of his heaviest displeasure in case of refusal, that the door should be opened.

A committee of the whole house immediately sat upon the question, and it was at length resolved, *nemine contradicente*, that the request should be complied with. A fresh bowl of punch, in honor of our expected guest, was immediately concocted, a new broil put on the gridiron, and, having seated ourselves with as great a semblance of decorum as four bottles a man admits of, Curtis, the junior Captain, being most drunk, was at once deputed to receive the Bursar at the door, and introduce him into our august presence.

Mike's instructions were, that immediately on Dr. Stone (the Bursar) entering, the door was to be slammed to, and none of his followers admitted. This done, the Doctor was to be ushered in, and left to our own polite attentions.

A fresh thundering from without scarcely left time for further deliberation; and at last Curtis moved towards the door, in execution of his mission.

"Is there any one there?" said Mike, in a tone of most unsophisticated innocence, to a rapping that, having lasted three-quarters of an hour, threatened now to break in the panel. "Is there any one there?"

"Open the door this instant—the senior Bursar desires you—this instant."

"Sure it's night, and we're all in bed," said Mike.

"Mr. Webber—Mr. O'Malley," said the Bursar, now boiling with indignation, "I summon you, in the name of the Board, to admit me."

"Let the gemman in," hiccupped Curtis; and at the same instant the heavy bars were withdrawn, and the doors opened, but so sparingly as with difficulty to permit the passage of the burly figure of the Bursar.

Forcing his way through, and regardless of what became of the rest, he pushed on vigorously through the ante-chamber, and before Curtis could perform his functions of usher, stood in the midst of us. What were his feelings at the scene before him, Heaven knows. The number of figures in uniform at once betrayed how little his jurisdiction extended to the great mass of the company, and he immediately turned towards me.

"Mr. Webber——"

"O'Malley, if you please, Mr. Bursar," said I, bowing with most ceremonious politeness.

"No matter, sir; *arcades ambo*, I believe."

"Both Archdeacons," said Melville, translating, with a look of withering contempt upon the speaker.

The Doctor continued, addressing me:

"May I ask, sir, if you believe yourself possessed of any privilege for converting this University into a common tavern?"

"I wish to Heaven he did," said Curtis; "capital tap your old commons would make."

"Really, Mr. Bursar," replied I, modestly, "I had begun to flatter myself that our little innocent gayety had inspired you with the idea of joining our party."

"I humbly move that the old cove in the gown do take the chair," sang out one. "All who are of this opinion say 'Aye.'" . A perfect yell of ayes followed this. "All who are of the contrary say 'No.' The ayes have it."

Before the luckless Doctor had a moment for thought, his legs were lifted from under him, and he was jerked, rather than placed, upon a chair, and put sitting upon the table.

"Mr. O'Malley, your expulsion within twenty-four hours——"

"Hip, hip, hurra, hurra, hurra!" drowned the rest, while Power, taking off the Doctor's cap, replaced it by a foraging cap, very much to the amusement of the party.

"There is no penalty that the law permits of that I shall not——"

"Help the Doctor," said Melville, placing a glass of punch in his unconscious hand.

"Now for a 'Viva la Compagnie!'" said Telford, seating himself at the piano, and playing the first bars of that well-known air, to which, in our meetings, we were accustomed to improvise a doggerel in turn:

> "I drink to the graces, Law, Physic, Divinity,
> Viva la Compagnie!
> And here's to the worthy old Bursar of Trinity,
> Viva la Compagnie!"

"Viva, viva la va!" &c., was chorused with a shout that shook the old walls, while Power took up the strain:

> "Though with lace caps and gowns they look so like asses,
> Viva la Compagnie!
> They'd rather have punch than the springs of Parnassus,
> Viva la Compagnie!"

> "What a nose the old gentleman has, by the way,
> Viva la Compagnie!
> Since he smelt out the devil from Botany Bay,*
> Viva la Compagnie!"

Words cannot give even the faintest idea of the poor Bursar's feelings while these demoniacal orgies were enacting around him. Held fast in his chair by Lechmere and another, he glowered on the

---

* Botany Bay was the slang name given by college men to a new square rather remotely situated from the remainder of the college.

10

riotous mob around like a maniac, and astonishment that such liberties could be taken with one in his situation seemed to have surpassed even his rage and resentment; and every now and then a stray thought would flash across his mind that we were mad,—a sentiment which, unfortunately, our conduct was but too well calculated to inspire.

"So you're the morning lecturer, old gentleman, and have just dropped in here in the way of business; pleasant life you must have of it," said Casey, now by far the most tipsy man present.

"If you think, Mr. O'Malley, that the events of this evening are to end here——"

"Very far from it, Doctor," said Power; "I'll draw up a little account of the affair for 'Saunders.' They shall hear of it in every corner and nook of the kingdom."

"The Bursar of Trinity shall be a proverb for a good fellow that loveth his lush," hiccupped out Fegan.

"And if you believe that such conduct is academical," said the Doctor, with a withering sneer.

"Perhaps not," lisped Melville, tightening his belt; "but yet it's devilish convivial—eh, Doctor?"

"Is that like him?" said Moreton, producing a caricature, which he had just sketched.

"Capital—very good—perfect. M'Cleary shall have it in his window by noon to-day," said Power.

At this instant some of the combustibles disposed among the rejected habiliments of my late vocation caught fire, and squibs, crackers, and detonating shots went off on all sides. The Bursar, who had not been deaf to several hints and friendly suggestions about setting fire to him, blowing him up, &c., with one vigorous spring burst from his antagonists, and, clearing the table at a bound, reached the floor. Before he could be seized, he had gained the door, opened it, and was away. We gave chase, yelling like so many devils; but wine and punch, songs and speeches, had done their work, and more than one among the pursuers measured his length upon the pavement; while the terrified Bursar, with the speed of terror, held on his way, and gained his chambers, by about twenty yards in advance of Power and Melville, whose pursuit only ended when the oaken panel of the door shut them out from their victim. One loud cheer beneath his window served for our farewell to our friend, and we returned to my rooms. By this time a regiment of those classic functionaries yclept porters had assembled around the door, and seemed bent upon giving battle in honor of their maltreated ruler; but Power explained to them, in a neat speech, replete with Latin quotations, that their cause was a weak one, that we were more than their match, and, finally, proposed to them to finish the punch-bowl—to which we were really incompetent—a motion that met immediate acceptance; and old Duncan, with his helmet in one hand and a goblet in the other, wished·me many happy days, and every luck in this life, as I stepped from the massive archway, and took my last farewell of Old Trinity.

Should any kind reader feel interested as to the ulterior course assumed by the Bursar, I have only to say that the terrors of the "Board" were never fulminated against me, harmless and innocent as I should have esteemed them. The threat of giving publicity to the entire proceedings by the papers, and the dread of figuring in a sixpenny caricature in M'Cleary's window, were too much for the worthy Doctor, and he took the wiser course, under the circumstances, and held his peace about the matter. I, too, have done so for many a year, and only now recall the scene among the wild transactions of early days and boyish follies.

CHAPTER XXI.

THE PHŒNIX PARK.

WHAT a glorious thing it is when our first waking thoughts not only dispel some dark depressing dream, but arouse us to the consciousness of a new and bright career suddenly opening before us, buoyant in hope, rich in promise for the future! Life has nothing better than this. The bold spring by which the mind clears the depth that separates misery from happiness, is ecstasy itself; and, then, what a world of bright visions come teeming before us—what plans we form—what promises we make to ourselves in our own hearts—how prolific is the dullest imagination—how excursive the tamest fancy, at such a moment! In a few short and fleeting seconds, the events of a whole life are planned and pictured before us. Dreams of happiness and visions of bliss, of which all our after years are insufficient to eradicate the prestige come in myriads about us; and from that narrow aperture through which this new hope pierces into our heart, a flood of light is poured that illumes our path to the very verge of the grave. How many a success in after-days is reckoned but as one step in that ladder of ambition some boyish review has framed,—perhaps, after all, destined to be the first and only one! With what triumph we hail some goal attained, some object of our wishes gained, less for its present benefit than as the accomplishment of some youthful prophecy, when, picturing to our hearts all that we would have in life, we whispered within us the flattery of success.

Who is there who has not had some such moment? and who would exchange it, with all the delusive and deceptive influences by which it comes surrounded, for the greatest actual happiness he has partaken of? Alas! alas! it is only in the boundless expanse of such imaginations, unreal and fictitious as they are, that we are truly blessed. Our choicest blessings in life come even so associated with some sources of care, that the cup of enjoyment is not pure, but dregged in bitterness.

To such a world of bright anticipation did I awake on the morning after the events I have detailed in my last chapter. The first thing my eyes fell upon was an official letter from the Horse Guards:—

"The Commander of the Forces desires that Mr. O'Malley will report himself, immediately on receipt of this letter, at the headquarters of the regiment to which he is gazetted."

Few and simple as the lines were, how brimful of pleasure they sounded to my ears. The regiment to which I was gazetted! And so I was a soldier at last! the first wish of my boyhood was then really accomplished. And my uncle—what will he say?—what will he think?

"A letter, sir, by the post," said Mike, at the moment.

I seized it eagerly; it came from home, but was in Considine's handwriting. How my heart failed me as I turned to look at the seal. "Thank God!" said I, aloud, on perceiving that it was a red one. I now tore it open and read:

"MY DEAR CHARLEY:—Godfrey being laid up with the gout, has desired me to write to you by this day's post. Your appointment to the 14th, notwithstanding all his prejudices about the army, has given him sincere pleasure. I believe, between ourselves, that your college career, of which he has heard something, convinced him that your forte did not lie in the classics; you know I said so always, but nobody minded me. Your new prospects are all that your best friends could wish for you. You begin early; your corps is a crack one; you are ordered for service. What could you have more?

"Your uncle hopes, if you can get a few days' leave, that you will come down here before you join, and I hope so too; for he is unusually low-spirited, and talks about never seeing you again, and all that sort of thing.

"I have written to Merivale, your colonel, on this subject, as well

as generally on your behalf; we were cornets together forty years
ago; a strict fellow you'll find him, but a trump on service. If you
can't manage the leave, write a long letter home, at all events; and
so God bless you, and all success.

" Yours, sincerely,

" W. CONSIDINE.

" I had thought of writing you a long letter of advice for your
new career, and, indeed, half accomplished one. After all, however,
I can tell you little that your own good sense will not teach you as
you go on, and experience is ever better than precept. I know of
but one rule in life which admits of scarcely any exception, and
having followed it upwards of sixty years, approve of it only the
more. Never quarrel when you can help it; but meet any man—
your tailor, your hairdresser—if he wishes to have you out.

" W. C."

I had scarcely come to the end of this very characteristic epistle,
when two more letters were placed upon my table. One was from
Sir George Dashwood, inviting me to dinner, to meet some of my
" brother officers." How my heart beat at the expression. The
other was a short note, marked " Private," from my late tutor, Dr.
Mooney, saying, " that if I made a suitable apology to the Bursar
for the late affair at my room, he might probably be induced to
abandon any further step; otherwise"—then followed innumerable
threats about fine, penalties, expulsion, &c., that fell harmlessly
upon my ears. I accepted the invitation; declined the apology;
and, having ordered my horse, cantered off to the barracks to consult my friend Power as to all the minor details of my career.

As the dinner hour drew near, my thoughts became again fixed
upon Miss Dashwood, and a thousand misgivings crossed my mind
as to whether I should have nerve enough to meet her, without disclosing in my manner the altered state of my feelings—a possibility
which I now dreaded fully as much as I had longed some days before
to avow my affection for her, however slight its prospects of return.
All my valiant resolves, and well-contrived plans for appearing unmoved and indifferent in her presence, with which I stored my mind
while dressing, and when on the way to dinner, were, however,
needless, for it was a party exclusively of men; and as the coffee was
served in the dining-room, no move was made to the drawing-room
by any of the company. " Quite as well as it is!" was my muttered
opinion, as I got into my cab at the door. " All is at an end as regards me in her esteem, and I must not spend my days sighing for a
young lady that cares for another." Very reasonable, very proper
resolutions these; but, alas! I went home to bed only to think half

the night long of the fair Lucy, and dream of her the remainder of it.

When morning dawned, my first thought was, Shall I see her once more? shall I leave her forever thus abruptly? or, rather, shall I not unburden my bosom of its secret, confess my love, and say farewell? I felt such a course much more in unison with my wishes than the day before; and, as Power had told me that before a week we should present ourselves at Fermoy, I knew that no time was to be lost.

My determination was taken. I ordered my horse, and, early as it was, rode out to the Royal Hospital. My heart beat so strongly as I rode up to the door, that I half resolved to return. I rang the bell. Sir George was in town. Miss Dashwood had just gone five minutes before to spend some days at Carton. "It is fate!" thought I, as I turned from the spot, and walked slowly beside my horse towards Dublin.

In the few days that intervened before my leaving town, my time was occupied from morning to night; the various details of my uniform, outfit, &c., were undertaken for me by Power. My horses were sent for to Galway, and I myself, with innumerable persons to see, and a mass of business to transact, contrived, at least three times a day, to ride out to the Royal Hospital, always to make some trifling inquiry for Sir George, and always to hear repeated that Miss Dashwood had not returned.

Thus passed five of my last six days in Dublin, and as the morning of the last opened, it was with a sorrowing spirit that I felt my hour of departure approach, without one only opportunity of seeing Lucy, even to say good-bye.

While Mike was packing in one corner, and I in another was concluding a long letter to my poor uncle, my door opened and Webber entered.

"Eh, O'Malley, I'm only in time to say adieu! it seems. To my surprise this morning I found you had cut the 'Silent Sister.' I feared I should be too late to catch one glimpse of you ere you started for the wars."

"You are quite right, Master Frank, and I scarcely expected to have seen you. Your last brilliant achievement at Sir George's very nearly involved me in a serious scrape."

"A mere trifle. How confoundedly silly Power must have looked, eh? Should have liked so much to have seen his face. He booked up next day—very proper fellow. By the bye, O'Malley, I rather like the little girl; she is decidedly pretty; and her foot—did you remark her foot?—capital."

"Yes, she's very good-looking," said I, carelessly.

"I'm thinking of cultivating her a little," said Webber, pulling up his cravat and adjusting his hair at the glass. "She's spoiled by all the tinsel vaporing of her hussar and aide-de-camp acquaintances; but something may be done for her, eh?"

"With your most able assistance and kind intentions."

"That's what I mean exactly. Sorry you're going—devilish sorry. You served out Stone gloriously: perhaps it's as well, though; you know they'd have expelled you. But still something might turn up; soldiering is a bad style of thing, eh? How the old General did take his sister-in-law's presence to heart. But he must forgive and forget, for I'm going to be very great friends with him and Lucy. Where are you going now?"

"I'm about to try a new horse before troops," said I. "He's staunch enough with the cry of the fox-pack in his ears, but I don't know how he'll stand a peal of artillery."

"Well, come along," said Webber; "I'll ride with you." So saying, we mounted and set off to the Park, where two regiments of cavalry and some horse artillery were ordered for inspection.

The review was over when we reached the exercising ground, and we slowly walked our horses towards the end of the Park, intending to return to Dublin by the road. We had not proceeded far, when, some hundred yards in advance, we perceived an officer riding with a lady, followed by an orderly dragoon.

"There he goes," said Webber; "I wonder if he'd ask me to dinner if I were to throw myself in his way?"

"Whom do you mean?" said I.

"Sir George Dashwood, to be sure, and, *la voilà*, Miss Lucy. The little darling rides well, too. How squarely she sits her horse. O'Malley, I've a weakness there; upon my soul I have."

"Very possible," said I; "I am aware of another friend of mine participating in the sentiment."

"One Charles O'Malley, of his Majesty's——"

"Nonsense, man—no, no. I mean a very different person, and, for all I can see, with some reason to hope for success."

"Oh, as to that, we flatter ourselves the thing does not present any very considerable difficulties."

"As how, pray?"

"Why, of course, like all such matters, a very decisive determination to be, to do, and to suffer, as Lindley Murray says, carries the day. Tell her she's an angel every day for three weeks. She may laugh a little at first, but she'll believe it in the end. Tell her that you have not the slightest prospect of obtaining her affection, but still persist in loving her. That, finally, you must die from the effects of despair, &c., but rather like the notion of it than otherwise. That you know she has no fortune; that you haven't a six-pence; and who should marry, if people whose position in the world was similar did not?"

"But halt; pray, how are you to get time and place for all such interesting conversations?"

"'Time and place! Good heavens, what a question! Is not every hour of the twenty-four the fittest? Is not every place the most suitable? A sudden pause in the organ of St. Patrick's did, it is true, catch me once in a declaration of love, but the choir came in to my aid, and drowned the lady's answer. My dear O'Malley, what could prevent you this instant, if you are so disposed, from doing the amiable to the darling Lucy, there?"

"With the father for an umpire, in case we disagreed," said I.

"Not at all. I should soon get rid of him."

"Impossible, my dear friend."

"Come, now, just for the sake of convincing your obstinacy. If you like to say good-bye to the little girl without a witness, I'll take off the he-dragon."

"You don't mean——"

"I do, man—I do mean it." So saying, he drew a crimson silk handkerchief from his pocket, and fastened it round his waist like an officer's sash. This done, and telling me to keep in their wake for some minutes, he turned from me, and was soon concealed by a copse of whitethorn near us.

I hadn't gone above a hundred yards farther when I heard Sir George's voice calling for the orderly. I looked, and saw Webber at a considerable distance in front, curveting and playing all species of antics. The distance between the General and myself was now so short, that I overheard the following dialogue with his orderly:

"He's not in uniform, then?"

"No, sir; he has a round hat."

"A round hat!"

"His sash——"

"A sword and sash. This is too bad. I'm determined to find him out."

"How d'ye do, General?" cried Webber, as he rode towards the trees.

"Stop, sir!" shouted Sir George.

"Good day, Sir George," replied Webber, retiring.

"Stay where you are, Lucy," said the General, as dashing spurs into his horse, he sprang forward at a gallop, incensed beyond en-durance that his most strict orders should be so openly and insult-ingly transgressed.

Webber led on to a deep hollow, where the road passed between two smooth slopes, covered with furze trees, and from which it emerged afterwards in the thickest and most intricate part of the Park. Sir George dashed boldly after, and in less than half a minute both were lost to my view, leaving me in breathless amazement at Master Frank's ingenuity, and some puzzle as to my own future movements.

"Now, then, or never," said I, as I pushed boldly forward, and in an instant was alongside of Miss Dashwood.

Her astonishment at seeing me so suddenly, increased the confusion from which I felt myself suffering, and for some minutes I could scarcely speak. At last I plucked up courage a little, and said,—

"Miss Dashwood, I have looked most anxiously, for the last four days, for the moment which chance has now given me. I wished, before I parted forever with those to whom I owe already so much, that I should at least speak my gratitude ere I said good-bye."

"But when do you think of going?"

"To-morrow. Captain Power, under whose command I am, has received orders to embark immediately for Portugal."

I thought—perhaps it was but a thought—that her cheek grew somewhat paler as I spoke; but she remained silent; and I, scarcely knowing what I had said, or whether I had finished, spoke not either.

"Papa, I'm sure, is not aware," said she, after a long pause, "of your intention of leaving so soon; for only last night he spoke of some letters he meant to give you to some friends in the Peninsula; besides, I know"—here she smiled faintly—"that he destined some excellent advice for your ears, as to your new path in life, for he has an immense opinion of the value of such to a young officer."

"I am indeed most grateful to Sir George, and truly never did any one stand more in need of counsel than I do." This was said half musingly, and not intended to be heard.

"Then, pray, consult papa," said she, eagerly; "he is much attached to you, and will, I am certain, do all in his power——"

"Alas! I fear not, Miss Dashwood."

"Why, what can you mean? Has anything so serious occurred?"

"No, no; I'm but misleading you, and exciting your sympathy with false pretences. Should I tell you all the truth, you would not pardon, perhaps not hear me."

"You have, indeed, puzzled me; but if there is anything in which my father——"

"Less him than his daughter," said I, fixing my eyes full upon her as I spoke. "Yes, Lucy, I feel I must confess it, cost what it may,—I love you. Stay, hear me out. I know the fruitlessness, the utter despair, that awaits such a sentiment. My own heart tells me that I am not, cannot be, loved in return; yet would I rather cherish in its core my affection slighted and unblessed, such as it is, than own another heart. I ask for nothing, I hope for nothing; I merely entreat that, for my truth, I may meet belief, and for my heart's worship of her whom alone I can love, compassion. I see that you at least pity me. Nay, one word more. I have one favor more to ask; it is my last, my only one. Do not, when time and distance may have separated us—perhaps forever—think that the expressions I now use are prompted by a mere sudden ebullition of boyish feeling—do not attribute to the circumstance of my youth alone the warmth of the attachment I profess; for I swear to you, by every hope I have, that, in my heart of hearts, my love to you is the source and spring of every action in my life, of every aspiration in my heart; and when I cease to love you, I shall cease to feel.

"And now, farewell—farewell forever!" I pressed her hand to my lips, gave one long, last look, turned my horse rapidly away, and ere a minute was far out of sight of where I had left her.

CHAPTER XXII.

THE ROAD.

POWER was detained in town by some orders from the Adjutant-General, so that I started for Cork the next morning, with no other companion than my servant Mike. For the first few stages upon the road, my own thoughts sufficiently occupied me to render me insensible or indifferent to all else. My opening career—the prospects my new life as a soldier held out —my hopes of distinction—my love of Lucy, with all its train of doubts and fears—passed in review before me, and I took no note of time till far past noon. I now looked to the back part of the coach, where Mike's voice had been, as usual, in the ascendant for some time, and perceived that he was surrounded by an eager auditory of four raw recruits, who, under the care of a sergeant, were proceeding to Cork to be enrolled in their regiment. The sergeant, whose minutes of wakefulness were only those when the coach stopped to change horses and when he got down to mix a "summat hot," paid little attention to his followers, leaving them perfectly free in all their movements, to listen to Mike's eloquence, and profit by his suggestions, should they deem fit. Master Michael's services to his new acquaintances, I began to perceive, were not exactly of the same nature as Dibdin is reported to have rendered to our navy in the late war. Far from it; his theme was no contemptuous disdain for danger—no patriotic enthusiasm to fight for home and country—no proud consciousness of British valor, mingled with the appropriate hatred of our mutual enemies; on the contrary, Mike's eloquence was enlisted for the defendant. He detailed, and in no unimpressive way either, the hardships of a soldier's life,—its dangers, its vicissitudes, its chances, its possible penalties, its inevitably small rewards; and, in fact, so completely did he work on the feelings of his hearers, that I perceived more than one glance exchanged between the victims, that certainly betokened anything save the resolve to fight for King George. It was at the close of a long and most powerful appeal upon the superiority of any other line of life, petty larceny and small felony inclusive, that he concluded with the following quotation:

"Thrue for ye, boys!

> ' With your red scarlet coat,
>   You're as proud as a goat,
>   And your long cap and feather.'

But, by the piper that played before Moses! it's more whipping nor gingerbread is going on amongst them, av ye knew but all, and heerd the misfortune that happened to my father."

"And was he a sodger?" inquired one.

"Troth was he—more sorrow to him; and wasn't he a'most whipped one day, for doing what he was bid?"

"Musha, but that was hard."

"To be sure it was hard; but, faix, when my father seen that they didn't know their own minds, he thought, anyhow, he knew his, so he ran away, and devil a bit of him they ever cotch afther. Maybe ye might like to hear the story, and there's instruction in it for yez too."

A general request to this end being preferred by the company, Mike took a shrewd look at the sergeant, to be sure that he was still sleeping, settled his coat comfortably across his knees, and began:

"Well, it's a good many years ago my father 'listed in the North Cork, just to oblige Mr. Barry, the landlord there; 'for,' says he, ' Phil,' says he, ' it's not a soldier ye'll be at all, but my own man, to brush my clothes and go errands, and the like o' that; and the King, —long life to him!—will help to pay ye for your trouble. Ye understand me?' Well, my father agreed, and Mr. Barry was as good as his word. Never a guard did my father mount, nor as much as a drill had he, nor a roll-call, nor anything at all, save and except wait on the Captain, his master, just as pleasant as need be, and no inconvenience in life.

"Well, for three years this went on as I am telling, and the regiment was ordered down to Bantry, because of a report that the 'boys' was rising down there; and the second evening there was a night party patrolling with Captain Barry for six hours in the rain, and the Captain—God be marciful to him!—tuk cowld and died; more by token, they said it was drink, but my father says it wasn't; 'for,' says he, 'after he tuk eight tumblers comfortable,' my father mixed the ninth, and the Captain waved his hand this way, as much as to say he'd have no more. 'Is it that ye mean?' says my father. And the Captain nodded. 'Musha, but it's sorry I am,' says my father, 'to see you this way, for ye must be bad entirely to leave off in the beginning of the evening.' And thrue for him, the Captain was dead in the morning.

"A sorrowful day it was for my father when he died. It was the finest place in the world; little to do; plenty of divarsion; and a kind man he was—when he was drunk. Well, then, when the Captain was buried and all was over, my father hoped they'd be for letting him away, as he said, 'Sure, I'm no use in life to anybody, save the man that's gone, for his ways are all I know, and I never was a sodger.' But, upon my conscience, they had other thoughts in their heads; for they ordered him into the ranks to be drilled just like the recruits they took the day before.

"'Musha, isn't this hard?' said my father. Here I am, an ould vitrin that ought to be discharged on a pension, with two-and-sixpence a day, obliged to go capering about the barrack-yard, practising the goose-step, or some other nonsense not becoming my age nor my habits.' But so it was. Well, this went on for some time, and, sure, if they were hard on my father, hadn't he his revenge, for he nigh broke their hearts with his stupidity. Oh! nothing in life could equal him; devil a thing, no matter how easy, he could learn at all, and so far from caring for being in confinement, it was that he liked best. Every sergeant in the regiment had a trial of him, but all to no good; and he seemed striving so hard to learn all the while that they were loath to punish him, the ould rogue!

"This was going on for some time, when one day news came in that a body of the rebels, as they called them, was coming down from the Gap of Mulnavick to storm the town and burn all before them. The whole regiment was of course under arms, and great preparations were made for a battle. Meanwhile, patrols were ordered to scour the roads, and sentries posted at every turn of the way and every rising ground to give warning when the boys came in sight; and my father was placed at the Bridge of Drumsnag, in the wildest and bleakest part of the whole country, with nothing but furze mountains on every side, and a straight road going over the top of them.

"'This is pleasant,' says my father, as soon as they left him there alone by himself, with no human creature to speak to, nor a whisky-shop within ten miles of him; 'cowld comfort,' says he, 'on a winter's day, and faix, but I have a mind to give ye the slip.'

"Well, he put his gun down on the bridge, and he lit his pipe, and he sat down under an ould tree and began to ruminate upon his affairs.

"'Oh, then, it's wishing it well I am,' says he, 'for sodgering; and bad luck to the hammer that struck the shilling that 'listed me, that's all,' for he was mighty low in his heart.

"Just then a noise came rattling down near him. He listened, and, before he could get on his legs, down comes the General, ould Cohoon, with an orderly after him.

"'Who goes that?' says my father.

"'The round,' says the General, looking about all the time to see where was the sentry, for my father was snug under the tree.

"'What round?' says my father.

"'The grand round,' says the General, more puzzled than afore.

"'Pass on, grand round, and God save you kindly!' says my father, putting his pipe in his mouth again, for he thought all was over.

"'D—n your soul, where are you?' says the General, for sorra bit of my father could he see yet.

"'It's here I am,' says he, 'and a cowld place I have of it; and if it wasn't for the pipe I'd be lost entirely.'

"The words wasn't well out of his mouth when the General began laughing till ye'd think he'd fall off his horse; and the dragoon behind him—more by token, they say it wasn't right for him—laughed as loud as himself.

"'Yer a droll sentry,' says the General, as soon as he could speak.

"'Be-gorra, it's little fun there's left in me,' says my father, 'with this drilling, and parading, and blackguarding about the roads all night.'

"'And is this the way you salute your officer?' says the General.

"'Just so,' says my father; 'devil a more politeness ever they taught me.'

"'What regiment do you belong to?' says the General.

"'The North Cork, bad luck to them!' says my father, with a sigh.

"'They ought to be proud of ye,' says the General.

"'I'm sorry for it,' says my father, sorrowfully, 'for maybe they'll keep me the longer.'

"'Well, my good fellow,' says the General, 'I haven't more time to waste here; but let me teach you something before I go. Whenever your officer passes, it's your duty to present to him.'

"'Arrah, it's jokin' ye are,' says my father.

"'No, I'm in earnest,' says he, 'as ye might learn, to your cost, if I brought you to a court-martial.'

"'Well, there's no knowing,' says my father, 'what they'd be up to; but sure, if that's all, I'll do it, with all "the veins," whenever yer coming this way again.'

"The General began to laugh again here; but said,—

"'I'm coming back in the evening,' says he, 'and mind you don't forget your respects to your officer.'

"'Never fear, sir,' says my father: 'and many thanks to you for your kindness for telling me.'

"Away went the General, and the orderly after him, and in ten minutes they were out of sight.

"The night was falling fast, and one half of the mountain was quite dark already, when my father began to think they were forgetting him entirely. He looked one way, and he looked another, but sorra bit of a sergeant's guard was coming to relieve him. There he was, fresh and fasting, and daren't go for the bare life. 'I'll give you a quarter of an hour more,' says my father, 'till the light leaves that rock up there; after that,' says he, 'by the mass! I'll be off, av it cost me what it may.'

"Well, sure enough, his courage was not needed this time; for what did he see at the same moment, but a shadow of something coming down the road opposite the bridge. He looked again; and then he made out the General himself, that was walking his horse down the steep part of the mountain, followed by the orderly. My father immediately took up his musket off the wall, settled his belts, shook the ashes out of his pipe, and put it into his pocket, making himself as smart and neat-looking as he could be, determining, when ould Cohoon came up, to ask him for leave to go home, at least for the night. Well, by this time the General was turning a sharp part of the cliff that looks down upon the bridge, from where you might look five miles round on every side. 'He sees me,' says my father; 'but I'll be just as quick as himself.' No sooner said than done; for, coming forward to the parapet of the bridge, he up with his musket to his shoulder, and presented it straight at the General. It wasn't well there, when the officer pulled up his horse quite short, and shouted out, 'Sentry! sentry!'

"'Anan?' said my father, still covering him.

"'Down with your musket, you rascal. Don't you see it's the grand round?'

"'To be sure I do,' says my father, never changing for a minute.

"'The ruffian will shoot me,' says the General.

"'Devil a fear,' says my father, 'av it doesn't go off of itself.'

"'What do you mean by that, you villain?' says the General, scarcely able to speak with fright, for, every turn he gave on his horse, my father followed with the gun—'what do you mean?'

"'Sure, ain't I presenting?' says my father. 'Blood an' ages! do you want me to fire next?'

"With that the General drew a pistol from his holster, and took deliberate aim at my father; and there they both stood for five minutes, looking at each other, the orderly all the while breaking his heart laughing behind a rock; for, ye see, the General knew av he retreated that my father might fire on purpose, and, av he came on, that he might fire by chance; and sorra bit he knew what was best to be done.

"'Are ye going to pass the evening up there, grand round?' says my father; 'for it's tired I'm getting houldin' this so long.'

"'Port arms!' shouted the General, as if on parade.

"'Sure I can't, till yer past,' says my father, angrily, 'and my hand's trembling already.'

"'By heavens! I shall be shot,' says the General.

"'Be-gorra, it's what I'm afraid of,' says my father; and the words wasn't out of his mouth before off went the musket—bang— and down fell the General, smack on the ground, senseless. Well, the orderly ran out at this, and took him up and examined his wound; but it wasn't a wound at all, only the wadding of the gun; for my father—God be kind to him!—ye see, could do nothing right; and so he bit off the wrong end of the cartridge when he put it in the gun, and, by reason, there was no bullet in it. Well, from that day after they never got a sight of him; for the instant that the General dropped, he sprang over the bridge-wall and got away; and what between living in a lime-kiln for two months, eating nothing but blackberries and sloes, and other disguises, he never returned to the army, but ever after took to a civil situation, and driv a hearse for many years."

How far Mike's narrative might have contributed to the support of his theory, I am unable to pronounce; for his auditory were, at some distance from Cork, made to descend from their lofty position, and join a larger body of recruits, all proceeding to the same destination, under a strong escort of infantry. For ourselves, we reached the "beautiful city" in due time, and took up our quarters at the Old George Hotel.

CHAPTER XXIII.

CORK.

THE undress rehearsal of a new piece, with its dirty-booted actors, its cloaked and hooded actresses *en papillote*, bears about the same relation to the gala, wax-lit, and bespangled ballet as the raw young gentleman of yesterday to the epauletted, belted, and sabretasched dragoon, whose transformation is due to a few hours of headquarters, and a few interviews with the adjutant.

So, at least, I felt it; and it was with a very perfect concurrence in his Majesty's taste in a uniform, and a most entire approval of the regimental tailor, that I strutted down George's street a few days after my arrival in Cork. The transports had not as yet come round; there was a great doubt of their doing so for a week or so longer; and I found myself, as the dashing Cornet, the centre of a thousand polite attentions and most kind civilities.

The officer under whose orders I was placed for the time was a great friend of Sir George Dashwood's, and paid me, in consequence, much attention. Major Dalrymple had been on the staff from the commencement of his military career—had served in the Commissariat for some time—was much on foreign stations, but never, by any of the many casualties of his life, had seen what could be called service. His idea of the soldier's profession was, therefore, what might almost be as readily picked up by a commission in the battle-axe guards, as one in his Majesty's 50th. He was now a species of distinct paymaster employed in a thousand ways, either inspecting recruits, examining accounts, revising sick certificates, or receiving contracts for mess beef. Whether the nature of his manifold occupations had enlarged the sphere of his talents and ambition, or whether the abilities had suggested the variety of his duties, I know not; but truly the Major was a man of all work. No sooner did a young ensign join his regiment at Cork, than Major Dalrymple's card was left at his quarters; the next day came the Major himself; the third brought an invitation to dinner; on the fourth he was told to drop in, in the evening; and from thenceforward he was the *ami de la maison*, in company with numerous others as newly-fledged and inexperienced as himself.

One singular feature of the society at the house was, that although the Major was as well known as the flag on Spike Island, yet, somehow, no officer above the rank of an ensign was ever to be met there. It was not that he had not a large acquaintance; in fact, the "How are you, Major?"—"How goes it, Dalrymple?" that kept everlastingly going on as he walked the streets, proved the reverse; but,

strange enough, his predilections leaned towards the newly-gazetted,
far before the bronzed and scared campaigners who had seen the
world, and knew more about it. The reasons for this line of conduct were two-fold. In the first place, there was not an article of
outfit, from a stock to a sword-belt, that he could not and did not
supply to the young officer; from the gorget of the infantry, to the
shako of the grenadier, all came within his province; not that he
actually kept a *magasin* of these articles, but he had so completely
interwoven his interests with those of numerous shopkeepers in
Cork, that he rarely entered a shop over whose door Dalrymple and
Co. might not have figured on the signboard. His stables were
filled with a perfect infirmary of superannuated chargers, fattened
and conditioned up to a miracle, and groomed to perfection. He
could get you—*only you*—about three dozen of sherry, to take out
with you as sea-store; he knew of such a servant; he chanced upon
such a camp-furniture yesterday in his walks; in fact, why want
for anything? His resources were inexhaustible—his kindness unbounded.

Then money was no object—hang it, you could pay when you
liked—what signified it? In other words, a bill at thirty-one days,
cashed and discounted by a friend of the Major's, would always do.
While such were the unlimited advantages his acquaintance conferred, the sphere of his benefits took another range. The Major
had two daughters. Matilda and Fanny were as well known in the
army as Lord Fitzroy Somerset or Picton, from the Isle of Wight to
Halifax, from Cape Coast to Chatham, from Belfast to the Bermudas.
Where was the subaltern who had not knelt at the shrine of one or the
other, if not of both, and vowed eternal love until a change of quarters? In plain words, the Major's solicitude for the service was such
that, not content with providing the young officer with all the necessary outfit of his profession, he longed also to supply him with a
comforter for his woes, a charmer for his solitary hours, in the person of one of his amiable daughters. Unluckily, however, the necessity for a wife is not enforced by " general orders," as is the cut
of your coat, or the length of your sabre; consequently, the Major's
success in the home department of his diplomacy was not destined
for the same happy results that awaited it when engaged about drill
trousers and camp kettles, and the Misses Dalrymple remained
Misses through every clime and every campaign. And yet, why
was it so? It is hard to say. What would men have? Matilda was
a dark-haired, dark-eyed, romantic-looking girl, with a tall figure
and a slender waist, with more poetry in her head than would have
turned any ordinary brain; always unhappy; in need of consolation;
never meeting with the kindred spirit that understood her; destined

11

to walk the world alone, her fair thoughts smothered in the recesses of her own heart. Devilish hard to stand this, when you began in a kind of platonic friendship on both sides. More than one poor fellow nearly-succumbed, particularly when she came to quote Cowley, and told him with tears in her eyes,—

"There are hearts that live and love alone," &c.

I'm assured that this *coup de grace* rarely failed in being followed by a downright avowal of open love, which, somehow, what between the route coming, what with waiting for leave from home, &c., never got further than a most tender scene, and exchange of love tokens; in fact, such became so often the termination, that Powers swears Matty had to make a firm resolve about cutting off any more hair, fearing a premature baldness during the recruiting season.

Now, Fanny had selected another arm of the service. Her hair was fair; her eyes blue,—laughing, languishing, mischief-loving blue—with long lashes, and a look in them that was wont to leave its impression rather longer than you exactly knew of; then, her figure was *petite*, but perfect; her feet Canova might have copied; and her hand was a study for Titian; her voice, too, was soft and musical, but full of that *gaiété de cœur* that never fails to charm. While her sister's style was *il penseroso*, hers was *l'allegro;* every imaginable thing, place, or person supplied food for her mirth, and her sister's lovers all came in for their share. She hunted with Smith Barry's hounds; she yachted with the Cove Club; she coursed, practised at a mark with a pistol, and played chicken hazard with all the cavalry; for, let it be remarked as a physiological fact, Matilda's admirers were almost invariably taken from the infantry, while Fanny's adorers were as regularly dragoons. Whether the former be the romantic arm of the service, and the latter be more adapted to dull realities, or whether the phenomenon had any other explanation, I leave to the curious. Now this arrangement, proceeding upon that principle which has wrought such wonders in Manchester and Sheffield—the division of labor—was a most wise and equitable one; each having her one separate and distinct field of action, interference was impossible; not but that when, as in the present instance, cavalry was in the ascendant, Fanny would willingly spare a dragoon or two to her sister, who likewise would repay the debt when occasion offered.

The mamma—for it is time I should say something of the head of the family—was an excessively fat, coarse-looking, dark-skinned personage of some fifty years, with a voice like a boatswain in a quinsy. Heaven can tell, perhaps, why the worthy Major allied his fortunes with hers, for she was evidently of a very inferior rank in society ; could never have been aught than downright ugly ; and I never heard that she brought him any money. " Spoiled five," the national amusement of her age and sex in Cork, scandal, the changes in the army list, the failures in speculation of her luckless husband, the forlorn fortunes of her daughters, kept her in occupation ; and her days were passed in one perpetual, unceasing current of dissatisfaction and ill-temper with all around, that formed a heavy counterpoise to the fascinations of the young ladies. The repeated jiltings to which they had been subject had blunted any delicacy upon the score of their marriage, and if the newly-introduced cornet or ensign was not coming forward, as became him, at the end of the requisite number of days, he was sure of receiving a very palpable admonition from Mrs. Dalrymple. Hints, at first dimly shadowed, that Matilda was not in spirits this morning ; that Fanny, poor child, had a headache,—directed especially at the culprit in question,— grew gradually into those little motherly fondnesses in mamma, that, like the fascinations of the rattlesnake, only lure on to ruin. The doomed man was pressed to dinner when all others were permitted to take their leave ; he was treated like one of the family— God help him ! After dinner, the Major would keep him an hour over his wine, discussing the misery of an ill-assorted marriage ; detailing his own happiness in marrying a woman like the Tonga Islander I have mentioned ; hinting that girls should be brought up not only to become companions to their husbands, but with ideas fitting their station ; if his auditor were a military man, that none but an old officer (like him) could know how to educate girls (like his) ; and that, feeling he possessed two such treasures, his whole aim in life was to guard and keep them,—a difficult task, when proposals of the most flattering kind were coming constantly before him. Then followed a fresh bottle, during which the Major would consult his young friend upon a very delicate affair—no less than a proposition for the hand of Miss Matilda, or Fanny, whichever he was supposed to be soft upon. This was generally a *coup de maître ;* should he still resist, he was handed over to Mrs. Dalrymple, with a strong indictment against him, and rarely did he escape a heavy sentence. Now, is it not strange that two really pretty girls, with fully enough of amiable and pleasing qualities to have excited the attention and won the affections of many a man, should have gone on for years—for, alas ! they did so in every climate under every sun—to waste their sweetness in this miserable career of intrigue and man-trap, and yet nothing come of it ? But so it was. The first question a newly-landed regiment was asked, if coming where they resided, was, " Well, how are the girls ?" " Oh, gloriously. Matty is there." " Ah, indeed ! poor thing !" " Has Fan sported a new habit ?"

"Is it the old gray, with the hussar braiding? Confound it, that was seedy when I saw them in Corfu. And is Mother Dal as fat and vulgar as ever?" "Dawson of ours was the last, and was called up for sentence when we were ordered away: of course he bolted," &c. Such was the invariable style of question and answer concerning them; and although some few, either from good feeling or fastidiousness, relished but little the mode in which it had become habitual to treat them, I grieve to say that, generally, they were pronounced fair game for every species of flirtation and love-making, without any "intentions" for the future. I should not have trespassed so far upon my readers' patience, were I not, in recounting these traits of my friends above, narrating matters of history. How many are there who may cast their eyes upon these pages, that will say, "Poor Matilda, I knew her at Gibraltar. Little Fanny was the life and soul of us all in Quebec."

"Mr. O'Malley," said the Adjutant, as I presented myself in the afternoon of my arrival in Cork, to a short, punchy, little red-faced gentleman, in a short jacket and ducks, "you are, I perceive, appointed to the 14th; you will have the goodness to appear on parade to-morrow morning. The riding-school hours are ————. The morning drill is —— ——; evening drill, —— ——. Mr. Minchin, you are a 14th man, I believe; no, I beg your pardon, a Carbineer; but no matter. Mr. O'Malley—Mr. Minchin; Captain Dounie—Mr. O'Malley. You'll dine with us to-day, and to-morrow you shall be entered at the mess."

"Yours are at Santarem, I believe?" said an old weather-beaten looking officer with one arm.

"I'm ashamed to say I know nothing whatever of them; I received my gazette unexpectedly enough."

"Ever in Cork before, Mr. O'Malley?"

"Never," said I.

"Glorious place!" lisped a white-eyelashed, knock-kneed Ensign; "splendid *gals*, eh?"

"Ah, Brunton," said Minchin, "you may boast a little, but we poor devils——"

"Know the Dals?" said the hero of the lisp, addressing me.

"I haven't that honor," I replied, scarcely able to guess whether what he alluded to were objects of the picturesque or a private family.

"Introduce him, then, at once," said the Adjutant; "we'll all go in the evening. What will the old squaw think?"

"Not I," said Minchin. "She wrote to the Duke of York about my helping Matilda at supper, and not having any honorable intentions afterwards."

" We dine at 'The George' to-day, Mr. O'Malley, sharp seven. Until then——"

So saying, the little man bustled back to his accounts, and I took my leave with the rest, to stroll about the town till dinner-time.

CHAPTER XXIV.

THE ADJUTANT'S DINNER.

THE Adjutant's dinner was as professional an affair as need be. A circuit or a learned society could not have been more exclusively devoted to their own separate and immediate topics than were we. Pipeclay in all its varieties came on the *tapis;* the last regulation cap—the new button—the promotions—the general orders—the Colonel, and the Colonel's wife—stoppages, and the mess fund, were all well and ably discussed; and, strange enough, while the conversation took this wide range, not a chance allusion, not one stray hint, ever wandered to the brave fellows who were covering the army with glory in the Peninsula, nor one souvenir of him that was even then enjoying a fame, as a leader, second to none in Europe. This surprised me not a little at the time; but I have since that learned how little interest the real services of an army possess for the ears of certain officials, who, stationed at home quarters, pass their inglorious lives in the details of drill, parade, mess-room gossip and barrack scandal. Such, in fact, were the dons of the present dinner. We had a Commissary-General, an inspecting Brigade-Major of something, a Physician to the Forces, the Adjutant himself, and Major Dalrymple; the *oi polloi* consisting of the raw Ensign, a newly-fledged Cornet (Mr. Sparks), and myself.

The Commissary told some very pointless stories about his own department, the Doctor read a dissertation upon Walcheren fever, the Adjutant got very stupidly tipsy, and Major Dalrymple succeeded in engaging the three juniors of the party to tea, having previously pledged us to purchase nothing whatever of outfit without his advice, he well knowing (which he did) how young fellows like us were cheated, and resolving to be a father to us (which he certainly tried to be).

As we rose from the table about ten o'clock, I felt how soon a few such dinners would succeed in disenchanting me of all my military illusions; for, young as I was, I saw that the Commissary was a vulgar bore, the Doctor a humbug, the Adjutant a sot, and the Major himself I greatly suspected to be an old rogue.

" You are coming with us, Sparks?" said Major Dalrymple, as he took me by one arm and the Ensign by the other. "We are going to have a little tea with the ladies ; not five minutes' walk."

"Most happy, sir," said Mr. Sparks, with a very flattered expression of countenance.

"O'Malley, you know Sparks, and Burton too."

This served for a species of triple introduction, at which we all bowed, simpered, and bowed again. We were very happy to have the pleasure, &c.

" How pleasant to get away from these fellows!" said the Major; "they are so uncommonly prosy, That Commissary, with his mess beef, and old Pritchard, with black doses and rigors—nothing so insufferable. Besides, in reality, a young officer never needs all that nonsense. A little medicine chest—I'll get you one each to-morrow for five pounds ; no, five pounds ten : the same thing—that will see you all through the Peninsula. Remind me of it in the morning." This we all promised to do, and the Major resumed : "I say, Sparks, you've got a real prize in that gray horse; such a trooper as he is ! O'Malley, you'll be wanting something of that kind, if we can find it out for you."

" Many thanks, Major, but my cattle are on the way here already. I've only three horses, but I think they are tolerably good ones."

The Major now turned to Burton, and said something in a low tone, to which the other replied,—

" Well, if you say so, I'll get it, but it's devilish dear."

"Dear ! my young friend ; cheap, dog cheap."

"Only think, O'Malley, a whole brass-bed, camp-stool, basin-stand, all complete for sixty pounds ! If it was not that a widow was disposing of it in great distress, one hundred could not buy it. Here we are; come along—no ceremony. Mind the two steps; that's it. Mrs. Dalrymple, Mr. O'Malley ; Mr. Sparks, Mr. Burton, my daughters. Is tea over, girls?"

" Why, papa, it's near eleven o'clock," said Fanny, as she rose to ring the bell, displaying, in so doing, the least possible portion of a very well-turned ankle.

Miss Matilda Dal laid down her book, but, seemingly lost in abstraction, did not deign to look at us. Mrs. Dalrymple, however, did the honors with much politeness, and having, by a few adroit and well-put queries, ascertained everything concerning our rank and position, seemed perfectly satisfied that our intrusion was justifiable.

While my *confrère* Mr. Sparks was undergoing his examination, I had time to look at the ladies, whom I was much surprised at finding so very well-looking; and as the Ensign had opened a conversation with Fanny, I approached my chair towards the other, and having carelessly turned over the leaves of the book she had been reading, drew her on to talk of it. As my acquaintance with young ladies hitherto had been limited to those who had "no soul," I felt some difficulty at first in keeping up with the exalted tone of my fair companion, but by letting her take the lead for some time, I got to know more of the ground. We went on tolerably together, every moment increasing my stock of technicals, which were all that was needed to sustain the conversation. How often have I found the same plan succeed, whether discussing a question of law or medicine, with a learned professor of either; or, what is still more difficult, canvassing the merits of a preacher, or a doctrine, with a serious young lady, whose "blessed privileges" were at first a little puzzling to comprehend.

I so contrived it, too, that Miss Matilda should seem as much to be making a convert to her views as to have found a person capable of sympathizing with her; and thus, long before the little supper with which it was the Major's practice to regale his friends every evening made its appearance, we had established a perfect understanding together—a' circumstance that, a bystander might have remarked, was productive of a more widely-diffused satisfaction than I could have myself seen any just cause for. Mr. Burton was also progressing, as the Yankees say, with the sister. Sparks had booked himself as purchaser of military stores enough to make the campaign of the whole globe, and we were thus all evidently fulfilling our various vocations, and affording perfect satisfaction to our entertainers.

Then came the spatch-cock, and the sandwiches, and the negus, which Fanny first mixed for papa, and, subsequently, with some little pressing, for Mr. Burton; Matilda, the romantic, assisted me. Sparks helped himself. Then we laughed and told stories; pressed Sparks to sing, which as he declined to do so, we only pressed the more. How invariably, by the bye, is it the custom to show one's appreciation of anything like a butt, by pressing him for a song.

The Major was in great spirits, told us anecdotes of his early life in India, and how he once contracted to supply the troops with milk, and made a purchase, in consequence, of some score of cattle, which turned out to be bullocks. Matilda recited some lines from Pope in my ear. Fanny challenged Burton to a rowing match. Sparks listened to all around him, and Mrs. Dalrymple mixed a very little weak punch, which Dr. Lucas had recommended to her, to take the last thing at night—*Noctes cænæque*. Say what you will, these were very jovial little *réunions.* The girls were decidedly very pretty. We were in high favor, and when we took leave at the door, with a very cordial shake hands, it was with no *arrière pensée* we promised to see them in the morning.

CHAPTER XXV.

THE ENTANGLEMENT.

WHEN we think for a moment over all the toils, all the anxieties, all the fevered excitement of a *grande passion*, it is not a little singular that love should so frequently be elicited by a state of mere idleness; and yet nothing, after all, is so predisposing a cause as this. Where is the man between eighteen and eight-and-thirty—might I not say forty?—who, without any very pressing duns, and having no taste for strong liquor and *rouge et noir*, can possibly lounge through the long hours of his day without at least fancying himself in love? The thousand little occupations it suggests become a necessity of existence; its very worries are like the wholesome opposition that purifies and strengthens the frame of a free state. Then, what is there half so sweet as the reflective flattery which results from our appreciation of an object who, in return, deems us the *ne plus ultra* of perfection? There it is, in fact—that confounded bump of self-esteem does it all, and has more imprudent matches to answer for than all the occipital protuberances that ever scared poor Harriet Martineau.

Now, to apply my moralizing. I very soon, to use the mess phrase, got "devilish spooney" about the "Dals." The morning drill, the riding-school, and the parade, were all most fervently consigned to a certain military character that shall be nameless, as detaining me from some appointment made the evening before; for, as I supped there each night, a party of one kind or another was always planned for the day following. Sometimes we had a boating excursion to Cove; sometimes a picnic at Foaty; now a rowing party to Glanmire, or a ride, at which I furnished the cavalry. These doings were all under my especial direction, and I thus became speedily the organ of the Dalrymple family; and the simple phrase, "It was Mr. O'Malley's arrangement," "Mr. O'Malley wished it," was like the "*Moi le roi*" of Louis XIV.

Though all this while we continued to carry on most pleasantly, Mrs. Dalrymple, I could perceive, did not entirely sympathize with our projects of amusement. As an experienced engineer might feel, when watching the course of some storming projectile—some brilliant congreve—flying over a besieged fortress, yet never touching the walls, nor harming the inhabitants, so she looked on all these demonstrations of attack with no small impatience, and wondered when the breach would be reported practicable. Another puzzle also contributed its share of anxiety—which of the girls was it? To be sure, he spent three hours every morning with Fanny; but, then, he never left Matilda the whole evening. He had given his miniature to one; a locket with his hair was a present to the sister. The Major thinks he saw his arm round Matilda's waist in the garden; the housemaid swears she saw him kiss Fanny in the pantry. Matilda smiles when we talk of his name with her sister's; Fanny laughs outright, and says, "Poor Matilda, the man never dreamed of her." This is becoming uncomfortable; the Major must ask his intentions—it is certainly one or the other; but then we have a right to know which. Such was a very condensed view of Mrs. Dalrymple's reflections on this important topic—a view taken with her usual tact and clear-sightedness.

Matters were in this state, when Power at length arrived in Cork, to take command of our detachment, and make the final preparations for our departure. I had been, as usual, spending the evening at the Major's, and had just reached my quarters, when I found my friend sitting at my fire, smoking his cigar and solacing himself with a little brandy-and-water.

"At last," said he, as I entered—"at last! Why, where the deuce have you been till this hour—past two o'clock? There is no ball, no assembly going on, eh?"

"No," said I, half blushing at the eagerness of the inquiry; "I've been spending the evening with a friend."

"Spending the evening! say, rather, the night. Why, confound you, man, what is there in Cork to keep you out of bed till near three?"

"Well, if you must know, I've been supping at a Major Dalrymple's—a devilish good fellow—with two such daughters!"

"Ahem!" said Power, shutting one eye knowingly, and giving a look like a Yorkshire horse-dealer. "Go on."

"Why, what do you mean?"

"Go on—continue."

"I've finished—I've nothing more to tell."

"So, they're here, are they!" said he, reflectively

"Who?" said I.

"Matilda and Fanny, to be sure."

"Why, you know them, then?"

"I should think I do."

" Where have you met them ?"

" Where have I not ?   When I was in the Rifles, they were quartered at Zante.   Matilda was just then coming it rather strong with Villiers, of ours, a regular greenhorn.   Fanny, also, nearly did for Harry Nesbitt, by riding a hurdle-race.   They then left for Gibraltar, in the year—what year was it ?"

" Come, come," said I, " this is a humbug : the girls are quite young ; you just have heard their names."

" Well, perhaps so ; only tell me which is your peculiar weakness, as they say in the west, and maybe I'll convince you."

" Oh ! as to that," said I, laughing, " I'm not very far gone on either side."

" Then Matilda, probably, has not tried you with Cowley, eh ?— you look a little pink—' There are hearts that live and love alone.' Oh ! poor fellow, you've got it.   By Jove ! how you've been coming it, though, in ten days !   She ought not to have got to that for a month, at least; and how like a young one it was, to be caught by the poetry.   Oh ! Master Charley, I thought that the steeple-chaser might have done most with your Galway heart—the girl in the gray habit, that sings ' Moddirederoo,' ought to have been the prize. Halt ! by St. George, but that tickles you also !   Why, zounds, if I go on, probably, at this rate, I'll find a tender spot occupied by the black lady herself."

It was no use concealing, or attempting to conceal, anything from my inquisitive friend ; so I mixed my grog, and opened my whole heart ; told how I had been conducting myself for the entire preceding fortnight ; and, when I concluded, sat silently awaiting Power's verdict, as though a jury were about to pronounce upon my life.

" Have you ever written ?"

" Never ; except, perhaps, a few lines, with tickets for the theatre, or something of that kind."

" Have you copies of your correspondence ?"

" Of course not.   Why, what do you mean ?"

" Has Mrs. Dal ever been present, or, as the French say, has she assisted, at any of your tender interviews with the young ladies ?"

" I'm not aware that one kisses a girl before mamma."

" I'm not speaking of that ; I merely allude to flirtation."

" Oh ! I suppose she has seen me attentive."

" Very awkward, indeed !   There is only one point in your favor; for, as your attentions were not decided, and as the law does not, as yet, permit polygamy——"

" Come, come, you know I never thought of marrying."

"Ah ! but they did."

" Not a bit of it."

"Ay, but they did. What do you wager but that the Major asks your intentions, as he calls it, the moment he hears the transport has arrived?"

" By Jove! now you remind me, he asked this evening when he could have a few minutes' private conversation with me to-morrow, and I thought it was about some confounded military chest or sea store, or one of his infernal contrivances that he every day assures me are indispensable; though, if every officer had only as much baggage as I have got, under his directions, it would take two armies at least to carry the effects of the fighting one."

" Poor fellow!" said he, starting upon his legs; "what a burst you've made of it!" So saying, he began, in a nasal twang,—

" I publish the banns of marriage between Charles O'Malley, late of his Majesty's 14th Dragoons, and —— Dalrymple, spinster, of this city ——"

" I'll be hanged if you do, though," said I, seeing pretty clearly by this time something of the estimation my friends were held in. " Come, Power, pull me through, like a dear fellow—pull me through, without doing anything to hurt the girls' feelings."

" Well, we'll see about it," said he—" we'll see about it in the morning, but, at the same time, let me assure you, the affair is not so easy as you may, at first blush, suppose. These worthy people have been so often 'done'—to use the cant phrase—before, that scarcely a *ruse* remains untried. It is of no use pleading that your family won't consent—that your prospects are null—that you are ordered for India—that you are engaged elsewhere—that you have nothing but your pay—that you are too young or too old—all such reasons, good and valid with any other family, will avail you little here. Neither will it serve your cause that you may be warranted by a doctor subject to periodical fits of insanity; monomaniacal tendencies to cut somebody's throat, &c. Bless your heart, man, they have soul above such littlenesses. They care nothing for consent of friends, means, age, health, climate, prospects, or temper. Firmly believing matrimony to be a lottery, they are not superstitious about the number they pitch upon; provided only that they get a ticket, they are content."

" Then it strikes me, if what you say is correct, that I have no earthly chance of escape, except some kind friend will undertake to shoot me."

" That has been also tried."

" Why, how do you mean?"

"A mock duel, got up at mess—we had one at Malta, Poor Vickers was the hero of that affair. It was right well planned, too. One of the letters was suffered, by mere accident, to fall into Mrs. Dal's hands, and she was quite prepared for the event, when he was reported shot the next morning. Then the young lady, of course, whether she cared or not, was obliged to be perfectly unconcerned, lest the story of engaged affections might get wind, and spoil another market. The thing went on admirably, till one day, some few months later, they saw, in a confounded army-list, that the late George Vickers was promoted to the 18th Dragoons, so that the trick was discovered, and is, of course, stale at present."

"Then could I not have a wife already, and a large family of interesting babes?"

"No go—only swell the damages, when they come to prosecute. Besides, your age and looks forbid the assumption of such a fact. No, no; we must go deeper to work."

"But where shall we go?" said I, impatiently; "for it appears to me these good people have been treated to every trick and subterfuge that ever ingenuity suggested."

"Come, I think I have it; but it will need a little more reflection. So, now, let us to bed. I'll give you the result of my lucubrations at breakfast; and, if I mistake not, we may get you through this without any ill consequences. Good-night, then, old boy; and now dream away of your lady-love till our next meeting."

CHAPTER XXVI.

THE PREPARATION.

TO prevent needless repetitions in my story, I shall not record here the conversation which passed between my friend Power and myself on the morning following at breakfast. Suffice it to say that the plan proposed by him for my rescue was one I agreed to adopt, reserving to myself, in case of failure, a *pis aller*, of which I knew not the meaning, but of whose efficacy Power assured me I need not doubt.

"If all fail," said he—"if every bridge break down beneath you, and no road of escape be left, why, then, I believe you must have recourse to another alternative. Still, I should wish to avoid it if possible, and I put it to you in honor, not to employ it unless as a last expedient. You promise me this."

"Of course," said I, with great anxiety for the dread final measure. "What is it?"

He paused, smiled dubiously, and resumed,—

"And, after all—but, to be sure, there will not be need for it—the other plan will do—must do. Come, come, O'Malley, the Admiralty say that nothing encourages drowning in the navy like a life-buoy. The men have such a prospect of being picked up, that they don't mind falling overboard; so, if I give you this life-preserver of mine, you'll not swim an inch. Is it not so, eh?"

"Far from it," said I. "I shall feel in honor bound to exert myself the more, because I now see how much it costs you to part with it."

"Well, then, hear it. When everything fails—when all your resources are exhausted—when you have totally lost your memory, in fact, and your ingenuity in excuses, say—but mind, Charley, not till then—say that you must consult your friend Captain Power, of the 14th—that's all."

"And is this it?" said I, quite disappointed at the lame and impotent conclusion to all the high-sounding exordium; "is this all?"

"Yes," said he, "that is all. But stop, Charley; is not that the Major crossing the street there? Yes, to be sure it is; and, by Jove! he has got on the old braided frock this morning. Had you not told me one word of your critical position, I should have guessed there was something in the wind from that. That same vestment has caused many a stout heart to tremble that never quailed before shot or shell."

"How can that be? I should like to hear."

"Why, my dear boy, that's his explanation coat, as we called it at Gibraltar. He was never known to wear it except when asking some poor fellow's 'intentions.' He would no more think of sporting it as an every-day affair than the Chief Justice would go cock-shooting in his black cap and ermine. Come, he is bound for your quarters, and, as it will not answer our plans to let him see you now, you had better hasten down stairs, and get round by the back way into George's street, and you'll be at his house before he can return."

Following Power's directions, I seized my foraging cap, and got clear out of the premises before the Major reached them. It was exactly noon as I sounded my loud and now well-known summons at the Major's knocker. The door was quickly opened; but instead of dashing up stairs, four steps at a time, as was my wont, to the drawing-room, I turned short into the dingy-looking little parlor on the right, and desired Matthew, the venerable servitor of the house, to say that I wished particularly to see Mrs. Dalrymple for a few minutes, if the hour were not inconvenient.

There was something perhaps of excitement in my manner—some

flurry in my look, or some trepidation in my voice; or perhaps it was the unusual hour, or the still more remarkable circumstance of my not going at once to the drawing-room, that raised some doubts in Matthew's mind as to the object of my visit; and, instead of at once complying with my request to inform Mrs. Dalrymple that I was there, he cautiously closed the door, and, taking a quick but satisfactory glance round the apartment, to assure himself that we were alone, he placed his back against it, and heaved a deep sigh.

We were both perfectly silent; I in total amazement at what the old man could possibly mean; he, following up the train of his own thoughts, comprehended little or nothing of my surprise, and evidently was so engrossed by his reflections that he had neither ears nor eyes for aught around him. There was a most singular semi-comic expression in the old withered face that nearly made me laugh at first; but as I continued to look steadily at it, I perceived that, despite the long-worn wrinkles that low Irish drollery and fun had furrowed around the angles of his mouth, the real character of his look was one of sorrowful compassion.

Doubtless my readers have read many interesting narratives, wherein the unconscious traveller in some remote land has been warned of a plan to murder him, by some mere passing wink, a look, a sign, which some one, who is less steeped in crime, less hardened in iniquity than his fellows, has ventured for his rescue. Sometimes, according to the taste of the narrator, the interesting individual is an old woman, sometimes a young one, sometimes a black-bearded bandit, sometimes a child, and not unfrequently a dog is humane enough to do this service. One thing, however, never varies; be the agent biped or quadruped, dumb or speechful, young or old, the stranger almost invariably takes the hint, and gets off scot free for his sharpness. This never-varying trick on the doomed man I had often been skeptical enough to suspect; however, I had not been many minutes a spectator of the old man's countenance, when I most thoroughly recanted my errors, and acknowledged myself wrong. If ever the look of a man conveyed a warning, his did; but there was more in it than even that—there was a tone of sad and pitiful compassion, such as an old gray-bearded rat might be supposed to put on at seeing a young and inexperienced one opening the hinge of an iron trap, to try its efficacy upon its neck. Many a little occasion had presented itself, during my intimacy with the family, of doing Matthew some small services, of making him some trifling presents, so that, when he assumed before me the gesture and look I have mentioned, I was not long in deciphering his intentions.

"Matthew!" screamed a sharp voice, which I recognized at

once for that of Mrs. Dalrymple. "Matthew! Where is the old fool?"

But Matthew heard not, or heeded not.

"Matthew! Matthew! I say."

"I'm comin', ma'am," said he, with a sigh, as, opening the parlor door, he turned upon me one look of such import, that only the circumstances of my story can explain its force, or my reader's own ingenious imagination can supply.

"Never fear, my good old friend," said I, grasping his hand warmly, and leaving a guinea in the palm—"never fear."

"God grant it, sir!" said he, settling on his wig in preparation for his appearance in the drawing-room.

"Matthew! the old wretch!"

"Mr. O'Malley," said the often-called Matthew, as, opening the door, he announced me unexpectedly among the ladies there assembled, who, not hearing of my approach, were evidently not a little surprised and astonished.

Had I really been the enamored swain that the Dalrymple family were willing to believe, I half suspect that the prospect before me might have cured me of my passion. A round bullet head, *papilloté* with the *Cork Observer*, where still-born babes and maids of all work were descanted upon in very legible type, was now the substitute for the classic front and Italian ringlets of *la belle* Matilda, while the chaste Fanny herself, whose feet had been a fortune for a statuary, was, in the most slatternly and slipshod attire, pacing the room in a towering rage, at some thing, place, or person, unknown to me. If the ballet-master at the *Académie* could only learn to get his imps, demons, angels and goblins "off" half as rapidly as the two young ladies retreated on my being announced, I answer for the piece so brought out having a run for half the season. Before my eyes had gained their position parallel to the plane of the horizon, they were gone, and I found myself alone with Mrs. Dalrymple. Now she stood her ground, partly to cover the retreat of the main body, partly, too, because—representing the baggage-wagons, ammunition stores, hospital staff, &c.—her retirement from the field demanded more time and circumspection than the light brigade.

Let not my readers suppose that the *mère* Dalrymple was so perfectly faultless in costume that her remaining was a matter of actual indifference; far from it. She evidently had a struggle for it; but a sense of duty decided her, and as Ney doggedly held back to cover the retreating forces on the march from Moscow, so did she resolutely lurk behind till the last flutter of the last petticoat assured her that the fugitives were safe. Then did she hesitate for a moment what course to take; but as I assumed my chair beside her, she composedly sat down, and, crossing her hands before her, waited for an explanation of this ill-timed visit.

Had the Horse Guards, in the plenitude of their power and the perfection of their taste, ordained that the 79th and 42d regiments should in future, in lieu of their respective tartans, wear flannel kilts and black worsted hose, I could readily have fallen into the error of mistaking Mrs. Dalrymple for a field-officer in the new regulation dress—the philibeg finding no mean representation in a capacious pincushion that hung down from her girdle, while a pair of shears (not scissors) corresponded to the dirk. After several ineffectual efforts upon her part to make her vestment (I know not its fitting designation) cover more of her legs than its length could possibly effect, and after some most bland smiles and half blushes at dishabille, &c., were over, and that I had apologized most humbly for the unusually early hour of my call, I proceeded to open my negotiations, and unfurl my banner for the fray.

"The old *Racehorse* has arrived at last," said I, with a half sigh, "and I believe that we shall not obtain a very long time for our leave-taking; so that, trespassing upon your very great kindness, I have ventured upon an early call."

"The *Racehorse* surely can't sail to-morrow," said Mrs. Dalrymple, whose experience of such matters made her a very competent judge; "her stores——"

"Are taken in already," said I; "and an order from the Horse Guards commands us to embark in twenty-four hours; so that, in fact, we scarcely have time to look about us."

"Have you seen the Major?" inquired Mrs. Dalrymple, eagerly.

"Not to-day," I replied, carelessly; "but, of course, during the morning we are sure to meet. I have many thanks yet to give him for all his most kind attentions."

"I know he is most anxious to see you," said Mrs. Dalrymple, with a very peculiar emphasis, and evidently desiring that I should inquire the reasons of this anxiety. I, however, most heroically forbore indulging my curiosity, and added that I should endeavor to find him on my way to the barracks; and then, hastily looking at my watch, I pronounced it a full hour later than it really was, and, promising to spend the evening—my last evening—with them, I took my leave, and hurried away, in no small flurry, to be once more out of reach of Mrs. Dalrymple's fire, which I every moment expected to open upon me.

CHAPTER XXVII.

THE SUPPER.

POWER and I dined together *tête-à-tête* at the hotel, and sat chatting over my adventures with the Dalrymples till nearly nine o'clock.

"Come, Charley," said he at length, "I see your eye wandering very often towards the timepiece; another bumper, and I'll let you off. What shall it be?"

"What you like," said I, upon whom a share of three bottles of strong claret had already made a very satisfactory impression.

"Then champagne for the *coup de grace.* Nothing like your *vin mousseux* for a critical moment—every bubble that rises sparkling to the surface, prompts some bright thought, or elicits some brilliant idea, that would only have been drowned in your more sober fluids. Here's to the girl you love, whoever she be."

"To her bright eyes, then, be it," said I, clearing off a brimming goblet of nearly half the bottle, while my friend Power seemed multiplied into any given number of gentlemen standing amid something like a glass manufactory of decanters.

"I hope you feel steady enough for this business," said my friend, examining me closely with the candle.

"I'm an archdeacon," muttered I, with one eye involuntarily closing.

"You'll not let them double on you!"

"Trust me, old boy," said I, endeavoring to look knowing.

"I think you'll do," said he; "so now march; I'll wait for you here, and we'll go on board together; for old Bloater, the skipper, says he'll certainly weigh by daybreak."

"Till then," said I, as, opening the door, I proceeded very cautiously to descend the stairs, affecting all the time considerable *nonchalance*, and endeavoring, as well as my thickened utterance would permit, to hum,—

"Oh love is the soul of an Irish dragoon."

If I was not in the most perfect possession of my faculties in the house, the change to the open air, certainly, but little contributed to their restoration, and I scarcely felt myself in the street when my brain became absolutely one whirl of maddened and confused excitement. Time and space are nothing to a man thus enlightened, and so they appeared to me. Scarcely a second had elapsed when I found myself standing in the Dalrymples' drawing-room.

If a few hours had done much to metamorphose *me*, certes they

12

had done something for my fair friends also—anything more unlike what they appeared in the morning can scarcely be imagined. Matilda in black, with her hair in heavy madonna bands upon her fair cheek, now paler even than usual, never seemed so handsome; while Fanny, in a light blue dress, with blue flowers in her hair, and a blue sash, looked the most lovely piece of coquetry ever man set his eyes upon. The old Major, too, was smartened up, and put into an old regimental coat that he had worn during the siege of Gibraltar; and lastly, Mrs. Dalrymple herself was attired in a very imposing costume, that made her, to my not over-accurate judgment, look very like an elderly bishop in a flame-colored cassock. Sparks was the only stranger, and wore upon his countenance, as I entered, a look of very considerable embarrassment, that even my thick-sightedness could not fail of detecting.

Parlez-moi de l'amitié, my friends. Talk to me of the warm embrace of your earliest friend, after years of absence; the cordial and heartfelt shake-hands of your old school companion, when, in after-years, a chance meeting has brought you together, and you have had time and opportunity for becoming distinguished and in repute, and are rather a good hit to be known to than otherwise; of the close grip you give your second when he comes up to say that the gentleman with the loaded detonator opposite won't fire—that he feels he's in the wrong. Any or all of these together, very effective and powerful though they be, are light in the balance when compared with the two-handed compression you receive from the gentleman that expects you to marry one of his daughters.

"My dear O'Malley, how goes it? Thought you'd never come," said he, still holding me fast, and looking me full in the face, to calculate the extent to which my potations rendered his flattery feasible.

"Hurried to death with preparations, I suppose," said Mrs. Dalrymple, smiling blandly. "Fanny dear, some tea for him."

"Oh, mamma, he does not like all that sugar; surely not," said she, looking up with a most sweet expression, as though to say, "I at least know his tastes."

"I believed you were going without seeing us," whispered Matilda, with a very glassy look about the corner of her eyes.

Eloquence was not just then my forte, so that I contented myself with a very intelligible look at Fanny, and a tender squeeze of Matilda's hand, as I seated myself at the table.

Scarcely had I placed myself at the tea-table, with Matilda beside and Fanny opposite me, each vieing with the other in their delicate and kind attentions, when I totally forgot all my poor friend Power's injunctions and directions for my management. It is true, I remembered that there was a scrape of some kind or other to be got out of, and one requiring some dexterity too, but what, or with whom, I could not for the life of me determine. What the wine had begun the bright eyes completed; and, amid the witchcraft of silky tresses and sweet looks, I lost all my reflection, till the impression of an impending difficulty remained fixed in my mind, and I tortured my poor, weak, and erring intellect to detect it. At last, and by a mere chance, my eyes fell upon Sparks, and, by what mechanism I contrived it I know not, I immediately saddled him with the whole of my annoyances, and attributed to him and to his fault any embarrassment I labored under.

The physiological reason of the fact I'm very ignorant of, but for the truth and frequency I can well vouch, that there are certain people, certain faces, certain voices, certain whiskers, legs, waistcoats, and guard-chains, that inevitably produce the most striking effects upon the brain of a gentleman already excited by wine, and not exactly cognizant of his own peculiar fallacies.

These effects are not produced merely among those who are quarrelsome in their cups, for I call the whole 14th to witness that I am not such; but to any person so disguised, the inoffensiveness of the object is no security on the other hand, for I once knew an eight-day clock kicked down a barrack stairs by an old Scotch major, because he thought it was laughing at him. To this source alone, whatever it be, can I attribute the feeling of rising indignation with which I contemplated the luckless Cornet, who, seated at the fire, unnoticed and uncared for, seemed a very unworthy object to vent anger or ill-temper upon.

"Mr. Sparks, I fear," said I, endeavoring at the time to call up a look of very sovereign contempt—"Mr. Sparks, I fear, regards my visit here in the light of an intrusion."

Had poor Mr. Sparks been told to proceed incontinently up the chimney before him, he could not have looked more aghast. Reply was quite out of his power; so sudden and unexpectedly was this charge of mine made, that he could only stare vacantly from one to the other, while I, warming with my subject, and perhaps—but I'll not swear it—stimulated by a gentle pressure from a soft hand near me, continued,—

"If he thinks for one moment that my attentions in this family are in any way to be questioned by him, I can only say——"

"My dear O'Malley, my dear boy!" said the Major, with the look of a father-in-law in his eye.

"The spirit of an officer and a gentleman spoke there," said Mrs. Dalrymple, now carried beyond all prudence, by the hope that my attack might arouse my dormant friend into a counter declaration.

Nothing, however, was further from poor Sparks, who began to think he had been unconsciously drinking tea with five lunatics.

"If he supposes," said I, rising from my chair, "that his silence will pass with me as any palliation——"

"Oh dear! oh dear! there will be a duel. Papa, dear, why don't you speak to Mr. O'Malley?"

"There, now, O'Malley, sit down. Don't you see he is quite in error?"

"Then let him say so," said I fiercely.

"Ah, yes, to be sure," said Fanny; "do say it; say anything he likes, Mr. Sparks."

"I must say," said Mrs. Dalrymple, "however sorry I may feel in my own house to condemn any one, that Mr. Sparks is very much in the wrong."

Poor Sparks looked like a man in a dream.

"If he will tell Charles—Mr. O'Malley, I mean," said Matilda, blushing scarlet, "that he meant nothing by what he said——"

"But I never spoke—never opened my lips!" cried out the wretched man, at length sufficiently recovered to defend himself.

"Oh, Mr. Sparks!"

"Oh, Mr. Sparks!"

"Oh, Mr. Sparks!" chorused the three ladies.

While the old Major brought up the rear with an "Oh, Sparks, I must say——"

"Then, by all the saints in the calendar, I must be mad," said he; "but if I have said anything to offend you, O'Malley, I am sincerely sorry for it."

"That will do, sir," said I with a look of royal condescension at the *amende* I considered as somewhat late in coming, and resumed my seat.

This little *intermezzo*, it might be supposed, was rather calculated to interrupt the harmony of our evening: not so, however. I had apparently acquitted myself like a hero, and was evidently in a white heat, in which I could be fashioned into any shape. Sparks was humbled so far, that he would probably feel it a relief to make any proposition; so that by our opposite courses, we had both arrived at a point at which all the dexterity and address of the family had been long since aiming without success. Conversation then resumed its flow, and in a few minutes every trace of our late fracas had disappeared.

By degrees I felt myself more and more disposed to turn my attention towards Matilda, and dropping my voice into a lower tone, opened a flirtation of a most determined kind. Fanny had, meanwhile, assumed a place beside Sparks, and, by the muttered tones that passed between them, I could plainly perceive they were similarly occupied. The Major took up the *Southern Reporter*, of which he appeared deep in the contemplation, while Mrs. Dal buried her head in her embroidery, and neither saw nor heard anything around her.

I know, unfortunately, but very little what passed between myself and my fair companion: I can only say that when supper was announced, at twelve (an hour later than usual), I was sitting upon the sofa, with my arm round her waist, my cheek so close, that already her lovely tresses brushed my forehead, and her breath fanned my burning brow.

"Supper at last," said the Major, with a loud voice, to arouse us from our trance of happiness, without taking any mean opportunity of looking unobserved. "Supper, Sparks: O'Malley, come now—it will be some time before we all meet this way again."

"Perhaps not so long, after all," said I, knowingly.

"Very likely not," echoed Sparks, in the same key.

"I've proposed for Fanny," said he, whispering in my ear.

"Matilda's mine," replied I, with the look of an emperor.

"A word with you, Major," said Sparks, his eye flashing with enthusiasm, and his cheek scarlet—"one word: I'll not detain you."

They withdrew into a corner for a few seconds, during which Mrs. Dalrymple amused herself by wondering what the secret could be; why Mr. Sparks couldn't tell her; and Fanny, meanwhile, pretended to look for something at a side-table, and never turned her head round.

"Then give me your hand," said the Major, as he shook Sparks's with a warmth of whose sincerity there could be no question. "Bess, my love," said he, addressing his wife; the remainder was lost in a whisper; but whatsoever it was, it evidently redounded to Sparks's credit, for the next moment a repetition of the hand-shaking took place, and Sparks looked the happiest of men.

"*A mon tour*," thought I, "now," as I touched the Major's arm, and led him towards the window. What I said may be one day matter for Major Dalrymple's memoirs, if he ever writes them; but for my part, I have not the least idea. I only know that, while I was yet speaking, he called over Mrs. Dal, who, in a frenzy of joy, seized me in her arms and embraced me. After which, I kissed her, shook hands with the Major, kissed Matilda's hand, and laughed prodigiously, as though I had done something confoundedly droll—a sentiment evidently participated in by Sparks, who laughed too, as did the others, and a merrier, happier party never sat down to supper.

"Make your company pleased with themselves," says Mr. Walker, in his *original* work upon dinner-giving, "and everything goes on well."   Now, Major Dalrymple, without having read the authority in question, probably because it was not written at the time, understood the principle fully as well as the police magistrate, and certainly was a proficient in the practice of it.

To be sure he possessed one grand requisite for success—he seemed most perfectly happy himself.   There was that *air dégagé* about him which, when an old man puts it on among his juniors, is so very attractive.   Then the ladies, too, were evidently well pleased; and the usually austere mamma had relaxed her "rigid front" into a smile, in which any *habitué* of the house could have read our fate.

We ate, we drank, we ogled, smiled, squeezed hands beneath the table, and, in fact, so pleasant a party had rarely assembled round the Major's mahogany.   As for me, I made a full disclosure of the most burning love, backed by a resolve to marry my fair neighbor, and settle upon her a considerably larger part of my native county than I had ever even ridden over.   Sparks, on the other side, had opened his fire more cautiously; but whether taking courage from my boldness, or perceiving with envy the greater estimation I was held in, he was now going the pace fully as fast as myself, and had commenced explanations of his intentions with regard to Fanny that evidently satisfied her friends.   Meanwhile, the wine was passing very freely, and the hints half uttered an hour before began now to be more openly spoken and canvassed.

Sparks and I hob-nobbed across the table, and looked unspeakable things at each other; the girls held down their heads; Mrs. Dal wiped her eyes; and the Major pronounced himself the happiest father in Europe.

It was now wearing late, or rather early; some gray streaks of dubious light were faintly forcing their way through the half-closed curtains, and the dread thought of parting first presented itself.   A cavalry trumpet, too, at this moment sounded a call that aroused us from our trance of pleasure, and warned us that our moments were few.   A dead silence crept over all, the solemn feeling which leave-taking ever inspires was uppermost, and none spoke.   The Major was the first to break it.

"O'Malley, my friend, and you, Mr. Sparks, I must have a word with you, boys, before we part."

"Here let it be, then, Major," said I, holding his arm as he turned to leave the room; "here, now; we are all so deeply interested, no place is so fit."

"Well, then," said the Major, "as you desire it, now that I'm to regard you both in the light of my sons-in-law—at least, as pledged to become so—it is only fair as respects——"

"I see—I understand perfectly," interrupted I, whose passion for conducting the whole affair myself was gradually gaining on me. "What you mean is, that we should make known our intentions before some mutual friends ere we part—eh, Sparks? eh, Major?"

"Right, my boy—right on every point."

"Well, then, I thought of all that; and if you'll just send your servant over to my quarters for our Captain—he's the fittest person, you know, at such a time——"

"How considerate!" said Mrs. Dalrymple.

"How perfectly just his idea is!" said the Major.

"We'll, then, in his presence, avow our present and unalterable determination as regards your fair daughters; and as the time is short——"

Here I turned towards Matilda, who placed her arm within mine; Sparks possessed himself of Fanny's hand, while the Major and his wife consulted for a few seconds.

"Well, O'Malley, all you propose is perfect. Now, then, for the Captain. Who shall he inquire for?"

"Oh, an old friend of yours," said I, jocularly; "you'll be glad to see him."

"Indeed!" said all together.

"Oh yes, quite a surprise, I'll warrant it."

"Who can it be? who on earth is it?"

"You can't guess," added I, with a very knowing look; "knew you at Corfu. He was a very intimate friend indeed, if he tell the truth."

A look of something like embarrassment passed around the circle at these words, while I, wishing to end the mystery, resumed:

"Come, then, who can be so proper for all parties, at a moment like this, as our mutual friend, Captain Power?"

Had a shell fallen into the cold grouse pie in the midst of us, scattering death and destruction on every side, the effect could scarcely have been more frightful than that my last words produced. Mrs. Dalrymple fell with a sough upon the floor, motionless as a corpse; Fanny threw herself, screaming, upon a sofa; Matilda went off into strong hysterics upon the hearth-rug; while the Major, after giving me a look a maniac might have envied, rushed from the room in search of his pistols, with a most terrific oath to shoot somebody, whether Sparks or myself, or both of us, on his return, I cannot say. Fanny's sobs and Matilda's cries, assisted by a drumming process by Mrs. Dal's heels upon the floor, made a most infernal concert, and effectually prevented anything like thought or reflection; and, in all probability, so overwhelmed was I at the sudden catastrophe I had so innocently caused, I should have waited in due patience for the Major's return, had not Sparks seized my arm, and cried out,—

"Run for it, O'Malley; cut like fun, my boy, or we're done for."

"Run—why?—what for?—where?" said I, stupefied by the scene before me.

"Here he is!" called out Sparks, as, throwing up the window, he sprang out upon the stone sill, and leaped into the street. I followed mechanically, and jumped after him, just as the Major had reached the window. A ball whizzed by me, that soon determined my further movements; so putting on all speed, I flew down the street, turned the corner, and regained the hotel breathless and without a hat, while Sparks arrived a moment later, pale as a ghost, and trembling like an aspen-leaf.

"Safe, by Jove!" said Sparks, throwing himself into a chair, and panting for breath.

"Safe at last," said I, without well knowing why or for what.

"You've had a sharp run for it apparently," said Power, coolly, and without any curiosity as to the cause; "and, now, let us on board; there goes the trumpet again. The Skipper is a surly old fellow, and we must not lose his tide for him." So saying, he proceeded to collect his cloaks, cane, &c., and get ready for departure.

CHAPTER XXVIII.

THE VOYAGE.

WHEN I awoke from the long, sound sleep which succeeded my last adventure, I had some difficulty in remembering where I was, or how I had come there. From my narrow berth I looked out upon the now empty cabin, and at length some misty and confused sense of my situation crept slowly over me. I opened the little shutter beside me, and looked out. The bold headlands of the southern coast were frowning, in sullen and dark masses, about a couple of miles distant, and I perceived that we were going fast through the water, which was beautifully calm and still. I now looked at my watch; it was past eight o'clock; and as it must evidently be evening, from the appearance of the sky, I felt that I had slept soundly for above twelve hours.

In the hurry of departure, the cabin had not been set to rights, and there lay every species of lumber and luggage in all imaginable confusion. Trunks, gun-cases, baskets of eggs, umbrellas, hampers of sea-store, cloaks, foraging-caps, maps, and sword-belts, were scattered on every side—while the débris of a dinner, not over remarkable for its propriety in table equipage, added to the ludicrous effect. The heavy tramp of a foot overhead denoted the step of some one taking his short walk of exercise; while the rough voice of the Skipper, as he gave the word to "Go about!" all convinced me that we were at last under weigh, and off to "the wars."

The confusion our last evening on shore produced in my brain was such, that every effort I made to remember anything about it only increased my difficulty, and I felt myself in a web so tangled and inextricable, that all endeavors to escape free was impossible. Sometimes I thought that I had really married Matilda Dalrymple; then I supposed that the father had called me out, and wounded me in a duel; and finally, I had some confused notion about a quarrel with Sparks, but what for, when, and how it ended, I knew not. How tremendously tipsy I must have been! was the only conclusion I could draw from all these conflicting doubts; and, after all, it was the only thing like fact that beamed upon my mind. How I had come on board and reached my berth, was a matter I reserved for future inquiry, resolving that about the real history of my last night on shore I would ask no questions, if others were equally disposed to let it pass in silence.

I next began to wonder if Mike had looked after all my luggage, trunks, &c., and whether he himself had been forgotten in our hasty departure. About this latter point I was not destined for much doubt; for a well known voice, from the foot of the companion-ladder, at once proclaimed my faithful follower, and evidenced his feelings at his departure from his home and country.

Mr. Free was, at the time I mention, gathered up like a ball, opposite a small, low window, that looked upon the bluff headlands now fast becoming dim and misty as the night approached. He was apparently in low spirits, and hummed in a species of low, droning voice, the following ballad, at the end of each verse of which came an Irish chorus, which, to the erudite in such matters, will suggest the air of Moddirederoo :—

"MICKEY FREE'S LAMENT.

"Then fare ye well, ould Erin dear;
 To part—my heart does ache well:
From Carrickfergus to Cape Clear,
 I'll never see your equal.
And though to foreign parts we're bound,
 Where cannibals may ate us,
We'll ne'er forget the holy ground
 Of poteen and potatoes.

   Moddirederoo aroo, aroo, &c.

> "When good St. Patrick banished frogs,
> And shook them from his garment,
> He never thought we'd go abroad,
> To live upon such varmint,
> Nor quit the land where whisky grew,
> To wear King George's button,
> Take vinegar for mountain dew,
> And toads for mountain mutton.
>
> Moddirederoo aroo, aroo," &c.

"I say, Mike, stop that confounded keen, and tell me where are we?"

"Off the ould head of Kinsale, sir."

"Where is Captain Power?"

"Smoking a cigar on deck, with the Captain, sir."

"And Mr. Sparks?"

"Mighty sick in his own state-room. Oh! but it's himself has enough of glory—bad luck to it!—by this time. He'd make your heart break to look at him."

"Who have you got on board besides?"

"The Adjutant's here, sir, and an old gentleman they call the Major."

"Not Major Dalrymple?" said I, starting up with terror at the thought, "eh, Mike?"

"No, sir, another Major; his name is Mulroon, or Mundoon, or something like that."

"Monsoon, you son of a lumper potato," cried out a surly, gruff voice from a berth opposite, "Monsoon. Who's at the other side?"

"Mr. O'Malley, 14th," said I, by way of introduction.

"My service to you, then," said the voice. "Going to join your regiment?"

"Yes; and you—are you bound on a similar errand?"

"No, Heaven be praised! I'm attached to the Commissariat, and only going to Lisbon. Have you had any dinner?"

"Not a morsel; have you?"

"No more than yourself; but I always lie by for three or four days this way, till I get used to the confounded rocking and pitching; and, with a little grog and some sleep, get over the time gayly enough. Steward, another tumbler like the last; there—very good—that will do. Your good health, Mr. —— what was it you said?"

"O'Malley."

"O'Malley—your good health—good night." And so ended our brief colloquy, and in a few minutes more, a very decisive snore pronounced my friend to be fulfilling his precept for killing the hours.

I now made the effort to emancipate myself from my crib, and at last succeeded in getting on the floor, where, after one *chassez* at a small looking-glass opposite, followed by a very impetuous rush at a little brass stove, in which I was interrupted by a trunk, and laid prostrate, I finally got my clothes on, and made my way to the deck. Little attuned as was my mind at the moment to admire anything like scenery, it was impossible to be unmoved by the magnificent prospect before me. It was a beautiful evening in summer; the sun had set above an hour before, leaving behind him in the west one vast arch of rich and burnished gold, stretching along the whole horizon, and tipping all the summits of the heavy rolling sea, as it rolled on, unbroken by foam or ripple, in vast moving mountains from the far coast of Labrador. We were already in blue water, though the bold cliffs that were to form our departing point were but a few miles to leeward. There lay the lofty bluff of Old Kinsale, whose crest, overhanging, peered from a summit of some hundred feet into the deep water that swept its rocky base, many a tangled lichen and straggling bough trailing in the flood beneath. Here and there, upon the coast, a twinkling gleam proclaimed the hut of a fisherman, whose swift hookers had more than once shot by us, and disappeared in a moment. The wind, which began to fall at sunset, freshened as the moon rose; and the good ship, bending to the breeze, lay gently over, and rushed through the water with a sound of gladness. I was alone upon the deck; Power and the Captain, whom I expected to have found, had disappeared somehow, and I was, after all, not sorry to be left to my own reflections uninterrupted.

My thoughts turned once more to my home—to my first, my best, earliest friend, whose hearth I had rendered lonely and desolate, and my heart sunk within me as I remembered it. How deeply I reproached myself for the selfish impetuosity with which I had ever followed any rising fancy, any new and sudden desire, and never thought of him whose every hope was in, whose every wish was for me. Alas! my poor uncle! how gladly would I resign every prospect my soldier's life may hold out, with all its glittering promise, and all the flattery of success, to be once more beside you; to feel your warm and manly grasp; to see your smile; to hear your voice; to be again where all our best feelings are born and nurtured, our cares assuaged, our joys more joyed in, and our griefs more wept— at home! These very words have more music to my ears than all the softest strains that ever syren sung. They bring us back to all we have loved, by ties that are never felt but through such simple associations. And in the earlier memories called up, our childish feelings come back once more to visit us, like better spirits, as we walk amid the dreary desolation that years of care and un-easiness have spread around us.

Wretched must be he who ne'er has felt such bliss; and thrice happy he who, feeling it, knows that still there lives for him that same early home, with all its loved inmates, its every dear and devoted object waiting his coming, and longing for his approach.

Such were my thoughts as I stood gazing at the bold line of coast now gradually growing more and more dim while evening fell, and we continued to stand farther out to sea. So absorbed was I all this time in my reflections, that I never heard the voices which now suddenly burst upon my ears quite close beside me. I turned, and saw for the first time that at the end of the quarter-deck stood what is called a roundhouse, a small cabin, from which the sound in question proceeded. I walked gently forward, and peeped in, and certainly anything more in contrast with my late reverie need not be conceived. There sat the Skipper, a bluff, round-faced, jolly-looking little tar, mixing a bowl of punch at the table, at which sat my friend Power, the Adjutant, and a tall, meagre-looking Scotchman, whom I once met in Cork, and heard that he was the doctor of some infantry regiment. Two or three black bottles, a paper of cigars, and a tallow candle, were all the table equipage; but, certainly, the party seemed not to want for spirits and fun, to judge from the hearty bursts of laughter that every moment pealed forth, and shook the little building that held them. Power, as usual with him, seemed to be taking the lead, and was evidently amusing himself with the peculiarities of his companions.

"Come, Adjutant, fill up. Here's to the campaign before us; we, at least, have nothing but pleasure in the anticipation,—no lovely wife behind—no charming babes to fret, and be fretted for, eh?"

"Vara true," said the Doctor, who was mated with a *tartar*. "Ye maun hae less regrets at leavin' hame; but a married man is no' entirely denied his ain consolations."

"Good sense in that," said the Skipper; "a wide berth and plenty of sea-room are not bad things now and then."

"Is that your experience also?" said Power, with a knowing look. "Come, come, Adjutant, we're not so ill off, you see; but, by Jove, I can't imagine how it is a man ever comes to thirty without having at least one wife—without counting his colonial possessions, of course."

"Yes," said the Adjutant, with a sigh, as he drained his glass to the bottom. "It is devilish strange—woman, lovely woman!" Here he filled and drank again, as though he had been proposing a toast for his own peculiar drinking.

"I say, now," resumed Power, catching at once that there was something working in his mind—"I say, now, how happened it that you, a right good-looking, soldier-like fellow, that always made his way among the fair ones, with that confounded roguish eye and slippery tongue—how the deuce did it come to pass that you never married?"

"I've been more than once on the verge of it," said the Adjutant, smiling blandly at the flattery.

"And nae bad notion yours just to stay there," said the Doctor, with a very peculiar contortion of countenance.

"No pleasing you—no contenting a fellow like you," said Power, returning to the charge; "that's the thing; you get a certain ascendency; you have a kind of success that renders you, as the French say, *tête montée*, and you think no woman rich enough, or good-looking enough, or high enough."

"No; by Jove, you're wrong," said the Adjutant, swallowing the bait, hook and all—"quite wrong there; for, somehow, all my life I was decidedly susceptible. Not that I cared much for your blushing sixteen, or budding beauties in white muslin, fresh from a backboard and a governess; no, my taste inclined rather to the more sober charms of two or three-and-thirty—the *embonpoint*, a good foot and ankle, a sensible breadth about the shoulders——"

"Somewhat Dutch-like, I take it," said the Skipper, puffing out a volume of smoke; "a little bluff in the bows, and great stowage, eh?"

"You leaned, then, towards the widows?" said Power.

"Exactly. I confess a widow always was my weakness. There was something I ever liked in the notion of a woman who had got over all the awkward girlishness of early years, and had that self-possession which habit and knowledge of the world confer, and knew enough of herself to understand what she really wished, and where she would really go."

"Like the trade winds," puffed the Skipper.

"Then, as regards fortune, they have a decided superiority over the spinster class. I defy any man breathing—let him be half police magistrate, half chancellor—to find out the figure of a young lady's dower. On your first introduction to the house, some kind friend whispers, 'Go it, old boy; forty thousand—not a penny less.' A few weeks later, as the siege progresses, a maiden aunt, disposed to puffing, comes down to twenty; this diminishes again one-half; but then 'the money is in bank stock, hard Three-and-a-Half.' You go a little further, and as you sit one day over your wine with papa, he certainly promulgates the fact that his daughter has five thousand pounds, two of which turn out to be in Mexican bonds and three in an Irish mortgage."

"Happy for you," interrupted Power, "that it be not in Galway, where a proposal to foreclose would be a signal for your being called out, and shot without benefit of clergy."

"Bad luck to it, for Galway," said the Adjutant. "I was nearly taken in there once to marry a girl that her brother-in-law swore had eight hundred a year, and it came out afterwards that so she had, but it was for one year only; and he challenged me for doubting his word too."

"There's an old formula for finding out an Irish fortune," says Power, "worth all the algebra they ever taught in Trinity. Take the half of the assumed sum, and divide it by three; the quotient will be a flattering representative of the figure sought for."

"Not in the north," said the Adjutant firmly—"not in the north, Power; they are all well off there. There's a race of canny, thrifty, half-Scotch niggers—your pardon, Doctor, they are all Irish—linen-weaving, Presbyterian, yarn-factoring, long-nosed, hard-drinking fellows, that lay by rather a snug thing now and then. Do you know, I was very near it once in the north. I've half a mind to tell you the story, though perhaps you'll laugh at me."

The whole party at once protested that nothing could induce them to deviate so widely from the line of propriety; and the Skipper having mixed a fresh bowl, and filled all the glasses round, the cigars were lighted, and the Adjutant began.

CHAPTER XXIX.

THE ADJUTANT'S STORY—LIFE IN DERRY.

IT is now about eight, maybe ten, years since we were ordered to march from Belfast, and take up our quarters in Londonderry. We had not been more than a few weeks altogether in Ulster when the order came; and as we had been for the preceding two years doing duty in the south and west, we concluded that the island was tolerably the same in all parts. We opened our campaign in the maiden city, exactly as we had been doing with 'unparalleled success' in Cashel, Fermoy, Tuam, &c.—that is to say, we announced garrison balls and private theatricals; offered a cup to be run for in steeple-chase; turned out a four-in-hand drag, with mottled grays, and brought over two Deal boats to challenge the north."

"The 18th found the place stupid," said his companions.

"To be sure they did; slow fellows like them must find any place stupid. No dinners; but they gave none. No fun; but they had none in themselves. In fact, we knew better. We understood how the thing was to be done, and resolved that as a mine of rich ore lay unworked, it was reserved for us to produce the shining metal that others, less discerning, had failed to discover. Little we knew of the matter; never was there a blunder like ours. Were you ever in Derry?"

"Never," said the three listeners.

" Well, then, let me inform you that the place has its own peculiar features. In the first place, all the large towns in the south and west have, besides the country neighborhood that surrounds them, a certain sprinkling of gentlefolk, who, though with small fortunes and not much usage of the world, are still a great accession to society, and make up the blank which, even in the most thickly-peopled country, would be sadly felt without them. Now, in Derry there is none of this. After the great guns—and, *per Baccho !* what great guns they are !—you have nothing but the men engaged in commerce—sharp, clever, shrewd, well-informed fellows. They are deep in flaxseed, cunning in molasses, and not to be excelled in all that pertains to coffee, sassafras, cinnamon, gum, oakum, and elephants' teeth. The place is a rich one, and the spirit of commerce is felt throughout it.. Nothing is cared for, nothing is talked of, nothing alluded to that does not bear upon this; and, in fact, if you haven't a venture in Smyrna figs, Memel timber, Dutch dolls, or some such commodity, you are absolutely nothing, and might as well be at a ball with a cork leg, or go deaf to the opera !

" Now, when I've told thus much, I leave you to guess what impression our triumphal entry into the city produced. Instead of the admiring crowds that awaited us elsewhere, as we marched gayly into quarters, here we saw nothing but grave, sober-looking, and (I confess it) intelligent-looking faces, that scrutinized our appearance closely enough, but evidently with no great approval, and less enthusiasm. The men passed on hurriedly to the counting-houses and the wharfs; the women, with almost as little interest, peeped at us from the windows, and walked away again. Oh, how we wished for Galway—glorious Galway ! that paradise of the infantry, that lies west of the Shannon. Little we knew, as we ordered the band, in lively anticipation of the gayeties before us, to strike up ' Payne's first set,' that, to the ears of the fair listeners in Ship Quay street, the rumble of a sugar hogshead or the creak of a weighing crane was more delightful music."

." By Jove !" interrupted Power, "you are quite right. Women are strongly imitative in their tastes. The lovely Italian, whose very costume is a natural following of a Raphael, is no more like the pretty Liverpool damsel than Genoa is to Glasnevin; and yet what the deuce have they, dear souls! with their feet upon a soft carpet, and their eyes upon the pages of Scott or Byron, to do with all the cotton or dimity that ever was printed? But let us not repine: that very plastic character is our greatest blessing."

"I'm not so sure that it always exists," said the Doctor, dubiously, as though his own experience pointed otherwise.

"Well, go ahead!" said the Skipper, who evidently disliked the digression thus interrupting the Adjutant's story.

"Well, we marched along, looking right and left at the pretty faces—and there were plenty of them, too—that a momentary curiosity drew to the windows; but, although we smiled, and ogled, and leered, as only a newly-arrived regiment can smile, ogle, or leer, by all that's provoking, we might as well have wasted our blandishments upon the Presbyterian meeting-house that frowned upon us with its high-pitched roof and round windows.

"'Droll people, these,' said one; 'Rayther rum ones,' cried another; 'The black north, by Jove!' said a third: and so we went along to the barracks, somewhat displeased to think that, though the 18th were slow, they might have met their match.

"Disappointed, as we undoubtedly felt, at the little enthusiasm that marked our *entrée*, we still resolved to persist in our original plan, and, accordingly, early the following morning, announced our intention of giving amateur theatricals. The Mayor, who called upon our Colonel, was the first to learn this, and received the information with pretty much the same kind of look the Archbishop of Canterbury might be supposed to assume if requested by a friend to ride 'a Derby.' The incredulous expression of the poor man's face as he turned from one of us to the other, evidently canvassing in his mind whether we might not, by some special dispensation of Providence, be all insane, I shall never forget.

"His visit was a very short one; whether concluding that we were not quite safe company, or whether our notification was too much for his nerves, I know not.

"We were not to be baulked, however; our schemes for gayety, long planned and conned over, were soon announced in all form; and though we made efforts almost superhuman in the cause, our plays were performed to empty benches, our balls were unattended, our picnic invitations politely declined, and, in a word, all our advances treated with a cold and chilling politeness, that plainly said, 'We'll none of you.'

"Each day brought some new discomfiture, and as we met at mess, instead of having, as heretofore, some prospect of pleasure and amusement to chat over, it was only to talk gloomily over our miserable failures, and lament the dreary quarters that our fates had doomed us to.

"Some months wore on in this fashion, and at length—what will not time do?—we began by degrees to forget our woes. Some of us took to late hours and brandy-and-water; others got sentimental, and wrote journals, and novels, and poetry; some made acquaintances among the townspeople, and cut in to a quiet rubber to pass the evening; while another detachment, among which I was, got up a little love affair to while away the tedious hours, and cheat the lazy sun.

"I have already said something of my taste in beauty; now, Mrs. Boggs was exactly the style of woman I fancied. She was a widow; she had black eyes—not your jet-black, sparkling, Dutch-doll eyes, that roll about and twinkle, but mean nothing—no; hers had a soft, subdued, downcast, pensive look about them, and were fully as melting a pair of orbs as any blue eyes you ever looked at.

"Then she had a short upper lip, and sweet teeth; by Jove, they were pearls! and she showed them, too, pretty often. Her figure was well rounded, plump, and what the French call *nette*. To complete all, her instep and ankle were unexceptionable; and lastly, her jointure was seven hundred pounds per annum, with a trifle of eight thousand more, that the late lamented Boggs bequeathed, when, after four months of uninterrupted bliss, he left Derry for another world.

"When chance first threw me in the way of the fair widow, some casual coincidence of opinion happened to raise me in her estimation, and I soon afterwards received an invitation to a small evening party at her house, to which I alone of the regiment was asked.

"I shall not weary you with the details of my intimacy; it is enough that I tell you I fell desperately in love. I began by visiting twice or thrice a week, and in less than two months spent every morning at her house, and rarely left it till the 'Roast Beef' announced mess.

"I soon discovered the widow's cue; she was serious. Now, I had conducted all manner of flirtations in my previous life,—timid young ladies, manly young ladies, musical, artistical, poetical, and hysterical. Bless you, I knew them all by heart; but never before had I to deal with a serious one, and a widow to boot. The case was a trying one. For some weeks it was all very up-hill work; all the red shot of warm affection I used to pour in on other occasions was of no use here. The language of love, in which I was no mean proficient, availed me not. Compliments and flattery, those rare shirmishers before the engagement, were denied me; and I verily think that a tender squeeze of the hand would have cost me my dismissal.

"'How very slow, all this!' thought I, as, at the end of two months' siege, I found myself seated in the trenches, and not a single breach in the fortress; 'but, to be sure, it's the way they have in the north, and one must be patient.'

"While thus I was in no very sanguine frame of mind as to my prospects, in reality my progress was very considerable. Having become a member of Mr. M'Phun's congregation, I was gradually rising in the estimation of the widow and her friends, whom my constant attendance at meeting, and my very serious demeanor, had so far impressed, that very grave deliberation was held whether I should not be made an elder at the next brevet.

"If the Widow Boggs had not been a very lovely and wealthy widow,—had she not possessed the eyes, hips, and ankles, and jointure aforesaid,—I honestly avow that neither the charms of that sweet man Mr. M'Phun's eloquence, not even the flattering distinction in store for me, would have induced me to prolong my suit. However, I was not going to despair when in sight of land. The widow was evidently softened. A little time longer, and the most scrupulous moralist, the most rigid advocate for employing time wisely, could not have objected to my daily system of courtship. It was none of your sighing, dying, ogling, hand-squeezing, waist-pressing, oath-swearing, everlasting-adoring affairs, with an interchange of rings and lockets,—not a bit of it. It was confoundedly like a controversial meeting at the Rotundo, and I myself had a far greater resemblance to Father Tom Maguire than a gay Lothario.

"After all, when mess-time came, when the 'Roast Beef' played and we assembled at dinner, and the soup and fish had gone round, with two glasses of sherry in, my spirits rallied, and a very jolly evening consoled me for all my fatigues and exertions, and supplied me with energy for the morrow; for let me observe here that I only made love before dinner. The evenings I reserved for myself, assuring Mrs. Boggs that my regimental duties required all my time after mess hour, in which I was perfectly correct; for at six we dined; at seven I opened the claret No. 1; at eight I had uncorked my second bottle; by half-past eight I was returning to the sherry; and at ten, punctual to the moment, I was repairing to my quarters on the back of my servant, Tim Daly, who had carried me safely for eight years, without a single mistake, as the fox-hunters say. This was a way we had in the —th. Every man was carried away from mess, some sooner, some later. I was always an early riser, and went betimes.

"Now, although I had very abundant proof, from circumstantial evidence, that I was nightly removed from the mess-room to my bed in the mode I mention, it would have puzzled me sorely to prove the fact in any direct way, inasmuch as by half-past nine, as the clock chimed and Tim entered to take me, I was very innocent of all that was going on, and, except a vague sense of regret at leaving the decanter, felt nothing whatever.

"It so chanced—what mere trifles are we ruled by in our destiny! —that just as my suit with the widow had assumed its most favorable footing, old General Hinks, that commanded the district, announced his coming over to inspect our regiment. Over he came accordingly, and, to be sure, we had a day of it. We were paraded for six mortal hours; then we were marching and countermarching; moving into line; back again into column; now forming open column, then into square; till at last we began to think that the old General was like the Flying Dutchman, and was probably condemned to keep on drilling us to the day of judgment. To be sure, he enlivened the proceeding to me by pronouncing the regiment the worst-drilled and appointed corps in the service, and the Adjutant (me!) the stupidest dunderhead—those were his words—he had ever met with.

"'Never mind,' thought I; 'a few days more, and it's little I'll care for the eighteen manœuvres. It's small trouble your eyes right, or your left shoulders forward, will give me. I'll sell out, and with the Widow Boggs and seven hundred a year—but no matter.'

"This confounded inspection lasted till half-past five in the afternoon, so that our mess was delayed a full hour in consequence, and it was past seven as we sat down to dinner. Our faces were grim enough as we met together at first; but what will not a good dinner and good wine do for the surliest party? By eight o'clock we began to feel somewhat more convivially disposed; and before nine the decanters were performing a quickstep round the table, in a fashion very exhilarating and very jovial to look at.

"'No flinching to-night,' said the senior Major. 'We've had a severe day; let us also have a merry evening.'

"'By Jove! Ormond,' cried another, 'we must not leave this to-night. Confound the old humbugs and their musty whist party; throw them over.'

"'I say, Adjutant,' said Forbes, addressing me, 'you've nothing particular to say to the fair widow this evening? You'll not bolt, I hope?'

"'That he shan't,' said one near me; 'he must make up for his absence to-morrow, for to-night we all stand fast.'

"'Besides,' said another, 'she's at meeting by this. Old—whatd'ye-call-him?—is at fourteenthly before now.'

"'A note for you, sir,' said the mess waiter, presenting me with a rose-colored three-cornered billet. It was from *la chère* Boggs herself, and ran thus :—

"'Dear Sir :—Mr. M'Phun and a few friends are coming to tea at my house after meeting; perhaps you will also favor us with your company.　　　　　　　Yours truly,

"'Eliza Boggs.'

"What was to be done? Quit the mess—leave a jolly party just at the jolliest moment—exchange Lafitte and red hermitage for a *soirée* of elders, presided over by that sweet man, Mr. M'Phun! It was too bad! But then, how much was in the scale? What would the widow say if I declined? What would she think? I well knew that the invitation meant nothing less than a full-dress parade of me before her friends, and that to decline was perhaps to forfeit all my hopes in that quarter forever.

"'Any answer, sir?' said the waiter.

"'Yes,' said I, in a half-whisper, 'I'll go—tell the servant I'll go.'

"At this moment my tender epistle was subtracted from before me, and, ere I had turned round, had made the tour of half the table. I never perceived the circumstance, however, and filling my glass, professed my resolve to sit to the last, with a mental reserve to take my departure at the very first opportunity. Ormond and the Paymaster quitted the room for a moment, as if to give orders for a broil at twelve, and now all seemed to promise a very convivial and well-sustained party for the night.

"'Is that all arranged?' inquired the Major, as Ormond entered.

"'All right,' said he; 'and now let us have a bumper and a song. Adjutant, old boy, give us a chant.'

"'What shall it be, then?' inquired I, anxious to cover my intended retreat by an appearance of joviality.

"'Give us—

'When I was in the Fusiliers
Some fourteen years ago.' "

"'No, no; confound it! I've heard nothing else since I joined the regiment. Let us have the "Paymaster's Daughter." '

"'Ah! that's pathetic; I like that,' lisped a young ensign.

"'If I'm to have a vote,' grunted out the senior Major, 'I pronounce for "West India Quarters." '

"'Yes, yes,' said half a dozen voices together; 'let's have "West India Quarters." Come, give him a glass of sherry, and let him begin.'

"I had scarcely finished off my glass, and cleared my throat for my song, when the clock on the chimney-piece chimed half-past nine, and the same instant I felt a heavy hand fall upon my shoulder. I turned, and beheld my servant, Tim. This, as I have already mentioned, was the hour at which Tim was in the habit of taking me home to my quarters; and though we had dined an hour later, he took no notice of the circumstance, but, true to his custom, he was behind my chair. A very cursory glance at my 'familiar' was quite sufficient to show me that we had somehow changed sides; for Tim, who was habitually the most sober of mankind, was on the present occasion exceedingly drunk, while I, a full hour before that consummation, was perfectly sober.

"'What d'ye want, sir?' inquired I, with something of severity in my manner.

"'Come home,' said Tim, with a hiccup that set the whole table in a roar.

"'Leave the room this instant,' said I, feeling wrath at being thus made a butt for his offences. 'Leave the room, or I'll kick you out of it.' Now, this, let me add, in a parenthesis, was somewhat of a boast, for Tim was six feet three, and strong in proportion, and, when in liquor, fearless as a tiger.

"'You'll kick me out of the room—eh! will you? Try—only try it, that's all.' Here a new roar of laughter burst forth, while Tim, again placing an enormous paw upon my shoulder, continued, 'Don't be sitting there, making a baste of yourself, when you've got enough. Don't you see you're drunk?'

" I sprang to my legs on this, and made a rush to the fireplace, to secure the poker; but Tim was beforehand with me, and seizing me by the waist with both hands, flung me across his shoulder, as though I were a baby, saying, at the same time, 'I'll take you away at half-past eight to-morrow, av you're as rampageous again.' I kicked, I plunged, I swore, I threatened, I even begged and implored to be set down; but whether my voice was lost in the uproar around me, or that Tim only regarded my denunciations in the light of cursing, I know not, but he carried me bodily down the stairs, steadying himself by one hand on the banisters, while with the other he held me as in a vice. I had but one consolation all this while; it was this, that, as my quarters lay immediately behind the mess-room, Tim's excursion would soon come to an end, and I should be free once more; but guess my terror to find that the drunken scoundrel, instead of going, as usual, to the left, turned short to the right hand, and marched boldly into Ship Quay street. Every window in the mess-room was filled with our fellows, absolutely shouting with laughter. 'Go it, Tim!—that's the fellow!—hold him tight!—never let go!' cried a dozen voices; while the wretch, with the tenacity of drunkenness, gripped me still harder, and took his way down the middle of the street.

"It was a beautiful evening in July, a soft summer night, as I made this pleasing excursion down the most frequented thoroughfare in the maiden city; my struggles every moment exciting·roars of laughter from an increasing crowd of spectators, who seemed scarcely less amused than puzzled at the exhibition. In the midst of a torrent of imprecations against my torturer, a loud noise attracted me. I turned my head, and saw—horror of horrors!—the door of the meeting-house just flung open, and the congregation issuing forth *en masse.* Is it any wonder if I remember no more? There I was, the chosen one of the Widow Boggs—the elder elect—the favored friend and admired associate of Mr. M'Phun, taking an airing on a summer's evening on the back of a drunken Irishman. Oh! the thought was horrible; and, certainly, the short and pithy epithets by which I was characterized in the crowd neither improved my temper nor assuaged my wrath; and I feel bound to confess that my own language was neither serious nor becoming. Tim, however, cared little for all this, and pursued the even tenor of his way through the whole crowd, nor stopped till, having made half the circuit of the wall, he deposited me safe at my own door, adding, as he set me down, 'Oh! av you're as throublesome every evening, it's a wheelbarrow I'll be obleeged to bring for you.'

"The next day I obtained a short leave of absence, and ere a fortnight expired, exchanged into the —th, preferring Halifax itself to the ridicule that awaited me in Londonderry."

CHAPTER XXX.

FRED POWER'S ADVENTURE IN PHILIPSTOWN.

THE lazy hours of the long summer day crept slowly over. The sea, unbroken by foam or ripple, shone like a broad blue mirror, reflecting here and there some fleecy patches of snow-white cloud, as they stood unmoved in the sky. The good ship rocked to and fro with a heavy lumbering motion; the cordage rattled; the bulkheads creaked; the sails flapped lazily against the masts; the very sea-gulls seemed to sleep as they rested on the long swell that bore them along; and everything in sea and sky bespoke the calm. No sailor trod the deck; no watch was stirring; the very tiller ropes were deserted; and, as they traversed backward and forward with every roll of the vessel, told that we had no steerage way, and lay a mere log upon the water.

I sat alone in the bow, and fell into a musing fit upon the past and the future. How happily for us is it ordained that, in the most stirring existences, there are every here and there such little resting-spots of reflection, from which, as from some eminence, we look back upon the road we have been treading in life, and cast a wistful glance at the dark vista before us! When first we set upon our worldly pilgrimage, these are, indeed, precious moments, when, with buoyant heart and spirit high, believing all things, trusting all things, our very youth comes back to us, reflected from every object we meet, and, like Narcissus, we are but worshipping our own image in the water. As we go on in life, the cares, the anxieties, and the business of the world, engross us more and more, and such moments become fewer and shorter. Many a bright dream has been dissolved, many a fairy vision replaced, by some dark reality; blighted hopes, false friendships, have gradually worn callous the heart once alive to every gentle feeling, and time begins to tell upon us. Yet still, as the well-remembered melody to which we listened with delight in infancy brings to our mature age a touch of early years, so will the very association of these happy moments recur to us in our reverie, and make us young again in thought. Then it is that, as we look back upon our worldly career, we become convinced how truly is the child the father of the man, how frequently are the projects of our manhood the fruit of some boyish predilection, and that, in the emulative ardor that stirs the schoolboy's heart, we may read the prestige of that high daring that makes a hero of its possessor.

These moments, too, are scarcely more pleasurable than they are salutary to us. Disengaged for the time from every worldly anxiety, we pass in review before our own selves, and in the solitude of our own hearts are we judged. That still small voice of conscience, unheard and unlistened to amid the din and bustle of life, speaks audibly to us now; and while chastened on one side by regrets, we are sustained on the other by some approving thought, and, with many a sorrow for the past, and many a promise for the future, we begin to feel "how good it is for us to be here."

The evening wore later; the red sun sank down upon the sea, growing larger and larger; the long line of mellow gold that sheeted along the distant horizon grew first of a dark ruddy tinge, then paler and paler, till it became almost gray; a single star shone faintly in the east, and darkness soon set in. With night came the wind, for almost imperceptibly the sails swelled slowly out, a slight rustle at the bow followed, the ship lay gently over, and we were once more in motion. It struck four bells; some slight resemblance in the sound to the old pendulum that marked the hour at my uncle's house startled me, so that I actually knew not where I was. With lightning speed my once home rose up before me, with its happy hearts. The old familiar faces were there; the gay laugh was in my cars; there sat my dear old uncle, as with bright eye and mellow voice he looked a very welcome to his guests; there Boyle; there Considine; there the grim-visaged portraits that graced the old walls, whose black oak wainscot stood in broad light and shadow, as the blazing turf fire shone upon it; there was my own place, now vacant. Methought my uncle's eye was turned towards it, and that I heard him say, "My poor boy! I wonder where he is now!" My heart swelled; my chest heaved; the tears coursed slowly down my cheeks, as I asked myself, "Shall I ever see them more?" Oh! how little, how very little, to us are the accustomed blessings of our life, till some change has robbed us of them! and how dear are they when lost to us! My uncle's dark foreboding that we should never meet again on earth came, for the first time, forcibly to my mind, and my heart was full to bursting. What could repay me for the agony of that moment, as I thought of him—my first, my best, my only friend—whom I had deserted? and how gladly would I have resigned my bright day-dawn of ambition to be once more beside his chair, to hear his voice, to see his smile, to feel his love for me! A loud laugh from the cabin roused me from my sad, depressing reverie, and at the same instant Mike's well-known voice informed me that the Captain was looking for me everywhere, as supper was on the table. Little as I felt disposed to join the party at such a moment, as I knew there was no escaping Power, I resolved to make the best of matters; so, after a few minutes, I followed Mickey down the companion, and entered the cabin.

The scene before me was certainly not calculated to perpetuate depressing thoughts. At the head of a rude, old-fashioned table, upon which figured several black bottles, and various ill-looking drinking vessels of every shape and material, sat Fred Power; on his right was placed the Skipper; on his left the Doctor, the bronzed, merry-looking, weather-beaten features of the one contrasting ludicrously with the pale, ascetic, acute-looking expression of the other. Sparks, more than half-drunk, with the mark of a red-hot cigar upon his nether lip, was lower down; while Major Monsoon, to preserve the symmetry of the party, had protruded his head, surmounted by a huge red nightcap, from the berth opposite, and held out his goblet to be replenished from the punch-bowl.

"Welcome, thrice welcome, thou man of Galway," cried out

Power, as he pointed to a seat, and pushed a wine-glass towards me. "Just in time, too, to pronounce upon a new brewing. Taste that; a little more of the lemon you would say, perhaps? Well, I agree with you; rum and brandy; Glenlivet and guava jelly; limes, green tea, and a slight suspicion of preserved ginger—nothing else, upon honor—and the most simple mixture for the cure, the radical cure, of blue devils and debt I know of; eh, Doctor? You advise it yourself, to be taken before bed-time; nothing inflammatory in it; nothing pugnacious; a mere circulation of the better juices and more genial spirits of the marly clay, without arousing any of the baser passions; whisky is the devil for that."

"I canna say that I dinna like whisky-toddy," said the Doctor; "in the cauld winter nights it's no sae bad."

"Ah! that's it," said Power; "there's the pull you Scotch have upon us poor Patlanders; cool, calculating, long-headed fellows, you only come up to the mark after fifteen tumblers; whereas, we hot-brained devils, with a blood at 212 degrees of Fahrenheit, and a high-pressure engine of good spirits always ready for an explosion, we go clean mad when tipsy; not but I am fully convinced that a mad Irishman is worth two sane people of any other country under heaven."

"If you mean by that insin—insin—sinuation to imply any disrespect to the English," stuttered out Sparks, "I am bound to say that I for one, and the Doctor, I am sure, for another——"

"Na, na," interrupted the Doctor, "ye mauna coont upon me; I'm no disposed to fecht ower our liquor."

"Then, Major Monsoon, I'm certain——"

"Are ye, faith?" said the Major, with a grin; "blessed are they who expect nothing—of which number you are not—for most decidedly you shall be disappointed."

"Never mind, Sparks, take the whole fight to your own proper self, and do battle like a man; and here I stand, ready at all arms to prove my position—that we drink better, sing better, court better, fight better, and make better punch, than ever John Bull from Berwick to the Land's End."

Sparks, however, who seemed not exactly sure how far his antagonist was disposed to quiz, relapsed into a half-tipsy expression of contemptuous silence, and sipped his liquor without reply.

"Yes," said Power, after a pause, "bad luck to it for whisky; it nearly got me broke once, and poor Tom O'Reilly of the 5th, too, the best-tempered fellow in the service; we were as near it as touch and go; and all for some confounded Loughrea spirits, that we believed to be perfectly innocent, and used to swill away freely without suspicion of any kind."

"Let's hear the story," said I, "by all means."

"It's not a long one," said Power; "so I don't care if I tell it; and, besides, if I make a clean breast of my own sins, I'll insist upon Monsoon's telling you afterwards how he stocked his cellar in Cadiz; eh, Major? there's worse tipple than the King of Spain's sherry?"

"You shall judge for yourself, old boy," said Monsoon, good-humoredly; "and as for the narrative; it is equally at your service. Of course, it goes no farther. The Commander-in-Chief—long life to him!—is a glorious fellow; but he has no more idea of a joke than the Archbishop of Canterbury, and it might chance to reach him."

"Recount, and fear not!" cried Power; "we are discreet as the worshipful company of apothecaries."

"But you forget you are to lead the way."

"Here goes, then," said the jolly Captain; "not that the story has any merit in it, but the moral is beautiful.

"Ireland, to be sure, is a beautiful country, but somehow it would prove a very dull one to be quartered in if it were not that the people seem to have a natural taste for the army. From the belle of Merrion square down to the innkeeper's daughter in Tralee, the loveliest part of the creation seem to have a perfect appreciation of our high acquirements and advantages; and in no other part of the globe, the Tonga Islands included, is a red coat more in favor. To be sure they would be very ungrateful if it were not the case; for we, upon our sides, leave no stone unturned to make ourselves agreeable. We ride, drink, play, and make love to the ladies, from Fairhead to Killarney, in a way greatly calculated to render us popular; and, as far as making the time pass pleasantly, we are the boys for the 'greatest happiness' principle. I repeat it, we deserve our popularity. Which of us does not get head and ears in debt, with garrison balls and steeple-chases, picnics, regattas, and the thousand-and-one inventions to get rid of one's spare cash, so called for being so sparingly dealt out by our governors? Now and then, too, when all else fails, we take a newly-joined ensign, and make him marry some pretty but penniless lass, in a country town, just to show the rest that we are not joking, but have serious ideas of matrimony, in the midst of all our flirtations. If it were all like this, the Green Isle would be a paradise; but, unluckily, every now and then one is condemned to some infernal place, where there is neither a pretty face nor tight ankle; where the priest himself is not a good fellow; and long, ill-paved, straggling streets, filled, on market days, with booths of striped calico and soapy cheese, are the only promenade, and a ruinous barrack, with mouldy walls and a tumbling chimney, the only quarters.

"In vain, on your return from your morning stroll or afternoon canter, you look on the chimney-piece for a shower of visiting cards and pink notes of invitation; in vain you ask your servant has any one called. Alas! your only visitor has been the gauger, to demand a party to assist in still-hunting, amid that interesting class of the population who, having nothing to eat, are engaged in devising drink, and care as much for the life of a red coat as you do for that of a crow or a curlew. This may seem overdrawn; but I would ask you, were you ever for your sins quartered in that capital city of the Bog of Allen they call Philipstown? Oh, but it is a romantic spot! They tell us somewhere that much of the expression of the human face divine depends upon the objects which constantly surround us. Thus the inhabitants of mountain districts imbibe, as it were, a certain bold and daring character of expression from the scenery, very different from the placid and monotonous looks of those who dwell in plains and valleys; and I can certainly credit the theory in this instance, for every man, woman, and child you meet has a brown, baked, scruffy, turf-like face, that fully satisfies you that if Adam were formed of clay, the Philipstown people were worse treated, and only made of bog mould.

"Well, one fine morning, poor Tom and myself were marched off from Birr, where one might 'live and love forever,' to take up our quarters at this sweet spot. Little we knew of Philipstown, and, like my friend the Adjutant there, when he laid siege to Derry, we made our *entrée* with all the pomp we could muster, and though we had no band, our drums and fifes did duty for it; and we brushed along through turf-creels and wicker-baskets of new brogues that obstructed the street till we reached the barrack, the only testimony of admiration we met with being, I feel bound to admit, from a ragged urchin of ten years, who, with a wattle in his hand, imitated me as I marched along, and, when I cried halt, took his leave of us by dexterously fixing his thumb to the side of his nose and outstretching his fingers, as if thus to convey a very strong hint that were not half so fine fellows as we thought ourselves. Well, four mortal summer months of hot sun and cloudless sky went over, and still we lingered in that vile village, the everlasting monotony of our days being marked by the same brief morning drill, the same blue-legged chicken dinner, the same smoky Loughrea whisky, and the same evening stroll along the canal bank to watch for the Dublin packet-boat, with its never-varying cargo of cattle-dealers, priests, and peelers on their way to the west country, as though the demand for such colonial productions in those parts were insatiable. This was pleasant, you will say; but what was to be done? We had nothing else. Now, nothing saps a man's temper like ennui. The cranky, peevish people one meets with would be excellent folk if they only had something to do. As for us, I'll venture to say two men more disposed to go pleasantly down the current of life it were hard to meet with; and yet such was the consequence of these confounded four months' sequestration from all other society, we became sour and cross-grained, everlastingly disputing about trifles, and continually arguing about matters which neither was interested in, nor, indeed, knew anything about. There were, it is true, few topics to discuss; newspapers we never saw; sporting there was none; but, then, the drill, the return of duty, the probable chances of our being ordered for service, were all daily subjects to be talked over, and usually with considerable asperity and bitterness. One point, however, always served us when hard pushed for a bone of contention, and which, begun by a mere accident at first, gradually increased to a sore and peevish subject, and finally led to the consequences which I have hinted at in the beginning. This was no less than the respective merits of our mutual servants; each everlastingly indulging in a tirade against the other for awkwardness, incivility, unhandiness—charges, I am bound to confess, most amply proved on either side.

" 'Well, I am sure, O'Reilly, if you can stand that fellow,—it's no affair of mine, but such an ungainly savage I never met,' I would say.

"To which he would reply, 'Bad enough he is, certainly; but, by Jove! when I only think of your Hottentot, I feel grateful for what I've got.'

"Then ensued a discussion, with attack, rejoinder, charge, and re-crimination, till we retired for the night, wearied with our exertions, and not a little ashamed of ourselves at bottom for our absurd warmth and excitement. In the morning the matter would be rigidly avoided by each party until some chance occasion had brought it on the *tapis*, when hostilities would be immediately renewed, and carried on with the same vigor, to end as before.

"In this agreeable state of matters we sat, one warm summer evening, before the mess-room, under the shade of a canvas awning, discussing, by way of refrigerant, our eighth tumbler of whisky-punch. We had, as usual, been jarring away about everything under heaven. A lately arrived post-chaise, with an old, stiff-looking gentleman in a queue, had formed a kind of 'godsend' for debate, as to who he was, whither he was going, whether he really had intended to spend the night there, or only put up because the chaise was broken; each, as was customary, maintaining his own opinion with an obstinacy we have often since laughed at, though at the time we had few mirthful thoughts about the matter.

"As the debate waxed warm, O'Reilly asserted that he positively knew the individual in question to be a United Irishman, travelling with instructions from the French Government, while I laughed him to scorn by swearing that he was the rector of Tyrrell's Pass; that I knew him well; and, moreover, that he was the worst preacher in Ireland. Singular enough it was, that all this while the disputed identity was himself standing coolly at the inn window, with his snuff-box in his hand, leisurely surveying us as we sat, appearing, at least, to take a very lively interest in our debate.

"'Come, now,' said O'Reilly, 'there's only one way to conclude this, and make you pay for your obstinacy. What will you bet that he's the rector of Tyrrell's Pass?'

"'What odds will you take that he's Wolfe Tone?' inquired I, sneeringly.

"'Five to one against the rector,' said he, exultingly.

"'An elephant's molar to a toothpick against Wolfe Tone,' cried I.

"'Ten pounds even that I'm nearer the mark than you,' said Tom, with a smash of his fist upon the table.

"'Done,' said I—'done. But how are we to decide the wager?'

"'That's soon done,' said he. At the same instant he sprang to his legs, and called out, 'Pat—I say, Pat—I want you to present my respects to——'

"'No, no, I bar that—no *ex parte* statements. Here, Jem, do you simply tell that——'

"'That fellow can't deliver a message. Do come here, Pat. Just beg of——'

"'He'll blunder it, the confounded fool; so, Jem, do you go.'

"The two individuals thus addressed were just in the act of conveying a tray of glasses and a spiced round of beef for supper into the mess-room; and, as I may remark that they fully entered into the feelings of jealousy their respective masters possessed, each eyed the other with a look of very unequivocal dislike.

"Arrah! ye needn't be pushing me that way,' said Pat, 'an' the round o' beef in my hands.'

"'Devil's luck to ye! it's the glasses you'll be breaking with your awkward elbow.'

"'Then why don't ye leave the way? Ain't I your suparior?'

"'Ain't I the Captain's own man?'

"'Ay, and if you war. Don't I belong to his betters? Isn't my master the two Liftenants?'

"This, however strange it may sound, was so far true, as I held a commission in an African corps, with my Lieutenancy in the 5th.

"'Be-gorra, av he was six—there now, you done it!'

"At the same moment a tremendous crash took place, and a large dish fell in a thousand pieces on the pavement, while the spiced round rolled pensively down the yard.

"Scarcely was the noise heard, when, with one vigorous kick, the tray of glasses was sent spinning into the air, and the next moment the disputants were engaged in bloody battle. It was at this moment that our attention was first drawn towards them, and I need not say with what feelings of interest we looked on.

"'Hit him, Pat—there, Jem, under the guard—that's it—go in—well done, left hand—by Jove, that was a facer—his eye's closed—he's down—not a bit of it—how do you like that?—unfair, unfair—no such thing—I say it was—not at all—I deny it.'

"By this time we had approached the combatants, each man patting his own fellow on the back, and encouraging him by the most lavish promises. Now it was, but in what way I never could exactly tell, that I threw out my right hand to stop a blow that I saw coming rather too near me, when, by some unhappy mischance, my double fist lighted upon Tom O'Reilly's nose. Before I could express my sincere regret for the accident, the blow was returned with double force, and the next moment we were at it harder than the others. After five minutes' sharp work, we both stopped for breath, and incontinently burst out a-laughing. There was Tom, with a nose as large as three; a huge cheek on one side, and the whole head swinging round like a harlequin's; while I, with one eye closed, and the other like a half-shut cockle-shell, looked scarcely less rueful. We had not much time for mirth, for at the same instant a sharp, full voice called out close beside us,—

"'To your quarters, sirs. I put you both under arrest, from which you are not to be released until the sentence of a court-martial decide if such conduct as this becomes officers and gentlemen.'

"I looked round, and saw the old fellow in the queue.

"'Wolfe Tone, by all that's unlucky!' said I, with an attempt at a smile.

"'The rector of Tyrrell's Pass,' cried out Tom, with a snuffle; 'the worst preacher in Ireland—eh, Fred?'

"We had not much time for further commentaries upon our friend, for he at once opened his frock coat, and displayed to our horrified gaze the uniform of a general officer.

"'Yes, sir, General Johnston, if you will allow me to present him to your acquaintance; and now, guard, turn out.'

"In a few minutes more the orders were issued, and poor Tom and myself found ourselves fast confined to our quarters, with a sentinel at the door, and the pleasant prospect that in the space of about ten days we should be broke, and dismissed the service—which verdict, as the general order would say, the Commander of the Forces has been graciously pleased to approve.

"However, when morning came, the old General, who was really a trump, inquired a little further into the matter, saw it was partly accidental, and, after a severe reprimand, and a caution about Loughrea whisky after the sixth tumbler, released us from arrest, and forgave the whole affair."

CHAPTER XXXI.

THE VOYAGE.

UGH! what a miserable thing is a voyage! Here we are now eight days at sea, the eternal sameness of all around growing every hour less supportable. Sea and sky are beautiful things when seen from the dark woods and waving meadows on shore; but their picturesque effect is sadly marred from want of contrast; besides that, the "*toujours* pork," with crystals of salt as long as your wife's fingers; the potatoes, that seemed varnished in French polish; the tea, seasoned with geological specimens from the basin of London, yclept maple sugar; and the butter—ye gods!—the butter! But why enumerate these smaller features of discomfort, and omit the more glaring ones? The utter selfishness which blue water suggests, as inevitably as the cold fit follows the ague; the good fellow that shares his knapsack or his last guinea on land, here forages out the best corner to hang his hammock; jockeys you into a comfortless crib, where the uncaulked deck-butt filters every rain from heaven on your head; he votes you the corner at dinner, not only that he may place you with your back to the thorough draft of the gangway ladder, but that he may eat, drink, and lie down before you have even begun to feel the qualmishness that the dinner of a troop-ship is well calculated to suggest; cuts his pencil with your best razor; wears your shirts, as washing is scarce; and winds up all by having a good story of you every evening for the edification of the other "sharp gentlemen," who, being too wide awake to be humbugged themselves, enjoy his success prodigiously. This, gentle reader, is neither confession nor avowal of mine. The passage I have here presented to you. I have taken from the journal of my brother officer, Mr. Sparks, who, when not otherwise occupied, usually employed his time in committing to paper his thoughts upon men, manners, and things at sea in general; though, sooth to say, his was not an idle life; being voted by unanimous consent "a junior," he was condemned to offices that the veriest fag in Eton or Harrow had rebelled against. In the morning, under the pseudonym of *Mrs. Sparks*, he presided at breakfast, having previously made tea, coffee, and chocolate for the whole cabin, besides boiling about twenty eggs at various degrees of hardness; he was under heavy recognizances to provide a plate of buttered toast of very alarming magnitude, fried ham, kidneys, &c., to no end. Later on, when others sauntered about the deck, vainly endeavoring to fix their attention upon a novel or a review, the poor Cornet might be seen, with a white apron tucked gracefully round his spare proportions, whipping eggs for pancakes, or, with upturned shirt sleeves, fashioning dough for a pudding. As the day waned, the cook's galley became his haunt, where, exposed to a roasting fire, he inspected the details of a *cuisine* for which, whatever his demerits, he was sure of an ample remuneration in abuse at dinner. Then came the dinner itself, that dread ordeal, where nothing was praised, and everything censured. This was followed by the punch-making, where the tastes of six different and differing individuals were to be exclusively consulted in the self-same beverage; and lastly, the supper at night, when Sparkie (as he was familiarly called), towards evening, quite exhausted, became the subject of unmitigated wrath and unmeasured reprobation.

"I say, Sparks, it's getting late; the spatch-cock, old boy; don't be slumbering."

"By the bye, Sparkie, what a mess you made of that pea-soup to-day! By Jove! I never felt so ill in my life."

"Na, na, it was na the soup; it was something he pit in the punch, that's burnin' me ever since I tuk it. Ou, man, but ye're an awfu' creture wi' vittals."

"He'll improve, Doctor, he'll improve; don't discourage him; the boy's young. Be alive now, there; where's the toast? Confound you—where's the toast?"

"There, Sparks, you like a drumstick, I know—mustn't muzzle the ox, eh? Scripture for you, old boy. Eat away; hang the expense. Hand him over the jug. Empty—eh, Charley? Come, Sparkie, bear a hand; the liquor's out."

"But won't you let me eat?"

"Eat! heavens, what a fellow for eating! By George, such an appetite is clean against the articles of war! Come, man, it's drink we're thinking of. There's the rum, sugar, limes; see to the hot water. Well, Skipper, how are we getting on?"

"Lying our course; eight knots off the log. Pass the rum. Why, Mister Sparks!"

"Eh, Sparks, what's this?"

"Sparks, my man, confound it!" And then, *omnes* chorusing,

"Sparks!" in every key of the gamut, the luckless fellow would be obliged to jump up from his meagre fare, and set to work at a fresh brewage of punch for the others. The bowl and the glasses filled, by some little management on Power's part, our friend the Cornet would be *drawn out*, as the phrase is, into some confession of his early years, which seemed to have been exclusively spent in love-making—devotion to the fair being as integral a portion of his character as tippling was of the worthy Major's.

Like most men who pass their lives in over-studious efforts to please,—however ungallant the confession be,—the amiable Sparks had had little success. His love, if not, as it generally happened, totally unrequited, was invariably the source of some awkward catastrophe, there being no imaginable error he had not, at some time or other, fallen into, nor any conceivable mischance to which he had not been exposed. Inconsolable widows, attached wives, fond mothers, newly-married brides, engaged young ladies, were, by some *contretemps*, continually the subjects of his attachments; and the least mishap which followed the avowal of his passion was to be heartily laughed at, and obliged to leave the neighborhood. Duels, apologies, actions at law, compensations, &c., were of every-day occurrence, and to such an extent, too, that any man blessed with a smaller bump upon the occiput would eventually have long since abandoned the pursuit, and taken to some less expensive pleasure; but poor Sparks, in the true spirit of a martyr, only gloried the more, the more he suffered, and, like the worthy man who continued to purchase tickets in the lottery for thirty years, with nothing but a succession of blanks, he ever imagined that fortune was only trying his patience, and had some cool forty thousand pounds of happiness waiting his perseverance in the end. Whether this prize ever did turn up in the course of years, I am unable to say; but, certainly, up to the period of his history I now speak of, all had been as gloomy and unrequiting as need be. Power, who knew something of every man's adventures, was aware of so much of poor Sparks's career, and usually contrived to lay a trap for a confession that generally served to amuse us during an evening, as much, I acknowledge, from the manner of the recital as anything contained in the story. There was a species of serious matter-of-fact simplicity in the detail of the most ridiculous scenes, that left you convinced that his bearing upon the affair in question must have greatly heightened the absurdity, nothing, however comic or droll in itself, ever exciting in him the least approach to a smile. He sat with his large light-blue eyes, light hair, long upper lip, and retreating chin, lisping out an account of an adventure, with a look of Liston about him that was inconceivably amusing.

14

"Come, Sparks," said Power, "I claim a promise you made me the other night, on condition that we let you off making the oyster-patties at ten o'clock; you can't forget what I mean." Here the Captain knowingly touched the tip of his ear, at which signal the Cornet colored slightly, and drank off his wine in a hurried, confused way. "He promised to tell us, Major, how he lost the tip of his left ear. I have myself heard hints of the circumstance, but would much rather hear Sparks's own version of it."

"Another love story," said the Doctor, with a grin, "I'll be bound."

"Shot off in a duel?" said I, inquiringly; "close work, too."

"No such thing," replied Power; "but Sparks will enlighten you. It is, without exception, the most touching and beautiful thing I ever heard; as a simple story, it beats the 'Vicar of Wakefield' to sticks."

"You don't say so?" said poor Sparks, blushing.

"Ay, that I do, and maintain it too. I'd rather be the hero of that little adventure, and be able to recount it as you do,—for, mark me, that's no small part of the effect,—than I'd be full colonel of the regiment. Well, I am sure I always thought it affecting; but, somehow, my dear friend, you don't know your powers; you have that within you which would make the fortune of half the periodicals going. Ask Monsoon or O'Malley there if I did not say so at breakfast, when you were grilling the old hen,—which, by the bye, let me remark, was not one of your *chefs-d'œuvre.*"

"A tougher beastie I never put a tooth in."

"But the story—the story," said I.

"Yes," said Power, with a tone of command: "the story, Sparks."

"Well, if you really think it worth telling, as I have always felt it a very remarkable incident, here goes."

<hr>

CHAPTER XXXII.

MR. SPARKS'S STORY.

I SAT at breakfast one beautiful morning at the Goat Inn at Barmouth, looking out of a window upon the lovely vale of Barmouth, with its tall trees and brown trout-stream struggling through the woods, then turning to take a view of the calm sea, that, speckled over with white-sailed fishing-boats, stretched away in the distance. The eggs were fresh; the trout newly caught; the cream delicious; before me lay the *Plwdwddlwn Advertiser*, which, among the fashionable arrivals at the sea-side, set forth Mr. Sparks, nephew of Sir Toby Sparks, of Manchester,—a paragraph, by the way, I always inserted. The English are naturally an aristocratic people, and set a due value upon a title."

"A very just observation," remarked Power, seriously, while Sparks continued.

" However, as far as any result from the announcement, I might as well have spared myself the trouble, for not a single person called; not one solitary invitation to dinner; not a picnic; not a breakfast; no, nor even a tea-party was heard of. Barmouth, at the time I speak of, was just in that transition state at which the caterpillar may be imagined, when, having abandoned his reptile habits, he still has not succeeded in becoming a butterfly. In fact, it had ceased to be a fishing-village, but had not arrived at the dignity of a watering-place. Now, I know nothing as bad as this. You have not, on one hand, the quiet retirement of a little peaceful hamlet, with its humble dwellings and cheap pleasures, nor have you the gay and animated tableau of fashion in miniature on the other; but you have noise, din, bustle, confusion, beautiful scenery, and lovely points of view, marred and ruined by vulgar associations. Every bold rock and jutting promontory has its citizen occupants; every sandy cove or tide-washed bay has its myriads of squalling babes and red baize-clad bathing women—those veritable descendants of the nymphs of old. Pink parasols, donkey-carts, baskets of bread-and-butter, reticules, guides to Barmouth, specimens of ore, fragments of gypsum, meet you at every step, and destroy every illusion of the picturesque.

" 'I shall leave this,' thought I. 'My dreams, my long-cherished dreams of romantic walks upon the sea-shore, of evening strolls by moonlight, through dell and dingle, are reduced to a short promenade through an alley of bathing-boxes, amid a screaming population of nursery-maids and sick children, with a thorough-bass of "Fresh Shrimps!" discordant enough to frighten the very fish from the shores. There is no peace, no quiet, no romance, no poetry, no love.' Alas! that most of all was wanting; for, after all, what is it which lights up the heart, save the flame of a mutual attachment? what gilds the fair stream of life, save the bright ray of warm affection? what——"

" In a word," said Power, "it is the sugar in the punch-bowl of our existence. *Perge*, Sparks; push on."

" I was not long in making up my mind. I called for my bill; I packed my clothes; I ordered post-horses; I was ready to start; one item in the bill alone detained me. The frequent occurrence of the enigmatical word 'crw' following my servant's name demanded an explanation, which I was in the act of receiving, when a chaise-and-four drove rapidly up to the house. In a moment the blinds were drawn up, and such a head appeared at the window! Let me pause for one moment to drink in the remembrance of that lovely being; eyes, where heaven's own blue seemed concentrated, were shaded by long, deep lashes of the darkest brown; a brow fair, noble, and expansive, at each side of which masses of dark-brown hair waved half in ringlets, half in loose falling bands, shadowing her pale and downy cheek, where one faint rosebud tinge seemed lingering; lips slightly parted, which, so to speak, gave to the features all the play of animation which completed this intellectual character, and made up——"

"What I should say was a devilish pretty girl," interrupted Power.

"Back the widow against her at long odds, any day," murmured the Adjutant.

"She was an angel! an angel!" cried Sparks, with enthusiasm.

"So was the widow, if you go to that," said the Adjutant, hastily.

"And so is Matilda Dalrymple," said Power, with a sly look at me. "We are all honorable men—eh, Charley?"

"Go ahead with the story," said the Skipper; "I'm beginning to feel an interest in it."

"'Isabella,' said a man's voice, as a large, well-dressed personage assisted her to alight—'Isabella, love, you must take a little rest here before we proceed farther.'

"'I think she had better, sir,' said a matronly-looking woman, with a plaid cloak and a black bonnet.

"They disappeared within the house, and I was left alone. The bright dream was past; she was there no longer; but in my heart her image lived, and I almost felt she was before me. I thought I heard her voice; I saw her move; my limbs trembled; my hands tingled; I rang the bell, ordered my trunks back again to No. 5, and, as I sank upon the sofa, murmured to myself, 'This is indeed love at first sight.'"

"How devilish sudden it was," said the Skipper.

"Exactly like camp fever," responded the Doctor. "One moment ye are vara well; the next ye are seized wi' a kind of shivering; then comes a kind of mandering, dandering, travelling a'overness."

"D— the camp fever," interrupted Power.

"Well, as I observed, I fell in love; and here let me take the opportunity of observing that all we are in the habit of hearing about single or only attachments is mere nonsense. No man is so capable of feeling deeply as he who is in the daily practice of it. Love, like everything else in this world, demands a species of cultivation. The mere tyro in an affair of the heart thinks he has exhausted all its pleasures and pains; but only he who has made it his daily study for years, familiarizing his mind with every phase of the passion, can properly or adequately appreciate it. Thus, the more you love, the better you love; the more frequently has your heart yielded——"

"It's vara like the mucous membrane," said the Doctor.

"I'll break your neck with the decanter if you interrupt him again!" exclaimed Power.

"For days I scarcely ever left the house," resumed Sparks, "watching to catch one glance of the lovely Isabella. My farthest excursion was to the little garden of the inn, where I used to set every imaginable species of snare, in the event of her venturing to walk there. One day I would leave a volume of poetry; another a copy of Paul and Virginia with a marked page; sometimes my guitar, with a broad blue ribbon, would hang pensively from a tree; but, alas! all in vain; she never appeared. At length, I took courage to ask the waiter about her. For some minutes he could not comprehend what I meant; but, at last, discovering my object, he cried out, 'Oh! No. 8, sir; it is No. 8 you mean.'

"'It may be,' said I. 'What of her, then?' ·

"'Oh, sir, she's gone these three days.'

"'Gone!' said I, with a groan.

"'Yes, sir; she left this early on Tuesday with the same old gentleman and the old woman in a chaise-and-four. They ordered horses at Dolgelly to meet them; but I don't know which road they took afterwards.'

"I fell back on my chair unable to speak. Here was I enacting Romeo for three mortal days to a mere company of Welsh waiters and chamber-maids, sighing, serenading, reciting, attitudinizing, rose-plucking, soliloquizing, half-suiciding, and all for the edification of a set of savages, with about as much civilization as their own goats.

"'The bill,' cried I, in a voice of thunder; 'my bill this instant.'

"I had been imposed upon, shamefully, grossly imposed upon, and would not remain another hour in the house. Such were my feelings, at least, and so thinking, I sent for my servant, abused him for not having my clothes ready packed. He replied; I reiterated; and, as my temper was mounted, vented every imaginable epithet upon his head, and concluded by paying him his wages and sending him about his business. In one hour more I was upon the road.

" ' What road, sir?' said the postilion, as he mounted into the saddle.

" ' To the devil, if you please,' said I, throwing myself back in the carriage.

" ' Very well, sir,' replied the boy, putting spurs to his horse.

" That evening I arrived in Bedgellert.

" The little humble inn of Bedgellert, with its thatched roof and earthen floor, was a most welcome sight to me, after eleven hours' travelling on a broiling July day. Behind the very house itself rose the mighty Snowdon, towering high above the other mountains, whose lofty peaks were lost amid the clouds; before me was the narrow valley——"

" Wake me up when he's under weigh again," said the Skipper, yawning fearfully.

" Go on, Sparks," said Power, encouragingly; " I was never more interested in my life; eh, O'Malley?"

" Quite thrilling," responded I, and Sparks resumed.

" Three weeks did I loiter about that sweet spot, my mind filled with images of the past and dreams of the future, my fishing-rod my only companion; not, indeed, that I ever caught anything, for, somehow, my tackle was always getting foul of some willow-tree or water-lily, and at last I gave up even the pretence of whipping the streams. Well, one day,—I remember it as well as though it were but yesterday—it was the 4th of August,—I had set off upon an excursion to Llanberris. I had crossed Snowdon early, and reached the little lake on the opposite side by breakfast-time. There I sat down near the ruined tower of Dolbadern, and, opening my knapsack, made a hearty meal. I have ever been a day-dreamer; and there are few things I like better than to lie, upon some hot and sunny day, in the tall grass beneath the shade of some deep boughs, with running water murmuring near, hearing the summer bee buzzing monotonously, and in the distance the clear, sharp tingle of the sheep-bell. In such a place, at such a time, one's fancy strays playfully, like some happy child, and none but pleasant thoughts present themselves. Fatigued by my long walk, and overcome by heat, I fell asleep. How long I lay there I cannot tell, but the deep shadows were half-way down the tall mountain when I awoke. A sound had startled me; I thought I heard a voice speaking close to me. I looked up, and for some seconds I could not believe that I was not dreaming. Beside me, within a few paces, stood Isabella, the beautiful vision that I had seen at Barmouth, but far, a thousand times, more beautiful. She was dressed in something like a peasant's dress, and wore the round hat which, in Wales at least, seems to suit the character of the female face so well; her long and waving ringlets fell carelessly upon her shoulders, and her cheek flushed from walking. Before I had a moment's notice to recover my roving thought, she spoke. Her voice was full and round, but soft and thrilling, as she said,—

"'I beg pardon, sir, for having disturbed you unconsciously; but having done so, may I request you will assist me to fill this pitcher with water?'

"She pointed at the same time to a small stream which trickled down a fissure in the rock, and formed a little well of clear water beneath. I bowed deeply, and murmuring something,—I know not what,—took the pitcher from her hand, and scaling the rocky cliff, mounted to the clear source above, where having filled the vessel, I descended. When I reached the ground beneath, I discovered that she was joined by another person, whom in an instant I recognized to be the old gentleman I had seen with her at Barmouth, and who in the most courteous manner apologized for the trouble I had been caused. He informed me that a party of his friends were enjoying a little picnic quite near, and invited me to make one of them.

"I need not say that I accepted the invitation, nor that with delight I seized the opportunity of forming an acquaintance with Isabella, who, I must confess, upon her part, showed no disinclination to the prospect of my joining the party.

"After a few minutes' walking, we came to a small rocky point which projected for some distance into the lake, and offered a view for several miles of the vale of Llanberris. Upon this lovely spot we found the party assembled. They consisted of about fourteen or fifteen persons, all busily engaged in the arrangement of a very excellent cold dinner, each individual having some peculiar province allotted to him or her, to be performed by their own hands. Thus, one elderly gentleman was whipping cream under a chestnut-tree, while a very fashionably-dressed young man was washing radishes in the lake; an old lady with spectacles was frying salmon over a wood fire, opposite to a short, pursy man, with a bald head and drab shorts, deep in the mystery of a chicken salad, from which he never lifted his eyes, when I came up. It was thus I found how the fair Isabella's lot had been cast, as a drawer of water; she, with the others, contributing her share of exertion for the common good. The old gentleman who accompanied her seemed the only unoccupied person, and appeared to be regarded as the ruler of the feast; at least, they all called him General, and implicitly followed every suggestion he threw out. He was a man of a certain grave and quiet manner, blended with a degree of mild good-nature and courtesy, that struck me much at first, and gained greatly on me, even in the few minutes I conversed with him as we came along. Just before he presented me to his friends, he gently touched my arm, and, drawing me aside, whispered in my ear,—

" ' Don't be surprised at anything you may hear to-day here; for I must inform you that this is a kind of club, as I may call it, where every one assumes a certain character, and is bound to sustain it under a penalty. We have these little meetings every now and then, and as strangers are never present, I feel some explanation necessary, that you may be able to enjoy the thing; you understand?'

" ' Oh, perfectly,' said I, overjoyed at the novelty of the scene, and anticipating much pleasure from my chance meeting with such very original characters.

" ' Mr. Sparks, Mrs. Winterbottom. Allow me to present Mr. Sparks.'

" ' Any news from Batavia, young gentleman?' said the sallow old lady addressed. 'How is coffee?'

" The General passed on, introducing me rapidly as he went.

" ' Mr. Doolittle, Mr. Sparks.'

" ' Ah, how do you do, old boy?' said Mr. Doolittle; 'sit down beside me. We have forty thousand acres of pickled cabbage spoiling for want of a little vinegar.'

" ' Fie, fie! Mr. Doolittle,' said the General, and passed on to another.

" ' Mr. Sparks, Captain Crosstree.'

" ' Ah, Sparks, Sparks! son of old Blazes? Ha, ha, ha!' and the Captain fell back in an immoderate fit of laughter.

" ' *Le Roi est servi*,' said the thin, meagre figure in nankeens, bowing, cap in hand, before the General; and, accordingly, we all assumed our places upon the grass.

" ' Say it again! say it again! and I'll plunge this dagger in your heart!' said a hollow voice, tremulous with agitation and rage, close beside me. I turned my head, and saw an old gentleman, with a wart on his nose, sitting opposite a meat pie, which he was contemplating with a look of fiery indignation. Before I could witness the sequel of the scene, I felt a soft hand pressed upon mine. I turned. It was Isabella herself, who, looking at me with an expression I shall never forget, said,—

" ' Don't mind poor Faddy; he never hurts any one.'

" Meanwhile the business of dinner went on rapidly. The servants, of whom enormous numbers were now present, ran hither and thither; and duck, ham, pigeon-pie, cold veal, apple tarts, cheese, pickled salmon, melon and rice-pudding, flourished on every side. As for me, whatever I might have gleaned from the conversation around, under other circumstances, I was too much occupied with Isabella to think of any one else. My suit—for such it was—progressed rapidly. There was evidently something favorable in the circumstances we last met under, for her manner had all the warmth and cordiality of old friendship. It is true that more than once I caught the General's eye fixed upon us, with anything but an expression of pleasure, and I thought that Isabella blushed and seemed confused also. 'What care I?' however, was my reflection; 'my views are honorable; and the nephew and heir of Sir Toby Sparks :——' Just in the very act of making this reflection, the old man in the shorts hit me in the eye with a roasted apple, calling out at the moment,—

"'When did you join, thou child of the pale faces?'

"'Mr. Murdocks!' cried the General, in a voice of thunder, and the little man hung down his head and spoke not.

"'A word with you, young gentleman,' said a fat old lady, pinching my arm above the elbow.

"'Never mind her,' said Isabella, smiling; 'poor dear old Dorkin, she thinks she's an hour-glass. How droll, isn't it?''

"'Young man, have you any feelings of humanity?' inquired the old lady, with tears in her eyes as she spoke; 'will you—dare you—assist a fellow-creature under my sad circumstances?'

"'What can I do for you, madam?' said I, really feeling for her distress.

"'Just, like a good dear soul, just turn me up, for I'm nearly run out.'

"Isabella burst out a-laughing at the strange request—an excess which, I confess, I was unable myself to repress; upon which the old lady, putting on a frown of the most ominous blackness, said,—

"'You may laugh, madam; but first, before you ridicule the misfortunes of others, ask yourself are you, too, free from infirmity? When did you see the ace of spades, madam? answer me that.'

"Isabella became suddenly pale as death, her very lips blanched, and her voice, almost inaudible, muttered,—

"'Am I, then, deceived? Is not this he?' So saying, she placed her hand upon my shoulder.

"'That the ace of spades!' exclaimed the old lady, with a sneer—'that the ace of spades!'

"'Are you, or are you not, sir?' said Isabella, fixing her deep and languid eyes upon me. 'Answer, as you are honest; are you the ace of spades?'

"'He is the King of Tuscarora. Look at his war-paint!' cried an elderly gentleman, putting a streak of mustard across my nose and cheek.

"' Then am I deceived,' said Isabella. And, flying at me, she plucked a handful of hair out of my whiskers.

"' Cuckoo, cuckoo !' shouted one ; ' Bow, wow, wow !' roared another ; ' Phiz !' went a third ; and, in an instant, such a scene of commotion and riot ensued! Plates, dishes, knives, forks, and decanters flew right and left ; every one pitched into his neighbor with the most fearful cries, and hell itself seemed let loose. The hourglass and the Moulah of Oude had got me down, and were pummelling me to death, when a short, thickset man came on all fours slap down upon them, shouting out, ' Way, make way for the royal Bengal tiger !' at which they both fled like lightning, leaving me to the encounter single-handed. Fortunately, however, this was not of very long duration, for some well-disposed Christians pulled him from off me ; not, however, before he had seized me in his grasp, and bitten off a portion of my right ear, leaving me, as you see, thus mutilated for the rest of my days."

"What an extraordinary club !" broke in the Doctor.

"Club ! sir, club ! it was a lunatic asylum. The General was no other than the famous Doctor Andrew Moorville, that had the great madhouse at Bangor, and who was in the habit of giving his patients every now and then a kind of country party ; it being one remarkable feature of their malady that, when one takes to his peculiar flight, whatever it be, the others immediately take the hint, and go off at score. Hence my agreeable adventure, the Bengal tiger being a Liverpool merchant, and the most vivacious madman in England ; while the hour-glass and the Moulah were both on an experimental tour to see whether they should not be pronounced totally incurable for life."

"And Isabella ?" inquired Power.

"Ah ! poor Isabella had been driven mad by a card-playing aunt at Bath, and was, in fact, the most hopeless case there. The last words I heard her speak confirmed my mournful impression of her case :—

"' Yes,' said she, as they removed her to her carriage, ' I must, indeed, have but weak intellects, when I could have taken the nephew of a Manchester cotton-spinner, with a face like a printed calico, for a trump card, and the best in the pack !' "

Poor Sparks uttered these last words with a faltering accent, and finishing his glass at one draught, withdrew without wishing us good night.

CHAPTER XXXIII.

THE SKIPPER.

IN such like gossipings passed our days away, for our voyage itself had nothing of adventure or incident to break its dull monotony. Save some few hours of calm, we had been steadily following our seaward track with a fair breeze, and the long pennant pointed ever to the land where our ardent expectations were hurrying before it.

The latest accounts which had reached us from the Peninsula told us that our regiment was almost daily engaged; and we burned with impatience to share with the others the glory they were reaping. Power, who had seen service, felt less on this score than we who had not "fleshed our maiden swords;" but even he sometimes gave way; and when the wind fell, towards sunset, he would break out into some exclamation of discontent, half-fearing we should be too late; "for," said he, "if we go on in this way, the regiment will be relieved, and ordered home before we reach it."

"Never fear, my boys, you'll have enough of it. Both sides like the work too well to give in; they've got a capital ground, and plenty of spare time," said the Major.

"Only to think," cried Power, "that we should be lounging away our idle hours, when these gallant fellows are in the saddle late and early. It is too bad; eh, O'Malley? You'll not be pleased to go back with the polish on your sabre? What will Lucy Dashwood say?"

This was the first allusion Power had ever made to her, and I became red to the very forehead.

"By the bye," added he, "I have a letter for Hammersley, which should rather have been entrusted to your keeping."

At these words I felt cold as death, while he continued:

"Poor fellow! certainly he is most desperately smitten; for, mark me, when a man at his age takes the malady, it is forty times as severe as with a younger fellow, like you. But then, to be sure, he began at the wrong end in the matter; why commence with papa? When a man has his own consent for liking a girl, he must be a contemptible fellow if he can't get her! and as to anything else being wanting, I don't understand it. But the moment you begin by influencing the heads of the house, good-bye to your chances with the dear thing herself, if she have any spirit whatever. It is, in fact, calling on her to surrender without the honors of war; and what girl would stand that?"

"It's vara true," said the Doctor; "there's a strong speerit of opposition in the sex, from physiological causes."

" Curse your physiology, old Galen: what you call opposition is that piquant resistance to oppression that makes half the charm of the sex. It is with them—with reverence be it spoken—as with horses: the dull, heavy-shouldered ones, that bore away with the bit in their teeth, never caring whether you are pulling to the right or to the left, are worth nothing; the real luxury is in the management of your arching-necked curveter, springing from side to side with every motion of your wrist, madly bounding at restraint; yet to the practised hand, held in check with a silk thread; eh, Skipper —am I not right?"

" Well, I can't say I've had much to do with horse-beasts, but I believe you're not far wrong. The lively craft that answers the helm quick, goes round well in stays, luffs up close within a point or two, when you want her, is always a good sea-boat, even though she pitches and rolls a bit; but the heavy lugger that never knows whether your helm is up or down, whether she's off the wind or on it, is only fit for firewood—you can do nothing with a ship or a woman if she hasn't got steerage way on her."

" Come, Skipper, we've all been telling our stories; let us hear one of yours?"

" My yarn won't come so well after your sky-scrapers of love and courting, and all that. But if you like to hear what happened to me once, I have no objection to tell you.

" I often think how little we know what's going to happen to us any minute of our lives. To-day we have the breeze fair in our favor; we are going seven knots, studding-sails set, smooth water, and plenty of sea-room ; to-morrow the wind freshens to half a gale, the sea gets up, a rocky coast is seen from the bow, and maybe—to add to all—we spring a leak forward; but then, after all, bad as it looks, mayhap we rub through even this, and with the next day, the prospect is as bright and cheering as ever. You'll perhaps ask me what has all this moralizing to do with women and ships at sea? Nothing at all with them, except that I was a-going to say that when matters look worst, very often the best is in store for us, and we should never say strike when there is a timber together. Now for my story :—

" It's about four years ago, I was strolling one evening down the side of the harbor at Cove, with my hands in my pockets, having nothing to do, nor no prospect of it, for my last ship had been wrecked off the Bermudas, and nearly all the crew lost ; and, somehow, when a man is in misfortune, the underwriters won't have him at any price. Well, there I was, looking about me at the craft that lay on every side waiting for a fair wind to run down channel. All was active and busy ; every one getting his vessel ship-shape and tidy, tarring, painting, mending sails, stretching new bunting, and getting in sea-store; boats were plying on every side, signals flying, guns firing from the men-of-war, and everything was lively as might be; all but me. There I was, like an old water-logged timber-ship, never moving a spar, but looking for all the world as though I were a-settling fast to go down stern foremost; maybe as how I had no objection to that same; but that's neither here nor there. Well, I sat down on the fluke of an anchor, and began a-thinking if it wasn't better to go before the mast than live on that way. Just before me, where I sat down, there was an old schooner, that lay moored in the same place for as long as I could remember. She was there when I was a boy, and never looked a bit the fresher nor newer as long as I recollected; her old bluff bows, her high poop, her round stern, her flush deck, all Dutch-like, I knew them well, and many a time I delighted to think what a queer kind of a chap he was that first set her on the stocks, and pondered in what trade she ever could have been. All the sailors about the port used to call her Noah's Ark, and swear she was the identical craft that he stowed away all the wild beasts in during the rainy season. Be that as it might, since I fell into misfortune, I got to feel a liking for the old schooner; she was like an old friend; she never changed to me, fair weather or foul; there she was, just the same as thirty years before, when all the world were forgetting and steering wide away from me. Every morning I used to go down to the harbor and have a look at her, just to see that all was right, and nothing stirred; and if it blew very hard at night, I'd get up and go down to look how she weathered it, just as if I was at sea in her. Now and then I'd get some of the watermen to row me aboard of her, and leave me there for a few hours, when I used to be quite happy walking the deck, holding the old worm-eaten wheel, looking out ahead, and going down below, just as though I was in command of her. Day after day this habit grew on me, and at last my whole life was spent in watching her and looking after her; there was something so much alike in our fortunes, that I always thought of her. Like myself, she had had her day of life and activity; we had both braved the storm and the breeze; her shattered bulwarks and worn cutwater attested that she had, like myself, not escaped her calamities. We both had survived our dangers, to be neglected and forgotten, and to lie rotting on the stream of life till the crumbling hand of Time should break us up, timber by timber. Is it any wonder if I loved the old craft? or if, by any chance, the idle boys would venture aboard of her to play and amuse themselves, that I hallooed them away? or, when a newly-arrived ship, not caring for the old boat, would run foul of her, and carry away some spar or piece of running rigging, I would suddenly call out to them to sheer off and not damage us? By degrees they came all to notice this; and I found that they thought me out of my senses, and many a trick was played off upon old Noah—for that was the name the sailors gave me.

"Well, this evening, as I was saying, I sat upon the fluke of the anchor, waiting for a chance boat to put me aboard. It was past sunset, the tide was ebbing, and the old craft was surging to the fast current that ran by with a short, impatient jerk, as though she were well weary, and wished to be at rest; her loose stays creaked mournfully, and, as she yawed over, the sea ran from many a breach in her worn sides, like blood trickling from a wound. 'Ay, ay,' thought I, 'the hour is not far off; another stiff gale, and all that remains of you will be found high and dry upon the shore.' My heart was very heavy as I thought of this, for, in my loneliness, the old Ark— though that was not her name, as I'll tell you presently—was all the companion I had. I've heard of a poor prisoner who for many and many years watched a spider that wove his web within his window, and never lost sight of him from morning till night, and, somehow, I can believe it well; the heart will cling to something, and if it has no living object to press on, it will find a lifeless one—it can no more stand alone than the shrouds can without the mast. The evening wore on, as I was thinking thus; the moon shone out, but no boat came, and I was just determining to go home again for the night, when I saw two men standing on the steps of the wharf below me, and looking straight at the Ark. Now, I must tell you I always felt uneasy when any one came to look at her, for I began to fear that some shipowner or other would buy her to break up, though, except the copper fastenings, there was little of any value about her. Now, the moment I saw the two figures stop short, and point to her, I said to myself, 'Ah! my old girl, so they won't even let the blue water finish you, but they must set their carpenters and dockyard people to work upon you.' This thought grieved me more and more. Had a stiff sou'-wester laid her over, I should have felt it more natural, for her sand was run out; but, just as this passed through my mind, I heard a voice from one of the persons, that I at once knew to be the Port Admiral's:—

"'Well, Dawkins,' said he to the other, 'if you think she'll hold together, I'm sure I've no objection. I don't like the job, I confess; but still the Admiralty must be obeyed.'

"'Oh, my lord,' said the other, 'she's the very thing; she's a rakish-looking craft, and will do admirably; any repair we want, a few days will effect; secrecy is the great thing.'

"'Yes,' said the Admiral, after a pause, 'as you observe, secrecy is the great thing.'

"'Ho! ho!' thought I, 'there's something in the wind here;' so I laid myself out upon the anchor-stock, to listen better, unobserved.

"'We must find a crew for her, give her a few carronades, make her as ship-shape as we can, and, if the Skipper——'

"'Ay, but there is the real difficulty,' said the Admiral, hastily; 'where are we to find a fellow that will suit us? We can't every day find a man willing to jeopardize himself in such a cause as this, even though the reward be a great one.'

"'Very true, my lord; but I don't think there's any necessity for our explaining to him the exact nature of the service.'

"'Come, come, Dawkins, you can't mean that you'll lead a poor fellow into such a scrape blindfolded?'

"'Why, my lord, you never think it requisite to give a plan of your cruise to your ship's crew before clearing out of harbor.'

"'This may be perfectly just, but I don't like it,' said the Admiral.

"'In that case, my lord, you are imparting the secrets of the Admiralty to a party who may betray the whole plot.'

"'I wish, with all my soul, they'd given the order to any one else,' said the Admiral, with a sigh; and for a few moments neither spoke a word.

"'Well, then, Dawkins, I believe there is nothing for it but what you say; meanwhile, let the repairs be got in hand, and see after a crew.'

"'Oh, as to that,' said the other, 'there are plenty of scoundrels in the fleet here fit for nothing else. Any fellow who has been thrice up for punishment in six months, we'll draft on board of her; the fellows who have only been once to the gangway, we'll make the officers.'

"'A pleasant ship's company,' thought I, 'if the devil would only take the command.'

"'And with a skipper proportionate to their merit,' said Dawkins.

"'Begad, I'll wish the French joy of them,' said the Admiral.

"'Ho, ho!' thought I, 'I've found you out, at last; so this is a secret expedition; I see it all; they're fitting her out as a fire-ship, and going to send her slap in among the French fleet at Brest. Well,' thought I, 'even that's better; that, at least, is a glorious end, though the poor fellows have no chance of escape.'

"'Now, then,' said the Admiral, 'to-morrow you'll look out for the fellow to take the command. He must be a smart seaman, a bold fellow, too; otherwise the ruffianly crew will be too much for him; he may bid high: we'll come to his price.'

" 'So you may,' thought I, 'when you are buying his life.'

" 'I hope sincerely,' continued the Admiral, 'that we may light upon some one without wife or child. I never could forgive my-self——'

" 'Never fear, my lord,' said the other. 'My care shall be to pitch upon one whose loss no one would feel—some one without friend or home, who, setting his life at naught, cares less for the gain than the very recklessness of the adventure.'

" 'That's me,' said I, starting up from the anchor stock, and springing between them ; 'I'm that man.'

" Had the very devil himself appeared at the moment, I doubt if they would have been more scared. The Admiral started a pace or two backward, whilst Dawkins, the first surprise over, seized me by the collar, and held me fast.

" 'Who are you, scoundrel, and what brings you here ?' said he, in a voice hoarse with passion.

" 'I'm old Noah,' said I ; for, somehow, I had been called by no other name for so long, I never thought of my real one.

" 'Noah !' said the Admiral—'Noah ! ·Well, but, Noah, what were you doing down here at this time of night ?'

" 'I was watching the Ark, my lord,' said I, bowing, as I took off my hat.

" 'I've heard of this fellow before, my lord,' said Dawkins ; 'he's a poor lunatic that is always wandering about the harbor, and I believe has no harm in him.'

" 'Yes ; but he has doubtless been listening to our conversation,' said the Admiral. 'Eh, have you heard all we have been say-ing ?'

" 'Every word of it, my lord.'

" At this the Admiral and Dawkins looked steadfastly at each other for some minutes, but neither spoke. At last Dawkins said, 'Well, Noah, I've been told you are a man to be depended on ; may we rely upon your not repeating anything you overheard this evening—at least for a year to come ?'

" 'You may,' said I.

" 'But, Dawkins,' said the Admiral, in a half-whisper, 'if the poor fellow be mad ?'

" 'My lord,' said I boldly, 'I am not mad. Misfortune and calamity I have had enough of to make me so ; but, thank God ! my brain has been tougher than my poor heart. I was once the part owner and commander of a goodly craft, that swept the sea, if not with a broad pennon at her mast-head, with as light a spirit as ever lived beneath one. I was rich ; I had a home and a child. I am now poor, houseless, childless, friendless, and an outcast. If, in my solitary wretchedness, I have loved to look upon that old bark, it is because its fortune seemed like my own. It had outlived all that needed or cared for it. For this reason they have thought me mad, though there are those, and not few either, who can well bear testimony if stain or reproach lie at my door, and if I can be reproached with aught save bad luck. I have heard by chance what you have said this night; I know that you are fitting out a secret expedition; I know its dangers, its inevitable dangers, and I here offer myself to lead it. I ask no reward, I look for no price. Alas! who is left to me for whom I can labor now? Give me but the opportunity to end my days with honor on board the old craft, where my heart still clings; give me but that. Well, if you will not do so much, let me serve among the crew; put me before the mast. My lord, you'll not refuse this; it is an old man who asks—one whose gray hairs have floated many a year before the breeze.'

" 'My poor fellow! you know not what you ask; this is no uncommon case of danger.'

" 'I know it all, my lord; I have heard it all.'

" 'Dawkins, what is to be done here?' inquired the Admiral.

" 'I say, friend,' inquired Dawkins, laying his hand upon my arm, 'what is your real name? Are you he who commanded the *Dwarf* privateer in the Isle of France?' ,

" 'The same.'

" 'Then you are known to Lord Collingwood?'

" 'He knows me well, and can speak to my character.'

" 'What he says of himself is all true, my lord.'

" 'True,' said I—'true! You did not doubt it, did you?'

" 'We,' said the Admiral, 'must speak together again; be here to-morrow night at this hour. Keep your own counsel of what has passed; and now, good-night.' So saying, the Admiral took Dawkins by the arm, and returned slowly towards the town, leaving me where I stood, meditating on this singular meeting, and its possible consequences.

" The whole of the following day was passed by me in a state of feverish excitement, which I cannot describe. This strange adventure breaking in so suddenly upon the dull monotony of my daily existence, had so aroused and stimulated me, that I could neither rest nor eat. How I longed for night to come! for, sometimes, as the day wore-later, I began to fear that the whole scene of my meeting with the Admiral had been merely some excited dream of a tortured and fretted mind; and, as I stood examining the ground where I believed the interview to have occurred, I endeavored to recall the position of different objects as they stood around, to corroborate my own failing remembrance.

15

"At last the evening closed in; but, unlike the preceding one, the sky was covered with masses of dark and watery cloud, that drifted hurriedly across; the air felt heavy and thick, and unnaturally still and calm; the water of the harbor looked of a dull, leaden hue, and all the vessels seemed larger than they were, and stood out from the landscape more clearly than usual. Now and then a low rumbling noise was heard, somewhat alike in sound, but far too faint, for distant thunder, while occasionally the boats and smaller craft rocked to and fro, as though some ground swell stirred them, without breaking the languid surface of the sea above.

"A few drops of thick, heavy rain fell just as the darkness came on, and then all felt still and calm as before. I sat upon the anchor-stock, my eyes fixed upon the old Ark, until gradually her outline grew fainter and fainter against the dark sky, and her black hull could scarcely be distinguished from the water beneath. I felt that I was looking towards her, for long after I had lost sight of the tall mast and high-pitched bowsprit, I feared to turn away my head, lest I should lose the place where she lay.

"The time went slowly on, and, although in reality I had not been long there, I felt as if years themselves had passed over my head. Since I had come there, my mind brooded over all the misfortunes of my life. As I contrasted its outset, bright with hope and rich in promise, with the sad reality, my heart grew heavy and my chest heaved painfully; so sunk was I in my reflections, so lost in thought, that I never knew that the storm had broken loose, and that the heavy rain was falling in torrents. The very ground, parched with long drought, smoked as it pattered upon it, while the low, wailing cry of the sea-gull, mingled with the deep growl of far-off thunder, told that the night was a fearful one for those at sea. Wet through and shivering, I sat still—now listening, amid the noise of the hurricane and the creaking of the cordage, for any footstep to approach, and now relapsing back into a half-despairing dread, that my heated brain alone had conjured up the scene of the day before. Such were my dreary reflections, when a loud crash aboard the schooner told me that some old spar had given way. I strained my eyes through the dark to see what had happened, but in vain; the black vapor, thick with falling rain, obscured everything, and all was hid from view. I could hear that she worked violently as the waves beat against her worn sides, and that her iron cable creaked as she pitched to the breaking sea. The wind was momentarily increasing, and I began to fear lest I should have taken my last look at the old craft, when my attention was called off by hearing a loud voice cry out, 'Halloo there! Where are you?'

"'Ay, ay, sir; I'm here.' In a moment the Admiral and his friend were beside me.

"'What a night!' exclaimed the Admiral, as he shook the rain from the heavy boat-cloak, and cowered in beneath some tall blocks of granite near. 'I began half to hope that you might not have been here, my poor fellow,' said the Admiral. 'It's a dreadful time for one so poorly clad for a storm. I say, Dawkins, let him have a pull at your flask.' The brandy rallied me a little, and I felt that it cheered my drooping courage.

"'This is not a time nor is it a place for much parley,' said the Admiral, 'so that we must even make short work of it. Since we met here last night, I have satisfied myself that you are to be trusted, that your character and reputation have nothing heavier against them than misfortune, which, certainly, if I have been rightly informed, has been largely dealt out to you. Now, then, I am willing to accept of your offer of service, if you are still of the same mind as when you made it, and if you are willing to undertake what we have to do, without any question or inquiry as to points on which we must not and dare not inform you. Whatever you may have overheard last night, may or may not have put you in possession of our secret. If the former, your determination can be made at once; if the latter, you have only to decide whether you are ready to go blindfolded in the business.'

"'I am ready, my lord,' said I.

"'You perhaps are then aware what is the nature of the service?'

"'I know it not,' said I. 'All that I heard, sir, leads me to suppose it one of danger, but that's all.'

"'I think, my lord,' said Dawkins, 'that no more need now be said. Cupples is ready to engage, we are equally so to accept; the thing is pressing. When can you sail?'

"'To-night,' said I, 'if you will.'

"'Really, Dawkins,' said the Admiral, 'I don't see why——'

"'My lord, I beg of you,' said the other, interrupting, 'let me now complete the arrangement. This is the plan,' said he, turning towards me as he spoke: 'As soon as that old craft can be got ready for sea, or some other, if she be not worth it, you will sail from this port with a strong crew, well armed and supplied with ammunition. Your destination is Malta, your object to deliver to the Admiral stationed there the despatches with which you will be entrusted; they contain information of immense importance, which, for certain reasons, cannot be sent through a ship of war, but must be forwarded by a vessel that may not attract peculiar notice. If you be attacked, your orders are to resist; if you be taken, on no account destroy the papers, for the French vessel can scarcely escape recapture from our frigates,

and it is of great consequence these papers should remain. Such is
a brief sketch of our plan; the details can be made known to you
hereafter.'

"'I am quite ready, my lord. I ask for no terms; I make no
stipulations. If the result be favorable, it will be time enough to
speak of that. When am I to sail?'

"As I spoke, the Admiral turned suddenly round, and said something in a whisper to Dawkins, who appeared to overrule it, whatever it might be, and finally brought him over to his own opinion.

"'Come, Cupples,' said Dawkins, 'the affair is now settled;
to-morrow a boat will be in waiting for you opposite Spike Island
to convey you on board the *Semiramis*, where every step in the
whole business shall be explained to you; meanwhile, you have
only to keep your own counsel, and trust the secret to no one.'

"'Yes, Cupples,' said the Admiral, 'we rely upon you for that,
so good-night.' As he spoke, he placed within my hands a crumpled
note for ten pounds, and, squeezing my fingers, departed.

"My yarn is spinning out to a far greater length than I intended,
so I'll try and shorten it a bit. The next day I went aboard the
Semiramis, where, when I appeared upon the quarter-deck, I found
myself an object of some interest. The report that I was the man
about to command the *Brian*—that was the real name of the old
craft—had caused some curiosity among the officers, and they all
spoke to me with great courtesy. After waiting a short time, I was
ordered to go below, where the Admiral, his Flag-Captain Dawkins,
and the others were seated. They repeated at greater length the
conversation of the night before, and finally decided that I was to
sail in three weeks; for, although the old schooner was sadly dam-
aged, they had lost no time, but had her already high in dock, with
two hundred ship carpenters at work upon her.

"I do not shorten sail here to tell you what reports were circulated about Cove as to my extraordinary change in circumstances,
nor how I bore my altered fortunes. It is enough if I say that in
less than three weeks I weighed anchor, stood out to sea one beautiful morning in autumn, and set out upon my expedition.

"I have already told you something of the craft. Let me complete
the picture by informing you that, before twenty-four hours passed
over, I discovered that so ungainly, so awkward, so unmanageable a
vessel never put to sea. In light winds she scarcely stirred, or moved
as if she were water-logged; if it came to blow upon the quarter,
she fell off from her helm at a fearful rate; in wearing, she endangered every spar she had; and when you put her in stays, when half
way round she would fall back, and nearly carry away every stitch
of canvas with the shock. If the ship was bad, the crew were ten

times worse. What Dawkins had said turned out to be literally true: every ill-conducted, disorderly fellow who had been up the gangway once a week or so, every unreclaimed landsman of bad character and no seamanship, was sent on board of us; and in fact, except that there was scarcely any discipline and no restraint, we appeared like a floating penitentiary of convicted felons.

"So long as we ran down channel, with a slack sea and fair wind, so long all went on tolerably well; to be sure, they only kept watch when they were tired below; when they came up, reeled about the deck, did all just as they pleased, and treated me with no manner of respect. After some vain efforts to repress their excesses—vain, for I had but one to second me—I appeared to take no notice of their misconduct, and contented myself with waiting for the time when, my dreary voyage over, I should quit the command, and part company with such associates forever. At last, however, it came on to blow, and the night we passed the Lizard was indeed a fearful one. As morning broke, a sea running mountains high, a wind strong from the northwest was hurrying the old craft along at a rate I believed impossible. I shall not stop to recount the frightful scenes of anarchy, confusion, drunkenness, and insubordination which our crew exhibited; the recollection is too bad already, and I would spare you and myself the recital; but from the fourth day of the setting in of the gale, as we entered the Bay of Biscay, some one aloft descried a strange sail to windward, bearing down as if in pursuit of us. Scarcely did the news reach the deck, when, bad as it was before, matters became now ten times worse, some resolving to give themselves up if the chase happened to be French, and vowing that, before surrendering, the spirit-room should be forced, and every man let drink as he pleased. Others proposed, if there were anything like equality in the force, to attack, and convert the captured vessel if they succeeded, into a slaver, and sail at once for Africa. Some were for blowing up the old *Brian* with all on board; and, in fact, every counsel that drunkenness, insanity, and crime combined could suggest was offered and descanted on. Meanwhile the chase gained rapidly upon us, and before noon we discovered her to be a French letter-of-marque, with four guns, and a long brass swivel upon the poop deck. As for us, every sheet of canvas we could crowd was crammed on, but in vain; and, as we labored through the heavy sea, our riotous crew grew every moment worse, and, sitting down sulkily in groups upon the deck, declared that, come what might, they would neither work the ship nor fight her; that they had been sent to sea in a rotten craft, merely to effect their destruction, and that they cared little for the disgrace of a flag they detested. Half furious with the taunting sarcasm I heard on every side, and nearly mad from passion, and bewildered, my first impulse was to rush amongst them with my drawn cutlass, and, ere I fell their victim, take heavy vengeance upon the ringleaders, when suddenly a sharp booming noise came thundering along, and a round shot went flying over our heads.

"'Down with the ensign; strike at once!' cried eight or ten voices together, as the ball whizzed through the rigging. Anticipating this, and resolving, whatever might happen, to fight her to the last, I had made the mate, a staunch-hearted, resolute fellow, to make fast the signal sailyard aloft, so that it was impossible for any one on deck to lower the bunting. Bang went another gun, and, before the smoke cleared away, a third, which, truer in its aim than the rest, went clean through the lower part of our mainsail.

"'Steady, then, boys, and clear for action,' said the mate. 'She's a French smuggling craft that will sheer off when we show fight, so that we must not fire a shot till she comes alongside.'

"'And harkee, lads,' said I, taking up the tone of encouragement he spoke with, 'if we take her, I promise to claim nothing of the prize. Whatever we capture you shall divide amongst yourselves.'

"'It's very easy to divide what we never had,' said one; 'Nearly as easy as to give it,' cried another; 'I'll never light match or draw cutlass in the cause,' said a third.

"'Surrender!' 'Strike the flag!' 'Down with the colors!' roared several voices together.

"By this time the Frenchman was close up, and ranging his long gun to sweep our decks; his crew were quite perceptible—about twenty bronzed, stout-looking fellows, stripped to the waist, and carrying pistols in broad, flat belts, slung over the shoulder.

"'Come, my lads,' said I, raising my voice, as I drew a pistol from my side and cocked it, 'our time is short now; I may as well tell you that the first shot that strikes us amidship blows up the whole craft and every man on board. We are nothing less than a fire-ship, destined for Brest harbor to blow up the French fleet. If you are willing to make an effort for your lives, follow me!'

"The men looked aghast. Whatever recklessness crime and drunkenness had given them, the awful feeling of inevitable death at once repelled. Short as was the time for reflection, they felt that there were many circumstances to encourage the assertion; the nature of the vessel, her riotous, disorderly crew, the secret nature of the service, all confirmed it, and they answered with a shout of despairing vengeance, 'We'll board her; lead us on.' As the cry rose up, the long swivel from the chase rang sharply in our ears, and a tremendous discharge of grape flew through our rigging; none of our men, however, fell; and, animated now with the desire for battle, they sprang to the binnacle, and seized their arms.

"In an instant the whole deck became a scene of excited bustle; and scarcely was the ammunition dealt out, and the boarding-party drawn up, when the Frenchman broached to, and lashed his bowsprit to our own.

"One terrific yell burst from our fellows as they sprang from the rigging and the poop upon the astonished Frenchmen, who thought that the victory was already their own. With death and ruin behind, their only hope before, they dashed forward like madmen to the fray.

"The conflict was bloody and terrific, though not a long one; nearly equal in number, but far superior in personal strength, and stimulated by their sense of danger, our fellows rushed onward, carrying all before them to the quarter-deck. Here the Frenchmen rallied, and for some minutes had rather the advantage, until the mate, turning one of their guns against them, prepared to sweep them down in a mass. Then it was that they ceased their fire, and cried out for quarter,—all save their captain, a short, thick-set fellow, with a grizzly beard and moustache, who, seeing his men fall back, turned on them one glance of scowling indignation, and, rushing forward, clove our boatswain to the deck with one blow. Before the example could have been followed, he lay a bloody corpse upon the deck, while our people, roused to madness by the loss of a favorite among the men, dashed impetuously forward, and, dealing death on every side, left not one man living among their unresisting enemies. My story is soon told now. We brought our prize safe into Malta, which we reached in five days. In less than a week our men were drafted into different men-of-war on the station. I was appointed a warrant officer in the *Sheerwater,* forty-four guns; and, as the Admiral opened the despatch, the only words he spoke puzzled me for many a day after.

"'You have accomplished your orders too well,' said he; 'that privateer is but a poor compensation for the whole French navy.'"

"Well," inquired Power, "and did you never hear the meaning of the words?"

"Yes," said he; "many years after, I found out that our despatches were false ones, intended to have fallen into the hands of the French, and mislead them as to Lord Nelson's fleet, which at that time was cruising to the southward to catch them. This, of course, explained what fate was destined for us—a French prison, if not death; and, after all, either was fully good enough for the crew that sailed in the old *Brian.*"

CHAPTER XXXIV.

THE LAND.

IT was late when we separated for the night, and the morning was already far advanced ere I awoke; the monotonous tramp overhead showed me that the others were stirring, and I gently moved the shutter of the narrow window beside me to look out.

The sea, slightly rippled upon its surface, shone like a plate of fretted gold; not a wave, not a breaker appeared; but the rushing sound close by showed that we were moving fast through the water.

"Always calm, hereabouts," said a gruff voice on deck, which I soon recognized as the Skipper's; "no sea whatever."

"I can make nothing of it," cried out Power from the forepart of the vessel; "it appears to me all cloud."

"No, no, sir; believe me, it's no fog-bank, that large dark mass to leeward there: that's Cintra."

"Land!" cried I, springing up and rushing upon deck; "where, Skipper,—where is the land?"

"I say, Charley," said Power, "I hope you mean to adopt a little more clothing on reaching Lisbon; for though the climate is a warm one——"

"Never mind, O'Malley," said the Major; "the Portuguese will only be flattered by the attention, if you land as you are."

"Why, how so?"

"Surely you remember what the niggers said when they saw the 79th Highlanders landing at St. Lucie. They had never seen a Scotch regiment before, and were consequently somewhat puzzled at the costume; till, at last, one more cunning than the rest explained it by saying, 'They are in such a hurry to kill the poor black man, that they come away without their breeches.'"

"Now, what say you?" cried the Skipper, as he pointed with his telescope to a dark blue mass in the distance; "see there!"

"Ah, true enough, that's Cintra!"

"Then we shall probably be in the Tagus before morning?"

"Before midnight, if the wind holds," said the Skipper.

We breakfasted on deck, beneath an awning; the vessel scarcely seemed to move as she cut her way through the calm water.

The misty outline of the coast grew gradually more defined, and at length the blue mountains could be seen, at first but dimly; but as the day wore on, there many-colored hues shone forth, and patches of green verdure, dotted with sheep, or sheltered by dark foliage, met the eye. The bulwarks were crowded with anxious faces; each looked pointedly towards the shore, and many a stout

heart beat high as the land drew near, fated to cover with its earth
more than one amongst us.

"And that's Portiugale, Mister Charles," said a voice behind me.
I turned, and saw my man Mike, as, with anxious joy, he fixed his
eyes upon the shore.

"They tell me it's a beautiful place, with wine for nothing, and
spirits for less. Isn't it a pity they won't be raisonable, and make
peace with us?"

"Why, my good fellow, we are excellent friends; it's the French
who want to beat us all."

"Upon my conscience, that's not right. There's an ould saying
in Connaught,—it's not fair for one to fall upon twenty. Sergeant
Haggarty says that I'll see none of the diversion at all."

"I don't well understand——"

"He does be telling me that, as I'm only your footboy, he'll send
me away to the rear, where there's nothing but wounded, and wagons,
and women."

"I believe the sergeant is right there; but, after all, Mike, it's a
safe place."

"Ah! then, musha for the safety; I don't think much of it; sure
they might circumvint us. And, av it wasn't displazing to you, I'd
rather list."

"Well, I've no objection, Mickey; would you like to join my
regiment?"

"By coorse, your honor. I'd like to be near yourself; bekase, too,
if anything happens to you—the Lord be between us and harm,"—
here he crossed himself piously,—"sure I'd like to be able to tell
the master how you died; and, sure, there's Mr. Considine—God
pardon him!—he'll be beating my brains out av I couldn't explain
it all."

"Well, Mike, I'll speak to some of my friends here about you,
and we'll settle it all properly. Here's the Doctor."

"Arrah, Mr. Charles, don't mind him; he's a poor crayture entirely; divil a thing he knows."

"Why, what do you mean, man? he's physician to the forces."

"Oh, be-gorra, and so he may be," said Mike, with a toss of his
head; "those army docthers isn't worth their salt. It's thruth I'm
tellin' you; sure, didn't he come see me when I was sick below in
the hould?

"'How do you feel?' says he.

"'Terribly dhry in the mouth,' says I.

"'But your bones,' says he; 'how's them?'

"'As if cripples was kicking me,' says I.

"Well, with that he wint away, and brought back two powthers.

" ' Take them,' says he, 'and you'll be cured in no time.'

" ' What's them ?' says I.

" ' They're ematics,' says he.

" ' Blood and ages,' says I, ' are they ?'

" ' Devil a lie,' says he; ' take them immediately.'

" And I tuk them, and, would you believe me, Mister Charles ?—it's thruth I'm telling you—devil a one o' them would stay on my stomach. So you see what a docther he is !"

I could not help smiling at Mike's ideas of medicine, as I turned away to talk to the Major, who was busily engaged beside me. His occupation consisted in furbishing up a very tarnished and faded uniform, whose white seams and threadbare lace betokened many years of service.

"Getting up our traps, you see, O'Malley," said he, as he looked with no small pride at the faded glories of his old vestment; "astonish them at Lisbon, we flatter ourselves. I say, Power, what a bad style of dress they've got into latterly, with their tight waists and strapped trousers—nothing free, nothing easy, nothing *dégagé* about it. When in a campaign, a man ought to be able to stow prog for twenty-four hours about his person, and no one the wiser. A very good rule, I assure you, though it sometimes leads to awkward results. At Vimeira, I got into a sad scrape that way. Old Sir Harry, who commanded there, sent for the sick return. I was at dinner when the orderly came; so I packed up the eatables about me, and rode off. Just, however, as I came up to the quarters, my horse stumbled, and threw me slap on my head.

" ' Is he killed ?' said Sir·Harry.

" ' Only stunned, your excellency,' said some one.

" ' Then he'll come to, I suppose. Look for the papers in his pocket.'

"So they turned me on my back, and plunged a hand into my side-pocket, but, the devil take it, they pulled out a roast hen. Well, the laugh was scarcely over at this, when another fellow dived into my coat behind, and lugged out three sausages; and so they went on, till the ground was covered with ham, pigeon-pie, veal, kidney, and potatoes, and the only thing like a paper was a mess roll of the 4th, with a droll. song about Sir Harry, written in pencil on the back of it. Devil of a bad affair for me; I was nearly broke for it; but they only reprimanded me a little, and I was afterwards attached to the victualling department."

What an anxious thing is the last day of a voyage ! How slowly creep the hours, teeming with memories of the past and expectations of the future !

Every plan, every well-devised expedient to cheat the long and weary days, is at once abandoned; the chess-board and the new novel are alike forgotten, and the very quarter-deck walk, with its merry gossip and careless chit-chat, becomes distasteful. One blue and misty mountain, one faint outline of the far-off shore, has dispelled all thought of these, and with straining eye and anxious heart we watch for land.

As the day wears on apace, the excitement increases; the faint and shadowy forms of distant objects grow gradually clearer. Where before some tall and misty mountain-peak was seen, we now descry patches of deepest blue and sombre olive; the mellow corn and the waving woods, the village spire and the lowly cot, come out of the landscape; and, like some well-remembered voice, they speak of home. The objects we have seen, the sounds we have heard a hundred times before without interest, become to us now things that stir the heart.

For a time the bright glare of the noonday sun dazzles the view, and renders indistinct the prospect; but, as evening falls, once more is all fair, and bright, and rich before us. Rocked by the long and rolling swell, I lay beside the bowsprit, watching the shore-birds that came to rest upon the rigging, or following some long and tangled sea-weed as it floated by,—my thoughts now wandering back to the brown hills and the broad river of my early home—now straying off in dreary fancies of the future.

How flat and unprofitable does all ambition seem at such moments as these! how valueless, how poor, in our estimation, those worldly distinctions we have so often longed and thirsted for, as with lowly heart and simple spirit we watch each humble cottage, weaving to ourselves some story of its inmates as we pass!

The night at length closed in, but it was a bright and starry one, lending to the landscape a hue of sombre shadow, while the outline of the objects were still sharp and distinct as before. One solitary star twinkled near the horizon. I watched it as, at intervals disappearing, it would again shine out, marking the calm sea with a tall pillar of light.

"Come down, Mr. O'Malley," cried the Skipper's well-known voice,—"come down below, and join us in a parting glass. That's the Lisbon light to leeward, and before two hours we drop our anchor in the Tagus."

CHAPTER XXXV.

MAJOR MONSOON.

OF my travelling companions I have already told my readers something. Power is now an old acquaintance; to Sparks I have already presented them; of the Adjutant they are not entirely ignorant; and it therefore only remains for me to introduce to their notice Major Monsoon. I should have some scruple for the digression which this occasions in my narrative, were it not that with the worthy Major I was destined to meet subsequently, and indeed served under his orders for some months in the Peninsula. When Major Monsoon had entered the army, or in what precise capacity, I never yet met the man who could tell. There were traditionary accounts of his having served in the East Indies and in Canada, in times long past. His own peculiar reminiscences extended to nearly every regiment in the service—"horse, foot, and dragoons." There was not a clime he had not basked in, not an engagement he had not witnessed. His memory, or, if you will, his invention, was never at fault; and from the siege of Seringapatam to the battle of Corunna he was perfect. Besides this, he possessed a mind retentive of even the most trifling details of his profession: from the formation of a regiment to the introduction of a new button—from the laying down of a parallel to the price of a camp-kettle, he knew it all. To be sure, he had served in the Commissary-General's department for a number of years, and nothing instills such habits as this.

"The commissaries are to the army what the special pleaders are to the bar," observed my friend Power—"dry dogs, not over-creditable, on the whole, but devilish useful."

The Major had begun life a two-bottle man, but by a studious cultivation of his natural gifts, and a steady determination to succeed, he had at the time I knew him attained to his fifth. It need not be wondered at, then, that his countenance bore some traces of his habits. It was of a deep, sunset purple, which, becoming tropical, at the tip of the nose verged almost upon a plum color; his mouth was large, thick-lipped, and good-humored; his voice rich, mellow and racy, and contributed, with the aid of a certain dry, chuckling laugh, greatly to increase the effect of the stories which he was ever ready to recount; and, as they most frequently bore in some degree against some of what he called his little failings, they were ever well received, no man being so popular with the world as he who flatters its vanity at his own expense. To do this the Major was ever ready, but at no time more so than when the evening wore late, and the last bottle of his series seemed to imply that any caution regarding the nature of his communication was perfectly unnecessary. Indeed, from the commencement of his evening to its close, he seemed to pass through a number of mental changes, all in a manner preparing him for this final consummation, when he confessed anything and everything; and so well-regulated had these stages become, that a friend dropping in upon him suddenly could at once pronounce, from the tone of his conversation, on what precise bottle the Major was then engaged.

Thus, in the outset he was gastronomic; discussed the dinner, from the soup to the Stilton; criticised the cutlets; pronounced upon the merits of the mutton; and threw out certain vague hints that he would one day astonish the world by a little volume upon cookery.

With bottle No. 2 he took leave of the *cuisine*, and opened his battery upon the wine. Bordeaux, Burgundy, hock, and hermitage, all passed in review before him; their flavor discussed, their treatment descanted upon, their virtues extolled; from humble port to imperial tokay, he was thoroughly conversant with all; and not a vintage escaped as to when the sun had suffered eclipse or when a comet had wagged his tail over it.

With No. 3 he became pipeclay; talked army list and eighteen manœuvres; lamented the various changes in equipments which modern innovation had introduced; and feared that the loss of pigtails might sap the military spirit of the nation.

With No. 4 his anecdotic powers came into play; he recounted various incidents of the war, with his own individual adventures and experience, told with an honest *naïveté* that proved personal vanity; indeed, self-respect never marred the interest of the narrative; besides, as he had ever regarded a campaign something in the light of a foray, and esteemed war as little else than a pillage excursion, his sentiments were singularly amusing.

With his last bottle, those feelings that seem inevitably connected with whatever is last appeared to steal over him. A tinge of sadness for pleasures fast passing and nearly passed, a kind of retrospective glance at the fallacy of all our earthly enjoyments, insensibly suggesting moral and edifying reflections, led him by degrees to confess that he was not quite satisfied with himself, though "not very bad for a commissary;" and, finally, as the decanter waxed low, he would interlard his meditations by passages of Scripture, singularly perverted, by his misdescription, from their true meaning, and alternately throwing out prospects of censure or approval. Such was Major Monsoon; and to conclude in his own words this brief sketch, he "would have been an excellent officer if Providence had not made him such a confounded drunken old scoundrel."

"Now, then, for the King of Spain's story. Out with it, old boy, we are all good men and true here," cried Power, as we slowly came along upon the tide up the Tagus, "so you've nothing whatever to fear."

"Upon my life," said the Major, "I don't half like the tone of our conversation. There is a certain freedom young men affect nowadays regarding morals that is not at all to my taste. When I was five or six and twenty——"

"You were the greatest scamp in the service," cried Power.

"Fie, fie, Fred. If I was a little wild or so"—here the Major's eyes twinkled maliciously—"it was the ladies that spoiled me; I was always something of a favorite, just like our friend Sparks there. Not that we fared very much alike in our little adventures; for, somehow, I believe I was generally in fault in most of mine, as many a good man and many an excellent man has been before." Here his voice dropped into a moralizing key, as he added, "David, you know, didn't behave well to old Uriah. Upon my life he did not, and he was a very respectable man."

"The King of Spain's sherry! the sherry!" cried I, fearing that the Major's digression might lose us a good story.

"You shall not have a drop of it," replied the Major.

"But the story, Major, the story."

"Nor the story either."

"What," said Power, "will you break faith with us?"

"There's none to be kept with reprobates like you. Fill my glass."

"Hold there!—stop!" cried Power. "Not a spoonful till he redeems his pledge."

"Well, then, if you must have a story—for most assuredly I must drink—I have no objection to give you a leaf from my early reminiscences; and, in compliment to Sparks there, my tale shall be of love."

"I dinna like to lose the King's story. I hae my thoughts it was na a bad ane."

"Nor I neither, Doctor; but——"

"Come, come, you shall have that too, the first night we meet in a bivouac, and, as I fear the time may not be very far distant, don't be impatient; besides, a love-story——"

"Quite true," said Power; "a love-story claims precedence— *place aux dames.* There's a bumper for you, old Wickedness; so go along."

The Major cleared off his glass, refilled it, sipped twice, and ogled it as though he would have no peculiar objection to sip once more, took a long pinch of snuff from a box nearly as long as, and something the shape of, a child's coffin, looked around to see that we were all attention, and thus began:

"When I have been in a moralizing mood, as I very frequently am about this hour in the morning, I have often felt surprised by what little, trivial, and insignificant circumstances our lot in life seems to be cast; I mean especially as regards the fair sex. You are prospering, as it were, to-day; to-morrow a new cut of your whiskers, a novel tie of your cravat, mars your destiny and spoils your future *varium et mutabile*, as Horace has it. On the other hand, some equally slight circumstance will do what all your ingenuity may have failed to effect. I knew a fellow who married the greatest fortune in Bath, from the mere habit he had of squeezing one's hand. The lady in question thought it particular, looked conscious, and all that; he followed up the blow; and, in a word, they were married in a week. So a friend of mine, who could not help winking his left eye, once opened a flirtation with a lively widow which cost him a special license and a settlement. In fact, you are never safe. They are like the guerillas, and they pick you off when you least expect it, and when you think there is nothing to fear. Therefore, as young fellows beginning life, I would caution you. On this head you can never be too circumspect. Do you know, I was once nearly caught by so slight a habit as sitting thus, with my legs across."

Here the Major rested his right foot on his left knee, in illustration, and continued:

"We were quartered in Jamaica. I had not long joined, and was about as raw a young gentleman as you could see; the only very clear ideas in my head being that we were monstrous fine fellows in the 50th, and that the planters' daughters were deplorably in love with us. Not that I was much wrong on either side. For brandy-and-water, sangaree, Manilla cigars, and the ladies of color, I'd have backed the corps against the service. Proof was, of eighteen only two ever left the island; for what with the seductions of the coffee plantations, the sugar-canes, the new rum, the brown skins, the rainy season, and the yellow fever, most of us settled there.

"It's very hard to leave the West Indies if once you've been quartered there."

"So I have heard," said Power.

"In fine, if you don't knock under to the climate, you become soon totally unfit for living anywhere else. Preserved ginger, yams, flannel jackets, and grog won't bear exportation; and the free-and-easy chuck under the chin, cherishing, waist-pressing kind of way we get with the ladies, would be quite misunderstood in less-favored regions, and lead to very unpleasant consequences.

"It is singular how much climate has to do with love-making. In our cold country the progress is lamentably slow: fogs, east winds, sleet-storms, and cutting March weather, nip many a budding flirtation; whereas warm, sunny days, and bright moonlight nights, with genial air and balmy zephyrs, open the heart, like the cup of a camelia, and let us drink in the soft dew of——"

"Devilish poetical, that!" said Power, evolving a long blue line of smoke from the corner of his mouth.

"Isn't it, though?" said the Major, smiling graciously. "'Pon my life, I thought so myself. Where was I?"

"Out of my latitude altogether," said the poor Skipper, who often found it hard to follow the thread of a story.

"Yes, I remember. I was remarking that sangaree and calipash, mangoes and Guava jelly, dispose the heart to love, and so they do. I was no more than six weeks in Jamaica when I felt it myself. Now, it was a very dangerous symptom, if you had it strong in you, for this reason. Our colonel, the most cross-grained old crabstick that ever breathed, happened himself to be taken in when young, and resolving, like the fox who lost his tail, and said it was not the fashion to wear one, to pretend he did the thing for fun, resolved to make every fellow marry upon the slightest provocation. Begad, you might as well enter a powder magazine with a branch of candles in your hand as go into society in the island with a leaning towards the fair sex. Very hard this was for me particularly; for, like poor Sparks there, my weakness was ever for the petticoats. I had, besides, no petty, contemptible prejudices as to nation, habits, language, color, or complexion—black, brown, or fair, from the Muscovite to the Malabar, from the voluptuous *embonpoint* of the Adjutant's widow—don't be angry, old boy—to the fairy form of Isabella herself, I loved them all round. But were I to give a preference anywhere, I should certainly do so to the West Indians, if it were only for the sake of the planters' daughters. I say it fearlessly, these colonies are the brightest jewels in the crown. Let's drink their health, for I'm as husky as a lime-kiln."

This ceremony being performed with suitable enthusiasm, the Major cried out, "Another cheer for Polly Hackett, the sweetest girl in Jamaica. By Jove, Power, if you only saw her, as I did, five-and-forty years ago, with eyes black as jet, twinkling, ogling, leering, teasing, and imploring, all at once, do you mind, and a mouthful of downright pearls pouting and smiling at you, why, man, you'd have proposed for her in the first half-hour, and shot yourself the next when she refused you. She was, indeed, a perfect little beauty; *rayther* dark, to be sure—a little upon the rosewood tinge, but beautifully polished, and a very nice piece of furniture for a cottage *orné*,

as the French call it. Alas, alas! how these vanities do catch hold
of us! My recollections have made me quite feverish and thirsty;
is there any cold punch in the bowl? Thank you, O'Malley, that
will do—merely to touch my lips. Well, well, it's all past and
gone now. But I was very fond of Polly Hackett, and she was of
me. We used to take our little evening walks together through the
coffee plantations; very romantic little strolls they were: she in
white muslin, with a blue sash, and blue shoes; I in a flannel jacket
and trousers, straw hat and cravat; a Virginia cigar, as long as a
walking-stick, in my mouth, puffing and courting between times;
then we'd take a turn to the refining-house, look in at the big boilers,
quiz the niggers, and come back to Twangberry Moss to supper,
where old Hackett, the father, sported a glorious table at eleven
o'clock. Great feeding it was. You were always sure of a preserved
monkey, a baked land-crab, or some such delicacy. And such
Madeira! it makes me dry to think of it!

"Talk of West India slavery, indeed! It's the only land of
liberty. There is nothing to compare with the perfect free-and-easy,
devil-may-care kind of a take-yourself way that every one has there.
If it would be any peculiar comfort for you to sit in the saddle of
mutton, and put your legs in a soup tureen at dinner, there would
be found very few to object to it. There is no nonsense of any kind
about etiquette. You eat, drink, and are merry, or, if you prefer,
are sad; just as you please. You may wear uniform, or you may
not—it's your own affair; and consequently, it may be imagined
how insensibly such privileges gain upon one, and how very reluctant we become ever to resign or abandon them.

"I was the man to appreciate it all. The whole course of proceeding seemed to have been invented for my peculiar convenience, and
not a man on the island enjoyed a more luxurious existence than
myself, not knowing all the while how dearly I was destined to pay
for my little comforts. Among my plenary after-dinner indulgences
I had contracted an inveterate habit of sitting cross-legged, as I
showed you. Now, this was become a perfect necessity of existence
to me. I could have dispensed with cheese, with my glass of port,
my pickled mango, my olive, my anchovy toast, my nutshell of
curaçoa, but not my favorite lounge. You may smile; but I've read
of a man who could never dance except in the room with an old
hair-brush. Now I'm certain my stomach would not digest if my
legs were perpendicular. I don't mean to defend the thing. The
attitude was not graceful; it was not imposing; but it suited me
somehow, and I liked it.

"From what I have already mentioned, you may suppose that
West India habits exercised but little control over my favorite prac-

tice, which I indulged in every evening of my life. Well, one day, old Hackett gave us a great blow-out—a dinner of two-and-twenty souls; six days' notice; turtle from St. Lucie, guinea-fowl, claret of the year forty, Madeira *à discrétion*, and all that. Very well done the whole thing: nothing wrong, nothing wanting. As for me, I was in great feather. I took Polly in to dinner, greatly to the discomfiture of old Belson, our Major, who was making up in that quarter; for, you must know, she was an only daughter, and had a very nice thing of it in molasses and niggers. The papa preferred the Major, but Polly looked sweetly upon me. Well, down we went, and really a most excellent feed we had. Now, I must mention here that Polly had a favorite Blenheim spaniel the old fellow detested; it was always tripping him up and snarling at him; for it was, except to herself, a beast of rather vicious inclinations. With a true Jamaica taste, it was her pleasure to bring the animal always into the dinner-room, where, if papa discovered him, there was sure to be a row—servants sent in one direction to hunt him out; others endeavoring to hide him, and so on; in fact, a tremendous hubbub always followed his introduction and accompanied his exit, upon which occasions I invariably exercised my gallantry by protecting the beast, although I hated him like the devil all the time.

"To return to our dinner. After two hours of hard eating, the pace slackened, and as evening closed in, a sense of peaceful repose seemed to descend upon our labors. Pastilles shed an aromatic vapor through the room. The well-iced decanters went with measured pace along; conversation, subdued to the meridian of after-dinner comfort, just murmured; the open *jalousies* displayed upon the broad verandah the orange tree in full blossom, slightly stirring with the cool sea-breeze.'

"And the piece of white muslin beside you, what of her?"

"Looked twenty times more bewitching than ever. Well, it was just the hour when, opening the last two buttons of your white waistcoat (remember we were in Jamaica), you stretch your legs to the full extent, throw your arm carelessly over the back of your chair, look contemplatively towards the ceiling, and wonder, within yourself, why it is not all 'after dinner' in this same world of ours. Such, at least, were my reflections as I assumed my attitude of supreme comfort, and inwardly ejaculated a health to Sneyd and Barton. Just at this moment I heard Polly's voice gently whisper,—

"'Isn't he a love? isn't he a darling?'

"'Zounds!' thought I, as a pang of jealousy shot through my heart, 'is it the Major she means?' for old Belson, with his bag wig and rouged cheeks, was seated on the other side of her.

"'What a dear old thing it is!' said Polly.

"'Worse and worse,' said I; 'it must be him.'

"'I do so love his muzzy face.'

"'It is him!' said I, throwing off a bumper, and almost boiling over with passion at the moment.

"'I wish I could take one look at him,' said she, laying down her head as she spoke.

"The Major whispered something in her ear, to which she replied,—

"'Oh! I dare not; papa will see me at once.'

"'Don't be afraid, madam,' said I, fiercely; 'your father perfectly approves of your taste.'

"'Are you sure of it?' said she, giving me such a look.

"'I know it,' said I, struggling violently with my agitation.

"The Major leaned over, as if to touch her hand beneath the cloth. I almost sprang from my chair, when Polly, in her sweetest accents, said,—

"'You must be patient, dear thing, or you may be found out, and then there will be such a piece of work. Though, I'm sure, Major, you would not betray me.' The Major smiled till he cracked the paint upon his cheeks. 'And I am sure that Mr. Monsoon ——'

"'You may rely upon me,' said I, half-sneeringly.

"The Major and I exchanged glances of defiance, while Polly continued,—

"'Now, come, don't be restless. You are very comfortable there. Isn't he, Major?' The Major smiled again more graciously than before, as he added,—

"'May I take a look?'

"'Just one peep, then,—no more!' said she, coquettishly; 'poor dear Wowski is so timid.'

"Scarcely had these words borne balm and comfort to my heart—for I now knew that to the dog, and not to my rival, were all the flattering expressions applied—when a slight scream from Polly, and a tremendous oath from the Major, roused me from my dream of happiness.

"'Take your foot down, sir. Mr. Monsoon, how could you do so?' cried Polly.

"'What the devil, sir, do you mean?' shouted the Major.

"'Oh! I shall die of shame,' sobbed she.

"'I'll shoot him like a riddle,' muttered old Belson.

"By this time the whole table had got at the story, and such peals of laughter, mingled with suggestions for my personal maltreatment, I never heard. All my attempts at explanation were in vain. I was not listened to, much less believed, and the old colonel finished the scene by ordering me to my quarters, in a voice I shall never forget, the whole room being, at the time I made my exit, one scene of tumultuous laughter from one end to the other. Jamaica after this became too hot for me. The story was repeated on every side; for it seems I had been sitting with my foot on Polly's lap; but so occupied was I with my jealous vigilance of the Major, I was not aware of the fact until she herself discovered it.

"I need not say how the following morning brought with it every possible offer of *amende* upon my part; anything, from a written apology to a proposition to marry the lady, I was ready for, and how the matter might have ended I know not; but in the middle of the negotiations we were ordered off to Halifax, where, be assured, I abandoned my oriental attitude for many a long day after."

CHAPTER XXXVI.

THE LANDING.

WHAT a contrast to the dull monotony of our life at sea did the scene present which awaited us on landing in Lisbon. The whole quay was crowded with hundreds of people eagerly watching the vessel which bore from her mast the broad ensign of Britain. Dark-featured, swarthy, moustached faces, with red caps rakishly set on one side, mingled with the Saxon faces and fair-haired natives of our own country. Men-of-war boats plied unceasingly to and fro across the tranquil river, some slender reefer in the stern-sheets, while behind him trailed the red pennon of some "tall admiral."

The din and clamor of a mighty city mingled with the far-off sounds of military music, and in the vistas of the opening street masses of troops might be seen, in marching order. All betokened the near approach of war.

Our anchor had scarcely been dropped, when an eight-oar gig, with a midshipman steering, came alongside.

"Ship ahoy, there! You've troops on board?"

"Ay, ay, sir."

Before the answer could be spoken, he was on deck.

"May I ask," said he, touching his cap slightly, "who is the officer in command of the detachment?"

"Captain Power—very much at your service," said Fred, returning the salute.

"Rear-Admiral Sir Edward Douglas requests that you will do

him the favor to come on board immediately, and bring your despatches with you."

"I'm quite ready," said Power, as he placed his papers in his sabretasche; "but first tell us what's doing here. Anything new lately?"

"I have heard nothing, except of some affair with the Portuguese. They've been drubbed again; but our people have not been engaged. I say, we had better get under way; there's our first lieutenant, with his telescope up; he's looking straight at us. So, come along. Good-evening, gentlemen." And in another moment the sharp craft was cutting the clear water, where Power gayly waved us a good-bye.

"Who's for shore?" said the Skipper, as half a dozen boats swarmed around the side, or held on by their boat-hooks to the rigging.

"Who is not?" said Monsoon, who now appeared in his old blue frock covered with tarnished braiding, and a cocked hat that might have roofed a pagoda. "Who is not, my old boy? Is not every man amongst us delighted with the prospect of fresh prog, cool wine, and a bed somewhat longer than four feet six? I say, O'Malley, Sparks! where's the Adjutant? Ah, there he is. We'll not mind the Doctor; he's a very jovial little fellow, but an infernal bore; *entre nous;* and we'll have a cosy little supper at the Rua di Toledo. I know the place well. Whew, now! Get away, boy. Sit steady, Sparks; she's only a cockle-shell. There—that's the Plaza de la Regna—there, to the left. There's the great cathedral—you can't see it now. Another seventy-four! why, there's a whole fleet here! I wish old Power joy of his afternoon with old Douglas."

"Do you know him, then, Major?"

"Do I!—I should rather think I do. He was going to put me in irons here in this river once. A great shame it was; but I'll tell you the story another time. There—gently now; that's it. Thank God! once more upon land. How I do hate a ship! Upon my life, a sauce-boat is the only boat endurable in this world."

We edged our way with difficulty through the dense crowd, and at last reached the Plaza. . Here the numbers were still greater, but of a different class. Several pretty and well-dressed women, with their dark eyes twinkling above their black mantillas, as they held them across their faces, watched with an intense curiosity one of the streets that opened upon the square.

In a few moments the band of a regiment was heard, and very shortly after the regular tramp of troops followed, as the 87th marched into the Plaza, and formed a line.

The music ceased; the drums rolled along the line; the next moment all was still. It was really an inspiriting sight, to one whose heart was interested in the career, to see those gallant fellows as, with their bronzed faces and stalwart frames, they stood motionless as a rock. All continued to look; the band marched into the square, and struck up "Garryowen." Scarcely was the first part played, when a tremendous cheer burst from the troop-ship in the river. The welcome notes had reached the poor fellows there; the well-known sounds, that told of home and country, met their ears, and the loud cry of recognition bespoke their hearts' fullness.

"There they go. Your wild countrymen have heard their *Ranz des vaches*, it seems. Lord, how they frightened the poor Portuguese! Look how they're running!"

Such was actually the case. The loud cheer uttered from the river was taken up by others straggling on shore, and one universal shout betokened that fully one-third of the red-coats around came from the dear island, and in their enthusiasm had terrified the natives to no small extent.

"Is not that Ferguson there?" cried the Major, as an officer passed us with his arm in a sling. "I say, Joe—Ferguson! Oh! knew it was."

"Monsoon, my hearty, how goes it?—only just arrived, I see. Delighted to meet you out here once more. Why, we've been dull as a veteran battalion without you. These your friends? Pray present me." The ceremony of introduction over, the Major invited Ferguson to join our party at supper. "No, not to-night, Major," said he; "you must be my guests this evening. My quarters are not five minutes' walk from this. I shall not promise you very luxurious fare."

"A carbonade of olives, a roast duck, a bowl of bishop, and, if you will, a few bottles of Burgundy," said the Major; "don't put yourself out for us—soldier's fare, eh?"

I could not help smiling at the *naïve* notion of simplicity so cunningly suggested by old Monsoon. As I followed the party through the streets, my step was light, my heart not less so; for what sensations are more delightful than those of landing after a voyage?—the escape from the durance vile of shipboard, with its monotonous days and dreary nights, its ill-regulated appointments, its cramped accommodations, its uncertain duration, its eternal round of unchanging amusements, for the freedom of the shore, with a land breeze, and a firm footing to tread upon; and, certainly, not least of all, the sight of that brightest part of creation, whose soft eyes and tight ankles are, perhaps, the greatest of all imaginable pleasures to him who has been the dweller on blue water for several weeks long.

"Here we are," cried out Ferguson, as we stopped at the door of a large and handsome house. We followed up a spacious stair into an ample room, sparingly but not uncomfortably furnished. Plans of sieges, maps of the seat of war, pistols, sabres, and belts, decorated the white walls, and a few books and a stray army-list betokened the habits of the occupant.

While Ferguson disappeared to make some preparations for supper, Monsoon commenced a congratulation to the party upon the good fortune that had befallen them. " Capital fellow is Joe—never without something good, and a rare one to pass the bottle. Oh ! here he comes. Be alive there, Sparks ; take a corner of the cloth. How deliciously juicy that ham looks ! Pass the Madeira down there ; what's under that cover—stewed kidneys ? While Monsoon went on thus, we took our places at table, and set to with an appetite which only a newly-landed traveller ever knows.

"Another spoonful of the gravy ? Thank you. And so they say we've not been faring over well latterly ?" said the Major.

" No truth in the report. Our people have not been engaged. The only thing lately was a smart brush we had at the Tamega. Poor Patrick, a countryman of ours, and myself were serving with the Portuguese brigade, when Laborde drove us back upon the town, and actually routed us. The Portuguese general, caring for little or anything save his own safety, was making at once for the mountains, when Patrick called upon his battalion to face about and charge ; and nobly they did it, too. Down they came upon the advancing masses of the French, and literally hurled them back upon the main body. The other regiments, seeing this gallant stand, wheeled about, and poured in a volley, and then, fixing bayonets, stormed a little mount beside the hedge, which commanded the whole suburb of Villa Real. The French, who soon recovered their order, now prepared for a second attack, and came on in two dense columns, when Patrick, who had little confidence in the steadiness of his people for any lengthened resistance, resolved upon once more charging with the bayonet. The order was scarcely given when the French were upon us, their flank defended by some of La Houssaye's heavy dragoons. For an instant the conflict was doubtful, until poor Patrick fell mortally wounded upon the parapet ; when the men, no longer hearing his bold cheer, nor seeing his noble figure in the advance, turned and fled, pell-mell, back upon the town. As for me, blocked up amid the mass, I was cut down from the shoulder to the elbow by a young fellow of about sixteen, who galloped about like a schoolboy on a holiday. The wound was only dangerous from the loss of blood, and so I contrived to reach Amacante without much difficulty, from whence, with three or four others, I was ordered here until fit for service."

"But what news from our own head-quarters?" inquired I.

"All imaginable kind of rumors are afloat. Some say that Craddock is retiring; others, that a part of the army is in motion upon Caldas."

"Then we are not going to have a very long sojourn here after all, eh, Major? Donna Maria de Tormes will be inconsolable. By the bye, their house is just opposite us. Have you never heard Monsoon mention his friends there?"

"Come, come, Joe, how can you be so foolish?"

"But, Major, my dear friend, what signifies your modesty? there is not a man in the service does not know it, save those in the last *Gazette.*"

"Indeed, Joe, I am very angry with you."

"Well, then, by Jove! I must tell it myself; though, faith, lads, you lose not a little for want of Monsoon's tact in the narrative."

"Anything is better than trusting to such a biographer," cried the Major; "so here goes:

"When I was Acting Commissary-General to the Portuguese forces, some few years ago, I obtained great experience of the habits of the people; for though naturally of an unsuspecting temperament myself, I generally contrive to pick out the little foibles of my associates, even upon a short acquaintance. Now, my appointment pleased me very much on this score; it gave me little opportunities of examining the world. 'The greatest study of mankind is man,—Sparks would say woman—but no matter.

"Now, I soon discovered that our ancient and very excellent allies, the Portuguese, with a beautiful climate, delicious wines, and very delightful wives and daughters, were the most infernal rogues and scoundrels ever met with. 'Make yourself thoroughly acquainted with the leading features of the natives,' said old Sir Harry to me, in a despatch from head-quarters; and, faith, it was not difficult; such open, palpable, undisguised rascals never were heard of. I thought I knew a thing or two myself, when I landed; but, Lord love you! I was a babe; I was an infant in swaddling clothes compared with them; and they humbugged me,—ay, *me!*— till I began to suspect that I was only walking in my sleep.

"'Why, Monsoon,' said the General, 'they told me you were a sharp fellow, and yet the people here seem to work round you every day. This will never do. You must brighten up a little, or I shall be obliged to send you back.'

"'General,' said I, 'they used to call me no fool in England, but, somehow, here——'

"'I understand,' said he, 'you don't know the Portuguese; there's but one way with them—strike quickly, and strike home. Never give them time for roguery ; for, if they have a moment's reflection, they'll cheat the devil himself; but when you see the plot working, come slap down and decide the thing your own way.'

" Well, now, there never was anything so true as this advice, and, for the eighteen months I acted upon it, I never knew it fail.

" ' I want a thousand measures of wheat.'

" ' Senhor Excellenza, the crops have been miserably deficient, and——'

" ' Sergeant-major,' I would say, ' these poor people have no corn ; it's a wine country ; let them make up the rations that way.'

" The wheat came in that evening.

" ' One hundred and twenty bullocks wanted for the reserve.'

" ' The cattle are all up the mountains.'

" ' Let the alcalde catch them before night, or I'll catch *him*.'

" Lord bless you ! I had beef enough to feed the Peninsula. And in this way, while the forces were eating short allowance and half-rations elsewhere, our brigade were plump as aldermen.

" When we lay in Andalusia, this was easy enough. What a country, to be sure ! Such vineyards, such gardens, such delicious valleys, waving with corn, and fat with olives ; actually it seemed a kind of dispensation of Providence to make war in. There was everything you could desire ; and, then, the people, like all your wealthy ones, were so timid, and so easily frightened, you could get what you pleased out of them by a little terror. My scouts managed this very well.

" ' He's coming,' they would say, ' after to-morrow.'

" ' *Madre de Dios !* '

" ' I hope he won't burn the village.'

" ' *Questos infernales Ingleses !* how wicked they are.'

" ' You'd better try what a sack of moidores or doubloons might do with him ; he may refuse them, but make the effort.'

" Ha !" said the Major, with a long-drawn sigh, " those were pleasant times ; alas ! that they should ever come to an end. Well, among the old hidalgos I met there was one Don Emanuel Selvio de Tormes, an awful old miser, rich as Crœsus, and suspicious as the arch-fiend himself. Lord, how I melted him down ! I quartered two squadrons of horse and a troop of flying artillery upon him. How the fellows did eat ! Such a consumption of wines was never heard of; and as they began to slacken a little, I took care to re-place them by fresh arrivals—fellows from the mountains—*caçadores* they call them. At last my friend Don Emanuel could stand it no longer, and he sent me a diplomatic envoy to negotiate terms, which, upon the whole, I must say were fair enough. In a few days after, the *caçadores* were withdrawn, and I took up my quarters at the chateau. I have had various chances and changes in this wicked world, but I am free to confess that I never passed a more agreeable time than the seven weeks I spent there. Don Emanuel, when properly managed, became a very pleasant little fellow. Donna Maria, his wife, was a sweet creature. You need not be winking that way. Upon my life she was; rather fat, to be sure, and her age something verging upon the fifties; but she had such eyes, black as sloes, and luscious as ripe grapes; and she was always smiling, and ogling, and looking so sweet. Confound me, if I think she wasn't the most enchanting being in this world, with about ten thousand pounds' worth of jewels upon her fingers and in her ears. I have her before me at this instant, as she used to sit in the little arbor in the garden, with a Manilla cigar in her mouth, and a little brandy-and-water—quite weak, you know—beside her.

"'Ah! General,' she used to say,—she always called me General,—'what a glorious career yours is! A soldier is *indeed* a man.'

"Then she would look at poor Emanuel, who used to sit in a corner, holding his hand to his face for hours, calculating interest and cent. per cent. till he fell asleep.

"Now, he labored under a very singular malady—not that I ever knew it at the time—a kind of luxation of the lower jaw, which, when it came on, happened somehow to press upon some vital nerve or other, and left him perfectly paralyzed till it was restored to its proper place. In fact, during the time the agony lasted, he was like one in a trance; for though he could see and hear, he could neither speak nor move, and looked as if he had done with both for many a day to come.

"Well, as I was saying, I knew nothing of all this, till a slight circumstance made it known to me. I was sitting one evening in the little arbor I mentioned with Donna Maria. There was a little table before us, covered with wines and fruits, a dish of olives, some Castile oranges, and a fresh pine. I remember it well. My eye roved over the little dessert, set out in old-fashioned, rich silver dishes, then turned towards the lady herself, with rings, brooches, ear-rings, and chains enough to reward one for sacking a town; and I said to myself, 'Monsoon, Monsoon, this is better than long marches in the Pyrenees, with a cork-tree for a bed-curtain and wet grass for a mattress. How pleasantly one might jog on in this world with this little country-house for his abode, and Donna Maria for a companion!'

"I tasted the port—it was delicious. Now, I knew very little Portuguese, but I made some effort to ask if there was much of it in the cellar.

"She smiled, and said, 'Oh! yes.'

" ' What a luxurious life one might lead here !' thought I ; 'and, after all, perhaps Providence might remove Don Emanuel.'

" I finished the bottle as I thus meditated.   The next was, if possible, more crusty.

" ' This is a delicious retreat,' said I, soliloquizing.

" Donna Maria seemed to know what was passing in my mind, for she smiled too.

" ' Yes,' said I, in broken Portuguese, 'one ought to be very happy here, Donna Maria.'

" She blushed, and I continued :

" ' What can one want for more in this life ?—all the charms that rendered Paradise what it was'—I took her hand here—'and made Adam blessed.'

" ' Ah, General !' said she, with a sigh, ' you are such a flatterer.'

" ' Who could flatter,' said I, with enthusiasm, ' when there are not words enough to express what he feels ?'   This was true, for my Portuguese was fast failing me.   ' But if ever I was happy, it is now.'

" I took another pull at the port.

" ' If I only thought,' said I, ' that my presence here was not thought unwelcome——'

" ' Fie, General,' said she, ' how could you say such a thing ?'

" ' If I only thought I was not hated,' said I, tremblingly.

" ' Oh !' said she again.

" ' Despised.'

" ' Oh !'

" ' Loathed.'

" She pressed my hand—I kissed hers; she hurriedly snatched it from me, and pointed towards a lime-tree near, beneath which, in the cool enjoyment of his cigar, sate the spare and detested figure of Don Emanuel.

" ' Yes,' thought I, ' there he is—the only bar to my good fortune. Were it not for him, I should not be long before I became possessor of this excellent old chateau, with a most indiscretionary power over the cellar.   Don Mauricius Monsoon would speedily assume his place among the grandees of Portugal.'

" I know not how long my reverie lasted, nor, indeed, how the evening passed; but I remember well the moon was up, and a sky bright with a thousand stars was shining, as I sat beside the fair Donna Maria, endeavoring, with such Portuguese as it had pleased fate to bestow on me, to instruct her touching my warlike services and deeds of arms.   The fourth bottle of port was ebbing beneath my eloquence, as responsively her heart beat, when I heard a slight rustle in the branches near.   I looked, and, heavens ! what a sight did I behold. There was little Don Emanuel stretched upon the grass, with his mouth wide open, his face pale as death, his arms stretched out at either side, and his legs stiffened straight out. I ran over and asked if he were ill, but no answer came. I lifted up an arm, but it fell heavily upon the ground as I let it go; the leg did likewise. I touched his nose—it was cold.

"'Hallo,' thought I, 'is it so? This comes of mixing water with your sherry. I saw where it would end.

"Now, upon my life, I felt sorry for the little fellow; but, somehow, one gets so familiarized with this sort of thing in a campaign, that one only half feels in a case like this.

"'Yes,' said I, 'man is but grass; but I, for one, must make hay when the sun shines. Now for the Donna Maria,' for the poor thing was asleep in the arbor all this while.

"'Donna,' said I, shaking her by the elbow,—'Donna, don't be shocked at what I'm going to say.'

"'Ah! General,' said she, with a sigh, 'say no more; I must not listen to you.'

"'You don't know that,' said I, with a knowing look,—'you don't know that.'

"'Why, what can you mean?'

"'The little fellow is done for.' The port was working strong now, and destroyed all my fine sensibility. 'Yes, Donna,' said I, 'you are free,'—here I threw myself upon my knees,—'free to make me the happiest of commissaries, and the jolliest grandee of Portugal that ever——'

"'But Don Emanuel?'

"'Run out—dry—empty,' inverting a finished decanter, to typify my words as I spoke.

"'He is not dead?' said she, with a scream.

"'Even so,' said I, with a hiccup; 'ordered for service in a better world, where there are neither inspections nor arrears.'

"Before the words were well out, she sprang from the bench and rushed over to the spot where the little Don lay. What she said or did I know not, but the next moment he sat bolt upright on the grass, and, as he held his jaw with one hand and supported himself on the other, vented such a torrent of abuse and insult at me, that, for want of Portuguese enough to reply, I rejoined in English, in which I swore pretty roundly for five minutes. Meanwhile the Donna had summoned the servants, who removed Don Emanuel to the house, where on my return I found my luggage displayed before the door, with a civil hint to deploy in orderly time, and take ground elsewhere.

"In a few days, however, his anger cooled down, and I received a polite note from Donna Maria that the Don at length began to understand the joke, and begged that I would return to the chateau, and that he would expect me at dinner the same day."

"With which, of course, you complied?"

"Which of course I did. Forgive your enemies, my dear boy; it is only Christian-like; and, really, we lived very happily ever after. The Donna was a mighty clever woman, and a dear good soul besides."

If was late when the Major concluded his story; so after wishing Ferguson a good night, we took our leave, and retired for the night to our quarters.

CHAPTER XXXVII.

LISBON.

THE tramp of horses' feet and the sound of voices beneath my window roused me from a deep sleep. I sprang up, and drew aside the curtain. What a strange confusion beset me as I looked forth! Before me lay a broad and tranquil river, whose opposite shore, deeply wooded, and studded with villas and cottages, rose abruptly from the water's edge; vessels of war lay tranquilly in the stream, their pennants trailing in the tide. The loud boom of a morning gun rolled along the surface, awaking a hundred echoes as it passed, and the lazy smoke rested for some minutes on the glassy water as it blended with the thin air of the morning.

"Where am I?" was my first question to myself, as I continued to look from side to side, unable to collect my scattered senses.

One word sufficed to recall me to myself, as I heard Power's voice from without, call out,—

"Charley! O'Malley, I say! Come down here!"

I hurriedly threw on my clothes, and went to the door.

"Well, Charley! I've been put in harness rather sooner than I expected. Here's old Douglas has been sitting up all night, writing despatches; and I must hasten on to head-quarters without a moment's delay. There's work before us—that's certain; but when, where, and how, of that I know nothing. You may expect the route every moment; the French are still advancing. Meanwhile, I have a couple of commissions for you to execute. First, here's a packet for Hammersley; you are sure to meet him with the regiment, in a day or two. I have some scruples about asking you this—but, confound it!—you're too sensible a fellow to care——"

Here he hesitated, and, as I colored to the eyes, for some minutes he seemed uncertain how to proceed. At length, recovering himself, he went on:

"Now for the other. This is a most loving epistle from a poor devil of a midshipman, written last night, by a tallow candle, in the cockpit, containing vows of eternal adoration and a lock of hair. I promised faithfully to deliver it myself: for the *Thunderer* sails for Gibraltar next tide, and he cannot go ashore for an instant. However, as Sir Arthur's billet may be of more importance than the reefer's, I must entrust its safe keeping to your hands. Now, then, don't look so devilish sleepy, but seem to understand what I am saying. This is the address:—'La Senhora Inez da Silviero, Rua Nuova, opposite the barber's;' you'll not neglect it. So now, my dear boy, till our next meeting, *adios!*"

"Stop! for heaven's sake, not so fast, I pray. Where's the street?"

"The Rua Nuova. Remember Figaro, my boy. Cinque perruche."

"But what am I to do?"

"To do! what a question! Anything—everything. Be a good diplomate; speak of the torturing agony of the lover, for which I can vouch (the boy is only fifteen); swear that he is to return in a month first lieutenant of the *Thunder Bomb*, with intentions that even Madame Dalrymple would approve."

"What nonsense," said I, blushing to the eyes.

"And if that suffice not, I know of but one resource."

"Which is—"

"Make love to her yourself. Ay, even so. Don't look so confoundedly vinegar; the girl, I hear, is a devilish pretty one, the house pleasant, and I sincerely wish I could exchange duties with you, leaving you to make your bows to his Excellency the C. O. F., and myself free to make mine to la Senhora. And now, push along, old red cap."

So saying, he made a significant cut of his whip at the Portuguese guide, and in another moment was out of sight.

My first thought was one of regret at Power's departure. For some time past we had been inseparable companions; and, notwithstanding the reckless and wild gayety of his conduct, I had ever found him ready to assist me in every difficulty, and that with an address and dexterity a more calculating adviser might not have possessed. I was now utterly alone; for though Monsoon and the Adjutant were still in Lisbon, as was also Sparks, I never could make intimates of them.

I ate my breakfast with a heavy heart, my solitary position again suggesting thoughts of home and kindred. Just at this moment my eyes fell upon the packet destined for Hammersley; I took it up and weighted it in my hand. "Alas!" thought I, "how much of my destiny may lie within that envelope! how fatally may my after-life be influenced by it!" It felt heavy, as though there was something besides letters. True, too true; there was a picture; Lucy's portrait! The cold drops of perspiration stood upon my forehead as my fingers traced the outline of a miniature-case in the parcel. I became deadly weak, and sank half-fainting upon a chair. And such is the end of my first dream of happiness! How have I duped, how have I deceived myself! For, alas! though Lucy had never responded to my proffered vows of affection, yet had I ever nurtured in my heart a secret hope that I was not altogether uncared for. Every look she had given me, every word she had spoken, the tone of her voice, her step, her every gesture—all were before me, confirming my delusion; and yet—I could bear no more, and burst into tears.

The loud call of a cavalry trumpet aroused me.

How long I had passed in this state of despondency I knew not; but it was long past noon when I rallied myself. My charger was already awaiting me; and a second blast of the trumpet told that the inspection in the Plaza was about to commence.

As I continued to dress, I gradually rallied from my depressing thoughts; and ere I belted my sabretasche, the current of my ideas had turned from their train of sadness to one of hardihood and daring. Lucy Dashwood had treated me like a wilful schoolboy. Mayhap I may prove myself as gallant a soldier as even him she has preferred before me.

A third sound of the trumpet cut short my reflections. I sprang into the saddle, and hastened towards the Plaza. As I dashed along the streets, my horse, maddened with the impulse that stirred my own heart, curveted and plunged unceasingly. As I reached the Plaza the crowd became dense, and I was obliged to pull up. The sound of the music, the parade, the tramp of the infantry, and the neighing of the horses, were, however, too much for my mettlesome steed, and he became nearly unmanageable; he plunged fearfully, and twice reared as though he would have fallen back. As I scattered the foot passengers right and left with terror, my eye fell upon one lovely girl, who, tearing herself from her companion, rushed wildly towards an open doorway for shelter; suddenly, however, changing her intention, she came forward a few paces, and then, as if overcome by fear, stood stock-still, her hands clasped upon her bosom, her eyes upturned, her features deadly pale, while her knees seemed bending beneath her. Never did I behold a more beautiful object. Her dark hair had fallen loose upon her shoulder, and she stood the very ideal of the "Madonna Supplicating." My glance was short as a lightning flash, for the same instant my horse swerved, and dashed forward right at the place where she was standing. One terrific cry rose from the crowd who saw her danger. Beside her stood a muleteer, who had drawn up his mule and cart close beside the footway for safety; she made one effort to reach it, but her outstretched arms alone moved, and, paralyzed by terror, she sank motionless upon the pavement. There was but one course open to me now; collecting myself for the effort, I threw my horse upon his haunches, and then, dashing the spurs into his flanks, breasted him at the mule-cart. With one spring he rose, and cleared it at a bound, while the very air rang with the acclamations of the multitude, and a thousand bravos saluted me as I alighted upon the opposite side.

"Well done, O'Malley!" sang out the little Adjutant, as I flew past, and pulled up in the middle of the Plaza.

"Something devilish like Galway in that leap," said a very musical voice beside me; and at the same instant a tall, soldier-like man, in an undress dragoon frock, touched his cap, and said, "A 14th man, I perceive, sir. May I introduce myself?—Major O'Shaughnessy."

I bowed, and shook the Major's proffered hand, while he continued:

"Old Monsoon mentioned your name to us this morning. You came out together, if I mistake not?"

"Yes; but somehow, I've missed the Major since my landing."

"Oh, you'll see him presently; he'll be on parade. By the bye, he wishes particularly to meet you. We dine to-day at the 'Quai de Soderi,' and if you're not engaged—— Yes, this is the person," said he, turning at the moment towards a servant, who, with a card in his hand, seemed to search for some one in the crowd.

The man approached and handed it to me.

"What can this mean?" said I. "Don Emanuel de Blacas y Silviero, Rua Nuova."

"Why, that's the great Portuguese contractor, the intendant of half the army, the richest fellow in Lisbon. Have you known him long?"

"Never heard of him till now."

"By Jove, you're in luck! No man gives such dinners; he has such a cellar! I'll wager a fifty it was his daughter you took in the flying leap a while ago. I hear she is a beautiful creature."

"Yes," thought I, "that must be it; and yet, strange enough, I think the name and address are familiar to me."

"Ten to one, you've heard Monsoon speak of him; he's most intimate there. But here comes the Major."

As he spoke, the illustrious Commissary came forward, holding a vast bundle of papers in one hand and his snuff-box in the other, followed by a long string of clerks, contractors, assistant-surgeons, paymasters, &c., all eagerly pressing forward to be heard.

"It's quite impossible; I can't do it to-day. Victualling and physicking are very good things, but must be done in season. I have been up all night at the accounts—haven't I, O'Malley?"—here he winked at me most significantly;—"and then I have the forage and stoppage fund to look through" ("We dine at six, sharp," said he, *sotto voce*), "which will leave me without one minute unoccupied for the next twenty-four hours. Look to your toggery this evening ; I've something in my eye for you, O'Malley."

"Officers unattached to their several corps will fall into the middle of the Plaza," said a deep voice among the crowd. In obedience to the order, I rode forward, and placed myself with a number of others, apparently newly-joined, in the open square. A short gray-haired old colonel, with a dark, eagle look, proceeded to inspect us, reading from a paper as he came along :

"Mr. Hepton, 6th foot; commission bearing date 11th January; drilled; proceed to Ovar, and join his regiment.

"Mr. Gronow, Fusilier Guards; remains with the depôt.

"Captain Mortimer, 1st Dragoons; appointed aide-de-camp to the General commanding the cavalry brigade.

"Mr. Sparks—where is Mr. Sparks? Mr. Sparks absent from parade; make a note of it.

"Mr. O'Malley, 14th Light Dragoons. Mr. O'Malley—oh, I remember; I have received a letter from Sir George Dashwood concerning you. You will hold yourself in readiness to march. Your friends desire that, before you may obtain any staff appointment, you should have the opportunity of seeing some service. Am I to understand such is your wish ?"

"Most certainly."

"May I have the pleasure of your company at dinner to day ?"

"I regret that I have already accepted an invitation to dine with Major Monsoon."

"With Major Monsoon ? ah, indeed! Perhaps it might be as well I should mention—— But no matter. I wish you good morning."

So saying, the little colonel rode off, leaving me to suppose that my dinner engagement had not raised me in his estimation, though why, I could not exactly determine.

17

OUR dinner was a long and uninteresting one, and as I found that the Major was likely to prefer his seat, as chairman of the party, to the seductions of ladies' society, I took the first opportunity of escaping, and left the room.

It was a rich moonlight night, as I found myself in the street. My way, which led along the banks of the Tagus, was almost as light as in daytime, and crowded with walking parties, who sauntered carelessly along, in the enjoyment of the cool, refreshing night air. On inquiring, I discovered that the Rua Nuova was at the extremity of the city; but, as the road led along by the river, I did not regret the distance, but walked on with increasing pleasure at the charms of so heavenly a climate and country.

After three-quarters of an hour's walk, the streets became by degrees less and less crowded. A solitary party passed me now and then; the buzz of distant voices succeeded to the gay laughter and merry tones of the passing groups, and at length my own footsteps alone awoke the echoes along the deserted pathway. I stopped every now and then to gaze upon the tranquil river, whose eddies were circling in the pale silver of the moonlight. I listened with attentive ear, as the night breeze wafted to me the far-off sounds of a guitar, and the deep tones of some lover's serenade; while again the tender warbling of the nightingale came borne across the stream, on a wind rich with the odor of the orange-tree.

As thus I lingered on my way, the time stole on, and it was near midnight ere I had roused myself from the reverie surrounding objects had thrown about me. I stopped suddenly, and for some minutes I struggled with myself to discover if I was really awake. As I walked along, lost in my reflections, I had entered a little garden beside the river. Fragrant plants and lovely flowers bloomed on every side: the orange, the camelia, the cactus, and the rich laurel of Portugal were blending their green and golden hues around me, while the very air was filled with delicious music. "Was it a dream? Could such ecstasy be real?" I asked myself, as the rich notes swelled upward in their strength, and sank in soft cadence to tones of melting harmony; now bursting forth in the full force of gladness, the voices blended together in one stream of mellow music, and suddenly ceasing, the soft but thrilling shake of a female voice rose upon the air, and, in its plaintive beauty, stirred the very heart. The proud tramp of martial music succeeded to the low wailing cry of agony; then came the crash of battle, the clang of steel; the thunder of the fight rolled on in all its majesty, increasing in its maddening excitement till it ended in one loud shout of victory.

All was still; not a breath moved, not a leaf stirred, and again was I relapsing into my dreamy skepticism, when again the notes swelled upward in concert. But now their accents were changed, and, in low, subdued tones, faintly and slowly uttered, the prayer of thanksgiving rose to heaven, and spoke their gratefulness. I almost fell upon my knees, and already the tears filled my eyes, as I drank in the sounds. My heart was full to bursting, and even now as I write it, my pulse throbs as I remember the hymn of the Abencerrages.

When I rallied from my trance of excited pleasure, my first thought was—where was I, and how came I there? Before I could resolve my doubts upon the question, my attention was turned in another direction, for close beside me the branches moved forward, and a pair of arms were thrown around my neck, while a delicious voice cried out, in an accent of childish delight, "*Trovado!*" At the same instant a lovely head sank upon my shoulder, covering it with tresses of long brown hair. The arms pressed me still more closely, till I felt her very heart beating against my side.

"*Mio fradre,*" said a soft, trembling voice, as her fingers played in my hair and patted my temples.

What a situation was mine! I well knew some mistaken identity had been the cause; but, still, I could not repress my inclination to return the embrace, as I pressed my lips upon the fair forehead that leaned upon my bosom; at the same moment she threw back her head, as if to look me more fully in the face. One glance sufficed; blushing deeply over her cheeks and neck, she sprang from my arms, and, uttering a faint cry, staggered against a tree. In an instant I saw it was the lovely girl I had met in the morning; and, without losing a second, I poured out apologies for my intrusion with all the eloquence I was master of, till she suddenly interrupted me by asking if I spoke French. Scarcely had I recommenced my excuses in that language, when a third party appeared upon the stage. This was a short, elderly man, in a green uniform, with several decorations upon his breast, and a cocked hat, with a flowing plume, in his right hand.

"May I beg to know whom I have the honor of receiving?" inquired he, in very excellent English, as he advanced with a look of very ceremonious and distant politeness.

I immediately explained that, presuming upon the card which his servant had presented me, I had resolved on paying my respects, when a mistake had led me accidentally into his garden.

My apologies had not come to an end, when he folded me in his arms and overwhelmed me with thanks, at the same time saying a few words in Portuguese to his daughter; she stooped down, and taking my hand gently within her own, touched it with her lips.

This piece of touching courtesy—which I afterwards found meant little or nothing—affected me deeply at the time, and I felt the blood rush to my face and forehead, half in pride, half in a sense of shame. My confusion was, however, of short duration, for, taking my arm, the old gentleman led me along a few paces, and turning round a small clump of olives, entered a little summer-house. Here a considerable party were assembled, which for their picturesque effect could scarcely have been better managed on the stage.

Beneath the mild lustre of a large lamp of stained glass, half hid in the overhanging boughs, was spread a table covered with vessels of gold and silver plate of gorgeous richness; drinking cups and goblets of antique pattern shone among cups of Sèvres china or Venetian glass; delicious fruit, looking a thousand times more tempting for being contained in baskets of silver foliage, peeped from amid a profusion of fresh flowers, whose odor was continually shed around by a slight *jet d'eau* that played among the leaves. Around, upon the grass, seated upon cushions, or reclining on Genoa carpets, were several beautiful girls, in most becoming costumes, their dark locks and darker .eyes speaking of "the soft south," while their expressive gestures and animated looks betokened a race whose temperament is glowing as their clime. There were several men also, the greater number of whom appeared in uniform—bronzed, soldier-like fellows, who had the jaunty air and easy carriage of their calling—among whom was one Englishman, or at least so I guessed from his wearing the uniform of a heavy dragoon regiment.

"This is my daughter's fête," said Don Emanuel, as he ushered me into the assembly,—"her birthday: a sad day it might have been for us had it not been for your courage and forethought." So saying, he commenced a recital of my adventure to the bystanders, who overwhelmed me with civil speeches and a shower of soft looks that completed the fascination of the fairy scene. Meanwhile, the fair Inez had made room for me beside her, and I found myself at once the lion of the party, each vieing with her neighbor who should show me the most attention, la Senhora herself directing her conversation exclusively to me—a circumstance which, considering the awkwardness of our first meeting, I felt no small surprise at, and which led me, somewhat maliciously, I confess, to make a half allusion to it, feeling some interest in ascertaining for whom the flattering reception was really intended.

" I thought you were Charles," said she, blushing in answer to my question.

"And you were right," said I, "I am Charles."

" Nay, but I meant *my* Charles."

There was something of touching softness in the tones of these few words that made me half wish I were *her* Charles. Whether my look evinced as much or not, I cannot tell, but she speedily added,—

" He is my brother; he is a captain in the *caçadores*, and I expected him here this evening. Some one saw a figure pass the gate and conceal himself in the trees, and I was sure it was he."

" What a disappointment," said I.

" Yes, was it not?" said she, hurriedly; and then, as if remembering how ungracious was the speech, she blushed more deeply and hung down her head.

Just at this moment, as I looked up, I caught the eye of the English officer fixed steadily upon me. He was a tall, fine-looking fellow, of about two or three and thirty, with marked and handsome features, which, however, conveyed an expression of something sneering and sinister, that struck me the moment I saw him. His glass was fixed in his eye, and I perceived that he regarded us both with a look of no common interest. My attention did not, however, dwell long upon the circumstance, for Don Emanuel, coming behind my shoulder, asked me if I would not take out his daughter in the bolero they were just forming.

To my shame I was obliged to confess that I had not even seen the dance ; and while I continued to express my resolve to correct the errors of my education, the Englishman came up and asked the Senhora to be his partner. This put the very keystone upon my annoyance, and I half turned angrily away from the spot, when I heard her decline his invitation, and avow her determination not to dance.

There was something which pleased me so much at this refusal, that I could not help turning upon her a look of most grateful acknowledgment ; but as I did so, I once more encountered the gaze of the Englishman, whose knitted brows and compressed lips were bent upon me in a manner there was no mistaking. This was neither the fitting time nor place to seek any explanation of the circumstance ; so wisely resolving to wait a better occasion, I turned away and resumed my attentions towards my fair companion.

"Then you don't care for the bolero?" said I, as she re-seated herself upon the grass.

" Oh! I delight in it," said she, enthusiastically.

" But you refused to dance."

She hesitated, blushed, tried to mutter something, and was silent.

"I had determined to learn it," said I, half jestingly; "but if you will not dance with me——"

"Yes; that I will—indeed I will."

"But you declined my countryman. Is it because he is inexpert?"

The Senhora hesitated; looked confused for some minutes; at length, coloring slightly, she said, "I have already made one rude speech to you this evening; I fear lest I should make a second. Tell me, is Captain Trevyllian your friend?"

"If you mean that gentleman yonder, I never saw him before."

"Nor heard of him?"

"Nor that either. We are total strangers to each other."

"Well, then, I may confess it. I do not like him. My father prefers him to any one else, invites him daily here, and, in fact, installs him as his first favorite. But still, I cannot like him; and yet I have done my best to do so."

"Indeed!" said I, pointedly. "What are his chief demerits? Is he not agreeable? is he not clever?"

"Oh! on the contrary, most agreeable; fascinating, I should say, in conversation; has travelled; seen a great deal of the world; is very accomplished, and has distinguished himself on several occasions; he wears, as you see, a Portuguese order."

"And, with all that——"

"And, with all that, I cannot bear him. He is a duellist, a notorious duellist. My brother, too, knows more of him, and always avoids him. But let us not speak further: I see his eyes are again fixed on us; and, somehow, I fear him, without well knowing wherefor."

A movement among the party; shawls and mantillas were sought for on all sides, and the preparations for leave-taking appeared general. Before, however, I had time to express my thanks for my hospitable reception, the guests had assembled in a circle around the Senhora, and, toasting her with a parting bumper, they commenced in concert a little Portuguese song of farewell, each verse concluding with a Good-night! which, as they separated and held their way homeward, might now and then be heard rising upon the breeze, and wafting their last thoughts back to her. The concluding verse, which struck me much, I have essayed to translate. It ran somehow thus:—

> "The morning breezes chill
> Now close our joyous scene,
> And yet we linger still,
> Where we've so happy been.

<blockquote>
How blest were it to live
With hearts like ours so light,
And only part to give
One long and last Good-night !
Good-night !"
</blockquote>

With many an invitation to renew my visit, most kindly proffered by Don Emanuel, and warmly seconded by his daughter, I, too, wished my Good-night! and turned my steps homeward.

CHAPTER XXXIX.

THE VILLA.

THE first object that presented itself to my eye the next morning was the midshipman's packet, entrusted to my care by Power. I turned it over to read the address more carefully, and what was my surprise to find that the name was that of my fair friend Donna Inez!

"This certainly thickens the plot," thought I; "and so I have now fallen upon the real Simon Pure, and the reefer has had the good fortune to distance the dragoon. Well, thus far, I cannot say that I regret it. Now, however, for the parade, and then for the villa."

"I say, O'Malley," cried out Monsoon, as I appeared on the Plaza, "I have accepted an invitation for you to-day. We dine across the river. Be at my quarters a little before six, and we'll go together."

I should rather have declined the invitation, but, not well knowing why, and having no ready excuse, acceded, and promised to be punctual.

"You were at Don Emanuel's last night; I heard of you!"

"Yes; I spent a most delightful evening."

"That's your ground, my boy; a million of moidores, and such a campagna in Valencia—a better thing than the Dalrymple affair. Don't blush. I know it all. But stay; here they come."

As he spoke, the general commanding, with a numerous staff, rode forward. As they passed, I recognized a face which I had certainly seen before, and in a moment remembered it was that of the dragoon of the evening before. He passed quite close, and fixing his eyes steadily on me, evinced no sign of recognition.

The parade lasted above two hours, and it was with a feeling of impatience that I mounted a fresh horse to canter out to the villa.

When I arrived, the servant informed me that Don Emanuel was in the city, but that the Senhora was in the garden, offering at the same time to escort me. Declining this honor, I entrusted my horse to his keeping, and took my way towards the arbor where last I had seen her.

I had not walked many paces, when the sound of a guitar struck on my ear. I listened. It was the Senhora's voice. She was sing-ing a Venetian canzonetta, in a low, soft, warbling tone, as one lost in a reverie—as though the music was a mere accompaniment to some pleasant thought. I peeped through the dense leaves, and there she sat upon a low garden seat, an open book on the rustic table before her; beside her, embroidery, which seemed only lately abandoned. As I looked, she placed her guitar upon the ground, and began to play with a small spaniel, that seemed to have waited with impatience for some testimony of favor. A moment more, and she grew weary of this; then, heaving a long but gentle sigh, leaned back upon her chair, and seemed lost in thought. I now had ample time to regard her, and certainly never beheld anything more lovely. There was a character of classic beauty, and her brow, though fair and ample, was still strongly marked upon the temples; the eyes, being deep and squarely set, imparted a look of intensity to her features which their own softness alone subdued, while the short upper lip, which trembled with every passing thought, spoke of a nature tender and impressionable, and yet impassioned. Her foot and ankle peeped from beneath her dark robe, and certainly nothing could be more faultless; while her hand, fair as marble, blue-veined and dimpled, played amid the long tresses of her hair, that, as if in the wantonness of beauty, fell carelessly upon her shoulders.

It was some time before I could tear myself away from the fasci-nation of so much beauty, and it needed no common effort to leave the spot. As I made a short *détour* in the garden before approach-ing the arbor, she saw me as I came forward, and kissing her hand gayly, made room for me beside her.

"I have been fortunate in finding you alone, Senhora," said I, as I seated myself by her side, "for I am the bearer of a letter to you. How far it may interest you I know not, but to the writer's feelings I am bound to testify."

"A letter to me? You jest, surely?"

"That I am in earnest, this will show," said I, producing the packet.

She took it from my hands, turned it about and about, examined the seal, while, half-doubtingly, she said,—

"The name is mine; but still——"

"You fear to open it; is it not so?   But, after all, you need not be surprised if it's from Howard; that's his name, I think."

"Howard! from little Howard!" exclaimed she, enthusiastically, and tearing open the letter, she pressed it to her lips, her eyes sparkling with pleasure, and her cheek glowing as she read.   I watched her as she ran rapidly over the lines; and I confess that more than once a pang of discontent shot through my heart that the midshipman's letter could have called up such interest; not that I was in love with her myself, but yet, I know not how it was, I had fancied her affections unengaged, and, without asking myself wherefor, I wished as much.

"Poor, dear boy!" said she, as she came to the end.

How these few and simple words sank into my heart as I remembered how they had once been uttered to myself, and in perhaps no very dissimilar circumstances.

"But where is the souvenir he speaks of?" said she.

"The souvenir!   I'm not aware ——"   ·

"Oh, I hope you have not lost the lock of hair he sent me!"

I was quite dumbfounded at this, and could not remember whether I had received it from Power or not; so I answered at random,—

"Yes; I must have left it on my table."

"Promise me, then, to bring it to-morrow with you?"

"Certainly," said I, with something of pique in my manner. "If I find such a means of making my visit an agreable one, I shall certainly not omit it."

"You are quite right," said she, either not noticing or not caring for the tone of my reply; "you will, indeed, be a welcome messenger.   Do you know he was one of my lovers?"

"One of them!   Indeed!   Then pray how many do you number at this moment?"

"What a question! as if I could possibly count them.   Besides, there are so many absent; some on leave, some deserters, perhaps, that I might be reckoning among my troops, but who possibly form part of the forces of the enemy.   Do you know little Howard?"

"I cannot say that we are personally acquainted, but I am enabled, through the medium of a friend, to say that his sentiments are not strange to me.   Besides, I have really pledged myself to support the prayer of his petition."

"How very good of you!   For which reason you've forgotten, if not lost, the lock of hair."

"That you shall have to-morrow," said I, pressing my hand solemnly to my heart.

"Well, then, don't forget it. But hush! here comes Captain Trevyllian. So you say Lisbon really pleases you?" said she, in a tone of voice totally changed, as the dragoon of the preceding evening approached.

"Mr. O'Malley, Captain Trevyllian."

We bowed stiffly and haughtily to each other, as two men salute who are unavoidably obliged to bow, with every wish on either side to avoid acquaintance. So, at least, I construed his bow; so I certainly intended my own.

It requires no common tact to give conversation the appearance of unconstraint and ease when it is evident that each person opposite is laboring under excited feelings; so that, notwithstanding the Senhora's efforts to engage our attention by the commonplaces of the day, we remained almost silent, and after a few observations of no interest, took our several leaves. Here again a new source of awkwardness arose; for as we walked together towards the house, where our horses stood, neither party seemed disposed to speak.

"You are probably returning to Lisbon?" said he, coldly.

I assented by a bow; upon which, drawing his bridle within his arm, he bowed once more, and turned away in an opposite direction; while I, glad to be relieved of an unsought-for companionship, returned alone to the town.

CHAPTER XL.

THE DINNER.

IT was with no peculiar pleasure that I dressed for our dinner party. Major O'Shaughnessy, our host, was one of that class of my countrymen I cared least for, — a riotous, good-natured, noisy, loud-swearing, punch-drinking western; full of stories of impossible fox-hunts, and unimaginable duels, which all were acted either by himself or some member of his family. The company consisted of the Adjutant, Monsoon, Ferguson, Trevyllian, and some eight or ten officers with whom I was unacquainted. As is usual on such occasions, the wine circulated freely, and, amid the din and clamor of excited conversation, the fumes of Burgundy, and the vapor of cigar smoke, we most of us became speedily mystified. As for me, my evil destiny would have it that I was placed exactly opposite Trevyllian, with whom, upon more than one occasion, I happened to differ in opinion; the question was in itself some trivial and unimportant one, yet the tone which he assumed, and of which

I, too, could not divest myself in reply, boded anything rather than an amicable feeling between us. The noise and turmoil about prevented the others remarking the circumstance; but I could perceive in his manner what I deemed a studied determination to provoke a quarrel, while I felt within myself a most unchristian-like desire to indulge his fancy.

"Worse fellows at passing the bottle than Trevyllian and O'Malley, there, I have rarely sojourned with," cried the Major; "look, if they haven't got eight decanters between them, and here we are in a state of African thirst."

"How can you expect him to think of thirst when such perfumed billets as that come showering upon him?" said the Adjutant, alluding to a rose-colored epistle a servant had placed within my hands.

"Eight miles of a stone-wall country in fifteen minutes!—devil a lie in it!" said O'Shaughnessy, striking the table with his clenched fist; "show me the man would deny it!"

"Why, my dear fellow——"

"Don't be dearing me. Is it no you'll be saying to me?"

"Listen, now: there's O'Reilly, there——"

"Where is he?"

"He's under the table!"

"Well, it's the same thing. His mother had a fox—bad luck to you, don't scald me with the jug!—his mother had a fox-cover in Shinrohan."

When O'Shaughnessy had got thus far in his narrative, I had the opportunity of opening my note, which merely contained the following words: "Come to the ball at the Casino, and bring the cadeau you promised."

I had scarcely read this over once, when a roar of laughter at something said attracted my attention. I looked up, and perceived Trevyllian's eyes bent upon me with the fierceness of a tiger; the veins in his forehead were swollen and distorted, and the whole expression of his face betokened rage and passion. Resolved no longer to submit to such evident determination to insult, I was rising from my place at table, when, as if anticipating my intention, he pushed back his chair, and left the room. Fearful of attracting attention by immediately following him, I affected to join in the conversation around me, while my temples throbbed, and my hands tingled with impatience to get away.

"Poor M'Manus!" said O'Shaughnessy—"rest his soul!—he'd have puzzled the bench of bishops for hard words. Upon my conscience, I believe he spent his mornings looking for them in the Old Testament. Sure ye might have heard what happened to him at

Banagher, when he commanded the Kilkennys,—ye never heard the story? well, then, ye shall. Push the sherry along first, though—old Monsoon, there, always keeps it lingering beside his left arm!

"Well, when Peter was Lieutenant-Colonel of the Kilkennys,—who, I may remark, *en passant*, as the French say, were the seediest-looking devils in the whole service,—he never let them alone from morning till night, drilling and pipeclaying, and polishing them up. 'Nothing will make soldiers of you,' said Peter; 'but by the rock of Cashel, I'll keep you as clean as a new musket!' Now, poor Peter himself was not a very warlike figure; he measured five feet one in his tallest boots; but certainly, if Nature denied him length of stature, she compensated for it in another way, by giving him a taste for the longest words in the language. An extra syllable or so in a word was always a strong recommendation; and whenever he could not find one to his mind, he'd take some quaint outlandish one, that more than once led to very awkward results. Well, the regiment was one day drawn up for parade in the town of Banagher, and as M'Manus came down the lines, he stopped opposite one of the men, whose face, hands, and accoutrements exhibited a most woeful contempt of his orders. The fellow looked more like a turf-stack than a light-company man!

"'Stand out, sir!' cried M'Manus, in a boiling passion. 'Sergeant O'Toole, inspect this individual.' Now, the sergeant was rather a favorite with Mac; for he always pretended to understand his phraseology, and, in consequence, was pronounced by the colonel a very superior man for his station in life. 'Sergeant,' said he, 'we shall make an exemplary illustration of our system here.'

"'Yes, sir,' said the sergeant, sorely puzzled at the meaning of what he spoke.

"'Bear him to the Shannon, and lave him there!' This he said in a kind of Coriolanus tone, with a toss up of his head, and a wave of his right arm, signs, whenever he made them, incontestably showing that further parley was out of the question, and that he had summed up, and charged the jury for good and all.

"'*Lave* him in the river?' said O'Toole, his eyes starting from the sockets, and his whole face working in strong anxiety; 'is it *lave* him in the river, yer honor means?'

"'I have spoken!' said the little man, bending an ominous frown upon the sergeant, which, whatever construction he might have put upon his words, there was no mistaking.

"'Well, well, av it's God's will he's drowned, it will not be on my head,' says O'Toole, as he marched the fellow away, between two rank and file.

"The parade was nearly over, when Mac happened to see the

sergeant coming up, all splashed with water, and looking quite tired.

"'Have you obeyed my orders?' said he.

"'Yes, yer honor; and tough work we had of it, for he struggled hard!'"

"'And where is he now?'

"'Oh, troth, he's there safe! Divil a fear he'll get out!'

"'Where?' said Mac.

"'In the river, yer honor.'

"'What have you done, you scoundrel?'

"'Didn't I do as you bid me?' says he; 'didn't I throw him in, and *lave* [leave] him there?'

"And faith so they did; and if he wasn't a good swimmer, and get over to Moystown, there's little doubt but he'd have been drowned, and all because Peter M'Manus could not express himself like a Christian."

In the laughter which followed O'Shaughnessy's story, I took the opportunity of making my escape from the party, and succeeded in gaining the street unobserved. Though the note I had just read was not signed, I had no doubt from whom it came; so I hastened at once to my quarters, to make search for the lock of Ned Howard's hair, to which the Senhora alluded. What was my mortification, however, to discover that no such thing could be found anywhere! I searched all my drawers; I tossed about my papers and letters; I hunted every likely, every unlikely spot I could think of, but in vain; now cursing my carelessness for having lost it; now swearing most solemnly to myself that I never could have received it. What was to be done? It was already late; my only thought was how to replace it. If I only knew the color, any other lock of hair would doubtless do just as well. The chances were, as Howard was young, and an Englishman, that his hair was light—light-brown, probably; something like my own. Of course it was! why didn't that thought occur to me before? how stupid I was. So saying, I seized a pair of scissors, and cut a long lock beside my temple; this in a calm moment I might have hesitated about. "Yes," thought I, "she'll never discover the cheat; and, besides, I do feel—I know not exactly why—rather gratified to think that I shall have left this souvenir behind me, even though it call up other recollections than of me." So thinking, I wrapped my cloak about me, and hastened towards the Casino.

CHAPTER XLI.

THE ROUTE.

I HAD scarcely gone a hundred yards from my quarters, when a great tramp of horses' feet attracted my attention. I stopped to listen, and soon heard the jingle of dragoon accoutrements, as the noise came nearer. The night was dark, but perfectly still; and before I stood many minutes I heard the tones of a voice which I well knew could belong to but one, and that Fred Power.

"Fred Power!" said I, shouting at the same time at the top of my voice—"Power!"

"Ah, Charley, is that you? come along to the Adjutant-General's quarters. I'm charged with some important despatches, and can't stop till I've delivered them. Come along, I've glorious news for you!" So saying, he dashed spurs to his horse, and, followed by two mounted dragoons, galloped past. Power's few and hurried words had so excited my curiosity, that I turned at once to follow him, questioning myself, as I walked along, to what he could possibly allude. He knew of my attachment to Lucy Dashwood—could he mean anything of her? But what could I expect there? by what flattery could I picture to myself any chance of success in that quarter? and yet, what other news could I care for or value than what bore upon her fate upon whom my own depended? Thus ruminating, I reached the door of the spacious building in which the Adjutant-General had taken up his abode, and soon found myself among a crowd of persons whom the rumor of some important event had assembled there, though no one could tell what had occurred. Before many minutes the door opened, and Power came out; bowing hurriedly to a few, and whispering a word or two as he passed down the steps, he seized me by the arm and led me across the street. "Charley," said he, "the curtain's rising; the piece is about to begin; a new commander-in-chief is sent out; Sir Arthur Wellesley, my boy, the finest fellow in England, is to lead us on, and we march to-morrow. There's news for you!" A raw boy, unread, uninformed as I was, I knew but little of his career whose name had even then shed such lustre upon our army; but the buoyant tone of Power as he spoke, the kindling energy of his voice, roused me, and I felt every inch a soldier. As I grasped his hand, in delightful enthusiasm, I lost all memory of my disappointment, and, in the beating throb that shook my head, I felt how deeply slept the ardor of military glory that first led me from my home to see a battle-field.

"'There goes the news!" said Frederick, pointing, as he spoke, to a rocket that shot up into the sky, and, as it broke into ten thousand stars, illuminated the broad stream where the ships of war lay darkly resting. In another moment the whole air shone with similar fires, while the deep roll of the drum sounded along the silent streets, and the city, so lately sunk in sleep, became, as if by magic, thronged with crowds of people; the sharp clang of the cavalry trumpet blended with the gay carol of the light-infantry bugle, and the heavy tramp of the march was heard in the distance. All was excitement, all bustle; but in the joyous tone of every voice was spoken the longing anxiety to meet the enemy. The gay, reckless tone of an Irish song would occasionally reach us, as some Connaught Ranger, or some 78th man, passed, his knapsack on his back; or the low monotonous pibroch of the Highlander, swelling into a war-cry, as some kilted corps drew up their ranks together. We turned to regain our quarters, when, at the corner of a street, we came suddenly upon a merry party, seated around a table before a little inn; a large street lamp, unhung for the occasion, had been placed in the midst of them, and showed us the figures of several soldiers in undress; at the end, and raised a little above his compeers, sat one whom, by the unfair proportion he assumed of the conversation, not less than by the musical intonation of his voice, I soon recognized as my man Mickey Free.

"I'll be hanged if that's not your fellow there, Charley," said Power, as he came to a dead stop a few yards off. "What an impertinent varlet he is: only to think of him there, presiding among a set of fellows that have fought all the battles in the Peninsular war. At this moment, I'll be hanged if he is not going to sing."

Here a tremendous thumping upon the table announced the fact, and after a few preliminary observations from Mike, illustrative of his respect for the service in which he had so often distinguished himself, he began, to the air of the "Young May Moon," a ditty of which I only recollect the following verses:

> "The pickets are fast retreating, boys,
>   The last tattoo is beating, boys;
>   So let every man
>   Finish his can,
>   And drink to our next merry meeting, boys!
>
> "The colonel so gayly prancing, boys,
>   Has a wonderful trick of advancing, boys;
>   When he sings out so large,
>   ' Fix bayonets and charge,'
>   He sets all the Frenchmen a-dancing, boys!
>
> "Let Mounseer look ever so big, my boys,
>   Who cares for fighting a fig, my boys?
>   When we play Garryowen,
>   He'd rather go home;
>   For somehow, he's no taste for a jig, my boys!"

This admirable lyric seemed to be a perfect success, if one were only to judge from the thundering of voices, hands, and drinking vessels which followed; while a venerable gray-haired sergeant rose to propose Mr. Free's health, and speedy promotion to him.

We stood for several minutes in admiration of the party, when the loud roll of the drums beating to arms awakened us to the thought that our moments were numbered.

"Good-night, Charley!" said Power, as he shook my hand warmly; 'good-night! It will be your last night under a curtain for some months to come; make the most of it! Adieu!"

So saying, we parted: he to his quarters, and I to all the confusion of my baggage, which lay in most admired disorder about my room.

CHAPTER XLII.

THE FAREWELL.

THE preparations for the march occupied me till near morning; and, indeed, had I been disposed to sleep, the din and clamor of the world without would have totally prevented it. Before daybreak the advanced guard was already in motion, and some squadrons of heavy cavalry had begun their march.

I looked around my now dismantled room, as one does usually for the last time ere leaving, and bethought me if I had not forgotten anything. Apparently all was remembered; but stay—what is this? To be sure, how forgetful I had become! It was the packet I destined for Donna Inéz, and which, in the confusion of the night before, I had omitted to take to the Casino.

I immediately despatched Mike to the Commissary with my luggage, and orders to ascertain when we were expected to march. He soon returned, with the intelligence that our corps was not to move before noon; so that I had yet some hours to spare, and make my adieux to the Senhora.

I cannot exactly explain the reason, but I certainly did bestow a more than common attention upon my toilette that morning. The Senhora was nothing to me. It is true she had, as she lately most candidly informed me, a score of admirers, among whom I was not even reckoned. She was evidently a coquette, whose greatest pleasure was to sport and amuse herself with the passions she excited in others. And even if she were not—if her heart were to be won to-morrow—what claims, what right, had I to seek it? My affections were already pledged; promised, it is true, to one who gave nothing in return, and who, perhaps, even loved another. Ah! there was the rub: that one confounded suspicion, lurking in the rear, chilled my courage and wounded my spirit.

If there be anything more disheartening to an Irishman, in his little *affaires de cœur*, than another, it is the sense of rivalry. The obstinacy of fathers, the ill will of mothers, the coldness, the indifference of the lovely object herself,—obstacles though they be,—he has tact, spirit, and perseverance to overcome them; but when a more successful candidate for the fair presents himself; when the eye that remains downcast at *his* suit lights up with animation at *another's* coming; when the features whose cold and chilling apathy to him have blended in one smile of welcome to another,—it is all up with him: he sees the game lost, and throws his cards upon the table. And yet, why is this? why is it that he, whose birthright it would seem to be sanguine when others despond,—to be confident when all else are hopeless,—should find his courage fail him here? The reason is, simply—— But, in good sooth, I am ashamed to confess it!

Having jogged on so far with my reader, in all the sober seriousness which the matter-of-fact material of these memoirs demands, I fear lest a seeming paradox may cause me to lose my good name for veracity, and that, while merely maintaining a national trait of my country, I may appear to be asserting some unheard-of and absurd proposition; so far have mere vulgar prejudices gone to sap our character as a people.

The reason, then, is this,—for I have gone too far to retreat,—the Irishman is essentially bashful. Well, laugh if you wish, for I conclude that by this time you have given way to a most immoderate excess of risibility; but still, when you have perfectly recovered your composure, I beg to repeat, the Irishman is essentially a bashful man!

Do not for a moment fancy that I would by this imply that in any new or unexpected situation—that from any unforeseen conjuncture of events—the Irishman would feel confused or abashed, more than any other; far from it. The cold and habitual reserve of the Englishman; the studied caution of the North Tweeder himself, would exhibit far stronger evidences of awkwardness in such circumstances as these. But, on the other hand, when measuring his capacity, his means of success, his probabilities of being preferred, with those of the natives of any other country, I back the Irishman against the world for distrust of his own powers, for an under-estimate of his real merits; in one word, for his bashfulness. But let us return to Donna Inez.

18

As I rode up to the villa, I found the family assembled at. break-fast. Several officers were also present, among whom I was not sorry to recognize my friend Monsoon.

"Ah, Charley!" cried he, as I seated myself beside him, "what a pity all our fun is so soon to have an end! Here's this confounded Soult won't be quiet and peaceable; but he must march upon Oporto, and Heaven knows where besides, just as we were really beginning to enjoy life. I had got such a contract for blankets! and now they've ordered me to join Beresford's corps in the mountains; and you,"—here he dropped his voice,—"and you were getting on so devilish well in this quarter; upon my life, I think you'd have carried the day; old Don Emanuel—you know he's a friend of mine—likes you very much. And then, there's Sparks——"

"Ay, Major, what of him? I have not seen him for some days."

"Why, they've been frightening the poor devil out of his life, O'Shaughnessy and a set of them. They tried him by court-martial yesterday, and sentenced him to mount guard with a wooden sword and a shooting jacket, which he did. Old Colbourne, it seems, saw him; and faith, there would be the devil to pay if the route had not come. Some of them would certainly have got a long leave to see their friends."

"Why is not the Senhora here, Major? I don't see her at table."

"A cold; a sore throat; a wet-feet affair of last night, I believe. Pass that cold pie down here. Sherry, if you please. You didn't see Power to-day?"

"No: we parted late last night; I have not been to bed."

"Very bad preparation for a march. Take some burnt brandy in your coffee."

"Then you don't think the Senhora will appear?"

"Very unlikely. But stay, you know her room—the small draw-ing-room that looks out upon the flower-garden; she usually passes the morning there. Leap the little wooden paling round the corner, and the chances are ten to one you find her."

I saw from the occupied air of Don Emanuel that there was little fear of interruption on his part; so, taking an early moment to escape unobserved, I rose and left the room. When I sprang over the oak fence, I found myself in a delicious little garden, where roses, grown to a height never seen in our colder climate, formed a deep bower of rich blossom.

The Major was right. The Senhora was in the room, and in one moment I was beside her.

"Nothing but my fears of not bidding you farewell could palliate my thus intruding, Donna Inez; but as we are ordered away——"

"When? not so soon, surely?"

"Even so; to-day, this very hour. But you see that, even in the hurry of departure, I have not forgotten my trust; this is the packet I promised you."

So saying, I placed the paper with the lock of hair within her hand, and bending downwards, pressed my lips upon her taper fingers. She hurriedly snatched her hand away, and tearing open the enclosure, took out the lock. She looked steadily for a moment at it, then at me, and again at it, and, at length, bursting into a fit of laughter, threw herself upon a chair in a very ecstasy of mirth.

"Why you don't mean to impose this auburn ringlet upon me for one of poor Howard's jetty curls? What downright folly to think of it! and then, with how little taste the deception was practised— upon your very temples, too! One comfort is, you are utterly spoiled by it."

Here she again relapsed into a fit of laughter, leaving me perfectly puzzled what to think of her, as she resumed:

"Well, tell me now, am I to reckon this as a pledge of your own allegiance, or am I still to believe it to be Edward Howard's? Speak, and truly."

"Of my own, most certainly," said I, "if it will be accepted."

"Why, after such treachery, perhaps it ought not; but, still, as you have already done yourself such injury, and look so very silly withal——"

"That you are even resolved to give me cause to look more so," added I.

"Exactly," said she; "for here, now, I reinstate you among my true and faithful admirers. Kneel down, sir knight! in token of which you will wear this scarf——"

A sudden start which the Donna gave at these words brought me to my feet. She was pale as death and trembling.

"What means this?" said I. "What has happened?"

She pointed with her finger towards the garden; but though her lips moved, no voice came forth. I sprang through the open window. I rushed into the copse, the only one which might afford concealment for a figure, but no one was there. After a few minutes' vain endeavor to discover any trace of an intruder, I returned to the chamber. The Donna was there still; but how changed! Her gayety and animation were gone; her pale cheek and trembling lip bespoke fear and suffering, and her cold hand lay heavily beside her.

"I thought—perhaps it was merely fancy, but I thought I saw Trevyllian beside the window."

"Impossible!" said I. "I have searched every walk and alley.

It was nothing but imagination—believe me, no more. There, be assured; think no more of it."

While I endeavored thus to reassure her, I was very far from feeling perfectly at ease myself; the whole bearing and conduct of this man had inspired me with a growing dislike of him, and I felt already half-convinced that he had established himself as a spy upon my actions.

"Then you really believe I was mistaken?" said the Donna, as she placed her hand within mine.

"Of course I do; but speak no more of it. You must not forget how few my moments are here. Already I have heard the tramp of horses without. Ah! there they are. In a moment more I shall be missed; so, once more, fairest Inez—— Nay, I beg pardon if I have dared to call you thus; but think, if it be the first, it may also be the last time I shall ever speak it."

Her head gently drooped as I said these words, till it sunk upon my shoulder, her long and heavy hair falling upon my neck and across my bosom. I felt her heart almost beat against my side. I muttered some words, I know not what; I felt them like a prayer. I pressed her cold forehead to my lips, rushed from the room, cleared the fence at a spring, and was far upon the road to Lisbon ere I could sufficiently collect my senses to know whither I was going. Of little else was I conscious; my heart was full to bursting, and, in the confusion of my excited brain, fiction and reality were so inextricably mingled as to defy every endeavor at discrimination. But little time had I for reflection; as I reached the city, the brigade to which I was attached was already under arms, and Mike impatiently waiting my arrival with the horses.

CHAPTER XLIII.

THE MARCH.

WHAT a strange spectacle did the road to Oliveira present upon the morning of the 7th of May! A hurried or incautious observer might at first sight have pronounced the long line of troops which wended their way through the valley as the remains of a broken and routed army, had not the ardent expression and bright eye that beamed on every side assured him that men who looked thus could not be beaten ones. Horse, foot, baggage, artillery, dismounted dragoons, even the pale and scarcely-recovered inhabitants of the hospital, might have been seen hurrying on; for the order, "Forward!" had been given at Lisbon, and those whose wounds did not permit their joining were more pitied for their loss than its cause. More than one officer was seen at the head of his troop with an arm in a sling, or a bandaged forehead; while among the men similar evidences of devotion were not unfrequent. As for me, long years and many reverses have not obliterated—scarcely blunted—the impression that sight made on me. The splendid spectacle of a review had often excited and delighted me; but here there was the glorious reality of war,—the bronzed faces, the worn uniforms, the well-tattered flags, the roll of the heavy guns mingling with the wild pibroch of the Highlander, or scarcely less wild recklessness of the Irish quickstep; while the long line of cavalry, their helmets and accoutrements shining in the morning sun, brought back one's boyish dreams of joust and tournament, and made the heart beat high with chivalrous enthusiasm.

"Yes," said I, half aloud, "this is indeed a realization of what I longed and thirsted for," the clang of the music and the tramp of the cavalry responding to my throbbing pulses as we moved along.

"Close up there,—trot!" cried out a deep and manly voice, and immediately a general officer rode by, followed by an aide-de-camp.

"There goes Cotton," said Power; "you may feel easy in your mind now, Charley; there's some work before us."

"You have not heard our destination?" said I.

"Nothing is yet known for certain. The report goes that Soult is advancing upon Oporto, and the chances are that Sir Arthur intends to hasten on to its relief. Our fellows are at Ovar, with General Murray."

"I say, Charley, old Monsoon is in a devil of a flurry. He expected to have been peaceably settled down in Lisbon for the next six months, and he has received orders to set out for Beresford's head-quarters immediately; and from what I hear, they have no idle time."

. "Well, Sparks, how goes it, man? Better fun this than the cook's galley, eh?"

"Why, do you know, these hurried movements put me out confoundedly. I found Lisbon very interesting, the little I could see of it last night."

"Ah! my dear fellow, think of the lovely Andalusian lasses, with their brown transparent skins and liquid eyes; why, you'd have been over head and ears in love in twenty-four hours more, had we stayed."

"Are they really so pretty?"

"Pretty!—downright lovely, man. Why, they have a way of looking at you, over their fans—just one glance, short and fleeting, but so melting, by Jove——. Then their walk—if it be not profane to call that springing, elastic gesture by such a name—why, it's regular witchcraft. Sparks, my man, I tremble for you. Do you know, by the bye that same pace of theirs is a devilish hard thing to learn? I never could come it; and yet, somehow, I was formerly rather a crack fellow at a ballet. Old Alberto used to select me for a *pas de zéphyr* among a host; but there's a kind of a hop, and a slide, and a spring—in fact, you must have been wearing petticoats for eighteen years, and have an Andalusian instep, and an india-rubber sole to your foot, or it's no use trying it. How I used to make them laugh at the old San Josef convent, formerly, by my efforts in the cause!"

"Why, how did it ever occur to you to practise it?"

"Many a man's legs have saved his head, Charley, and I put it to mine to do a similar office for me."

"True; but I never heard of a man that performed a *pas seul* before the enemy."

"Not exactly; but still you're not very wide of the mark. If you'll only wait till we reach Portalegre, I'll tell you the story; not that it is worth the delay, but talking at this brisk pace I don't admire."

"You leave a detachment here, Captain Power," said an aide-de-camp, riding hastily up; "and General Cotton requests you will send a subaltern and two sergeants forward towards Berar, to reconnoitre the pass. Franchesca's cavalry are reported in that quarter." So speaking, he dashed spurs to his horse, and was out of sight in an instant.

Power at the same moment wheeled to the rear, from which he returned in an instant, accompanied by three well-mounted light dragoons. "Sparks," said he, "now for an occasion of distinguishing yourself. You heard the order—lose no time; and as your horse is an able one, and fresh, lose not a second, but forward."

No sooner was Sparks despatched on what it was evident he felt to be anything but a pleasant duty, than I turned towards Power, and said, with some tinge of disappointment in the tone, "Well, if you really felt there was anything worth doing there—I flattered myself—that——"

"Speak out, man. That I should have sent you, eh—is it not so?"

"Yes, you've hit it."

"Well, Charley, my peace is easily made on this head. Why, I selected Sparks simply to spare you one of the most unpleasant duties that can be imposed upon a man—a duty which, let him discharge it to the uttermost, will never be acknowledged, and the slightest failure in which will be remembered for many days against him, besides the pleasant and very probable prospect of being selected as a bull's eye for a French rifle, or carried off a prisoner; eh, Charley? there's no glory in that, devil a ray of it! Come, come, old fellow, Fred Power's not the man to keep his friend out of the *mélée* if only anything can be made by being in it. Poor Sparks, I'd swear, is as little satisfied with the arrangement as yourself, if one knew but all."

"I say, Power," said a tall, dashing-looking man of about five-and forty, with a Portuguese order on his breast—"I say, Power, dine with us at the halt."

"With pleasure, if I may bring my young friend here."

"Of course; pray introduce us."

"Major Hixley, Mr. O'Malley,—a 14th man, Hixley."

"Delighted to make your acquaintance, Mr. O'Malley. Knew a famous fellow in Ireland of your name, a certain Godfrey O'Malley, member for some county or other."

"My uncle," said I, blushing deeply, with a pleasurable feeling at even this slight praise of my oldest friend.

"Your uncle! give me your hand! By Jove, his nephew has a right to good treatment at my hands; he saved my life in the year '98. And how is old Godfrey?"

"Quite well, when I left him some months ago; a little gout now and then."

"To be sure he has; no man deserves it better; but it's a gentlemanlike gout, that merely jogs his memory in the morning of the good wine he has drunk over night. By the bye, what became of a friend of his, a devilish eccentric fellow, who held a command in the Austrian service?"

"Oh, Considine—the Count?"

"The same."

"As eccentric as ever; I left him on a visit with my uncle. And Boyle—did you know Sir Harry Boyle?"

"To be sure I did; shall I ever forget him, and his capital blunders, that kept me laughing the whole time I spent in Ireland. I was in the house when he concluded a panegyric upon a friend, by calling him 'the father to the poor, and uncle to Lord Donoughmore.'"

"He was the only man who could render by a bull what it was impossible to convey more correctly," said Power. "You've heard of his duel with Dick Toler?"

"Never; let's hear it."

"It was a bull from beginning to end. Boyle took it into his head that Dick was a person with whom he had a serious row in Cork. Dick, on the other hand, mistook Boyle for Old Caples, whom he had been pursuing with horse-whipping intentions for some months; they met in Kildare street Club, and very little colloquy satisfied them that they were right in their conjectures, each party being so eagerly ready to meet the views of the other. It never was a difficult matter to find a friend in Dublin; and to do them justice, Irish seconds, generally speaking, are perfectly free from any imputation upon the score of mere delay. No men have less impertinent curiosity as to the cause of the quarrel; wisely supposing that the principals know their own affairs best, they cautiously abstain from indulging any prying spirit, but proceed to discharge their functions as best they may. Accordingly, Sir Harry and Dick were 'set up,' as the phrase is, at twelve paces, and, to use Boyle's own words, for I have heard him relate the story,—

"' We blazed away, sir, for three rounds. I put two in his hat, and one in his neckcloth; his shots went all through the skirt of my coat.'

"' We'll spend the day here,' says Considine, ' at this rate. Couldn't you put them closer?'

"' And give us a little more time in the word,' says I.

"' Exactly,' said Dick.

"Well, they moved us forward two paces, and set to loading the pistols again.

"By this time we were so near, that we had full opportunity to scan each other's faces; well, sir, I stared at him, and he at me.

"' What!' said I.

"' Eh!' said he.

"' How's this?' said I.

"' You're not Billy Caples?' said he.

"' Devil a bit,' said I, ' nor I don't think you're Archy Devine;' and, faith, sir, so it appeared we were fighting away all the morning for nothing; for, somehow, it turned out *it was neither of us!*"

What amused me most in this anecdote was the hearing it at such a time and place. That poor Sir Harry's eccentricities should turn up for discussion on a march in Portugal was singular enough; but, after all, life is full of such incongruous incidents. I remember once supping with King Calzoo on the Blue Mountains, in Jamaica. By way of entertaining his guests, some English officers, he ordered one of his suite to sing. We were of course pleased at the opportunity of hearing an Indian war-chant, with a skull and thigh-bone accompaniment; but what was our astonishment to hear the Indian—

a ferocious-looking dog, with an awful scalp-lock, and two streaks of red paint across his chest—clear his voice well for a few seconds, and then begin, without discomposing a muscle of his gravity, "The Laird of Cockpen !" I need not say that the "Great Racoon" was a Dumfries man, who had quitted Scotland forty years before, and, with characteristic prosperity, had attained his present rank in a foreign service.

"Halt, halt !" cried a deep-toned, manly voice in the leading column, and the word was repeated from mouth to mouth to the rear.

We dismounted, and picketing our horses beneath the broad-leaved foliage of the cork-trees, stretched ourselves out at full length upon the grass, while our messmen prepared the dinner. Our party at first consisted of Hixley, Power, the Adjutant, and myself; but our number was soon increased by three officers of the 6th Foot, about to join their regiment.

"Barring the ladies,—God bless them !"—said Power, "there's no such picnics as campaigning presents ; the charms of the scenery are greatly enhanced by their coming unexpectedly on you. Your chance good fortune in the prog has an interest that no ham-and-cold-chicken affair, prepared by your servants beforehand, and got ready with a degree of fuss and worry that converts the whole party into an assembly of cooks, can ever afford ; and, lastly, the excitement that this same life of ours is never without, gives a zest——"

"There you've hit it," cried Hixley ; "it's that same feeling of uncertainty that those who meet now may never do so again, full as it is of sorrowful reflection, that still teaches us, as we become inured to war, to economize our pleasures, and to be happy when we may. Your health, O'Malley, and your uncle Godfrey's, too."

"A little more of the pastry ?"

"What a capital guinea fowl this is !"

"That's some of old Monsoon's old particular port."

"Pass it round here ; really this is pleasant."

"My blessing on the man who left that vista yonder ; see what a glorious valley stretches out there, undulating in its richness ; and look at those dark trees, where just one streak of soft sunlight is kissing their tops, giving them one chaste good night——"

"Well done, Power !"

"Confound you, you've pulled me short, and I was about becoming downright pastoral. *À propos* of kissing, I understand Sir Arthur won't allow the convents to be occupied by troops."

"And *à propos* of convents," said I, "let's hear your story ; you promised it a while ago."

"My dear Charley, it's far too early in the evening for a story ; I should rather indulge my poetic fancies here, under the shade of melancholy boughs. And, besides, I am not half screwed up yet!"

"Come, Adjutant, let's have a song."

"I'll sing you a Portuguese serenade when the next bottle comes in. What capital port! Have you much of it?"

"Only three dozen. We got it late last night; forged an order from the commanding officer, and sent it up to old Monsoon—'for hospital use.' He gave it with a tear in his eye, saying, as the sergeant marched away, 'Only think of such wine for fellows that may be in the next world before morning. It's a downright sin!'"

"I say, Power, there's something going on there."

At this instant the trumpet sounded "boot and saddle," and, like one man, the whole mass rose up, when the scene, late so tranquil, became one of excited bustle and confusion. An aide-de-camp galloped past towards the river, followed by two orderly sergeants, and the next moment Sparks rode up, his whole equipment giving evidence of a hurried ride, while his cheek was deadly pale and haggard.

Power presented to him a goblet of sherry, which having emptied at a draught, he drew a long breath and said,—

"They are coming—coming in force."

"Who are coming?" said Power. "Take time, man, and collect yourself."

"The French! I saw them a devilish deal closer than I liked; they wounded one of the orderlies and took the other prisoner."

"Forward!" cried out a hoarse voice in the front. "March—trot!"

Before we could obtain any further information from Sparks, whose faculties seemed to have received a terrific shock, we were once more in the saddle, and moving onward at a brisk pace.

Sparks had barely time to tell us that a large body of French cavalry occupied the pass of Berar, when he was sent for by General Cotton to finish his report.

"How frightened the fellow is!" said Hixley.

"I don't think the worse of poor Sparks for all that," said Power; "he saw these fellows for the first time, and no bird's-eye view of them either."

"Then we are in for a skirmish, at least," said I.

"It would appear not from that," said Hixley, pointing to the head of the column, which, leaving the high road upon the left, entered the forest by a deep cleft that opened upon a valley traversed by a broad river.

"That looks very like taking up a position, though," said Power.

"Look—look down yonder!" cried Hixley, pointing to a dip in the plain beside the river; "is there not a cavalry picket there?"

"Right, by Jove! I say, Fitzroy," said Power to an aide-de-camp as he passed; "what's going on?"

"Soult has carried Oporto," cried he, "and Franchesca's cavalry have escaped."

"And who are these fellows in the valley?"

"Our own people coming up."

In less than half an hour's brisk trotting we reached the stream, the banks of which were occupied by two cavalry regiments, advancing to the main army; and what was my delight to find that one of them was our own corps, the 14th Light Dragoons.

"Hurrah!" cried Power, waving his cap as he came up. "How are you, Sedgwick? Baker, my hearty, how goes it? How are Hampton and the Colonel?"

In an instant we were surrounded by our brother officers, who all shook me cordially by the hand, and welcomed me to the regiment with most gratifying warmth.

"One of us," said Power, with a knowing look, as he introduced me, and the freemasonry of these few words secured me a hearty greeting.

"Halt! halt! Dismount!" sounded again from front to rear; and in a few minutes we were once more stretched upon the grass, beneath the deep and mellow moonlight, while the bright stream ran placidly beside us, reflecting on its calm surface the varied groups as they lounged or sat around the blazing fires of the bivouac.

CHAPTER XLIV.

THE BIVOUAC.

WHEN I contrasted the gay and lively tone of the conversation which ran on around our bivouac fire with the dry monotony and prosaic tediousness of my first military dinner at Cork, I felt how much the spirit and adventure of a soldier's life can impart of chivalrous enthusiasm to even the dullest and least susceptible. I saw even many who under common circumstances would have possessed no interest, nor excited any curiosity, but now, connected as they were with the great events occurring around them, absolutely became heroes; and it was with a strange, wild throbbing of excitement that I listened to the details of movements and marches, whose objects I knew not, but in which the magical words Corunna, Vimeira, were mixed up, and gave to the circumstances an interest of the highest character. How proud, too, I felt to be the companions in arms of such fellows! Here they sat, the tried and proved soldiers of a hundred fights, treating me as their brother and their equal. Who need wonder if I felt a sense of excited pleasure? Had I needed such a stimulant, that night beneath the cork-trees had been enough to arouse a passion for the army in my heart, and an irrepressible determination to seek for a soldier's glory.

"Fourteenth!" called out a voice from the wood behind, and in a moment after the aide-de-camp appeared with a mounted orderly.

"Colonel Merivale?" said he, touching his cap to the stalwart, soldier-like figure before him.

The Colonel bowed.

"Sir Stapleton Cotton desires me to request that at an early hour to-morrow you will occupy the pass, and cover the march of the troops. It is his wish that all the reinforcements should arrive at Oporto by noon. I need scarcely add that we expect to be engaged with the enemy."

These few words were spoken hurriedly, and, again saluting our party, he turned his horse's head and continued his way towards the rear.

"There's news for you, Charley," said Power, slapping me on the shoulder. "Lucy Dashwood or Westminster Abbey!"

"The regiment never was in finer condition, that's certain," said the Colonel, "and most eager for a brush with the enemy."

"How your old friend the Count would have liked this work" said Hixley; "gallant fellow he was."

"Come," cried Power, "here's a fresh bowl coming. Let's drink to the ladies, wherever they be; we most of us have some soft spot on that score."

"Yes," said the Adjutant, singing:

> "'Here's to the maiden of blushing fifteen,
> Here's to the damsel that's merry,
> Here's to the flaunting, extravagant quean——"

"And," said Power, interrupting,—

> "Here's to the 'Widow of Derry.'"

"Come, come, Fred, no more quizzing on that score. It's the only thing ever gives me a distaste to the service, the souvenir of that adventure. When I reflect what I might have been, and think what I am,—when I contrast a Brussels carpet with wet grass, silk hangings with a canvas tent, Sneyd's claret with ration brandy, and Sir Arthur for a Commander-in-Chief *vice* Boggs, a widow ——"

"Stop there," cried Hixley; "without disparaging the fair widow, there's nothing beats campaigning, after all: eh, Fred?"

"And to prove it," said the Colonel, "Power will sing us a song."

Power took his pencil from his pocket, and, placing the back of a letter across his shako, commenced inditing his lyric; saying, as he did so,—

"I'm your man in five minutes: just fill my glass in the meantime."

"That fellow beats Dibdin hollow," whispered the Adjutant. "I'll be hanged if he'll not knock you off a song like lightning."

"I understand," said Hixley, "they have some intention at the Horse Guards of having all the general orders set to popular tunes, and sung at every mess in the service. You've heard that, I suppose, Sparks?"

"I confess I had not before."

"It will certainly come very hard upon the subalterns," continued Hixley, with much gravity; "they'll have to brush up their *sol, mi, fas;* all the solos are to be their part."

"What rhymes with slaughter?" said Power.

"Brandy-and-water," said the Adjutant.

"Now, then," said Power, "are you all ready?"

"Ready!"

"You must chorus, mind; and, mark me, take care you give the hip, hip, hurrah! well, as that's the whole force of the chant. Take the time from me. Now for it. Air, 'Garryowen,' with spirit, but not too quick:—

> "Now that we've pledged each eye of blue,
> And every maiden fair and true,
> And our green island home—to you
> The ocean's waves adorning,
> Let's give one hip, hip, hip, hurrah!
> And drink e'en to the coming day,
> When, squadron square,
> We'll all be there,
> To meet the French in the morning.

> "May his bright laurels never fade,
> Who leads our fighting fifth brigade,
> Those lads so true in heart and blade,
> And famed for danger scorning:
> So join me in one hip, hurrah!
> And drink e'en to the coming day,
> When, squadron square,
> We'll all be there,
> To meet the French in the morning.

"And, when with years and honors crowned,
You sit some homeward hearth around,
And hear no more the stirring sound
That spoke the trumpet's warning,—
You'll fill, and drink, one hip, hurrah!
And pledge the memory of the day,
When, squadron square,
They all were there,
To meet the French in the morning."

"Gloriously done, Fred!" cried Hixley. "If I ever get my deserts in this world, I'll make you Laureate to the Forces, with a hogshead of your own native whisky for every victory of the army."

"A devilish good chant," said Merivale; "but the air surpasses anything I ever heard: thoroughly Irish, I take it."

"Irish! upon my conscience, I believe you!" shouted O'Shaughnessy, with an energy of voice and manner that created a hearty laugh on all sides. "It's few people ever mistook it for a Venetian melody. Hand over the punch—the sherry I mean. When I was in the Clare militia, we always went in to dinner to 'Tatter Jack Walsh,' a sweet air, and had 'Garryowen' for a quickstep. Ould M'Manus, when he got the regiment, wanted to change; he said they were d— vulgar tunes, and wanted to have 'Rule Britannia,' or the 'Hundredth Psalm;' but we would not stand it; there would have been a mutiny in the corps."

"The same fellow, wasn't he, that you told the story of, the other evening, in Lisbon?" said I.

"The same. Well, what a character he was! As pompous and conceited a little fellow as ever you met with; and then, he was so bullied by his wife, he always came down to revenge it on the regiment. She was a fine, showy, vulgar woman, with a most cherishing affection for all the good things in this life, except her husband, whom she certainly held in due contempt. 'Ye little crayture,' she'd say to him with a sneer, 'it ill becomes you to drink and sing, and be making a man of yourself. If you were like O'Shaughnessy there, six foot three in his stockings——' Well, well, it looks like boasting; but no matter: here's her health, anyway"

"I knew you were tender in that quarter," said Power, "I heard it when quartered in Limerick."

"Maybe you heard, too, how I paid off Mac, when he came down on a visit to that county."

"Never; let's hear it now."

"Ay, O'Shaughnessy, now's your time; the fire's a good one, the night fine, the liquor plenty."

"I'm *convanient*," said O'Shaughnessy, as, depositing his enormous legs on each side of the burning fagots, and placing a bottle between his knees, he began his story :—

"It was a cold rainy night in January, in the year '98, I took my place in the Limerick mail, to go down for a few days to the west country. As the waiter of the Hibernian came to the door with a lantern, I just caught a glimpse of the other insides, none of whom were known to me, except Colonel M'Manus, that I met once in a boarding-house in Molesworth street. I did not at the time think him a very agreeable companion; but, when morning broke, and we began to pay our respects to each other in the coach, I leaned over, and said, 'I hope you're well, Colonel M'Manus,' just by way of civility like. He didn't hear me at first; so that I said it again, a little louder.

"I wish you saw the look he gave me; he drew himself up to the height of his cotton umbrella, put his chin inside his cravat, pursed up his dry, shrivelled lips, and, with a voice he meant to be awful, replied,—

"'You appear to have the advantage of me.'

"'Upon my conscience, you're right,' said I, looking down at myself, and then over at him, at which the other travellers burst out a-laughing—'I think there's few will dispute that point.' When the laugh was over, I resumed—for I was determined not to let him off so easily. 'Sure I met you at Mrs. Cayle's,' said I; 'and by the same token—it was a Friday, I remember it well,—maybe you didn't pitch into the salt cod? I hope it didn't disagree with you ?'

"'I beg to repeat, sir, that you are under a mistake,' said he.

"'Maybe so, indeed,' said I. 'Maybe you're not Colonel M'Manus at all; maybe you wasn't in a passion for losing seven-and-six-pence at loo with Mrs. Moriarty; maybe you didn't break the lamp in the hall with your umbrella, pretending you touched it with your head, and wasn't within three foot of it; maybe Counsellor Brady wasn't going to put you in the box of the Foundling Hospital, if you wouldn't behave quietly in the streets——'

"Well, with this the others laughed so heartily that I could not go on; and the next stage the bold Colonel got outside with the guard, and never came in till we reached Limerick. I'll never forget his face, as he got down at Swinburne's Hotel. 'Good-bye, Colonel,' said I; but he wouldn't take the least notice of my politeness, but, with a frown of utter defiance, he turned on his heel and walked away.

"'I haven't done with you yet,' says I; and, faith, I kept my word.

"I hadn't gone ten yards down the street, when I met my old friend Darby O'Grady.

"'Shaugh, my boy,' says he,—he called me that way for short-ness,—'dine with me to-day at Mosey's: a green goose and goose-berries; six to a minute.'

"'Who have you?' says I.

"'Tom Keane and the Wallers, a counsellor or two, and one M'Manus, from Dublin.'

"'The Colonel?'

"'The same,' said he.

"'I'm there, Darby!' said I; 'but mind, you never saw me before.'

"'What!' said he.

"'You never set eyes on me before; mind that.'

"'I understand,' said Darby, with a wink; and we parted.

"I certainly was never very particular about dressing for dinner, but on this day I spent a considerable time at my toilette, and when I looked in my glass at its completion, was well satisfied that I had done myself justice. A waistcoat of brown rabbit-skin with flaps, a red worsted comforter round my neck, an old gray shooting-jacket, with a brown patch on the arm, corduroys and leather gaiters, with a tremendous oak cudgel in my hand, made me a most presentable figure for a dinner-party.

"'Will I do, Darby?' says I, as he came into my room before dinner.

"'If it's for robbing the mail you are,' says he, 'nothing could be better. Your father wouldn't know you!'

"'Would I be the better of a wig?'

"'Leave your hair alone,' said he. 'It's painting the lily to alter it.'

"'Well, God's will be done,' said I, 'so come now.'

"Well, just as the clock struck six I saw the Colonel come out of his room, in a suit of most accurate sable, stockings, and pumps. Down stairs he went, and I heard the waiter announce him.

"'Now's my time,' thought I, as I followed slowly after.

"When I reached the door, I heard several voices within, among which I recognized some ladies. Darby had not told me about them; 'but no matter,' said I; 'it's all as well;' so I gave a gentle tap at the door with my knuckles.

"'Come in,' said Darby.

"I opened the door slowly, and putting in only my head and shoulders, took a cautious look round the room.

"'I beg pardon, gentlemen,' said I, 'but I was only looking for one Colonel M'Manus, and as he is not here——'

"'Pray walk in, sir,' said O'Grady, with a polite bow. 'Colonel M'Manus is here. There's no intrusion whatever. I say, Colonel,' said he, turning round, 'a gentleman here desires to——'

"'Never mind it now,' said I, as I stepped cautiously into the room; 'he's going to dinner; another time will do just as well.'

"'Pray come in.'

"'I could not think of intruding——'

"'I must protest,' said M'Manus, coloring up, 'that I cannot understand this gentleman's visit.'

"'It's a little affair I have to settle with him,' said I, with a fierce look, that I saw produced its effect.

"'Then perhaps you would do me the very great favor to join him at dinner,' said O'Grady. 'Any friend of Colonel M'Manus——'

"'You are really too good,' said I; 'but as an utter stranger——'

"'Never think of that for a moment. My friend's friend, as the adage says.'

"'Upon my conscience, a good saying,' said I, 'but you see there's another difficulty. I've ordered a chop and potatoes up in No. 5.'

"'Let that be no obstacle,' said O'Grady. 'The waiter shall put it in my bill, if you will only do me the pleasure.'

"'You're a trump,' said I. 'What's your name?'

"'O'Grady, at your service.'

"'Any relation of the counsellor?' said I. 'They're all one family, the O'Gradys. I'm Mr. O'Shaughnessy, from Ennis; won't you introduce me to the ladies?'

"While the ceremony of presentation was going on, I caught one glance at M'Manus, and had hard work not to roar out laughing. Such an expression of surprise, amazement, indignation, rage, and misery, never was mixed up in one face before. Speak he could not; and I saw that, except for myself, he had neither eyes, ears, nor senses for anything around him. Just at this moment dinner was announced, and in we went. I never was in such spirits in my life; the trick upon M'Manus had succeeded perfectly; he believed in his heart that I had never met O'Grady in my life before, and that, upon the faith of our friendship, I had received my invitation. As for me, I spared him but little. I kept up a running fire of droll stories; had the ladies in fits of laughing, made everlasting allusions to the Colonel; in a word, ere the soup had disappeared, except himself, the company were entirely with me.

"'O'Grady,' said I, 'forgive the freedom, but I feel as if we were old acquaintances.'

"'As Colonel M'Manus's friend,' said he, 'you can take no liberty here to which you are not perfectly welcome.'

"'Just what I expected,' said I. 'Mac and I,'—I wish you saw his face when I called him Mac—'Mac and I were schoolfellows five-and-thirty years ago; though he forgets me, I don't forget him; to

19

be sure it would be hard for me. I'm just thinking of the day Bishop Oulahan came over to visit the college. Mac was coming in at the door of the refectory as the Bishop was going out. 'Take off your caubeen, you young scoundrel, and kneel down for his reverence to bless you,' said one of the masters, giving his hat a blow at the same moment that sent it flying to the other end of the room, and with it about twenty ripe pears that Mac had just stolen in the orchard, and had in his hat. I wish you only saw the Bishop; and Mac himself he was a picture. Well, well, you forget it all now, but I remember it as if it was only yesterday. Any champagne, Mr. O'Grady? I'm mighty dry.'

" 'Of course,' said Darby. 'Waiter, some champagne here.'

" 'Ah, it's himself was the boy for every kind of fun and devilment, quiet and demure as he looks over there. Mac, your health. It's not every day of the week we get champagne.'

"He laid down his knife and fork as I said this: his face and temples grew deep purple, his eyes started as if they would spring from his head, and he put both his hands to his forehead, as if trying to assure himself that it was not some horrid dream.

" 'A little slice more of the turkey,' said I, 'and then, O'Grady, I'll try your hock. It's a wine I'm mighty fond of, and so is Mac there. Oh! it's seldom, to tell you the truth, it troubles us. There, fill up the glass; that's it. Here now, Darby—that's your name, I think—you'll not think I'm taking a liberty in giving a toast. Here, then, I'll give M'Manus's health, with all the honors; though it's early yet, to be sure, but we'll do it again, by-and-by, when the whisky comes. Here's M'Manus's good health! and, though his wife, they say, does not treat him well, and keeps him down——'

"The roar of laughing that interrupted me here was produced by the expression of poor Mac's face. He had started up from the table, and, leaning with both his hands upon it, stared round upon the company like a maniac—his mouth and eyes wide open, and his hair actually bristling with amazement. Thus he remained for a full minute, gasping like a fish in a landing-net. It seemed a hard struggle for him to believe he was not deranged. At last his eyes fell upon me; he uttered a deep groan, and with a voice tremulous with rage, thundered out:

" 'The scoundrel! I never saw him before.'

"He rushed from the room and gained the street. Before our roar of laughter was over he had secured post-horses, and was galloping towards Ennis at the top speed of his cattle.

"He exchanged at once into the line; but they say that he caught a glimpse of my name in the army list, and sold out the next morning; be that as it may, we never met since."

I have related O'Shaughnessy's story here, rather from the memory I have of how we all laughed at it at the time, than from any feeling as to its real desert; but when I think of the voice, look, accent, and gesture of the narrator, I can scarcely keep myself from again giving way to laughter.

CHAPTER XLV.

THE DOURO.

NEVER did the morning break more beautifully than on the 12th of May, 1809. Huge masses of fog-like vapor had succeeded to the starry, cloudless night, but one by one they moved onwards towards the sea, disclosing, as they passed, long tracts of lovely country, bathed in a rich golden glow. The broad Douro, with its transparent current, shone out like a bright-colored ribbon, meandering through the deep garment of fairest green ; the darkly-shadowed mountains, which closed the background, loomed even larger than they were, while the summits were tipped with the yellow glory of the morning. The air was calm and still, and the very smoke that arose from the peasant's cot labored as it ascended through the perfumed air, and, save the ripple of the stream, all was silent as the grave.

The squadron of the 14th with which I was had diverged from the road beside the river, and, in order to obtain a shorter path, had entered the skirts of a dark pine wood. Our pace was a sharp one; an orderly had been already despatched to hasten our arrival, and we pressed on at a brisk trot. In less than' an hour we reached the verge of the wood, and as we rode out upon the plain, what a spectacle met our eyes! Before us, in a narrow valley, separated from the river by a low ridge, were picketed three cavalry regiments, their noiseless gestures and perfect stillness bespeaking at once that they were intended for a surprise party. Farther down the stream, and upon the opposite side, rose the massive towers and tall spires of Oporto, displaying from their summits the broad ensign of France; while, far as the eye could reach, the broad dark masses of troops might be seen, the intervals between the columns glittering with the bright equipments of their cavalry, whose steel caps and lances were sparkling in the sunbeams. The bivouac fires were still smouldering, marking where some part of the army had passed the night; for, early as it was, it was evident that their position had been changed; and even now the dark masses of infantry might be seen moving from place to place, while the long line of the road to Vallonga was marked with a vast cloud of dust. The French drum and the light infantry bugle told from time to time that orders were passing among the troops, while the glittering uniform of a staff officer, as he galloped from the town, bespoke the note of preparation.

"Dismount! Steady—quietly, my lads," said the Colonel, as he alighted upon the grass. "Let the men have their breakfast."

The little amphitheatre we occupied hid us entirely from all observation on the part of the enemy, but equally so excluded us from perceiving their movements. It may readily be supposed, then, with what impatience we waited here, while the din and clangor of the French force, as they marched and countermarched so near us, were clearly audible. The orders were, however, strict that none should approach the bank of the river, and we lay anxiously awaiting the moment when this inactivity should cease. More than one orderly had arrived among us, bearing despatches from head-quarters; but where our main body was, or what the nature of the orders, no one could guess. As for me, my excitement was at its height, and I could not speak for the very tension of my nerves. The officers stood in little groups of two and three, whispering anxiously together; but all I could collect was, that Soult had already begun his retreat upon Amarante, and that, with the broad stream of the Douro between us, he defied our pursuit.

"Well, Charley," said Power, laying his arm upon my shoulder, "the French have given us the slip this time. They are already on the march, and even if we dared force a passage in the face of such an enemy, it seems there is not a boat to be found. I have just seen Hammersley."

"Indeed! Where is he?" said I.

"He's gone back to Villa de Conde; he asked after you most particularly. Don't blush, man; I'd rather have your chance than his, notwithstanding the long letter that Lucy sends him. Poor fellow! he has been badly wounded, but it seems declines going back to England."

"Captain Power," said an orderly, touching his cap, "General Murray desires to see you."

Power hastened away, but returned in a few moments.

"I say, Charley, there's something in the wind here. I have just been ordered to try where the stream is fordable. I've mentioned your name to the General, and I think you'll be sent for soon. Good-bye."

I buckled on my sword, and, looking to my girths, stood watching the groups around me, when suddenly a dragoon pulled his horse short up, and asked a man standing near me if Mr. O'Malley was there.

"Yes; I am he."

"Orders from General Murray, sir," said the man, and rode off at a canter.

I opened and saw that the despatch was addressed to Sir Arthur Wellesley, with the mere words "With haste!" on the envelope.

Now, which way to turn I knew not. Springing into the saddle, I galloped to where Colonel Merivale was standing talking to the colonel of a heavy dragoon regiment.

"May I ask, sir, by which road I am to proceed with this despatch?"

"Along the river, sir," said a heavy, large, dark-browed man, with a most forbidding look. "You'll soon see the troops. You'd better stir yourself, sir, or Sir Arthur is not very likely to be pleased with you."

Without venturing a reply to what I felt a somewhat unnecessary taunt, I dashed spurs into my horse, and turned towards the river. I had not gained the bank above a minute, when the loud ringing of a rifle struck upon my ear. Bang went another and another. I hurried on, however, at the top of my speed, thinking only of my mission, and its pressing haste. As I turned an angle of the stream, the vast column of the British came in sight, and scarcely had my eye rested upon them when my horse staggered forward, plunged twice with his head nearly to the earth, and then, rearing madly up, fell backward upon the ground. Crushed and bruised as I felt by my fall, I was soon aroused to the necessity of exertion; for as I disengaged myself from the poor beast, I discovered that he had been killed by a bullet in the counter; and scarcely had I recovered my legs, when a shot struck my shako and grazed my temples. I quickly threw myself to the ground, and creeping on for some yards, reached at last some rising ground, from which I rolled gently downward into a little declivity, sheltered by the bank from the French fire.

When I arrived at head-quarters, I was dreadfully fatigued and heated; but, resolving not to rest till I had delivered my despatches, I hastened towards the convent of La Sierra, where I was told the Commander-in-Chief was.

As I came into the court of the convent, filled with general officers and people of the staff, I was turning to ask how I should proceed, when Hixley caught my eye.

"Well, O'Malley, what brings you here?"

"Despatches from General Murray."

"Indeed; oh! follow me."

He hurried me rapidly through the buzzing crowd, and ascending a large gloomy stair, introduced me into a room, where about a dozen persons in uniform were writing at a long deal table.

"Captain Gordon," said he, addressing one of them, "despatches requiring immediate attention have just been brought by this officer."

Before the sentence was finished, the door opened, and a short, slight man, in a gray undress coat, with a white cravat and a cocked hat, entered. The dead silence that ensued was not necessary to assure me that he was one in authority. The look of command his bold and stern features presented, the sharp, piercing eye, the compressed lip, the impressive expression of the whole face, told plainly that he was one who held equally himself and others in mastery.

"Send General Sherbrooke here," said he to an aide-de-camp. "Let the light brigade march into position;" and then, turning suddenly to me, "Whose despatches are these?"

"General Murray's, sir."

I needed no more than that look to assure me that this was he of whom I had heard so much, and of whom the world was still to hear so much more.

He opened them quickly, and glancing his eye across the contents, crushed the paper in his hand. Just as he did so, a spot of blood upon the envelope attracted his attention.

"How's this—are you wounded?"

"No, sir; my horse was killed——"

"Very well, sir; join your brigade. But stay, I shall have orders for you. Well, Waters, what news?"

This question was addressed to an officer in a staff uniform, who entered at the moment, followed by the short and bulky figure of a monk, his shaven crown and large cassock strongly contrasting with the gorgeous glitter of the costumes around him.

"I say, who have we here?"

"The Prior of Amarante, sir," replied Waters, "who has just come over. We have already, by his aid, secured three large barges——"

"Let the artillery take up position in the convent at once," said Sir Arthur, interrupting. "The boats will be brought round to the small creek beneath the orchard. You, sir," turning to me, "will convey to General Murray—but you appear weak—— You, Gordon, will desire Murray to effect a crossing at Avintas with the Germans and the 14th. Sherbrooke's division will occupy the Villa Nuova. What number of men can that seminary take?"

"From three to four hundred, sir. The padre mentions that

all the vigilance of the enemy is limited to the river below the town."

"I perceive it," was the short reply of Sir Arthur, as, placing his hands carelessly behind his back, he walked towards the window, and looked out upon the river.

All was still as death in the chamber; not a lip murmured. The feeling of respect for him in whose presence we were standing checked every thought of utterance, while the stupendous gravity of the events before us engrossed every mind and occupied every heart. I was standing near the window; the effect of my fall had stunned me for a time, but I was gradually recovering, and watched with a thrilling heart the scene before me. Great and absorbing as was my interest in what was passing without, it was nothing compared with what I felt as I looked at him upon whom our destiny was then hanging. I had ample time to scan his features and canvass their every lineament. Never before did I look upon such perfect impassibility; the cold, determined expression was crossed by no show of passion or impatience. All was rigid and motionless, and whatever might have been the workings of the spirit within, certainly no external sign betrayed them; and yet what a moment for him must that have been! Before him, separated by a deep and rapid river, lay the conquering legions of France, led on by one second alone to him whose very name had been the prestige of victory. Unprovided with every regular means of transport, in the broad glare of day, in open defiance of their serried ranks and thundering artillery, he dared the deed. What must have been his confidence in the soldiers he commanded! What must have been his reliance upon his own genius! As such thoughts rushed through my mind, the door opened, and an officer entered hastily. After whispering a few words to Colonel Waters, he left the room.

"One boat is already brought up to the crossing-place, and entirely concealed by the wall of the orchard."

"Let the men cross," was the brief reply.

No other word was spoken as, turning from the window, he closed his telescope, and, followed by all the others, descended to the court-yard.

This simple order was enough; an officer, with a company of the Buffs, embarked, and thus began the passage of the Douro.

So engrossed was I in my vigilant observation of our leader, that I would gladly have remained at the convent, when I received an order to join my brigade, to which a detachment of artillery was already proceeding.

As I reached Avintas, all was in motion. The cavalry was in readiness beside the river; but as yet no boats had been discovered,

and such was the impatience of the men to cross, it was with difficulty they were prevented trying the passage by swimming, when
suddenly Power appeared, followed by several fishermen. Three or
four small skiffs had been found, half sunk in mud, among the
rushes, and with such frail assistance we commenced to cross.

"There will be something to write home to Galway soon,
Charley, or I'm terribly mistaken," said Fred, as he sprang into
the boat beside me. "Was I not a true prophet when I told you
'We'd meet the French in the morning?'"

"They're at it already," said Hixley, as a wreath of blue smoke
floated across the stream below us, and the loud boom of a large gun
resounded through the air.

Then came a deafening shout, followed by a rattling volley of
small arms, gradually swelling into a hot, sustained fire, through
which the cannon pealed at intervals. Several large meadows lay
along the river-side, where our brigade was drawn up as the detachments landed from the boats; and here, although nearly a league
distant from the town, we now heard the din and crash of battle,
which increased every moment. The cannonade from the Sierra
convent, which at first was merely the fire of single guns, now thundered away in one long roll, amid which the sounds of falling walls
and crashing roofs were mingled. It was evident to us, from the
continual fire kept up, that the landing had been effected, while the
swelling tide of musketry told that fresh troops were momentarily
coming up.

In less than twenty minutes our brigade was formed, and we now
only waited for two light four-pounders to be landed, when an officer
galloped up in haste, and called out,—

"The French are in retreat!" and, pointing at the same moment
to the Vallonga road, we saw a long line of smoke and dust leading
from the town, through which, as we gazed, the colors of the enemy
might be seen as they defiled, while the unbroken lines of the wagons
and heavy baggage proved that it was no partial movement, but the
army itself retreating.

"Fourteenth, threes about, close up, trot!" called out the loud
and manly voice of our leader, and the heavy tramp of our squadrons shook the very ground, as we advanced towards the road to Vallonga.

As we came on, the scene became one of overwhelming excitement; the masses of the enemy that poured unceasingly from the
town could now be distinguished more clearly; and, amid all the
crash of gun-carriages and caissons, the voices of the staff officers
rose high as they hurried along the retreating battalions. A troop
of flying artillery galloped forth at top speed, and, wheeling their

guns into position with the speed of lightning, prepared by a flanking fire to cover the retiring column. The gunners sprang from their seats, the guns were already unlimbered, when Sir George Murray, riding up at our left, called out,—

"Forward—close up—charge !"

The word was scarcely spoken, when the loud cheer answered the welcome sound, and the same instant the long line of shining helmets passed with the speed of a whirlwind; the pace increased at every stride, the ranks grew closer, and, like the dread force of some mighty engine, we fell upon the foe. I have felt all the glorious enthusiasm of a fox-hunt, when the loud cry of the hounds, answered by the cheers of the joyous huntsman, stirred the very heart within, but never till now did I know how far higher the excitement reaches when, man to man, sabre to sabre, arm to arm, we ride forward to the battle-field. On we went, the loud shout of " Forward !" still ringing in our ears. One broken, irregular discharge from the French guns shook the head of our advancing column, but stayed us not as we galloped madly on.

I remember no more. The din, the smoke, the crash—the cry for quarter, mingled with the shout of victory—the flying enemy—the agonizing shrieks of the wounded—all are commingled in my mind, but leave no trace of clearness or connection between them ; and it was only when the column wheeled to re-form, behind the advancing squadrons, that I awoke from my trance of maddening excitement, and perceived that we had carried the position, and cut off the guns of the enemy.

" Well done, 14th !" said an old gray-headed colonel, as he rode along our line—"gallantly done, lads !" The blood trickled from a sabre-cut on his temple, along his cheek, as he spoke; but he either knew it not or heeded it not.

"There go the Germans !" said Power, pointing to the remainder of our brigade, as they charged furiously upon the French infantry, and rode them down in masses.

Our guns came up at this time, and a plunging fire was opened upon the thick and retreating ranks of the enemy. The carnage must have been terrific, for the long breaches in their lines showed where the squadrons of the cavalry had passed, or the most destructive tide of the artillery had swept through them. The speed of the flying columns momentarily increased ; the road became blocked up, too, by broken carriages and wounded ; and, to add to their discomfiture, a damaging fire now opened from the town upon the retreating columns, while the brigade of Guards and the 29th pressed hotly on their rear.

The scene was now beyond anything maddening in its interest.

From the walls of Oporto the English infantry poured forth in pursuit, while the whole river was covered with boats, as they still continued to cross over. The artillery thundered from the Sierra, to protect the landing, for it was even still contested, in places; and the cavalry, charging in flank, swept the broken ranks, and bore down upon the squares.

It was now, when the full tide of victory ran highest in our favor, that we were ordered to retire from the road. Column after column passed before us, unmolested and unassailed, and not even a cannon-shot arrested their steps.

Some unaccountable timidity of our leader directed this movement; and while before our very eyes the gallant infantry were charging the retiring columns, we remained still and inactive.

How little did the sense of praise we had already won repay us for the shame and indignation we experienced at this moment, as, with burning cheek and compressed lip, we watched the retreating files. "What can he mean?" "Is there not some mistake?" "Are we never to charge?" were the muttered questions around, as a staff officer galloped up with the order to take ground still further back, and nearer to the river.

The word was scarcely spoken, when a young officer, in the uniform of a general, dashed impetuously up; he held his plumed cap high above his head, as he called out, "14th, follow me! Left face— wheel—charge!"

So, with the word, we were upon them. The French rear-guard was at this moment at the narrowest part of the road which opened by a bridge upon a large open space; so that, forming with a narrow front, and favored by a declivity in the ground, we actually rode them down. Twice the French formed, and twice were they broken. Meanwhile the carnage was dreadful on both sides; our fellows dashing madly forward where the ranks were thickest,—the enemy resisting with the stubborn courage of men fighting for their last spot of ground. So impetuous was the charge of our squadrons, that we stopped not till, piercing the dense column of the retreating mass, we reached the open ground beyond. Here we wheeled, and prepared once more to meet them; when suddenly some squadrons of Cuirassiers debouched from the road, and, supported by a field-piece, showed front against us. This was the moment that the remainder of our brigade should have come to our aid; but not a man appeared. However, there was not an instant to be lost; already the plunging fire of the four-pounder had swept through our files, and every moment increased our danger.

"Now, my lads, forward!" cried our gallant leader, Sir Charles Stewart, as, waving his sabre, he dashed into the thickest of the fray.

So sudden was our charge, that we were upon them before they were prepared. And here ensued a terrific struggle; for, as the cavalry of the enemy gave way before us, we came upon the close ranks of the infantry, at half-pistol distance, who poured a withering volley into us as we approached. But what could arrest the sweeping torrent of our brave fellows, though every moment falling in numbers?

Harvey, our major, lost his arm near the shoulder. Scarcely an officer was not wounded. Power received a deep sabre-cut in the cheek, from an aide-de-camp of General Foy, in return for a wound he gave the General; while I, in my endeavor to save General Laborde, when unhorsed, was cut down through the helmet, and so stunned that I remembered no more around me. I kept my saddle, it is true, but I lost every sense of consciousness; my first glimmering of reason coming to my aid as I lay upon the river bank, and felt my faithful follower Mike bathing my temples with water, as he kept up a running fire of lamentations for my being *murthered* so young.

"Are you better, Mister Charles? Spake to me, alanah; say that you're not kilt, darlin'; do now. Oh, wirra! what'll I ever say to the master? and you doing so beautiful! Wouldn't he give the best baste in his stable to be looking at you to-day? There, take a sup; it's only water. Bad luck to them, but it's hard work beatin' them. They're only gone now. That's right: now you're coming to."

"Where am I, Mike?"

"It's here you are, darlin', restin' yourself."

"Well, Charley, my poor fellow, you've got sore bones, too," cried Power, as, his face swathed in bandages and covered with blood, he lay down on the grass beside me. "It was a gallant thing while it lasted, but has cost us dearly. Poor Hixley——"

"What of him?" said I, anxiously.

"Poor fellow! he has seen his last battle-field. He fell across me as we came out upon the road. I lifted him up in my arms, and bore him along above fifty yards; but he was stone dead. Not a sigh, not a word escaped him; shot through the forehead." As Power spoke, his lips trembled, and his voice sank to a mere whisper at the last words,—"You remember what he said last night. Poor fellow! he was every inch a soldier."

Such was the epitaph.

I turned my head towards the scene of our late encounter. Some dismounted guns and broken wagons alone marked the spot; while, far in the distance, the dust of the retreating columns showed the beaten enemy, as they hurried towards the frontiers of Spain.

CHAPTER XLVI.

THE MORNING.

THERE are few sadder things in life than the day after a battle. The high-beating hopes, the bounding spirits, have passed away, and in their stead comes the depressing reaction by which every overwrought excitement is followed. With far different eyes do we look upon the compact ranks and glistening files,—

> "With helm arrayed,
> And lance and blade,
> And plume in the gay wind dancing!"

and upon the cold and barren heath, whose only memory of the past is the blood-stained turf, the mangled corpse, the broken gun, the shattered wall, the well-trodden earth where columns stood, the cut up ground where cavalry had charged,—these are the sad relics of all the chivalry of yesterday.

*   *   *   *   *   *   *   *

The morning which followed the battle of the Douro was one of the most beautiful I ever remember. There was that kind of freshness and elasticity in the air which certain days possess, and communicate by some magic their properties to ourselves. The thrush was singing gayly out from every grove and wooded dell; the very river had a sound of gladness, as it rippled on against its sedgy banks; the foliage, too, sparkled in the fresh dew, as in its robes of holiday, and all looked bright and happy.

We were picketed near the river, upon a gently rising ground, from which the view extended for miles in every direction. Above us, the stream came winding down amid broad and fertile fields of tall grass and waving corn, backed by deep and mellow woods, which were lost to the view upon the distant hills; below, the river, widening as it went, pursued a straighter course or turned with bolder curves, till, passing beneath the town, it spread into a large sheet of glassy water, as it opened to the sea. The sun was just rising as I looked upon this glorious scene, and already the tall spires of Oporto were tipped with a bright rosy hue, while the massive towers and dark walls threw their lengthened shadows far across the plain.

The fires of the bivouac still burned, but all slept around them. Not a sound was heard save the tramp of a patrol, or the short, quick cry of the sentry. I sat lost in meditation, or rather in that state of dreamy thoughtfulness in which the past and present are combined, and the absent are alike before us as are the things we look upon.

One moment I felt as though I were describing to my uncle the battle of the day before, pointing out where we stood and how we charged. Then, again, I was at home, beside the broad, bleak Shannon, and the brown hills of Scariff. I watched with beating heart the tall Sierra, where our path lay for the future, and then turned my thoughts to him whose name was so soon to be received in England with a nation's pride and gratitude, and panted for a soldier's glory.

As thus I followed every rising fancy, I heard a step approach. It was a figure muffled in a cavalry cloak, which I soon perceived to be Power.

"Charley!" said he, in a half whisper, "get up and come with me. You are aware of the general order, that while in pursuit of an enemy all military honors to the dead are forbidden; but we wish to place our poor comrade in the earth before we leave."

I followed down a little path, through a grove of tall beech-trees, that opened upon a little grassy terrace beside the river. A stunted olive-tree stood by itself in the midst, and there I found five of our brother officers standing, wrapped in their wide cloaks. As we pressed each other's hand, not a word was spoken. Each heart was full, and hard features, that never quailed before the foe, were now shaken with the convulsive spasm of agony, or compressed with a stern determination to seem calm.

A cavalry helmet and a large blue cloak lay upon the ground. The narrow grave was already dug beside it, and in the deathlike stillness around the service for the dead was read. The last words were over. We stooped and placed the corpse, wrapped up in the broad mantle, in the earth; we replaced the mould, and stood silently around the spot. The trumpet of our regiment at this moment sounded the call; its clear notes rang sharply through the thin air; it was the soldier's requiem! We turned away without speaking, and returned to our quarters.

I had never known poor Hixley till a day or two before; but, somehow, my grief for him was deep and heartfelt. It was not that his frank and manly bearing, his bold and military air, had gained upon me. No; these were indeed qualities to attract and delight me, but he had obtained a stronger and faster hold upon my affections—he spoke to me of home.

Of all the ties that bind us to the chance acquaintances we meet with in life, what can equal this one? What a claim upon your love has he who can, by some passing word, some fast-flitting thought, bring back the days of your youth! What interest can he not excite by some anecdote of your boyish days, some well-remembered trait of youthful daring or early enterprise! Many a year of sunshine and of storm has passed over my head. I have not been without my moments of gratified pride and rewarded ambition; but my heart has never responded so fully, so thankfully, so proudly, to these, such as they were, as to the simple, touching words of one who knew my early home, and loved its inmates.

"Well, Fitzroy, what news?" cried I, roused from my musing, as an aide-de-camp galloped up at full speed.

"Tell Merivale to get the regiment under arms at once. Sir Arthur Wellesley will be here in less than half an hour. You may look for the route immediately. Where are the Germans quartered?"

"Lower down, beside that grove of beech-trees, next the river."

Scarcely was my reply spoken, when he dashed spurs into his horse, and was soon out of sight. Meanwhile, the plain beneath me presented an animated and splendid spectacle. The different corps were falling into position to the enlivening sounds of their quickstep, the trumpets of the cavalry rang loudly through the valley, and the clatter of sabres and sabretasches, joined with the hollow tramp of the horses, as the squadron came up.

I had not a moment to lose, so, hastening back to my quarters, I found Mike waiting with my horse.

"Captain Power's before you, sir," said he, "and you'll have to make haste. The regiments are under arms already."

From the little mound where I stood, I could see the long line of cavalry as they deployed into the plain, followed by the horse artillery, which brought up the rear.

"This looks like a march," thought I, as I pressed forward to join my companions.

I had not advanced above a hundred yards, through a narrow ravine, when the measured tread of infantry fell upon my ears. I pulled up to slacken my pace, just as the head of a column turned round the angle of the road, and came in view. The tall caps of a grenadier company were the first things I beheld, as they came on without roll of drum or sound of fife. I watched with a soldier's pride the manly bearing and gallant step of the dense mass as they defiled before me. I was struck no less by them than by a certain look of a steady but sombre cast which each man wore.

"What can this mean?" thought I.

My first impression was that a military execution was about to take place; the next moment solved my doubt, for as the last files of the grenadiers wheeled round, a dense mass behind came in sight, whose unarmed hands and downcast air at once bespoke them prisoners of war.

What a sad sight it was! There was the old and weather-beaten grenadier, erect in frame and firm in step, his gray moustache scarcely concealing the scowl that curled his lip, side by side with the young and daring conscript, even yet a mere boy. Their march was regular, their gaze steadfast; no look of flinching courage there. On they came, a long unbroken line. They looked not less proudly than their captors around them. As I looked with heavy heart upon them, my attention was attracted to one who marched alone behind the rest. He was a middle-sized but handsome youth of some eighteen years at most; his light helmet and waving plume bespoke him a *chasseur à cheval*, and I could plainly perceive, in his careless, half-saucy air, how indignantly he felt the position to which the fate of war had reduced him. He caught my eyes fixed upon him, and for an instant turned upon me a gaze of open and palpable defiance, drawing himself up to his full height, and crossing his arms upon his breast; but probably perceiving in my look more of interest than of triumph, his countenance suddenly changed, a deep blush suffused his cheek, his eye beamed with a softened and kindly expression, and, carrying his hand to his helmet, he saluted me, saying, in a voice of singular sweetness,—

"Je vous souhaite un meilleur sort, camarade."

I bowed, and, muttering something in return, was about to make some inquiry concerning him, when the loud call of the trumpet rang through the valley, and apprised me that in my interest for the prisoners I had forgotten all else, and was probably incurring censure for my absence.

CHAPTER XLVII.

THE REVIEW.

WHEN I joined the group of my brother officers, who stood gayly chatting and laughing together before our lines, I was much surprised—nay, almost shocked—to find how little seeming impression had been made upon them by the sad duty we had performed that morning.

When last we met, each eye was downcast, each heart was full. Sorrow for him we had lost from amongst us forever, mingling with the awful sense of our own uncertain tenure here, had laid its impress on each brow; but now, scarcely an hour elapsed, and all were cheerful and elated. The last shovelful of earth upon the grave seemed to have buried both the dead and the mourning. And such is war! and such the temperament it forms! Events so strikingly opposite in their character and influences succeed so rapidly one upon another, that the mind is kept in one whirl of excitement, and at length accustoms itself to change with every phase of circumstances; and between joy and grief, hope and despondency, enthusiasm and depression, there is neither breadth nor interval; they follow each other as naturally as morning succeeds to night.

I had not much time for such reflections. Scarcely had I saluted the officers about me, when the loud prolonged roll of the drums along the line of infantry in the valley, followed by the sharp clatter of muskets as they were raised to the shoulder, announced that the troops were under arms, and the review begun.

"Have you seen the general order this morning, Power?" inquired an old officer beside me.

"No; they say, however, that ours are mentioned."

"Harvey is going on favorably," cried a young cornet, as he galloped up to our party.

"Take ground to the left!" sung out the clear voice of the Colonel, as he rode along in front. "Fourteenth! I am happy to inform you that your conduct has met approval in the highest quarter. I have just received the general orders, in which this occurs:—

"'The timely passage of the Douro, and subsequent movements upon the enemy's flank, by Lieutenant-General Sherbroke with the Guards and 29th Regiment, and the bravery of the two squadrons of the 14th Light Dragoons under the command of Major Harvey, and led by the Honorable Brigadier-General Charles Stewart, obtained the victory'—Mark that, my lads!—obtained the victory—'which has contributed so much to the honor of the troops on this day.'"

The words were hardly spoken, when a tremendous cheer burst from the whole line at once.

"Steady, Fourteenth! steady, lads!" said the gallant old Colonel, as he raised his hand gently; "the staff is approaching."

At the same moment, the white plumes appeared rising above the brow of the hill. On they came, glittering in all the splendor of aiguillettes and orders; all, save one. He rode foremost, upon a small compact black horse; his dress, a plain gray frock, fastened at the waist by a red sash. His cocked-hat alone bespoke, in its plume, the general officer. He galloped rapidly on till he came to the centre of the line: then, turning short round, he scanned the ranks from end to end with an eagle glance.

"Colonel Merivale, you have made known to your regiment my opinion of them, as expressed in general orders?"

The Colonel bowed low in acquiescence.

"Fitzroy, you have got the memorandum, I hope?"

The aide-de-camp here presented to Sir Arthur a slip of paper, which he continued to regard attentively for some minutes.

"Captain Powel—Power, I mean. Captain Power!"

Power rode out from the line.

"Your very distinguished conduct yesterday has been reported to me. I shall have sincere pleasure in forwarding your name for the vacant majority."

"You have forgotten, Colonel Merivale, to send in the name of the officer who saved General Laborde's life."

"I believe I have mentioned it, Sir Arthur. Mr. O'Malley."

"True, I beg pardon; so you have—Mr. O'Malley; a very young officer indeed—ha, an Irishman! the south of Ireland, eh?"

"No, sir, the west."

"Oh! yes. Well, Mr. O'Malley, you are promoted. You have the lieutenancy in your own regiment. By the bye, Merivale,"— here his voice changed into a half-laughing tone,—" ere I forget it, pray let me beg of you to look into this honest fellow's claim; he has given me no peace the entire morning."

As he spoke, I turned my eyes in the direction he pointed, and, to my utter consternation, beheld my man Mickey Free standing among the staff; the position he occupied, and the presence he stood in, having no more perceptible effect upon his nerves than if he were assisting at an Irish wake; but so completely was I overwhelmed with shame at the moment, that the staff were already far down the lines ere I recovered my self-possession, to which, certainly, I was in some degree recalled by Master Mike's addressing me in a somewhat imploring voice:

"Arrah, spake for me, Master Charles, alanah; sure they might do something for me now, av it was only to make me a gauger."

Mickey's ideas of promotion, thus insinuatingly put forward, threw the whole party around into one burst of laughter.

"I have him down there," said he, pointing as he spoke to a thick grove of cork-trees at a little distance.

"Who have you got there, Mike?" inquired Power.

"Divil a one o' me knows his name," replied he; "maybe it's Bony himself."

"And how do you know he's there still?"

"How do I know, is it? Didn't I tie him last night?"

Curiosity to find out what Mickey could possibly allude to, induced Power and myself to follow him down the slope to the clump of trees I have mentioned. As we came near, the very distinct denunciations that issued from the thicket proved pretty clearly the nature of the affair. It was nothing less than a French officer of cavalry, that Mike had unhorsed in the *mêlée*, and wishing, probably, to preserve

20

some testimony of his prowess, had made prisoner, and tied fast to a cork-tree, the preceding evening.

"Sacrebleu!" said the poor Frenchman, as we approached, "ce sont des sauvages!"

"Av it's making your sowl ye are," said Mike, "you're right; for maybe they won't let me keep you alive."

Mike's idea of a tame prisoner threw me into a fit of laughing, while Power asked,—

"And what do you want to do with him, Mickey?"

"The sorra one o' me knows, for he spakes no dacent tongue. Thighum thu," said he, addressing the prisoner, with a poke in the ribs at the same moment; "but sure, Master Charles, he might tache me French."

There was something so irresistibly ludicrous in his tone and look as he said these words, that both Power and myself absolutely roared with laughter. We began, however, to feel not a little ashamed of our position in the business, and explained to the Frenchman that our worthy countryman had but little experience in the usages of war, while we proceeded to unbind him, and liberate him from his miserable bondage.

"It's letting him loose you are, Captain! Master Charles, take care; be-gorra, av you had as much trouble in catching him as I had, you'd think twice about letting him out. Listen to me now,"—here he placed his closed fist within an inch of the poor prisoner's nose,— "listen to me; av you say peas, by the morteal, I'll not lave a whole bone in your skin."

With some difficulty we persuaded Mike that his conduct, so far from leading to his promotion, might, if known in another quarter, procure him an acquaintance with the Provost-Marshal,—a fact which, it was plain to perceive, gave him but a very poor impression of military gratitude.

"Oh, then, if they were in swarms forninst me, divil resave the prisoner I'll take again."

So saying, he slowly returned to the regiment, while Power and I, having conducted the Frenchman to the rear, cantered towards the town to learn the news of the day.

The city on that day presented a most singular aspect. The streets filled with the town's-people and the soldiery, were decorated with flags and garlands; the cafés were crowded with merry groups, and the sounds of music and laughter resounded on all sides. The houses seemed to be quite inadequate to afford accommodation to the numerous guests, and, in consequence, bullock cars and forage wagons were converted into temporary hotels, and many a jovial party was collected in both. Military music, church bells, drinking choruses, were all commingled in the din and turmoil; processions in honor of " Our Lady of Succor" were jammed up among bacchanalian orgies, and their very chant half-drowned in the cries of the wounded, as they passed on to the hospitals. With difficulty we pushed our way through the dense mob, as we turned our steps towards the seminary. We both felt naturally curious to see the place where our first detachment landed, and to examine the opportunities of defence it presented. The building itself was a large and irregular one, of an oblong form, surrounded by a high wall of solid masonry, the only entrance being by a heavy iron gate.

At this spot the battle appeared to have raged with violence; one side of the massive gate was torn from its hinges, and lay flat upon the ground; the walls were breached in many places; and pieces of torn uniforms, broken bayonets, and bruised shakos, attested that the conflict was a close one. The seminary itself was in a falling state; the roof, from which Paget had given his orders, and where he was wounded, had fallen in. The French cannon had fissured the building from top to bottom, and it seemed only awaiting the slightest impulse to crumble into ruin. When we regarded the spot, and examined the narrow doorway which, opening upon a flight of a few steps to the river, admitted our first party, we could not help feeling struck anew with the gallantry of that mere handful of brave fellows who thus threw themselves amid the overwhelming legions of the enemy, and at once, without waiting for a single reinforcement, opened a fire upon their ranks. Bold as the enterprise unquestionably was, we still felt with what consummate judgment it had been planned;—a bend of the river concealed entirely the passage of the troops, the guns of the Sierra covered their landing, and completely swept one approach to the seminary. The French, being thus obliged to attack by the gate, were compelled to make a considerable *détour* before they reached it, all of which gave time for our divisions to cross; while the brigade of Guards, under General Sherbroke, profiting by the confusion, passed the river below the town, and took the enemy unexpectedly in the rear.

Brief as was the struggle within the town, it must have been a terrific one. The artillery were firing at musket-range; cavalry and infantry were fighting hand to hand in the narrow streets, a destructive musketry pouring all the while from window and house-tops.

At the Amarante gate, where the French defiled, the carnage was also great; their light artillery unlimbered some guns here to cover the columns as they deployed; but Murray's cavalry having carried these, the flank of the infantry became entirely exposed to the galling fire of small-arms from the seminary, and the far more destructive shower of grape that poured unceasingly from the Sierra.

Our brigade did the rest; and in less than one hour from the landing of the first man, the French were in full retreat upon Vallonga.

"A glorious thing, Charley," said Power, after a pause, "and a proud souvenir for hereafter."

A truth I felt deeply at the time, and one my heart responds to not less fully as I am writing.

CHAPTER XLVIII.

THE QUARREL.

ON the evening of the 12th, orders were received for the German brigade and three squadrons of our regiment to pursue the French upon the Terracinthe road by daybreak on the following morning.

I was busily occupied in my preparations for a hurried march, when Mike came up to say that an officer desired to speak with me; and the moment after Captain Hammersley appeared. A sudden flush colored his pale and sickly features, as he held out his hand, and said,—

"I've come to wish you joy, O'Malley. I just this instant heard of your promotion. I am sincerely glad of it; pray tell me the whole affair."

"That is the very thing I am unable to do. I have some very vague, indistinct remembrance of warding off a sabre-cut from the head of a wounded and unhorsed officer in the *mêlée* of yesterday; but more I know not. In fact, it was my first day under fire; I've a tolerably clear recollection of all the events of the morning, but the word 'Charge!' once given, I remember very little more. But you, where have you been? How have we not met before?"

"I've exchanged into a heavy dragoon regiment, and am now employed upon the staff."

"You are aware that I have letters for you?"

"Power hinted, I think, something of the kind. I saw him very hurriedly."

These words were spoken with an effort at *nonchalance* that evidently cost him much.

As for me, my agitation was scarcely less, as, fumbling for some seconds in my portmanteau, I drew forth the long destined packet. As I placed it in his hands he grew deadly pale, and a slight spasmodic twitch in his upper lip bespoke some unnatural struggle. He broke the seal suddenly, and as he did so, the morocco case of a miniature fell upon the ground; his eyes fell rapidly across the letter; the livid color of his lips, as the blood forced itself to them, added to the corpse-like hue of his countenance.

"You probably are aware of the contents of this letter, Mr. O'Malley?" said he, in an altered voice, whose tones, half in anger, half in suppressed irony, cut to my very heart.

"I am in complete ignorance of them," said I, calmly.

"Indeed, sir!" replied he, with a sarcastic curl of his mouth as he spoke. "Then, perhaps, you will tell me, too, that your very success is a secret to you?"

"I'm really not aware——"

"You probably think, sir, that the pastime is an amusing one, to interfere where the affections of others are concerned. I've heard of you, sir. Your conduct at Lisbon is known to me; and though Captain Trevyllian may bear——"

"Stop, Captain Hammersley!" said I, with a tremendous effort to be calm; "stop; you have said enough, quite enough, to convince me of what your object was in seeking me here to-day. You shall not be disappointed. I trust that assurance will save you from any further display of temper."

"I thank you; most humbly I thank you for the quickness of your apprehension; and I shall now take my leave. Good evening, Mr. O'Malley. I wish you much joy; you have my very fullest congratulations upon *all* your good fortune."

The sneering emphasis the last words were spoken with remained fixed in my mind long after he took his departure; and, indeed, so completely did the whole seem like a dream to me, that were it not for the fragments of the miniature that lay upon the ground, where he had crushed them with his heel, I could scarcely credit myself that I was awake.

My first impulse was to seek Power, upon whose judgment and discretion I could with confidence rely.

I had not long to wait; for scarcely had I thrown my cloak around me, when he rode up. He had just seen Hammersley, and learned something of our interview.

"Why, Charley, my dear fellow, what is this? How have you treated poor Hammersley?"

"Treated *him!* say, rather, how has he treated *me.*"

I here entered into a short but accurate account of our meeting, during which Power listened with great composure, while I could perceive, from the questions he asked, that some very different impression had been previously made upon his mind.

"And this was all that passed?"

"All."

"But what of the business at Lisbon ?"

"I don't understand."

"Why, he speaks—he has heard some foolish account of your having made some ridiculous speech there about your successful rivalry of him in Ireland—Lucy Dashwood, I suppose, is referred to. Some one has been good-natured enough to repeat the thing to him."

"But it never occurred. I never did."

"Are you sure, Charley ?"

"I am sure; I know I never did."

"The poor fellow, he has been duped! Come, Charley, you must not take it ill. Poor Hammersley has never recovered from a sabre-wound he received some months since upon the head; his intellects are really affected by it. Leave it all to me. Promise not to leave your quarters till I return, and I'll put everything right again."

I gave the required pledge, while Power, springing into the saddle, left me to my own reflections.

My frame of mind as Power left me was by no means an enviable one. A quarrel is rarely a happy incident in a man's life, still less is it so when the difference arises with one we are disposed to like and respect. Such was Hammersley. His manly, straightforward character had won my esteem and regard, and it was with no common scrutiny I taxed my memory to think what could have given rise to the impression he labored under of my having injured him. His chance mention of Trevyllian suggested to me some suspicion that his dislike of me, wherefore arising I knew not, might have its share in the matter. In this state of doubt and uncertainty I paced impatiently up and down, anxiously watching for Power's return, in the hope of at length getting some real insight into the difficulty.

My patience was fast ebbing; Power had been absent above an hour, and no appearance of him could I detect, when suddenly the tramp of a horse came rapidly up the hill. I looked out, and saw a rider coming forward at a very fast pace. Before I had time for even a guess as to who it was, he drew up, and I recognized Captain Trevyllian. There was a certain look of easy impertinence and half-smiling satisfaction about his features I had never seen before, as he touched his cap in salute, and said,—

"May I have the honor of a few moments' conversation with you ?"

I bowed silently, while he dismounted, and passing his bridle beneath his arm, walked on beside me.

"My friend Captain Hammersley has commissioned me to wait upon you about this unpleasant affair——"

"I beg pardon for the interruption, Captain Trevyllian, but as I have yet to learn to what you and your friend allude, perhaps it may facilitate matters if you will explicitly state your meaning."

He grew crimson on the cheek as I said this, while, with a voice perfectly unmoved, he continued,—

"I am not sufficiently in my friend's confidence to know the whole of the affair in question, nor have I his permission to enter into any of it, he probably presuming, as I certainly did myself, that your sense of honor would have deemed further parley and discussion both unnecessary and unseasonable."

"In fact, then, if I understand, it is expected that I should meet Captain Hammersley for some reason unknown——"

"He certainly desires a meeting with you," was the dry reply.

"And as certainly I shall not give it before understanding upon what grounds."

"And such I am to report as your answer?" said he, looking at me at the moment with an expression of ill-repressed triumph as he spoke.

There was something in these few words, as well as in the tone in which they were spoken, that sunk deeply in my heart. Was it that by some trick of diplomacy he was endeavoring to compromise my honor and character? Was it possible that my refusal might be construed into any other than the real cause? I was too young, too inexperienced in the world, to decide the question for myself, and no time was allowed me to seek another's counsel. What a trying moment was that for me! My temples throbbed, my heart beat almost audibly, and I stood afraid to speak, dreading, on the one hand, lest my compliance might involve me in an act to embitter my life forever, and fearful, on the other, that my refusal might be reported as a trait of cowardice.

He saw, he read my difficulty at a glance, and, with a smile of most supercilious expression, repeated coolly his former question. In an instant all thought of Hammersley was forgotten. I remembered no more. I saw him before me, he who had, since my first meeting, continually contrived to pass some inappreciable slight upon me. My eyes flashed, my hands tingled with ill-repressed rage, as I said,—

"With Captain Hammersley I am conscious of no quarrel, nor have I ever shown by any act or look an intention to provoke one. Indeed, such demonstrations are not always successful. There are persons most rigidly scrupulous for a friend's honor little disposed to guard their own."

"You mistake," said he, interrupting me,—as I spoke these words with a look as insulting as I could make it,—"you mistake. I have sworn a solemn oath never to *send* a challenge."

The emphasis upon the word "send" explained fully his meaning, when I said,—

"But you will not decline——"

"Most certainly not," said he, again interrupting, while with sparkling eye and elated look he drew himself up to his full height.

"Your friend is——"

"Captain Power; and yours——"

"Sir Harry Beaufort. I may observe that, as the troops are in marching order, the matter had better not be delayed."

"There shall be none on my part."

"Nor mine," said he, as, with a low bow, and a look of most ineffable triumph, he sprang into his saddle; then, "*Au revoir*, Mr. O'Malley," said he, gathering up his reins. "Beaufort is on the staff, and quartered at Oporto." So saying, he cantered easily down the slope, and once more I was alone.

CHAPTER XLIX.

THE ROUTE.

I WAS leisurely examining my pistols—poor Considine's last present to me on leaving home—when an orderly sergeant rode rapidly up, and delivered into my hands the following order:—

"Lieutenant O'Malley will hold himself in immediate readiness to proceed on a particular service. By order of his Excellency the Commander of the Forces.

"S. GORDON, Military Secretary."

"What can this mean?" thought I. "It is not possible that any rumor of my intended meeting could have got abroad, and that my present destination could be intended as a punishment?"

I walked hurriedly to the door of the little hut which formed my quarters. Below me, in the plain, all was activity and preparation; the infantry were drawn up in marching order; baggage wagons, ordnance stores and artillery seemed all in active preparation; and some cavalry squadrons might be already seen, with forage allowances behind the saddle, as if only waiting the order to set out. I strained my eyes to see if Power was coming, but no horseman approached in the direction. I stood, and·I hesitated whether I should not rather seek him at once, than continue to wait on in my present uncertainty. But then, what if I should miss him? and I had pledged myself to remain till he returned.

While I deliberated thus with myself, weighing the various chances for and against each plan, I saw two mounted officers coming towards me at a brisk trot. As they came nearer, I recognized one as my Colonel; the other was an officer of the staff.

Supposing that their mission had some relation to the order I had so lately received, and which until now I had forgotten, I hastily returned, and ordered Mike to my presence.

"How are the horses, Mike?" said I.

"Never better, sir. Badger was wounded slightly by a spent shot in the counter, but he's never the worse this morning, and the black horse is capering like a filly."

"Get ready my pack, feed the cattle, and be prepared to set out at a moment's warning."

"Good advice, O'Malley," said the Colonel, as he overheard the last direction to my servant. "I hope the nags are in condition."

"Why, yes, sir, I believe they are."

"All the better; you've a sharp ride before you. Meanwhile, let me introduce my friend; Captain Beaumont—Mr. O'Malley. I think we had better be seated."

"These are your instructions, Mr. O'Malley," said Captain Beau-- mont, unfolding a map as he spoke. "You will proceed from this, with half a troop of your regiment, by forced marches, towards the frontier, passing through the town of Calenco, and Guarda, and the Estrella pass. On arriving at the head-quarters of the Lusitanian Legion, which you will find there, you are to put yourself under the orders of Major Monsoon, commanding that force. Any Portuguese cavalry he may have with him will be attached to yours, and under your command; your rank, for the time, being that of captain. You will, as far as possible, acquaint yourself with the habits and capabilities of the native cavalry, and make such report as you judge necessary thereupon to his Excellency the Commander of the Forces. I think it only fair to add that you are indebted to my friend Colonel Merivale for the very flattering position thus opened to your skill and enterprise."

"My dear Colonel, let me assure you——"

"Not a word, my boy. I knew the thing would suit you, and I am sure I can count upon your not disappointing my expectations of you. Sir Arthur perfectly remembers your name. He only asked two questions—

"'Is he well mounted?'

"'Admirably,' was my answer.

"'Can you depend upon his promptitude?'

"'He'll leave in half an hour.'

"So you see, O'Malley, I have already pledged myself for you. And now I must say adieu; the regiments are about to take up a more advanced position, so good-bye. I hope you will have a pleasant time of it till we meet again."

"It is now twelve o'clock, Mr. O'Malley," said Beaumont; "we may rely upon your immediate departure. Your written instructions and despatches will be here within a quarter of an hour."

I muttered something—what, I cannot remember; I bowed my thanks to my worthy Colonel, shook his hand warmly, and saw him ride down the hill, and disappear in the crowd of soldiery beneath, before I could recall my faculties and think over my situation.

Then all at once did the full difficulty of my position break upon me. If I accepted my present employment, I must certainly fail in my engagement to Trevyllian. But I had already pledged myself to its acceptance. What was to be done? No time was left for deliberation. The very minutes I should have spent in preparation were fast passing. Would that Power might appear. Alas! he came not. My state of doubt and uncertainty increased every moment; I saw nothing but ruin before me, even at a moment when fortune promised most fairly for the future, and opened a field of enterprise my heart had so often and so ardently desired. Nothing was left me but to hasten to Colonel Merivale and decline the appointment; to do so was to prejudice my character in his estimation forever, for I dared not allege my reasons, and in all probability my conduct might require my leaving the army.

"Be it so, then," said I, in an accent of despair; "the die is cast."

I ordered my horse round; I wrote a few words to Power, to explain my absence, should he come while I was away, and leaped into the saddle. As I reached the plain, my pace became a gallop, and I pressed my horse with all the impatience my heart was burning with. I dashed along the lines towards Oporto, neither hearing nor seeing aught around me, when suddenly the clank of cavalry accoutrements behind induced me to turn my head, and I perceived an orderly dragoon at full gallop in pursuit. I pulled up till he came alongside.

"Lieutenant O'Malley, sir," said the man, saluting, "these despatches are for you."

I took them hurriedly, and was about to continue my route, when the attitude of the dragoon arrested my attention. He had reined in his horse to the side of the narrow causeway, and, holding him still and steadily, sat motionless as a statue. I looked behind, and saw the whole staff approaching at a brisk trot. Before I had a moment for thought they were beside me.

"Ah! O'Malley," cried Merivale, "you have your orders; don't wait; his Excellency is coming up."

"Get along, I advise you," said another, "or you'll catch it, as some of us have done this morning."

"All is right, Charley; you can go in safety," said a whispering voice, as Power passed in a sharp canter.

That one sentence was enough; my heart bounded like a deer, my cheek beamed with the glow of delighted pleasure, I closed my spurs upon my gallant gray, and dashed across the plain.

When I arrived at my quarters, the men were drawn up in waiting, and provided with rations for three days' march: Mike was also prepared for the road, and nothing more remained to delay me.

"Captain Power has been here, sir, and left a note."

I took it and thrust it hastily into my sabretasche. I knew from the few words he had spoken that my present step involved me in no ill consequences; so, giving the word to wheel into column, I rode to the front, and set out upon my march to Alcantara.

CHAPTER L.

THE WATCH-FIRE.

THERE are few things so inspiriting to a young soldier as the being employed with a separate command; the picket and out-post duty have a charm for him no other portion of his career possesses. The field seems open for individual boldness and heroism: success, if obtained, must redound to his own credit; and what can equal, in its spirit-stirring enthusiasm, that first moment when we become in any way the arbiter of our own fortunes?

Such were my happy thoughts as, with a proud and elated heart, I set forth upon my march. The notice the Commander-in-Chief had bestowed upon me had already done much: it had raised me in my own estimation, and implanted within me a longing desire for further distinction. I thought, too, of those far, far away, who were yet to hear of my successes.

I fancied to myself how they would severally receive the news. My poor uncle, with tearful eye and quivering lip, was before me, as

I saw him read the despatch, then wipe his glasses, and read on, till at last, with one long-drawn breath, his manly voice, tremulous with emotion, would break forth—"My boy! my own Charley!" Then I pictured Considine, with port erect and stern features, listening silently; not a syllable, not a motion betraying that he felt interested in my fate, till, as if impatient, at length he would break in—"I knew it—I said so; and yet you thought to make him a lawyer!" And then old Sir Harry: his warm heart glowing with pleasure, and his good-humored face beaming with happiness. How many a blunder he would make in retailing the news, and how many a hearty laugh his version of it would give rise to!

I passed in review before me the old servants, as they lingered in the room to hear the story. Poor old Matthew, the butler, fumbling with his corkscrew to gain a little time; then looking in my uncle's face, half entreatingly, as he asked,—"Any news of Master Charles, sir, from the wars?"

While thus my mind wandered back to the scenes and faces of my early home, I feared to ask myself how *she* would feel to whom my heart was now turning. Too deeply did I know how poor my chances were in that quarter to nourish hope, and yet I could not bring myself to abandon it altogether. Hammersley's strange conduct suggested to me that he, at least, could not be *my* rival, while I plainly perceived that he regarded me as *his*. There was a mystery in all this I could not fathom, and I ardently longed for my next meeting with Power, to learn the nature of his interview, and also in what manner the affair had been arranged.

Such were my passing thoughts as I pressed forward. My men, picked no less for themselves than their horses, came rapidly along, and ere evening we had accomplished twelve leagues of our journey.

The country through which we journeyed, though wild and romantic in its character, was singularly rich and fertile,—cultivation reaching to the very summits of the rugged mountains, and patches of wheat and Indian corn peeping amid masses of granite rock and tangled brushwood. The vine and the olive grew wild on every side; while the orange and the arbutus, loading the air with perfume, were mingled with prickly pear-trees and variegated hollies. We followed no regular track, but cantered along over hill and valley, through forest and prairie; now in long file through some tall field of waving corn, now in open order upon some level plain, our Portuguese guide riding a little in advance of us, upon a jet-black mule, carolling merrily some wild Galician melody as he went.

As the sun was setting, we arrived beside a little stream, that, flowing along a rocky bed, skirted a vast forest of tall cork trees.

Here we called a halt; and, picketing our horses, proceeded to make our arrangements for a bivouac.

Never do I remember a more lovely night. The watch-fires sent up a delicious odor from the perfumed shrubs; while the glassy water reflected on its still surface the starry sky that, unshadowed and unclouded, stretched above us. I wrapped myself in my trooper's mantle, and lay down beneath a tree,—but not to sleep. There was a something so exciting, and withal so tranquillizing, that I had no thought of slumber, but fell into a musing reverie. There was a character of adventure in my position that charmed me much. My men were gathered in groups beside the fires; some were sunk in slumber, others sat smoking silently, or chatting, in a low and undertone, of some bygone scene of battle or bivouac; here and there were picketed the horses, the heavy panoply and piled carbines flickering in the red glare of the watch-fires, which ever and anon threw a flitting glow upon the stern and swarthy faces of my bold troopers. Upon the trees around, sabres and helmets, holsters and cross-belts, were hung like armorial bearings in some antique hall, the dark foliage spreading its heavy shadow around us. Farther off, upon a little rocky ledge, the erect figure of the sentry, with his short carbine resting in the hollow of his arm, was seen slowly pacing in measured tread, or standing for a moment silently, as he looked upon the fair and tranquil sky,—his thoughts doubtless far, far away, beyond the sea, to some humble home, where

> "The hum of the spreading sycamore,
> That grew beside his cottage door,"

was again in his ears, while the merry laugh of his children stirred his bold heart. It was a Salvator-Rosa scene, and brought me back in fancy to the bandit legends I had read in boyhood. By the uncertain light of the wood embers I endeavored to sketch the group that lay before me.

The night wore on. One by one the soldiers stretched themselves to sleep, and all was still. As the hours rolled by, a drowsy feeling crept gradually over me. I placed my pistols by my side, and having replenished the fire by some fresh logs, disposed myself comfortably before it.

It was during that half-dreamy state that intervenes between waking and sleep that a rustling sound of the branches behind attracted my attention. The air was too calm to attribute this to the wind, so I listened for some minutes; but sleep, too long deferred, was over-powerful; my head sank upon my grassy pillow, and I was soon sound asleep. How long I remained thus, I know not, but I awoke suddenly. I fancied some one had shaken me rudely by the shoulder; but yet all was tranquil. My men were sleeping soundly, as I saw them last. The fires were becoming low, and a gray streak in the sky, as well as a sharp cold feeling of the air, betokened the approach of day. Once more I heaped some dry branches together, and was about again to stretch myself to rest, when I felt a hand upon my shoulder. I turned quickly round, and, by the imperfect light of the fire, saw the figure of a man standing motionless, beside me. His head was bare, and his hair fell in long curls over his shoulders; one hand was pressed upon his bosom, and with the other he motioned me to silence. My first impression was that our party was surprised by some French patrol; but as I looked again, I recognized, to my amazement, that the individual before me was the young French officer I had seen that morning a prisoner beside the Douro.

"How came you here?" said I, in a low voice, to him in French.

"Escaped. One of my own men threw himself between me and the sentry; I swam the Douro, received a musket-ball through my arm, lost my shako, and here I am!"

"You are aware you are again a prisoner?"

"If you desire it, of course I am," said he, in a voice full of feeling, that made my very heart creep. "I thought you were a party of Lorge's dragoons, scouring the country for forage; tracked you the entire day, and have only now come up with you."

The poor fellow, who had neither eaten nor drunk since daybreak, wounded and footsore, had accomplished twelve leagues of a march, only once more to fall into the hands of his enemies. His years could scarcely have numbered nineteen; his countenance was singularly prepossessing; and, though bleeding and torn, with tattered uniform, and without a covering to his head, there was no mistaking for a moment that he was of gentle blood. Noiselessly and cautiously I made him sit down beside the fire, while I spread before him the sparing remnant of my last night's supper, and shared my solitary bottle of sherry with him.

From the moment he spoke, I never entertained a thought of making him a prisoner; but, as I knew not how far I was culpable in permitting, if not actually facilitating, his escape, I resolved to keep the circumstance a secret from my party, and, if possible, get him away before daybreak.

No sooner did he learn my intentions regarding him, than in an instant all memory of his past misfortune, all thoughts of his present destitute condition, seemed to have fled; and while I dressed his wound and bound-up his shattered arm, he chatted away as unconcernedly about the past and the future as though seated beside the fire of his own bivouac, surrounded by his own brother officers.

"You took us by surprise the other day," said he. "Our Marshal looked for the attack from the mouth of the river; we received information that your ships were expected there. In any case, our retreat was an orderly one, and must have been effected with slight loss."

I smiled at the self-complacency of this reasoning, but did not contradict him.

"Your loss must indeed have been great; your men crossed under the fire of a whole battery."

"Not exactly," said I; "our first party were quietly stationed in Oporto before you knew anything about it."

"*Ah! sacré Dieu!* Treachery!" cried he, striking his forehead with his clenched fist.

"Not so; mere daring—nothing more. But come, tell me something of your own adventures. How were you taken?"

"Simply thus: I was sent to the rear with orders to the artillery to cut their traces and leave the guns; when coming back, my horse grew tired in the heavy ground, and I was spurring him to the utmost, when one of your heavy dragoons—an officer, too—dashed at me, and actually rode me down, horse and all. I lay for some time bruised by the fall, when an infantry soldier, passing by, seized me by the collar, and brought me to the rear. No matter, however, here I am now. You will not give me up; and perhaps I may one day live to repay the kindness."

"You have not long joined?"

"It was my first battle; my epaulettes were very smart things yesterday, though they do look a little *passées* to-day. You are advancing, I suppose?"

I smiled, without answering this question.

"Ah, I see you don't wish to speak; never mind, your discretion is thrown away upon me; for if I rejoined my regiment to-morrow, I should have forgotten all you told me—all but your great kindness." These last words he spoke bowing slightly his head, and coloring as he said them.

"You are a dragoon, I think?" said I, endeavoring to change the topic.

"I was, two days ago, *chasseur à cheval,* a sous-lieutenant in the regiment of my father, the General St. Croix."

"The name is familiar to me," I replied; "and I am sincerely happy to be in a position to serve the son of so distinguished an officer."

"The son of so distinguished an officer is most deeply obliged, but wishes with all his heart and soul he had never sought glory under such very excellent auspices. You look surprised, *mon cher;*

but, let me tell you, my military ardor is considerably abated in the
last three days. Hunger, thirst, imprisonment, and this"—lifting
his wounded limb as he spoke—"are sharp lessons in so short a
campaign, and for one, too, whose life hitherto had much more of
ease than adventure to boast of. Shall I tell you how I became a
soldier?"

"By all means; give me your glass first; and now, with a fresh
log to the fire, I'm your man."

"But stay; before I begin, look to this."

The blood was flowing rapidly from his wound, which with some
difficulty I succeeded in stanching. He drank off his wine hastily,
held out his glass to be refilled, and then began his story.

"You have never seen the Emperor?"

"Never."

"*Sacrebleu!* What a man he is! I'd rather stand under the fire
of your grenadiers than meet his eye. When in a passion, he does
not say much, it is true; but what he does, comes with a kind of
hissing, rushing sound, while the very fire seems to kindle in his
look. I have him before me this instant, and though you will confess that my present condition has nothing very pleasing in it, I
should be sorry indeed to change it for the last time I stood in his
presence.

"Two months ago, I sported the gay light blue and silver of a
page to the Emperor, and certainly, what with balls, bonbons, flirtation, gossip, and champagne suppers, led a very gay, reckless, and
indolent life of it. Somehow—I may tell you more accurately at
another period, if we ever meet—I got myself into disgrace, and, as
a punishment, was ordered to absent myself from the Tuileries, and
retire for some weeks to Fontainebleau. Siberia to a Russian would
scarcely be a heavier infliction than was this banishment to me.
There was no court, no levée, no military parade, no ball, no opera.
A small household of the Emperor's chosen servants quietly kept
house there. The gloomy walls re-echoed to no music; the dark
alleys of the dreary garden seemed the very impersonation of solitude and decay. Nothing broke the dull monotony of the tiresome
day, except when occasionally, near sunset, the clash of the guard
would be heard turning out, and the clank of presenting arms, followed by the roll of a heavy carriage into the gloomy court-yard.
One lamp, shining like a star, in a small chamber on the second
floor, would remain till near four, sometimes five o'clock in the
morning. The same sounds of the guard and the same dull roll of
the carriage would break the stillness of the early morning; and the
Emperor—for it was he—would be on his road back to Paris.

"We never saw him—I say we, for, like myself, some half-dozen others were also there, expiating their follies by a life of cheerless *ennui.*

" It was upon a calm evening in April, we sat together chatting over the various misdeeds which had consigned us to exile, when some one proposed, by way of passing the time, that we should visit the small flower-garden that was parted from off the rest, and reserved for the Emperor alone. It was already beyond the hour he usually came; besides that, even should he arrive, there was abundant time to get back before he could possibly reach it. The garden we had often seen, but there was something in the fact that our going there was a transgression that so pleased us all, that we agreed at once, and set forth. For above an hour we loitered about the lonely and deserted walks, where already the Emperor's foot-tracks had worn a marked pathway, when we grew weary, and were about to return, just as one of the party suggested, half in ridicule of the sanctity of the spot, that we should have a game of leap-frog ere we left it. The idea pleased us, and was at once adopted. Our plan was this: each person stationed himself in some by-walk or alley, and waited till the other, whose turn it was, came and leaped over him; so that, besides the activity displayed, there was a knowledge of the locale necessary; for to any one passed over, a forfeit was to be paid. Our game began at once, and certainly I doubt if ever those green alleys and shady groves rang to such hearty laughter. Here would be seen a couple rolling over together on the grass; there some luckless wight counting out his pocket-money, to pay his penalty. The hours passed quietly over, and the moon rose, and at last it came my turn to make the tour of the garden. As I was supposed to know all its intricacies better than the rest, a longer time was given for them to conceal themselves; at length the word was given, and I started.

" Anxious to acquit myself well, I hurried along at top speed, but guess my surprise to discover that nowhere could I find one of my companions; down one walk I scampered, up another, across a third, but all was still and silent; not a sound, not a breath, could I detect. There was still one part of the garden unexplored; it was a small open space before a little pond, which usually contained the gold fish the Emperor was so fond of. Thither I bent my steps, and had not gone far when, in the pale moonlight, I saw, at length, one of my companions waiting patiently for my coming, his head bent forward and his shoulders rounded. Anxious to repay him for my own disappointment, I crept silently forward on tiptoe till quite near him, when, rushing madly on, I sprang upon his back; just, however, as I rose to leap over, he raised his head, and, staggered by the impulse of my spring, he was thrown forward, and, after an ineffec-

21

tual effort to keep his legs, fell flat upon his face in the grass. Bursting with laughter, I fell over him on the ground, and was turning to assist him, when suddenly he sprang upon his feet, and—horror of horrors!—it was Napoleon himself; his usually pale features were purple with rage, but not a word, not a syllable escaped him.

"'*Qui êtes-vous ?*' said he, at length.

"'St. Croix, sire,' said I, still kneeling before him, while my very heart leaped into my mouth.

"'St. Croix! *toujours* St. Croix! Come here; approach me,' cried he, in a voice of stifled passion.

"I rose; but before I could take a step forward he sprang at me, and tearing off my epaulettes, trampled them beneath his feet, and then he shouted out, rather than spoke, the word '*Allez!*'

"I did not wait for a second intimation, but clearing the paling at a spring, was many a mile from Fontainebleau before daybreak."

CHAPTER LI.

THE MARCH.

TWICE the *réveille* sounded; the horses champed impatiently their heavy bits; my men stood waiting for the order to mount ere I could arouse myself from the deep sleep I had fallen into. The young Frenchman and his story were in my dreams, and when I awoke, his figure, as he lay sleeping beside the wood embers, was the first object I perceived. There he lay, to all seeming as forgetful of his fate as though he still inhabited the gorgeous halls and gilded saloons of the Tuileries; his pale and handsome features wore even a placid smile as, doubtless, some dream of other days flitted across him; his long hair waved in luxurious curls upon his neck, and his light brown moustache, slightly curled at the top, gave to his mild and youthful features an air of saucy *fierté* that heightened their effect. A narrow blue ribbon which he wore round his throat gently peeped from his open bosom. I could not resist the curiosity I felt to see what it meant, and drawing it softly forth, I perceived that a small miniature was attached to it. It was beautifully painted, and surrounded with brilliants of some value. One glance showed me—for I had seen more than one engraving before of her—that it was the portrait of the Empress Josephine. Poor boy! he doubtless was a favorite at court; indeed everything in his air and manner bespoke him such. I gently replaced the precious locket, and turned from the spot, to think over what was best to be done for him. Knowing the vindictive feeling of the Portuguese towards their invaders, I feared to take Pietro, our guide, into my confidence. I accordingly summoned my man Mike to my aid, who, with all his country's readiness, soon found out an expedient. It was to pretend to Pietro that the prisoner was merely an English officer, who had made his escape from the French army, in which, against his will, he had been serving for some time.

This plan succeeded perfectly; and when St. Croix, mounted upon one of my led horses, set out upon his march beside me, none was more profuse of his attentions than the dark-brown guide, whose hatred of a Frenchman was beyond belief.

By thus giving him safe-conduct through Portugal, I knew that when we reached the frontier he could easily manage to come up with some part of Marshal Victor's force, the advanced guard of which lay on the left bank of the Tagus.

To me the companionship was the greatest boon; the gay and buoyant spirit, that no reverse of fortune, no untoward event, could subdue, lightened many an hour of the journey; and though at times the gasconading tone of the Frenchman would peep through, there was still such a fund of good-tempered raillery in all he said, that it was impossible to feel angry with him. His implicit faith in the Emperor's invincibility also amused me. Of the unbounded confidence of the nation in general, and the army particularly, in Napoleon, I had till then no conception. It was not that in the profound skill and immense resources of the general they trusted, but they actually regarded him as one placed above all the common accidents of fortune, and revered him as something more than human.

"*Il viendra, et puis——*" was the continued exclamation of the young Frenchman. Any notion of our successfully resisting the overwhelming might of the Emperor, he would have laughed to scorn, and so I let him go on prophesying our future misfortunes till the time when, driven back upon Lisbon, we should be compelled to evacuate the Peninsula, and, under favor of a convention, be permitted to return to England. All this was sufficiently ridiculous, coming from a youth of nineteen, wounded, in misery, a prisoner; but further experience of his nation has shown me that St. Croix was not the exception, but the rule. The conviction in the ultimate success of their army, whatever be the merely momentary mishap, is the one present thought of a Frenchman; a victory with them is a conquest; a defeat—if they are by any chance driven to acknowledge one—a *fatalité.*

I was too young a man, and, still more, too young a soldier, to bear with this absurd affectation of superiority as I ought, and consequently was glad to wander whenever I could from the contested point of our national superiority to other topics. St. Croix, although young, had seen much of the world, as a page in the splendid court of the Tuileries. The scenes passing before his eyes were calculated to make a strong impression; and by many an anecdote of his former life he lightened the road as we passed along.

"You promised, by the bye, to tell me of your banishment. How did that occur, St. Croix?"

"*Ah! par Dieu!* that was an unfortunate affair for me: then began all my mishaps; but for that, I should never have been sent to Fontainebleau—never have played leap-frog with the Emperor—never have been sent a soldier into Spain. True," said he, laughing, "I should never have had the happiness of your acquaintance. But still, I'd much rather have met you first in the Places des Victoires than in the Estrella Mountains."

"Who knows?" said I; "perhaps your good genius prevailed in all this."

"Perhaps," said he, interrupting me; "that's exactly what the Empress said—she was my godmother—'Jules will be a *Maréchal de France* yet.' But certainly it must be confessed I have made a bad beginning. However, you wish to hear of my disgrace at court., *Allons, donc.* But had we not better wait for a halt?"

"Agreed," said I; "and so let us now press forward."

CHAPTER LII.

THE PAGE.

UNDER the deep shade of some tall trees, sheltered from the noonday sun, we lay down to rest ourselves, and enjoy a most patriarchal dinner. Some dry biscuits, a few bunches of grapes, and a little weak wine, savoring more of the boraccio-skin than the vine-juice, were all we boasted; yet they were not unacceptable at such a time and place.

"Whose health did you pledge then?" inquired St. Croix, with a half-malicious smile, as I raised the glass silently to my lips.

I blushed deeply and looked confused.

"*A ses beaux yeux!* whoever she be," said he, gayly, tossing off his wine; "and now, if you feel disposed, I'll tell you my story. In good truth, it is not worth relating, but it may serve to set you asleep, at all events.

"I have already told you that I was a page. Alas! the impressions you may feel of that functionary, from having seen Cherubino, give but a faint notion of him when pertaining to the household of the Emperor Napoleon.

"The *farfallone amoroso* basked in the soft smiles and sunny looks of the Countess Almaviva; we met but the cold, impassive look of Talleyrand, the piercing and penetrating stare of Savary, or the ambiguous smile, half menace, half mockery, of Monsieur Fouché. While on service, our days were passed in the ante-chamber, beside the *salle d'audience* of the Emperor, reclining against the closed door, watching attentively for the gentle tinkle of the little bell which summoned us to open for the exit of some haughty diplomate, or the *entrée* of some redoubted general. Thus passed we the weary hours. The illustrious visitors by whom we were surrounded had no novelty, consequently no attraction for us, and the names already historical were but household words with us.

"We often remarked, too, the proud and distant bearing the Emperor assumed to those of his generals who had been his former companions in arms. Whatever familiarity or freedom may have existed in the campaign or in the battle-field, the air of the Tuileries certainly chilled it. I have often heard that the ceremonious observances and rigid etiquette of the old Bourbon court were far preferable to the stern reserve and unbending stiffness of the Imperial one.

"The ante-chamber is but the reflection of the reception-room; and whatever be the whims, the caprices, the littleness of the Great Man, they are speedily assumed by his inferiors, and the dark temper of one casts a lowering shadow on every menial by whom he is surrounded.

"As for us, we were certainly not long in catching somewhat of the spirit of the Emperor; and I doubt much if the impertinence of the waiting-room was not more dreaded and detested than the abrupt speech and searching look of Napoleon himself.

"What a malicious pleasure have I not felt in arresting the step of M. de Talleyrand, as he approached the Emperor's closet! With what easy insolence have I lisped out, 'Pardon, monsieur, but his Majesty cannot receive you;' or, 'Monsieur le Duc, his Majesty has given no orders for your admission.' How amusing it was to watch the baffled look of each, as he retired once more to his place among the crowd—the wily diplomate covering his chagrin with a practised smile, while the stern marshal would blush to his very eyes with indignation. This was the great pleasure our position afforded us, and, with a boyish spirit of mischief, we cultivated it to perfection, and became at last the very horror and detestation of all who frequented the levées; and the ambassador whose fearless voice was heard among the councils of kings became soft and conciliating in his approaches to us; and the hardy general, who would have charged upon a brigade of artillery, was timid as a girl in addressing us a mere question.

"Among the amiable class thus characterized I was most conspicuous. Preserving cautiously a tone of civility that left nothing openly to complain of, I assumed an indifference and impartiality of manner that no exigency of affairs, no pressing haste, could discompose or disturb; and my bow of recognition to Soult or Massena was as coolly measured as my monosyllabic answer was accurately conned over.

"Upon ordinary occasions, the Emperor, at the close of each person's audience, rang his little bell for the admission of the next in order as they arrived in the waiting-room; yet when anything important was under consideration, a list was given us in the morning of the names to be presented in rotation, which no casual circumstance was ever suffered to interfere with.

"It is now about four months since, one fine morning, such a list was placed within my hands. His Majesty was just then occupied with an inquiry into the naval force of the kingdom. As I cast my eyes carelessly over the names, I read little else than Vice-Admiral so-and-so, Commander such-a-one, and Chef d'Escadron such another, and the levée presented, accordingly, instead of its usual brilliant array of gorgeous uniform and aiguilletted marshals, the simple blue-and-gold of the naval service.

"The marine was not in high favor with the Emperor, and truly my reception of these unfrequent visitors was anything but flattering. The early part of the morning was, as usual, occupied by the audience of the Minister of Police and the Duc de Bassano, who evidently, from the length of time they remained, had matter of importance to communicate. Meanwhile, the ante-chamber filled rapidly, and before noon was actually crowded. It was just at this moment that the folding-door slowly opened, and a figure entered such as I had never before seen in our brilliant saloon. He was a man of five or six-and-fifty, short, thick-set, and strongly built, with a bronzed and weather-beaten face, and a broad, open forehead, deeply scarred with a sabre-cut; a shaggy gray moustache curled over and concealed his mouth, while eyebrows of the same color shaded his dark and piercing eyes. His dress was a coarse coat of blue cloth, such as the fishermen wear in Bretagne, fastened at the waist by a broad belt of black leather, from which hung a short broad-bladed cutlass; his loose trousers, of the same material, were turned up at the ankles, to show a pair of strong legs, coarsely cased

in blue stockings and thick-soled shoes; a broad-leaved oil-skin hat
was held in one hand, and the other stuck carelessly in his pocket,
as he entered. He came in with a careless air, and, familiarly saluting one or two officers in the room, he sat himself down near the
door, appearing lost in his own reflections.

"'Who can you be, my worthy friend?' was my question to myself, as I surveyed this singular apparition. At the same time,
casting my eyes down the list, I perceived that several pilots of the
coast of Havre, Calais, and Boulogne had been summoned to Paris,
to give some information upon the soundings and depth of water
along the shore.

"'Ha,' thought I, 'I have it; the good man has mistaken his
place, and instead of remaining without, has walked boldly forward
to the ante-chamber.' There was something so strange and so original in the grim look of the old fellow, as he sat there alone, that I
suffered him to remain quietly in his delusion, rather than order him
back to the waiting-room without; besides, I perceived that a kind
of sensation was created among the others by his appearance there,
which amused me greatly.

"As the day wore on, the officers formed into little groups of three
or four, chatting together in an undertone of voice, all save the old
pilot; he had taken a huge tobacco-box from his capacious breast-
pocket, and inserting an immense piece of the bitter weed in his
mouth, began to chew it as leisurely as though he were walking the
quarter-deck. The cool *insouciance* of such a proceeding amused me
much, and I resolved to draw him out a little.

"His strong, broad Breton features, his deep voice, his dry, blunt
manner, were all in admirable keeping with his exterior, and amused
me highly.

"'*Par Dieu!* my lad,' said he, after chatting some time, 'had you
not better tell the Emperor that I am waiting? It's now past noon,
and I must eat something.'

"'Have a little patience,' said I; 'his Majesty is going to invite
you to dinner.'

"'Be it so,' said he, gravely; 'provided the hour be an early one,
I'm his man.'

"With difficulty did I keep down my laughter as he said this, and
continued,—

"'So you know the Emperor already, it seems?'

"'Yes, that I do! I remember him when he was no higher than
yourself.'

"'How delighted he'll be to find you here. I hope you have
brought up some of your family with you, as the Emperor would be
so flattered by it?'

"'No, I've left them at home; this place don't suit us over well. We have plenty to do, besides spending our time and money among all you fine folks here.'

"'And not a bad life of it, either,' added I, 'fishing for cod and herrings—stripping a wreck now and then.'

"He stared at me as I said this, like a tiger on the spring, but spoke not a word.

"'And how many young sea-wolves may you have in your den at home?'

"'Six; and all o' them able to carry you with one hand at arm's length!'

"'I have no doubt; I shall certainly not test their ability. But you yourself, how do you like the capital?'

"'Not over well, and I'll tell you why——'

"As he said this, the door of the audience-chamber opened, and the Emperor appeared. His eyes flashed fire, as he looked hurriedly around the room.

"'Who is in waiting here?'

"'I am, please your Majesty,' said I, bowing deeply, as I started from my seat.

"'And where is the Admiral Truguet? Why was he not admitted?'

"'Not present, your Majesty,' said I, trembling with fear.

"'Hold there, young fellow. Not so fast; here he is.'

"'Ah, Truguet, *mon ami!*' cried the Emperor, placing both-hands on the old fellow's shoulders; 'how long have you been in waiting?'

"'Two hours and a half,' said he, producing in evidence a watch like a saucer.

"'What! two hours and a half, and I not know it?'

"'No matter; I am always happy to serve your Majesty. But if that fine fellow had not told me that you were going to ask me to dinner——'

"'He! he said so, did he?' said Napoleon, turning on me a glance like a wild beast. 'Yes, Truguet, so I am; you shall dine with me to-day. And you, sir,' said he, dropping his voice to a whisper, as he came closer towards me, 'and you have dared to speak thus? Call in a guard there. Capitaine, put this person under arrest; he is disgraced; he is no longer page of the palace. Out of my presence! away, sir!'

"The room wheeled round; my legs tottered, my senses reeled; and I saw no more.

"'Three weeks' bread and water in St. Pélagie, however, brought me to my recollection; and at last my kind, my more than kind friend, the Empress, obtained my pardon and sent me to Fontaine-bleau, till the Emperor should forget all about it. How I contrived again to refresh his memory I have already told you; and certainly you will acknowledge that I have not been fortunate in my interviews with Napoleon."

·I am conscious how much St. Croix's story loses in my telling. The simple expressions, the grace of the narrative, were its charm; and these, alas! I can neither translate nor imitate, no more than I can convey the strange mixture of deep feeling and levity, shrewdness and simplicity, that constituted the manner of the narrator.

With many a story of his courtly career he amused me as we trotted along; when, towards nightfall of the third day, a peasant informed us that a body of French cavalry occupied the convent of San Cristoval, about three leagues off. The opportunity of his return to his own army pleased him far less than I expected; he heard without any show of satisfaction that the time of his liberation had arrived, and when the moment of leave-taking drew near, he became deeply affected.

"*Eh bien*, Charles," said he, smiling sadly through his dimmed and tearful eyes. "You've been a kind friend to me. Is the time never to come when I can repay you?"

"Yes, yes; we'll meet again, be assured of it. ‑ Meanwhile, there is one way you can more than repay anything I have done for you."

"Oh! name it at once."

"Many a brave fellow of ours is now, and, doubtless, many more will be, prisoners with your army in this war. Whenever, therefore, your lot brings you in contact with such——"

"They shall be my brothers," said he, springing towards me, and throwing his arms round my neck. "Adieu, adieu!" With that he rushed from the spot, and before I could speak again, was mounted upon the peasant's horse, and waving his hand to me in farewell.

I looked after him as he rode at a fast gallop down the slope of the green mountain, the noise of the horse's feet echoing along the silent plain. I turned at length to leave the spot, and then perceived, for the first time, that, when taking his farewell of me, he had hung round my neck his miniature of the Empress. Poor boy! how sorrowful I felt thus to rob him of what he held so dear! How gladly would I have overtaken him to restore it! It was the only keepsake he possessed; and knowing that I would not accept it if offered, he took this way of compelling me to keep it.

Through the long hours of the summer's night I thought of him; and, when at last I slept, towards morning, my first thought on waking was of the solitary day before me. The miles no longer slipped imperceptibly along; no longer did the noon and night seem fast to follow. Alas! that one should grow old! The very sorrows of our early years have something soft and touching in them. Arising less from deep wrong than slight mischances, the grief they cause comes ever with an alloy of pleasant thoughts, telling of the tender past, and, 'mid the tears they call up, forming some bright rainbow of future hope.

Poor St. Croix had already won greatly upon me, and I felt lonely and desolate when he departed.

CHAPTER LIII.

ALVAS.

NOTHING of incident marked our further progress towards the frontier of Spain, and at length we reached the small town of Alvas. It was past sunset as we arrived, and, instead of the usual quiet and repose of a little village, we found the streets crowded with people, on horseback and on foot; mules, bullocks, carts, and wagons blocked up the way, and the oaths of the drivers and the screaming of women and children resounded on all sides.

With what little Spanish I possessed, I questioned some of those near me, and learned, in reply, that a dreadful engagement had taken place that day between the advanced guard of the French, under Victor, and the Lusitanian legion; that the Portuguese troops had been beaten and completely routed, losing all their artillery and baggage; that the French were rapidly advancing, and expected hourly to arrive at Alvas, in consequence of which the terror-stricken inhabitants were packing up their possessions and hurrying away.

Here, then, was a point of considerable difficulty for me at once. My instructions had never provided for such a conjuncture, and I was totally unable to determine what was best to be done; both my men and their horses were completely tired by a march of fourteen leagues, and had a pressing need of some rest; on every side of me the preparations for flight were proceeding with all the speed that fear inspires; and to my urgent request for some information as to food and shelter, I could obtain no other reply than muttered menaces of the fate before me if I remained, and exaggerated accounts of French cruelty.

Amid all this bustle and confusion, a tremendous fall of heavy rain set in, which at once determined me, come what might, to house my party, and provide forage for our horses.

As we pushed our way slowly through the encumbered streets, looking on every side for some appearance of a village inn, a tremendous shout rose in our rear, and a rush of the people towards us induced us to suppose that the French were upon us. For some minutes the din and uproar were terrific—the clatter of horses' feet, the braying of trumpets, the yelling of the mob, all mingling in one frightful concert.

I formed my men in close column, and waited steadily for the attack, resolving, if possible, to charge through the advancing files, any retreat through the crowded and blocked-up thoroughfares being totally out of the question. The rain was falling in such torrents that nothing could be seen a few yards off, when suddenly a pause of a few seconds occurred, and, from the clash of accoutrements and the hoarse tones of a loud voice, I judged that the body of men before us were forming for attack.

Resolving, therefore, to take them by surprise, I gave the word to charge, and, spurring our jaded cattle, onward we dashed. The mob fled right and left from us as we came on; and through the dense mist we could just perceive a body of cavalry before us.

In an instant we were among them; down they went on every side, men and horses rolling pell-mell over each other—not a blow, not a shot striking us as we pressed on. Never did I witness such total consternation; some threw themselves from their horses, and fled towards the houses; others turned and tried to fall back, but the increasing pressure from behind held them, and finally succeeded in blocking us up amongst them.

It was just at this critical moment that a sudden gleam of light from a window fell upon the disordered mass, and to my astonishment—I need not say, to my delight—I perceived that they were Portuguese troops. Before I had well time to halt my party, my convictions were pretty well strengthened by hearing a well-known voice in the rear of the mass call out:—

"Charge, ye devils! charge, will ye? illustrious Hidalgos! cut them down; *los infidelos, sacrificiados los*—scatter them like chaff!"

One roar of laughter was my only answer to this energetic appeal for my destruction, and the moment after, the dry features and pleasant face of old Monsoon beamed on me by the light of a pine-torch he carried in his right hand.

"Are they prisoners?—have they surrendered?" inquired he, riding up. "It is well for them; we'd have made mincemeat of them otherwise; now they shall be well treated, and ransomed if they prefer."

"*Gracias excellenze!*" said I, in a feigned voice.

"Give up your sword," said the Major, in an undertone. "You behaved gallantly, but you fought against invincibles. Lord love them! but they are the most terrified invincibles."

I nearly burst aloud at this.

"It was a close thing which of us ran first," muttered the Major, as he turned to give some directions to an aide-de-camp. "Ask them who they are," said he, in Spanish.

By this time I came close alongside of him, and placing my mouth close to his ear, holloed out,—

"Monsoon, old fellow, how goes the King of Spain's sherry?"

"Eh!—what—why—upon my life, and so it is—Charley, my boy, so it's you, is it—egad, how good; and we were so near being the death of you! My poor fellow, how came you here?"

A few words of explanation sufficed to inform the Major why we were there, and still more to comfort him with the assurance that he had not been charging the General's staff, and the Commander-in-Chief himself.

"Upon my life, you gave me a great start; though, as long as I thought you were French, it was very well."

"True, Major, but certainly the invincibles were merciful as they were strong."

"They were tired, Charley—nothing more; why, lad, we've been fighting since daybreak—beat Victor at six o'clock—drove him back behind the Tagus—took a cold dinner, and had at him again in the afternoon... Lord love you! we've immortalized ourselves; but you must never speak of this little business here; it tells devilish ill for the discipline of your fellows, upon my life it does."

This was rather an original turn to give the transaction, but I did not oppose; and thus chatting, we entered the little inn, where, confidence once restored, some semblance of comfort already appeared.

"And so you're come to reinforce us?" said Monsoon; "there was never anything more opportune; though we surprised ourselves to-day with valor, I don't think we could persevere."

"Yes, Major, the appointment gave me sincere pleasure; I greatly desired to see a little service under your orders. Shall I present you with my despatches?"

"Not now, Charley—not now, my lad. Supper is the first thing at this moment; besides, now that you remind me, I must send off a despatch myself. Upon my life, it's a great piece of fortune that you're here; you shall be Secretary at War, and write it for me; here now—how lucky that I thought of it, to be sure! and that was just a mere chance; one has so many things——" Muttering such broken, disjointed sentences, the Major opened a large portfolio with writing materials, which he displayed before me as he rubbed his hands with satisfaction, and said, "Write away, lad."

"But, my dear Major, you forget; I was not in the action. You must describe; I can only follow you."

"Begin then thus:—

"'Head-Quarters, Alvas, June 26.

"'YOUR EXCELLENCY,

"'Having learned from Don Alphonzo Xaviero da Minto, an officer upon my personal staff——'

"Luckily sober at that moment——

"'That the advanced guard of the eighth corps of the French army——'

"Stay, though, was it the eighth? Upon my life, I'm not quite clear as to that; blot the word a little and go on——

"'That the —— corps, under Marshal Victor, had commenced a forward movement towards Alcantara, I immediately ordered a flank movement of the light infantry regiment to cover the bridge over the Tagus. After breakfast——'"

"I'm afraid, Major, that is not precise enough."

"Well, 'About eleven o'clock, the French skirmishers attacked, and drove in our pickets that were posted in front of our position, and following rapidly up with cavalry, they took a few prisoners, and killed old Alphonzo; he ran like a man, they say, but they caught him in the rear.'

"You needn't put that in, if you don't like.

"'I now directed a charge of the cavalry brigade under Don Asturias Y'Hajos, that cut them up in fine style. Our artillery, posted on the heights, mowed away at their columns like fun.

"'Victor didn't like this, and got into a wood, when we all went to dinner: it was about two o'clock then.

"'After dinner, the Portuguese light corps, under Silva da Onorha, having made an attack upon the enemy's left, without my orders, got devilishly well trounced, and served them right; but, coming up to their assistance, with the heavy brigade of guns, and the cavalry, we drove back the French, and took several prisoners, none of whom we put to death.'

"Dash that—Sir Arthur likes respect for the usages of war.—Lord, how dry I'm getting!

"'The French were soon seen to retire their heavy guns, and speedily afterwards retreated. We pursued them for some time, but they showed fight; and as it was getting dark, I drew off my forces, and came here to supper. Your Excellency will perceive, by the enclosed return, that our loss has been considerable.

"'I send this despatch by Don Emmanuel Forgalcs, whose services——'

"I back him for mutton hash with onions against the whole regiment——

"'Have been of the most distinguished nature, and beg to recommend him to your Excellency's favor.

"'I have the honor, &c.'

"Is it finished, Charley? Egad, I'm glad of it, for here comes supper."

The door opened as he spoke, and displayed a tempting tray of smoking viands, flanked by several bottles; an officer of the Major's staff accompanied it, and showed, by his attentions to the etiquette of the table, and the proper arrangement of the meal, that his functions in his superior's household were more than military.

We were speedily joined by two others in rich uniform, whose names I now forget, but to whom the Major presented me in all form, introducing me, as well as I could interpret his Spanish, as his most illustrious ally and friend, Don Carlos O'Malley.

CHAPTER LIV.

THE SUPPER.

I HAVE often partaken of more luxurious cookery and rarer wines; but never do I remember enjoying a more welcome supper than on this occasion.

Our Portuguese guests left us soon, and the Major and myself were once more *tête-à-tête* beside a cheerful fire; a well-chosen array of bottles guaranteeing that, for some time at least, no necessity of leave-taking should arise from any deficiency of wine.

"That sherry is very near the thing, Charley; a little, a very little sharp, but the after-taste perfect. And now, my boy, how have you been doing since we parted?"

"Not so badly, Major. I have already got a step in promotion. The affair at the Douro gave me a lieutenancy."

"I wish you joy with all my heart. I'll call you Captain always while you're with me. Upon my life I will. Why, man, they style me your Excellency here. Bless your heart! we are great folk among the Portuguese, and no bad service after all."

"I should think not, Major. You seem to have always made a good thing of it."

"No, Charley; no, my boy. They overlook us greatly in general orders and despatches. Had the brilliant action of to-day been fought by the British—but no matter; they may behave well in England, after all; and, when I'm called to the Upper House as Baron Monsoon of the Tagus—— is that better than Lord Alcantara?"

"I prefer the latter."

"Well, then, I'll have it. Lord! what a treaty I'll move for with Portugal, to let us have wine cheap. Wine, you know, as David says, gives us a pleasant countenance; and oil, I forget what oil does,—pass over the decanter. And how is Sir Arthur, Charley? A fine fellow, but sadly deficient in the knowledge of supplies.— Never would have made any character in the commissariat. Bless your heart, he pays for everything here, as if he were in Cheapside."

"How absurd, to be sure!"

"Isn't it, though? That was not my way, when I was commissary-general about a year or two ago. To be sure, how I did puzzle them! They tried to audit my accounts; and what do you think I did? I brought them in three thousand pounds in my debt. They never tried on that game any more. 'No! no!' said the Junta; 'Beresford and Monsoon are great men, and must be treated with respect.' Do you think we'd let them search our pockets? But the rogues doubled on us, after all; they sent us to the northward,—a poor country——"

"So that, except a little commonplace pillage of the convents and nunneries, you had little or nothing?"

"Exactly so; and then I got a great shock about that time, that affected my spirits for a considerable while."

"Indeed, Major! some illness?"

"No, I was quite well; but—Lord! how thirsty it makes me to think of it! my throat is absolutely parched,—I was near being hanged!"

"Hanged!"

"Yes. Upon my life it's true—very horrible, ain't it? It had a great effect upon my nervous system; and they never thought of any little pension to me, as a recompense for my sufferings."

"And who was barbarous enough to think of such a thing, Major?"

"Sir Arthur Wellesley himself; none other, Charley."

"Oh, it was a mistake, Major, or a joke."

"It was devilish near being a practical one, though. I'll tell you how it occurred. After the battle of Vimeira, the brigade to which I was attached had their head-quarters at San Pietro, a large convent where all the church plate for miles around was stored up for safety. A sergeant's guard was accordingly stationed over the refectory, and every precaution taken to prevent pillage, Sir Arthur himself having given particular orders on the subject. Well, some-how,—I never could find out how,—but in leaving the place all the wagons of our brigade had got some trifling articles of small value scattered, as it might be, among their stores—gold cups, silver-candlesticks, Virgin Marys, ivory crucifixes, saints' eyes set in topazes, and martyrs' toes in silver filigree, and a hundred other similar things.

"One of these confounded bullock-cars broke down just at the angle of the road where the Commander-in-Chief was standing with his staff to watch the troops defile, and out rolled, among bread rations and salt beef, a whole avalanche of precious relics and church ornaments. Every one stood aghast! Never was there such a misfortune. No one endeavored to repair the mishap, but all looked on in terrified amazement as to what was to follow.

"'Who has command of this detachment?' shouted out Sir Arthur, in a voice that made more than one of us tremble.

"'Monsoon, your Excellency—Major Monsoon, of the Portuguese brigade.'

"'The d— old rogue!—I know him.' Upon my life that's what he said. 'Hang him up on the spot,' pointing with his finger as he spoke; 'we shall see if this practice cannot be put a stop to.' And with these words he rode leisurely away, as if he had been merely ordering dinner for a small party.

"When I came up to the place, the halberts were fixed, and Gronow, with a company of the Fusiliers, under arms beside them.

"'Devilish sorry for it, Major,' said he. 'It's confoundedly unpleasant, but it can't be helped. We've got orders to see you hanged!'

"Faith it was just so he said it, tapping his snuff-box as he spoke, and looking carelessly about him. Now had it not been for the fixed halberts and the Provost-Marshal, I'd not have believed him; but one glance at them, and another at the bullock-cart with all the holy images, told me at once what had happened.

"'He only means to frighten me a little. Isn't that all, Gronow?' cried I, in a supplicating voice.

"'Very possibly, Major,' said he; 'but I must execute my orders.'

"'You'll surely not——' Before I could finish, up came Dan Mackinnon, cantering smartly. 'Going to hang old Monsoon, eh, Gronow? What fun!'

"'Ain't it, though?' said I, half blubbering.

" ' Well, if you're a good Catholic, you may have your choice of a saint, for, by Jupiter! there's a strong muster of them here.' This cruel allusion was made in reference to the gold and silver effigies that lay scattered about the highway.

" ' Dan,' said I, in a whisper, ' intercede for me—do, like a good, kind fellow. You have influence with Sir Arthur.'

" ' You old sinner,' said he, ' it's useless.'

" ' Dan, I'll forgive you the fifteen pounds.'

" ' That you owe *me*,' said Dan, laughing.

" ' Who'll ever be the father to you I have been? Who'll mix your punch with burnt Madeira, when I'm gone ?' said I.

" ' Well, really, I am sorry for you, Monsoon. I say, Gronow, don't tuck him up for a few minutes; I'll speak for the old villain, and if I succeed, I'll wave my handkerchief.'

" Well, away went Dan at a full gallop. Gronow sat down on a bank, and I fidgeted about in no very enviable frame of mind, the confounded Provost-Marshal eyeing me all the while.

" ' I can only give you five minutes more, Major,' said Gronow, placing his watch beside him on the grass. I tried to pray a little, and said three or four of Solomon's proverbs, when he again called out,—' There, you see it won't do! Sir Arthur is shaking his head.'

" ' What's that waving yonder ?

" ' The colors of the Sixth Foot. Come, Major, off with your stock.'

" ' Where is Dan now—what is he doing ?'—for I could see nothing myself.

" ' He's riding beside Sir Arthur. They all seem laughing.'

" ' God forgive them ! What an awful retrospect this will prove to some of them.'

" ' Time's up !' said Gronow, jumping up and replacing his watch in his pocket.

" ' Provost-Marshal, be quick now ——'

" ' Eh ? what's that?—there, I see it waving !—there's a shout, too !'

" ' Ay, by Jove! so it is. Well, you're saved this time, Major,— that's the signal.'

" So saying, Gronow formed his fellows in line and resumed his march quite coolly, leaving me alone on the roadside, to meditate over martial law and my pernicious taste for relics.

" Well, Charley, this gave me a great shock, and I think, too, it must have had a great effect upon Sir Arthur himself; but, upon my life, he has wonderful nerves. I met him one day afterwards at dinner in Lisbon ; he looked at me very hard for a few seconds— ' Eh, Monsoon ! Major Monsoon, I think ?'

22

" ' Yes, your Excellency,' said I, briefly, thinking how painful it must be for him to meet me.

" ' Thought I had hanged you—know I intended it. No matter—a glass of wine with you ?'

" Upon my life, that was all. How easily some people can forgive themselves. But, Charley, my hearty, we are getting on slowly with the tipple. Are they all empty ? So they are ! Let us make a sortie on the cellar. Bring a candle with you, and come along."

We had scarcely proceeded a few steps from the door, when a most vociferous sound of mirth, arising from a neighboring apartment, arrested our progress.

" Are the Dons so convivial, Major ?" said I, as a hearty burst of laughter broke forth at the moment.

" Upon my life, they surprise me ; I begin to fear they have taken some of our wine."

We now perceived that the sounds of merriment came from the kitchen, which opened upon a little court-yard. Into this we crept stealthily, and approaching noiselessly to the window, obtained a peep at the scene within.

Around a blazing fire, over which hung by a chain a massive iron pot, sat a goodly party of some half-dozen people. One group lay in dark shadow, but the others were brilliantly lighted up by the cheerful blaze, and showed us a portly Dominican friar, with a beard down to his waist; a buxom, dark-eyed girl of some eighteen years; and between the two, most comfortably leaning back, with an arm round each, no less a person than my trusty man, Mickey Free.

It was evident from the alternate motion of his head that his attentions were evenly divided between the Church and the fair sex ; although, to confess the truth, they seemed much more favorably received by the latter than the former—a brown earthen flagon appearing to absorb all the worthy monk's thoughts that he could spare from the contemplation of heavenly objects.

" Mary, my darlin', don't be looking at me that way,. through the corner of your eye. I know you're fond of me—but the girls always was. You think I'm joking, but troth I wouldn't say a lie before the holy man beside me ; sure I wouldn't, father."

The friar grunted out something in reply, not very unlike, in sound at least, a hearty anathema.

" Ah, then, isn't it yourself has the illigant time of it, father dear !" said he, tapping him familiarly upon his ample paunch, " and nothing to trouble you; the best of divarsion wherever you go, and whether it's Badahos or Ballykilruddery, it's all one; the women is fond of ye. Father Murphy, the coadjutor in Scariff, was just such another as yourself, and he'd coax the birds off the trees with the tongue of him. Give us a pull at the pipkin before it's all gone, and I'll give you a chant."

With this he seized the jar, and drained it to the bottom—the smack of his lips as he concluded, and the disappointed look of the friar, as he peered into the vessel, throwing the others once more into a loud burst of laughter.

"And now, your rev'rance, a good chorus is all I'll ask, and you'll not refuse it for the honor of the Church."

So saying, he turned a look of most droll expression upon the monk, and began the following ditty, to the air of "St. Patrick was a gentleman."

> "What an illigant life a friar leads,
>   With a fat round paunch before him;
> He mutters a prayer and counts his beads,
>   And all the women adore him.
> It's little he's troubled to work or to think,
>   Wherever devotion leads him;
> A 'pater' pays for his dinner and drink,
>   For the Church—good luck to her!—feeds him.
>
> "From the cow in the field to the pig in the sty,
>   From the maid to the lady in satin,
> They tremble wherever he turns an eye;
>   He can talk of the devil in Latin!
> He's mighty severe to the ugly and ould,
>   And curses like mad when he's near 'em;
> But one beautiful trait of him I've been tould,
>   The innocent craytures don't fear him.
>
> "It's little for spirits or ghosts he cares;
>   For 'tis true as the world supposes,
> With an *ave* he'd make them march down stairs,
>   Av they dared to show their noses.
> The devil himself's afraid, 'tis said,
>   And dares not to deride him;
> For 'angels make each night his bed,
>   And then—lie down beside him.'"

A perfect burst of laughter from Monsoon prevented my hearing how Mike's minstrelsy succeeded within doors, but when I looked again, I found that the friar had decamped, leaving the field open to his rival—a circumstance, I could plainly perceive, not disliked by either party.

"Come back, Charley; that villain of yours has given me the cramp, standing here on the cold pavement. We'll have a little warm posset—very small and thin, as they say in 'Tom Jones,'—and then to bed."

Notwithstanding the abstemious intentions of the Major it was daybreak ere we separated, neither party being in a condition for performing upon the tight-rope.

CHAPTER LV.

THE LEGION.

MY services while with the Legion were of no very distinguished character, and require no lengthened chronicle. Their great feat of arms, the repulse of an advanced guard of Victor's corps, had taken place the very morning I had joined them, and the ensuing month was passed in soft repose upon their laurels.

For the first few days, indeed, a multiplicity of cares beset the worthy Major. There was a despatch to be written to Beresford, another to the Supreme Junta, a letter to Wilson, at that time with a corps of observation to the eastward. There were some wounded to be looked after, a speech to be made to the conquering heroes themselves, and, lastly, a few prisoners were taken, whose fate seemed certainly to partake of the most uncertain of war's proverbial chances.

The despatches gave little trouble; with some very slight alterations, the great original, already sent forward to Sir Arthur, served as a basis for the rest. The wounded were forwarded to Alcantara, with a medical staff, to whom Monsoon, at parting, pleasantly hinted that he expected to see all the sick at their duty by an early day, or he would be compelled to report the doctors. The speech, which was intended as a kind of general order, he deferred for some favorable afternoon, when he could get up his Portuguese; and, lastly, came to the prisoners, by far the most difficult of all his cares. As for the few common soldiers taken, they gave him little uneasiness; as Sir John has it, they were "mortal men, and food for powder;" but there was a staff officer among them, aiguilletted and epauletted. The very decorations he wore were no common temptation. Now, the Major deliberated a long time with himself whether the usages of modern war might not admit of the ancient, time-honored practice of ransom. The battle, save in glory, had been singularly unproductive; plunder there was none; the few ammunition-wagons and gun-carriages were worth little or nothing; so that, save the prisoners, nothing remained. It was late in the evening—the mellow hour of the Major's meditations—when he ventured to open his heart to me upon the matter.

"I was just thinking, Charley, how very superior they were in olden time to us moderns, in many matters, and nothing more than in their treatment of prisoners. They never took them away from their friends and country; they always ransomed them—if they had wherewithal to pay their way. So good-natured—upon my life it was a most excellent custom. They took any little valuables they found about them, and then put them up at auction. Moses and Eleazar, a priest, we are told, took every piece of gold, and their wrought jewels—meaning their watches and earrings. You needn't laugh; they all wore earrings, those fellows did. Now, why shouldn't I profit by their good example? I have taken Agag, the king of the Amalekites—no, but, upon my life, I have got a French Major, and I'd let him go for fifty doubloons."

It was not without much laughing and some eloquence that I could persuade Monsoon that Sir Arthur's military notions might not accept of even the authority of Moses; and, as our head-quarters were at no great distance, the danger of such a step as he meditated was too considerable at such a moment.

As for ourselves, no fatiguing drills, no harassing field-days, and no provoking inspections, interfered with the easy current of our lives. Foraging parties there were, it is true, and some occasional outpost duty was performed; but the officers for both were selected with a tact that proved the Major's appreciation of character; for while the gay, joyous fellow that sung a jovial song and loved his *liquor* was certain of being entertained at head-quarters, the less gifted and less congenial spirit had the happiness of scouring the country for forage, and presenting himself as a target to a French rifle.

My own endeavors to fulfil my instructions met with but little encouragement or support; and although I labored hard at my task, I must confess that the soil was a most ungrateful one. The cavalry were, it is true, composed mostly of young fellows well appointed, and in most cases well mounted; but a more disorderly, careless, undisciplined set of good-humored fellows never formed a corps in the world.

Monsoon's opinions were felt in every branch of the service, from the adjutant to the drummer-boy—the same reckless, indolent, plunder-loving spirit prevailed everywhere. And although under fire they showed no lack of gallantry or courage, the moment of danger past, discipline departed with it, and their only conception of benefiting by a victory consisted in the amount of pillage that resulted from it.

From time to time the rumors of great events reached us. We heard that Soult, having succeeded in reorganizing his beaten army, was, in conjunction with Ney's corps, returning from the North; that the Marshals were consolidating their forces in the neighborhood of Talavera, and that King Joseph himself, at the head of a large army, had marched for Madrid.

Menacing as such an aspect of affairs was, it had little disturbed the Major's equanimity; and when our advanced posts reported daily the intelligence that the French were in retreat, he cared little with what object of concentrating they retired, provided the interval between us grew gradually wider. His speculations upon the future were singularly prophetic. "You'll see, Charley, what will happen; old Cuesta will pursue them and get thrashed. The English will come up, and perhaps get thrashed too;' but we—God bless us! are only a small force, partially organized and ill to depend on; we'll go up the mountains till all is over!" Thus did the Major's discretion not only extend to the avoidance of danger, but he actually disqualified himself from even making its acquaintance.

Meanwhile, our operations consisted in making easy marches to Almarez, halting wherever the commissariat reported a well-stocked cellar or well-furnished hen-roost; taking the primrose path in life, and being, in the words of the Major, "contented and grateful, even amid great perils!"

CHAPTER LVI.

THE DEPARTURE.

ON the morning of the 10th July, a despatch reached us announcing that Sir Arthur Wellesley had taken up his head-quarters at Placentia, for the purpose of communicating with Cuesta, then at Casa del Puerto, and ordering me immediately to repair to the Spanish head-quarters, and await Sir Arthur's arrival, to make my report upon the effective state of our corps. As for me, I was heartily tired of the inaction of my present life, and, much as I relished the eccentricities of my friend the Major, longed ardently for a different sphere of action.

Not so Monsoon; the prospect of active employment, and the thoughts of being left once more alone,—for his Portuguese staff afforded him little society,—depressed him greatly, and, as the hour of my departure drew near, he appeared lower in spirits than I had ever seen him.

"I shall be very lonely without you, Charley," said he, with a sigh, as we sat the last evening together beside our cheerful wood fire. "I have little intercourse with the Dons; for my Portuguese is none of the best, and only comes when the evening is far advanced; and, besides, the villains, I fear, may remember the sherry affair. Two of my present staff were with me then."

"Is that the story Power so often alluded to, Major, the King of Spain's ——?"

"There, Charley, hush—be cautious, my boy. I'd rather not speak about that till we get amongst our own fellows."

"Just as you like, Major; but, do you know, I have a strong curiosity to hear the narrative?"

"If I'm not mistaken, there is some one listening at the door—gently—that's it, eh?"

"No, we are perfectly alone; the night's early—who knows when we shall have as quiet an hour again together? Let me hear it by all means."

"Well, I don't care. The thing, Heaven knows! is tolerably well known; so, if you'll amuse yourself making a devil of the turkey's legs there, I'll tell you the story. It's very short, Charley, and there's no moral; so you're not likely to repeat it."

So saying, the Major filled up his glass, drew a little closer to the fire, and began :—

"When the French troops under Laborde were marching upon Alcobaca, in concert with Loison's corps, I was ordered to convey a very valuable present of sherry the Duc d'Albuquerque was making to the Supreme Junta—no less than ten hogsheads of the best sherry the royal cellars of Madrid had formerly contained.

"It was stored in the San Vincente convent; and the Junta, knowing a little about monkish tastes and the wants of the Church, prudently thought it would be quite as well at Lisbon. I was accordingly ordered with a sufficient force to provide for its safe-conduct and secure arrival, and set out upon my march one lovely morning in April with my precious convoy.

"I don't know, I never could understand, why temptations are thrown in our way in this life, except for the pleasure of yielding to them. As for me, I'm a stoic when there's nothing to be had; but, let me get a scent of a well-kept haunch, the odor of a wine-bin once in my nose, I forget everything except appropriation.—That bone smells deliciously, Charley; a little garlic would improve it vastly.

"Our road lay through cross paths and mountain tracts—for the French were scouring the country on every side—and my fellows, only twenty altogether, trembled at the very name of them; so that our only chance was to avoid falling in with any forage parties. We journeyed along for several days, rarely making more than a few leagues between sunrise and sunset, a scout always in advance to assure us that all was safe. The road was a lonesome one, and the way weary,—for I had no one to speak to or converse with,—so I fell into a kind of musing fit about the old wine in the great brown casks. I thought on its luscious flavor, its rich straw tint, its oily look as it flowed into the glass, the mellow after-taste, warming the heart as it went down, and I absolutely thought I could smell it through the wood.

"How I longed to broach one of them, if it were only to see if my dreams about it were correct. 'Maybe it's brown sherry,' thought I, 'and I am all wrong.' This was a very distressing reflection. I mentioned it to the Portuguese Intendant, who travelled with us as a kind of supercargo; but the villain only grinned, and said something about the Junta and the galleys for life; so I did not recur to it afterwards. Well, it was upon the third evening of our march that the scout reported that at Merida, about a league distant, he had fallen in with an English cavalry regiment, who were on their march to the northern provinces, and remaining that night in the village. As soon, therefore, as I had made all my arrangements for the night, I took a fresh horse, and cantered over to have a look at my countrymen, and hear the news. When I arrived it was dark night; but I was not long in finding out our fellows. They were the 11th Light Dragoons, commanded by my old friend Bowes, and with as jolly a mess as any in the service.

"Before half an hour's time I was in the midst of them, hearing all about the campaign, and telling them in return about my convoy—dilating upon the qualities of the wine, as if I had been drinking it every day at dinner.

"We had a very mellow night of it, and before four o'clock the senior major and four captains were under the table, and all the subs. in a state unprovided for by the articles of war. So I thought I'd be going, and, wishing the sober ones a good-bye, set out on my road to join my own party.

"I had not gone above a hundred yards, when I heard some one running after me, and calling out my name.

"'I say, Monsoon; Major, confound you, pull up.'

"'Well, what's the matter? has any more lush turned up?' inquired I—for we had drunk the tap dry when I left.

"'Not a drop, old fellow,' said he; 'but I was thinking of what you've been saying about that sherry.'

"'Well! what then?'

"'Why, I want to know how we could get a taste of it?'

"'You'd better get elected one of the Cortes,' said I, laughing; 'for it does not seem likely you'll do so in any other way.'

"'I'm not so sure of that,' said he, smiling. 'What road do you travel to-morrow?'

"'By Cavalhos and Reina.'

"'Whereabouts may you happen to be towards sunset?'

"'I fear we shall be in the mountains,' said I, with a knowing look, 'where ambuscades and surprise parties would be highly dangerous.'

"'And your party consists of——?'

"'About twenty Portuguese, all ready to run at the first shot.'

"'I'll do it, Monsoon! I'll be hanged if I don't.'

"'But Tom,' said I, 'don't make any blunder; only blank cartridge, my boy.'

"'Honor bright!' cried he; 'your fellows are armed, of course?'

"'Never think of that; they may shoot each other in the confusion; but if you only make plenty of noise coming on, they'll never wait for you.'

"'What capital fellows they must be!'

"'Crack troops, Tom; so don't harm them. And now, good-night.'

"As I cantered off, I began to think over O'Flaherty's idea, and, upon my life, I didn't half like it. He was a reckless, devil-may-care fellow, and it was just as likely he would really put his scheme into practice.

"When morning broke, however, we got under way again, and I amused myself all the forenoon in detailing stories of French cruelty; so that, before we had marched ten miles, there was not a man amongst us not ready to run at the slightest sound of attack on any side. As evening was falling, we reached Morento, a little mountain pass which follows the course of a small river, and where in many places the mule-carts had barely space enough to pass between the cliffs and the stream. 'What a place for Tom O'Flaherty and his foragers!' thought I, as we entered the little mountain gorge; but all was silent as the grave; except the tramp of our party, not a sound was heard. There was something solemn and still in the great brown mountain, rising like a vast wall on either side, with a narrow streak of gray sky at top, and in the dark sluggish stream, that seemed to awe us, and no one spoke; the muleteer ceased his merry song, and did not crack or flourish his long whip as before, but chid his beasts in a half-muttered voice, and urged them faster, to reach the village before nightfall.

"Egad, somehow I felt uncommonly uncomfortable; I could not divest my mind of the impression that some disaster was impending, and I wished O'Flaherty and his project in a very warm climate. 'He'll attack us,' thought I, 'where we can't run; fair play forever; but if they are not able to get away, even the militia will fight.' However, the evening crept on, and no sign of his coming appeared on any side. To my sincere satisfaction, I could see, about half a league distant, the twinkling light of the little village where we were to halt for the night. It was just at this time that a scout I had sent out some few hundred yards in advance came galloping up, almost breathless.

"'The French, captain—the French are upon us!' said he, with a face like a ghost.

"'Whew! Which way? how many?' said I, not at all sure that he might not be telling the truth.

"'Coming in force!' said the fellow: 'dragoons—by this road.'

"'Dragoons? By this road?' repeated every man of the party, looking at each other like men sentenced to be hanged.

"Scarcely had they spoken, when we heard the distant noise of cavalry advancing at a brisk trot. Lord, what a scene ensued! The soldiers ran hither and thither like frightened sheep; some pulled out crucifixes and began to say their prayers; others fired off their muskets in a panic; the mule-drivers cut their traces, and endeavored to get away by riding; and the Intendant took to his heels, screaming out to us, as he went, to fight manfully to the last, and that he'd report us favorably to the Junta.

"Just at this moment the dragoons came in sight; they came galloping up, shouting like madmen. One look was enough for my fellows; they sprang to their legs from their devotions; fired a volley straight at the new moon, and ran like men.

"I was knocked down in the rush. As soon as I regained my legs, Tom O'Flaherty was standing beside me, laughing like mad.

"'Eh, Monsoon! I've kept my word, old fellow! What legs they have! We shall make no prisoners, that's certain. Now, lads, here it is; put the horses to, here. We shall take but one, Monsoon, so that your gallant defence of the rest will please the Junta. Good-night! good-night! I will drink your health every night these two months.'

"So saying, Tom sprang to his saddle, and in less time than I've been telling it the whole was over, and I sitting by myself in the gray moonlight, meditating on all I saw, and now and then shouting to my Portuguese friends to come back again. They came in time, by twos and threes, and at last the whole party reassembled, and we set forth again,—every man, from the Intendant to the drummer, lauding my valor, and saying that Don Monsoon was a match for the Cid."

"And how did the Junta behave?"

"Like trumps, Charley. Made me a Knight of Battalha, and kissed me on both cheeks, having sent twelve dozen of the rescued wine to my quarters, as a small testimony of their esteem. I have laughed very often at it since. But, hush, Charley! What's that I hear without there?"

"Oh, it's my fellow Mike. He asked my leave to entertain his friends before parting, and I perceive he is delighting them with a song."

"But what a confounded air it is! Are the words Hebrew?"

"Irish, Major—most classical Irish, too, I'll be bound."

"Irish! I think I've heard most tongues; but that certainly surprises me. Call him in, however, Charley, and let us have the canticle."

In a few minutes more Mr. Free appeared, in a state of very satisfactory elevation, his eyebrows alternately rising and falling, his mouth a little drawn to one side, and a side motion in his knee-joints that might puzzle a physiologist to account for.

"A sweet little song of yours, Mike," said the Major,—"a very sweet thing indeed. Wet your lips, Mickey."

"Long life to your honor, and Master Charles there too, and them that belongs to both of yez. May a gooseberry skin make a night-cap for the man would harm either of ye."

"Thank you, Mike. And now about that song."

"It's the ouldest tune ever was sung," said Mike, with a hiccup, "barrin' Adam had a taste for music; but the words—the poethry —is not so ould."

" And how comes that?"

" The poethry, ye see, was put to it by one of my ancesthors,—he was a great inventhor in times past, and made beautiful songs,—and ye'd never guess what it's all about."

" Love, mayhap?" quoth Monsoon.

"Sorra taste of kissin' from beginning to end."

" A drinking song?" said I.

" Whisky is never mentioned." .

"Fighting is the only other national pastime. It must be in praise of sudden death."

"You're out again; but sure you'd never guess it," said Mike. "Well, ye see, here's what it is. It's the praise and glory of ould Ireland in the great days that's gone, when we were all Phenay-ceans and Armanians, and when we worked all manner of beautiful contrivances in goold and silver—bracelets, and collars, and tea-pots, illigant to look at; and read Roosian and Latin, and playcd the harp and the barrel-organ; and ate and drank of the best, for nothing but asking."

"Blessed times, upon my life!" quoth the Major; "I wish we had them back again."

"There's more of your mind," said Mike, steadying himself. "My ancesthors was great people in them days; and sure it isn't in my present situation I'd be av we had them back again—sorra bit, faith! It isn't 'Come here, Mickey, bad luck to you, Mike!' or, 'That blackguard, Mickey Free!' people'd be calling me. But no matter; here's your health again, Major Monsoon——"

"Never mind vain regrets, Mike. Let us hear your song; the Major has taken a great fancy to it."

"Ah, then, it's joking you are, Misther Charles," said Mike, affecting an air of most bashful coyness.

"By no means; we want to hear you sing it."

"To be sure we do. Sing it, by all means; never be ashamed. King David was very fond of singing—upon my life he was."

"But you'd never understand a word of it, sir."

"No matter; we know what it's about. That's the way with the Legion; they don't know much English, but they generally guess what I'm at."

This argument seemed to satisfy all Mike's remaining scruples, so, placing himself in an attitude of considerable pretension as to grace, he began, with a voice of no very measured compass, an air, of which, neither by name nor otherwise, can I give any conception, my principal amusement being derived from a tol-de-rol chorus of the Major, which concluded each verse, and, indeed, in a lower key, accompanied the singer throughout.

Since that I have succeeded in obtaining a free-and-easy transla- tion of the lyric; but in my anxiety to preserve the metre and something of the spirit of the original, I have made several blunders and many anachronisms. Mr. Free, however, pronounces my ver- sion to be a very good one, and the world must take his word till some more worthy translator shall have consigned it to immortal verse.

With this apology, therefore, I present Mr. Free's song, which is set to the air—"Na Guilloch y' Goulen."

> "Oh! once we were illigant people,
>   Though we now live in cabins of mud;
> And the land that ye see from the steeple
>   Belonged to us all from the flood.
> My father was then king of Connaught,
>   My grand-aunt viceroy of Tralee;
> But the Sassenach came, and, signs on it,
>   The devil an acre have we.

> "The least of us then were all earls,
>   And jewels we wore without name;
> We drank punch out of rubies and pearls—
>   Mr. Petrie can tell you the same.
> But, except some turf mould and potatoes,
>   There's nothing our own we can call;
> And the English—bad luck to them!—hate us,
>   Because we've more fun than them all!

> "My grand-aunt was niece to St. Kevin,
>   That's the reason my name's Mickey Free!
> Priest's nieces—but sure he's in heaven,
>   And his failins is nothing to me.
> And we still might get on without doctors,
>   If they'd let the ould island alone;
> And if purple men, priests, and tithe-proctors,
>   Were crammed down the great gun of Athlone."

As Mike's melody proceeded, the Major's thorough bass waxed beautifully less—now and then, it's true, roused by some momentary strain, it swelled upward in full chorus; but gradually these passing flights grew rarer, and finally all ceased, save a long, low, droning sound, like the expiring sigh of a wearied bagpipe. His fingers still continued mechanically to beat time upon the table, and still his head nodded sympathetically to the music; his eyelids closed in sleep, and, as the last verse concluded, a full-drawn snore announced that Monsoon, if not in the land of dreams, was, at least, in a happy oblivion of all terrestrial concerns, and caring as little for the woes of green Erin and the altered fortunes of the Free family as any Saxon that ever oppressed them.

There he sat, the finished decanter and empty goblet testifying that his labors had only ceased from the pressure of necessity; but the broken, half-uttered words that fell from his lips evinced that he reposed on the last bottle of the series.

"Oh, thin, he's a fine ould gentleman," said Mike, after a pause of some minutes, during which he had been contemplating the Major with all the critical acumen Chantrey or Canova would have bestowed upon an antique statue—"a fine ould gentleman, every inch of him; and it's the master would like to have him up at the castle."

"Quite true, Mike; but let us not forget the road. Look to the cattle, and be ready to start within an hour."

When he left the room for this purpose, I endeavored to shake the Major into momentary consciousness ere we parted.

"Major, Major," said I, "time is up. I must start."

"Yes, it's all true, your Excellency; they pillaged a little; and, if they did change their facings, there was a great temptation. All the red velvet they found in the churches——"

"Good-bye, old fellow, good-bye!"

"Stand at ease!"

"Can't, unfortunately, yet awhile; so farewell. I'll make a capital report of the Legion to Sir Arthur. Shall I add anything particularly from yourself?"

This, and the shake that accompanied it, aroused him. He started up, and looked about him for a few seconds.

"Eh, Charley! You didn't say Sir Arthur was here, did you?"

"No, Major; don't be frightened; he's many a league off. I asked if you had anything to say when I met him."

"Oh yes, Charley. Tell him we're capital troops in our own little way in the mountains; would never do in pitched battles; skirmishing's our forte; and for cutting off stragglers or sacking a town, back them at any odds."

"Yes, yes, I know all that: you've nothing more?"

"Nothing," said he, once more closing his eyes and crossing his hands before him, while his lips continued to mutter on, "Nothing more, except you may say from me,—he knows me, Sir Arthur does. Tell him to guard himself from intemperance: a fine fellow if he wouldn't drink."

"You horrid old humbug, what nonsense are you muttering there?"

"Yes, yes; Solomon says, ' Who hath red eyes and carbuncles?' —they that mix their lush. Pure *Sneyd* never injured any one. Tell him so from me: it's an old man's advice, and I have drunk some hogsheads of it."

With these words he ceased to speak, while his head, falling gently forward upon his chest, proclaimed him sound asleep.

"Adieu! then, for the last time," said I, slapping him gently on the shoulder; "and now for the road."

<hr>

CHAPTER LVII.

CUESTA.

THE second day of our journey was drawing to a close as we came in view of the Spanish army. The position they occupied was an undulating plain beside the Teitar river. The country presented no striking feature of picturesque beauty; but the scene before us needed no such aid to make it one of the most interesting kind. From the little mountain path we travelled, we beheld beneath a force of thirty thousand men drawn up in battle array; dense columns of infantry, alternating with squadrons of horse or dark masses of artillery, dotted the wide plain, the bright steel glittering in the rich sunset of a July evening. Not a breath of air was stirring; the very banners hung down listlessly, and not a sound broke the solemn stillness of the hour. All was silent. So impressive and so strange was the spectacle of a vast army thus resting mutely under arms, that I reined in my horse, and almost doubted the reality of the scene as I gazed upon it. The dark shadows of the tall mountain were falling across the valley, and a starry sky was already replacing the ruddy glow of sunset as we reached the plain ; but still no change took place in the position of the Spanish army.

"Who goes there?" cried a hoarse voice, as we issued from the mountain gorge, and in a moment we found ourselves surrounded by an outpost party. Having explained, as well as I was able, who I was, and for what reason I was there, I proceeded to accompany the officer towards the camp.

On my way thither I learned the reason of the singular display of troops which had been so puzzling to me. From an early hour of that day Sir Arthur Wellesley's arrival had been expected, and old Cuesta had drawn up his men for inspection, and remained thus for several hours patiently awaiting his coming; he himself, overwhelmed with years and infirmity, sitting upon his horse the entire time.

As it was not necessary that I should be presented to the General, my report being for the ear of Sir Arthur himself, I willingly availed myself of the hospitality proffered by a Spanish officer of cavalry. Having provided for the comforts of my tired cattle and taken a hasty supper, I issued forth to look at the troops, which, although it was now growing late, were still in the same attitude.

Scarcely had I been half an hour thus occupied, when the stillness of the scene was suddenly interrupted by the loud report of a large gun, immediately followed by a long roll of musketry, while at the same moment the bands of the different regiments struck up, and, as if by magic, a blaze of red light streamed across the dark ranks. This was effected by pine-torches held aloft at intervals, throwing a lurid glow upon the grim and swarthy features of the Spaniards, whose brown uniforms and slouching hats presented a most picturesque effect as the red light fell upon them.

The swell of the thundering cannon grew louder and nearer ; the shouldering of muskets, the clash of sabres, and the hoarse roll of the drum, mingling in one common din. .I at once guessed that Sir Arthur had arrived, and as I turned the flank of a battalion, I saw the staff approaching.

Nothing can be conceived more striking than their advance. In the front rode old Cuesta himself, clad in the costume of a past century, his slashed doublet and trunk hose reminding one of a more chivalrous period ; his heavy, unwieldy figure, looming from side to side, and threatening at each moment to fall from his saddle. On each side of him walked two figures gorgeously dressed, whose duty appeared to be to sustain the chief in his seat. At his side rode a far different figure. Mounted upon a slight-made, active thorough-bred, whose drawn flanks bespoke a long and weary journey, sat Sir Arthur Wellesley, a plain blue frock and gray trousers being his unpretending costume; but the eagle glance which he threw around on every side, the quick motion of his hand as he pointed hither and thither among the dense battalions, bespoke him every inch a soldier. Behind them came a brilliant staff, glittering in aiguillettes and golden trappings, among whom I recognized some well-remembered faces, our gallant leader at the Douro, Sir Charles Stewart, among the number.

As they passed the spot where I was standing, the torch of a foot soldier behind me flared suddenly up, and threw a strong flash upon the party. Cuesta's horse grew frightened, and plunged so fearfully for a minute, that the poor old man could scarcely keep his seat. A smile shot across Sir Arthur's features at the moment, but the next instant he was grave and steadfast as before.

A wretched hovel, thatched and in ruins, formed the head-quarters of the Spanish army, and thither the staff now bent their steps; a supper being provided there for our Commander-in-Chief and the officers of his suite. Although not of the privileged party, I lingered round the spot for some time, anxiously expecting to find some friend or acquaintance, who might tell me the news of our people, and what events had occurred in my absence.

CHAPTER LVIII.

THE LETTER.

THE hours passed slowly over, and I at length grew weary of waiting. For some time I had amused myself with observing the slouching gait and unsoldier-like air of the Spaniards as they lounged carelessly about, looking, in dress, gesture, and appointment, far more like a guerilla than a regular force. Then, again, the strange contrast of the miserable hut, with falling chimneys and ruined walls, to the glitter of the mounted guard of honor who sat motionless beside it, served to pass the time; but as the night was already far advanced, I turned towards my quarters, hoping that the next morning might gratify my curiosity about my friends.

Beside the tent where I was billeted, I found Mike in waiting, who, the moment he saw me, came hastily forward with a letter in his hand. An officer of Sir Arthur's staff had left it while I was absent, desiring Mike on no account to omit its delivery the first instant he met me. The hand—not a very legible one—was perfectly unknown to me, and the appearance of the billet such as betrayed no over-scrupulous care in the writer.

I trimmed my lamp leisurely, threw a fresh log upon the fire, disposed myself completely at full length beside it, and then proceeded to form acquaintance with my unknown correspondent. I will not attempt any description of the feelings which gradually filled me as I read on; the letter itself will suggest them to those who know my story. It ran thus.

PLACENTIA, July 8, 1809.

"DEAR O'MALLEY :—Although I'd rather march to Lisbon barefoot than write three lines, Fred Power insists upon my turning scribe, as he has a notion you'll be up at Cuesta's head-quarters about this time. You're in a nice scrape—devil a lie in it! Here has Fred been fighting that fellow Trevyllian for you—all because you would not have patience and fight him yourself the morning you left the Douro—so much for haste! Let it be a lesson to you for life.

"Poor Fred got the ball in his hip, and the devil a one of the doctors can find it. But he's getting better anyway, and going to Lisbon for change of air. Meanwhile, since Power's been wounded, Trevyllian's speaking very hardly of you, and they all say here you must come back—no matter how—and put matters to rights. Fred has placed the matter in my hands, and I'm thinking we'd better call out the 'heavies' by turns; for most of them stand by Trevyllian. Maurice Quill and myself sat up considering it last night; but, somehow, we don't clearly remember to-day a beautiful plan we hit upon. However, we'll have at it again this evening. Meanwhile, come over here, and let us be doing something. We hear that old Monsoon has blown up a town, a bridge, and a big convent. They must have been hiding the plunder very closely, or he'd never have been reduced to such extremities. We'll have a brush with the French soon.   Yours most eagerly,

"D. O'SHAUGHNESSY."

My first thought, as I ran my eyes over these lines, was to seek for Power's note, written on the morning we parted. I opened it, and to my horror found that it only related to my quarrel with Hammersley. My meeting with Trevyllian had been during Fred's absence; and when he assured me that all was satisfactorily ar-

23

ranged and a full explanation tendered—that nothing interfered with my departure—I utterly forgot that he was only aware of one half my troubles, and in the haste and bustle of my departure, had not a moment left me to collect myself and think calmly on the matter. The two letters lay before me, and as I thought over the stain upon my character thus unwittingly incurred,—the blast I had thrown upon my reputation, the wound of my poor friend, who exposed himself for my sake,—I grew sick at heart, and the bitter tears of agony burst from my eyes.

That weary night passed slowly over; the blight of all my prospects, when they seemed fairest and brightest, presented itself to me in a hundred shapes; and when, overcome by fatigue and exhaustion, I closed my eyes to sleep, it was only to follow up in my dreams my waking thoughts. Morning came at length, but its bright sunshine and balmy air brought no comfort to me. I absolutely dreaded to meet my brother officers; I felt that, in such a position as I stood, no half or partial explanation could suffice to set me right in their estimation; and yet, what opportunity had I for aught else? Irresolute how to act, I sat leaning my head upon my hands, when I heard a footstep approach. I looked up, and saw before me no other than my poor friend Sparks, from whom I had been separated so long. Any other adviser at such a moment would, I acknowledge, have been more welcome, for the poor fellow knew but little of the world, and still less of the service. However, one glance convinced me that his heart at least was true, and I shook his outstretched hand with delight. In a few words he informed me that Merivale had secretly commissioned him to come over, in the hope of meeting me; that although all the 14th men were persuaded that I was not to blame in what had occurred, yet that reports so injurious had gone abroad, so many partial and imperfect statements were circulated, that nothing but my return to head-quarters would avail, and that I must not lose a moment in having Trevyllian out, with whom all the misrepresentations had originated.

"This, of course," said Sparks, "is to be a secret; Merivale, being our Colonel——"

"Of course," said I, "he cannot countenance, much less counsel, such a proceeding. Now, then, for the road."

"Yes; but you cannot leave before making your report. Gordon expects to see you at eleven; he told me so last night."

"I cannot help it; I shall not wait; my mind is made up. My career here matters but little in comparison with this horrid charge. I shall be broken, but I shall be avenged."

"Come, come, O'Malley; you are in our hands now, and you must be guided. You *shall* wait: you shall see Gordon. Half an hour will make your report, and I have relays of horses along the road, and we shall reach Placentia by nightfall."

There was a tone of firmness in this so unlike anything I ever looked for in the speaker, and withal so much of foresight and precaution, that I could scarcely credit my senses as he spoke. Having at length agreed to his proposal, Sparks left me to think over my return to the Legion, promising that immediately after my interview with the Military Secretary, we should start together for headquarters.

CHAPTER LIX.

MAJOR O'SHAUGHNESSY.

THIS is Major O'Shaughnessy's quarters, sir, said a sergeant, as he stopped short at the door of a small low house in the midst of an olive plantation. An Irish wolf-dog—the well-known companion of the Major—lay stretched across the entrance, watching with eager and bloodshot eyes the process of cutting up a bullock, which two soldiers in undress jackets were performing within a few yards of the spot.

Stepping cautiously across the savage-looking sentinel, I entered the little hall, and, finding no one near, passed into a small room, the door of which lay half open.

A very palpable odor of cigars and brandy proclaimed, even without his presence, that this was O'Shaughnessy's sitting-room; so I sat myself down upon an old-fashioned sofa to wait patiently for his return, which I heard would be immediately after the evening parade. Sparks had become knocked up during our ride, so that for the last three leagues I was alone; and, like most men in such circumstances, pressed on only the harder. Completely worn out for want of rest, I had scarcely placed myself on the sofa when I fell sound asleep. When I awoke, all was dark around me, save the faint flickering of the wood embers on the hearth, and for some moments I could not remember where I was. By degrees recollection came, and as I thought over my position and its possible consequences, I was again nearly dropping asleep, when the door suddenly opened, and a heavy step sounded on the floor.

I lay still and spoke not, as a large figure in a cloak approached the fireplace, and stooping down, endeavored to light a candle at the fast expiring fire.

I had little difficulty in detecting the Major even by the half-light; a muttered execration upon the candle, given with an energy that only an Irishman ever bestows upon slight matters, soon satisfied me on this head.

"May the devil fly away with the commissary and the chandler to the forces! Ah! you've lit at last."

With these words he stood up, and his eyes falling on me at the moment, he sprang a yard or two backward, exclaiming, as he did so, "The blessed Virgin be near us, what's this?" a most energetic crossing of himself accompanying his words. My pale and haggard face, thus suddenly presented, having suggested to the worthy Major the impression of a supernatural visitor, a hearty burst of laughter, which I could not resist, was my only answer; and the next moment O'Shaughnessy was wrenching my hand in a grasp like a steel vice.

"Upon my conscience, I thought it was your ghost; and if you kept quiet a little longer, I was going to promise you Christian burial, and as many masses for your soul as my uncle the bishop could say between this and Easter. How are you, my boy?—a little thin and something paler, I think, than when you left us."

Having assured him that fatigue and hunger were in a great measure the cause of my sickly looks, the Major proceeded to place before me the remains of his day's dinner, with a sufficiency of bottles to satisfy a mess-table, keeping up as he went a running fire of conversation.

"I'm as glad as if the Lord took the senior Major to see you here this night. With the blessing of Providence we'll shoot Trevyllian in the morning, and any more of the heavies that like it. You are an ill-treated man, that's what it is, and Dan O'Shaughnessy says it. Help yourself, my boy: crusty old port in that bottle as ever you touched your lips to. Power's getting all right; it was contract powder, warranted not to kill. Bad luck to the commissaries once more! With such ammunition Sir Arthur does right to trust most to the bayonet. And how is Monsoon, the old rogue?"

"Gloriously; living in the midst of wine and olives."

"No fear of him, the old sinner; but he is a fine fellow, after all. Charley, you are eating nothing, boy."

"To tell you the truth, I'm far more anxious to talk with you at this moment than aught else."

"So you shall—the night's young. Meanwhile, I had better not delay matters. You want to have Trevyllian out—is not that so?"

"Of course; you are aware how it happened?"

"I know everything. Go on with your supper, and don't mind me; I'll be back in twenty minutes or less."

Without waiting for any reply, he threw his cloak around him, and strode out of the room. Once more I was alone; but already my frame of mind was altered. The cheering tone of my reckless, gallant countryman had raised my spirits, and I felt animated by his very manner.

An hour elapsed before the Major returned, and when he did come, his appearance and gestures bespoke anger and disappointment. He threw himself hurriedly into a seat, and for some minutes never spoke.

"The world's beautifully changed, anyhow, since I began it, O'Malley—when you thanked a man civilly that asked you to fight him. The devil take the cowards! say I."

"What has happened? Tell me, I·beseech you!"

"He won't fight," said the Major, blurting out the words as if they would choke him.

"He'll not fight! And why?"

The Major was silent: he seemed confused and embarrassed; he turned from the fire to the table, from the table to the fire, filled out a glass of wine, drank ʼit hastily off, and, springing from his chair, paced the room with long, impatient strides.

"My dear O'Shaughnessy, explain, I beg of you. Does he refuse to meet me for any reason——"

"He does," said the Major, turning on me a look of deep feeling as he spoke; "and he does it to ruin you, my boy; but, as sure as my name is Dan, he'll fail this time. He was sitting with his friend Beaufort when I reached his quarters, and received me with all the ceremonious politeness he well knows how to assume. I told him in a few words the object of my visit; upon which Trevyllian, standing up, referred me to his friend for a reply, and left the room. I thought that all was right, and sat down to discuss, as I believed, preliminaries, when the cool puppy, with his back to the fire, carelessly lisped out, 'It can't be, Major: your friend is too late.'

"'Too late! too late!' said I.

"'Yes, precisely so. Not up to time; the affair should have come off some weeks since. We won't meet him now.'

"'This is really your answer?'

"'This is really my answer; and not only so, but the decision of our mess.'

"What I said after this *he* may remember. Devil take me if *I* can; but I have a vague recollection of saying something that the aforesaid mess will never petition the Horse Guards to put on their regimental colors: and here I am——"

With these words the Major gulped down a full goblet of wine, and once more resumed his walk through the room. I shall not attempt to record the feelings which agitated me during the Major's recital. In one rapid glance I saw the aim of my vindictive enemy. My honor, not my life, was the object he sought for; and ten thousand times more than ever did I pant for the opportunity to confront him in a deadly combat.

"Charley," said O'Shaughnessy, at length, placing his hand upon my shoulder, "you must get to bed now—nothing more can be done to-night in any way. Be assured of one thing, my boy—I'll not desert you; and if that assurance can give you a sound sleep, you'll not need a lullaby."

CHAPTER LX.

PRELIMINARIES.

I AWOKE refreshed on the following morning, and came down to breakfast with a lighter heart than I had even hoped for; a secret feeling that all would go well had somehow taken possession of me, and I longed for O'Shaughnessy's coming, trusting that he might be able to confirm my hopes. His servant informed me that the Major had been absent since daybreak, and left orders that he was not to be waited for at breakfast.

I was not destined, however, to pass a solitary time in his absence, for every moment brought some new arrival to visit me, and during the morning the Colonel and every officer of the regiment not on actual duty came over. I soon learned that the feeling respecting Trevyllian's conduct was one of unmixed condemnation among my corps; but a kind of party spirit, which had subsisted for some months between the regiment he belonged to and the 14th, had given a graver character to the affair, and induced many men to take up his views of the transaction; and although I heard of none who attributed my absence to any dislike to a meeting, yet there were several who conceived that, by my not going at the time, I had forfeited all claim to satisfaction at his hands.

"Now that Merivale is gone," said an officer to me, as the Colonel left the room, "I may confess to you that he sees nothing to blame in your conduct throughout; and, even had you been aware of how matters were circumstanced, your duty was too imperative to have preferred your personal consideration to it!"

"Does any one know where Conyers is?" said Baker.

"The story goes that Conyers can assist us here. Conyers is at Zarza la Mayor, with the 28th; but what can he do?"

"That I'm not able to tell you! but I know O'Shaughnessy heard something at parade this morning, and has set off in search of him on every side."

"Was Conyers ever out with Trevyllian?"

"Not as a principal, I believe. The report is, however, that he knows more about him than other people, as Tom certainly does of everybody."

"It is rather a new thing for Trevyllian to refuse a meeting. They say, O'Malley, he has heard of your shooting!"

"No, no," said another, "he cares very little for any man's pistol. If the story be true, he fires a second or two before his adversary; at least, it was in that way he killed Carysfort."

"Here comes the great O'Shaughnessy!" cried some one at the window; and the next moment the heavy gallop of a horse was heard along the causeway.

In an instant we all rushed to the door to receive him.

"It's all right, lads," cried he, as he came up: "we have him this time."

"How? when? why? in what way have you managed?" fell from a dozen voices, as the Major elbowed his way through the crowd to the sitting-room.

"In the first place," said O'Shaughnessy, drawing a long breath, "I have promised secrecy as to the steps of this transaction; secondly, if I hadn't, it would puzzle me to break it, for I'll be hanged if I know more than yourselves. Tom Conyers wrote me a few lines for Trevyllian, and Trevyllian pledges himself to meet our friend; and that's all we need know or care for."

"Then you have seen Trevyllian this morning?"

"No; Beaufort met me at the village; but even now it seems this affair is never to come off. Trevyllian has been sent with a forage party towards Lesco; however, that can't be a long absence. But, for Heaven's sake! let me have some breakfast."

While O'Shaughnessy proceeded to the attack of the viands before him, the others chatted about in little groups; but all wore the pleased and happy looks of men who had rescued their friend from a menaced danger. As for myself, my heart swelled with gratitude to the kind fellows around me.

"How has Conyers assisted us at this juncture?" was my first question to O'Shaughnessy, when we were once more alone.

"I am not at liberty to speak on that subject, Charley. But be satisfied the reasons for which Trevyllian meets you are fair and honorable."

"I am content."

"The only thing now to be done is, to have the meeting as soon possible."

"We are all agreed upon that point," said I; "and the more so as the matter had better be decided before Sir Arthur's return."

"Quite true; and now, O'Malley, you had better join your people as soon as may be, and it will put a stop to all talking about the matter."

The advice was good, and I lost no time in complying with it. When I joined the regiment that day at mess, it was with a light heart and a cheerful spirit; for, come what might of the affair, of one thing I was certain—my character was now put above any reach of aspersion, and my reputation beyond attack.

CHAPTER LXI.

ALL RIGHT.

SOME days after coming back to head-quarters, I was returning from a visit I had been making to a friend at one of the outposts, when an officer, whom I knew slightly, overtook me and informed me that Major O'Shaughnessy had been to my quarters in search of me, and had sent persons in different directions to find me.

Suspecting the object of the Major's haste, I hurried on at once. As I rode up to the spot, I found him in the midst of a group of officers, engaged, to all appearance, in most eager conversation. "Oh, here he comes!" cried he, as I cantered up. "Come, my boy, doff the blue frock, as soon as you can, and turn out in your best fitting black. Everything has been settled for this evening at seven o'clock, and we have no time to lose."

"I understand you," said I, "and shall not keep you waiting." So saying, I sprang from my saddle and hastened to my quarters. As I entered the room, I was followed by O'Shaughnessy, who closed the door after him as he came in, and having turned the key in it, sat down beside the table, and, folding his arms, seemed buried in reflection. As I proceeded with my toilet, he returned no answers to the numerous questions I put to him, either as to the time of Trevyllian's return, the place of the meeting, or any other part of the transaction.

His attention seemed to wander far from all around and about him; and as he muttered indistinctly to himself, the few words I could catch bore not in the remotest degree upon the matter before us.

"I have written a letter or two here, Major," said I, opening my writing-desk; "in case anything happens, you will look to a few things I have mentioned here. Somehow, I could not write to poor Fred Power; but you must tell him from me that his rude conduct towards me was the last thing I spoke of."

"What confounded nonsense you are talking!" said O'Shaughnessy, springing from his seat and crossing the room with tremendous strides; "croaking away there as if the bullet was in your thorax. Hang it, man, bear up!"

"But, Major, my dear friend, what the deuce are you thinking of? The few things I mentioned——"

"The devil! you are not going over it all again, are you?" said he, in a voice of no measured tone.

I now began to feel irritated in turn, and really looked at him for some seconds in considerable amazement. That he should have mistaken the directions I was giving him, and attributed them to any cowardice, was too insulting a thought to bear; and yet how otherwise was I to understand the very coarse style of his interruption?

At length my temper got the victory, and, with a voice of most measured calmness, I said, "Major O'Shaughnessy, I am grateful, most deeply grateful, for the part you have acted towards me in this difficult business; at the same time, as you now appear to disapprove of my conduct and bearing, when I am most firmly determined to alter nothing, I shall beg to relieve you of the unpleasant office of my friend."

"Heaven grant that you could do so!" said he, interrupting me, while his clasped hands and eager look attested the vehemence of the wish. He paused for a moment; then, springing from his chair, rushed towards me, and threw his arms around me. "No, my boy, I can't do it—I can't do it. I have tried to bully myself into insensibility for this evening's work—I have endeavored to be rude to you, that you might insult me, and steel my heart against what might happen; but it won't do, Charley—it won't do."

With these words the big tears rolled down his stern cheeks, and his voice became thick with emotion.

"But for me, all this need not have happened. I know it—I feel it. I hurried on this meeting. Your character stood fair and unblemished without that—at least they tell me so now; and I still have to assure you——"

"Come, my dear, kind friend, don't give way in this fashion. You have stood manfully by me through every step of the road; don't desert me on the threshold of——"

"The grave, O'Malley?"

"I don't think so, Major; but see, it is now half-past six! Look to these pistols for me. Are they likely to object to hair-triggers?"

A knocking at the door turned off our attention, and the next moment Baker's voice was heard.

"O'Malley, you'll be close run for time; the meeting-place is full three miles from this."

I seized the key and opened the door. At the same instant, O'Shaughnessy rose and turned towards the window, holding one of the pistols in his hand.

"Look at that, Baker,—what a sweet tool it is!" said he, in a voice that actually made me start. Not a trace of his late excitement remained; his usually dry, half-humorous manner had returned, and his droll features were as full of their own easy, devil-may-care fun as ever.

"Here comes the drag," said Baker. "We can drive nearly all the way, unless you prefer riding."

"Of course not. Keep your hand steady, Charley, and if you don't bring him down with that saw-handle, you're not your uncle's nephew."

With these words we mounted into the tax-cart, and set off for the meeting-place.

CHAPTER LXII.

THE DUEL.

A SMALL and narrow ravine between two furze-covered dells led to the open space where the meeting had been arranged for. As we reached this, therefore, we were obliged to descend from the drag, and proceed the remainder of the way afoot. We had not gone many yards when a step was heard approaching, and the next moment Beaufort appeared. His usually easy and *dégagé* air was certainly tinged with somewhat of constraint, and though his soft voice and half smile were as perfect as ever, a slightly flurried expression about the lip, and a quick and nervous motion of his eyebrow, bespoke a heart not completely at ease. He lifted his foraging-cap most ceremoniously to salute us as we came up, and casting an anxious look to see if any others were following, stood quite still.

"I think it right to mention, Major O'Shaughnessy," said he, in a voice of most dulcet sweetness, "that I am the only friend of Captain Trevyllian on the ground; and though I have not the slightest objection to Captain Baker being present, I hope you will see the propriety of limiting the witnesses to the three persons now here."

"Upon my conscience, as far as I am concerned, or my friend either, we are perfectly indifferent if we fight before three or three thousand. In Ireland we rather like a crowd."

"Of course, then, as you see no objection to my proposition, I may count upon your co-operation in the event of any intrusion; I mean that while we upon our sides will not permit any of our friends to come forward, you will equally exert yourself with yours."

"Here we are—Baker and myself—neither more nor less. We expect no one, and want no one, so that I humbly conceive all the preliminaries you are talking of will never be required."

Beaufort tried to smile, and bit his lips, while a small red spot upon his cheek spoke that some deeper feeling of irritation than the mere careless manner of the Major could account for still rankled in his bosom. We now walked on without speaking, except when occasionally some passing observation of Beaufort upon the fineness of the evening, or the rugged nature of the road, broke the silence. As we emerged from the little mountain pass into the open meadow land, the tall and soldier-like figure of Trevyllian was the first object that presented itself. He was standing beside a little stone cross that stood above a holy well, and seemed occupied in deciphering the inscription. He turned at the noise of our approach, and calmly awaited our coming. His eye glanced quickly from the features of O'Shaughnessy to those of Baker; but, seemingly rapidly reassured as he walked forward, his face at once recovered its usual severity, and its cold, impassive look of sternness.

"All right!" said Beaufort in a whisper, the tones of which I overheard as he drew near to his friend. Trevyllian smiled in return, but did not speak. During the few moments which passed in conversation between the seconds, I turned from the spot with Baker, and had scarcely time to address a question to him, when O'Shaughnessy called out, "Hallo, Baker!—come here a moment!" The three seemed now in eager discussion for some minutes, when Baker walked towards Trevyllian, and saying something, appeared to wait for his reply. This being obtained, he joined the others, and the moment afterwards came to where I was standing. "You are to toss for first shot, O'Malley. O'Shaughnessy has made that proposition, and the others agree that, with two crack marksmen, it is perhaps the fairest way. I suppose you have no objection?"

"Of course, I shall make none. Whatever O'Shaughnessy decides for me I am ready to abide by."

"Well, then, as to the distance," said Beaufort, loud enough to be heard by me where I was standing. O'Shaughnessy's reply I could not catch, but it was evident, from the tone of both parties, that some difference existed on the point.

"Captain Baker shall decide between us," said Beaufort at length, and they all walked away to some distance. During all the while I could perceive that Trevyllian's uneasiness and impatience seemed extreme; he looked from the speakers to the little mountain pass, and strained his eyes in every direction. It was clear that he dreaded some interruption. At last, unable any longer to control his feeling, he called out, "Beaufort, I say, what the devil are we waiting for now?"

"Nothing at present," said Beaufort, as he came forward with a dollar in his hand. "Come, Major O'Shaughnessy, you shall call for your friend."

As he spoke, he pitched the piece of money high into the air, and watched it as it fell on the soft grass beneath.

"Head! for a thousand," cried O'Shaughnessy, running over and stooping down; "and head it is!"

"You've won the first shot," whispered Baker; "for Heaven's sake be cool!"

Beaufort grew deadly pale as he bent over the crown piece, and seemed scarcely to have courage to look his friend in the face. Not so Trevyllian; he pulled off his gloves without the slightest semblance of emotion, buttoned up his well-fitting black frock to the throat, and, throwing a rapid glance around, seemed only eager to begin the combat.

"Fifteen paces, and the words 'One—two.'"

"Exactly. My cane shall mark the spot."

"Devilish long paces you make them," said O'Shaughnessy, who did not seem to approve of the distance. "They have some confounded advantage in this, depend upon it," said the Major in a whisper to Baker.

"Are you ready?" inquired Beaufort.

"Ready—quite ready!"

"Take your ground, then!"

As Trevyllian moved forward to his place, he muttered something to his friend. I did not hear the first part, but the latter words which met me were ominous enough,—"for as I intend to shoot him, 'tis just as well as it is."

Whether this was intended to be overheard and intimidate me I knew not; but its effect proved directly opposite. My firm resolution to hit my antagonist was now confirmed, and no compunctious visiting unnerved my arm. As we took our places, some little delay again took place, the flint of my pistol having fallen; and thus we remained full ten or twelve seconds steadily regarding each other. At length O'Shaughnessy came forward, and, putting my weapon in my hand, whispered low, "Remember, you have but one chance."

"You are both ready?" cried Beaufort.

"Ready!"

"Then, One—two——"

The last word was lost in the report of my pistol, which went off at the instant. For a second, the flash and smoke obstructed my view; but the moment after I saw Trevyllian stretched upon the ground, with his friend kneeling beside him. My first impulse was to rush over, for now all feeling of enmity was buried in most heartfelt anxiety for his fate; but as I was stepping forward, O'Shaughnessy called out, "Stand fast, boy, he's only wounded!" and the same moment he rose slowly from the ground, with the assistance of his friend, and looked with the same wild gaze around him. Such a look! I shall never forget it; there was that intense expression of searching anxiety, as if he sought to trace the outlines of some visionary spirit as it receded before him. Quickly reassured, as it seemed by the glance he threw on all sides, his countenance lighted up, not with pleasure, but with a fiendish expression of revengeful triumph, which even his voice evinced as he called out, "It's my turn now."

I felt the words in their full force, as I stood silently awaiting my death wound. The pause was a long one. Twice did he interrupt his friend, as he was about to give the word, by an expression of suffering, pressing his hand upon his side, and seeming to writhe with torture; and yet this was mere counterfeit.

O'Shaughnessy was now coming forward to interfere and prevent these interruptions, when Trevyllian called out in a firm tone, "I am ready!" The words "One—two!" the pistol slowly rose, his dark eye measured me coolly, steadily; his lip curled, and just as I felt that my last moment of life had arrived, the heavy sound of a horse galloping along the rocky causeway seemed to take off his attention. His frame trembled, his hand shook, and jerking upward his weapon, the ball passed high above my head.

"You bear me witness I fired in the air," said Trevyllian, while the large drops of perspiration rolled from his forehead, and his features worked as if in a fit.

"You saw it, sir; and you, Beaufort, my friend,—you also. Speak! Why will you not speak?"

"Be calm, Trevyllian; be calm, for Heaven's sake! What's the matter with you?"

"The affair is then ended," said Baker, "and most happily so. You are, I hope, not dangerously wounded."

As he spoke, Trevyllian's features grew deadly livid; his half-open mouth quivered slightly; his eyes became fixed, and his arm dropped heavily beside him, and with a low moan he fell fainting to the ground.

As we bent over him, I perceived that another person had joined our party; he was a short, determined-looking man of about forty, with black eyes and aquiline features. Before I had time to guess who it might be, I heard O'Shaughnessy address him as Colonel Conyers.

"He is dying!" said Beaufort, still stooping over his friend, whose cold hand he grasped within his own. "Poor, poor fellow!"

"He fired in the air," said Baker, as he spoke in reply to a question from Conyers.

What he answered I heard not, but Baker rejoined,—

"Yes, I am certain of it. We all saw it."

"Had you not better examine his wounds?" said Conyers, in a tone of sarcastic irony I could almost have struck him for. "Is your friend not hit? Perhaps he is bleeding."

"Yes," said O'Shaughnessy, "let us look to the poor fellow now." So saying, with Beaufort's aid he unbuttoned his frock, and succeeded in opening the waistcoat. There was no trace of blood anywhere, and the idea of internal hemorrhage at once occurred to us; when Conyers, stooping down, pushed me aside, saying at the same time, "Your fears for his safety need not distress you much—look here!" As he spoke, he tore open his shirt, and disclosed to our almost doubting senses a vest of chain mail armor fitting close next the skin and completely pistol proof.

I cannot describe the effect this sight produced upon us. Beaufort sprang to his feet with a bound as he screamed out, rather than spoke, "No man believes me to have been aware——"

"No, no, Beaufort; your reputation is very far removed from such a stain," said Conyers.

O'Shaughnessy was perfectly speechless. He looked from one to the other, as though some unexplained mystery still remained, and only seemed restored to any sense of consciousness as Baker said, "I can feel no pulse at his wrist—his heart, too, does not beat." Conyers placed his hand upon his bosom, then felt along his throat, lifted up an arm, and, letting it fall heavily upon the ground, he muttered, "He is dead!"

It was true. No wound had pierced him—the pistol bullet was found within his clothes. Some tremendous conflict of the spirit within had snapped the cords of life, and the strong man had perished in his agony.

CHAPTER LXIII.

NEWS FROM GALWAY.

I HAVE but a vague and most imperfect recollection of the events which followed this dreadful scene. For some days my faculties seemed stunned and paralyzed, and my thoughts clung to the minute detail of the ground—the persons about—the mountain path—and, most of all, the half-stifled cry that spoke the broken heart, with a tenacity that verged upon madness.

A court-martial was appointed to inquire into the affair; and although I have been since told that my deportment was calm, and my answers were firm and collected, yet I remember nothing of the proceedings.

The inquiry, through a feeling of delicacy for the friends of him who was no more, was made as brief and as private as possible. Beaufort proved the facts which exonerated me from any imputation in the matter; and upon the same day the court delivered the decision, "that Lieutenant O'Malley was not guilty of the charges preferred against him, and that he should be released from arrest and join his regiment."

Nothing could be more kind and considerate than the conduct of my brother officers; a hundred little plans and devices for making me forget the late unhappy event were suggested and practised; and I look back to that melancholy period, marked, as it was, by the saddest circumstance of my life, as one in which I received more of truly friendly companionship than even my palmiest days of prosperity boasted.

While, therefore, I deeply felt the good part my friends were performing towards me, I was still totally unsuited to join in the happy current of their daily pleasures and amusements. The gay and unreflecting character of O'Shaughnessy—the careless merriment of my brother officers—jarred upon my nerves, and rendered me irritable and excited; and I sought, in lonely rides and unfrequented walks, the peace of spirit that calm reflection, and a firm purpose for the future, rarely fail to lead to.

There is in deep sorrow a touch of the prophetic. It is at seasons when the heart is bowed down with grief, and the spirit wasted with suffering, that the veil which conceals the future seems to be removed, and a glance, short and fleeting as the lightning flash, is permitted us into the gloomy valley before us.

Misfortunes, too, come not singly—the seared heart is not suffered to heal from one affliction ere another succeeds it; and this anticipation of the coming evil is perhaps one of the most poignant features of grief—the ever watchful apprehension—the ever rising question, " What next?" is a torture that never sleeps.

This was the frame of my mind for several days after I returned to my duty—a morbid sense of some threatened danger being my last thought at night and my first on awakening. I had not heard from home since my arrival in the Peninsula. A thousand vague fancies haunted me now that some brooding misfortune awaited me. My poor uncle never left my thoughts. Was he well,—was he happy? Was he, as he ever used to be, surrounded by the friends he loved,—the old familiar faces, around the hospitable hearth his kindliness had hallowed in my memory as something sacred? Oh! could I but see his manly smile, or hear his voice! Could I but feel his hand upon my head, as he was wont to press it, while words of comfort fell from his lips, and sunk into my heart!

Such were my thoughts one morning as I sauntered unaccompanied from my quarters. I had not gone far, when my attention was aroused by the noise of a mule-cart, whose jingling bells and clattering timbers announced its approach by the road I was walking. Another turn of the way brought it into view ; and I saw from the gay costume of the driver, as well as a small orange flag which decorated the conveyance, that it was the mail-cart, with letters from Lisbon.

Full as my mind was with the thoughts of home, I turned hastily back, and retraced my steps towards the camp. When I reached the Adjutant-General's quarters, I found a considerable number of officers assembled ; the report that the post had come was a rumor of interest to all, and, accordingly, every moment brought fresh arrivals, pouring in from all sides, and eagerly inquiring " if the bag had been opened?" The scene of riot, confusion, and excitement, when that event did take place, exceeded all belief, each man reading his letter half aloud, as if his private affairs and domestic concerns must interest his neighbors, amid a volley of exclamations of surprise, pleasure, or occasionally anger, as the intelligence severally suggested,—the disappointed expectants cursing their idle correspondents, bemoaning their fate about remittances that never arrived, or drafts never honored ; while here and there some public benefactor, with an outspread *Times* or *Chronicle*, was retailing the narrative of our own exploits in the Peninsula, or the more novel changes in the world of politics, since we left England. A cross-fire of news and London gossip ringing on every side, made up a perfect Babel, most difficult to form an idea of. The jargon partook of every accent and intonation the empire boasts of, and, from the sharp precision of the North Tweeder to the broad Doric of Kerry, every portion, almost every county, of Great Britain had its representative. Here was a Scotch Paymaster, in a lugubrious tone, detailing to his friend the apparently not over-welcome news that Mistress M'Elwain had just been safely delivered of twins, which, with their mother, were doing as well as possible. Here an eager Irishman, turning over the pages rather than reading his letter, while he exclaimed to his friend,

"Oh, the devil a rap she's sent me. The old story about runaway tenants and distress notices—sorrow else tenants seem to do in Ireland than run away every half year."

A little apart some sentimental-looking cockney was devouring a very crossed epistle, which he pressed to his lips whenever any one looked at him; while a host of others satisfied themselves by reading in a kind of buzzing undertone, every now and then interrupting themselves with some broken exclamation as commentary—such as "Of course she will!"—"Never knew him better!"—"That's the girl for my money!"—"Fifty per cent.—the devil!"—and so on. At last I was beginning to weary of the scene, and finding that there appeared to be nothing for me, was turning to leave the place, when I saw a group of two or three endeavoring to spell out the address of a letter.

"That's an Irish post-mark, I'll swear," said one; "but who can make anything of the name? It's devilish like Otaheite—isn't it?"

"I wish my tailor wrote as illegibly," said another; "I'd keep up a most animated correspondence with him."

"Here, O'Shaughnessy, you know something of savage life—spell us this word here."

"Show it here—what nonsense—it's as plain as the nose on my face!—'Master Charles O'Malley, in foreign parts!'"

A roar of laughter followed this announcement, which, at any other time, perhaps, I should have joined in, but which now grated sadly on my ruffled feelings.

"Here, Charley, this is for you," said the Major; and added in a whisper—"and upon my conscience, between ourselves, your friend, whoever he is, has a strong action against his writing-master—devil such a fist ever I looked at!"

One glance satisfied me as to my correspondent. It was from Father Rush, my old tutor. I hurried eagerly from the spot. Regaining my quarters, I locked the door, and with a beating heart broke the seal and began, as well as I was able, to decipher his letter. The hand was cramped and stiffened with age, and the bold upright letters were gnarled and twisted like a rustic fence, and demanded great patience and much time in unravelling. It ran thus:

The Priory, Lady-day, 1809.

"My Dear Master Charles:—Your uncle's feet are so big and so uneasy that he can't write, and I am obliged to take up the pen
24

myself, to tell you how we are doing here since you left us. And, first of all, the master lost the lawsuit in Dublin, all for the want of a Galway jury; but they don't go up to town for strong reasons they had; and the Curranolick property is gone to Ned M'Manus, and—may the devil do him good with it! Peggy Maher left this on Tuesday; she was complaining of a weakness; she's gone to consult the doctors. I'm sorry for poor Peggy.

"Owen M'Neil beat the Slatterys out of Portumna on Saturday, and Jem, they say, is fractured. I trust it's true, for he never was good, root nor branch, and we've strong reasons to suspect him for drawing the river with a net at night. Sir Harry Boyle sprained his wrist, breaking open his bed-room, that he locked when he was inside. The Count and the master were laughing all the evening at him. Matters are going very hard in the country; the people paying their rents regularly, and not caring half as much as they used about the real gentry and the old families.

"We kept your birthday at the Castle in great style, had the militia band from the town, and all the tenants. Mr. James Daly danced with your old friend Mary Green, and sang a beautiful song, and was going to raise the devil, but I interfered; he burnt down half the blue drawing-room the last night with his tricks; not that your uncle cares,—God preserve him to us!—it's little anything like that would fret him. The Count quarrelled with a young gentleman in the course of the evening, but found out that he was only an attorney from Dublin, so he didn't shoot him, but he was ducked in the pond by the people, and your uncle says he hopes they have a true copy of him at home, as they'll never know the original.

"Peter died soon after you went away, but Tim hunts the dogs just as well; they had a beautiful run last Wednesday, and the Lord* sent for him and gave him a five-pound note; but he says he'd rather see yourself back again than twice as much. They killed near the big turnip field, and all went down to see where you leaped Badger over the sunk fence; they call it 'Hammersley's Nose' ever since. Bodkin was at Ballinasloe the last fair, limping about with a stick; he's twice as quiet as he used to be, and never beat any one since that morning.

"Nelly Guire, at the cross-roads, wants to send you four pair of stockings she knitted for you; and I have a keg of potteen of Barney's own making this two months, not knowing how to send it; may be Sir Arthur himself would like a taste; he's an Irishman himself, and one we're proud of too! The Maynooth chaps are flying all about the country, and making us all uncomfortable—

---

* To excuse Father Rush for any apparent impiety, I must add, that by the "Lord," he means "Lord Clanricarde."

God's will be done, but we used to think ourselves good enough ! Your foster sister, Kitty Doolan, had a fine boy ; it's to be called after you, and your uncle's to give a christening. He bids me tell you to draw on him when you want money, and that there's £400 ready for you now somewhere in Dublin, I forget the name, and as he's asleep I don't like asking him. There was a droll devil down here in the summer that knew you well—a Mr. Webber. The master treated him like the Lord Lieutenant; had dinner parties for him, and gave him Oliver Cromwell to ride over to Meelish. He is expected again for the cock-shooting, for the master likes him greatly. I'm done at last, for my paper is finished and the candle just out ; so with every good wish and every good thought, remember your old friend,

" Peter Rush.

"P.S.—It's Smart and Sykes, Fleet street, who has the money. Father O'Shaughnessy, of Ennis, bids me ask if you ever met his nephew. If you do, make him sing 'Larry M'Hale.' I hear it's a treat.

"How is Mickey Free going on? There are three decent young women in the parish he promised to marry, and I suppose he's pursuing the same game with the Portuguese. But he was never remarkable for minding his duties. Tell him I am keeping my eye on him.

"P. R."

Here concluded this long epistle, and though there were many parts I could not help smiling at, yet upon the whole, I felt sad and disappointed. What I had long foreseen and anticipated was gradually being accomplished—the wreck of an old and honored house—the fall of a name once the watchword for all that was benevolent and hospitable in the land. The termination of the lawsuit I knew must have been a heavy blow to my poor uncle, who, every consideration of money apart, felt in a legal combat all the enthusiasm and excitement of a personal conflict. With him there was less a question of to whom the broad acres reverted, so much as whether that "scoundrel Tom Bassett, the attorney at Athlone, should triumph over us ;" or "M'Manus live in the house as master, where his father had officiated as butler." It was at this his Irish pride took offence ; and straitened circumstances and narrowed fortunes bore little upon him in comparison with this feeling.

I could see, too, that with breaking fortunes, bad health was making heavy inroads upon him ; and while, with the reckless desperation of ruin, he still kept open house, I could picture to myself his cheerful eye and handsome smile, but ill concealing the slow but certain march of a broken heart.

My position was doubly painful; for my advice, had I been calculated to give it, would have seemed an act of indelicate interference from one who was to benefit by his own counsel; and although I had been reared and educated as my uncle's heir, I had no title nor pretension to succeed him other than his kind feelings respecting me. I could therefore only look on in silence, and watch the painful progress of our downfall, without a power to arrest it.

These were sad thoughts, and came when my heart was already bowed down with its affliction. That my poor uncle might be spared the misery which sooner or later seemed inevitable, was now my only wish; that he might go down to the grave without the embittering feelings which a ruined fortune and a fallen house bring home to the heart, was all my prayer. Let him but close his eyes in the old wainscoted bedroom, beneath the old roof where his fathers and grandfathers have done so for centuries. Let the faithful followers he has known since his childhood stand round his bed, while his fast-failing sight recognizes each old and well-remembered object, and the same bell which rang its farewell to the spirit of his ancestors, toll for him, the last of his race. As for me, there was the wide world before me, and a narrow resting-place would suffice for a soldier's sepulchre.

As the mail-cart was returning the next day to Lisbon, I immediately sat down and replied to the worthy Father's letter, speaking as encouragingly as I could of my own prospects. I dwelt much upon what was nearest my heart, and begged of the good priest to watch over my uncle's health, to cheer his spirits, and support his courage; and that I trusted the day was not far distant when I should be once more amongst them, with many a story of fray and battle-field to enliven their firesides. Pressing him to write frequently to me, I closed my hurried letter; and, having despatched it, sat sorrowfully down to muse over my fortunes.

CHAPTER LXIV.

AN ADVENTURE WITH SIR ARTHUR.

THE events of the last few days had impressed me with the weight of years. The awful circumstances of that evening lay heavily at my heart, and though guiltless of Trevyllian's blood, the reproach that conscience ever carries when one has been involved in a death-scene never left my thoughts. For some time previously I had been depressed and dispirited, and the awful shock I had sustained broke my nerve and unmanned me greatly.

There are times when our sorrows tinge all the coloring of our thoughts, and one pervading hue of melancholy spreads like a pall upon what we have of fairest and brightest on earth. So was it now; I had lost hope and ambition—a sad feeling that my career was destined to misfortune and mishap gained hourly upon me; and all the bright aspirations of a soldier's glory, all my enthusiasm for the pomp and circumstance of glorious war, fell coldly upon my heart; and I looked upon the chivalry of a soldier's life as the empty pageant of a dream.

In this sad frame of mind I avoided all intercourse with my brother officers; their gay and joyous spirits only jarred upon my brooding thoughts, and, feigning illness, I kept almost entirely to my quarters.

The inactivity of our present life weighed also heavily upon me. The stirring events of a campaign—the march, the bivouac, the picket—call forth a certain physical exertion that never fails to react upon the torpid mind.

Forgetting all around me, I thought of home; I thought of those whose hearts I felt were now turning towards me, and considered within myself how I could have exchanged home—the days of peaceful happiness there—for the life of misery and disappointment I now endured.

A brooding melancholy gained daily more and more upon me. A wish to return to Ireland, a vague and indistinct feeling that my career was not destined for aught of great and good, crept upon me, and I longed to sink into oblivion, forgetting and forgot.

I record this painful feeling here, while it is still a painful memory, as one of the dark shadows that cross the bright sky of our happiest days.

Happy, indeed, are they, as we look back to them, and remember the times we have pronounced ourselves "the most miserable of mankind." This somehow is a confession we never make later on in life, when real troubles and true afflictions assail us. Whether we call in moral philosophy to our aid, or that our senses become less acute and discerning, I'm sure I know not.

As for me, I confess that by far the greater portion of my sorrows seemed to come in that budding period of existence when life is ever fairest and most captivating. Not, perhaps, that the fact was really so, but the spoiled and humored child, whose caprices were a law, felt heavily the threatening difficulties of his first voyage; while, as he continued to sail over the ocean of life, he braved the storm and the squall, and felt only gratitude for the favoring breeze that wafted him upon his course.

What an admirable remedy for misanthropy is the being placed in a subordinate condition in life! Had I, at the period of which I write, been Sir Arthur Wellesley—had I even been Marshal Beresford, to all certainty I'd have played the very devil with his Majesty's forces. I'd have brought my rascals to where they'd have been well peppered—that's certain.

But as, luckily for the sake of humanity in general and the well-being of the service in particular, I was merely Lieutenant O'Malley, 14th Light Dragoons, the case was very different. With what heavy censure did I condemn the Commander of the Forces in my own mind for his want of daring and enterprise! Whole nights did I pass in endeavoring to account for his inactivity and lethargy. Why he did not *seriatim* fall upon Soult, Ney, and Victor, annihilate the French forces, and sack Madrid, I looked upon as little less than a riddle; and yet there we waited, drilling, exercising, and foraging, as if we were at Hounslow. Now, most fortunately, here again I was not Sir Arthur.

Something in this frame of mind, I was one evening taking a solitary ride some miles from the camp. Without noticing the circumstance, I had entered a little mountain tract, when the ground being broken and uneven, I dismounted and proceeded afoot, with the bridle within my arm. I had not gone far when the clatter of a horse's hoofs came rapidly towards me, and though there was something startling in the pace over such a piece of road, I never lifted my eyes as the horseman came up, but continued my slow progress onward, my head sunk upon my bosom.

" Holloa, sir !" cried a sharp voice, whose tones seemed somehow not heard for the first time. I looked up, saw a slight figure closely buttoned up in a blue horseman's cloak, the collar of which almost entirely hid his features; he wore a plain cocked hat without a feather, and was mounted upon a sharp, wiry-looking hack.

" Holloa, sir ! What regiment do you belong to ?"

As I had nothing of the soldier about me, save a blue foraging cap, to denote my corps, the tone of the demand was little calculatcd to elicit a very polished reply; but preferring, as was most impertinent, to make no answer, I passed on without speaking.

"Did you hear, sir?" cried the same voice, in a still louder key. "What's your regiment?"

I now turned round, resolved to question the other in turn, when, to my inexpressible shame and confusion, he had lowered the collar of his cloak, and I saw the features of Sir Arthur Wellesley.

"Fourteenth Light Dragoons, sir," said I, blushing as I spoke.

"Have you not read the general order, sir? Why have you left the camp?"

Now I had not read a general order, nor even heard of one, for above a fortnight. So I stammered out some bungling answer.

"To your quarters, sir, and report yourself under arrest. What's your name?"

"Lieutenant O'Malley, sir."

"Well, sir, your passion for rambling shall be indulged. You shall be sent to the rear with despatches; and as the army is in advance, probably the lesson may be serviceable." So saying, he pressed spurs to his horse, and was out of sight in a moment.

CHAPTER LXV.

TALAVERA.

HAVING been despatched to the rear with orders for General Craufurd, I did not reach Talavera till the morning of the 28th. Two days' hard fighting had left the contending armies still face to face, and without any decided advantage on either side.

When I arrived upon the battle-field, the combat of the morning was over. It was then ten o'clock, and the troops were at breakfast, if the few ounces of wheat sparingly dealt out amongst them could be dignified by that name. All was, however, life and animation on every side. The merry laugh, the passing jest, the careless look, bespoke the free and daring character of the soldiery, as they sat in groups upon the grass; and except when a fatigue party passed by, bearing some wounded comrade to the rear, no touch of seriousness rested upon their hardy features. The morning was indeed a glorious one; a sky of unclouded blue stretched above a landscape unsurpassed in loveliness. Far to the right rolled on in placid stream the broad Tagus, bathing in its eddies the very walls of Talavera, the ground from which to our position gently undulated across a plain of most fertile richness, and terminated on our extreme left in a bold height, protected in front by a ravine, and flanked by a deep and rugged valley.

The Spaniards occupied the right of the line, connecting with our troops at a rising ground, upon which a strong redoubt had been hastily thrown up. The fourth division and the Guards were stationed here, next to whom came Cameron's brigade and the Germans. Mackenzie and Hill held the extreme left of all, which might be called the key of our position. In the valley beneath the latter were picketed three cavalry regiments, among which I was not long in detecting my gallant friends of the Twenty-third.

As I rode rapidly past, saluting some old familiar face at each moment, I could not help feeling struck at the evidence of the desperate battle that so lately had raged there. The whole surface of the hill was one mass of dead and dying, the bearskin of the French grenadier lying side by side with the tartan of the Highlander. Deep furrows in the soil showed the track of the furious cannonade, and the terrible evidences of a bayonet charge were written in the mangled corpses around.

The fight had been maintained without any intermission from daybreak till near nine o'clock that morning, and the slaughter on both sides was dreadful. The mounds of fresh earth on every side told of the soldier's sepulchre, and the unceasing tramp of the pioneers struck sadly upon the ear, as the groans of the wounded blended with the funeral sounds around them.

In front were drawn up the dark legions of France, massive columns of infantry, with dense bodies of artillery alternating along the line. They, too, occupied a gently rising ground, the valley between the two armies being crossed half way by a little rivulet; and here, during the sultry heat of the morning, the troops on both sides met and mingled to quench their thirst ere the trumpet again called them to the slaughter.

In a small ravine, near the centre of our line, was drawn up Cotton's brigade, of whom the Fusiliers formed a part. Directly in front of this was Campbell's brigade, to the left of which, upon a gentle slope, the staff were now assembled. Thither, accordingly, I bent my steps. As I came up the little scarp, I found myself among the generals of division, hastily summoned by Sir Arthur to deliberate upon a forward movement. The council lasted scarcely a quarter of an hour, and when I presented myself to deliver my report, all the dispositions for the battle had been decided upon, and the Commander of the Forces, seated on the grass at his breakfast, looked by far the most unconcerned and uninterested man I had seen that morning.

He turned his head rapidly as I came up, and, before the aide-de-camp could announce me, called out,—

" Well, sir, what news of the reinforcements?"

" They cannot reach Talavera before to-morrow, sir."

" Then, before that time we shall not want them. That will do, sir."

So saying, he resumed his breakfast, and I retired, more than ever struck with the surprising coolness of the man upon whom no disappointment seemed to have the slightest influence.

I had scarcely rejoined my regiment, and was giving an account to my brother officers of my journey, when an aide-de-camp came galloping at full speed down the line, and communicated with the several commanding officers as he passed.

What might be the nature of the orders we could not guess at, for no word to fall in followed, and yet it was evident that something of importance was at hand. Upon the hill where the staff were assembled, no unusual bustle appeared, and we could see the bay cob of Sir Arthur still being led up and down by the groom, with a dragoon's mantle thrown over him. The soldiers, completely overcome by the heat and fatigue of the morning, lay stretched around upon the grass, and everthing bespoke a period of rest and refreshment.

" We are going to advance, depend upon it!" said a young officer beside me; " the repulse of this morning has been a smart lesson to the French, and Sir Arthur won't leave them without impressing it upon them."

" Hark! what's that?" cried Baker; " listen."

As he spoke, a strain of most delicious music came wafted across the plain. It was from the band of a French regiment, and, mellowed by the distance, it seemed, in the calm stillness of the morning air, like something less of earth than heaven. As we listened, the notes swelled upward yet fuller, and one by one the different bands seemed to join, till at last the whole air seemed full of the rich flood of melody.

We could now perceive that the stragglers were rapidly falling back, while high above all other sounds the clanging notes of the trumpet were heard along the line. The hoarse drum now beat to arms, and soon after a brilliant staff rode slowly from between two dense bodies of infantry, and advancing some distance into the plain, seemed to reconnoitre us. A cloud of Polish cavalry, distinguished by their long lances and floating banners, loitered in their rear.

We had not time for further observation, when the drums on our side beat to arms, and the hoarse cry, "Fall in—fall in there, lads !" resounded along the line.

It was now one o'clock, and before half an hour the troops had resumed the position of the morning, and stood silent and anxious spectators of the scene before them.

Upon the table land to the rear of the French position we could descry the gorgeous tent of King Joseph, around which a large and splendidly-accoutred staff were seen standing. Here, too, the bustle and excitement seemed considerable, for to this point the dark masses of the infantry seemed converging from the extreme right ; and here we could perceive the royal guards and the reserve now forming in column of attack.

From the crest of the hill down to the very valley, the dark, dense ranks extended, the flanks protected by a powerful artillery and deep masses of heavy cavalry. It was evident that the attack was not to commence on our side, and the greatest and most intense anxiety pervaded us as to what part of our line was first to be assailed.

Meanwhile, Sir Arthur Wellesley, who from the height had been patiently observing the field of battle, despatched an aide-de-camp at full gallop towards Campbell's brigade, posted directly in advance of us. As he passed swiftly along, he called out, "You're in for it, Fourteenth ; you'll have to open the ball to-day."

Scarcely were the words spoken, when a signal gun from the French boomed heavily through the still air. The last echo was growing fainter, and the heavy smoke breaking into mist, when the most deafening thunder ever my ears heard came pealing around us ; eighty pieces of artillery had opened upon us, sending a very tempest of balls upon our line, while midst the smoke and dust we could see the light troops advancing at a run, followed by the broad and massive columns in all the terror and majesty of war.

"What a splendid attack ! How gallantly they come on !" cried an old veteran officer beside me, forgetting all rivalry in his noble admiration of our enemy.

The intervening space was soon passed, and the tirailleurs falling back as the columns came on, the towering masses bore down upon Campbell's division with a loud cry of defiance. Silently and steadily the English infantry awaited the attack, and returning the fire with one withering volley, were ordered to charge. Scarcely were the bayonets lowered, when the head of the advancing column broke and fled, while Mackenzie's brigade, overlapping the flank, pushed boldly forward, and a scene of frightful carnage followed. For a moment a hand-to-hand combat was sustained, but the unbroken files and impregnable bayonets of the English conquered, and the French fled, leaving six guns behind them.

The gallant enemy were troops of tried and proved courage, and scarcely had they retreated when they again formed, but just as they prepared to come forward, a tremendous shower of grape opened upon them from our batteries, while a cloud of Spanish horse assailed them in flank, and nearly cut them in pieces.

While this was passing on the right, a tremendous attack menaced the hill upon which our left was posted. Two powerful columns of French infantry, supported by some regiments of light cavalry, came steadily forward to the attack; Anson's brigade were ordered to charge.

Away they went at top speed, but had not gone above a hundred yards when they were suddenly arrested by a deep chasm; here the German hussars pulled short up, but the 23d dashing impetuously forward, a scene of terrible carnage ensued, men and horses rolled indiscriminately together under a withering fire from the French squares. Even here, however, British valor quailed not, for Major Francis Ponsonby, forming all who came up, rode boldly upon a brigade of French chasseurs in the rear. Victor, who from the first had watched the movement, at once despatched a lancer regiment against them, and then these brave fellows were absolutely cut to atoms, the few who escaped having passed through the French columns and reached Bassecour's Spanish division on the far right.

During this time the hill was again assailed, and even more desperately than before, while Victor himself led on the fourth corps to an attack upon our right and centre.

The Guards waited without flinching the impetuous rush of the advancing columns, and when at length within a short distance, dashed forward with the bayonet, driving everything before them. The French fell back upon their sustaining masses, but, rallying in an instant, again came forward, supported by a tremendous fire from their batteries. The Guards drew back, and the German Legion, suddenly thrown into confusion, began to retire in disorder. This was the most critical moment of the day, for although successful upon the extreme right and left of our line, our centre was absolutely broken. Just at this moment Gordon rode up to our brigade; his face was pale and his look hurried and excited.

"The Forty-eighth are coming; here they are—support them, Fourteenth."

These words were all he spoke; and the next moment the measured tread of a column was heard behind us. On they came like one man, their compact and dense formation looking like some massive wall; wheeling by companies, they suffered the Guards and

Germans to retire behind them, and then re-forming into line, they rushed forward with the bayonet. Our artillery opened with a deafening thunder behind them, and then we were ordered to charge.

We came on at a trot. The Guards, who had now recovered their formation, cheered us as we proceeded. The smoke of the cannonade obscured everything until we had advanced some distance, but just as we emerged beyond the line of the gallant Forty-eighth, the splendid panorama of the battle-field broke suddenly upon us.

"Charge! forward!" cried the hoarse voice of our Colonel; and we were upon them. The French infantry, already broken by the withering musketry of our people, gave way before us, and, unable to form a square, retired fighting, but in confusion, and with tremendous loss, to their position. One glorious cheer from left to right of our line proclaimed the victory, while a deafening discharge of artillery from the French replied to this defiance, and the battle was over. Had the Spanish army been capable of a forward movement, our successes at this moment would have been much more considerable; but they did not dare to change their position, and the repulse of our enemy was destined to be all our glory. The French, however, suffered much more severely than we did. Retiring during the night, they fell back behind the Alberche, leaving us the victory and the battle-field.

CHARLES O'MALLEY,

THE IRISH DRAGOON.

———

VOLUME II.

CHARLES O'MALLEY,

The Irish Dragoon.

CHAPTER I.

NIGHT AFTER TALAVERA.

THE night which followed the battle was a sad one. Through the darkness, and under a fast-falling rain, the hours were spent searching for our wounded comrades amid the heap of slain upon the field; and the glimmering of the lanterns, as they flickered far and near across the wide plain, bespoke the track of the fatigue parties in their mournful round; while the groans of the wounded rose amid the silence with an accent of heartrending anguish; so true was it, as our great commander said, "there is nothing more sad than a victory except a defeat!"

Around our bivouac fires the feeling of sorrowful depression was also evident. We had gained a great victory, it was true; we had beaten the far-famed legions of France upon a ground of their own choosing, led by the most celebrated of their Marshals, and under the eyes of the Emperor's own brother; but still we felt all the hazardous danger of our position, and had no confidence whatever in the courage or discipline of our allies; and we saw that in the very *mêlée* of the battle the efforts of the enemy were directed almost exclusively against our line, so confidently did they undervalue the efforts of the Spanish troops. Morning broke at length, and scarcely was the heavy mist clearing away before the red sunlight, when the sounds of fife and drum were heard from a distant part of the field. The notes swelled or sank as the breeze rose or fell, and many a conjecture was hazarded as to their meaning, for no object was well visible for more than a few hundred yards off; gradually, however, they grew nearer and nearer, and at length, as the air cleared, and the hazy vapor evaporated, the bright scarlet uniform of a British regiment was seen advancing at a quick step.

(383)

As they came nearer, the well-known march of the gallant Forty-third was recognized by some of our people, and immediately the rumor flew like lightning,—"It is Craufurd's brigade!" and so it was; the noble fellow had marched his division the unparalleled distance of sixty English miles in twenty-seven hours. Over a burning soil, exposed to a raging sun, without rations, almost without water, these gallant troops pressed on in the unwearied hope of sharing the glory of the battle-field. One tremendous cheer welcomed the head of the column as they marched past, and continued till the last file had deployed before us.

As these splendid regiments moved by, we could not help feeling what signal service they might have rendered us but a few hours before; their soldier-like bearing, their high and effective state of discipline, their well-known reputation, were in every mouth; and I scarcely think that any corps who stood the brunt of the mighty battle were the subject of more encomiums than the brave fellows who had just joined us.

The mournful duties of the night were soon forgotten in the gay and buoyant sounds on every side. Congratulations, shaking of hands, kind inquiries, went round; and, as we looked to the hilly ground where so lately were drawn up in battle array the dark columns of our enemy, and where not one sentinel now remained, the proud feeling of our victory came home to our hearts with the ever-thrilling thought, "What will they say at home?"

I was standing amid a group of my brother officers, when I received an order from the Colonel to ride down to Talavera for the return of our wounded, as the arrival of the Commander-in-Chief was momentarily looked for. I threw myself upon my horse, and setting out at a brisk pace, soon reached the gates.

On entering the town, I was obliged to dismount and proceed on foot. The streets were completely filled with people, treading their way among wagons, forage-carts, and sick-litters. Here was a booth filled with all imaginable wares for sale; there a temporary gin-shop established beneath a broken baggage-wagon; here might be seen a merry party throwing dice for a turkey or a kid—there, a wounded man, with bloodless cheek and tottering step, inquiring the road to the hospital; the accents of agony mingled with the drunken chorus, and the sharp crack of the Provost-Marshal's whip was heard above the boisterous revelling of the debauchee. All was confusion, bustle, and excitement. The staff-officer, with his flowing plume and glittering epaulettes, wended his way on foot amid the din and bustle, unnoticed and uncared for; while the little drummer amused an admiring audience of simple country-folk by some wondrous tale of the great victory.

My passage through this dense mass was necessarily a slow one.
No one made way for another; discipline for the time was at an
end, and with it all respect for rank or position. It was what nothing
of mere vicissitude in the fortune of war can equal—the wild orgies
of an army the day after a battle.

On turning the corner of a narrow street, my attention was
attracted by a crowd which, gathered round a small fountain,
seemed, as well as I could perceive, to witness some proceeding with
more than ordinary interest. Exclamations in Portuguese, expressive of surprise and admiration, were mingled with English oaths
and Irish ejaculations, while high above all rose other sounds—the
cries of some one in pain and suffering. Forcing my way through
the dense group, I at length reached the interior of the crowd, when,
to my astonishment, I perceived a short, fat, punchy-looking man,
stripped of his coat and waistcoat, and with his shirt sleeves rolled
up to his shoulders, busily employed in operating upon a wounded
soldier. Amputation knives, tourniquets, bandages, and all other
imaginable instruments for giving or alleviating torture, were strewed
about him, and, from the arrangement and preparation, it was clear
that he had pitched upon this spot as a hospital for his patients.
While he continued to perform his functions with a singular speed
and dexterity, he never for a moment ceased a running fire of small
talk, now addressed to the patient in particular, now to the crowd at
large—sometimes a soliloquy to himself, and not unfrequently, ab-
stractedly, upon things in general. These little specimens of oratory, delivered in such a place at such a time, and, not least of all,
in the richest imaginable Cork accent, were sufficient to arrest my
steps, and I stopped for some time to observe him.

The patient, who was a large, powerfully-built fellow, had been
wounded in both legs by the explosion of a shell, but yet not so
severely as to require amputation.

" Does that plaze you, then ?" said the doctor, as he applied some
powerful caustic to a wounded vessel ; " there's no satisfying the like
of you. Quite warm and comfortable ye'll be this morning after
that. I saw that same shell coming, and I called out to Maurice
Blake, ' By your leave, Maurice, let that fellow pass, he's in a hurry !'
and faith, I said to myself, ' there's more where you came from—
you're not an only child, and I never liked the family.' What are
ye grinning for, ye brown thieves ?" This was addressed to the
Portuguese. " There, now, keep the limb quiet and easy. Upon
my conscience, if that shell fell into ould Lundy Foot's shop this
morning, there'd be plenty of sneezing in Sackville street. Who's
next ?" said he, looking round with an expression that seemed to
threaten that, if no wounded man was ready, he was quite prepared

25

to carve out a patient for himself. Not exactly relishing the invitation in the searching that accompanied it, I backed my way through the crowd, and continued my path towards the hospital.

Here the scene which presented itself was shocking beyond belief—frightful and ghastly wounds from shells and cannon-shot were seen on all sides, every imaginable species of suffering that man is capable of was presented to view, while amid the dead and dying, operations the most painful were proceeding with a haste and bustle that plainly showed how many more waited their turn for similar offices. The stairs were blocked up with fresh arrivals of wounded men, and even upon the corridors and landing-places the sick were strewn on all sides.

I hurried to that part of the building where my own people were, and soon learned that our loss was confined to about fourteen wounded, five of whom were officers; but, fortunately, we lost not a man of our gallant fellows, and Talavera brought us no mourning for a comrade, to damp the exultation we felt in our victory,

---

CHAPTER II.

THE OUTPOST.

DURING the three days which succeeded the battle, all things remained as they were before. The enemy had gradually withdrawn all his forces, and our most advanced pickets never came in sight of a French detachment. Still, although we had gained a great victory, our situation was anything but flattering. The most strenuous exertions of the commissariat were barely sufficient to provision the troops, and we had even already but too much experience of how little trust or reliance could be reposed in the most lavish promises of our allies. It was true our spirits failed us not, but it was rather from an implicit and never-failing confidence in the resources of our great leader, than that any amongst us could see his way through the dense cloud of difficulty and danger that seemed to envelope us on every side.

To add to the pressing emergencies of our position, we learned on the evening of the 31st that Soult was advancing from the north, and, at the head of fourteen thousand chosen troops, in full march upon Placentia, thus threatening our rear, at the very moment, too, when any further advance was evidently impossible.

On the morning of the 1st of August, I was ordered with a small party to push forward in the direction of the Alberche, upon the left bank of which it was reported that the French were again concentrating their forces, and, if possible, to obtain information as to their future movements. Meanwhile, the army was about to fall back upon Oropesa, there to await Soult's advance, and, if necessary, to give him battle—Cuesta engaging with his Spaniards to secure Talavera, with its stores and hospitals, against any present movement from Victor.

After a hearty breakfast, and a kind "Good-bye!" from my brother officers, I set out. My road along the Tagus, for several miles of the way, was a narrow path scarped from the rocky ledge of the river, shaded by rich olive plantations, that threw a friendly shade over us during the noonday heat.

We travelled along silently, sparing our cattle from time to time, but endeavoring ere nightfall to reach Torrijos, in which village we had heard several French soldiers were in hospital. Our information leading us to believe them very inadequately guarded, we hoped to make some prisoners, from whom the information we sought could in all likelihood be obtained. More than once during the day our road was crossed by parties similar to our own, sent forward to reconnoitre; and towards evening a party of the Twenty-third Light Dragoons, returning towards Talavera, informed us that the French had retired from Torrijos, which was now occupied by an English detachment, under my old friend O'Shaughnessy.

I need not say with what pleasure I heard this piece of news, and eagerly pressed forward, preferring the warm shelter and hospitable board the Major was certain of possessing, to the cold blast and dripping grass of a bivouac. Night, however, fell fast; darkness, without an intervening twilight, set in, and we lost our way. A bleak table-land, with here and there a stunted, leafless tree, was all that we could discern by the pale light of a new moon. An apparently interminable heath, uncrossed by path or foot-track, was before us, and our jaded cattle seemed to feel the dreary uncertainty of the prospect as sensitively as ourselves, stumbling and overreaching at every step.

Cursing my ill-luck for such a misadventnre, and once more picturing to my mind the bright blazing hearth and smoking supper I had hoped to partake of, I concluded to call a halt, and prepared to pass the night. My decision was hastened by finding myself suddenly in a little grove of pine-trees, whose shelter was not to be despised; besides that, our bivouac fires were now sure of being supplied.

It was fortunate the night was fine, though dark. In a calm, still atmosphere, when not a leaf moved nor a branch stirred, we picketed our tired horses, and, shaking out their forage, heaped up in the midst a blazing fire of the fir-tree. Our humble supper was produced, and even with the still lingering reverie of the Major and his happier destiny, I began to feel comfortable.

My troopers, who probably had not been flattering their imaginations with such *gourmand* reflections and views, sat happily around their cheerful blaze, chatting over the great battle they had so lately witnessed, and mingling their stories of some comrade's prowess with sorrows for the dead and proud hopes for the future. In the midst, upon his knees beside the flame, was Mike, disputing, detailing, guessing, and occasionally inventing, all his arguments only tending to one view of the late victory,—"that it was the Lord's mercy the most of the Forty-eighth was Irish, or we wouldn't be sitting there now!"

Despite Mr. Free's conversational gifts, however, his audience one by one dropped off in sleep, leaving him sole monarch of the watch-fire, and—what he thought more of—a small brass kettle nearly full of brandy and water. This latter, I perceived, he produced when all was tranquil, and seemed, as he cast a furtive glance around, to assure himself that he was the only company present.

Lying some yards off, I watched him for about an hour, as he sat rubbing his hands before the blaze, or lifting the little vessel to his lips, his droll features ever and anon seeming acted upon by some passing dream of former devilment, as he smiled and muttered some sentences in an under-voice. Sleep at length overpowered me; but my last waking thoughts were haunted with a single ditty by which Mike accompanied himself as he kept burnishing the buttons of my jacket before the fire, now and then interrupting the melody by a recourse to the copper.

"Well, well, you're clean enough now; and sure it's little good brightening you up, when you'll be as bad to-morrow. Like his father's son, devil a lie in it! Nothing would serve him but his best blue jacket to fight in, as if the French was particular what they killed us in. Pleasant trade, upon my conscience! Well, never mind. That's beautiful *spercts* anyhow. Your health, Mickey Free; it's yourself that stands to me.

> 'It's little for glory I care;
>   Sure ambition is only a fable;
> I'd as soon be myself as Lord Mayor,
>   With lashings of drink on the table.
> I like to lie down in the sun,
>   And *drame*, when my *faytures* is scorchin',
> That when I'm too *ould* for more fun,
>   Why, I'll marry a wife with a fortune.

> 'And in winter, with bacon and eggs,
>   And a place at the turf-fire basking,
> Sip my punch as I roasted my legs,
>   Oh! the devil a more I'd be asking!
> For I haven't a *janius* for work,—
>   It was never a gift of the Bradies,—
> But I'd make a most *illigant* Turk,
>   For I'm fond of tobacco and ladies.' "

This confounded *refrain* kept ringing through my dream, and "tobacco and ladies" mingled with my thoughts of storm and battle-field, long after their very gifted author had composed himself to slumber.

Sleep, and sound sleep, came at length, and many hours elapsed ere I awoke. When I did so, my fire was reduced to its last embers. Mike, like the others, had sunk in slumber, and mid the gray dawn that precedes the morning, I could just perceive the dark shadows of my troopers as they lay in groups around.

The fatigues of the previous day had so completely overcome me, that it was with difficulty I could arouse myself so far as to heap fresh logs upon the fire. This I did with my eyes half closed, and in that listless, dreamy state which seems the twilight of sleep.

I managed so much, however, and was returning to my couch beneath a tree, when suddenly an object presented itself to my eyes that absolutely rooted me to the spot. At about twenty or thirty yards distant, where but the moment before the long line of horizon terminated the view, there now stood a huge figure of some ten or twelve in height; two heads—which surmounted this colossal personage—moved alternately from side to side, while several arms waved loosely to and fro in the most strange and uncouth manner. My first impression was that a dream had conjured up this distorted image; but when I had assured myself by repeated pinchings and shakings that I was really awake, still it remained there. I was never much given to believe in ghosts; but even had I been so, this strange apparition must have puzzled me as much as ever, for it could not have been the representative of anything I ever heard of before.

A vague suspicion that some French trickery was concerned, induced me to challenge it in French, so without advancing a step, I halloed out, "*Qui va là?*"

My voice aroused a sleeping soldier, who, springing up beside me, had his carbine at the cock; while, equally thunderstruck with myself, he gazed at the monster.

"*Qui va là?*" shouted I again, and no answer was returned, when suddenly the huge object wheeled rapidly around, and without waiting for any further parley, made for the thicket.

The tramp of a horse's feet now assured me as to the nature of at least part of the spectacle, when click went the trigger behind me, and the trooper's ball rushed whistling through the brushwood.　In a moment the whole party were up and stirring.

"This way, lads!" cried I, as, drawing my sabre, I dashed into the pine wood.

For a few moments all was as dark as midnight; but as we proceeded farther, we came out upon a little open space which commanded the plain beneath for a great extent.

"There it goes!" said one of the men, pointing to a narrow, beaten path, in which the tall figure moved at a slow and stately pace, while still the same wild gestures of heads and limbs continued.

"Don't fire, men! don't fire!" I cried, "but follow me," as I set forward as hard as I could.

As we neared it, the frantic gesticulations grew more and more remarkable, while some stray words which we half caught, sounded like English in our ears.　We were now within pistol-shot distance, when suddenly the horse—for that much at least we were assured of —stumbled and fell forward, precipitating the remainder of the object headlong into the road.

In a second we were upon the spot, when the first sounds which greeted me were the following, uttered in an accent by no means new to me:—

"Oh, blessed Virgin!　Wasn't it yourself that threw me in the mud, or my nose was done for?　Shaugh, Shaugh, my boy! since we are taken, tip them the blarney, and say we're generals of division!"

I need not say with what a burst of laughter I received this very original declaration.

"I ought to know that laugh," cried a voice I at once knew to be that of my friend O'Shaughnessy.　"Are you Charles O'Malley, by any chance in life?"

"The same, Major, and delighted to meet you; though, faith, we were near giving you a rather warm reception.　What in the devil's name did you represent just now?"

"Ask Maurice, there, bad luck to him!　I wish the devil had him when he persuaded me into it."

"Introduce me to your friend," replied the other, rubbing his shins as he spoke.　"Mr. O'Mealey,"—so he called me—"I think. Happy to meet you.　My mother was a Ryan of Killdooley, married to a first cousin of your father's, before she took Mr. Quill, my respected progenitor.　I'm Dr. Quill, of the 48th, more commonly called Maurice Quill.　Tear and ages! how sore my back is!　It was all the fault of the baste, Mr. O'Mealey. We set out in search of you this morning, to bring you back with us to Torrijos, but we fell in with a very pleasant funeral at Barcaventer, and joined them; they invited us, I may say, to spend the day; and a very jovial day it was. I was the chief mourner, and carried a very big candle through the village, in consideration of as fine a meat-pie and as much lush as my grief permitted me to indulge in afterwards. But, my dear sir, when it was all finished, we found ourselves nine miles from our quarters, and as neither of us was in a very befitting condition for pedestrian exercise, we stole one of the leaders out of the hearse—velvet, plumes, and all—and set off home.

"When we came upon your party, we were not over clear whether you were English, Portuguese, or French, and that was the reason I called out to you, 'God save all here!' in Irish. Your polite answer was a shot, which struck the old horse in the knee, and although we wheeled about in double quick, we never could get him out of his professional habits on the road. He had a strong notion he was engaged in another funeral—as he was very likely to be—and the devil a bit faster than a dead march could we get him to, with all our thrashing. Orderly time, for men in a hurry, with a whole platoon blazing away behind them! But long life to the cavalry, they never hit anything!"

While he continued to run on in this manner, we reached our watch-fire, when what was my surprise to discover, in my newly-made acquaintance, the worthy Doctor I had seen a day or two before, operating at the fountain at Talavera!

"Well, Mr. O'Mealey," said he, as he seated himself before the blaze, "what is the state of the larder? Anything savory—anything drink-inspiring to be had?"

"I fear, Doctor, my fare is of the very humblest; but still——"

"What are the fluids, Charley?" cried the Major; "the cruel performance I have been enacting on that cursed beast has left me in a fever."

"This was a pigeon-pie formerly," said Dr. Quill, investigating the ruined walls of a pastry; "and—but come, here's a duck; and if my nose deceive me not, a very tolerable ham. Peter—Larry—Patsy—What's the name of your familiar there?"

"Mickey—Mickey Free."

"Mickey Free, then; come here, avick! Devise a little drink, my son—none of the weakest—no lemon—hot! You understand, hot! That chap has an eye for punch; there's no mistaking an Irish fellow; nature has endowed them richly—fine features, and a beautiful absorbent system! That's the gift! Just look at him, blowing up the fire—isn't he a picture? Well, O'Mealey, I was fretting that

we hadn't you up at Torrijos; we were enjoying life very respectably; we established a little system of small tithes upon fowl, sheep,
pigs' heads and wine skins, that throve remarkably for the time.
Here's the lush! Put it down there, Mickey, in the middle; that's
right. Your health, Shaugh. O'Mealey, here's a troop to you; and
in the meantime I'll give you a chant:

> 'Come, ye jovial souls, don't o'er the bowl be sleeping,
> Nor let the grog go round like a cripple creeping;
> If your care comes up—in the liquor sink it,
> Pass along the lush—I'm the boy can drink it.
> Isn't that so, Mrs. Mary Callaghan?
> Isn't that so, Mrs. Mary Callaghan?'

"Shaugh, my hearty, this begins to feel comfortable."

"Your man, O'Mealey, has a most judicious notion of punch for
a small party; and though one has prejudices about a table, chairs,
and that sort of thing, take my word for it, it's better than fighting
the French any day!"

"Well, Charley, it certainly did look quite awkward enough the
other day towards three o'clock, when the Legion fell back before
that French column, and broke the Guards behind them."

"Yes, you're quite right; but I think every one felt that the confusion was but momentary; the gallant 48th was up in an instant."

"Faith! I can answer for their alacrity," said the Doctor; "I was
making my way to the rear with all convenient despatch, when an
aide-de-camp called out,—

"'Cavalry coming! take care, 48th.'

"'Left face, wheel! Fall in there, fall in there!' I heard on
every side, and soon found myself standing in a square, with Sir
Arthur himself, and Hill, and the rest of them, all around me.

"'Steady, men! Steady, now!' said Hill, as he rode around the
ranks, while we saw an awful column of cuirassiers forming on the
rising ground to our left.

"'Here they come!' said Sir Arthur, as the French came powder-
ing along, making the very earth tremble beneath them.

"My first thought was, 'The devils are mad! and they'll ride
down into us, before they know they're kilt!' And sure enough,
smash into our first rank they pitched, sabring and cutting all
before them! when at last the word 'Fire!' was given, and the whole
head of the column broke like a shell, and rolled horse over man on
the earth.

"'Very well done! very well, indeed!' said Sir Arthur, turning
as coolly round to me as if he were asking for more gravy.

"'Mighty well done!' said I in reply; and resolving not to be
out lone in coolness, I pulled out my snuff-box and offered him a

pinch, saying, 'The real thing, Sir Arthur; our own countryman—blackguard.'

"He gave a little grim kind of a smile, took a pinch, and then called out,—

"'Let Sherbroke advance!' while turning again towards me, he said, 'Where are your people, Colonel?'

"'Colonel!' thought I; 'is it possible he's going to promote me?' But before I could answer, he was talking to another. Meanwhile, Hill came up, and, looking at me steadily, burst out with,—

"'Why the devil are you here, sir? Why ain't you at the rear?'

"'Upon my conscience,' said I, 'that's the very thing I'm puzzling myself about this minute! but if you think it's pride in me, you're greatly mistaken, for I'd rather the greatest scoundrel in Dublin was kicking me down Sackville street than be here now!'

"You'd think it was fun I was making, if you heard how they all laughed, Hill and Cameron and the others louder than any.

"'Who is he?' said Sir Arthur, quickly.

"'Dr. Quill, surgeon of the 33d, where I exchanged, to be near my brother, sir, in the 34th.'

"'A doctor,—a surgeon! That fellow a surgeon! D— him, I took him for Colonel Grosvenor! I say, Gordon, these medical officers must be docked of their fine feathers, there's no knowing them from the staff; look to that in the next general order.'

"And sure enough they left us bare and naked the next morning; and if the French sharpshooters pick us down now, devil mend them for wasting powder, for if they look in the orderly books, they'll find their mistake."

"Ah, Maurice, Maurice!" said Shaugh, with a sigh, "you'll never improve—you'll never improve!"

"Why the devil would I?" said he; "ain't I at the top of my profession—full surgeon—with nothing to expect—nothing to hope for? Oh, if I only remained in the light company, what wouldn't I be now?"

"Then you were not always a doctor?" said I.

"Upon my conscience I wasn't," said he. "When Shaugh knew me first, I was the Adonis of the Roscommon militia, with more heiresses in my list than any man in the regiment; but Shaugh and myself were always unlucky."

"Poor Mrs. Rogers!" said the Major, pathetically, drinking off his glass and heaving a profound sigh.

"Ah, the darling!" said the Doctor; "if it wasn't for a jug of punch that lay on the hall table, our fortune in life would be very different."

"True for you, Maurice!" quoth O'Shaughnessy.

"I should like much to hear that story," said I, pushing the jug briskly round.

"He'll tell it you," said O'Shaughnessy, lighting his cigar, and leaning pensively back against a tree,—"he'll tell it you."

"I will with pleasure," said Maurice. "Let Mr. Free meantime amuse himself with the punch-bowl, and I'll relate it."

CHAPTER III.

THE DOCTOR'S TALE.*

IT is now some fifteen years since—if it wasn't for O'Shaughnessy's wrinkles, I could not believe it five—we were quartered in Loughrea. There were besides our regiment the 50th, the 73d, and a troop or two of horse artillery; the whole town was literally a barrack, and, as you may suppose, the pleasantest place imaginable. All the young ladies, and indeed all those that had got their brevet some years before, came flocking into the town, not knowing but the devil might persuade a raw ensign or so to marry some of them.

"Such dinner parties—such routs and balls—never were heard of west of Athlone. The gayeties were incessant; and if good feeding, plenty of claret, short whist, country-dances, and kissing, could have done the thing, there wouldn't have been a bachelor with a red coat for six miles around.

"You know the west, O'Malley; so I needn't tell you what the Galway girls are like—fine, hearty, free-and-easy, talking, laughing devils; but as deep and as 'cute as a Master in Chancery—ready for any fun or merriment; but always keeping a sly look-out for a proposal or a tender acknowledgment, which—what between the heat of a ball-room, whisky-negus, white satin shoes, and a quarrel with your guardian—it's ten to one you fall into before you're a week in the same town with them.

"As for the men, I don't admire them so much; pleasant and cheerful enough, when they're handicapping the coat off your back,

---

* I cannot permit the reader to fall into the same blunder with regard to the worthy "Maurice" as my friend Charles O'Malley has done. It is only fair to state that the Doctor in the following tale was hoaxing the "Dragoon." A braver and a better fellow than Quill never existed, equally beloved by his brother officers as delighted in for his convivial talents. His favorite amusement was to invent some story or adventure, in which, mixing up his own name with that of some friend or companion, the veracity of the whole was never questioned. Of this nature was the pedigree he devised in the last chapter to impose upon O'Malley, who believed implicitly all he told him.

and your new tilbury for a spavined pony and a cotton umbrella; but regular devils if you come to cross them the least in life; nothing but ten paces—three shots a piece—to begin and end with something like Sir Roger de Coverley, when every one has a pull at his neighbor. I'm not saying they're not agreeable, well-informed, and mild in their habits; but they lean over-much to corduroys and coroners' inquests for one's taste farther south. However, they're a fine people, take them all in all; and, if they were not interfered with, and their national customs invaded with road making, petty sessions, grand jury laws, and a stray commission now and then, they are undoubtedly capable of great things, and would astonish the world.

" But, as I was saying, we were ordered to Loughrea, after being fifteen months in detachments about Birr, Tullamore, Kilbeggan, and all that country; the change was indeed a delightful one, and we soon found ourselves the centre of the most marked and determined civilities. I told you they were wise people in the west; this was their calculation: the line—ours was the Roscommon militia— are here to-day, there to-morrow; they may be flirting in Tralee this week, and fighting on the Tagus the next; not that there was any fighting there in those times, but then there was always Nova Scotia and St. John's, and a hundred other places that a Galway young lady knew nothing about, except that people never came back from them. Now, what good, what use was there in falling in love with them? mere transitory and passing pleasure that was. But as for us : there we were; if not in Kilkenny, we were in Cork. Safe cut and come again ; no getting away under pretence of foreign service; no excuse for not marrying by any cruel pictures of the colonies, where they make spatchcocks of the officers' wives, and scrape their infant families to death with a small tooth-comb. In a word, my dear O'Mealey, we were at a high premium; and even O'Shaughnessy, with his red head and the legs you see, had his admirers—there now, don't be angry, Dan—the men, at least, were mighty partial to you.

" Loughrea, if it was a pleasant, was a very expensive place. White gloves and car-hire—there wasn't a chaise in the town— short whist, too (God forgive me if I wrong them, but I wonder were they honest?), cost money; and as our popularity rose, our purses fell, till at length, when the one was at the flood, the other was something very like low water.

" Now, the Roscommon was a beautiful corps—no petty jealousies, no little squabbling among the officers, no small spleen between the Major's wife and the Paymaster's sister,—all was amiable, kind, brotherly, and affectionate. To proceed, I need only mention one

fine trait of them—no man ever refused to endorse a brother officer's bill. To think of asking the amount, or even the date, would
be taken personally ; and thus we went on mutually aiding and
assisting each other—the Colonel drawing on me, I on the Major,
the senior Captain on the Surgeon, and so on,—a regular cross-fire
of 'promises to pay,' all stamped and regular.

"Not but the system had its inconveniences, for sometimes an
obstinate tailor or bootmaker would make a row for his money, and
then we'd be obliged to get up a little quarrel between the drawer
and the acceptor of the bill ; they couldn't speak for some days,
and a mutual friend to both would tell the creditor that the slightest imprudence on his part would lead to bloodshed ; 'and the Lord
help him ! if there was a duel, he'd prove the whole cause of it.'
This and twenty other plans were employed, and finally the matter
would be left to arbitration among our brother officers, and I need
not say they behaved like trumps. But notwithstanding all this, we
were frequently hard pressed for cash ; as the Colonel said, 'It's a
mighty expensive corps.' Our dress was costly—not that it had
much lace and gold on it, but that, what between falling on the road
at night, shindies at mess, and other devilment, a coat lasted no
time. Wine, too, was heavy on us, for though we often changed
our wine merchant, and rarely paid him, there was an awful consumption at the mess.

"Now, what I have mentioned may prepare you for the fact that,
before we were eight weeks in garrison, Shaugh and myself, upon
an accurate calculation of our joint finances, discovered that, except
some vague promises of discounting here and there through the
town, and seven and fourpence in specie, we were innocent of any
pecuniary treasures. This was embarrassing. We had both embarked in several small schemes of pleasurable amusement ; had a
couple of hunters each, a tandem, and a running account—I think
it *galloped*—at every shop in the town.

" Let me pause for a moment here, O'Mealey, while I moralize a
little in a strain which I hope may benefit you. Have you ever
considered—of course you have not: you're too young and unreflecting—how beautifully every climate and every soil possesses some
one antidote or another to its own noxious influences ? The tropics
have their succulent and juicy fruits, cooling and refreshing ; the
northern latitudes have their beasts with fur and warm skin to keep
out the frost-bites. And so it is in Ireland ; nowhere on the face of
the habitable globe does a man contract such habits of small debt,
and nowhere, I'll be sworn, can he so easily get out of any scrape
concerning them. They have their tigers in the east, their ante-
lopes in the south, their white bears in Norway, their buffaloes in

America; but we have an animal in Ireland that beats them all hollow—a country attorney!

"Now, let me introduce you to Mr. Matthew Donevan. Mat, as he was familiarly called by his numerous acquaintances, was a short, florid, rosy little gentleman, of some four or five-and-forty, with a well-curled wig of the fairest imaginable auburn, the gentle wave of the front locks, which played in infantine loveliness upon his little bullet forehead, contrasting strongly enough with a cunning leer of his eye, and a certain *nisi prius* laugh that, however it might please a client, rarely brought pleasurable feelings to his opponent in a cause.

"Mat was a character in his way. Deep, double, and tricky in everything that concerned his profession, he affected the gay fellow; liked a jolly dinner at Brown's Hotel—would go twenty miles to see a steeple-chase and a coursing match—bet with any one, when the odds were strong in his favor, with an easy indifference about money that made him seem, when winning, rather the victim of good luck than anything else. As he kept a rather pleasant bachelor's house, and liked the military much, we soon became acquainted. Upon him, therefore, for reasons I can't explain, both our hopes reposed, and Shaugh and myself agreed that if Mat could not assist us in our distresses, the case was a bad one.

"A pretty little epistle was accordingly concocted, inviting the worthy attorney to a small dinner at five o'clock the next day, intimating that we were to be perfectly alone, and had a little business to discuss. True to the hour, Mat was there; and, as if instantly guessing that ours was no regular party of pleasure, his look, dress, and manner were all in keeping with the occasion—quiet, subdued, and searching.

"When the claret had been superseded by the whisky, and the confidential hours were approaching, by an adroit allusion to some heavy wager then pending, we brought our finances upon the *tapis*. The thing was done beautifully—an easy *adagio* movement—no violent transition; but hang me if old Mat didn't catch the matter at once.

"'Oh! it's there ye are, Captain,' said he, with his peculiar grin. 'Two-and-sixpence in the pound, and no assets.'

"'The last is nearer the mark, my old boy,' said Shaugh, blurting out the whole truth at once. The wily attorney finished his tumbler slowly, as if giving himself time for reflection, and then, smacking his lips in a preparatory manner, took a quick survey of the room with his piercing green eye.

"'A very sweet mare of yours that little mouse-colored one is, with the dip in the back; and she has a trifling curb—maybe it's a spavin, indeed—in the near hind leg. You gave five-and-twenty for her, now, I'll be bound?'

"'Sixty guineas, as sure as my name's Dan,' said Shaugh, not at all pleased at the value put upon his hackney; 'and as to the spavin and curb, I'll wager double the sum she has neither the slightest trace of one nor the other.'

"'I'll not take the bet,' said Mat, dryly; 'money's scarce in these parts.'

"This hit silenced us both, and our friend continued :—

"'Then there's the bay horse—a great strapping, leggy beast he is for a tilbury; and the hunters—worth nothing here; they don't know this country. Them's neat pistols; and the tilbury is not bad——'

"'Confound you!' said I, losing all patience; 'we didn't ask you here to praise our movables; we want to raise the wind without that.'

"'I see—I perceive,' said Mat, taking a pinch of snuff very leisurely as he spoke; 'I see. Well, that is difficult—very difficult, just now. I've mortgaged every acre of ground in the two counties near us, and a sixpence more is not to be had that way. Are you lucky at the races?'

"'Never win a sixpence.'

"'What can you do at whist?'

"'Why, I revoke, and get cursed by my partner—the devil a bit more.'

"'That's mighty bad, for otherwise we might arrange something for you. Well, I only see one thing for it—you must marry. A wife with some money will get you out of your present difficulties, and we'll manage that easily enough.'

"'Come, Dan,' said I—for Shaugh was dropping asleep—'cheer up, old fellow. Donevan has found the way to pull us through our misfortunes—a girl with forty thousand pounds, the best cock-shooting in Ireland; an old family, a capital cellar—all awaits ye. Rouse up, there!'

"'I'm convanient,' said Shaugh, with a look intended to be knowing, but really very tipsy.

"'I didn't say much for her personal attractions, Captain,' said Mat; 'nor, indeed, did I specify the exact sum; but Mrs. Rogers Dooley, of Clonakilty, might be a princess——'

"'And so she shall be, Mat; the O'Shaughnessys were kings of Ennis in the time of Nero; and I'm only waiting for a trifle of money to revive the title. What's her name?'

"'Mrs. Rogers Dooley.'

"'Here's her health, and long life to her,—

> 'And may the devil cut the toes
>   Of all her foes,
> That we may know them by their limping.' "

" This benevolent wish uttered, Dan fell flat upon the hearth-rug, and was soon sound asleep. I must hasten on, so need only say that before we parted that night Mat and myself had finished the half-gallon bottle of Loughrea whisky, and concluded a treaty for the hand and fortune of Mrs. Rogers Dooley, he being guaranteed a very handsome percentage on the property, and the lady being reserved for choice between Dan and myself, which, however, I was determined should fall upon my more fortunate friend.

"The first object which presented itself to my aching senses the following morning was a very spacious card of invitation from Mr. Jonas Malone, requesting me to favor him with the seductions of my society the next evening to a ball; at the bottom of which, in Mr. Donevan's hand, I read,—

" ' Don't fail; you know who is to be there. I've not been idle since I saw you. Would the Captain take twenty-five for the mare ?'

" ' So far so good,' thought I, as entering O'Shaughnessy's quarters, I discovered him endeavoring to spell out his card, which, however, had no postscript. We soon agreed that Mat should have his price; so, sending a polite answer to the invitation, we despatched a still more civil note to the attorney, and begged of him, as a weak mark of esteem, to accept the mouse-colored mare as a present.

Here O'Shaughnessy sighed deeply, and even seemed affected by the souvenir.

"Come, Dan, we did it all for the best. Oh ! O'Mealey, he was a cunning fellow; but no matter. We went to the ball, and, to be sure, it was a great sight. Two hundred and fifty souls, where there was not good room for the odd fifty; such laughing, such squeezing, such pressing of hands and waists in the staircase ! and then such a row and riot at the top,—four fiddles, a key bugle, and a bagpipe, playing 'Haste to the Wedding,' amid the crash of refreshment trays, the tramp of feet, and the sounds of merriment on all sides !

" It's only in Ireland, after all, people have fun ; old and young, merry and morose, the gay and cross-grained, are crammed into a lively country dance; and, ill-matched, ill-suited, go jigging away together to the blast of a bad band, till their heads, half turned by the noise, the heat, the novelty, and the hubbub, they all get as tipsy as if they were really deep in liquor.

"Then there is that particularly free-and-easy tone in every one about; there go a couple capering daintily out of the ball-room to take a little fresh air on the stairs, where every step has its own separate flirtation party; there, a riotous old gentleman, with a boarding-school girl for his partner, has plunged smack into a party at loo, upsetting cards and counters, and drawing down curses innumerable. Here are a merry knot round the refreshments, and well they may be; for the negus is strong punch, and the biscuit tipsy cake,—and all this with a running fire of good stories, jokes, and witticisms on all sides, in the laughter for which even the droll-looking servants join as heartily as the rest.

"We were not long in finding out Mrs. Rogers, who sat in the middle of a very high sofa, with her feet just touching the floor. She was short, fat, wore her hair in a crop, had a species of shining yellow skin, and a turned-up nose, all of which were by no means prepossessing. Shaugh and myself were too hard-up to be particular, and so we invited her to dance alternately for two consecutive hours, plying her assiduously with negus during the lulls in the music.

"Supper was at last announced, and enabled us to recruit for new efforts; and so, after an awful consumption of fowl, pigeon-pie, ham, and brandy cherries, Mrs. Rogers brightened up considerably, and professed her willingness to join the dancers. As for us, partly from exhaustion, partly to stimulate our energies, and in some degree to drown reflection, we drank deep, and when we reached the drawing-room, not only the agreeable guests themselves, but even the furniture, the venerable chairs and the stiff old sofa, seemed performing 'Sir Roger de Coverley.' How we conducted ourselves till five in the morning, let our cramps confess, for we were both bedridden for ten days after. However, at last, Mrs. Rogers gave in; and, reclining gracefully upon a window-seat, pronounced it a most elegant party, and asked me to look for her shawl. While I perambulated the staircase with her bonnet on my head, and more wearing-apparel than would stock a magazine, Shaugh was roaring himself hoarse in the street, calling for Mrs. Rogers's coach.

"'Sure, Captain,' said the lady, with a tender leer, 'it's only a chair.'

"'And here it is,' said I, surveying a very portly-looking old sedan, newly painted and varnished, that blocked up half the hall.

"'You'll catch cold, my angel,' said Shaugh, in a whisper, for he was coming it very strong by this; 'get into the chair. Maurice, can't you find those fellows?' said he to me; for the chairmen had gone down stairs, and were making very merry among the servants.

"'She's fast now,' said I, shutting the door to. 'Let us do the gallant thing, and carry her home ourselves.' Shaugh thought this a great notion; and in a minute we mounted the poles and sallied forth, amid a great chorus of laughing from all the footmen, maids, and teaboys that filled the passage.

"'The big house, with the bow-window and the pillars, Captain,' said a fellow, as we issued upon our journey.

"'I know it,' said I. 'Turn to your left after you pass the square.'

"'Isn't she heavy?' said Shaugh, as he meandered across the narrow streets with a sidelong motion, that must have suggested to our fair inside passenger some notions of a sea voyage. In truth, I must confess our progress was rather a devious one; now zig-zagging from side to side, now getting into a sharp trot, and then suddenly pulling up at a dead stop, or running the machine chuck against a wall, to enable us to stand still and gain breath.

"'Which way now?' cried he, as we swung round the angle of a street, and entered the large market-place; 'I'm getting terribly tired.'

"'Never give in, Dan; think of Clonakilty, and the old lady herself;' and here I gave the chair a hoist that evidently astonished our fair friend, for a very imploring cry issued forth immediately after.

"'To the right, quick step, forward—charge!' cried I; and we set off at a brisk trot down a steep narrow lane.

"'Here it is now: the light in the window; cheer up!'

"As I said this, we came short up to a fine portly-looking doorway, with great stone pillars and cornice.

"'Make yourself at home, Maurice,' said he; 'bring her in;' and so saying we pushed forward—for the door was open—and passed boldly into a great flagged hall, silent and cold, and dark as the night itself.

"'Are you sure we're right?' said he.

"'All right,' said I; 'go ahead.'

"And so we did, till we came in sight of a small candle that burned dimly at a distance from us.

"'Make for the light,' said I; but just as I said so, Shaugh slipped and fell flat on the flagway. The noise of his fall sent up a hundred echoes in the silent building, and terrified us both dreadfully; after a minute's pause, by one consent we turned and made for the door, falling almost at every step; and frightened out of our senses, we came tumbling together into the porch, and out in the street, and never drew breath till we reached the barracks. Meanwhile, let me return to Mrs. Rogers. The dear old lady, who had passed an awful time since she left the ball, had just rallied out of a fainting fit when we took to our heels; so, after screaming and crying her best, she at last managed to open the top of the chair, and by dint of great exertions succeeded in forcing the door, and at

26

length freed herself from bondage. She was leisurely groping her way round it in the dark, when her lamentations being heard without, woke up the old sexton of the chapel—for it was there we placed her—who, entering cautiously with a light, no sooner caught a glimpse of the great black sedan and the figure beside it, than he also took to his heels, and ran like a madman to the priest's house.

"'Come, your reverence, come, for the love of marcy! Sure didn't I see him myself! O wirra, wirra!'

"'What is it, ye old fool?' said M'Kenny.

"'It's Father Con Doran, your reverence, that was buried last week, and there he is up now, coffin and all! saying a midnight mass as lively as ever.'

"Poor Mrs. Rogers, God help her! It was a trying sight for her, when the priest and the two coadjutors, and three little boys and the sexton, all came in to lay her spirit; and the shock she received that night, they say, she never got over.

"Need I say, my dear O'Mealey, that our acquaintance with Mrs. Rogers was closed? The dear woman had a hard struggle for it afterwards. Her character was assailed by all the elderly ladies in Loughrea for going off in our company, and her blue satin, piped with scarlet, utterly ruined by a deluge of holy water bestowed on her by the pious sexton. It was in vain that she originated twenty different reports to mystify the world; and even ten pounds spent in masses for the eternal repose of Father Con Doran only increased the laughter this unfortunate affair gave rise to. As for us, we exchanged into the.Line, and foreign service took us out of the road of duns, debts, and devilment, and we soon reformed, and eschewed such low company."

*   *   *   *   *   *   *   *

The day was breaking ere we separated, and amid the rich and fragrant vapors that exhaled from the earth, the faint traces of sunlight dimly stealing, told of the morning. My two friends set out for Torrijos, and I pushed forward in the direction of the Alberche.

It was a strange thing, that although but two days before the roads we were then travelling had been the line of retreat of the whole French army, not a vestige of their equipment, nor a trace of their *matériel*, had been left behind. In vain we searched each thicket by the wayside for some straggling soldier, some wounded or wearied man—nothing of the kind was to be seen. Except the deeply-rutted road, torn by the heavy wheels of the artillery, and the white ashes of a wood fire, nothing marked their progress.

Our journey was a lonely one. Not a man was to be met with. The houses stood untenanted; the doors lay open; no smoke wreathed from their deserted hearths; the peasantry had taken to the mountains, and although the plains were yellow with the ripe harvest, and the peaches hung temptingly upon the trees, all was deserted and forsaken. I had often seen the blackened walls and broken rafters, the traces of the wild revenge and reckless pillage of a retiring army—the ruined castle and the desecrated altar are sad things to look upon; but, somehow, a far heavier depression sunk into my heart as my eye ranged over the wide valleys and broad hills, all redolent of comfort, of beauty, and of happiness, and yet not one man to say, "This is my home; these are my household gods!" The birds carolled gayly in each leafy thicket, the bright stream sung merrily as it rippled through the rocks, the tall corn, gently stirred by the breeze, seemed to swell the concert of sweet sounds; but no human voice awoke the echoes there. It was as if the earth was speaking in thankfulness to its Maker; while man, ungrateful and unworthy man, pursuing his ruthless path of devastation and destruction, had left no being to say, " I thank Thee for all these."

The day was closing as we drew near the Alberche, and came in sight of the watch-fires of the enemy. Far as the eye could reach, their column extended; but in the dim twilight nothing could be seen with accuracy. Yet from the position their artillery occupied, and the unceasing din of baggage wagons and heavy carriages towards the rear, I came to the conclusion that a still further retreat was meditated. A picket of light cavalry was posted upon the river's bank, and seemed to watch with vigilance the approaches to the stream.

Our bivouac was a dense copse of pine trees, exactly opposite to the French advanced posts, and there we passed the night—fortunately, a calm and starlight one—for we dared not light fires, fearful of attracting attention.

During the long hours, I lay patiently watching the movements of the enemy till the dark shadows hid all from my sight; even then, as my ears caught the challenge of a sentry, or the footsteps of some officer on his round, my thoughts were riveted upon them, and a hundred fancies as to the future were based upon no stronger foundation than the click of a firelock or the low-muttered song of a patrol.

Towards morning I slept, and when day broke, my first glance was towards the river-side; but the French were gone—noiselessly —rapidly. Like one man, that vast army had departed; and a dense column of dust towards the horizon alone marked the long line of march where the martial legions were retreating.

My mission was thus ended. Hastily partaking of the humble breakfast my friend Mike provided for me, I once more set out, and took the road towards head-quarters.

CHAPTER IV.

THE SKIRMISH.

FOR several months after the battle of Talavera, my life presented nothing which I feel worth recording. Our good fortune seemed to have deserted us when our hopes were highest; for from the day of that splendid victory we began our retrograde movement upon Portugal. Pressed hard by overwhelming masses of the enemy, we saw the fortresses of Ciudad Rodrigo and Almeida fall successively into their hands. The Spaniards were defeated wherever they ventured upon a battle; and our own troops, thinned by sickness and desertion, presented but a shadow of that brilliant army which only a few months previous had followed the retiring French beyond the frontiers of Portugal.

However willing I now am—and who is not?—to recognize the genius and foresight of that great man who then held the destinies of the Peninsula within his hands, I confess, at the time I speak of, I could ill comprehend, and still less feel contented with, the successive retreats our forces made; and while the words Torres Vedras brought nothing to my mind but the last resting-place before embarkation, the sad fortunes of Corunna were now before me, and it was with a gloomy and desponding spirit I followed the routine of my daily duty.

During these weary months, if my life was devoid of stirring interest or adventure, it was not profitless. Constantly employed at the outposts, I became thoroughly inured to all the roughing of a soldier's life, and learned in the best of schools that tacit obedience which alone can form the subordinate, or ultimately fit its possessor for command himself.

Humble and unobtrusive as such a career must ever be, it was not without its occasional rewards. From General Craufurd I more than once obtained most kind mention in his despatches, and felt that I was not unknown or unnoticed by Sir Arthur Wellesley himself. At that time these testimonies, slight and passing as they were, contributed to the pride and glory of my existence; and even now—shall I confess it?—when some gray hairs are mingling with the brown, and when my old dragoon swagger is taming down into a kind of half-pay shamble, I feel my heart warm at the recollection of them.

Be it so. I care not who smiles at the avowal. I know of little better worth remembering as we grow old than what pleased us while we were young. With the memory of the kind words once spoken, come back the still kinder looks of those who spoke them, and, better than all, that early feeling of budding manhood when there was neither fear nor distrust. Alas! these are the things, and not weak eyes and tottering limbs, which form the burden of old age. Oh! if we could only go on believing, go on trusting, go on hoping to the last, who would shed tears for the bygone feats of his youthful days, when the spirit that evoked them lived young and vivid as before?

But to my story. While Ciudad Rodrigo still held out against the besieging French, its battered walls and breached ramparts sadly foretelling the fate inevitably impending, we were ordered, together with the 16th Light Dragoons, to proceed to Gallegos, to reinforce Craufurd's division, then forming a corps of observation upon Massena's movements.

The position he occupied was a most commanding one—the crown of a long mountain ridge, studded with pine copse and cork trees, presenting every facility for light infantry movements; and here and there, gently sloping towards the plain, offering a field for cavalry manœuvres. Beneath, in the vast plain, were encamped the dark legions of France, their heavy siege artillery planted against the doomed fortress, while clouds of their cavalry caracoled proudly before us, as if in taunting sarcasm at our inactivity.

Every artifice which his natural cunning could suggest, every taunt a Frenchman's vocabulary contains, had been used by Massena to induce Sir Arthur Wellesley to come to the assistance of the beleaguered fortress; but in vain. In vain he relaxed the energy of the siege, and affected carelessness. In vain he asserted that the English were either afraid, or else traitors to their allies. The mind of him he thus assailed was neither accessible to menace nor to sarcasm. Patiently abiding his time, he watched the progress of events, and provided for that future which was to crown his country's arms with success, and himself with undying glory.

Of a far different mettle was the general formed under whose orders we were now placed. Hot, passionate, and impetuous, relying upon bold and headlong heroism, rather than upon cool judgment and well-matured plans, Craufurd felt in war all the asperity and bitterness of a personal conflict. Ill brooking the insulting tone of the wily Frenchman, he thirsted for any occasion of a battle; and his proud spirit chafed against the colder counsels of his superior.

On the very morning we joined, the pickets brought in the intelligence that the French patrols were nightly in the habit of visiting the villages of the outposts, and committing every species of cruel indignity upon the wretched inhabitants. Fired at this daring insult, our General resolved to cut them off, and formed two ambuscades for that purpose.

Six squadrons of the 14th were despatched to Villa del Puerco, three of the 16th to Baguetto, while some companies of the 95th, and the caçadores, supported by artillery, were ordered to hold themselves in reserve, for the enemy were in force at no great distance from us.

The morning was just breaking as an aide-de-camp galloped up with the intelligence that the French had been seen near the Villa del Puerco, a body of infantry and some cavalry having crossed the plain, and disappeared in that direction. While our Colonel was forming us, with the intention of getting between them and their main body, the tramp of horses was heard in the wood behind, and in a few moments two officers rode up. The foremost, who was a short, stoutly-built man of about forty, with a bronzed face and eye of piercing black, shouted out as we wheeled into column,—

"Halt, there! Why, where the devil are you going? That's your ground!" So saying, and pointing straight towards the village with his hand, he would not listen to our Colonel's explanation that several stone fences and enclosures would interfere with cavalry movements, but added, "Forward, I say! Proceed!"

Unfortunately, the nature of the ground separated our squadron, as the Colonel anticipated; and although we came on at a topping pace, the French had time to form in square upon a hill to await us, and when we charged, they stood firmly, and firing with a low and steady aim, several of our troopers fell. As we wheeled round, we found ourselves exactly in front of their cavalry coming out of Baguilles; so, dashing straight at them, we revenged ourselves for our first repulse by capturing twenty-nine prisoners and wounding several others.

The French infantry were, however, still unbroken; and Colonel Talbot rode boldly up with five squadrons of the 14th; but the charge, pressed home with all its gallantry, failed also, and the Colonel fell mortally wounded, and fourteen of his troopers around him. Twice we rode round the square seeking for a weak point, but in vain; the gallant Frenchman who commanded, Captain Guache, stood fearlessly amid his brave followers, and we could hear him, as he called out from time to time,

"C'est ça, mes enfans! très bien fait, mes braves!"

And at length they made good their retreat, while we returned to the camp, leaving thirty-two troopers and our brave Colonel dead upon the field in this disastrous affair.

*   *   *   *   *   *   *   *

The repulse we had met with, so contrary to all our hopes and expectations, made that a most gloomy day to all of us. The brave fellows we had left behind us, the taunting cheer of the French infantry, the unbroken ranks against which we rode time after time in vain, never left our minds; and a sense of shame of what might be thought of us at head-quarters rendered the reflection still more painful.

Our bivouac, notwithstanding all our efforts, was a sad one, and when the moon rose, some drops of heavy rain falling at intervals in the still, unruffled air, threatened a night of storm; gradually the sky grew darker and darker, the clouds hung nearer to the earth, and a dense, thick mass of dark mist shrouded every object. The heavy cannonade of the siege was stilled; nothing betrayed that a vast army was encamped near us; their bivouac fires were even imperceptible, and the only sound we heard was the great bell of Ciudad Rodrigo as it struck the hour, and seemed, in the mournful cadence of its chime, like the knell of the doomed citadel.

The patrol which I commanded had to visit on its rounds the most advanced post of our position. This was a small farm-house, which, standing upon a little rising ledge of ground, was separated from the French lines by a small tributary stream to the Aguda. A party of the 14th were picketed here, and beneath them, in the valley, scarce five hundred yards distant, was a detachment of cuirassiers which formed the French outpost. As we neared our picket, the deep voice of the sentry challenged us, and, while all else was silent as the grave, we could hear from the opposite side the merry chorus of a French *chanson à boire*, with its clattering accompaniment of glasses, as some gay companions were making merry together.

Within the little hut which contained *our* fellows, the scene was a different one. The three officers who commanded sat moodily over a wretched fire of wet wood; a solitary candle dimly lighted the dismantled room, where a table but ill-supplied with cheer stood unminded and uncared for.

"Well, O'Malley," cried Baker, as I came in, "what is the night about? and what's Craufurd for next?"

"We hear," cried another, "that he means to give battle to-morrow; but surely Sir Arthur's orders are positive enough. Gordon himself told me that he was forbid to fight beyond the Coa, but to retreat at the first advance of the enemy."

"I'm afraid," replied I, "that retreating is his last thought just now. Ammunition has just been served out, and I know the horse artillery have orders to be in readiness by daybreak."

"All right," said Hampden, with a half-bitter tone. "Nothing like going through with it. If he is to be brought to court-martial for disobedience, he'll take good care we shan't be there to see it."

"Why, the French are fifty thousand strong!" said Baker.

"Look there! What does that mean, now? That's a signal from the town."

As he spoke, a rocket of great brilliancy shot up into the sky, and bursting, at length fell in millions of red lustrous sparks on every side, showing forth the tall fortress, and the encamped army around it, with all the clearness of noonday. It was a most splendid sight; and though the next moment all was dark as before, we gazed still fixedly into the gloomy distance, straining our eyes to observe what was hid from our view forever.

"That must be a signal," repeated Baker.

"Begad! if Craufurd sees it, he'll interpret it as a reason for fighting. I trust he's asleep by this time," said Hampden. "By the bye, O'Malley, did you see the fellows at work in the trenches? How beautifully clear it was towards the southward!"

"Yes, I remarked that; and what surprised me was the openness of their position in that direction. Towards the San Benito mole I could not see a man."

"Ah! they'll not attack on that side: but if we really are——"

"Stay, Hampden!" said I, interrupting him; "a thought has just struck me. At sunset I saw, through my telescope, the French engineers marking with their white tape the line of a new entrenchment in that quarter. Would it not be a glorious thing to move the tape, and bring the fellows under the fire of San Benito?"

"By Jove! O'Malley, that is a thought worth a troop to you."

"Far more likely to forward his promotion in the next world than in this," said Baker, smiling.

"By no means," added I; "I marked the ground this evening, and have it perfectly in my mind. If we were to follow the bend of the river, I'll be bound we'd come right upon the spot; by nearing the fortress we'll escape the sentries; and all this portion is open to us."

The project thus loosely thrown out was now discussed in all its bearings. Whatever difficulties it presented were combated so much to our own satisfaction, that at last its very facility damped our ardor. Meanwhile, the night wore on, and the storm of rain so long impending began to descend in very torrents; hissing along the parched ground, it rose in a mist, while overhead the heavy thunder rolled in long unbroken peals, the crazy door threatened to give way at each moment, and the whole building trembled to its foundation.

"Pass the brandy down here, Hampden, and thank your stars you're where you are. Eh, O'Malley? You'll defer your trip to San Benito for finer weather."

"Well, to come to the point," said Hampden, "I'd rather begin my engineering at a more favorable season; but if O'Malley's for it——"

"And O'Malley *is* for it," said I, suddenly.

"Then, faith, I'm not the man to baulk his fancy; and as Craufurd is so bent upon fighting to-morrow, it don't make much difference. Is it a bargain?"

"It is; here's my hand on it."

"Come, come, boys," said Baker, "I'll have none of this; we've been prettily cut up this morning already. You shall not go upon this foolish excursion."

"Confound it, old fellow! it's all very well for you to talk, with the majority before you next step; but here we are, if peace came to-morrow, scarcely better than we left England. No, no; if O'Malley's ready—and I see he is so before me——What have you got there? Oh! I see; that's our tape line; capital fun, by George! The worst of it is, they'll make us colonels of engineers. Now, then, what's your plan—on foot or mounted?"

"Mounted, and for this reason, the country is all open; if we are to have a run for it, our thorough-breds ought to distance them; and as we must expect to pass some of their sentries, our only chance is on horseback."

"My mind is relieved of a great load," said Hampden. "I was trembling in my skin lest you should make it a walking party. I'll do anything you like in the saddle, from robbing the mail to cutting out a frigate; but I never was much of a footpad."

"Well, Mike," said I, as I returned to the room with my trusty follower, "are the cattle to be depended on?"

"If we had a snaffle in Malachi Daly's mouth" (my brown horse), "I'd be afeared of nothing, sir; but if it comes to fencing, with that cruel bit—— but sure, you've a light hand, and let him have his head, if it's wall."

"By Jove, he thinks it a fox-chase!" said Hampden.

"Isn't it the same, sir?" said Mike, with a seriousness that made the whole party smile.

"Well, I hope we shall not be earthed, anyway," said I. "Now, the next thing is, who has a lantern?—ah! the very thing—nothing better. Look to your pistols, Hampden; and, Mike, here's a glass of grog for you; we'll want you. And now, one bumper for good luck. Eh, Baker, won't you pledge us?"

"And spare a little for me," said Hampden. "How it does rain! If one didn't expect to be waterproofed before morning, one really wouldn't go out in such weather."

While I busied myself in making my few preparations, Hampden proceeded gravely to inform Mike that we were going to the assistance of the besieged fortress, which could not possibly go on without us.

"Tare and ages!" said Mike, "that's mighty quare; and the blue rocket was a letter of invitation, I suppose?"

"Exactly," said Hampden; "and you see there's no ceremony between us. We'll just drop in, in the evening, in a friendly way."

"Well, then, upon my conscience, I'd wait, if I was you, till the family wasn't in confusion. They have enough on their hands just now."

"So you'll not be persuaded?" said Baker. "Well, I frankly tell you that, come what will of it, as your senior officer, I'll report you to-morrow. I'll not risk myself for any such hare-brained expeditions."

"A mighty pleasant lookout for me," said Mike; "if I'm not shot to-night, I may be flogged in the morning."

This speech once more threw us into a hearty fit of laughter, amid which we took leave of our friends, and set forth upon our way.

CHAPTER V.

THE LINES OF CIUDAD RODRIGO.

THE small twinkling lights which shone from the ramparts of Ciudad Rodrigo were our only guide as we issued forth upon our perilous expedition. The storm raged, if possible, even more violently than before, and gusts of wind swept along the ground with the force of a hurricane, so that at first our horses could scarcely face the tempest. Our path lay along the little stream for a considerable way, after which, fording the rivulet, we entered upon the open plain, taking care to avoid the French outpost on the extreme left, which was marked by a bivouac fire, burning under the heavy down-pour of rain, and looking larger through the dim atmosphere around it.

I rode foremost, followed closely by Hampden and Mike. Not a word was spoken after we crossed the stream. Our plan was, if challenged by a patrol, to reply in French and press on; so small a party could never suggest the idea of attack, and we hoped in this manner to escape.

The violence of the storm was such, that many of our precautions as to silence were quite unnecessary; and we had advanced to a considerable extent into the plain before any appearance of the cncampment struck us. At length, on mounting a little rising ground, we perceived several fires stretching far away to the northward, while still to our left there blazed one larger and brighter than the others. We now found that we had not outflanked their position as we intended, and learning, from the situation of the fires, that we were still only at the outposts, we pressed sharply forward, directing our course by the twin stars that shone from the fortress.

"How heavy the ground is here!" whispered Hampden, as our horses sunk above the fetlocks; "we had better stretch away to the right; the rise of the hill will favor us."

"Hark!" said I; "did you not hear something? Pull up. Silence now. Yes, there they come. It's a patrol; I hear their tramp." As I spoke, the measured tread of infantry was heard above the storm, and soon after a lantern was seen coming along the causeway near us. The column passed within a few yards of where we stood. I could even recognize the black covering of the shakos as the light fell on them. "Let us follow them," whispered I, and the next moment we fell in upon their track, holding our cattle well in hand, and ready to start at a moment.

"Qui va là?" a sentry demanded.

"La deuxième division," cried a hoarse voice.

"Halte là! la consigne?"

"Wagram!" repeated the same voice as before, while his party resumed their march; and the next moment the patrol was again upon his post, silent and motionless as before.

"En avant, messieurs!" said I aloud, as soon as the infantry had proceeded some distance; "en avant!"

"Qui va là?" demanded the sentry, as we came along at a sharp trot.

"L'état-major, Wagram!" responded I, pressing on without drawing rein; and in a moment we had regained our former position behind the infantry. We had scarcely time to congratulate ourselves upon the success of our scheme, when a tremendous clattering noise in front, mingled with the galloping of horses and the cracking of whips, announced the approach of the artillery as they came along by a narrow road which bisected our path. As they passed between us and the column, we could hear the muttered sentences of the drivers, cursing the unseasonable time for an attack, and swearing at their cattle in no measured tones.

"Did you hear that?" whispered Hampden; "the battery is about to be directed against the San Benito, which must be far away to the left. I heard one of the troop saying that they were to open their fire at daybreak."

"All right, now," said I; "look there!"

From the hill we now stood upon, a range of lanterns was distinctly visible, stretching away for nearly half a mile.

"There are the trenches; they must be at work, too; see how the lights are moving from place to place! Straight, now. Forward!"

So saying, I pressed my horse boldly on.

We had not proceeded many minutes, when the sounds of galloping were heard coming along behind us.

"To the right, in the hollow," cried I; "be still."

Scarcely had we moved off when several horsemen galloped up, and, drawing their reins to breathe their horses up the hill, we could hear their voices as they conversed together.

In the few broken words we could catch, we guessed that the attack upon San Benito was only a feint to induce Craufurd to hold his position, while the French, marching upon his flank and front, were to attack him with overwhelming masses and crush him.

"You hear what's in store for us, O'Malley," whispered Hampden. "I think we could not possibly do better than hasten back with the intelligence."

"We must not forget what we came for, first," said I; and the next moment we were following the horsemen, who, from their helmets, seemed horse-artillery officers.

The pace our guides rode at showed us that they knew their ground. We passed several sentries, muttering something at each time, and seeming as if only anxious to keep up with our party.

"They've halted," said I. "Now to the left there; gently here, for we must be in the midst of their lines. Ha! I knew we were right; see there!"

Before us, now, at a few hundred yards, we could perceive a number of men engaged upon the field. Lights were moving from place to place rapidly, while immediately in front a strong picket of cavalry were halted.

"By Jove, there's sharp work of it to-night!" whispered Hampden; "they do intend to surprise us to-morrow."

"Gently now, to the left," said I, as, cautiously skirting the little hill, I kept my eye firmly fixed upon the watch-fire.

The storm, which for some time had abated considerably, was now nearly quelled, and the moon again peeped forth amid masses of black and watery clouds.

"What good fortune for us!" thought I, at this moment, as I surveyed the plain before me.

"I say, O'Malley, what are those fellows at, yonder, where the blue light is burning?"

"Ah! the very people we want; these are the sappers. Now for it, that's our ground; we'll soon come upon their track now."

We pressed rapidly forward, passing an infantry party as we went. The blue light was scarcely one hundred yards off; we could even hear the shouting of the officers to their men in the trenches, when suddenly my horse came down upon his head, and rolling over, crushed me to the earth.

"Not hurt, my boy," cried I, in a subdued tone, as Hampden jumped down beside me.

It was the angle of a trench I had fallen into; and though both my horse and myself felt stunned for the moment, we rallied the next minute.

"Here is the very spot," said I. "Now, Mike, catch the bridles and follow us closely."

Guiding ourselves along the edge of the trench, we crept stealthily forward; the only watch-fire near was where the engineer party was halted, and our object was to get outside of this.

"My turn this time," said Hampden, as he tripped suddenly, and fell head foremost upon the grass.

As I assisted him to rise, something caught my ankle; and, on stooping, I found it was a cord pegged fast into the ground, and lying only a few inches above it.

"Now, steady! see here; this is their working line; pass your hand along it there, and let us follow it out."

While Hampden accordingly crept along on one side, I tracked the cord upon the other; here I found it terminating upon a small mound, where probably some battery was to be erected. I accordingly gathered it carefully up, and was returning towards my friend, when what was my horror to hear Mike's voice, conversing, as it seemed to me, with some one in French.

I stood fixed to the spot, my very heart beating almost in my mouth as I listened.

"Qui etes vous donc, mon ami?" inquired a hoarse, deep voice, a few yards off.

"Bon cheval, non *beast*, sacre nom de Dieu!" A hearty burst of laughter prevented my hearing the conclusion of Mike's French.

I now crept forward upon my hands and knees, till I could catch the dark outline of the horses, one hand fixed upon my pistol trigger, and my sword drawn in the other. Meanwhile the dialogue continued.

"Vous etes d'Alsace, n'est-ce-pas?" asked the Frenchman, kindly supposing that Mike's French savored of Strasburg.

"Oh, blessed Virgin! av I might shoot him," was the muttered reply.

Before I had time to see the effect of the last speech, I pressed forward with a bold spring, and felled the Frenchman to the earth; my hand had scarcely pressed upon his mouth, when Hampden was beside me. Snatching up the pistol I let fall, he held it to the man's chest, and commanded him to be silent. To unfasten his girdle, and bind the Frenchman's hands behind him, was the work of a moment; and, as the sharp click of the pistol-cock seemed to calm his efforts to escape, we soon succeeded in fastening his handkerchief tight across his mouth, and the next minute he was placed behind Mike's saddle, firmly attached to this worthy individual by his sword-belt.

"Now, a clear run home for it, and a fair start," said Hampden, as he sprang into the saddle.

"Now, then, for it," I replied, as, turning my horse's head towards our lines, I dashed madly forward.

The moon was again obscured, but still the dark outline of the hill which formed our encampment was discernible on the horizon. Riding side by side, on we hurried; now splashing through the deep and wet marshes, now plunging through small streams. Our horses were high in mettle, and we spared them not; by taking a wide *détour* we had outflanked the French pickets, and were almost out of all risk, when suddenly, on coming to the verge of a rather steep hill, we perceived beneath us a strong cavalry picket standing around a watch-fire; their horses were ready saddled, the men accoutred, and quite prepared for the field. While we conversed together in whispers as to the course to follow, our deliberations were very rapidly cut short. The French prisoner, who hitherto had given neither trouble nor resistance, had managed to free his mouth from the encumbrance of the handkerchief; and, as we stood quietly discussing our plans, with one tremendous effort he endeavored to hurl himself and Mike from the saddle, shouting out, as he did so,

"A moi camarades! a moi!"

Hampden's pistol leaped from the holster as he spoke, and, leveling it with a deadly aim, he pulled the trigger; but I threw up his arm, and the ball passed high above his head. To have killed the Frenchman would have been to lose my faithful follower, who struggled manfully with his adversary, and, at length, by throwing himself flatly forward upon the mane of his horse, completely disabled him. Meanwhile, the picket had sprung to their saddles, and looked wildly about on every side.

Not a moment was to be lost; so, turning our horse's heads towards the plain, away we went. One loud cheer announced to us that we had been seen, and the next instant the clash of the pursuing cavalry was heard behind us. It was now entirely a question of speed, and little need we have feared had Mike's horse not been doubly weighted. However, as we still had considerably the start, and the gray dawn of day enabled us to see the ground, the odds were in our favor. "Never let your horse's head go," was my often-repeated direction to Mike, as he spurred with all the desperation of madness. Already the low meadow-land was in sight which flanked the stream we had crossed in the morning; but, unfortunately, the heavy rains had swollen it now to a considerable depth, and the muddy current, choked with branches of trees and great stones, was hurrying down like a torrent. "Take the river: never flinch it!" was my cry to my companions, as I turned my head and saw a French dragoon, followed by two others, gaining rapidly upon us. As I spoke, Mike dashed in, followed by Hampden, and the same moment the sharp ring of a carbine whizzed past me. To take off the pursuit from the others, I wheeled my horse suddenly round, as if I feared to take the stream, and dashed along by the river's bank.

Beneath me, in the foaming current, the two horsemen labored; now stemming the rush of water, now reeling almost beneath. A sharp cry burst from Mike as I looked; and I saw the poor fellow bend nearly to his saddle. I could see no more, for the chase was now hot upon myself; behind me rode a French dragoon, his carbine pressed tightly to his side, ready to fire as he pressed on in pursuit. I had but one chance; so, drawing my pistol, I wheeled suddenly in my saddle, and fired straight at him. The Frenchman fell, while a regular volley from his party rung around me; one ball striking my horse, and another lodging in the pommel of my saddle. The noble animal reeled nearly to the earth, but as if rallying for a last effort, sprang forward with renewed energy and plunged boldly into the river.

For a moment, so sudden was my leap, my pursuers lost sight of me; but the bank being somewhat steep, the efforts of my horse to climb again discovered me, and before I reached the field, two pistol-balls took effect upon me: one slightly grazed my side, but my bridle-arm was broken by the other, and my hand fell motionless to my side. A cheer of defiance was, however, my reply, as I turned round in my saddle, and the next moment I was far beyond the range of their fire.

Not a man durst follow, and the last sight I had of them was the dismounted group who stood around their dead comrade; before me rode Hampden and Mike, still at top speed, and never turning their heads backward. I hastened after them; but my poor wounded horse, nearly hamstrung by the shot, became dead lame, and it was past daybreak ere I reached the first outposts of our lines.

CHAPTER VI.

THE DOCTOR.

AND his wound? Is it a serious one?" said a round full voice as the Doctor left my room at the conclusion of his visit.

"No, sir; a fractured bone is the worst of it; the bullet grazed, but did not cut the artery; and, as——"

"Well, how soon will he be about again?"

"In a few weeks, if no fever sets in."

"There is no objection to my seeing him?—a few minutes only—I'll be cautious." So saying, and, as it seemed to me, without waiting for a reply, the door was opened by an aide-de-camp, who announcing General Craufurd, closed it again and withdrew.

The first glance I threw upon the General enabled me to recognize the officer who on the previous morning had ridden up to the picket and given us the orders to charge. I essayed to rise a little as he came forward, but he motioned me with his hand to lie still, while, placing a chair close beside my bed, he sat down.

"Very sorry for your mishap, sir, but glad it is no worse. Moreton says that nothing of consequence is injured. There, you mustn't speak, except I ask you. Hampden has told me everything necessary; at least, as far as he knew. Is it your opinion, also, that any movement is in contemplation? and from what circumstance?"

I immediately explained, and as briefly as I was able, the reasons for suspecting such, with which he seemed quite satisfied. I detailed the various changes in the positions of the troops that were taking place during the night, the march of the artillery, and the strong bodies of cavalry that were posted in reserve along the river.

"Very well, sir; they'll not move; your prisoner, a quartermaster of an infantry battalion, says not, also. Yours was a bold stroke, but could not possibly have been of service, and the best thing I can do for you is not to mention it; a court-martial's but a poor recompense for a gun-shot wound. Meanwhile, when this blows over, I'll appoint you on my personal staff. There, not a word, I beg; and now, good-bye."

So saying, and waving me an adieu with his hand, the gallant veteran withdrew before I could express my gratitude for his kindness.

I had little time for reflecting over my past adventure, such numbers of my brother officers poured in upon me. All the Doctor's cautions respecting quietness and rest were disregarded, and a perfect levée sat the entire morning in my bedroom. I was delighted to learn that Mike's wound, though painful at the moment, was of no consequence; and, indeed, Hampden, who escaped both steel and shot, was the worst off amongst us, his plunge in the river having brought on an ague he had labored under years before.

"The illustrious Maurice has been twice here this morning, but they wouldn't admit him. Your Scotch physician is afraid of his Irish *confrère*, and they had a rare set-to about Galen and Hippocrates outside," said Baker.

"By the bye," said another, "did you see how Sparks looked when Quill joined us? Egad, I never saw a fellow in such a fright; he reddened up, then grew pale, turned his back, and slunk away at the very first moment."

"Yes, I remember it. We must find out the reason; for Maurice, depend upon it, has been hoaxing the poor fellow."

"Well, O'Malley," growled out the senior Major, "you certainly did give Hampden a benefit. He'll not trust himself in such company again; and, begad, he says the man is as bad as the master. That fellow of yours never let go his prisoner till he reached the Quartermaster-General, and they were both bathed in blood by that time."

"Poor Mike! we must do something for him."

"Oh! he's as happy as a king. Maurice has been in to see him, and they've had a long chat about Ireland, and all the national pastimes of whisky-drinking and smashing skulls. My very temples ache at the recollection."

"Is Mister O'Mealey at home?" said a very rich Cork accent, as the well-known and most droll features of Dr. Maurice Quill appeared at the door.

"Come in, Maurice," said the Major; "and, for Heaven's sake, behave properly. The poor fellow must not have a row about his bedside."

"A row—a row! Upon my conscience, it is little you know about a row, and there's worse things going than a row."

"Which leg is it?"

"It's an arm, Doctor, I'm happy to say."

"Not your punch hand, I hope. No; all's right. A neat fellow you have for a servant, that Mickey Free. I was asking him about a townsman of his own, one Tim Delany—the very cut of himself; the best servant I ever had. I never could make out what became of him. Old Hobson, of the 95th, gave him to me, saying, 'There he is for you, Maurice, and a bigger thief and a greater blackguard there's not in the 60th.'

"'Strong words,' said I.

"'And true,' said he; 'he'd steal your molar tooth while you were laughing at him.'

27

"'Let me have him, and try my hand on him, anyway. I've got no one just now. Anything is better than nothing.'

"Well, I took Tim, and sending for him to my room, I locked the door, and sitting down gravely before him, explained in a few words that I was quite aware of his little propensities.

"'Now,' said I, 'if you like to behave well, I'll think you as honest as the Chief Justice; but if I catch you stealing, if it be only the value of a brass snuff-box, I'll have you flogged before the regiment, as sure as my name's Maurice.'

"Oh! I wish you heard the volley of protestations that fell from him fast as hail. He was a calumniated man; the world conspired to wrong him; he was never a thief nor a rogue in his life. He had a weakness, he confessed, for the ladies; but, except that, he hoped he might die so thin that he could shave himself with his shin-bone if he ever so much as took a pinch of salt that wasn't his own.

"However this might be, nothing could be better than the way Tim and I got on together. Everything was in its place—nothing missing; and, in fact, for upwards of a year, I went on wondering when he was to show out in his true colors—for hitherto he had been a phœnix.

"At last—we were quartered at Limerick at the time—every morning used to bring accounts of all manner of petty thefts in the barrack. One fellow had lost his belt, another his shoes, a third had three-and-sixpence in his pocket when he went to bed, and woke without a farthing, and so on. Everybody save myself was mulcted of something. At length some rumors of Tim's former propensities got abroad; suspicion was excited; my friend Delany was rigidly watched, and some very dubious circumstances attached to the way he spent his evenings.

"My brother officers called upon me about the matter, and although nothing had transpired like proof, I sent for Tim, and opened my mind on the subject.

"You may talk of the look of conscious innocence, but I defy you to conceive of anything finer than the stare of offended honor Tim gave me as I began.

"'They say it's me, Doctor, do they?' said he. 'And you—you believe them. You allow them to revile me that way? Well, well, the world is come to a pretty pass, anyhow! Now, let me ask your honor a few questions. How many shirts had yourself when I entered your service? Two, and one was more like a fishing-net! And how many have ye now? Eighteen; ay, eighteen bran new cambric ones—devil a hole in one of them! How many pair of stockings had you? Three and an odd one. You have two dozen this minute. How many pocket-handkerchiefs? One—devil a more! You could only blow your nose two days in the week, and now may every hour of the twenty-four! And as to the trifling articles of small value, snuff-boxes, gloves, boot-jacks, night-caps, and ——'

" 'Stop, Tim, that's enough ——'

" 'No, sir, it is not,' said Tim, drawing himself up to his full height; 'you have wounded my feelings in a way I can't forget. It is impossible we can have that mutual respect our position demands. Farewell, farewell, Doctor, and forever !'

"Before I could say another word, the fellow had left the room, and closed the door after him; and from that hour to this I never set eyes on him."

In this vein did the worthy Doctor run on, till some more discreet friend suggested that however well-intentioned the visit, I did not seem to be fully equal to it—my flushed cheek and anxious eye betrayed that the fever of my wound had commenced; they left me, therefore, once more alone, and to my solitary musings over the vicissitudes of my fortune.

CHAPTER VII.

THE COA.

WITHIN a week from the occurrence of the events just mentioned, Ciudad Rodrigo surrendered, and Craufurd assumed another position beneath the walls of Almeida. The Spanish contingent having left us, we were reinforced by the arrival of two battalions, renewed orders having been sent not to risk a battle, but if the French should advance, to retire beyond the Coa.

On the evening of the 21st of July, a strong body of French cavalry advanced into the plain, supported by some heavy guns, upon which Craufurd retired upon the Coa, intending, as we supposed, to place that river between himself and the enemy. Three days, however, passed over without any movement upon either side, and we still continued, with a force of scarcely four thousand infantry and a thousand dragoons, to stand opposite to an army of nearly fifty thousand men. Such was our position as the night of the 24th set in. I was sitting alone in my quarters. Mike, whose wound had been severer than at first was supposed, had been sent to Almeida, and I was musing in solitude upon the events of the campaign, when the noise and bustle without excited my attention.

The roll of artillery wagons, the clash of musketry, and the distant sound of marching, all proved that the troops were effecting some new movement, and I burned with anxiety to learn what it was. My brother officers, however, came not as usual to my quarters, and although I waited with impatience while the hours rolled by, no one appeared.

Long, low, moaning gusts of wind swept along the earth, carrying the leaves as they tore them from the trees, and mingling their sad sounds with the noises of the retiring troops; for I could perceive that gradually the sounds grew more and more remote, and only now and then could I trace their position as the roll of a distant drum swelled upon the breeze, or the more shrill cry of a pibroch broke upon my ear. A heavy down-pour of rain followed soon after, and its unceasing plash drowned all other sounds.

As the little building shook beneath the peals of loud thunder, the lightning flashed in broad sheets upon the rapid river, which, swollen and foaming, dashed impetuously beside my window. By the uncertain but vivid glare of the flashes, I endeavored to ascertain where our force was posted, but in vain. Never did I witness such a night of storm. The deep booming of the thunder seemed never for a moment to cease, while the rush of the torrent grew gradually louder, till at length it swelled into one deep and sullen roar like that of distant artillery.

Weak and nervous as I felt from the effects of my wound, feverish and exhausted by days of suffering and sleepless nights, I paced my little room with tottering but impatient steps. The sense of my sad and imprisoned state impressed me deeply; and while from time to time I replenished my fire, and hoped to hear some friendly step upon the stair, my heart grew gradually heavier, and every gloomy and depressing thought suggested itself to my imagination. My most constant impression was that the troops were retiring beyond the Coa, and that, forgotten in the haste and confusion of a night march, I had been left behind to fall a prisoner to the enemy.

The sounds of the troops retiring gradually farther and farther favored the idea, in which I was still more strengthened on finding that the peasants who inhabited the little hut had departed, leaving me utterly alone. From the moment I ascertained this fact, my impatience knew no bounds; and in proportion as I began to feel some exertion necessary on my part, so much more did my nervousness increase my debility, and at last I sank exhausted upon my bed, while a cold perspiration broke out upon my temples.

I have mentioned that the Coa was immediately beneath the house; I must also add, that the little building occupied the angle of a steep but narrow gorge which descended from the plain to the bridge across the stream. This, as far as I knew, was the only means we possessed of passing the river, so that,when the last retiring sounds of the troops were heard by me, I began to suspect that Craufurd, in compliance with his orders, was making a backward movement, leaving the bridge open to the French, to draw them on to his line of march, while he should cross over at some more distant point.

As the night grew later, the storm seemed to increase; the waves of the foaming river dashed against the frail walls of the hut, while its roof, rent by the blast, fell in fragments upon the stream, and all threatened a speedy and perfect ruin.

How I longed for morning! The doubt and uncertainty I suffered nearly drove me distracted. Of all the casualties my career as a soldier opened, none had such horrors for me as imprisonment; the very thought of the long years of inaction and inglorious idleness was worse than any death. My wounds, and the state of fever I was in, increased the morbid dread upon me, and had the French captured me at the time, I know not that madness of which I was not capable. Day broke at last, but slowly and sullenly. The gray clouds hurried past upon the storm, pouring down the rain in torrents as they went, and the desolation and dreariness on all sides was scarcely preferable to the darkness and gloom of night. My eyes were turned ever towards the plain, across which the winter wind bore the plashing rain in vast sheets of water; the thunder crashed louder and louder; but except the sounds of the storm, none others met my ear. Not a man, not a human figure, could I see, as I strained my sight towards the distant horizon.

The morning crept over, but the storm abated not, and the same unchanged aspect of dreary desolation prevailed without. At times I thought I could hear, amidst the noises of the tempest, something like the roll of distant artillery; but the thunder swelled in sullen roar above all, and left me uncertain as before.

At last, in a momentary pause of the storm, a tremendous peal of heavy guns caught my ear, followed by a long rattling of small-arms. My heart bounded with ecstasy. The thought of the battle-field, with all its changing fortunes, was better, a thousand times better, than the despairing sense of desertion I labored under. I listened now with eagerness, but the rain bore down again in torrents, and the crumbling walls and falling timbers left no other sounds to be heard. Far as my eye could reach, nothing could still be seen save the dreary monotony of the vast plain, undulating slightly here and there, but unmarked by a sign of man.

Far away towards the horizon I had remarked for some time past that the clouds resting upon the earth grew blacker and blacker, spreading out to either side in vast masses, and not broken or wafted along like the rest. As I watched the phenomenon with an anxious eye, I perceived the dense mass suddenly appear, as it were rent asunder, while a volume of liquid flame rushed wildly out, throwing a lurid glare on every side. One terrific clap, louder than any thunder, shook the air at this moment, while the very earth trembled beneath the shock.

As I hesitated what it might be, the heavy din of great guns again was heard, and from the midst of the black smoke rode forth a dark mass, which I soon recognized as the horse-artillery at full gallop. They were directing their course towards the bridge.

As they mounted the little rising ground, they wheeled and unlimbered with the speed of lightning, just as a strong column of cavalry showed above the ridge. One tremendous discharge again shook the field, and ere the smoke cleared away they were again far in retreat.

So much was my attention occupied with this movement, that I had not perceived the long line of infantry that came from the extreme left, and were now advancing also towards the bridge at a brisk, quick step; scattered bodies of cavalry came up from different parts, while from the little valley, every now and then, a rifleman would mount the rising ground, turning to fire as he retreated. All this boded a rapid and disorderly retreat; and although as yet I could see nothing of the pursuing enemy, I knew too well the relative forces of each to have a doubt for the result.

At last the head of a French column appeared above the mist, and I could plainly distinguish the gestures of the officers as they hurried their men onwards. Meanwhile, a loud hurrah attracted my attention, and I turned my eyes towards the road which led to the river. Here a small body of the 95th had hurriedly assembled; and, formed again, were standing to cover the retreat of the broken infantry as they pressed on eagerly to the bridge; in a second after the French cuirassiers appeared. Little anticipating resistance from a flying and disordered mass, they rode headlong forward, and although the firm attitude and steady bearing of the Highlanders might have appalled them, they rode heedlessly down upon the square, sabring the very men in the front rank. Till now not a trigger had been pulled, when suddenly the word "Fire!" was given, and a withering volley of balls sent the cavalry column in shivers. One hearty cheer broke from the infantry in the rear, and I could hear "Gallant 95th!" shouted on every side along the plain.

The whole vast space before me was now one animated battle-ground. Our own troops retiring in haste before the overwhelming forces of the French, occupied every little vantage ground with their guns and light infantry, charges of cavalry coursing hither and thither; while, as the French pressed forward, the retreating columns again formed into squares to permit stragglers to come up. The rattle of small-arms, the heavy peal of artillery, the earthquake crash of cavalry, rose on every side, while the cheers which alternately told of the vacillating fortune of the fight rose amidst the wild pibroch of the Highlanders.

A tremendous noise now took place on the floor beneath me; and, looking down, I perceived that a sergeant and party of the Sappers had taken possession of the little hut, and were busily engaged piercing the walls for musketry; and before many minutes had elapsed, a company of the Rifles were thrown into the building, which, from its commanding position above, enfiladed the whole line of march. The officer in command briefly informed me that we had been attacked that morning by the French in force, and "devilishly well thrashed;" that we were now in retreat beyond the Coa, where we ought to have been three days previously, and desired me to cross the bridge and get myself out of the way as soon as I possibly could.

A twenty-four pounder from the French lines struck the angle of the house as he spoke, scattering the mortar and broken bricks about us on all sides. This was a warning sufficient for me, wounded and disabled as I was; so, taking the few things I could save in my haste, I hurried from the hut, and descending the path, now slippery by the heavy rain, I took my way across the bridge, and established myself on a little rising knoll of ground beyond, from which a clear view could be obtained of the whole field.

I had not been many minutes in my present position ere the pass which led down to the bridge became thronged with troops, wagons, ammunition carts, and hospital stores, pressing thickly forward amid shouting and uproar; the hills on either side of the way were crowded with troops, who formed as they came up, the artillery taking up their position on every rising ground. The firing had already begun, aud the heavy booming of the large guns was heard at intervals amid the rattling crash of musketry. Except the narrow road before me, and the high bank of the stream, I could see nothing; but the tumult and din, which grew momentarily louder, told that the tide of battle raged nearer and nearer. Still the retreat continued; and at length the heavy artillery came thundering across the narrow bridge, followed by stragglers of all arms, and wounded, hurrying to the rear. The sharpshooters and the Highlanders held the heights above the stream, thus covering the retiring columns; but I could plainly perceive that their fire was gradually slackening,

and that the guns which flanked their position were withdrawn, and
everything bespoke a speedy retreat. A tremendous discharge of
musketry at this moment, accompanied by a deafening cheer, announced the advance of the French, and soon the head of the Highland brigade was seen descending towards the bridge, followed by
the Rifles and the 95th ; the cavalry, consisting of the 11th and 14th
Light Dragoons, were now formed in column of attack, and the
infantry deployed into line; in an instant after, high above the din
and crash of battle, I heard the word "Charge !" The rising crest
of the hill hid them from my sight, but my heart bounded with
ecstasy as I listened to the clanging sound of the cavalry advance.
Meanwhile, the infantry pressed on, and forming upon the bank,
took up a strong position in front of the bridge ; the heavy guns
were also unlimbered, riflemen scattered through the low copse-
wood, and every precaution taken to defend the pass to the last.
For a moment all my attention was riveted to the movements upon
our own side of the stream, when suddenly the cavalry bugle
sounded the recall, and the same moment the staff came galloping
across the bridge. One officer I could perceive, covered with orders
and trappings ; his head was bare, and his horse, splashed with
blood and foam, moved lamely and with difficulty ; he turned in the
middle of the bridge, as if irresolute whether to retreat farther.
One glance at him showed me the bronzed, manly features of our
leader. Whatever his resolve, the matter was soon decided for him,
for the cavalry came galloping swiftly down the slope, and in an
instant the bridge was blocked up by the retreating forces, while the
French, as suddenly appearing above the height, opened a plunging
fire upon their defenceless enemies. Their cheer of triumph was
answered by our fellows from the opposite bank, and a heavy cannonade thundered along the rocky valley, sending up a hundred
echoes as it went.

The scene now became one of overwhelming interest. The French,
posting their guns upon the height, replied to our fire, while their
line, breaking into skirmishers, descended the banks to the river
edge, and poured in one sheet of galling musketry. The road to the
bridge, swept by our artillery, presented not a single file ; and
although a movement among the French announced the threat of
an attack, the deadly service of the artillery seemed to pronounce
it hopeless.

A strong cavalry force stood inactively, spectators of the combat,
on the French side, among whom I now remarked some bustle
and preparation. As I looked, an officer rode boldly to the river
edge, and spurring his horse forward, plunged into the stream.
The swollen and angry torrent, increased by the late rains, boiled

likc barm and foamed around him as he advanced; when suddenly his horse appcared to have lost its footing, and the rapid current, circling around him, bore him along with it. He labored madly, but in vain, to retrace his steps; the rolling torrent rose above his saddle, and all that his gallant steed could do was barely sufficient to keep afloat; both man and horse were carried down between the contending armies. I could see him wave his hand to his comrades as if in adieu. One deafening cheer of admiration rose from the French lines, and the next moment he was seen to fall from his seat, and his body, shattered with balls, floated mournfully upon the stream.

This little incident, to which both armies were witnesses, seemed to have called forth all the fiercer passions of the contending forces. A loud yell of taunting triumph rose from the Highlanders, responded to by a cry of vengeance from the French, and the same moment the head of a column was seen descending the narrow causeway to the bridge, while an officer, with a whole blaze of decorations and crosses, sprang from his horse and took the lead. The little drummer, a child scarcely ten years old, tripped gayly on, beating his little *pas de charge*, seeming rather like the play of infancy than the summons to death and carnage, as the heavy guns of the French opened a volume of fire and flame to cover the attacking column. For a moment all was hid from our eyes; the moment after the grapeshot swept along the narrow causeway; and the bridge, which but a second before was crowded with the life and courage of a noble column, was now one heap of dead and dying. The gallant fellow who led them on fell among the first rank, and the little child, as if kneeling, was struck dead beside the parapet; his fair hair floated across his cold features, and seemed in its motion to lend a look of life where the heart throb had ceased forever. The artillery again reopened upon us; and when the smoke had cleared away, we discovered that the French had advanced to the middle of the bridge and carried off the body of their general. Twice they essayed to cross, and twice the death-dealing fire of our guns covered the narrow bridge with slain, while by the wild pibroch of the 42d, swelling madly into notes of exultation and triumph, the Highlanders could scarcely be prevented from advancing hand to hand with the foe. Gradually the French slackened their fire, their great guns were one by one withdrawn from the heights, and a dropping, irregular musketry at intervals sustained the fight, which, ere sunset, ceased altogether; and thus ended "The Battle of the Coa!"

CHAPTER VIII.

THE NIGHT MARCH.

SCARCELY had the night fallen when our retreat commenced. Tired and weary as our brave fellows felt, but little repose was allowed them; their bivouac fires were blazing brightly, and they had just thrown themselves in groups around them, when the word to fall in was passed from troop to troop, and from battalion to battalion—no trumpet, no bugle, called them to their ranks. It was necessary that all should be done noiselessly and speedily; while, therefore, the wounded were marched to the front, and the heavy artillery with them, a brigade of light four-pounders, and two squadrons of cavalry, held the heights above the bridge, and the infantry, forming into three columns, began their march.

My wound, forgotten in the heat and excitement of the conflict, was now becoming excessively painful, and I gladly availed myself of a place in a wagon, where, stretched upon some fresh straw, with no other covering save the starry sky, I soon fell sound asleep, and neither the heavy jolting of the rough conveyance nor the deep and rutty road was able to disturb my slumbers. Still through my sleep I heard the sounds around me, the heavy tramp of infantry, the clash of the moving squadrons, and the dull roll of artillery; and ever and anon the half-stifled cry of pain, mingling with the reckless carol of some drinking song, all flitted through my dreams, lending to my thoughts of home and friends a memory of glorious war.

All the vicissitudes of a soldier's life passed then in review before me, elicited in some measure by the things about. The pomp and grandeur, the misery and meanness, the triumph, the defeat, the moment of victory, and the hour of death, were there, and in that vivid dream I lived a long life.

I awoke at length. The cold and chilling air which follows midnight blew around me, and my wounded arm felt as though it were frozen. I tried to cover myself beneath the straw, but in vain, and as my limbs trembled and my teeth chattered, I thought again of home, where, at that moment, the poorest menial of my uncle's house was better lodged than I, and, strange to say, something of pride mingled with the thought, and in my lonely heart a feeling of elation cheered me.

These reflections were interrupted by the sound of a voice near me, which I at once knew to be O'Shaughnessy's; he was on foot, and speaking evidently in some excitement.

"I tell you, Maurice, some confounded blunder there must be;

sure he was left in that cottage near the bridge, and no one saw him after."

"The French took it from the Rifles before we crossed the river. By Jove! I'll wager my chance of promotion against a pint of sherry he'll turn up somewhere in the morning; those Galway chaps have as many lives as a cat."

"See, now, Maurice, I wouldn't for a full colonelcy anything would happen to him—I like the boy."

"So do I myself; but I tell you there's no danger of him. Did you ask Sparks anything?"

"Ask Sparks! God help you! Sparks would go off in a fit at the sight of me. No, no, poor creature! it's little use it would be my speaking to him."

"Why so, Doctor?" cried I, from my straw couch.

"May I never, if it's not him! Charley, my son, I'm glad you're safe. 'Faith, I thought you were on your way to Verdun by this time."

"Sure, I told you he'd find his way here; but, O'Mealey, dear, you're mighty could—a rigor, as old M'Lauchlan would call it."

"E'en sae, Maister Quill," said a broad Scotch accent behind him; "and I canna see ony objection to giein' things their right names."

"The top of the morning to you!" said Quill, familiarly patting him on the back; "how goes it, old Brimstone?"

The conversation might not have taken a very amicable turn had M'Lauchlan heard the latter part of this speech; but as, happily, he was engaged unpacking a small canteen which he had placed in the wagon, it passed unnoticed.

"Ye'll no' dislike a toothfu' o' something warm, Major," said he, presenting a glass to O'Shaughnessy; "and if ye'll permit me, Mr. O'Mealey, to help you——"

"A thousand thanks, Doctor; but I fear a broken arm."

"There's naething in the whisky to prevent the proper formation of callus."

"By the rock of Cashel, it never made any one callous," said O'Shaughnessy, mistaking the import of the phrase.

"Ye are nae drinking frae the flask?" said the Doctor, turning in some agitation towards Quill.

"Devil a bit, my darling. I've a little horn convaniency here, that holds half a pint, nice measure."

I don't imagine that our worthy friend participated in Quill's admiration of the "convaniency," for he added, in a dry tone,

"Ye may as weel tak' your liquor frae a glass, like a Christian, as stick your nose in a coo's horn."

"By my conscience, you're no small judge of spirits, wherever you learned it," said the Major; "it's like Islay malt!"

"I was aye reckoned a gude ane," said the Doctor, "and my mither's brither, Caimbogie, hadna his like in the north country. Ye maybe heerd tell what he aince said to the Duchess of Argyle, when she sent for him to taste her claret."

""Never heard of it," quoth Quill; "let's have it by all means. I'd like to hear what the Duchess said to him."

"It wasna what the Duchess said to him, but what he said to the Duchess, ye ken. The way of it was this:—My uncle, Caimbogie, was aye up at the castle, for, besides his knowledge of liquor, there wasna his match for deer-stalking, or spearing a salmon, in those parts. He was a great, rough carle, it's true, but ane ye'd rather crack wi' than fight wi'.

"Weel, ae day they had a grand dinner at the Duke's, and there were plenty o' great southern lords and braw leddies in velvets and satin; and vara muckle surprised they were at my uncle, when he came in wi' his tartan kilt, in full Highland dress, as the head of a clan ought to do. Caimbogie, however, paid nae attention to them, but he ate his dinner and drank his wine, and talked away about fallow and red deer, and at last the Duchess—for she was aye fond o' him—addressed him frae the head o' the table:—

"'Caimbogie, I'd like to hae your opinion about that wine. It's some the Duke has just received, and we should like to hear what you think of it.'

"'It's no sae bad, my leddy,' said my uncle; for ye see he was a man o' few words, and never flattered onybody.

"'Then you don't much approve of it?' said the Duchess.

"'I've drank better, and I've drank waur,' quo' he.

"'I'm sorry you don't like it, Caimbogie,' said the Duchess, 'for it never can be popular now; we have such a dependence upon your taste.'

"'I canna say ower muckle for my *taste*, my leddy; but ae thing I *will* say, I've a most d— *smell!*'

"I hear that never since the auld walls stood was there ever the like o' the laughing that followed. The puir Duke himsel' was carried away, and nearly had a fit, and a' the grand lords and leddies a'most died of it. But, see here, the carle hasna left a drap o' whisky in the flask."

"The last glass I drained to your respectable uncle's health," said Quill, with a most professional gravity. "Now, Charley, make a little room for me in the straw."

The Doctor soon mounted beside me, and giving me a share of his ample cloak, considerably ameliorated my situation.

"So you knew Sparks, Doctor?" said I, with a strong curiosity to hear something of his early acquaintance.

"That I did. I knew him when he was an ensign in the 10th Foot; and, to say the truth, he is not much changed since that time,—the same lively look of a sick codfish about his gray eyes,—the same disorderly wave of his yellow hair,—the same whining voice, and that confounded apothecary's laugh."

"Come, come, Doctor, Sparks is a good fellow at heart; I won't have him abused. I never knew he had been in the infantry; I should think it must have been another of the same name."

"Not at all; there's only one like him in the service, and that's himself. Confound it, man, I'd know his skin upon a bush; he was only three weeks in the 10th, and, indeed, your humble servant has the whole merit of his leaving it so soon."

"Do let us hear how that happened."

"Simply thus: The jolly 10th were some four years ago the pleasantest corps in the army; from the lieutenant-colonel down to the last-joined sub., all were out-and-outers—real gay fellows. The mess was, in fact, like a pleasant club, and if you did not suit it, the best thing you could do was to sell out or exchange into a slower regiment; and, indeed, this very wholesome truth was not very long in reaching your ears some way or other, and a man that could remain after being given this hint, was likely to go afterwards without one."

Just as Doctor Quill reached this part of his story, an orderly dragoon galloped furiously past, and the next moment an aide-de-camp rode by, calling, as he passed us,—

"Close up, there—close up! Get forward, my lads—get forward!"

It was evident, from the stir and bustle about, that some movement was being made; and soon after a dropping, irregular fire from the rear showed that our cavalry were engaged with the enemy. The affair was scarcely of five minutes' duration, and our march resumed all its former regularity immediately after.

I now turned to the Doctor to resume his story, but he was gone; at what moment he left I could not say. O'Shaughnessy was also absent, nor did I again meet with them for a considerable time after.

Towards daybreak we halted at Bonares, when, my wound demanding rest and attention, I was billeted in the village, and consigned to all the miseries of a sick-bed.

CHAPTER IX.

THE JOURNEY.

WITH that disastrous day my campaigning was destined, for some time at least, to conclude. My wound, which grew from hour to hour more threatening, at length began to menace the loss of the arm, and, by the recommendation of the regimental surgeons, I was ordered back to Lisbon.

Mike, by this time perfectly restored, prepared everything for my departure, and on the third day after the battle of the Coa, I began my journey with downcast spirits and depressed heart. The poor fellow was, however, a kind and affectionate nurse, and, unlike many others, his cares were not limited to the mere bodily wants of his patient. He sustained, as well as he was able, my drooping resolution, rallied my spirits, and cheered my courage. With the very little Portuguese he possessed, he contrived to make every imaginable species of bargain, always managed a good billet, kept every one in good humor, and rarely left his quarters in the morning without a most affecting leave-taking, and reiterated promises to renew his visit.

Our journeys were usually short ones, and already two days had elapsed, when, towards nightfall, we entered the little hamlet of Jaffra. During the entire of that day, the pain of my wounded limb had been excruciating; the fatigue of the road and the heat had brought back violent inflammation, and when at last the little village came in sight, my reason was fast yielding to the torturing agonies of my wound. But the transports with which I greeted my resting-place were soon destined to a change, for as we drew near, not a light was to be seen, not a sound to be heard, not even a dog barked, as the heavy mule-cart rattled over the uneven road. No trace of any living thing was there. The little hamlet lay sleeping in the pale moonlight, its streets deserted and its homes tenantless; our own footsteps alone echoed along the dreary causeway. Here and there, as we advanced farther, we found some relics of broken furniture and house-gear; most of the doors lay open, but nothing remained within save bare walls; the embers still smoked in many places upon the hearth, and showed us that the flight of the inhabitants had been recent. Yet everything convinced us that the French had not been there; there was no trace of the reckless violence and wanton cruelty which marked their footsteps everywhere.

All proved that the desertion had been voluntary—perhaps in compliance with an order of our Commander-in-Chief, who fre-

quently desired any intended line of march of the enemy to be thus
left a desert. As we sauntered slowly on from street to street, half-
hoping that some one human being yet remained behind, and casting our eyes from side to side in search of quarters for the night,
Mike suddenly came running up, saying,—

"I have it, sir,—I've found it out. There's people living down
that small street there; I saw a light this minute as I passed."

I turned immediately, and, accompanied by the mule-driver, followed Mike across a little open square into a small and narrow
street, at the end of which a light was seen faintly twinkling. We
hurried on, and in a few minutes reached a high wall of solid
masonry, from a niche of which we now discovered, to our utter
disappointment, the light proceeded. It was a small lamp placed
before a little waxen image of the Virgin, and was probably the last
act of piety of some poor villager ere he left his home and hearth
forever. There it burned, brightly and tranquilly, throwing its
mellow ray upon the cold, deserted stones.

Whatever impatience I might have given way to in a moment of
chagrin was soon repressed, as I saw my two followers, uncovering
their heads in silent reverence, kneel down before the little shrine.
There was something at once touching and solemn in this simultaneous feeling of homage from the hearts of those removed in country,
language, and in blood; they bent meekly down, their heads bowed
upon their bosoms, while with muttering voices each offered up his
prayer. All sense of their disappointment, all memory of their
forlorn state, seemed to have yielded to more powerful and absorbing thoughts as they opened their hearts in prayer.

My eyes were still fixed upon them, when suddenly Mike, whose
devotion seemed to be briefest, sprang to his legs, and with a spirit
of levity but little in accordance with his late proceedings, commenced a series of kicking, rapping, and knocking at a small oak
postern sufficient to have aroused a whole convent from their cells.
"House there!—good people within!"—bang, bang, bang; but the
echoes alone responded to his call, and the sounds died away at
length in the distant streets, leaving all as silent and dreary as
before.

Our Portuguese friend, who by this time had finished his orisons,
now began a vigorous attack upon the small door, and, with the
assistance of Mike, armed with a fragment of granite about the size
of a man's head, at length separated the frame from the hinges and
sent the whole mass prostrate before us.

The moon was just rising as we entered the little park, where
gravelled walks, neatly kept and well trimmed, bespoke recent care
and attention; following a handsome alley of lime trees, we reached

a little jet d'eau, whose sparkling fountain shone, diamond-like, in the moonbeams; and, escaping from the edge of a vast shell, ran murmuring amid mossy stones and water lilies, that however naturally they seemed thrown around, bespoke also the hand of taste in their position. On turning from the spot, we came directly in front of an old but handsome château, before which stretched a terrace of considerable extent. Its balustraded parapet, lined with orange-trees, now in full blossom, scented the still air with their delicious odor; marble statues peeped here and there amid the foliage, while a rich acacia, loaded with flowers, covered the walls of the building, and hung in vast masses of variegated blossom across the tall windows.

As, leaning on Mike's arm, I slowly ascended the steps of the terrace, I was more than ever struck with the silence and death-like stillness around; except the gentle plash of the fountain, all was at rest; the very plants seemed to sleep in the yellow moonlight, and not a trace of any living thing was there.

The massive door lay open as we entered the spacious hall, flagged with marble, and surrounded with armorial bearings. We advanced farther, and came to a broad and handsome stair, which led us to a long gallery, from which a suite of rooms opened, looking towards the front part of the building. Wherever we went, the furniture appeared perfectly untouched; nothing was removed; the very chairs were grouped around the windows and the tables; books, as if they suddenly dropped from their readers' hands, were scattered upon the sofas and the ottomans; and in one small apartment, whose blue satin walls and damask drapery bespoke a boudoir, a rich mantilla of black velvet and a silk glove were thrown upon a chair. It was clear the desertion had been most recent; and everything indicated that no time had been given to the fugitives to prepare for flight. What a sad picture of war was there! To think of those whose home, endeared to them by all the refinements of cultivated life, and all the associations of years of happiness, sent out upon the wide world—wanderers and houseless; while their hearth, sacred by every tie that binds us to our kindred, was to be desecrated by the ruthless and savage hands of a ruffian soldiery. I thought of them. Perhaps at that very hour their thoughts were clinging round the old walls; remembering each well-beloved spot, while they took their lonely path through mountain and through valley; and I felt ashamed and abashed at my own intrusion there. While thus my reverie ran on, I had not perceived that Mike, whose views were very practical upon all occasions, had lighted a most cheerful fire upon the hearth, and disposing a large sofa before it, had carefully closed the curtains, and was, in fact, making himself and his master as much at home as though he had spent his life there.

"Isn't it a beautiful place, Misther Charles? and this little room, doesn't it remind you of the blue bedroom in O'Malley Castle, barrin' the illigant view out upon the Shannon and the mountain of Scariff?"

Nothing short of Mike's patriotism could forgive such a comparison; but, however, I did not contradict him, as he ran on:

"Faith, I knew well there was luck in store for us this evening; and ye see the handful of prayers I threw away outside wasn't lost. José's making the beasts comfortable in the stable, and I'm thinking we'll none of us complain of our quarters. But you're not eating your supper; and the beautiful hare pie that I stole this morning, won't you taste it? Well, a glass of Malaga?—not a glass of Malaga? Oh, mother of Moses! what's this for?"

Unfortunately, the fever produced by the long and toilsome journey had gained considerably on me, and except copious libations of cold water, I could touch nothing; my arm, too, was much more painful than before. Mike soon perceived that rest and quietness were most important to me at the moment, and having with difficulty been prevailed upon to swallow a few hurried mouthfuls, the poor fellow disposed cushions around me in every imaginable form for comfort; and then, placing my wounded limb in its easiest position, he extinguished the lamp, and sat silently down beside the hearth, without speaking another word.

Fatigue and exhaustion, more powerful than pain, soon produced their effects upon me, and I fell asleep, but it was no refreshing slumber which visited my heavy eyelids; the slow fever of suffering had been hour by hour increasing, and my dreams presented nothing but scenes of agony and torture. Now I thought that, unhorsed and wounded, I was trampled beneath the clanging hoofs of charging cavalry; now, I felt the sharp steel piercing my flesh, and heard the loud cry of a victorious enemy; then methought I was stretched upon a litter, covered by gore and mangled by a grapeshot. I thought I saw my brother officers approach and look sadly upon me, while one, whose face I could not remember, muttered, "I should not have known him." The dreadful hospital of Talavera, and all its scenes of agony, came up before me, and I thought that I lay waiting my turn for amputation. This last impression, more horrible to me than all the rest, made me spring from my couch, and I awoke; the cold drops of perspiration stood upon my brow, my mouth was parched and open, and my temples throbbed so, that I could count their beatings; for some seconds I could not throw off the frightful illusion I labored under, and it was only by degrees I recovered consciousness, and remembered where I was. Before me, and on one side of the bright wood fire, sat Mike, who,

28

apparently deep in thought, gazed fixedly at the blaze; the start I gave on awaking had not attracted his attention, and I could see, as the flickering glare fell upon his features, that he was pale and ghastly, while his eyes were riveted upon the fire; his lips moved rapidly, as if in prayer, and his locked hands were pressed firmly upon his bosom; his voice, at first inaudible, I could gradually distinguish, and at length heard the following muttered sentences:

" Oh, mother of mercy ! so far from his home and his people, and so young, to die in a strange land—there it is again." Here he appeared listening to some sounds without. " Oh, wirra, wirra, I know it well !—the winding-sheet, the winding-sheet! there it is, my own eyes saw it !" The tears coursed fast down his pale cheeks, and his voice grew almost inaudible, as, rocking to and fro, for some time he seemed in a very stupor of grief; when at last, in a faint, subdued tone, he broke into one of those sad and plaintive airs of his country, which only need the moment of depression to make them wring the very heart in agony.

His song was that to which Moore has appended the beautiful lines, " Come, rest on this bosom." The following imperfect translation may serve to convey some impression of the words, which in Mike's version were Irish:

> "The day was declining,
>   The dark night drew near,
> And the old lord grew sadder,
>   And paler with fear:
> ' Come listen, my daughter,
>   Come nearer—oh! near.
> Is't the wind or the water
>   That sighs in my ear?'
>
> " Not the wind nor the water
>   Now stirr'd the night air;
> But a warning far sadder—
>   The banshee was there!
> Now rising, now swelling,
>   On the night wind it bore,
> One cadence, still telling,—
>   'I want thee, Rossmore!'
>
> " And then fast came his breath,
>   And more fix'd grew his eye;
> And the shadow of death
>   Told his last hour was nigh.
> Ere the dawn of that morning
>   The struggle was o'er,
> For when thrice came the warning,
>   A corpse was Rossmore!"

The plaintive air to which these words were sung fell heavily upon my heart, and it needed but the low and nervous condition I was in to make me feel their application to myself. But so it is; the very superstition your reason rejects and your sense spurns has, from old association, from habit, and from mere nationality too, a hold upon your hopes and fears, that demands more firmness and courage than a sick-bed possesses to combat with success; and I now listened with an eager ear to mark if the banshee cried, rather than sought to fortify myself by any recurrence to my own convictions. Meanwhile, Mike's attitude became one of listening attention. Not a finger moved; he scarce seemed even to breathe; the state of suspense I suffered from was maddening; and at last, unable to bear it longer, I was about to speak, when suddenly, from the floor beneath us, one long-sustained note swelled upon the air and died away again, and immediately after, to the cheerful sounds of a guitar, we heard the husky voice of our Portuguese guide, indulging himself in a love-ditty.

Ashamed of myself for my fears, I kept silent; but Mike, who felt only one sensation—that of unmixed satisfaction at his mistake—rubbed his hands pleasantly, filled up his glass, drank it, and refilled; while with an accent of reassured courage he briefly remarked:

"Well, Mr. José, if that be singing, upon my conscience I wonder what crying is like!"

I could not forbear a laugh at the criticism, and in a moment the poor fellow, who up to that moment believed me sleeping, was beside me. I saw from his manner that he dreaded lest I had been listening to his melancholy song, and had overheard any of his gloomy forebodings; and as he cheered my spirits and spoke encouragingly, I could remark that he had made more than usual endeavors to appear light-hearted and at ease. Determined, however, not to let him escape so easily, I questioned him about his belief in ghosts and spirits, at which he endeavored, as he ever did when the subject was an unpleasant one, to avoid the discussion; but rather perceiving that I indulged in no irreverent disrespect of these matters, he grew gradually more open, treating the affair with that strange mixture of credulity and mockery which formed his estimate of most things—now seeming to suppose that any palpable rejection of them might entail sad consequences in future, now half ashamed to go the whole length in his credulity.

"And so, Mike, you never saw a ghost yourself?—that you acknowledge?"

"No, sir, I never saw a real ghost: but sure there's many a thing I never saw; but Mrs. Moore, the housekeeper, seen two. And your grandfather that's gone—the Lord be good to him!—used to walk once a year in Lurra Abbey; and sure you know the story about Tim Clinchy, that was seen every Saturday night coming out of the cellar with a candle and a mug of wine, and a pipe in his mouth, till Mr. Barry laid him. It cost his honor your uncle ten pounds in masses to make him easy, not to speak of a new lock and two bolts on the cellar door."

"I have heard all about that; but as you never yourself saw any of these things——"

"But sure my father did, and that's the same, any day. My father seen the greatest ghost that ever was seen in the county Cork, and spent the evening with him, that's more."

"Spent the evening with him!—what do you mean?"

"Just that, devil a more nor less. If your honor wasn't so weak, and the story wasn't a trying one, I'd like to tell it to you."

"Out with it, by all means, Mike; I am not disposed to sleep; and now that we are upon these matters, my curiosity is strongly excited by your worthy father's experience."

Thus encouraged, having trimmed the fire, and re-seated himself beside the blaze, Mike began; but as a ghost is no every-day personage in our history, I must give him a chapter to himself.

CHAPTER X.

THE GHOST.

WELL, I believe your honor heard me tell long ago how my father left the army, and the way that he took to another line of life that was more to his liking. And so it was, he was happy as the day was long; he drove a hearse for Mr. Callaghan of Cork, for many years, and a pleasant place it was; for, ye see, my father was a 'cute man, and knew something of the world; and though he was a droll devil, and could sing a funny song when he was among the boys, no sooner had he the big black cloak on him and the weepers, and he seated on the high box with the six long-tailed blacks before him, you'd really think it was his own mother was inside, he looked so melancholy and miserable. The sexton and gravedigger was nothing to my father; and he had a look about his eye—to be sure there was a reason for it—that you'd think he was up all night crying; though it's little indulgence he took that way.

"Well, of all Mr. Callaghan's men, there was none so great a favorite as my father. The neighbors were all fond of him.

"'A kind crayture, every inch of him!' the women would say. 'Did ye see his face at Mrs. Delany's funeral?'

"'True for you,' another would remark; 'he mistook the road with grief, and stopped at a shebeen house instead of Kilmurry church.'

"I need say no more, only one thing: that it was principally among the farmers and the country people my father was liked so much. The great people and the quality—I ax your pardon; but sure isn't it true, Misther Charles?—they don't fret so much after their fathers and brothers, and they care little who's driving them, whether it was a decent, respectable man like my father, or a chap with a grin on him like a rat-trap. And so it happened that my father used to travel half the county, going here and there wherever there was trade stirring; and, faix, a man didn't think himself rightly buried if my father wasn't there; for, ye see, he knew all about it; he could tell to a quart of spirits what would be wanting for a wake; he knew all the good criers for miles round; and I've heard it was a beautiful sight to see him standing on a hill, arranging the procession, as they walked into the churchyard, and giving the word like a captain.

"'Come on, the stiff—now the friends of the stiff—now the pop'lace.'

"That's what he used to say, and troth he was always repeating it when he was a little gone in drink—for that's the time his spirits would rise—and he'd think he was burying half Munster.

"And sure it was a rale pleasure and a pride to be buried in them times; for av it was only a small farmer with a potato garden, my father would come down with the black cloak on him, and three yards of crape behind his hat, and set all the children crying and yelling for half a mile round; and then the way he'd walk before them with a spade on his shoulder, and sticking it down in the ground, clap his hat on the top of it, to make it look like a chief mourner. It was a beautiful sight!"

"But, Mike, if you indulge much longer in this flattering recollection of your father, I'm afraid we shall lose sight of the ghost entirely."

"No fear in life, your honor; I'm coming to him now. Well, it was this way it happened: In the winter of the great frost, about forty-two or forty-three years ago, the ould priest of Tulloughmurray took ill and died; he was sixty years priest of the parish, and mightily beloved by all the people; and good reason for it—a pleasanter man, and a more social crayture, never lived. 'Twas himself was the life of the whole country-side. A wedding or a christening wasn't lucky av he wasn't there, sitting at the top of the table, with maybe his arm round the bride herself, or the baby on his lap, a smoking jug of punch before him, and as much kindness in his eye as would make the fortunes of twenty hypocrites if they had it among them. And then he was so good to the poor; the Priory was always full of ould men and ould women sitting around the big fire in the kitchen, that the cook could hardly get near it. There they were, eating their meals and burning their shins, till they were speckled like a trout's back, and grumbling all the time; but Father Dwyer liked them, and he would have them.

"'Where have they to go,' he'd say, 'av it wasn't to me? Give Molly Kinshela a lock of that bacon. Tim, it's a could morning; will ye have a taste of the dew?'

"Ah! that's the way he'd spake to them; but sure goodness is no warrant for living any more than devilment, and so he got could in his feet at a station, and he rode home in the heavy snow without his big coat—for he gave it away to a blind man on the road. In three days he was dead.

"I see you're getting impatient, so I'll not stop to say what grief was in the parish when it was known; but, troth, there never was seen the like before—not a crayture would lift a spade for two days, and there was more whisky-sold in that time than at the old spring fair. Well, on the third day the funeral set out, and never was the equal of it in them parts. First, there was my father—he came special from Cork with the six horses all in new black, and plumes like little poplar trees; then came Father Dwyer, followed by the two coadjutors in beautiful surplices, walking bare-headed, with the little boys of the Priory school, two and two."

"Well, Mike, I'm sure it was very fine; but, for Heaven's sake, spare me all these descriptions,.and get on to the ghost."

"'Faith, your honor's in a great hurry for the ghost—maybe ye won't like him when ye have him; but I'll go faster, av you plase. Well, Father Dwyer, ye see, was born at Aghan-lish, of an ould family, and he left it in his will that he was to be buried in the family vault; and as Aghan-lish was eighteen miles up the mountains, it was getting late when they drew near. By that time the great procession was all broke up and gone home. The coadjutors stopped to dine at the 'Blue Bellows,' at the cross-roads. The little boys took to pelting snowballs, there was a fight or two on the way besides, and, in fact, except an ould deaf fellow that my father took to mind the horses, he was quite alone. Not that he minded that same; for when the crowd was gone, my father began to sing a droll song, and tould the deaf chap that it was a lamentation. At last they came in sight of Aghan-lish. It was a lonesome, melancholy-looking place, with nothing near it except two or three ould fir-trees, and a small slated house with one window, where the sexton lived, and even that was shut up, and had a padlock on the door.

Well, my father was not over-much pleased with the look of matters, but as he was never hard put to what to do, he managed to get the coffin into the vestry; and then, when he unharnessed the horses, he sent the deaf fellow with them down to the village, to tell the priest that the corpse was there, and to come up early in the morning and perform mass. The next thing to do was to make himself comfortable for the night; and then he made a roaring fire on the ould hearth,—for there was plenty of bog-fir there,—closed the windows with the black cloaks, and, wrapping two round himself, he sat down to cook a little supper he brought with him in case of need.

"Well, you may think it was melancholy enough to pass the night up there alone, with a corpse in an old ruined church in the middle of the mountains, the wind howling about on every side and the snowdrift beating against the walls; but as the fire burned brightly, and the little plate of rashers and eggs smoked temptingly before him, my father mixed a jug of the strongest punch, and sat down as happy as a king. As long as he was eating away, he had no time to be thinking of anything else; but when all was done, and he looked about him, he began to feel very low and melancholy in his heart. There was the great black coffin on three chairs in one corner; and then the mourning cloaks that he had stuck up against the windows moved backward and forward like living things; and, outside, the wild cry of the plover as he flew past, and the night-owl sitting in a nook of the old church. 'I wish it was morning, anyhow,' said my father, 'for this is a lonesome place to be in; and, faix, he'll be a cunning fellow that catches me passing the night this way again.' Now, there was one thing distressed him most of all,—my father used always to make fun of the ghosts and sperits the neighbors would tell of, pretending there was no such thing; and now the thought came to him, 'Maybe they'll revenge themselves on me to-night when they have me up here alone;' and with that he made a jug stronger than the first, and tried to remember a few prayers in case of need, but somehow his mind was not too clear, and he said afterwards he was always mixing up ould songs and toasts with the prayers, and when he thought he had just got hold of a beautiful psalm, it would turn out to be 'Tatter Jack Welsh,' or 'Limping James,' or something like that. The storm, meanwhile, was rising every moment, and parts of the old abbey were falling, as the wind shook the ruin, and my father's spirits, notwithstanding the punch, were lower than ever.

"'I made it too weak,' said he, as he set to work on a new jorum; and, troth, this time that was not the fault of it, for the first sup nearly choked him.

"'Ah!' said he now, 'I knew what it was; this is like the thing;

and, Mr. Free, you are beginning to feel easy and comfortable. Pass the jug. Your very good health and song. I'm a little hoarse, it's true, but if the company will excuse——'

"And then he began knocking on the table with his knuckles as if there was a room full of people asking him to sing. In short, my father was drunk as a fiddler; the last brew finished him; and he began roaring away all kinds of droll songs, and telling all manner of stories, as if he was at a great party.

" While he was capering this way about the room, he knocked down his hat, and with it a pack of cards he put into it before leaving home, for he was mighty fond of a game.

"'Will ye take a hand, Mr. Free?' said he, as he gathered them up and sat down beside the fire.

"' I'm convanient,' said he, and began dealing out as if there was a partner forninst him.

"When my father used to get this far in the story, he became very confused. He says that once or twice he mistook the liquor, and took a pull at the bottle of potteen instead of the punch; and the last thing he remembers was asking poor Father Dwyer if he would draw near to the fire, and not be lying there near the door.

" With that he slipped down on the ground and fell fast asleep. How long he lay that way he could never tell. When he awoke and looked up, his hair nearly stood on an end with fright. What do you think he seen forninst him, sitting at the other side of the fire, but Father Dwyer himself. There he was, divil a lie in it, wrapped up in one of the mourning cloaks, trying to warm his hands at the fire.

"'*Salve hoc nomine patri!*' said my father, crossing himself; ' av it's your ghost, God presarve me !'

"' Good evening t'ye, Mr. Free,' said the ghost; 'and av I might be bould, what's in the jug ?'—for ye see my father had it under his arm fast, and never let it go when he was asleep.

"'*Pater noster qui es in*—potteen, sir,' said my father; for the ghost didn't look pleased at his talking Latin.

"' Ye might have had the politeness to ax if one had a mouth on him, then,' says the ghost.

"' Sure, I didn't think the like of you would taste sperits.'

"' Try me,' says the ghost; and with that he filled out a glass and tossed it off like a Christian.

"' Beamish !' says the ghost, smacking his lips.

"'The same,' says my father; 'and sure what's happened you has not spoiled your taste.'

"' If you'd mix a little hot,' says the ghost, ' I'm thinking it would be better; the night is mighty sevare.'

"'Anything that your reverance plases,' says my father, as he began to blow up a good fire to boil the water.

"'And what news is stirring?' says the ghost.

"'Devil a word, your reverance: your own funeral was the only thing doing last week; times is bad; except the measles, there's nothing in our parts.'

"'And we're quite dead hereabouts, too,' says the ghost.

"'There's some of us so, anyhow,' says my father, with a sly look. 'Taste that, your reverance.'

"'Pleasant and refreshing,' says the ghost. 'And now, Mr. Free, what do you say to a little spoilt five, or beggar my neighbor?'

"'What will we play for?' says my father; for a thought just struck him—'maybe it's some trick of the devil to catch my soul.'

"'A pint of Beamish,' says the ghost.

"'Done!' says my father; 'cut for deal; the ace of clubs; you have it.'

"Now, the whole time the ghost was dealing the cards my father never took his eyes off of him, for he wasn't quite asy in his mind at all; but when he saw him turn up the trump, and take a strong drink afterwards, he got more at ease, and began the game.

"How long they played it was never rightly known; but one thing is sure, they drank a cruel deal of sperits; three quart bottles my father brought with him were all finished, and by that time his brain was so confused with the liquor, and all he lost—for somehow he never won a game—that he was getting very quarrelsome.

"'You have your own luck to it,' says he, at last.

"'True for you; and, besides, we play a great deal where I come from.'

"'I've heard so,' says my father. 'I lead the knave, sir; spades! Bad cess to it, lost again!'

"Now it was really very distressing; for by this time, though they only began for a pint of Beamish, my father went on betting till he lost the hearse and all the six horses, mourning cloaks, plumes, and everything.

"'Are you tired, Mr. Free? Maybe you'd like to stop?'

"'Stop! faith it's a nice time to stop; of course not.'

"'Well, what will ye play for now?'

"The way he said these words brought a trembling all over my father, and his blood curdled in his heart. 'Oh, murther!' says he to himself, 'it's my sowl he is wanting all the time.'

"'I've mighty little left,' says my father, looking at him keenly, while he kept shuffling the cards quick as lightning.

"'Mighty little; no matter, we'll give you plenty of time to pay;

and if you can't do it, it shall never trouble you as long as you live.'

"'Oh, you murthering devil!' says my father, flying at him with a spade that he had behind his chair, 'I've found you out.'

"With one blow he knocked him down; and now a terrible fight began, for the ghost was very strong too; but my father's blood was up, and he'd have faced the devil himself then. They rolled over each other several times, the broken bottles cutting them to pieces, and the chairs and tables crashing under them. At last the ghost took the bottle that lay on the hearth, and levelled my father to the ground with one blow. Down he fell, and the bottle and the whisky were both dashed into the fire; that was the end of it, for the ghost disappeared that moment in a blue flame that nearly set fire to my father as he lay on the floor.

"Och! it was a cruel sight to see him next morning, with his cheek cut open and his hands all bloody, lying there by himself; all the broken glass, and the cards all round him; the coffin, too, was knocked down off the chair: maybe the ghost had trouble getting into it. However that was, the funeral was put off for a day; for my father couldn't speak; and as for the sexton, it was a queer thing, but when they came to call him in the morning, he had two black eyes, and a gash over his ear, and he never knew how he got them. It was easy enough to know the ghost did it; but my father kept the secret, and never told it to any man, woman or child in them parts."

CHAPTER XI.

LISBON.

I HAVE little power to trace the events which occupied the succeeding three weeks of my history. The lingering fever which attended my wound detained me during that time at the château; and when at last I did leave for Lisbon, the winter was already beginning, and it was upon a cold raw evening that I once more took possession of my old quarters at the Quay de Soderi.

My eagerness and anxiety to learn something of the campaign was ever uppermost, and no sooner had I reached my destination than I despatched Mike to the Quartermaster's office to pick up some news, and hear which of my friends and brother officers were then at Lisbon. I was sitting in a state of nervous impatience watching for his return, when at length I heard footsteps approaching my room, and the next moment Mike's voice, saying, "The ould room, sir, where he was before." The door suddenly opened, and my friend Power stood before me.

"Charley, my boy!"—"Fred, my fine fellow!" was all either could say for some minutes. Upon my part, the recollection of his bold and manly bearing in my behalf choked all utterance; while, upon his, my haggard cheek and worn look produced an effect so sudden and unexpected that he became speechless.

In a few minutes, however, we both rallied, and opened our store of mutual remembrances since we parted. My career I found he was perfectly familiar with, and his consisted of nothing but one unceasing round of gayety and pleasure. Lisbon had been delightful during the summer; parties to Cintra, excursions through the surrounding country, were of daily occurrence; and as my friend was a favorite everywhere, his life was one of continued amusement.

"Do you know, Charley, had it been any other man than yourself, I should not have spared him; for I have fallen head over ears in love with your little dark-eyed Portuguese."

"Ah! Donna Inez, you mean?"

"Yes, it is she I mean, and you need not affect such an air of uncommon *nonchalance*. She's the loveliest girl in Lisbon, and with fortune to pay off all the mortgages in Connemara."

"Oh, faith! I admire her-amazingly; but, as I never flattered myself upon any preference——"

"Come, come, Charley, no concealment, my old fellow; every one knows the thing's settled. Your old friend Sir George Dashwood told me yesterday."

"Yesterday! Why, is he here—at Lisbon?"

"To be sure he is; didn't I tell you that before? confound it! what a head I have! Why, man, he's come out as Deputy Adjutant-General; but for him I should not have got renewed leave."

"And Miss Dashwood, is she here?"

"Yes, she came with him. By Jove, how handsome she is! quite a different style of thing from our dark friend, but, to my thinking, even handsomer. Hammersley seems of my opinion, too."

"How! is Hammersley at Lisbon?"

"On the staff here. But, confound it, what makes you so red. you have no ill feeling towards him now. I know he speaks most warmly of you; no later than last night, at Sir George's——"

What Power was about to add I know not, for I sprang from my chair with a sudden start, and walked to the window to conceal my agitation from him.

"And so," said I, at length regaining my composure in some

measure, "Sir George also spoke of my name in connection with the Senhora?"

"To be sure he did. All Lisbon does. Why, what can you mean? But I see, my dear boy; you know you are not of the strongest; and we've been talking far too long. Come now, Charley, I'll say good-night. I'll be with you at breakfast to-morrow, and tell you all the gossip; meanwhile, promise me to get quietly to bed, and so good-night."

Such was the conflicting state of feeling I suffered from, that I made no effort to detain Power. I longed to be once more alone, to think—calmly, if I could—over the position I stood in, and to resolve upon my plans for the future.

My love for Lucy Dashwood had been long rather a devotion than a hope. My earliest dawn of manly ambition was associated with the first hour I met her. She it was who first touched my boyish heart, and suggested a sense of chivalrous ardor within me; and, even though lost to me forever, I could still regard her as the mainspring of my actions, and dwell upon my passion as the thing that hallowed every enterprise of my life.

In a word, my love, however little it might reach her heart, was everything to mine. It was the worship of the devotee to his protecting saint. It was the faith that made me rise above every misfortune and mishap, and led me onward; and in this way I could have borne anything, everything, rather than the imputation of fickleness.

Lucy might not—nay, I felt she did not—love me. It was possible that some other was preferred before me; but to doubt my own affection, to suspect my own truth, was to destroy all the charm of my existence, and to extinguish within me forever the enthusiasm that made me a hero to my own heart.

It may seem but poor philosophy, but, alas! how many of our happiest, how many of our brightest thoughts here are but delusions like this! This dayspring of youth gilds the tops of the distant mountains before us, and many a weary day through life, when clouds and storms are thickening around us, we live upon the mere memory of the past. Some fast-flitting prospect of a bright future, some passing glimpse of a sunlit valley, tinges all our after-years.

It is true that he will suffer fewer disappointments, he will incur fewer of the mishaps of the world, who indulges in no fancies such as these; but equally true is it that he will taste none of that exuberant happiness which is that man's portion who weaves out a story of his life, and who, in connecting the promise of early years with the performance of later, will seek to fulfil a fate and destiny.

Weaving such fancies, I fell sound asleep, nor woke before the stir and bustle of the great city aroused me. Power, I found, had been twice to my quarters that morning, but, fearing to disturb me, had merely left a few lines to say that, as he should be engaged on service during the day, we could not meet before the evening. There were certain preliminaries requisite regarding my leave which demanded my appearing before a board of medical officers, and I immediately set about dressing, resolving that, as soon as they were completed, I should, if permitted, retire to one of the small cottages on the opposite bank of the Tagus, there to remain until my restored health allowed me to rejoin my regiment.

I dreaded meeting the Dashwoods. I anticipated with a heavy heart how effectually one passing interview would destroy all my day-dreams of happiness, and I preferred anything to the sad conviction of hopelessness such a meeting must lead to.

While I thus balanced with myself how to proceed, a gentle step came to the door, and as it opened slowly, a servant in a dark livery entered.

"Mr. O'Malley, sir?"

"Yes," said I, wondering to whom my arrival could be thus early known.

"Sir George Dashwood requests you will step over to him as soon as you go out," continued the man; "he is so engaged that he cannot leave home, but is most desirous to see you."

"It is not far from here?"

"No, sir; scarcely five minutes' walk."

"Well, then, if you will show me the way, I'll follow you."

I cast one passing glance at myself to see that all was right about my costume, and sallied forth.

In the middle of the Black Horse-square, at the door of a large stone-fronted building, a group of military men were assembled, chatting and laughing away together; some were reading the lately-arrived English papers; others were lounging upon the stone parapet, carelessly puffing their cigars. None of the faces were known to me; so threading my way through the crowd, I reached the steps. Just as I did so, a half-muttered whisper met my ear:

"Who did you say?"

"O'Malley, the young Irishman who behaved so gallantly at the Douro."

The blood rushed hotly to my cheek; my heart bounded with exultation; my step, infirm and tottering but a moment before, became fixed and steady, and I felt a thrill of proud enthusiasm playing through my veins. How little did the speaker of those few and random words know what courage he had given to a drooping heart, what renewed energy to a breaking spirit! The voice of praise, too, coming from those to whom we had thought ourselves unknown, has a magic about it that must be felt to be understood. So it happened that in a few seconds a revolution had taken place in all my thoughts and feelings, and I, who had left my quarters dispirited and depressed. now walked confidently and proudly forward.

"Mr. O'Malley," said the servant to the officer in waiting, as we entered the ante-chamber.

"Ah! Mr. O'Malley," said the aide-de-camp, in blandest accent, "I hope you're better. Sir George is most anxious to see you; he is at present engaged with the staff——"

A bell rang at the moment, and cut short the sentence: he flew to the door of the inner room, and, returning in an instant, said,—

"Will you follow me? This way, if you please."

The room was crowded with general officers and aides-de-camp, so that for a second or two I could not distinguish the parties; but no sooner was my name announced, than Sir George Dashwood, forcing his way through, rushed forward to meet me.

"O'Malley, my brave fellow! delighted to shake your hand again! How much grown you are—twice the man I knew you! and the arm, too, is it getting on well?"

Scarcely giving me a moment to reply, and still holding my hand tightly in his grasp, he introduced me on every side.

"My young Irish friend, Sir Edward, the man of the Douro. My lord, allow me to present Lieutenant O'Malley, of the 14th."

"A very dashing thing, that of yours, sir, at Ciudad Rodrigo."

"A very senseless one, I fear, my lord."

"No, no, I don't agree with you at all; even when no great results follow, the *morale* of an army benefits by acts of daring."

A running fire of kind and civil speeches poured in on me from all quarters, and, amid all that crowd of bronzed and war-worn veterans, I felt myself the lion of the moment. Craufurd, it appeared, had spoken most handsomely of my name, and I was thus made known to many of those whose own reputations were then extending over Europe.

In this happy trance of excited pleasure I passed the morning. Amid the military chit-chat of the day around me, treated as an equal by the greatest and the most distinguished, I heard all the confidential opinions upon the campaign and its leaders; and in that most entrancing of all flatteries—the easy tone of companionship of our elders and betters—forgot my griefs, and half believed I was destined for great things.

Fearing at length that I had prolonged my visit too far, I approached Sir George to take my leave, when, drawing my arm within his, he retired towards one of the windows.

"A word, O'Malley, before you go. I've arranged a little plan for you; mind, I shall insist upon obedience. They'll make some difficulty about your remaining here, so that I have appointed you one of our extra aides-de-camp. That will free you from all trouble, and I shall not be very exacting in my demands upon you. You must, however, commence your duties to-day, and as we dine at seven precisely, I shall expect you. I am aware of your wish to stay in Lisbon, my boy, and, if all I hear be true, congratulate you sincerely; but more of this another time, and so good-bye." So saying, he shook my hand once more, warmly; and without well feeling how or why, I found myself in the street.

The last few words Sir George had spoken threw a gloom over all my thoughts. I saw at once that the report Power had alluded to had gained currency at Lisbon. Sir George believed it; doubtless Lucy, too; and, forgetting in an instant all the emulative ardor that so lately stirred my heart, I took my path beside the river, and sauntered slowly along, lost in my reflections.

I had walked for above an hour, before paying any attention to the path I followed. Mechanically, as it were, retreating from the noise and tumult of the city, I wandered towards the country. My thoughts fixed but upon one theme, I had neither ears nor eyes for aught around me; the great difficulty of my present position now appearing to me in this light—my attachment to Lucy Dashwood, unrequited and unreturned as I felt it, did not permit of my rebutting any report which might have reached her concerning Donna Inez. I had no right, no claim to suppose her sufficiently interested about me to listen to such an explanation, had I even the opportunity to make it. One thing was thus clear to me—all my hopes had ended in that quarter; and as this conclusion sank into my mind, a species of dogged resolution to brave my fortune crept over me, which only waited the first moment of my meeting her to overthrow and destroy forever.

Meanwhile I walked on; now rapidly, at some momentary rush of passionate excitement; now slowly, as some depressing and gloomy notion succeeded; when suddenly my path was arrested by a long file of bullock cars which blocked up the way. Some chance squabble had arisen among the drivers, and to avoid the crowd and collision, I turned into a gateway which opened beside me, and soon found myself in a lawn handsomely planted, and adorned with flowering shrubs and ornamental trees.

In the half-dreamy state my musings had brought me to, I struggled to recollect why the aspect of the place did not seem altogether new. My thoughts were, however, far away—now blending some memory of my distant home with scenes of battle and bloodshed, or resting upon my first interview with her whose chance word, carelessly and lightly spoken, had written the story of my life. From this reverie I was rudely awakened by a rustling noise in the trees behind me, and before I could turn my head, the two fore paws of a large stag-hound were planted upon my shoulders, while the open mouth and panting tongue were close beside my face. My daydream was dispelled quick·as lightning; it was Juan himself, the favorite dog of the Senhora, who gave me this rude welcome, and who now, by a thousand wild gestures and bounding caresses, seemed to do the honors of his house. There was something so like home in these joyful greetings, that I yielded myself at once his prisoner, and followed, or rather was accompanied by him towards the villa.

Of course, sooner or later, I should have called upon my kind friends, then why not now, when chance had already brought me so near? Besides, if I held to my resolution, which I meant to do—of retiring to some quiet and sequestered cottage till my health was restored—the opportunity might not readily present itself again. This line of argument perfectly satisfied my reason, while a strong feeling of something like curiosity piqued me to proceed, and before many minutes elapsed I reached the house. The door, as usual, lay wide open, and the ample hall, furnished like a sitting-room, had its customary litter of books, music, and flowers scattered upon the tables. My friend Juan, however, suffered me not to linger here, but rushing furiously at a door before me, began a vigorous attack for admittance.

As I knew this to be the drawing-room, I opened the door and walked in, but no one was to be seen; a half-open book lay upon an ottoman, and a fan, which I recognized as an old acquaintance, was beside it, but the owner was absent.

I sat down, resolved to wait patiently for her coming, without any announcement of my being there. I was not sorry, indeed, to have some moments to collect my thoughts, and restore my erring faculties to something like order.

As I looked about the room, it seemed as if I had been there but yesterday. The folding-doors lay open to the garden, just as I had seen them last, and save that the flowers seemed fewer, and those which remained of a darker and more sombre tint, all seemed unchanged. There lay the guitar, to whose thrilling chords my heart had bounded; there, the drawing, over which I had bent in admiring pleasure, suggesting some tints of light or shadow, as the fairy fingers traced them; every chair was known to me, and I greeted them as things I cared for.

While thus I scanned each object around me, I was struck by a little china vase, which, unlike its other brethren, contained a bouquet of dead and faded flowers; the blood rushed to my cheek; I started up; it was one I had myself presented to her the day before we parted. It was in that same vase I placed it; the very table, too, stood in the same position beside that narrow window. What a rush of thoughts came pouring on me! And oh! shall I confess it? how deeply did such a mute testimony of remembrance speak to my heart, at the moment that I felt myself unloved and uncared for by another! I walked hurriedly up and down, a maze of conflicting resolves combating in my mind, while one thought ever recurred—"Would that I had not come here!" and yet, after all, it may mean nothing; some piece of passing coquetry, which she will be the very first to laugh at. I remember how she spoke of poor Howard; what folly to take it otherwise! "Be it so, then," said I, half aloud; "and now for my part of the game;" and with this I took from my pocket the light blue scarf she had given me the morning we parted, and, throwing it over my shoulder, prepared to perform my part in what I had fully persuaded myself to be a comedy. The time, however, passed on, and she came not; a thousand high-flown Portuguese phrases had time to be conned over again and again by me, and I had abundant leisure to enact my coming part; but still the curtain did not rise. As the day was wearing, I resolved at last to write a few lines, expressive of my regret at not meeting her, and promising myself an early opportunity of paying my respects under more fortunate circumstances. I sat down, accordingly, and, drawing the paper towards me, began, in a mixture of French and Portuguese, as it happened, to indite my billet.

"Senhora Inez"—no—"Ma chère Mademoiselle Inez"—confound it, that's too intimate; well, here goes—"Monsieur O'Malley presente ses respects"—that will never do; and then, after twenty other abortive attempts, I began thoughtlessly sketching heads upon the paper, and scribbling with wonderful facility in fifty different ways—"Ma charmante amie—Ma plus chère Inez," &c., and in this most useful and profitable occupation did I pass another half hour.

How long I should have persisted in such an employment it is difficult to say, had not an incident intervened which suddenly but most effectually put an end to it. As the circumstance is one which, however little striking in itself, had the greatest and most lasting influence upon my future career, I shall perhaps be excused for devoting another chapter to its recital.

CHAPTER XII.

A PLEASANT PREDICAMENT.

WHILE I sat endeavoring to fix upon some suitable and appropriate epithet by which to commence my note, my back was turned towards the door of the garden; and so occupied was I in my meditations, that even had any one entered at the time, in all probability I should not have perceived it. At length, however, I was aroused from my study by a burst of laughter, whose girlish joyousness was not quite new to me. I knew it well; it was the Senhora herself; and the next moment I heard her voice.

"I tell you I'm quite certain I saw his face in the mirror as I passed. Oh, how delightful! and you'll be charmed with him; so, mind, you must not steal him from me; I shall never forgive you if you do; and look, only look! he has got the blue scarf I gave him when he marched to the Douro."

While I perceived that I was myself seen, I could see nothing of the speaker, and, wishing to hear something further, appeared more than ever occupied in the writing before me.

What her companion replied, I could not, however, catch, but only guess at its import by the Senhora's answer.

"*Fi donc!*—I really am very fond of him; but, never fear, I shall be as stately as a queen. You shall see how meekly he will kiss my hand, and with what unbending reserve I'll receive him."

"Indeed!" thought I; "mayhap I'll mar your plot a little; but let us listen."

"It is so provoking," continued Inez; "I never can remember names, and his was something too absurd; but, never mind, I shall make him a grandee of Portugal. Well, but come along, I long to present him to you."

Here a gentle struggle seemed to ensue; for I heard the Senhora coaxingly entreat her, while her companion steadily resisted.

"I know you think I shall be so silly, and perhaps wrong; is it not so? But you're mistaken. You'll be surprised at my cold and dignified manner. I shall draw myself proudly up, and, curtseying deeply, say, 'Monsieur, j'ai l'honneur de vous saluer.'"

A laugh twice as mirthful as before followed, while I could hear the tones of the friend evidently in expostulation.

"Well, then, to be sure, you are provoking, but you really promise to follow me. Be it so; then give me that moss-rose. How you have fluttered me; now for it!"

So saying, I heard her foot upon the gravel, and the next instant upon the marble step of the door. There is something in expecta-

tion that sets the heart beating, and mine throbbed against my side.
I waited, however, till she entered before lifting my head, and then
springing suddenly up, with one bound clasped her in my arms, and
pressing my lips upon her roseate cheek, said,—

"*Ma charmante amie!*" To disengage herself from me, and to
spring suddenly back, was her first effort; to burst into an immoderate
fit of laughing, her second; her cheek was, however, covered with a
deep blush, and I already repented that my malice had gone so far.

"Pardon, Mademoiselle," said I, in affected innocence, "if I have
so far forgotten myself as to assume a habit of my own country to a
stranger."

A half-angry toss of the head was her only reply, and, turning
towards the garden, she called to her friend:—

"Come here, dearest, and instruct my ignorance upon your national customs; but first let me present to you—I never knew his
name—the Chevalier de —— What is it?"

The glass door opened as she spoke; a tall and graceful figure
entered, and, turning suddenly round, showed me the features of
Lucy Dashwood. We both stood opposite each other, each mute
with amazement. *My* feelings let me not attempt to convey; shame,
for the first moment stronger than aught else, sent the blood rushing
to my face and temples, and the next I was cold and pale as death.
As for her, I cannot guess at what passed in her mind. She curt-
seyed deeply to me, and with a half-smile of scarce recognition
passed by me, and walked towards a window.

"*Comme vous êtes aimable!*" said the lively Portuguese, who comprehended little of this dumb show; "here have I been flattering
myself what friends you'd be the very moment you met, and now
you'll not even look at each other."

What was to be done? The situation was every instant growing
more and more embarrassing; nothing but downright effrontery
could get through with it now; and never did a man's heart more
fail him than did mine at this conjuncture. I made the effort, however, and stammered out certain unmeaning commonplaces. Inez
replied, and I felt myself conversing with the headlong recklessness
of one marching to a scaffold, a coward's fear at his heart, while he
essayed to seem careless and indifferent.

Anxious to reach what I estimated safe ground, I gladly adverted
to the campaign; and at last, hurried on by the impulse to cover
my embarrassment, was describing some skirmish with a French
outpost. Without intending, I had succeeding in exciting the Senhora's interest, and she listened with sparkling eye and parted lips
to the description of a sweeping charge in which a square was broken, and several prisoners carried off. Warming with the eager

avidity of her attention, I grew myself more excited, when just as my narrative reached its climax, Miss Dashwood walked gently towards the bell, rang it, and ordered her carriage. The tone of perfect *nonchalance* of the whole proceeding struck me dumb. I faltered, stammered, hesitated, and was silent. Donna Inez turned from one to the other of us with a look of unfeigned astonishment, and I heard her mutter to herself something like a reflection upon "national eccentricities." Happily, however, her attention was now exclusively turned towards her friend, and while assisting her to shawl, and extorting innumerable promises of an early visit, I got a momentary reprieve; the carriage drew up also, and as the gravel flew right and left beneath the horses' feet, the very noise and bustle relieved me.

"*Adios!*" then said Inez, as she kissed her for the last time, while she motioned to me to escort her to her carriage. I advanced— stopped—made another step forward, and again grew irresolute; but Miss Dashwood speedily terminated the difficulty; for, making me a formal curtsey, she declined my scarce-proffered attention, and left the room.

As she did so, I perceived that, on passing the table, her eyes fell upon the paper I had been scribbling over so long, and I thought that for an instant an expression of ineffable scorn seemed to pass across her features, save which—and perhaps even in this I was mistaken—her manner was perfectly calm, easy, and indifferent.

Scarce had the carriage rolled from the door, when the Senhora, throwing herself upon a chair, clapped her hands in childish ecstasy, while she fell into a fit of laughing that I thought would never have an end. "Such a scene!" cried she; "I would not have lost it for the world; what cordiality! what *empressement* to form an acquaintance! I shall never forget it, Monsieur le Chevalier; your national customs seem to run sadly in extremes. One would have thought you deadly enemies; and poor me! after a thousand delightful plans about you both."

As she ran on thus, scarce able to control her mirth at each sentence, I walked the room with impatient strides; now resolving to hasten after the carriage, stop it, explain in a few words how all had happened, and then fly from her forever; then, the remembrance of her cold, impassive look crossed me, and I thought that one bold leap into the Tagus might be the shortest and easiest solution to all my miseries; perfect abasement, thorough self-contempt, had broken all my courage, and I could have cried like a child. What I said, or how I comforted myself after, I know not; but my first consciousness came to me as I found myself running at the top of my speed far upon the road towards Lisbon.

CHAPTER XIII.

THE DINNER.

IT may be easily imagined that I had little inclination to keep my promise of dining that day with Sir George Dashwood. However, there was nothing else for it; the die was cast—my prospects as regarded Lucy were ruined forever. We were not, wo never could be, anything to each other; and as for me, the sooner I braved my altered fortunes the better; and, after all, why should I call them altered? She evidently never had cared for me; and even supposing that my fervent declaration of attachment had interested her, the apparent duplicity and falseness of my late conduct could only fall the more heavily upon me.

I endeavored to philosophize myself into calmness and indifference. One by one, I exhausted every argument for my defence, which, however ingeniously put forward, brought no comfort to my own conscience. I pleaded the unerring devotion of my heart—the uprightness of my motives—and when called on for the proofs—alas! except the blue scarf I wore in memory of another, and my absurd conduct at the villa, I had none. From the current gossip of Lisbon, down to my own disgraceful folly, all—all was against me.

Honesty of intention, rectitude of purpose, may be, doubtless they are, admirable supports to a rightly-constituted mind; but even then they must come supported by such claims to probability as make the injured man feel that he has not lost the sympathy of all his fellows. Now, I had none of these, had even my temperament, broken by sickness and harassed by unlucky conjectures, permitted my appreciating them.

I endeavored to call my wounded pride to my aid, and thought over the glance of haughty disdain she gave me as she passed on to her carriage; but even this turned against me, and a humiliating sense of my own degraded position sank deeply into my heart. "This impression at least," thought I, "must be effaced. I cannot permit her to believe——"

"His Excellency is waiting dinner, sir," said a lacquey, introducing a finely-powdered head gently within the door. I looked at my watch—it was eight o'clock; snatching my sabre, and shocked at my delay, I hastily followed the servant down stairs, and thus at once cut short my deliberations.

The man must be but little observant, or deeply sunk in his own reveries, who, arriving half an hour too late for dinner, fails to detect in the faces of the assembled and expectant guests a very palpable expression of discontent and displeasure. It is truly a moment of awkwardness, and one in which few are found to manage with success; the blushing, hesitating, blundering apology of the absent man, is scarcely better than the ill-affected surprise of the more practised offender. The bashfulness of the one is as distasteful as the cool impertinence of the other; both are thoroughly out of place, for we are thinking of neither; our thoughts are wandering to cold soups and rechauffé pâtés, and we neither care for nor estimate the cause, but satisfy our spleen by cursing the offender.

Happily for me, I was clad in a triple insensibility to such feelings, and, with an air of most perfect unconstraint and composure, walked into a drawing-room where about twenty persons were busily discussing what peculiar amiability in my character would compensate for my present conduct.

"At last, O'Malley, at last!" said Sir George. "Why, my dear boy, how very late you are!"

I muttered something about a long walk—distance from Lisbon, &c.

"Ah! that was it. I was right, you see!" said an old lady in a spangled turban, as she whispered something to her friend beside her, who appeared excessively shocked at the information conveyed; while a fat, round-faced little general, after eyeing me steadily through his glass, expressed a *sotto voce* wish that I was upon *his* staff. I felt my cheek reddening at the moment, and stared around me like one whose trials were becoming downright insufferable, when happily dinner was announced, and terminated my embarrassment.

As the party filed past, I perceived that Miss Dashwood was not amongst them; and, with a heart relieved for the moment by the circumstance, and inventing a hundred conjectures to account for it, I followed with the aides-de-camp and the staff to the dinner-room.

The temperament is very Irish, I believe, which renders a man so elastic that from the extreme of depression to the very climax of high spirits there is but one spring. To this I myself plead guilty, and thus scarcely was I freed from the embarrassment which a meeting with Lucy Dashwood must have caused, when my heart bounded with lightness.

When the ladies withdrew, the events of the campaign became the subject of conversation, and upon these, very much to my astonishment, I found myself consulted as an authority. The Douro, from some fortunate circumstance, had given me a reputation I never dreamed of, and I heard my opinions quoted upon topics of which my standing as an officer and my rank in the service could not imply a very extended observation. Power was absent on duty:

and, happily for my supremacy, the company consisted entirely of generals in the commissariat, or new arrivals from England, all of whom knew still less than myself.

What will not iced champagne and flattery do? Singly, they are strong impulses; combined, their power is irresistible. I now heard for the first time that our great leader had been elevated to the peerage by the title of Lord Wellington, and I sincerely believe—however now I may smile at the confession—that at the moment I felt more elation at the circumstance than he did. The glorious sensation of being in any way, no matter how remotely, linked with the career of those whose path is a high one, and whose destinies are cast for great events, thrilled through me; and, in all the warmth of my admiration and pride for our great captain, a secret pleasure stirred within me as I whispered to myself, "And I, too, am a soldier!"

I fear me that very little flattery is sufficient to turn the head of a young man of eighteen; and if I yielded to the "pleasant incense," let my apology be, that I was not used to it; and, lastly, let me avow, if I did get tipsy—I liked the liquor. And why not? It is the only tipple I know of that leaves no headache the next morning to punish you for the glories of the past night. It may, like all other strong potations, induce you to make a fool of yourself when under its influence; but, like the nitrous oxide gas, its effects are passing, and as the pleasure is an ecstasy for the time, and your constitution none the worse when it is over, I really see no harm in it.

Then the benefits are manifest; for while he who gives becomes never the poorer for his benevolence, the receiver is made rich indeed. It matters little that some dear, kind friend is ready with his bitter draught to remedy what he is pleased to call its unwholesome sweetness; you betake yourself with only the more pleasure to the "blessed elixir," whose fascinations neither the poverty of your pocket nor the penury of your brain can withstand, and by the magic of whose spell you are great and gifted. *"Vive la bagatelle!"* saith the Frenchman. "Long live Flattery!" say I, come from what quarter it will; the only wealth of the poor man,—the only reward of the unknown one; the arm that supports us in failure,— the hand that crowns us in success; the comforter in our affliction, —the gay companion in our hours of pleasure; the lullaby of the infant,—the staff of old age; the secret treasure we lock up in our own hearts, and which ever grows greater as we count it over. Let me not be told that the coin is fictitious, and the gold not genuine; its clink is as musical to the ear as though it bore the last impression of the mint, and I'm not the man to cast an aspersion upon its value.

This little digression, however seemingly out of place, may serve to illustrate what it might be difficult to convey in other words, namely, that if Charles O'Malley became in his own estimation a very considerable personage that day at dinner, the fault lay not entirely with himself, but with his friends, who told him he was such. In fact, my good reader, I was the lion of the party,—the man who saved Laborde,—who charged through a brigade of guns,—who performed feats which newspapers quoted, though he never heard of them himself. At no time is a man so successful in society as when his reputation heralds him, and it needs but little conversational eloquence to talk well, if you have but a willing and ready auditory. Of mine, I could certainly not complain; and as, drinking deeply, I poured forth a whole tide of campaigning recital, I saw the old colonels of recruiting districts exchanging looks of wonder and admiration with officers of the ordnance, while Sir George himself, evidently pleased at my *début*, went back to an early period of our acquaintance, and related the rescue of his daughter in Galway.

In an instant the whole current of my thoughts was changed. My first meeting with Lucy, my boyhood's dream of ambition, my plighted faith, my thoughts of our last parting in Dublin, when, in a moment of excited madness, I told my tale of love. I remembered her downcast look, as, her cheek now flushing, now growing pale, she trembled while I spoke. I thought of her as in the crash of battle her image flashed across my brain, and made me feel a rush of chivalrous enthusiasm to win her heart by "doughty deeds."

I forgot all around and about me. My head reeled; the wine, the excitement, my long previous illness, all pressed upon me; and, as my temples throbbed loudly and painfully, a chaotic rush of discordant, ill-connected ideas flitted across my mind. There seemed some stir and confusion in the room, but why or wherefore I could not think, nor could I recall my scattered senses, till Sir George Dashwood's voice roused me once again to consciousness.

"We are going to have some coffee, O'Malley. Miss Dashwood expects us in the drawing-room. You have not seen her yet?"

I know not my reply; but he continued:

"She has some letters for you, I think."

I muttered something, and suffered him to pass on; no sooner had he done so, however, than I turned towards the door, and rushed into the street. The cold night air suddenly recalled me to myself, and I stood for a moment, endeavoring to collect myself; as I did so a servant stopped, and, saluting me, presented me with a letter. For a second, a cold chill came over me; I knew not what fear beset me. The letter I at last remembered must be that one alluded to by Sir George, so I took it in silence, and walked on.

CHAPTER XIV.

THE LETTER.

HURRYING to my quarters, I made a hundred guesses from whom the letter could have come; a kind of presentiment told me that it bore in some measure upon the present crisis of my life, and I burned with anxiety to read it.

No sooner had I reached the light than all my hopes on this head vanished; the envelope bore the well-known name of my old college chum, Frank Webber, and none could at the moment have more completely dispelled all chance of interesting me. I threw it from me with disappointment, and sat moodily down to brood over my fate.

At length, however, and almost without knowing it, I drew the lamp towards me, and broke the seal. The reader being already acquainted with my amiable friend, there is the less indiscretion in communicating the contents, which ran thus:

> "TRINITY COLLEGE, DUBLIN, No. 2.
> "Oct. 5, 1810.

"MY DEAR O'MALLEY:—Nothing but your death and burial, with or without military honors, can possibly excuse your very disgraceful neglect of your old friends here. Nesbitt has never heard of you, neither has Smith. Ottley swears never to have seen your handwriting, save on the back of a protested bill. You have totally forgotten *me*, and the Dean informs me that you have never condescended a single line to him; which latter inquiry on my part nearly cost me a rustication.

"A hundred conjectures to account for your silence—a new feature in you since you were here—are afloat. Some assert that your soldiering has turned your head, and that you are above corresponding with civilians. Your friends, however, who know you better, and value your worth, think otherwise; and having seen a paragraph about a certain O'Malley being tried by court-martial for stealing a goose, and maltreating the woman that owned it, ascribe your not writing to other motives. Do, in any case, relieve our minds; say, is it yourself, or only a relative that's mentioned?

"Herbert came over from London with a long story about your doing wonderful things—capturing cannon and general officers by scores—but devil a word of it is extant; and if you have really committed these acts, they have 'misused the king's press infernally,' for neither in the *Times* nor the *Post* are you heard of. Answer this point, and say also if you have got promotion; for what precise sign you are algebraically expressed by at this writing may serve Fitzgerald for a fellowship question. And for us, we are jogging along, *semper eadem*—that is, worse and worse. Dear Cecil Cavendish, our gifted friend, slight of limb and soft of voice, has been rusticated for immersing four bricklayers in that green receptacle of stagnant water and duckweed, yclept the 'Haha.' Roper, equally unlucky, has taken to reading for honors, and obtained a medal, I fancy—at least his friends shy him, and it must be something of that kind. Belson—poor Belson (fortunately for him he was born in the nineteenth, not the sixteenth century, or he'd be most likely ornamenting a pile of fagots)—ventured upon some stray excursions into the Hebrew verbs—the professor himself never having transgressed beyond the declensions—and the consequence is, he is in disgrace among the seniors. And as for me, a heavy charge hangs over my devoted head, even while I write. The Senior Lecturer, it appears, has been for some time instituting some very singular researches into the original state of our goodly college at its founding. Plans and specifications showing its extent and magnificence have been continually before the board for the last month; and in such repute have been a smashed door-sill or an old arch, that freshmen have now abandoned conic sections for crowbars, and instead of the 'Principia' have taken up the pickaxe. You know, my dear fellow, with what enthusiasm I enter into any scheme for the aggrandizement of our Alma Mater, so I need not tell you how ardently I adventured into the career now opened to me. My time was completely devoted to the matter; neither means nor health did I spare, and in my search for antiquarian lore, I have actually undermined the old wall of the fellows' garden, and am each morning in expectation of hearing that the big bell near the commons-hall has descended from its lofty and noisy eminence, and is snugly reposing in the mud. Meanwhile, accident put me in possession of a most singular and remarkable discovery. Our chambers—I call them ours for old association sake—are, you may remember, in the Old Square. Well, I have been fortunate enough, within the very precincts of my own dwelling, to contribute a very wonderful fact to the history of the University; alone—unassisted—unaided, I labored at my discovery. Few can estimate the pleasure I felt—the fame and reputation I anticipated. I drew up a little memoir for the board, most respectfully and civilly worded, having for its title the following:

'ACCOUNT

Of a remarkable Subterranean Passage lately discovered in the
Old Building of Trinity College, Dublin:
With Observations upon its Extent, Antiquity, and Probable Use.
By F. WEBBER, Senior Freshman.'

"My dear O'Malley, I'll not dwell upon the pride I felt in my new character of antiquarian; it is enough to state that my very remarkable tract was well considered and received, and a commission appointed to investigate the discovery, consisting of the Vice-Provost, the Senior Lecturer, old Woodhouse, the Sub-Dean, and a few more.

"On Tuesday last they came accordingly in full academic costume, I being habited most accurately in the like manner, and conducting them with all form into my bed-room, where a large screen concealed from view the entrance to the tunnel alluded to. Assuming a very John Kembleish attitude, I struck this down with one hand, pointing with the other to the wall, as I exclaimed, 'There! look there!'

"I need only quote Barret's exclamation to enlighten you upon my discovery, as drawing in his breath with a strong effort, he burst out:

"'May the devil admire me, but it's a rat hole!'

"I fear, Charley, he's right, and, what's more, that the board will think so, for this moment a very warm discussion is going on among that amiable and learned body whether I shall any longer remain an ornament to the University. In fact, the terror with which they fled from my chambers, overturning each other in the passage, seemed to imply that they thought me mad; and I do believe my voice, look, and attitude would not have disgraced a blue cotton dressing-gown and a cell in 'Swifts'. Be this as it may, few men have done more for college than I have. The sun never stood still for Joshua with more resolution than I have rested in my career of freshman; and if I have contributed little to the fame, I have done much for the funds of the University; and when they come to compute the various sums I have paid in, for fines, penalties, and what they call properly 'impositions,' if they don't place a portrait of me in the examination-hall, between Archbishop Usher and Flood, then do I say there is no gratitude in mankind; not to mention the impulse I have given to the various artisans whose business it is to repair lamps, windows, chimneys, iron railings, and watchmen, all of which I have devoted myself to with an enthusiasm for political economy well known, and registered in the College-street police office.

"After all, Charley, I miss you greatly. Your second in a ballad is not to be replaced; besides, Carlisle Bridge has got low; medical students and young attorneys affect minstrelsy, and actually frequent haunts sacred to our muse.

"Dublin is, upon the whole, I think, worse; though one scarcely ever gets tired laughing at the small celebrities——"

Master Frank here gets indiscreet, so I shall skip.

*   *   *   *   *   *   *

"And so the Dashwoods are going too; this will make mine a pitiable condition, for I really did begin to feel tenderly in that quarter. You may have heard that she refused me; this, however, is not correct, though I have little doubt it might have been—had I asked her.

"Hammersley has, you know, got his dismissal. I wonder how the poor fellow took it, when Power gave him back his letters and his picture. How *you* are to be treated remains to be seen; in any case, you certainly stand first favorite."

I laid down the letter at this passage, unable to read further. Here, then, was the solution of the whole chaos of mystery—here the full explanation of what had puzzled my aching brain for many a night long. These were the very letters I had myself delivered into Hammersley's hands; this the picture he had trodden to dust beneath his heel the morning of our meeting. I now felt the reason of his taunting allusion to my "success," his cutting sarcasm, his intemperate passion. A flood of light poured at once across all the dark passages of my history; and Lucy, too—dare I think of her? A rapid thought shot through my brain. What if she had really cared for me! What if for me she had rejected another's love! What if, trusting to my faith—my pledged and sworn faith—she had given me her heart! Oh! the bitter agony of that thought, to think that all my hopes were shipwrecked, with the very land in sight.

I sprang to my feet with some sudden impulse, but as I did so, the blood rushed madly to my face and temples, which beat violently; a parched and swollen feeling came about my throat; I endeavored to open my collar and undo my stock, but my disabled arm prevented me. I tried to call my servant, but my utterance was thick, and my words would not come; a frightful suspicion crossed me that my reason was tottering. I made towards the door, but, as I did so, the objects around me became confused and mingled, my limbs trembled, and I fell heavily upon the floor; a pang of dreadful pain shot through me as I fell—my arm was rebroken. After this, I knew no more! All the accumulated excitement of the evening bore down with one fell swoop upon my brain. Ere day broke, I was delirious.

I have a vague and indistinct remembrance of hurried and anxious faces around my bed, of whispered words and sorrowful looks; but my own thoughts careered over the bold hill of the far west as I trod them in my boyhood, free and high of heart, or recurred to the din and crash of the battle-field, with the mad bounding of the war-horse, and the loud clang of the trumpet; perhaps the acute pain of my swollen and suffering arm gave the character to my mental aberration; for I have more than once observed among the wounded in battle that, even when torn and mangled by grape from a howitzer, their ravings have partaken of a high feature of enthusiasm, shouts of triumph, and exclamations of pleasure; even songs have I heard—but never once the low muttering of despair, or the half-stifled cry of sorrow and affliction.

Such were the few gleams of consciousness which visited me, and even to such as these I soon became insensible.

Few like to chronicle, fewer still to read, the sad history of a sick-bed. Of mine, I know but little. The throbbing pulses of the erring brain, the wild fancies of lunacy, take no note of time. There is no past nor future—a dreadful present, full of its hurried and confused impressions, is all that the mind beholds; and even when some gleams of returning reason flash upon the mad confusion of the brain, they come like sunbeams through a cloud, dimmed, darkened, and perverted.

It is the restless activity of the mind in fever that constitutes its most painful anguish; the fast-flitting thoughts that rush ever onward, crowding sensation on sensation, an endless train of exciting images, without purpose or repose; or even worse, the straining effort to pursue some vague and shadowy conception, which evades us ever as we follow, but which mingles with all around and about us—haunting us at midnight as in the noontime.

Of this nature was a vision which came constantly before me, till at length, by its very recurrence, it assumed a kind of real and palpable existence; and as I watched it, my heart thrilled with the high ardor of enthusiasm and delight, or sunk into the dark abyss of sorrow and despair. "The dawning of morning, the daylight sinking," brought no other image to my aching sight; and of this alone, of all the impressions of the period, has my mind retained any consciousness.

Methought I stood within an old and venerable cathedral, where the dim yellow light fell with a rich but solemn glow upon the fretted capitals, or the grotesque tracings of the oaken carvings, lighting up the faded gildings of the stately monuments, and tinting the varied hues of time-worn banners. The mellow notes of a deep organ filled the air, and seemed to attune the sénse to all the awe and reverence of the place, where the very footfall, magnified by its many echoes, seemed half a profanation. I stood before an altar, beside me a young and lovely girl, whose bright brown tresses waved in loose masses upon a neck of snowy whiteness; her hand, cold and pale, rested within my own; we knelt together, not in prayer, but a feeling of deep reverence stole over my heart, as she repeated some few half-uttered words after me; I knew that she was mine. Oh!

the ecstasy of that moment, as, springing to my feet, I darted forward to press her to my heart! when suddenly, an arm was interposed between us, while a low but solemn voice rung in my ears, "Stir not, for thou art false and traitorous, thy vow a perjury, and thy heart a lie!" Slowly and silently the fair form of my loved Lucy—for it was she—receded from my sight. One look, one last look of sorrow—it was scarce reproach—fell upon me, and I sank back upon the cold pavement broken-hearted and forsaken.

This dream came with daybreak, and with the calm repose of evening; the still hours of the waking night brought no other image to my eyes; and when its sad influence had spread a gloom and desolation over my wounded heart, a secret hope crept over me that again the bright moment of happiness would return, and once more beside that ancient altar I'd kneel, beside my bride, and call her mine.

*　　*　　*　　*　　*.　　*　　*　　*

For the rest, my memory retains but little; the kind looks which came around my bedside brought but a brief pleasure, for in their affectionate beaming I could read the gloomy prestige of my fate. The hurried but cautious step, the whispered sentences, the averted gaze of those who sorrowed for me, sank far deeper into my heart than my friends then thought of. Little do they think, who minister to the sick or dying, how each passing word, each flitting glance is noted, and how the pale and stilly figure, which lies all but lifeless before them, counts over the hours he has to live by the smiles or tears around him.

Hours, days, weeks rolled over, and still my fate hung in the balance; and while in the wild enthusiasm of my erring faculties I wandered far in spirit from my bed of suffering and pain, some well-remembered voice beside me would strike upon my ear, bringing me back, as if by magic, to all the realities of life, and investing my almost unconscious state with all the hopes and fears about me.

One by one, at length, these fancies fled from me, and to the delirium of fever succeeded the sad and helpless consciousness of illness, far, far more depressing; for as the conviction of sense came back, the sorrowful aspect of a dreary future came with it.

CHAPTER XV.

THE VILLA.

THE gentle twilight of an autumnal evening, calm, serene and mellow, was falling, as I opened my eyes to consciousness of life and being, and looked around me. I lay in a large and handsomely-furnished apartment, in which the hand of taste was as evident in all the decorations as the unsparing employment of wealth; the silk draperies of my bed, the inlaid tables, the ormolu ornaments which glittered upon the chimney, were one by one so many puzzles to my erring senses, and I opened and shut my eyes again and again, and essayed by every means in my power to ascertain if they were not the visionary creations of a fevered mind. I stretched out my hands to feel the objects; and even while holding freshly-plucked flowers in my grasp, I could scarce persuade myself that they were real. A thrill of pain at this instant recalled me to other thoughts, and I turned my eyes upon my wounded arm, which, swollen and stiffened, lay motionless beside me. Gradually, my memory came back, and to my weak faculties some passages of my former life were presented, not collectedly it is true, nor in any order, but scattered, isolated scenes. While such thoughts flew past, my ever rising question to myself was, " Where am I now?" The vague feeling which illness leaves upon the mind whispered to me of kind looks and soft voices; and I had a dreamy consciousness about me of being watched and cared for, but wherefore, or by whom, I knew not.

From a partly-open door, which led into a garden, a mild and balmy air fanned my temples, and soothed my heated brow; and as the light curtain waved to and fro with the breeze, the odor of the rose and the orange-tree filled the apartment.

There is something in the feeling of weakness which succeeds to long illness of the most delicious and refined enjoyment. The spirit, emerging as it were from the thraldom of its grosser prison, rises high and triumphant above the meaner thoughts and more petty ambitions of daily life. Purer feelings, more ennobling hopes, succeed; and gleams of our childhood, mingling with promises for the future, make up an ideal existence, in which the low passions and cares of ordinary life enter not or are forgotten. 'Tis then we learn to hold converse with ourselves; 'tis then we ask, how has our manhood performed the promises of its youth? or, have our ripened prospects borne out the pledges of our boyhood? 'Tis then, in the calm justice of our lonely hearts, we learn how our failures are but another name for our faults, and that what we looked on as the vicissitudes of fortune are but the fruits of our own vices. Alas! how short-lived are such intervals! Like the fitful sunshine in the wintry sky, they throw one bright and joyous tint over the dark landscape; for a moment the valley and the mountain-top are bathed in a ruddy glow; the leafless tree and the dark moss seem to feel a touch of spring; but the next instant it is past; the lowering clouds and dark shadows intervene, and the cold blast, the moaning wind, and the dreary waste are once more before us.

I endeavored to recall the latest events of my career, but in vain; the real and the visionary were inextricably mingled; and the scenes of my campaign were blended with hopes, and fears, and doubts, which had no existence save in my dreams. My curiosity to know where I was grew now my strongest feeling, and I raised myself with one arm to look around me. In the room all was still and silent, but nothing seemed to intimate what I sought for. As I looked, however, the wind blew back the curtain which half concealed the sash-door, and disclosed to me the figure of a man seated at a table; his back was towards me, but his broad sombrero hat and brown mantle bespoke his nation. The light blue curl of smoke which wreathed gently upward, and the ample display of long-necked, straw-wrapped flasks, also attested that he was enjoying himself with the true Peninsular gusto, having probably partaken of a long siesta.

It was a perfect picture in its way of the indolent luxury of the South. The rich and perfumed flowers, half closing to the night air, but sighing forth a perfumed "*buonas noches*" as they betook themselves to rest; the slender shadows of the tall shrubs, stretching motionless across the walks; the very attitude of the figure himself, was in keeping, as, supported by easy-chairs, he lounged at full length, raising his head ever and anon, as if to watch the wreath of eddying smoke as it rose upward from his cigar, and melted away in the distance.

"Yes," thought I, as I looked for some time, "such is the very type of his nation. Surrounded by every luxury of climate, blessed with all that earth can offer of its best and fairest, and yet only using such gifts as mere sensual gratifications." Starting with this theme, I wove a whole story for the unknown personage, whom, in my wandering fancy, I began by creating a grandee of Portugal, invested with rank, honors, and riches, but who, effeminated by the habits and usages of his country, had become the mere idle voluptuary, living a life of easy and inglorious indolence. My further musings were interrupted at this moment, for the individual to whom I had been so complimentary in my reverie slowly arose from his recumbent position, flung his loose mantle carelessly across his left shoulder, and pushing open the sash-door, entered my chamber. Directing his steps to a large mirror, he stood for some minutes contemplating himself with what, from his attitude, I judged to be no small satisfaction. Though his back was still towards me, and the dim twilight of the room too uncertain to see much, yet I could perceive that he was evidently admiring himself in the glass. Of this fact I had soon the most complete proof, for as I looked, he slowly raised his broad-leafed Spanish hat with an air of most imposing pretension, and bowed reverently to himself.

"*Comesta vostra senoria ?*" said he.

The whole gesture and style of this proceeding struck me as so ridiculous, that, in spite of all my efforts, I could scarcely repress a laugh. He turned quickly round, and approached the bed. The deep shadow of the sombrero darkened the upper part of his features, but I could distinguish a pair of fierce-looking moustaches beneath, which curled upward towards his eyes, while a stiff pointed beard stuck straight from his chin. Fearing lest my rude interruption had been overheard, I was framing some polite speech in Portuguese, when he opened the dialogue by asking in that language how I did.

I replied, and was about to ask some questions relative to where and under whose protection I then was, when my grave-looking friend, giving a pirouette upon one leg, sent his hat flying into the air, and cried out in a voice that not even my memory could fail to recognize,—

"By the rock of Cashel he's cured, he's cured!—the fever's over. Oh, Master Charles, dear! oh, master, darling! and you ain't mad, after all ?"

"Mad! no, faith! but I shrewdly suspect you must be."

"Oh, devil a taste! But spake to me, honey—spake to me, acushla."

"Where am I? Whose house is this? What do you mean by that disguise—that beard ——"

"Whisht! I'll tell you all, av you have patience. But are you cured ?—tell me that first. Sure they was going to cut the arm off you, till you got out of bed, and with your pistols sent them flying, one out of the window and the other down stairs; and I myself bate the little chap with the saw till he couldn't know himself in the glass."

While Mike ran on at this rate, I never took my eyes from him, and it was all my poor faculties were equal to, to convince myself that the whole scene was not some vision of a wandering intellect. Gradually, however, the well-known features recalled me to myself,

30

and as my doubts gave way at length, I laughed long and heartily at the masquerade absurdity of his appearance.

Mike, meanwhile, whose face expressed no small mistrust at the sincerity of my mirth, having uncloaked himself, proceeded to lay aside his beard and moustaches, saying, as he did so,—

"There now, darlin'! there now, master dear! Don't be grinnin' that way; I'll not be a Portigee any more av you'll be quiet and listen to reason."

"But, Mike, where am I? Answer me that question."

"You're at home, dear; where else would you be?"

"At home," said I, with a start, as my eye ranged over the various articles of luxury and elegance around, so unlike the more simple and unpretending features of my uncle's house—"at home!"

"Ay, just so; sure, isn't it the same thing? It's ould Don Emanuel that owns it; and won't it be your own when you're married to that lovely crayture herself?"

I started up, and placing my hand upon my throbbing temple, asked myself if I were really awake, or if some flight of fancy had not carried me away beyond the bounds of reason and sense. "Go on, go on!" said I, at length, in a hollow voice, anxious to gather from his words something like a clue to this mystery. "How did this happen?"

"Av ye mean how you came here, faith, it was just this way: After you got the fever, and bate the doctors, devil a one would go near you but myself and the Major."

"The Major—Major Monsoon?"

"No; Major Power himself. Well, he tould your friends up here how it was going very hard with you, and that you were like to die, and the same evening they sent down a beautiful litter, as like a hearse as two peas, for you, and brought you up here in state; devil a thing was wanting but a few people to raise the cry to make it as fine a funeral as ever I seen; and sure I set up a whillilew myself in the Black Horse square, and the devils only laughed at me.

"Well, you see they put you into a beautiful, elegant bed, and the young lady herself sat down beside you, between times fanning you with a big fan, and then drying her eyes, for she was weeping like a waterfall. 'Don Miguel,' says she to me,—for, ye see, I put your cloak on by mistake when I was leaving the quarters,—'Don Miguel, questa hidalgo é vostros amigo?'

"'My most particular friend,' says I; 'God spare him many years to be so.'

"'Then take up your quarters here,' said she, 'and don't leave him; we'll do everything in our power to make him comfortable.'

"'I'm not particular,' says I; 'the run of the house——'"

"Then this is the Villa Nuova?" said I, with a faint sigh.

"The same," replied Mike; "and a sweet place it is for eating and drinking—for wine in bucketfuls, av ye axed for it,—for dancing and singing every evening, with as pretty craytures as ever I set eyes upon. Upon my conscience, it's as good as Galway; and good manners it is they have. What's more, none of your liberties nor familiarities with strangers, but it's Don Miguel, devil a less. 'Don Miguel, av it's plazing to you to take a drop of Xeres before your meat?'—or, 'Would you have a shaugh of a pipe or cigar when you're done?' That's the way of it."

"And Sir George Dashwood," said I, "has he been here? has he inquired for me?"

"Every day, either himself or one of the staff comes galloping up at luncheon-time to ask after you; and then they have a bit of tender discourse with the Senhora herself. Oh! devil a bit need ye fear them, she's true blue; and it isn't the Major's fault,—upon my conscience it isn't; for he does be coming the blarney over her in beautiful style."

"Does Miss Dashwood ever visit here?" said I, with a voice faltering and uncertain enough to have awakened suspicion in a more practised observer.

"Never once; and that's what I call unnatural behavior, after you saving her life; and if she wasn't——"

"Be silent, I say."

"Well—well, there; I won't say any more; and sure it's time for me to be putting on my beard again. I'm going to the Casino with Catrina, and sure it's with real ladies I might be going av it wasn't for Major Power, that told them I wasn't an officer; but it's all right again. I gave them a great history of the Frees, from the time of Cuila na Toole, that was one of the family, and a cousin of Moses, I believe! and they behave well to one that comes from the ould stock."

"Don Miguel! Don Miguel!" said a voice from the garden.

"I'm coming, my angel! I'm coming, my turtle-dove!" said Mike, arranging his moustache and beard with amazing dexterity. "Ah, but it would do your heart good av you could take a peep at us about twelve o'clock, dancing 'Dirty James' for a bolero, and just see Miss Catrina, the lady's maid, doing 'Cover the Buckle' as neat as nature. There, now, there's the lemonade near your hand, and I'll leave you the lamp, and you may go asleep as soon as you please, for Miss Inez won't come in to-night to play the guitar, for the doctor said it might do you harm now."

So saying, and before I could summon presence of mind to ask another question, Don Miguel wrapped himself in the broad folds of his Spanish cloak, and strode from the room with the air of an hidalgo.

I slept little that night; a full tide of memory rushing in upon me, brought back the hour of my return to Lisbon and the wreck of all my hopes, which, from the narrative of my servant, I now perceived to be complete. I dare not venture upon recording how many plans suggested themselves to my troubled spirit, and were in turn rejected. To meet Lucy Dashwood—to make a full and candid declaration—to acknowledge that flirtation alone with Donna Inez—a mere passing, boyish flirtation—had given the coloring to my innocent passion, and that in heart and soul I was hers and hers only—this was my first resolve; but, alas! if I had not courage to sustain a common interview, to meet her in the careless crowd of a drawing-room, what could I do under circumstances like these? Besides, the matter would be cut very short by her coolly declaring that she had neither right nor inclination to listen to such a declaration. The recollection of her look as she passed me to her carriage came flashing across my brain, and decided this point. No, no! I'll not encounter that; however appearances for the moment had been against me, she should not have treated me thus coldly and disdainfully. It was quite clear she had never cared for me; wounded pride had been her only feeling. As I reasoned, I ended by satisfying myself that in that quarter all was at an end forever.

Now, then, for dilemma number two, I thought. The Senhora— my first impulse was one of anything but gratitude to her, by whose kind, tender care my hours of pain and suffering had been soothed and alleviated. But for her, I should have been spared all my present embarrassment—all my shipwrecked fortunes; but for her, I should now be the aide-de-camp residing in Sir George Dashwood's own house, meeting with Lucy every hour of the day, dining beside her, riding out with her, pressing my suit by every means and with every advantage of my position; but for her and her dark eyes—and, by-the-by, what eyes they are!—how full of brilliancy, yet how teeming with an expression of soft and melting sweetness; and her mouth, too, how perfectly chiselled those full lips—how different from the cold, unbending firmness of Miss Dashwood's— not but I have seen Lucy smile too, and what a sweet smile!—how it lighted up her fair cheek, and made her blue eyes darken and deepen till they looked like heaven's own vault. Yes, there is more poetry in a blue eye. But still Inez is a very lovely girl, and her foot never was surpassed; she is a coquette, too, about that foot and ankle—I rather like a woman to be so. What a sensation she would make in England—how she would be the rage! And then I thought of home and Galway, and the astonishment of some, the admiration

of others, as I presented her as my wife; the congratulations of my
friends, the wonder of the men, the tempered envy of the women.
Methought I saw my uncle, as he pressed her in his arms, say,
"Yes, Charley, this is a prize worth campaigning for."

The stray sounds of a guitar which came from the garden broke
in upon my musings at this moment. It seemed as if a finger was
straying heedlessly across the strings. I started up, and to my surprise perceived it was Inez. Before I had time to collect myself, a
gentle tap at the window aroused me; it opened softly, while from
an unseen hand a bouquet of fresh flowers was thrown upon my
bed; before I could collect myself to speak, the sash closed again
and I was alone.

CHAPTER XVI.

THE VISIT.

MIKE'S performances at the masquerade had doubtless been of
the most distinguished character, and demanded a compen-
sating period of repose, for he did not make his appearance
the entire morning. Towards noon, however, the door from the
garden gently opened, and I heard a step upon the stone terrace, and
something which sounded to my ears like the clank of a sabre. I
lifted my head, and saw Fred Power beside me.

I shall spare my readers the recital of my friend, which, however
full and explanatory of past events, contained in reality little more
than Mickey Free had already told me. In fine, he informed me
that our army, by a succession of retreating movements, had deserted
the northern provinces, and now occupied the entrenched lines of
Torres Vedras. Massena, with a powerful force, was still in march,
reinforcements pouring in upon him, and every expectation pointing to the probability that he would attempt to storm our position.

"The wise-heads," remarked Power, "talk of our speedy embarkation—the sanguine and the hot-brained rave of a great victory, and
the retreat of Massena; but I was up at head-quarters last week
with despatches, and saw Lord Wellington myself."

"Well, what did you make out? Did he drop any hint of his
own views?"

"Faith, I can't say he did. He asked me some questions about
the troops just landed—he spoke a little of the commissary department—cursed the blankets—said that the green forage was bad for
the artillery horses—sent me an English paper to read about the

O. P. riots, said the harriers would throw off about six o'clock, and that he hoped to see me at dinner."

I could not restrain a laugh at Power's catalogue of his lordship's topics. "So," said I, "he at least does not take any gloomy views of our present situation."

"Who can tell what he thinks? He's ready to fight, if fighting will do anything—and to retreat, if that be better. But that he'll sleep an hour less, or drink a glass of claret more—come what will of it—I'll believe from no man living.

"We've lost one gallant thing in any case, Charley," resumed Power. "Busaco was, I'm told, a glorious day, and our people were in the heat of it. So that if we do leave the Peninsula now, that will be a confounded chagrin. Not for you, my poor fellow, for you could not stir; but I was so cursed foolish to take the staff appointment: thus one folly ever entails another."

There was a tone of bitterness in which these words were uttered that left no doubt upon my mind some *arrière pensée* remained lurking behind them. My eyes met his—he bit his lip, colored deeply, rose from the chair, and walked towards the window.

The chance allusion of my man Mike flashed upon me at the moment, and I dared not trust myself to break silence. I now thought I could trace in my friend's manner less of that gay and careless buoyancy which ever marked him. There was a tone, it seemed, of more grave and sombre character, and even when he jested, the smile his features bore was not his usual frank and happy one, and speedily gave way to an expression I had never before remarked. Our silence, which had now lasted for some minutes, was becoming embarrassing—that strange consciousness that, to a certain extent, we were reading each other's thoughts, made us both cautious of breaking it; and when, at length, turning abruptly round, he asked, "When I hoped to be up and about again?" I felt my heart relieved from what I knew not well what load of doubt and difficulty that oppressed it. We chatted on for some little time longer, the news of Lisbon and the daily gossip finishing our topics.

"Plenty of gayety, Charley! dinners and balls to no end! so get well, my boy, and make the most of it."

"Yes," I replied, "I'll do my best; but be assured the first use I'll make of health will be to join the regiment. I am heartily ashamed of myself for all I have lost already—though not altogether my fault."

"And will you really join at once?" said Power, with a look of eager anxiety I could not possibly account for.

"Of course I will; what have I, what can I have, to detain me here?"

What reply he was about to make at this moment I know not, but the door opened, and Mike announced Sir George Dashwood.

"Gently! my worthy man, not so loud, if you please!" said the mild voice of the General, as he stepped noiselessly across the room, evidently shocked at the indiscreet tone of my follower. "Ah, Power, you here! and our poor friend, how is he?"

"Able to answer for himself at last, Sir George," said I, grasping his proffered hand.

"My poor lad! you've had a long bout of it; but you've saved your arm, and that's well worth the lost time. Well, I've come to bring you good news; there's been a very sharp cavalry affair, and our fellows have been the conquerors."

"There again, Power—listen to that! We are losing everything!"

"Not so, not so, my boy," said Sir George, smiling blandly, but archly. "There are conquests to be won here as well as there, and, in your present state, I rather think you better fitted for such as these."

Power's brow grew clouded; he essayed a smile, but it failed, and he rose and hurried towards the window.

As for me, my confusion must have led to a very erroneous impression of my real feelings, and I perceived Sir George anxious to turn the channel of the conversation.

"You see but little of your host, O'Malley," he resumed; "he is ever from home; but I believe nothing could be kinder than his arrangements for you. You are aware that he kidnapped you from us? I had sent Forbes over to bring you to us, your room was prepared, everything in readiness, when we met your man Mike, setting forth upon a mule, who told us you had just taken your departure for the villa. We both had a claim upon you, and, I believe, pretty much on the same score. By the bye, you have not seen Lucy since your arrival. I never knew it till yesterday, when I asked if she did not find you altered."

I blundered out some absurd reply, blushed, corrected myself, and got confused. Sir George, attributing this, doubtless, to my weak state, rose soon after, and, taking Power along with him, remarked, as he left the room,

"We are too much for him yet, I see that; so we'll leave him quiet some time longer."

Thanking him in my heart for his true appreciation of my state, I sank back upon my pillow to think over all I had heard and seen.

"Well, Mister Charles," said Mike, as he came forward with a smile, "I suppose you heard the news? The 14th bate the French down at Merca there, and took seventy prisoners; but, sure, it's little good it'll do, after all."

"And why not, Mike?"

"Musha! isn't Boney coming himself? He's bringing all the Roossians down with him, and going to destroy us entirely."

"Not at all, man; you mistake. He's nothing to do with Russia, and has quite enough on his hands at this moment."

"God grant it was truth you were talking! But, you see, I read it myself in the papers,—or Sergeant Haggarty did, which is the same thing,—that he's coming with the Cusacks."

"With who?—with what?"

"With the Cusacks."

"What the devil do you mean? Who are they?"

"Oh, Tower of Ivory! did you never hear of the Cusacks, with the red beards, and the red breeches, and long poles with pike-heads on them, that does all the devilment on horseback—piking and spitting the people like larks."

"The Cossacks is it, you mean? The Cossacks?"

"Ay, just so, the Cusacks. They're from Clare Island, and thereabouts; and there's more of them in Meath. They're my mother's people, and always was real devils for fighting."

I burst out into an immoderate fit of laughing at Mike's etymology, which thus converted Hetman Platoff into a Galway man.

"Oh, murder! isn't it cruel to hear you laugh that way! There now, alanna! be aisy, and I'll tell you more news. We've the house to ourselves to-day. The ould gentleman's down at Behlem, and the daughter's in Lisbon, making great preparations for a grand ball they're to give when you are quite well."

"I hope I shall be with the army in a few days, Mike; and certainly, if I'm able to move about, I'll not remain longer in Lisbon."

"Arrah! don't say so now! When was you ever so comfortable? Upon my conscience, it's more like Paradise than anything else. If ye see the dinner we set down to every day! and, as for drink— if it wasn't that I sleep on the ground-floor, I'd seldom see a blanket."

"Well, certainly, Mike, I agree with you, these are hard things to tear ourselves away from."

"Aren't they now, sir? And then Miss Catherine, I'm taching her Irish!"

"Teaching her Irish! for Heaven's sake, what use can she make of Irish?"

"Ah, the crayture, she doesn't know better; and as she was always bothering me to learn her English, I promised one day to do it; but ye see, somehow, I never was very proficient in strange tongues; so I thought to myself Irish will do as well. So, you perceive, we're taking a coorse of Irish literature, as Mr. Lynch says in Athlone; and, upon my conscience, she's an apt scholar."

"'Good-morning to you, Katey,' says Mr. Power to her the other day, as he passed through the hall. 'Good-morning, my dear! I hear you speak English perfectly now?'

"'*Honia mon diaoul*,' says she, making a curtsey.

"Be the powers, I thought he'd die with the laughing.

"'Well, my dear, I hope you don't mean it—do you know what you're saying?'

"'Honor bright, Major!' says I—'honor bright!' and I gave him a wink at the same time.

"'Oh, that's it!' said he, 'is it?' and so he went off holding his hands to his sides with the bare laughing; and your honor knows it wasn't a blessing she wished him for all that."

CHAPTER XVII.

THE CONFESSION.

WHAT a strange position this of mine!" thought I, a few mornings after the events detailed in the last chapter. "How very fascinating in some respects, how full of all the charm of romance, and how confoundedly difficult to see one's way through."

To understand my cogitation right, *figurez vous*, my dear reader, a large and splendidly-furnished drawing-room, from one end of which an orangery in full blossom opens; from the other is seen a delicious little boudoir, where books, bronzes, pictures and statues, in all the artistic disorder of a lady's sanctum, are bathed in a deep purple light from a stained-glass window of the seventeenth century.

At a small table beside the wood fire, whose mellow light is flirting with the sunbeams upon the carpet, stands an antique silver breakfast service, which none but the hand of Benvenuto could have chiselled; beside it sits a girl, young and beautiful; her dark eyes, beaming beneath their long lashes, are fixed with an expression of watchful interest upon a pale and sickly youth, who, lounging upon a sofa opposite, is carelessly turning over the leaves of a new journal, or gazing steadfastly on the fretted gothic of the ceiling, while his thoughts are travelling many a mile away,—the lady being the Senhora Inez; the nonchalant invalid, your unworthy acquaintance, Charles O'Malley.

What a very strange position, to be sure!

"Then you are not equal to this ball to-night?" said she, after a pause of some minutes.

I turned as she spoke; her words had struck audibly upon my ear, but, lost in my reverie, I could but repeat my own fixed thought—how strange to be so situated!

"You are really very tiresome, Signor; I assure you, you are. I have been giving you a most elegant description of the Casino fête, and the beautiful costumes of our Lisbon belles, but I can get nothing from you but this muttered something, which may be very shocking, for aught I know. I'm sure your friend Major Power would be much more attentive to me; that is," added she, archly, "if Miss Dashwood were not present."

"What—why—you don't mean that there is anything there—that Power is paying attention to——"

"*Madre divina*, how that seems to interest you, and how red you are! If it were not that you never met her before, and that your acquaintance did not seem to make rapid progress, then I should say you are in love with her yourself."

I had to laugh at this, but felt my face flushing more. "And so," said I, affecting a careless and indifferent tone, "the gay Fred Power is smitten at last!"

"Was it so very difficult a thing to accomplish?" said she, slyly.

"He seems to say so, at least. And the lady, how does she appear to receive his attentions?"

"Oh, I should say with evident pleasure and satisfaction, as all girls do the advances of men they don't care for, nor intend to care for."

"Indeed," said I, slowly; "indeed, Senhora?" looking into her eyes as I spoke, as if to read if the lesson were destined for my benefit.

"There, don't stare so!—every one knows that."

"So you don't think, then, that Lucy—I mean Miss Dashwood,—why are you laughing so?"

"How can I help it? your calling her Lucy is so good, I wish she heard it; she's the very proudest girl I ever knew."

"But to come back; you really think she does not care for him?"

"Not more than for you; and I may be pardoned for the simile, having seen your meeting. But let me give you the news of our own fête. Saturday is the day fixed; and you must be quite well—I insist upon it. Miss Dashwood has promised to come—no small concession; for, after all, she has never once been here since the day you frightened her. I can't help laughing at my blunder—the two people I had promised myself should fall desperately in love with each other, and who will scarcely meet."

"But I trusted," said I, pettishly, "that you were not disposed to resign your own interest in me?"

"Neither was I," said she, with an easy smile, "except that I have so many admirers. I might even spare you to my friends; though, after all, I should be sorry to lose you—I like you."

"Yes," said I, half bitterly, "as girls do those they never intend to care for; is it not so?"

"Perhaps yes, and perhaps——But is it going to rain? How provoking! and I have ordered my horse. Well, Signor Carlos, I leave you to your delightful newspaper, and all the magnificent descriptions of battles, and sieges, and skirmishes for which you seem doomed to pine without ceasing. There, don't kiss my hand twice; that's not right."

"Well, let me begin again——"

"I shall not breakfast with you any more; but, tell me, am I to order a costume for you in Lisbon; or will you arrange all that yourself? You must come to the fête, you know."

"If you would be so very kind."

"I will, then, be so very kind; and, once more, *adios*." So saying, with a slight motion of her hand, she smiled a good-bye, and left me.

"What a lovely girl!" thought I, as I rose and walked to the window, muttering to myself Othello's line,—

"When I love thee not, chaos is come again."

In fact, it was the perfect expression of my feeling—the only solution to all the difficulties surrounding me, being to fall desperately, irretrievably in love with the fair Senhora, which, all things considered, was not a very desperate resource for a gentleman in trouble. As I thought over the hopelessness of one attachment, I turned calmly to consider the favorable points of the other. She was truly beautiful, attractive in every sense; her manner most fascinating, and her disposition, so far as I could pronounce, perfectly amiable. I felt already something more than interest about her; how very easy would be the transition to a stronger feeling! There was an *éclat*, too, about being her accepted lover that had its charm. She was the belle *par excellence* of Lisbon; and then a sense of pique crossed my mind as I reflected, what would Lucy say of him whom she had slighted and insulted, when he became the husband of the beautiful and millionaire Senhora Inez?

As my meditations had reached thus far, the door opened stealthily, and Catherine appeared, her finger upon her lips, and her gesture indicating caution. She carried on her arm a mass of drapery covered by a large mantle, which throwing off as she entered, she displayed before me a rich blue domino with silver embroidery. It was large and loose in its folds, so as thoroughly to conceal the figure of any wearer. This she held up before me for an instant without speaking; when at length, seeing my curiosity fully excited, she said,—

"This is the Senhora's domino. I should be ruined if she knew I showed it; but I promised—that is, I told——"

"Yes, yes, I understand," relieving her embarrassment about the source of her civilities; "go on."

"Well, there are several others like it, but with this small difference, instead of a carnation, which all the others have embroidered upon the cuff, I have made it a rose—you perceive? La Senhora knows nothing of this—no one save yourself knows it. I'm sure I may trust you with the secret."

"Fear not in the least, Catherine; you have rendered me a great service. Let me look at it once more; ah! there's no difficulty in detecting it.   And you are certain she is unaware of it?"

"Perfectly so; she has several other costumes, but in this one I know she intends some surprise, so be upon your guard."

With these words, once more carefully concealing the rich dress beneath the mantle, she withdrew, while I strolled forth to wonder what mystery might lie beneath this scheme, and speculate how far I myself was included in the plot she spoke of.

*   *   *   *   *   *   *   *

For the few days which succeeded, I passed my time much alone. The Senhora was but seldom at home, and I remarked that Power rarely came to see me. A strange feeling of half-coolness had latterly grown between us, and instead of the open confidence we formerly indulged in when together, we appeared now rather to chat over things of mere every-day interest than of our own immediate plans and prospects. There was a kind of pre-occupation, too, in his manner that struck me; his mind seemed ever straying from the topics he talked of to something remote, and, altogether, he was no longer the frank and reckless dragoon I had ever known him. What could be the meaning of this change? Had he found out by any accident that I was to blame in my conduct towards Lucy—had any erroneous impression of my interview with her reached his ears? This was most improbable; besides, there was nothing in that to draw down his censure or condemnation, however represented; or was it that he was himself in love with her—that, devoted heart and soul to Lucy, he regarded me as a successful rival, preferred before him! Oh, how could I have so long blinded myself to the fact! This was the true solution of the whole difficulty. I had more than once suspected this to be so; now all the circumstances of proof poured in upon me. I called to mind his agitated manner the night of my arrival in Lisbon—his thousand questions concerning the reasons of my furlough; and then, lately, the look of unfeigned pleasure with which he heard me resolve to join my regiment the moment I was sufficiently recovered. I also remembered how assiduously he pressed his intimacy with the Senhora, Lucy's dearest friend here; his continual visits at the villa; those long walks in the garden, where his very look betokened some confidential mission of the heart. Yes, there was no doubt of it—he loved Lucy Dashwood! Alas! there seemed to be no end to the complication of my misfortunes; one by one, I appeared fated to lose whatever had a hold upon my affections, and to stand alone, unloved and uncared for in the world. My thoughts turned towards the Senhora, but I could not deceive myself into any hope there. My own feelings were untouched, and hers I felt to be equally so. Young as I was, there was no mistaking the easy smile of coquetry, the merry laugh of flattered vanity, for a deeper and holier feeling. And then I did not wish it otherwise. One only had taught me to feel how ennobling, how elevating, in all its impulses can be a deep-rooted passion for a young and beautiful girl! From her eyes alone had I caught the inspiration—that made me pant for glory and distinction. I could not transfer the allegiance of my heart, since it had taught that very heart to beat high and proudly. Lucy, lost to me forever as she must be, was still more than any other woman ever could be. All the past clung to her memory, all the prestige of the future must point to it also.

And Power, why had he not trusted—why had he not confided in me? Was this like my old and tried friend? Alas! I was forgetting that in his eyes I was the favored rival, and not the despised, rejected suitor.

"It is past now," thought I, as I rose and walked into the garden; "the dream that made life a fairy tale is dispelled; the cold reality of the world is before me, and my path lies a lonely and solitary one." My first resolution was to see Power, and relieve his mind of any uneasiness as regarded my pretensions; they existed no longer. As for me, I was no obstacle to his happiness; it was, then, but fair and honorable that I should tell him so; this done, I should leave Lisbon at once. The cavalry had for the most part been ordered to the rear; still there was always something going forward at the outposts.

The idea of active service, the excitement of a campaigning life, cheered me, and I advanced along the dark alley of the garden with a lighter and a freer heart. My resolves were not destined to meet delay. As I turned the angle of a walk, Power was before me. He was leaning against a tree, his hands crossed upon his bosom, his head bowed forward, and his whole air and attitude betokening deep reflection.

He started as I came up, and seemed almost to change color.

"Well, Charley," said he, after a moment's pause; "you look better this morning. How goes the arm?"

"The arm is ready for service again, and its owner most anxious for it. Do you know, Fred, I'm thoroughly weary of this life."

"They're little better, however, at the lines. The French are in position, but never venture a movement; and, except some few affairs at the pickets, there is really nothing to do."

"No matter; remaining here can never serve one's interests; and besides, I have accomplished what I came for——"

I was about to add, "the restoration of my health," when he suddenly interrupted me, eyeing me fixedly as he spoke.

"Indeed! indeed! Is that so?"·

"Yes," said I, half puzzled at the tone and manner of the speech; "I can join now when I please; meanwhile, Fred, I have been thinking of you. Yes, don't be surprised; at the very moment we met, you were in my thoughts."

I took his arm as I said this, and led him down the alley.·

"We are too old, and, I trust, too true friends, Fred, to have secrets from each other, and yet we have been playing this silly game for some weeks past. Now, my dear fellow, I have yours, and it is only fair justice you should have mine, and, faith, I feel you'd have discovered it long since, had your thoughts been as free as I have known them to be. Fred, you are in love. There, don't wince, man—I know it; but hear me out. You believe me to be so also; nay, more, you think that my chances of success are better, stronger than your own. Learn, then, that I have none—absolutely none. Don't interrupt me now, for this avowal cuts me deeply; my own heart alone knows what I suffer as I record my wrecked fortunes. But I repeat it, my hopes are at an end forever; but, Fred, my boy, I cannot lose my friend too. If I have been the obstacle to your path, I am so no more. Ask me not why; it is enough that I speak in all truth and sincerity. Ere three days I shall leave this, and with it all the hopes that once beamed upon my fortunes, and all the happiness,—nay, not all, my boy, for I feel some thrill at my heart yet, as I think that I have been true to you."

I know not what more I spoke, nor how he replied to me. I felt the warm grasp of his hand, I saw his delighted smile; the words of grateful acknowledgment his lips uttered conveyed but an imperfect meaning to my ear, and I remembered no more.

The courage which sustained me for the moment sank gradually as I meditated over my avowal, and I could scarce help accusing Power of a breach of friendship for exacting a confession which, in reality, I had volunteered to give him. How Lucy herself would think of my conduct was ever recurring to my thoughts, and I felt, as I ruminated upon the conjectures it might give rise to, how much more likely a favorable opinion might now be formed of me than when such an estimation could have crowned me with delight.

"Yes," thought I; "she will at last learn to know him who loved her with truth and with devoted affection; and when the blight of all his hopes is accomplished, the fair fame of his fidelity will be proved. The march, the bivouac, the battle-field, are now all to me, and the campaign alone presents a prospect which may fill up the aching void that disappointed and ruined hopes have left behind them."

How I longed for the loud call of the trumpet, the clash of the steel, the tramp of the war-horse, though the proud distinction of a soldier's life was less to me in the distance than the mad and whirlwind passion of a charge, and the loud din of the rolling artillery.

It was only some hours after, as I sat alone in my chamber, that all the circumstances of our meeting came back clearly to my memory, and I could not help muttering to myself: "It is indeed a hard lot, that to cheer the heart of my friend, I must bear witness to the despair that sheds darkness on my own."

CHAPTER XVIII.

MY CHARGER.

ALTHOUGH I felt my heart relieved of a heavy load by the confession I had made to Power, yet still I shrank from meeting him for some days after; a kind of fear lest he should in any way recur to our conversation continually beset me, and I felt that the courage which bore me up for my first effort would desert me on the next occasion.

My determination to join my regiment was now made up, and I sent forward a resignation of my appointment to Sir George Dashwood's staff, which I had never been in health to fulfil, and commenced with energy all my preparations for a speedy departure.

The reply to my rather formal letter was a most kind note written by himself. He regretted the unhappy cause which had so long separated us, and though wishing, as he expressed it, to have me near him, perfectly approved of my resolution.

"Active service alone, my dear boy, can ever place you in the position you ought to occupy, and I rejoice the more at your decision in this matter, as I feared the truth of certain reports here, which attributed to you other plans than those which a campaign suggests. My mind is now easy on this score, and I pray you forgive me if my congratulations are *mal à propos.*"

After some hints for my future management, and a promise of some letters to his friends at head-quarters, he concluded :—

"As this climate does not seem to suit my daughter, I have applied for a change, and am in daily hope of obtaining it. Before going, however, I must beg your acceptance of the charger which my groom will deliver to your servant with this. I was so struck with his figure and action, that I purchased him before leaving England, without well knowing why or wherefore. Pray let him see some service under your auspices, which he is most unlikely to do under mine. He has plenty of bone to be a weight-carrier, and they tell me also that he has speed enough for anything."

Mike's voice in the lawn beneath interrupted my reading further, and on looking out I perceived him and Sir George Dashwood's servant standing beside a large and striking-looking horse, which they were both examining with all the critical accuracy of adepts.

"Arrah, isn't he a darling, a real beauty, every inch of him ?"

" That 'ere splint don't signify nothing, he aren't the worse of it," said the English groom.

"Of coorse it doesn't," replied Mike. "What a forehand! and the legs, clean as a whip."

"There's the best of him, though," interrupted the other, patting the strong hind-quarters with his hand. "There's the stuff to push him along through heavy ground and carry him over timber."

" Or a stone wall," said Mike, thinking of Galway.

My own impatience to survey my present had now brought me into the conclave, and before many minutes were over I had him saddled, and was cantering around the lawn with a spirit and energy I had not felt for months long. Some small fences lay before me, and over these he carried me with all the ease and freedom of a trained hunter. My courage mounted with the excitement, and I looked eagerly around for some more bold and dashing leap.

"You may take him over the avenue gate," said the English groom, divining with a jockey's readiness what I looked for; " he'll do it, never fear him."

Strange as my equipment was, with an undress jacket flying

loosely open, and a bare head, away I went. The gate which the groom spoke of was a strongly barred one of oak timber, nearly five feet high—its difficulty as a leap only consisted in the winding approach, and the fact that it opened upon a hard road beyond it.

In a second or two a kind of half fear came across me. My long illness had unnerved me, and my limbs felt weak and yielding; but as I pressed into the canter, that secret sympathy between the horse and his rider shot suddenly through me, I pressed my spurs to his flanks, and dashed him at it.

Unaccustomed to such treatment, the noble animal bounded madly forward; with two tremendous plunges he sprang wildly in the air, and shaking his long mane with passion, stretched out at the gallop.

My own blood boiled now as tempestuously as his; and, with a shout of reckless triumph, I rose him at the gate. Just at the instant two figures appeared before it—the copse had concealed their approach hitherto—but they stood now, as if transfixed; the wild attitude of the horse, the not less wild cry of its rider, had deprived them for a time of all energy; and, overcome by the sudden danger, they seemed rooted to the ground. What I said, spoke, begged, or imprecated, Heaven knows—not I. But they stirred not! One moment more and they must lie trampled beneath my horse's hoofs—he was already on his haunches for the bound; when, wheeling half aside, I faced him at the wall. It was at least a foot higher, and of solid stone masonry, and as I did so, I felt I was perilling my life to save theirs. One vigorous dash of the spur I gave him, as I lifted him to the leap—he bounded beneath it quick as lightning—still, with a spring like a rocket, he rose into the air, cleared the wall, and stood trembling and frightened on the road outside.

"Safe, by Jupiter! and splendidly done too," cried a voice near me, that I immediately recognized as Sir George Dashwood's.

"Lucy, my love, look up—Lucy, my dear, there's no danger now. She has fainted. O'Malley, fetch some water—fast. Poor fellow—your own nerves seem shaken. Why, you've let your horse go! Come here, for Heaven's sake!—support her for an instant. I'll fetch some water."

It appeared to me like a dream—I leaned against the pillar of the gate—the cold and death-like features of Lucy Dashwood lay motionless upon my arm—her hand, falling heavily upon my shoulder, touched my cheek—the tramp of my horse, as he galloped onward, was the only sound that broke the silence, as I stood there, gazing steadfastly upon the pale brow and paler cheek, down which a solitary tear was slowly stealing. I knew not how the minutes passed—my memory took no note of time; but at length a gentle tremor

31

thrilled her frame, a slight, scarce-perceptible blush colored her fair face, her lips slightly parted, and heaving a deep sigh, she looked around her. Gradually her eyes turned and met mine. Oh, the bliss unutterable of that moment. It was no longer the look of cold scorn she had given me last—the expression was one of soft and speaking gratitude. She seemed to read my very heart, and know its truth; there was a tone of deep and compassionate interest in the glance; and forgetting all—everything that had passed—all save my unaltered, unalterable love, I kneeled beside her, and, in words burning as my own heart burned, poured out my tale of mingled sorrow and affection with all the eloquence of passion. I vindicated my unshaken faith—reconciling the conflicting evidences with the proofs I proffered of my attachment. If my moments were measured, I spent them not idly; I called to witness how every action of my soldier's life emanated from her—how her few and chance words had decided the character of my fate—if aught of fame or honor were my portion, to her I owed it. As, hurried onward by my ardent hopes, I forgot Power and all about him—a step up the gravel walk came rapidly nearer, and I had but time to assume my former attitude beside Lucy as her father came up.

"Well, Charley, is she better? Oh, I see she is. Here we have the whole household at our heels." So saying, he pointed to a string of servants pressing eagerly forward with every species of restorative that Portuguese ingenuity has invented.

The next moment we were joined by the Senhora, who, pale with fear, seemed scarcely less in need of assistance than her friend.

Amid questions innumerable—explanations sought for on all sides—mistakes and misconceptions as to the whole occurrence—we took our way towards the villa, Lucy walking between Sir George and Donna Inez, while I followed, leaning upon Power's arm.

"They've caught him again, O'Malley," said the General, turning half round to me; he, too, seemed as much frightened as any of us.

"It is time, Sir George, I should think of thanking you. I never was so mounted in my life——"

"A splendid charger, by Jove!" said Power; "but, Charley, my lad, no more feats of this nature, if you love me. No girl's heart will stand such continued assaults as your winning horsemanship submits it to."

I was about making some half-angry reply, when he continued:

"There, don't look sulky; I have news for you. Quill has just arrived; I met him at Lisbon. He has got leave of absence for a few days, and is coming to our masquerade here this evening."

"This evening!" said I, in amazement; "why, is it so soon?"

"Of course it is. Have you not got all your trappings ready? The Dashwoods came out here on purpose to spend the day. But come, I'll drive you into town. My tilbury is ready, and we'll both look out for our costumes." So saying, he led me along towards the house, when, after a rapid change of my toilet, we set out for Lisbon.

CHAPTER XIX.

MAURICE.

IT seemed a conceded matter between Power and myself that we should never recur to the conversation we held in the garden, and so, although we dined *tête à tête* that day, neither of us ventured, by any allusion the most distant, to what it was equally evident was uppermost in the minds of both.

All our endeavors, therefore, to seem easy and unconcerned were in vain; a restless anxiety to seem interested about things and persons we were totally indifferent to pervaded all our essays at conversation. By degrees we grew weary of the parts we were acting, and each relapsed into a moody silence, thinking over his plans and projects, and totally forgetting the existence of the other.

The decanter was passed across the table without speaking, a half nod intimated that the bottle was standing, and except an occasional malediction upon an intractable cigar, nothing was heard.

Such was the agreeable occupation we were engaged in, when, towards nine o'clock, the door opened, and the great Maurice himself stood before us.

"Pleasant fellows, upon my conscience, and jovial over their liquor! Confound your smoking! That may do very well in a bivouac. Let us have something warm!"

Quill's interruption was a most welcome one to both parties, and we rejoiced with a sincere pleasure at his coming.

"What shall it be, Maurice? Port or sherry mulled, and an anchovy?"

"Or what say you to a bowl of bishop?" said I.

"Hurrah for the Church, Charley! Let us have the bishop; and not to disparage Fred's taste, we'll be eating the anchovy while the liquor's concocting."

"Well, Maurice, and now for the news. How are matters at Torres Vedras? Anything like movement in that quarter?"

"Nothing very remarkable. Massena made a reconnaissance

some days since, and one of our batteries threw a shower of grape among the staff, which spoiled the procession, and sent them back in very disorderly time.　Then we've had a few skirmishes to the front, with no great results, a few. courts-martial, bad grub, and plenty of grumbling."

"Why, what would they have?　It's a great thing to hold the French army in check within a few marches of Lisbon."

"Charley, my man, who cares twopence for the French army, or Lisbon, or the Portuguese, or the Junta, or anything about it?— every man is pondering over his own affairs.　One fellow wants to get home again and be sent upon some recruiting station.　Another wishes to get a step or two in promotion, to come to Torres Vedras, where even the *grande armée* can't.　Then some of us are in love, and some of us are in debt.　There is neither glory nor profit to be had.　But here's the bishop, smoking and steaming with an odor of nectar!"

"And our fellows, have you seen them lately?"

"I dined with yours on Tuesday.—Was it Tuesday?　Yes; I dined with them.　By the bye, Sparks was taken prisoner that morning."

"Sparks taken prisoner!　Poor fellow!　I am sincerely sorry. How did it happen, Maurice?"

"Very simply.　Sparks had a forage patrol towards Vieda, and set out early in the morning with his party.　It seemed that they succeeded perfectly, and were returning to the lines, when poor Sparks, always susceptible where the sex are concerned, saw, or thought he saw, a lattice gently open as he rode from the village, and a very taper finger make a signal to him.　Dropping a little behind the rest, he waited till the men had debouched upon the road, when, riding quietly up, he coughed a couple of times to attract the fair unknown; a handkerchief waved from the lattice in reply, which was speedily closed, and our valiant Cornet accordingly dismounted and entered the house.

"The remainder of the adventure is soon told, for in a few seconds after, two men mounted on one horse were seen galloping at top speed towards the French lines,—the foremost being a French officer of the 4th Cuirassiers—the gentleman with his face to the tail, our friend Sparks.　The lovely unknown was a *vieille moustache* of Loison's corps, who had been wounded in a skirmish some days before, and lay waiting an opportunity of rejoining his party.　One of our prisoners knew the fellow well; he had been promoted from the ranks, and was an Hercules for feats of strength; so that, after all, Sparks could not help himself."

"Well, I'm really sorry; but, as you say, Sparks's tender nature is always the ruin of him."

"Of him! ay, and of you, and of Power, and of myself—of all of us. Isn't it the sweet creatures that make fools of us from Father Adam down to Maurice Quill, neither sparing age nor rank in the service, half-pay, nor the Veteran Battalion—it's all one? Pass the jug, there. O'Shaughnessy ——"

"Ah, by the bye, how's the Major?"

"Charmingly; only a little bit in a scrape just now. Sir Arthur—Lord Wellington, I mean—had him up for his fellows being caught pillaging, and gave him a devil of a rowing a few days ago.

"'Very disorderly corps yours, Major O'Shaughnessy,' said the General; 'more men up for punishment than any regiment in the service.'

"Shaugh muttered something; but his voice was lost in a loud cock-a-doo-do-doo, that some bold chanticleer set up at the moment.

"'If the officers do their duty, Major O'Shaughnessy, these acts of insubordination do not occur.'

"'Cock-a-doo-do-doo,' was the reply. Some of the staff found it hard not to laugh; but the General went on:

"'If, therefore, the practice does not cease, I'll draft the men into West India regiments.'

"'Cock-a-doo-do-doo.'

"'And if any articles pillaged from the inhabitants are detected in the quarters, or about the person of the troops ——"

"'Cock-a-doo-do-doo,' screamed louder here than ever.

"'D— that cock. Where is it?'

"There was a general look around on all sides, which seemed in vain, when a tremendous repetition of the cry resounded from O'Shaughnessy's coat pocket, thus detecting the valiant Major himself in the very practice of his corps. There was no standing this. Every one burst out into a peal of laughing, and Lord Wellington himself could not resist, but turned away, muttering to himself as he went, 'D— robbers, every man of them!' while a final war-note from the Major's pocket closed the interview."

"Confound you, Maurice, you've always some villainous narrative or other. You never crossed a street for shelter without making something out of it."

"True this time, as sure as my name's Maurice; but the bowl is empty."

"Never mind; here comes its successor. How long can you stay amongst us?"

"A few days at most. Just took a run off to see the sights. I was all over Lisbon this morning; saw the Inquisition and the cells, and the place where they tried the fellows—the kind of grand jury

room, with the great picture of Adam and Eve at the end of it.
What a beautiful creature she is! hair down to her waist; and such
eyes! 'Ah, ye darling!' said I to myself, 'small blame to him for
what he did.   Wouldn't I ate every crab in the garden, if ye asked
me!'"

"I must certainly go see her, Maurice.   Is she very Portuguese
in her style?"

"Devil a bit of it. She might be a Limerick woman, with elegant
brown hair, and blue eyes, and a skin like snow."

"Come, come, they've pretty girls in Lisbon too, Doctor."

"Yes, faith," said Power, "that they have."

"Nothing like Ireland, boys—not a bit of it; they're the girls for
my money; and where's the man can resist them? From St. Patrick, that had to go and live in the Wicklow mountains——"

"St. Kevin, you mean, Doctor."

"Sure it's all the same, they were twins. I made a little song
about them one evening last week—the women, I mean."

"Let us have it, Maurice; let us have it, old fellow.   What's the
measure?"

"Short measure; four little verses—devil a more."

"But the time, I mean?"

"Whenever you like to sing it; here it is.   The air is 'Teddy ye
Gander.'"

"THE GIRLS OF THE WEST."

"You may talk, if you please,
Of the brown Portuguese,
But, wherever you roam, wherever you roam,
You nothing will meet
Half so lovely or sweet
As the girls at home, the girls at home.

"Their eyes are not sloes,
Nor so long is their nose,
But, between me and you, between me and you,
They are just as alarming,
And ten times more charming,
With hazel and blue, with hazel and blue.

"They don't ogle a man,
O'er the top of their fan,
'Till his heart's in a flame, his heart's in a flame;
But though bashful and shy,
They've a look in their eye,
That just comes to the same, just comes to the same.

"No mantillas they sport,
But a petticoat short
Shows an ankle the best, an ankle the best,
And a leg—but, O murther!
I dare not go further,
So here's to the West; so here's to the West."

"Now that really is a sweet little thing. Moore's, isn't it."

"Not a bit of it; my own muse, every word of it."

"And the music?" said I.

"My own, too. Too much spice in that bowl; that's an invariable error in your devisers of drink, to suppose that the tipple you start with can please your palate to the last; they forget that as we advance either in years or lush, our tastes simplify."

"*Nous revenons à nos premières amours.* Isn't that it?"

"No, not exactly, for we go even further; for if you mark the progression of a sensible man's fluids, you'll find what an emblem of life it presents to you. What is his initiatory glass of 'Chublis' that he throws down with his oysters but the budding expectancy of boyhood—the appetizing sense of pleasure to come; then follows the sherry with his soup, that warming glow which strength and vigor in all their consciousness impart, as a glimpse of life is opening before him. Then youth succeeds—buoyant, wild, tempestuous youth—foaming and sparkling, like the bright champagne, whose stormy surface subsides into a myriad of bright stars."

"*Œil de perdrix.*"

"Not a bit of it; woman's own eye; brilliant, sparkling, and life-giving——"

"Devil take the fellow, he's getting poetical."

"Ah, Fred! if that could only last; but one must come to the burgundies with his maturer years. Your first glass of hermitage is the algebraic sign for five-and-thirty—the glorious burst is over; the pace is still good, to be sure, but the great enthusiasm is past. You can afford to look forward, but, confound it, you've a long way to look back also."

"I say, Charley, our friend has contrived to finish the bishop during his disquisition ; the bowl's quite empty."

"You don't say so, Fred. To be sure, how a man does forget himself in abstract speculations; but let us have a little more—I've not concluded my homily."

"Not a glass, Maurice ; it's already past nine; we are all pledged to the masquerade ; before we've dressed and got there, 'twill be late."

"But I'm not disguised yet, my boy, nor half."

"Well, they must take you *au naturel*, as our countrymen do their potatoes."

"Yes, Doctor, Fred's right; we had better start."

"Well, I can't help it; I've recorded my opposition to the motion, but I must submit; and now that I'm on my legs, explain to me what's that very dull-looking old lamp up there?"

"That's the moon, man—the full moon."

"Well, I've no objection; I'm full too; so come along, lads."

CHAPTER XX.

THE MASQUERADE.

TO form one's impression of a masked ball from the attempts at
this mode of entertainment in our country, is but to conceive
a most imperfect and erroneous notion. With us the first *coup
d'œil* is everything; the nuns, the shepherdesses, the Turks, sailors,
eastern princes, watchmen, moonshees, milestones, devils, and
Quakers, are all very well in their way as they pass in the review
before us,—but when we come to mix in the crowd, we discover that
except the turban and the cowl, the crook and the broad-brim, no
further disguise is attempted or thought of. The nun, forgetting
her vow and her vestments, is flirting with the devil; the watchman,
a very fastidious elegant, is ogling the fishwomen through his glass,
while the Quaker is performing a *pas seul* Alberti might be proud of
in a quadrille of riotous Turks and half-tipsy Hindoos; in fact, the
whole wit of the scene consists in absurd associations. Apart from
this, the actors have rarely any claims upon your attention; for even
supposing a person clever enough to sustain his character, whatever
it be, you must also supply the other personages of the drama, or, in
stage phrase, he'll have nothing to "play up to." What would be
Bardolph without Pistol? what Sir Lucius O'Trigger without Acres?
It is the relief which throws out the disparities and contradictions
of life that afford us most amusement; hence it is that one swallow
can no more make a summer than one well-sustained character can
give life to a masquerade. Without such sympathies, such points of
contact, all the leading features of the individual, making him act
and be acted upon, are lost; the characters being mere parallel
lines, which, however near they approach, never bisect or cross each
other.

This is not the case abroad. The domino, which serves for mere
concealment, is almost the only dress assumed, and the real disguise
is therefore thrown from necessity upon the talents, whatever they
be, of the wearer. It is no longer a question of a beard or a spangled
mantle, a Polish dress or a pasteboard nose; the mutation of voice,
the assumption of a different manner, walk, gesture, and mode of
expression, are all necessary, and no small tact is required to effect
this successfully.

I may be pardoned this little digression, as it serves to explain in
some measure how I felt on entering the splendidly lit-up *salons* of
the villa, crowded with hundreds of figures in all the varied costumes of a carnival. The sounds of laughter, mingled with the crash
of the music; the hurrying hither and thither of servants with re-

freshments; the crowds gathered around fortune-tellers, whose predictions threw the parties at each moment into shouts of merriment; the eager following of some disappointed domino, interrogating every one to find out a lost mask. For some time I stood an astonished spectator at the kind of secret intelligence which seemed to pervade the whole assemblage, when suddenly a mask, who for some time had been standing beside me, whispered in French,—

"If you pass your time in this manner, you must not feel surprised if your place be occupied."

I turned hastily round, but she was gone. She, I say, for the voice was clearly a woman's; her pink domino could be no guide, for hundreds of the same color passed me every instant; the meaning of the allusion I had little doubt of. I turned to speak to Power, but he was gone; and for the first moment of my life the bitterness of rivalry crossed my mind. It was true I had resigned all pretensions in his favor; my last meeting with Lucy had been merely to justify my own character against an impression that weighed heavily on me; still I thought he might have waited; another day and I should be far away, neither to witness nor grieve over his successes.

"You still hesitate," whispered some one near me.

I wheeled round suddenly, but could not detect the speaker, and was again relapsing into my own musings, when the same voice repeated,—

"The white domino with the blue cape. Adieu."

Without waiting to reflect upon the singularity of the occurrence, I now hurried along through the dense crowd, searching on every side for the domino.

"Isn't that O'Malley?" said an Englishman to his friend.

"Yes," replied the other; "the very man we want. O'Malley, find a partner; we have been searching a vis-à-vis this ten minutes."

The speaker was an officer I had met at Sir George Dashwood's.

"How did you discover me?" said I, suddenly.

"Not a very difficult thing, if you carry your mask in your hand that way," was the answer.

And now I perceived that in the abstraction of my thoughts I had been carrying my mask in this manner since my coming into the room.

"There now, what say you to the blue domino? I saw her foot, and a girl with such an instep must be a waltzer."

I looked round, a confused effort at memory passing across my mind; my eyes fell at the instant upon the embroidered sleeve of the domino, where a rosebud worked in silver at once reminded me of Catrina's secret. "Ah!" thought I, "la Senhora herself!" She was leaning upon the arm of a tall and portly figure in black; who this was I knew not, nor sought to discover, but at once advancing towards Donna Inez, asked her to waltz.

Without replying to me, she turned towards her companion, who seemed, as it were, to press her acceptance of my offer; she hesitated, however, for an instant, and, curtseying deeply, declined it. "Well," thought I, "she at least has not recognized me."

"And yet, Senhora," said I, half jestingly, "I *have* seen you join a bolero before now."

"You evidently mistake me," was the reply, but in a voice so well feigned as almost to convince me she was right.

"Nay, more," said I, "under your own fair auspices did I myself first adventure one."

"Still in error, believe me; I am not known to you."

"And yet I have a talisman to refresh your memory, should you dare me further."

At this instant my hand was grasped warmly by a passing mask. I turned round rapidly, and Power whispered in my ear,—

"Yours forever, Charley; you've made my fortune."

As he hurried on, I could perceive that he supported a lady on his arm, and that she wore a loose white domino with a deep blue cape. In a second all thought of Inez was forgotten, and anxious only to conceal my emotion, I turned away and mingled with the crowd. Lost to all around me, I wandered carelessly, heedlessly on, neither noticing the glittering throng around, nor feeling a thought in common with the gay and joyous spirits that flitted by. The night wore on, my melancholy and depression growing ever deeper; yet so spell-bound was I that I could not leave the place. A secret sense that it was the last time we were to meet had gained entire possession of me, and I longed to speak a few words ere we parted forever.

I was leaning at a window which looked out upon the court-yard, when suddenly the tramp of horses attracted my attention, and I saw by the clear moonlight a group of mounted men, whose long cloaks and tall helmets announced dragoons, standing around the porch. At the same moment the door of the saloon opened, and an officer in undress, splashed and travel-stained, entered. Making his way rapidly through the crowd, he followed the servant who introduced him towards the supper-room. Thither the dense mass now pressed to learn the meaning of the singular apparition, while my own curiosity, not less excited, led me towards the door; as I crossed the hall, however, my progress was interrupted by a group of persons, among whom I saw an aide-de-camp of Lord Wellington's staff, narrating, as it were, some piece of newly-arrived intelligence. I had no time for further inquiry, when a door opened near me, and Sir George Dashwood, accompanied by several general officers, came forth, the officer I had first seen enter the ball-room along with them. Every one was by this unmasked, and eagerly looking to hear what had occurred.

"Then, Dashwood, you'll send off an orderly at once?" said an old general officer beside me.

"This instant, my lord. I'll despatch an aide-de-camp. The troops shall be in marching order before noon. Oh, here's the man I want! O'Malley, come here. Mount your horse and dash into town. Send for Brotherton and M'Gregor to quarters, and announce the news as quickly as possible."

"But what am I to announce, Sir George?"

"That the French are in retreat—Massena in retreat, my lad."

A tremendous cheer at this instant burst from the hundreds in the salon, who now heard the glorious tidings. Another cheer and another followed—ten thousand vivas rose amid the crash of the band, as it broke into a patriotic war chant. Such a scene of enthusiasm and excitment I had never witnessed. Some wept for joy. Others threw themselves into their friends' arms.

"They're all mad, every mother's son of them!" said Maurice Quill, as he elbowed his way through the mass; "and here's an old vestal won't leave my arm. She has already embraced me three times, and we've finished a flask of Malaga between us."

"Come, O'Malley, are you ready for the road?"

My horse was by this time standing saddled at the front. I sprang at once to the saddle, and, without waiting for a second order, set out for Lisbon. Ten minutes had scarce elapsed—the very shouts of joy of the delighted city were still ringing in my ears—when I was once again back at the villa. As I mounted the steps into the hall, a carriage drew up; it was Sir George Dashwood's; he came forward—his daughter leaning upon his arm.

"Why, O'Malley, I thought you had gone."

"I have returned, Sir George. Colonel Brotherton is in waiting, and the staff also. I have received orders to set out for Benejos, where the 14th are stationed, and have merely delayed to say adieu."

"Adieu, my dear boy, and God bless you!" said the warm-hearted old man, as he pressed my hand between both his. "Lucy, here's your old friend about to leave; come and say good-bye."

Miss Dashwood had stopped behind to adjust her shawl. I flew to her assistance. "Adieu, Miss Dashwood, and forever!" said I, in a broken voice, as I took her hand in mine. "This is not your domino," said I eagerly, as a blue silk one peeped from beneath her mantle; "and the sleeve, too—did you wear this?" She blushed slightly, and assented.

"I changed with the Senhora, who wore mine all the evening."

"And Power, then, was not your partner?"

"I should think not—for I never danced."

"Lucy, my love, are you ready? Come, be quick."

"Good-bye, Mr. O'Malley, and *au revoir, n'est-ce pas?*"

I drew her glove from her hand as she spoke, and, pressing my lips upon her fingers, placed her within the carriage. "Adieu, and *au revoir!*" said I; the carriage turned away, and a white glove was all that remained to me of Lucy Dashwood!

The carriage had turned the angle of the road, and its retiring sounds were growing gradually fainter, ere I recovered myself sufficiently to know where I stood. One absorbing thought alone possessed me. Lucy was not lost to me forever; Power was not my rival in that quarter—that was enough for me. I needed no more to nerve my arm and steel my heart. As I reflected thus, the long loud blast of a trumpet broke upon the silence of the night, and admonished me to depart. I hurried to my room to make my few preparations for the road, but Mike had already anticipated everything here, and all was in readiness.

But one thing now remained—to make my adieu to the Senhora. With this intent, I descended a narrow winding stair which led from my dressing-room, and opened by a little terrace upon the flower-garden beside her apartments.

As I crossed the gravelled alley, I could not but think of the last time I had been there. It was on the eve of departure for the Douro. I recalled the few and fleeting moments of our leave-taking, and a thought flashed upon me—what if she cared for me! —what if, half in coquetry, half in reality, her heart was mixed up in those passages which daily associations give rise to?

I could not altogether acquit myself of all desire to make her believe me her admirer; nay, more, with the indolent *abandon* of my country, I had fallen into a thousand little schemes to cheat the long hours away, which having no other object than the happiness of the moment, might yet color all her after-life with sorrow.

Let no one rashly pronounce me a coxcomb, vain and pretentious, for all this. In my inmost heart I had no feeling of selfishness mingled with the consideration. It was from no sense of my own merits, no calculation of my own chances of success, that I thought thus. Fortunately, at eighteen one's heart is uncontaminated with such an alloy of vanity. The first emotions of youth are pure and holy things, tempering our fiercer passions, and calming the rude effervescence of our boyish spirit; and when we strive to please, and hope to win affection, we insensibly fashion ourselves to nobler and higher thoughts, catching from the source of our devotion a portion of that charm that idealizes daily life, and makes our path in it a glorious and a bright one.

Who would not exchange all the triumph of his later days, the proudest moments of successful ambition, the richest trophies of hard-won daring, for the short and vivid flash that first shot through his heart and told him he was loved? It is the opening consciousness of life, the first sense of power, that makes of the mere boy a man—a man in all his daring and his pride—and hence it is that in early life we feel ever prone to indulge those fancied attachments which elevate and raise us in our own esteem. Such was the frame of my mind as I entered the little boudoir, where once before I had ventured on a similar errand.

As I closed the sash-door behind me, the gray dawn of breaking day scarcely permitted my seeing anything around me, and I felt my way towards the door of an adjoining room, where I supposed it was likely I should find the Senhora. As I proceeded thus with cautious step and beating heart, I thought I heard a sound near me. I stopped and listened, and was again about to move on, when a half-stifled sob fell upon my ear. Slowly and silently guiding my steps towards the sounds, I reached a sofa, when, my eyes growing by degrees more accustomed to the faint light, I could detect a figure which, at a glance, I recognized as Donna Inez. A cashmere shawl was loosely thrown round her, and her face was buried in her hands. As she lay, to all seeming, still and insensible before me, her beautiful hair fell heavily upon her back and across her arm, and her whole attitude denoted the very abandonment of grief. A short convulsive shudder which slightly shook her frame alone gave evidence of life, except when a sob, barely audible, in the death-like silence, escaped her.

I knelt silently down beside her, and, gently withdrawing her hand, placed it within mine. A dreadful feeling of self-condemnation shot through me as I felt the gentle pressure of her taper fingers, which rested without a struggle in my grasp. My tears fell hot and fast upon that pale hand, as I bent in sadness over it, unable to utter a word. A rush of conflicting thoughts passed through my brain, and I knew not what to do. I now had no doubt upon my mind that she loved me, and that her present affliction was caused by my approaching departure.

"Dearest Inez!" I stammered out at length, as I pressed her hands to my lips; "dearest Inez!"—a faint sob, and a slight pressure of her hand, was the only reply. "I have come to say good-bye," continued I, gaining a little courage as I spoke; "a long good-bye, too, in all likelihood. You have heard that we are ordered away,—there, don't sob, dearest, and, believe me, I had wished ere we parted to have spoken to you calmly and openly; but alas! I cannot,—I scarcely know what I say."

"You will not forget me?" said she, in a low voice, that sank into my very heart. "You will not forget me?" As she spoke, her hand dropped heavily upon my shoulder, and her rich luxuriant hair fell upon my cheek. What a devil of a thing is proximity to a downy cheek and a black eyelash, more especially when they belong to one whom you are disposed to believe not indifferent to you! What I did at this precise moment there is no necessity for recording, even had not an adage interdicted such confessions, nor can I now remember what I said; but I can well recollect how, gradually warming with my subject, I entered into a kind of half-declaration of attachment, intended most honestly to be a mere *exposé* of my own unworthiness to win her favor, and my resolution to leave Lisbon and its neighborhood forever.

Let not any one blame me rashly if he has not experienced the difficulty of my position. The impetus of love-making is like the ardor of a fox-hunt. You care little that the six-bar gate before you is the boundary of another gentleman's preserves or the fence of his pleasure-ground. You go slap along at a smashing pace, with your head up, and your hand low, clearing all before you, the opposing difficulties to your progress giving half the zest, because all the danger, to your career. So it is with love. The gambling spirit urges one ever onward, and the chance of failure is a reason for pursuit, where no other argument exists.

"And you do love me?" said the Senhora, with a soft, low whisper, that most unaccountably suggested anything but comfort to me.

"Love you, Inez? By this kiss—I'm in an infernal scrape!" said I, muttering this last half of my sentence to myself.

"And you'll never be jealous again?"

"Never, by all that's lovely!—your own sweet lips. That's the very last thing to reproach me with."

"And you promise me not to mind that foolish boy? For, after all, you know it was mere flirtation—if even that."

"I'll never think of him again," said I, while my brain was burning to make out her meaning. "But, dearest, there goes the trumpet-call——"

"And, as for Pedro Mascarenhas, I never liked him."

"Are you quite sure, Inez?"

"I swear it!—so no more of him. Gonzales Cordenza—I've broke with him long since. So that you see, dearest Frederic——"

"Frederic!" said I, starting almost to my feet with amazement, while she continued:—

"I'm your own—all your own!"

"Oh! the coquette, the heartless jilt!" groaned I, half aloud. "And O'Malley, Inez, poor Charley!—what of him?"

"Poor thing! I can't help him. But he's such a puppy, the lesson may do him good."

"But perhaps he loved you, Inez?"

"To be sure he did; I wished him to do so,—I can't bear not to be loved. But, Frederic, tell me, may I trust you—will you keep faithful to me?"

"Sweetest Inez! by this last kiss I swear, that such as I kneel before you now, you'll ever find me."

A foot upon the gravel-walk without now called me to my feet. I sprang towards the door, and before Inez had lifted her head from the sofa, I had reached the garden. A figure muffled in a cavalry cloak passed near me, but without noticing me, and the next moment I had cleared the paling, and was hurrying towards the stable, where I had ordered Mike to be in waiting.

The faint streak of dull pink which announces the coming day, stretched beneath the dark clouds of the night, and the chill air of the morning was already stirring in the leaves.

As I passed along by a low beech hedge which skirted the avenue, I was struck by the sound of voices near me. I stopped to listen, and soon detected in one of the speakers my friend Mickey Free; of the other I was not long in ignorance.

"Love you, is it—bathershin? It's worship you—adore you, my darling—that's the word—there, acushla, don't cry—dry your eyes— oh, murther! it's a cruel thing to tear one's self away from the best of living, with the run of the house in drink and kissing. Bad luck to it for campaigning, anyway, I never liked it!"

Catrina's reply,—for it was she—I could not gather; but Mike resumed:—

"Ay, just so, sore bones and wet grass, accadenté and half rations. Oh, that I ever saw the day when I took to it! Listen to me now, honey; here it is, on my knees I am before you, and throth it's not more nor three, maybe four, young women I'd say the like to; bad scran to me if I wouldn't marry you out of a face this blessed morning just as soon as I'd look at ye. Arrah, there now, don't be screeching and bawling; what'll the neighbors think of us, and my own heart's destroyed with grief entirely."

Poor Catrina's voice returned an inaudible answer, and not wishing any longer to play the eavesdropper, I continued my path towards the stable. The distant noises from the city announced a state of movement and preparation, and more than one orderly passed the road near me at a gallop. As I turned into the wide court-yard, Mike, breathless and flurried with running, overtook me.

"Are the horses ready, Mike?" said I; "we must start this instant."

"They've just finished a peck of oats apiece, and faix that same may be a stranger to them this day six months."

"And the baggage, too?"

"On the cars, with the staff and the light brigade. It was down there I was now, to see all was right."

"Oh, I'm quite aware; and now bring out the cattle. I hope Catrina received your little consolations well. That seems a very sad affair."

"Murder, real murder, devil a less! It's no matter where you go, from Clonmel to Chayney, it's all one; they've a way of getting round you. Upon my soul, it's like the pigs they are."

"Like pigs, Mike? That appears a strange compliment you've selected to pay them."

"Ay, just like the pigs, no less. Maybe you never heard what happened to myself up at Moronha?"

"Look to that girth there. Well, go on."

"I was coming along one morning just as day was beginning to break, when I sees a slip of a pig trotting before me, with nobody near him; but as the road was lonely, and myself rather down in heart, I thought, Musha! but yer fine company, anyhow, av a body could only keep you with him. But, ye see, a pig—saving your presence—is a baste not easily flattered, so I didn't waste time and blarney upon him, but I took off my belt and put it round its neck as neat as need be; but as the devil's luck would have it, I didn't go half an hour when a horse came galloping up behind me. I turned round, and by the blessed light, it was Sir Dinny himself was on it!"

"Sir Dennis Pack?"

"Yes, bad luck to his hook nose. 'What are you doing there, my fine fellow?' says he. 'What's that you have dragging there behind you?'

"'A boneen, sir,' says I. 'Isn't he a fine crayture?—av he wasn't so troublesome.'

"'Troublesome, troublesome—what do you mean?'

"'Just so,' says I. 'Isn't he parsecuting the life out of me the whole mornin', following me about everywhere I go? Contrary bastes they always was.'

"'I advise you to try and part company, my friend, notwithstanding,' says he; 'or maybe it's the same end you'll be coming to, and not long either.' And, faix, I took his advice; and ye see,

Mister Charles, it's just as I was saying, they're like the women, the least thing in life is enough to bring them after us, av ye only put the '*comether*' upon them."

"And now adieu to the Villa Nuova," said I, as I rode slowly down the avenue, turning ever and anon in my saddle to look back on each well-known spot.

A heavy sigh from Mike responded to my words.

"A long, a last farewell!" said I, waving my hand towards the trellised walls, now half hidden by the trees; and as I spoke, that heaviness of the heart came over me that seems inseparable from leave-taking. The hour of parting seems like a warning to us that all our enjoyments and pleasures here are destined to a short and merely fleeting existence; and, as each scene of life passes away never to return, we are made to feel that youth and hope are passing with them; and that, although the fair world be as bright, and its pleasures as rich in abundance, our capacity of enjoyment is daily, hourly diminishing; and while all around us smiles in beauty and happiness, that we, alas! are not what we were.

Such was the tenor of my thoughts as I reached the road, when they were suddenly interrupted by my man Mike, whose meditations were following a somewhat similar channel, though at last inclining to different conclusions. He coughed a couple of times, as if to attract my attention, and then, as it were half thinking aloud, he muttered :—

"I wonder if we treated the young ladies well, anyhow, Mister Charles, for, faix, I've my doubts on it."

<hr>

CHAPTER XXI.

THE LINES.

WHEN we reached Lescas, we found that an officer of Lord Wellington's staff had just arrived from the lines, and was occupied in making known the general order from headquarters; this set forth, with customary brevity, that the French armies, under the command of Massena, had retired from their position, and were in full retreat; the second and third corps which had been stationed at Villa Franca, having marched during the night of the 15th, in the direction of Manal. The officers in command of divisions were ordered to repair instantly to Pero Negro to consult upon a forward movement, Admiral Berkeley being written to to pro-

32

vide launches to pass over General Hill's, or any other corps which might be selected, to the left bank of the Tagus. All was now excitement, heightened by the unexpected nature of an occurrence which not even speculation had calculated upon. It was but a few days before, and the news had reached Torres Vedras that a powerful reinforcement was in march to join Massena's army, and their advanced guard had actually reached Santarem. The confident expectation was, therefore, that an attack upon the lines was meditated. Now, however, this prospect existed no longer; for scarcely had the heavy mists of the lowering day disappeared, when the vast plain, so lately peopled by the thickened ranks and dark masses of a great army, was seen in its whole extent deserted and untenanted.

The smouldering fires of the pickets alone marked where the troops had been posted, but not a man of that immense force was to be seen. General Fane, who had been despatched with a brigade of Portuguese cavalry and, some artillery, hung upon the rear of the retiring army, and from him we learned that the enemy were continuing their retreat northward, having occupied Santarem with a strong force to cover the movement. Craufurd was ordered to the front with the light division, the whole army following in the same direction, except Hill's corps, which, crossing the river at Velada, was intended to harass the enemy's flank, and assist our future operations.

Such, in brief, was the state of affairs when I reached Villa Franca towards noon, and received orders to join my regiment, then forming part of Sir Stapleton Cotton's brigade.

It must be felt, to be thoroughly appreciated, the enthusiastic pleasure with which one greets his old corps after some months of separation; the bounding ecstasy with which the weary eye rests on the old familiar faces, dear by every association of affection and brotherhood; the anxious look for this one, and for that; the thrill of delight sent through the heart as the well-remembered march swells upon the ear; the very notes of that rough voice which we have heard amid the crash of battle and the rolling of artillery, speaks softly to our senses, like a father's welcome; from the well-tattered flag that waves above us, to the proud steed of the war-worn trumpeter—each has a niche in our affections.

If ever there was a corps calculated to increase and foster these sentiments, the 14th Light Dragoons was such. The warm affection, the truly heartfelt regard, which existed among my brother officers made of our mess a happy home. Our veteran Colonel, grown gray in campaigning, was like a father to us; while the senior officers, tempering the warm blood of impetuous youth with their hard-won experience, threw a charm of peace and tranquillity over all our intercourse that made us happy when together, and taught us to feel that, whether seated around the watch-fire, or charging amid the squadrons of the enemy, we were surrounded by those devoted heart and soul to aid us.

Gallant 14th !—ever first in every gay scheme of youthful jollity, as foremost in the van to meet the foe—how happy am I to recall the memory of your bright looks and bold hearts!—of your manly daring and your bold frankness—of your merry voices, as I have heard them in the battle or in the bivouac! Alas, and alas! that I should indulge such recollections alone! How few—how very few— are left of those with whom I trod the early steps of life! whose bold cheer I have heard above the clashing sabres of the enemy—whose broken voice I have listened to above the grave of a comrade! The dark pines of the Pyrenees wave over some, the burning sands of India cover others, and the wide plans of Salamanca are now your abiding-places.

"Here comes O'Malley!" shouted a well-known voice, as I rode down the little slope, at the foot of which a group of officers were standing beside their horses.

"Welcome, thou man of Galway!" cried Hampden, "delighted to have you once more amongst us. How confoundedly well the fellow is looking!"

"Lisbon beef seems better prog than commissariat biscuit!" said another.

"A'weel, Charley!" said my friend, the Scotch Doctor; " how's a' wi' ye, man ? Ye seem to thrive on your mishaps! How cam' ye by that braw beastie ye're mounted on ?"

"A present, Doctor ; the gift of a very warm friend."

"I hope you invited him to the mess, O'Malley! For, by Jove, our stables stand in need of his kind offices! There he goes! Look at him! What a slashing pace for a heavy fellow!" This observation was made with reference to a well-known officer on the Commander-in-Chief's staff, whose weight—some two-and-twenty stone— was never any impediment to his bold riding.

"Egad, O'Malley, you'll soon be as pretty a light-weight as our friend yonder. Ah! there's a storm going on there! Here comes the Colonel!"

"Well, O'Malley, are you come back to us? Happy to see you, boy!—hope we shall not lose you again in a hurry!—We can't spare the scapegraces! There's plenty of skirmishing going on!—Craufurd always asks for the scapegraces for the pickets!"

I shook my gallant Colonel's hand, while I acknowledged, as best I might, his ambiguous compliment.

"I say, lads," resumed the Colonel, "squad your men and form on the road! Lord Wellington's coming down this way to have a look at you! O'Malley, I have General Craufurd's orders to offer you your old appointment on his staff; without you prefer remaining with the regiment."

"I can never be sufficiently grateful, sir, to the General; but, in fact—I think—that is, I believe——"

"You'd rather be among your own fellows. Out with it, boy! I like you all the better! but come, we mustn't let the General know that; so that I shall forget to tell you all about it. Eh? isn't that best? But join your troop now; I hear the staff coming this way."

As he spoke a crowd of horsemen were seen advancing towards us at a sharp trot; their waving plumes and gorgeous aiguillettes denoting their rank as generals of division. In the midst, as they came nearer, I could distinguish one whom, once seen, there was no forgetting; his plain blue frock and his gray trousers unstrapped beneath his boots, not a little unlike the trim accuracy of costume around him. As he rode to the head of the leading squadron, the staff fell back and he stood alone before us; for a second there was a dead silence, but the next instant—by what impulse tell who can— one tremendous cheer burst from the entire regiment. It was like the act of one man—so sudden, so spontaneous. While every cheek glowed, and every eye sparkled with enthusiasm, he alone seemed cool and unexcited, as gently raising his hand, he motioned them to silence.

"Fourteenth, you are to be where you always desire to be—in the advanced guard of the army. I have nothing to say on the subject of your conduct in the field. I know *you;* but if, in pursuit of the enemy, I hear of any misconduct towards the people of the country, or any transgression of the general orders regarding pillage, by G—, I'll punish you as severely as the worst corps in the service, and you know *me.*"

"Oh! tear an' ages, listen to that; and there's to be no plunder after all!" said Mickey Free; and for an instant the most I could do was not to burst into a fit of laughter. The word "Forward!" was given at the moment, and we moved past in close column, while that penetrating eye, which seemed to read our very thoughts, scanned us from one end of the line to the other.

"I say, Charley," said the captain of my troop in a whisper—"I say, that confounded cheer we gave got us that lesson; he can't stand that kind of thing."

"By Jove! I never felt more disposed than to repeat it," said I.

"No, no, my boy, we'll give him the honors, nine times nine; but wait till evening. Look at old Merivale there. I'll swear he's saying something devilish civil to him. Do you see the old fellow's happy look ?"

And so it was ; the bronzed, hard-cast features of the veteran soldier. were softened into an expression of almost boyish delight, as he sat bare-headed, bowing to his very saddle, while Lord Wellington was speaking.

As I looked, my heart throbbed painfully against my side, my breath came quick, and I muttered to myself, "What would I not give to be in his place now !"

CHAPTER XXII.

THE RETREAT OF THE FRENCH.

IT is not my intention, were I even adequate to the task, to trace with anything like accuracy the events of the war at this period. In fact, to those who, like myself, were performing a mere subaltern character, the daily movements of our own troops, not to speak of the continual changes of the enemy, were perfectly unknown, and an English newspaper was more ardently longed for in the Peninsula than by the most eager crowd of a London coffee-room ; nay, the results of the very engagements we were ourselves concerned in, more than once, first reached us through the press of our own country. It is easy enough to understand this. The officer in command of the regiment, and, how much more the captain of a troop, or the subaltern under him, knows nothing beyond the sphere of his own immediate duty : by the success or failure of his own party his knowledge is bounded, but how far he or his may influence the fortune of the day, or of what is taking place elsewhere, he is totally ignorant ; and an old 14th man did not badly explain his ideas on the matter who described Busaco as "a great noise and a great smoke, booming artillery and rattling small-arms, infernal confusion, and, to all seeming, incessant blundering, orders and counter-orders, ending with a crushing charge, when, not being hurt himself nor having hurt anybody, he felt much pleased to learn that they had gained a victory." It is, then, sufficient for all the purposes of my narrative when I mention that Massena continued his retreat by Santarem and Thomar, followed by the allied army, who, however desirous of pressing upon the rear of their enemy, were still obliged to maintain their communication with the lines, and at the same time to watch the movement of the large armies which, under Ney and Soult, threatened at any unguarded moment to attack them in flank.

The position which Massena occupied at Santarem, naturally one of great strength, and further improved by intrenchments, defied any attack on the part of Lord Wellington, until the arrival of the long-expected reinforcements from England. These had sailed in the early part of January, but, delayed by adverse winds, only reached Lisbon on the 2d of March, and so correctly was the French Marshal apprised of the circumstance, and so accurately did he anticipate the probable result, that on the 4th he broke up his encampment, and recommenced his retrograde movement, with an army now reduced to forty thousand fighting men, and with two thousand sick, destroying all his baggage and guns that could not be horsed. By a demonstration of advancing upon the Zezere, by which he held the allies in check, he succeeded in passing his wounded to the rear, while Ney, appearing with a large force suddenly at Leiria, seemed bent upon attacking the lines. By these stratagems two days' march were gained, and the French retreated upon Torres Novas and Thomar, destroying the bridges behind them as they passed.

The day was breaking, on the 12th of March, when the British first came in sight of the retiring enemy. We were then ordered to the front, and, broken up into small parties, threw out our skirmishers. The French chasseurs, usually not indisposed to accept this species of encounter, showed now less of inclination than usual, and either retreated before us or hovered in masses to check our advance. In this way the morning was passed, when towards noon we perceived that the enemy was drawn up in battle array, occupying the height above the village of Redinha. This little straggling village is situated in a hollow, traversed by a narrow causeway, which opens by a long and dangerous defile upon a bridge, on either side of which a dense wood afforded a shelter for light troops, while upon the commanding eminence above a battery of heavy guns was seen in position.

In front of the village a brigade of artillery and a division of infantry were drawn up so skilfully as to give the appearance of a considerable force, so that when Lord Wellington came up, he spent some time in examining the enemy's position, Erskine's brigade was immediately ordered up, and the 52d and 94th, and a company of the 43d, were led against the wooded slopes upon the French right. Picton simultaneously attacked the left. In less than an hour both were successful, and Ney's position was laid bare. His skirmishers, however, continued to hold their ground in front, and La Ferrière, a colonel of hussars, dashing boldly forward at this very moment, carried off fourteen prisoners from the very front of our line. Deceived by the confidence of the enemy, Lord Wellington now prepared for an attack in force. The infantry were therefore formed into line, and, at the signal of three shots fired from the centre, began their forward movement.

Bending up a gentle curve, the whole plain glistened with the glancing bayonets, and the troops marched majestically onward, while the light artillery and the cavalry, bounding forward from the left and centre, rushed eagerly towards the foe. One deafening discharge from the French guns opened at the moment, with a general volley of small-arms. The smoke for an instant obscured everything, and when that cleared away, no enemy was to be seen.

The British pressed madly on, like heated bloodhounds; but when they descended the slope, the village of Redinha was in flames, and the French were in full retreat beyond it. A single howitzer seemed our only trophy, and even this we were not destined to boast of, for from the midst of the crashing flame and dense smoke of the burning village a troop of dragoons rushed forward, and, charging our infantry, carried it off. The struggle, though but for a moment, cost them dear—twenty of their comrades lay dead upon the spot; but they were resolute and determined, and the officer who led them on, fighting hand to hand with a soldier of the 42d, cheered them as they retired. His gallant bearing, and his coat covered with decorations, bespoke him one of note, and well it might; he who thus perilled his life to maintain the courage of his soldiers at the commencement of a retreat, was no other than Ney himself—*le plus brave des braves.* The British pressed hotly on, and the light troops crossed the river almost at the same time with the French. Ney, however, fell back upon Condeixa, where his main body was posted, and all further pursuit was for the present abandoned.

At Casa Noval and at Foz d'Aronce the allies were successful; but the French still continued to retire, burning the towns and villages in their rear, and devastating the country along the whole line of march by every expedient of cruelty the heart of man has ever conceived. In the words of one whose descriptions, however fraught with the most wonderful power of painting, are equally marked by truth,—"Every horror that could make war hideous attended this dreadful march. Distress, conflagration, death in all modes,—from wounds, from fatigue, from water, from the flames, from starvation, —vengeance, unlimited vengeance—was on every side. The country was a desert!"

Such was the exhaustion of the allies, who suffered even greater privations than the enemy, that they halted upon the 16th, unable to proceed farther, and the river Ceira, swollen and unfordable, flowed between the rival armies.

The repose of even one day was a most grateful interruption to the harassing career we had pursued for some time past; and it seemed that my comrades felt, like myself, that such an opportunity was by no means to be neglected. But while I am devoting so much space, and trespassing on my reader's patience thus far, with narrative of flood and field, let me steal a chapter for what will sometimes seem a scarcely less congenial topic, and bring back the recollection of a glorious night in the Peninsula.

CHAPTER XXIII.

PATRICK'S DAY IN THE PENINSULA.

THE *reveille* had not yet sounded, when I felt my shoulder shaken gently as I lay wrapped up in my cloak beneath a prickly pear-tree.

"Lieutenant O'Malley, sir; a letter, sir; a bit of a note, your honor," said a voice which bespoke that the bearer and myself were countrymen. I opened it, and, with difficulty, by the uncertain light read as follows :—

"DEAR CHARLEY :—As Lord Wellington, like a good Irishman as he is, wouldn't spoil Patrick's Day by marching, we've got a little dinner at our quarters to celebrate the holy times, as my uncle would call it. Maurice, Phil Grady, and some regular trumps, will all come, so don't disappoint us. I've been making punch all night, and Casey, who has a knack at pastry, has made a goose-pie as big as a portmanteau. Sharp seven, after parade. The second battalion of the Fusiliers are quartered at Melanté, and we are next them. Bring any of yours worth their liquor. Power is, I know, absent with the staff. Perhaps the Scotch Doctor would come—try him. Carry over a little mustard with you, if there be such in your parts.

"Yours,

"D. O'SHAUGHNESSY.

"Patrick's Day, and raining like blazes."

Seeing that the bearer expected an answer, I scrawled the words "I'm there" with my pencil on the back of the note, and again turned myself round to sleep. My slumbers were, however, soon interrupted once more, for the bugles of the light infantry and the hoarse trumpet of the cavalry sounded the call, and I found to my surprise that, though halted, we were by no means destined to a day of idleness. Dragoons were already mounted, carrying orders hither and thither, and staff officers were galloping right and left. A general order commanded an inspection of the troops, and within less than an hour from daybreak the whole army was drawn up under arms. A thin, drizzling rain continued to fall during the early part of the day, but the sun gradually dispelled the heavy vapor, and as the bright verdure glittered in its beams, sending up all the perfumes of a southern clime, I thought I had never seen a more lovely morning. The staff were stationed upon a little knoll beside the river, round the base of which the troops defiled, at first in orderly, then in quick time, the bands playing and the colors flying. In the same brigade with us the 88th came, and as they neared the Commander-in-Chief, their quick step was suddenly stopped, and after a pause of a few seconds, the band struck up " St. Patrick's Day ;" the notes were caught up by the other Irish regiments, and, amid one prolonged cheer from the whole line, the gallant fellows moved past.

The grenadier company was drawn up beside the road, and I was not long in detecting my friend O'Shaughnessy, who wore a tremendous shamrock in his shako.

"Left face, wheel! quick march! Don't forget the mustard!" said the bold Major; and a loud roar of laughter from my brother officers followed him off the ground: I soon explained the injunction, and, having invited some three or four to accompany me to the dinner, waited with all patience for the conclusion of the parade.

The sun was setting as I mounted, and, joined by Hampden, Baker, the Doctor, and another, set out for O'Shaughnessy's quarters. As we rode along, we were continually falling in with others bent upon the same errand as ourselves, and ere we arrived at Melanté our party was some thirty strong; and truly a most extraordinary procession did we form. Few of the invited came without some contribution to the general stock; and while a staff-officer flourished a ham, a smart hussar might be seen with a plucked turkey, trussed for roasting; most carried bottles, as the consumption of fluid was likely to be considerable; and one fat old major jogged along on a broken-winded pony, with a basket of potatoes on his arm. Good fellowship was the order of the day, and certainly a more jovial squadron seldom was met together than ours. As we turned the angle of a rising ground, a hearty cheer greeted us, and we beheld in front of an old ordnance marquee a party of some fifty fellows engaged in all the pleasing duties of the *cuisine.*

Maurice, conspicuous above all, with a white apron, and a ladle in his hand, was running hither and thither, advising, admonishing, instructing, and occasionally imprecating. Ceasing for a second his functions, he gave us a cheer and a yell like that of an Indian savage, and then resumed his duties beside a huge boiler, which, from the frequency of his explorations into its contents, we judged to be punch.

"Charley, my son, I've a place for you; don't forget. Where's my learned brother?—haven't you brought him with you? Ah, Doctor, how goes it?"

"Nae that bad, Master Quell, a' things considered; we've had an awfu' time of it lately."

"You know my friend Hampden, Maurice. Let me introduce Mr. Baker—Mr. Maurice Quill. Where's the Major?"

"Here I am, my darling, and delighted to see you. Some of yours, O'Malley, ain't they? Proud to have you, gentlemen. Charley, we are obliged to have several tables; but you are to be beside Maurice, so take your friends with you. There goes the 'Roast Beef;' my heart warms to that old tune."

Amid a hurried recognition, and shaking of hands on every side, I elbowed my way into the tent, and soon reached a corner, where, at a table for eight, I found Maurice seated at one end; a huge, purple-faced old major, whom he presented to us as Bob Mahon, occupied the other. O'Shaughnessy presided at the table next to us, but near enough to join in all the conviviality of ours.

One must have lived for some months upon hard biscuit and harder beef to relish as we did the fare before us, and to form an estimate of our satisfaction. If the reader cannot fancy Van Amburgh's lions in red coats and epaulettes, he must be content to lose the effect of the picture. A turkey rarely fed more than two people, and few were abstemious enough to be satisfied with one chicken. The order of the viands, too, observed no common routine, each party being happy to get what he could, and satisfied to follow up his pudding with fish, or his tart with a sausage. Sherry, champagne, London porter, Malaga, and even, I believe, Harvey's sauce, were hobnobbed in, while hot punch, in teacups or tin vessels, was unsparingly distributed on all sides. Achilles himself, they say, got tired of eating, and though he consumed something like a prize ox to his own cheek, he at length had to call for cheese, so that we at last gave in, and, having cleared away the broken tumbrels and baggage-carts of our army, cleared for a general action.

"Now, lads!" cried the Major, "I'm not going to lose your time and mine by speaking; but there are a couple of toasts I must insist upon you drinking with all the honors: and as I like despatch, we'll couple them. It so happens that our old island boasts of two of the finest fellows that ever wore Russia ducks. None of your non-sensical geniuses, like poets, or painters, or anything like that; but downright, straightforward, no-humbug sort of devil-may-care and bad-luck-to-you kind of chaps—real Irishmen! Now, it's a strange thing that they both had such an antipathy to vermin, they spent their life in hunting them down and destroying them; and whether they met toads at home, or Johnny Crapaud abroad, it was all one. (Cheers.) Just so, boys; they made them leave that. But I see you are getting impatient, so I'll not delay you, but fill to the brim, and, with the best cheer in your body, drink with me the two greatest Irishmen that ever lived, 'St. Patrick and Lord Wellington.'"

The Englishmen laughed long and loud, while we cheered with an energy that satisfied even the Major.

"Who is to give us the chant? Who is to sing St. Patrick?" cried Maurice. "Come, Bob, out with it."

"I'm four tumblers too low for that yet," growled out the Major.

"Well, then, Charley, be you the man; or why not Dennis himself? Come, Dennis, we cannot better begin our evening than with a song; let us have our old friend 'Larry M'Hale.'"

"Larry M'Hale!" resounded from all parts of the room, while O'Shaughnessy rose once more to his legs.

"Faith, boys, I'm always ready to follow your lead; but what analogy can exist between 'Larry M'Hale' and the toast we have just drunk, I can't see for the life of me; not but Larry would have made a strapping light company man had he joined the army."

"The song, the song!" cried several voices.

"Well, if you will have it, here goes."

"LARRY M'HALE."

"Oh! Larry M'Hale he had little to fear,
　And never could want when the crops didn't fail,
He'd a house and demesne and eight hundred a year,
　And the heart for to spend it, had Larry M'Hale!
The soul of a party,—the life of a feast,
　And an illigant song he could sing, I'll be bail;
He would ride with the rector, and drink with the priest,
　Oh! the broth of a boy was old Larry M'Hale.

"It's little he cared for the judge or recorder,
　His house was as big and as strong as a gaol;
With a cruel four-pounder he kept in great order,
　He'd murder the country, would Larry M'Hale.
He'd a blunderbuss, too; of horse-pistols a pair;
　But his favorite weapon was always a flail;
I wish you could see how he'd empty a fair,
　For he handled it neatly, did Larry M'Hale.

> "His ancestors were kings before Moses was born,
>   His mother descended from great Grana Uaile;
> He laughed all the Blakes and the Frenches to scorn;
>   They were mushrooms compared to old Larry M'Hale.
> He sat down every day to a beautiful dinner,
>   With cousins and uncles enough for a tail;
> And, though loaded with debt, oh! the devil a thinner
>   Could law or the sheriff make Larry M'Hale.
>
> "With a larder supplied and a cellar well stored,
>   None lived half so well, from Fair-Head to Kinsale;
> As he piously said, 'I've a plentiful board,
>   And the Lord he is good to old Larry M'Hale.'
> So fill up your glass, and a high bumper give him,
>   It's little we'd care for the tithes or repale;
> For ould Erin would be a fine country to live in,
>   If we only had plenty like Larry M'Hale."

"Very singular style of person your friend Mr. M'Hale," lisped a spoony-looking Cornet at the end of the table.

"Not in the country he belongs to, I assure you," said Maurice; "but I presume you were never in Ireland."

"You are mistaken there," resumed the other; "I was in Ireland though I confess not for a long time."

"If I might be so bold," cried Maurice, "how long?"

"Half an hour, by a stop-watch," said the other, pulling up his stock; "and I had quite enough of it in that time.

"Pray give us your experiences," cried out Bob Mahon. "They should be interesting, considering your opportunities."

"You are right," said the Cornet; "they were so; and as they illustrate a feature in your amiable country, you shall have them."

A general knocking upon the table announced the impatience of the company, and when silence was restored, the Cornet began:

"When the *Bermuda* transport sailed from Portsmouth for Lisbon, I happened to make one of some four hundred interesting individuals who, before they became food for powder, were destined to try their constitutions on pickled pork. The second day after our sailing, the winds became adverse; it blew a hurricane from every corner of the compass but the one it ought, and the good ship, that should have been standing straight for the Bay of Biscay, was scudding away under a double-reefed topsail towards the coast of Labrador. For six days we experienced every sea-manœuvre that usually preludes a shipwreck, and at length, when from sea-sickness and fear, we had become utterly indifferent to the result, the storm abated, the sea went down, and we found ourselves lying comfortably in the harbor of Cork, with a strange suspicion on our minds that the frightful scenes of the past week had been nothing but a dream.

"'Come Mr. Medlicot,' said the Skipper to me, 'we shall be here

for a couple of days to refit; had you not better go ashore and see
the country ?'

"I sprang to my legs with delight; visions of cowslips, larks,
daisies, and mutton chops floated before my excited imagination,
and in ten minutes I found myself standing at that pleasant little
inn at Cove which, opposite Spike Island, rejoices in the name of the
'Goat and Garters.'

"'Breakfast, waiter,' said I; 'a beefsteak—fresh beef, mark ye;
fresh eggs, bread, milk, and butter, all fresh.—No more hard tack,'
thought I; 'no salt butter, but a genuine land breakfast.'

"'Up stairs, No. 4, sir,' said the waiter, as he flourished a dirty
napkin, indicating the way.

"Up stairs I went, and in due time the appetizing little meal made
its appearance. Never did a minor's eye revel over his broad acres
with more complacent enjoyment than did mine skim over the beefsteak and the muffin, the teapot, the trout, and the devilled kidney,
so invitingly spread out before me. 'Yes,' thought I, as I smacked
my lips, 'this is the reward of virtue ! pickled pork is a probationary
state that admirably fits us for future enjoyments.' I arranged my
napkin upon my knee, seized my knife and fork, and proceeded with
most critical acumen to bisect a beefsteak. Scarcely, however, had
I touched it, when with a loud crash, the plate smashed beneath it,
and the gravy ran piteously across the cloth. Before I had time to
account for the phenomenon, the door opened hastily, and the waiter
rushed into the room, his face beaming with smiles, while he rubbed
his hands in an ecstasy of delight.

"'It's all over, sir,' said he; 'glory be to God ! it's all done.'

"'What's over? what's done?' inquired I, with impatience.

"'Mr. M'Mahon is satisfied,' replied he, 'and so is the other gentleman.'

"'Who and what the devil do you mean?'

"'It's over, sir, I say,' replied the waiter again; 'he fired in the
air.'

"'Fired in the air ! Was there a duel in the room below stairs?'

"'Yes, sir,' said the waiter, with a benign smile.

"'That will do,' said I, as, seizing my hat, I rushed out of the
house, and, hurrying to the beach, took a boat for the ship. Exactly
half an hour had elapsed since my landing, but even those short
thirty minutes had fully as many reasons that, although there may
be few more amusing, there are some safer places to live in than the
Green Isle."

A general burst of laughter followed the Cornet's story, which
was heightened in its effect by the gravity with which he told it.

"And, after all," said Maurice Quill, "now that people have given up making fortunes for the insurance companies, by living to the age of Methuselah, there's nothing like being an Irishman. In what other part of the habitable globe can you cram so much of adventure into one year? Where can you be so often in love, in liquor, or in debt? and where can you get so merrily out of the three? Where are promises to marry and promises to pay treated with the same gentlemanlike forbearance? and where, when you have lost your heart and your fortune, are people found so ready to comfort you in your reverses? Yes," said Maurice, as he filled his glass up to the brim, and eyed it lusciously for a moment—"yes, darling, here's your health; the only girl I ever loved—in that part of the country, I mean. Give her a bumper, lads, and I'll give you a chant!"

"Name! name! name!" shouted several voices from different parts of the table.

"Mary Draper!" said Maurice, filling his glass once more, while the name was re-echoed by every lip at table.

"The song! the song!"

"Faith, I hope I haven't forgotten it," quoth Maurice. "No; here it is."

So saying, after a couple of efforts to assure the pitch of his voice, the worthy Doctor began the following words to that very popular melody, "Nancy Dawson:"

"MARY DRAPER."

"Don't talk to me of London dames,
Nor rave about your foreign flames,
That never lived,—except in drames,
Nor shone, except on paper;
I'll sing you 'bout a girl I knew,
Who lived in Ballywhacmacrew,
And, let me tell you, mighty few
Could equal Mary Draper.

"Her cheeks were red, her eyes were blue,
Her hair was brown, of deepest hue,
Her foot was small, and neat to view,
Her waist was slight and taper;
Her voice was music to your ear,
A lovely brogue, so rich and clear,
Oh, the like I ne'er again shall hear,
As from sweet Mary Draper.

"She'd ride a wall, she'd drive a team,
Or with a fly she'd whip a stream,
Or may be sing you 'Rousseau's Dream,'
For nothing could escape her;
I've seen her, too—upon my word—
At sixty yards bring down her bird.
Oh! she charmed all the Forty-third,
Did lovely Mary Draper.

> "And at the spring assizes' ball,
>   The junior bar would one-and all
> For all her fav'rite dances call,
>   And Harry Deane would caper;
> Lord Clare would then forget his lore,
> King's Counsel, voting law a bore,
> Were proud to figure on the floor,
>   For love of Mary Draper.
>
> "The parson, priest, sub-sheriff too,
> Were all her slaves, and so would you,
> If you had only but one view
>   Of such a face and shape, or
> Her pretty ankles—but, ohone,
> It's only west of old Athlone
> Such girls were found—and now they're gone—
>   So here's to Mary Draper!"

"So here's to Mary Draper!" sang out every voice, in such efforts to catch the tune as pleased the taste of the motley assembly.

"For Mary Draper and Co., I thank you," said Maurice. "Quill drinks to Dennis," added he, in a grave tone, as he nodded to O'Shaughnessy. "Yes, Shaugh, few men better than ourselves know these matters; and few have had more experience of the three perils of Irishmen—love, liquor, and the law of arrest."

"It's little the latter has ever troubled my father's son," replied O'Shaughnessy; "our family have been writ proof for centuries, and he'd have been a bold man who would have ventured with an original or a true copy within the precincts of Killinahoula."

"Your father had a touch of Larry M'Hale in him," said I, "apparently."

"Exactly so," replied Dennis; "not but they caught him at last; and a scurvy trick it was, and well worthy of him who did it! Yes," said he, with a sigh, "it is only another among the many instances where the better features of our nationality have been used by our enemies as instruments for our destruction; and should we seek for the causes of unhappiness in our wretched country, we should find them rather in our virtues than in our vices, and in the bright rather than in the darker phases of our character."

"Metaphysics, by Jove!" cried Quill; "but all true at the same time. There was a messmate of mine in the Roscommon, who never paid car-hire in his life. 'Head or Harp, Paddy!' he would cry. 'Two tenpennies, or nothing. Harp! for the honor of ould Ireland,' was the invariable response, and my friend was equally sure to make head come uppermost; and, upon my soul, they seem to know the trick at the Home Office."

"That must have been the same fellow that took my father," cried O'Shaughnessy, with energy.

"Let us hear the story, Dennis," said I.

"Yes," said Maurice, "for the benefit of self and fellows, let us hear the stratagem!"

"The way of it was this," resumed O'Shaughnessy; "my father, who, for reasons registered in the King's Bench, spent a great many years of his life in that part of Ireland geographically known as lying west of the law, was obliged for certain reasons of family to come up to Dublin. This he proceeded to do with due caution. Two trusty servants formed an advanced guard, and patrolled the country for at least five miles in advance; after them came a skirmishing body of a few tenants, who, for the consideration of never paying rent, would have charged the whole Court of Chancery, if needful. My father himself, in an old chaise victualled like a fortress, brought up the rear; and, as I said before, he was a bold man who would have attempted to have laid siege to him. As the column advanced into the enemy's country, they assumed a closer order, the patrol and the picket falling back upon the main body; and in this way they reached that most interesting city called Kilbeggan. What a fortunate thing it is for us in Ireland that we can see so much of the world without foreign travel, and that any gentleman for six-and-eightpence can leave Dublin in the morning and visit Timbuctoo against dinner-time! Don't stare! it's truth I'm telling; for dirt, misery, smoke, unaffected behavior, and black faces, I'll back Kilbeggan against all Africa. Free-and-easy, pleasant people ye are, with a skin as begrimed and as rugged as your own potatoes! But, to resume. The sun was just rising in a delicious morning of June, when my father—whose loyal antipathies I have mentioned made him also an early riser—was preparing for the road. A stout escort of his followers were as usual under arms to see him safe in the chaise, the passage to and from which every day being the critical moment of my father's life.

"'It's all right, your honor,' said his own man, as, armed with a blunderbuss, he opened the bedroom door.

"'Time enough, Tim,' said my father; 'close the door, for I haven't finished my breakfast.'

"Now, the real truth was, that my father's attention was at that moment withdrawn from his own concerns, by a scene which was taking place in a field beneath his window.

"But a few minutes before, a hack-chaise had stopped upon the road-side, out of which sprang three gentlemen, who, proceeding into the field, seemed bent upon something, which, whether a survey or a duel, my father could not make out. He was not long, however, to remain in ignorance. One, with an easy, lounging gait, strode towards a distant corner; another took an opposite direction;

while a third, a short, pursy gentleman, in a red handkerchief and rabbit-skin waistcoat, proceeded to open a mahogany box, which, to the critical eyes of my respected father, was agreeably suggestive of bloodshed and murder.

"'A duel, by Jupiter!' said my father, rubbing his hands. 'What a heavenly morning the scoundrels have! not a leaf stirring, and a sod like a billiard-table!'

"Meanwhile, the little man who officiated as second, it would appear, to both parties, bustled about with an activity little congenial to his shape; and, what between snapping the pistols, examining the flints, and ramming down the charges, had got himself into a sufficient perspiration before he commenced to measure out the ground.

"'Short distance and no quarter!' shouted one of the combatants, from the corner of the field.

"'Across a handkerchief, if you like!' roared the other.

"'Gentlemen, every inch of them!' responded my father.

"'Twelve paces!' cried the little man. 'No more and no less. Don't forget that I am alone in this business.'

"'A very true remark!' observed my father; 'and an awkward predicament yours will be if they are not both shot!'

"By this time the combatants had taken their places, and the little man, having delivered the pistols, was leisurely retiring to give the word. My father, however, whose critical eye was never at fault, detected a circumstance which promised an immense advantage to one at the expense of the other; in fact, one of the parties was so placed with his back to the sun, that his shadow extended in a straight line to the very foot of his antagonist.

"'Unfair, unfair!' cried my father, opening the window as he spoke, and addressing himself to him of the rabbit-skin. 'I crave your pardon for the interruption,' said he; 'but I feel bound to observe that that gentleman's shadow is likely to make a shade of him.'

"'And so it is,' observed the short man; 'a thousand thanks for your kindness; but the truth is, I am totally unaccustomed to this kind of thing, and the affair will not admit of delay.'

"'Not an hour!' said one.

"'Not five minutes!' growled the other of the combatants.

"'Put them up north and south!' said my father.

"'Is it thus?'

"'Exactly so. But now again, the gentleman in the brown coat is covered with the ash-tree.'

"'And so he is!' said rabbit-skin, wiping his forehead with agitation.

33

"'Move them a little to the left,' said he.

"'That brings me upon an eminence,' said the gentleman in blue. 'I'll be d— if I'll be made a cock-shot of!'

"'What an awkward little thief it is in the hairy waistcoat!' said my father; 'he's lucky if he don't get shot himself!'

"'May I never, if I'm not sick of you both!' ejaculated rabbit-skin, in a passion. 'I've moved you round every point of the compass, and devil a nearer we are than ever.'

"'Give us the word,' said one.

"'The word!'

"'Downright murder,' said my father.

"'I don't care,' cried the little man; 'we shall be here till doomsday.'

"'I can't permit this,' said my father; 'allow me.' So saying, he stepped upon the window-sill, and leaped down into the field.

"'Before I can accept of your politeness,' said he of the rabbit-skin, 'may I beg to know your name and position in society?'

"'Nothing more reasonable,' said my father. 'I'm Miles O'Shaughnessy, Colonel of the Royal Raspers; here is my card.'

"The piece of pasteboard was complacently handed from one to the other of the party, who saluted my father with a smile of most courteous benignity.

"'Colonel O'Shaughnessy,' said one.

"'Miles O'Shaughnessy,' said the other.

"'Of Killinahoula Castle,' said the third.

"'At your service,' said my father, bowing as he presented his snuff-box; 'and now to business, if you please; for my time also is limited.'

"'Very true,' observed he of the rabbit-skin, 'and, as you observe, now to business; in virtue of which, Colonel Miles O'Shaughnessy, I hereby arrest you in the King's name. Here is the writ: it's at the suit of Barnaby Kelly, of Loughrea, for the sum of £1,482 19s. 7½d., which——'

"Before he could conclude the sentence, my father discharged one obligation, by implanting his closed knuckles in his face. The blow, well aimed and well intentioned, sent the little fellow summerset-ting like a sugar hogshead. But, alas! it was no use; the others, strong and able-bodied, fell both upon him, and after a desperate struggle succeeded in getting him down. To tie his hands and convey him to a chaise was the work of a few moments; and, as my father drove by the inn, the last object which caught his view was a bloody encounter between his own people and the myrmidons of the law, who, in great numbers, had laid siege to the house during his capture. Thus was my father taken; and thus, in reward for yielding to a virtuous weakness in his character, was he consigned to the ignominious durance of a prison. Was I not right, then, in saying that such is the melancholy position of our country, the most beautiful traits in our character are converted into the elements of our ruin?"

"I dinna think ye hae made out your case, Major," said the Scotch Doctor, who felt sorely puzzled at my friend's logic. "If your faither had nae gi'en the bond——"

"There is no saying what he wouldn't have done to the bailiffs," interrupted Dennis, who was following up a very different train of reasoning.

"I fear me, Doctor," observed Quill, "you are much behind us in Scotland. Not but that some of your chieftains are respectable men, and wouldn't get on badly even in Galway."

"I thank ye muckle for the compliment," said the Doctor, dryly; "but I hae my doubts they'd think it ane, and they're crusty carles that's no' ower safe to meddle wi'."

"I'd as soon propose a hand of spoiled five to the Pope of Rome, as a joke to one of them," returned Maurice.

"Maybe ye are na wrang there, Maister Quell."

"Well," cried Hampden, "if I may be allowed an opinion, I can safely aver I know no quarters like Scotland. Edinburgh beyond anything or anywhere I was ever placed in."

"Always after Dublin," interposed Maurice, while a general chorus of voices re-echoed the sentiment.

"You are certainly a strong majority," said my friend, "against me; but still I recant not my original opinion. Edinburgh before the world. For a hospitality that never tires; for pleasant fellows that improve every day of your acquaintance; for pretty girls that make you long for a repeal of the canon about being only singly blessed, and lead you to long for a score of them, Edinburgh, I say again, before the world."

"Their ankles are devilish thick," whispered Maurice.

"A calumny, a base calumny!"

"And then they drink——"

"Oh——"

"Yes; they drink very strong tea."

"Shall we hae a glass o' sherry together, Hampden?" said the Scotch Doctor, willing to acknowledge his defence of Auld Reekie.

"And we'll take O'Malley in," said Hampden; "he looks imploringly."

"And now to return to the charge," quoth Maurice. "In what particular dare ye contend the palm with Dublin? We'll not speak of beauty. I can't suffer any such profane turn in the conversation as to dispute the superiority of Irishwomen's lips, eyes, noses, and eyebrows, to anything under heaven. We'll not talk of gay fellows; egad, we needn't. I'll give you the garrison—a decent present; and I'll back the Irish bar for more genuine drollery, more wit, more epigram, more ready, sparkling fun, than the whole rest of the empire—ay, and all her colonies—can boast of."

"They are nae remarkable for passing the bottle, if they resemble their gifted advocate," observed the Scotchman.

"But they are for filling and emptying both, making its current, as it glides by, like a rich stream glittering in the sunbeams with the sparkling lustre of their wit. Lord, how I'm blown! Fill my pannikin, Charley. There's no subduing a Scot. Talk with him, drink with him, fight with him, and he'll always have the last of it: there's only one way of concluding the treaty——"

"And that is——"

"Blarney him. Lord bless you! he can't stand it. Tell him Holyrood's like Versailles, and the Trossachs finer than Mont Blanc; that Geordie Buchanan was Homer, and the Canongate, Herculaneum,—then ye have him on the hip. Now, ye can never humbug an Irishman that way; he'll know you're quizzing him when you praise his country."

"Ye are right, Hampden," said the Scotch Doctor, in reply to some observation. "We are vara primitive in the Hielands, and we keep to our ain national customs in dress and everything; and we are vara slow to learn; and even when we try, we are nae ower successfu' in our imitations, which sometimes cost us dearly enough. Ye may have heard, maybe, of the M'Nab o' that ilk, and what happened him with the King's equerry?"

"I am not quite certain," said Hampden, "if I ever heard the story."

"It's nae muckle of a story; but the way of it was this:—When Montrose came back from London, he brought with him a few Englishers to show them the Hielands, and let them see something of deer-stalking; among the rest, a certain Sir George Sowerby, an aide-de-camp or an equerry of the Prince. He was a vara fine gentleman, that never loaded his ain gun, and a'most thought it too much trouble to pull the trigger. He went out every morning to shoot with his hair curled like a woman, and dressed like a dancing-master. Now, there happened to be at the same time at the castle the Laird o' M'Nab; he was a kind of cousin of the Montrose, and a rough old tyke of the true Hieland breed, wha thought that the head of a clan was fully equal to any king or prince. He sat opposite to Sir George at dinner the day of his arrival, and could not conceal his surprise at the many new-fangled ways of feeding himself the Englisher adopted. He ate his saumon wi' his fork in ae hand and a bittock of bread in the other; he wouldna touch the whisky; helped himself to a cutlet wi' his fingers; but, what was maist extraordinary of all, he wore a pair of braw white gloves during the whole time o' dinner; and when they came to tak' away the cloth, he drew them off with a great air, and threw them into the middle of it, and then, leisurely-taking another pair off a silver salver which his ain man presented, he pat them on for the dessert. The M'Nab, who, although an auld-fashioned carle, was aye fond of bringing something new home to his friends, remarked the Englisher's proceeding with great care, and the next day he appeared at dinner wi' a huge pair of Hieland mittens, which he wore, to the astonishment of all and the amusement of most, through the whole three courses, and exactly as the Englishman changed his gloves, the M'Nab produced a fresh pair of goat's wool, four times as large as the first, which drawing on with prodigious gravity, he threw the others into the middle of the cloth, remarking as he did so,—

"'Ye see, Captain, we are never ower auld to learn.'

"All propriety was now at an end, and a hearty burst of laughter from one end of the table to the other convulsed the whole company; the M'Nab and the Englishman being the only two persons who did not join in it, but sat glowering at each other like twa tigers; and, indeed, it needed a' the Montrose's interferences that they hadna quarrelled upon it in the morning."

"The M'Nab was a man after my own heart," said Maurice; "there was something very Irish in the lesson he gave the Englishman."

"I'd rather ye'd told him that than me," said the Doctor, dryly; "he wouldna hae thanked ye for mistaking him for ane of your countrymen."

"Come, Doctor!" said Dennis, "could ye not give us a stave? Have ye nothing that smacks of the brown fern and the blue lakes in your memory?"

"I havena a sang in my mind just noo except Johnny Cope; which, maybe, might no' be ower pleasant for the Englishers to listen to."

"I never heard a Scotch song worth sixpence," quoth Maurice, who seemed bent on provoking the Doctor's ire. "They contain nothing save some puling sentimentality about lasses with lint-white locks, or some absurd laudations of the barley bree."

"Hear till him—hear till him!" said the Doctor, reddening with impatience.

"Show me anything," said Maurice, "like the 'Cruiskeen Lawn' or the 'Jug of Punch;' but who can blame them, after all? You can't expect much from a people with an imagination as naked as their own knees."

"Maurice! Maurice!" cried O'Shaughnessy, reprovingly, who saw that he was pushing the other's endurance beyond all bounds.

"I mind weel," said the Scotchman, "what happened to ane o' your countrymen wha took upon him to jest as you are doing now. It was to Laurie Cameron he did it."

"And what said the redoubted Laurie in reply?"

"He didna say muckle, but he did something."

"And what might it be?" inquired Maurice.

"He threw him ower the brig of Ayr into the water, and he was drowned."

"And did Laurie come to no harm about the matter?"

"Ay! they tried him for it, and found him guilty; but when they asked him what he had to say in his defence, he merely replied, 'When the carle sneered about Scotland, I didna suspect that he didna ken how to swim;' and so the end of it was, they did naething to Laurie."

"Cool that, certainly," said I.

"I prefer your friend with the mittens, I confess," said Maurice; "though I'm sure both were most agreeable companions. But come, Doctor, couldn't you give us,—

> "Sit ye down, my heartie, and gie us a crack,
> Let the wind tak' the care o' the world on its back."

"You maunna attempt English poetry, my freend Quell; for it must be confessed you've a d— accent of your ain."

"Milesian-Phœnician-Corkacian—nothing more, my boy; and a coaxing kind of recitative it is, after all. Don't tell me of your soft Etruscan—your plethoric Hoch-Deutsch—your flattering French. To woo and win the girl of your heart, give me a rich brogue and the least taste in life of blarney! There's nothing like it, believe me—every inflection of your voice suggesting some tender pressure of her soft hand or taper waist; every cadence falling on her gentle heart like a sea-breeze on a burning coast, or a soft sirocco over a rose-tree; and then think, my boys,—and it is a fine thought after all,—what a glorious gift that is, out of the reach of kings to give or to take, what neither depends upon the act of Union nor the *Habeas Corpus.* No! they may starve us—laugh at us—tax us—transport us. They may take our mountains, our valleys, and our bogs; but, bad luck to them, they can't steal our 'blarney;' that's the privilege one and indivisible with our identity; and while an Englishman raves of his liberty—a Scotchman of his oaten meal—blarney's *our* birthright, and a prettier portion I'd never ask to leave

behind me to my sons. If I'd as large a family as the ould gentleman called Priam we used to hear of at school, it's the only inheri-
tance I'd give them; and one comfort there would be besides—the
legacy duty would be only a trifle. Charley, my son, I see you're
listening to me, and nothing satisfies me more than to instruct
aspiring youth; so never forget the old song,—

> "If at your ease, the girls you'd please,
>   And win them, like Kate Kearney,
> There's but one way, I've heard them say,
>   Go kiss the 'Stone of Blarney.'"

"What do you say, Shaugh, if we drink it with all the honors?"
"But gently: do I hear a trumpet there?"
"Ah, there go the bugles. Can it be daybreak already?"
"How short the nights are at this season!" said Quill.
"What an infernal rumpus they're making! it's not possible the
troops are to march so early."
"It wouldn't surprise me in the least;" quoth Maurice; "there
is no knowing what the Commander-in-Chief's not capable of: the
reason's clear enough."
"And why, Maurice?"
"There's not a bit of blarney about him."
The *reveille* rang out from every brigade, and the drums beat to
fall in, while Mike came galloping up at full speed to say that the
bridge of boats was complete, and that the 12th were already ordered
to cross. Not a moment was therefore to be lost; one parting cup
was drained to our next meeting, and amid a hundred "good-byes"
we mounted our horses. Poor Hampden's brains being sadly confused by the wine and the laughing, he knew little of what was
going on around him, and passed the entire time of our homeward
ride in a vain endeavor to adapt Mary Draper to the air of "Rule
Britannia."

CHAPTER XXIV.

FUENTES D'ONORO.

FROM this period the French continued their retreat, closely
followed by the allied armies, and on the 5th of April Massena once more crossed the frontier into Spain, leaving thirty
thousand of his bravest troops behind him, fourteen thousand of
whom had fallen, or been taken prisoners; reinforcements, however,

came rapidly pouring in. Two divisions of the ninth corps had already arrived, and Drouet, with eleven thousand infantry and cavalry, was preparing to march to his assistance. Thus strengthened, the French army marched towards the Portuguese frontier, and Lord Wellington, who had determined not to hazard much by his blockade of Ciudad Rodrigo, fell back upon the large table-land beyond the Turones and the Dos Casas, with his left at Fort Conception, and his right resting upon Fuentes d'Onoro. His position extended to about five miles; and here, although vastly inferior in numbers, yet relying upon the bravery of the troops, and the moral ascendency acquired by their pursuit of the enemy, he finally resolved upon giving them battle.

Being sent with despatches to Pack's Brigade, which formed the blockading force at Almeida, I did not reach Fuentes d'Onoro until the evening of the 3d. The thundering of the guns, which, even at the distance I was at, was plainly heard, announced then an attack had taken place, but it by no means prepared me for the scene which presented itself on my return.

The village of Fuentes d'Onoro, one of the most beautiful in Spain, is situated in a lovely valley, where all the charms of verdure so peculiar to the Peninsula seemed to have been scattered with a lavish hand. The citron and the arbutus, growing wild, sheltered every cottage door, and the olive and the laurel threw their shadows across the little rivulet which traversed the village. The houses, observing no uniform arrangement, stood wherever the caprice or the inclination of the builder suggested, surrounded with little gardens, the inequality of the ground imparting a picturesque feature to even the lowliest hut, while, upon a craggy eminence above the rest, an ancient convent and a ruined chapel looked down upon the little peaceful hamlet with an air of tender protection.

Hitherto, this lovely spot had escaped all the ravages of war. The light division of our army had occupied it for months long; and every family was gratefully remembered by some one or other of our officers; and more than one of our wounded found in the kind and affectionate watching of these poor peasants the solace which sickness rarely meets with when far from home and country.

It was with an anxious heart that I pressed my horse forward into a gallop as the night drew near. The artillery had been distinctly heard during the day, and while I burned with eagerness to know the result, I felt scarcely less anxious for the fate of that little hamlet whose name many a kind story had implanted in my memory. The moon was shining brightly as I passed the outpost; leading my horse by the bridle, I descended the steep and rugged causeway to the village beneath me. The lanterns were moving rapidly to and fro; the measured tread of infantry at night—that ominous sound, which falls upon the heart so sadly—told me that they were burying the dead. The air was still and breathless; not a sound was stirring save the step of the soldiery, and the harsh clash of the shovel as it struck the earth. I felt sad, and sick at heart, and leaned against a tree. A nightingale concealed in the leaves was pouring forth its plaintive notes to the night air, and its low warble sounded like the dirge of the departed. Far beyond, in the plain, the French watch-fires were burning, and I could see from time to time the fatigue-parties moving in search of their wounded. At this moment the clock of the convent struck eleven, and a merry chime rang out, and was taken up by the echoes, till it melted away in the distance. Alas! where were those whose hearts were wont to feel cheered at that happy peal?—whose infancy it had gladdened, whose old age it has hallowed? The fallen walls, the broken roof-trees, the ruin and desolation on every side, told plainly that they had passed away forever. The smoking embers, the torn-up pathway, denoted the hard-fought struggle; and, as I passed along, I could see that every garden where the cherry and the apple-blossom were even still per-fuming the air, had now its sepulchre.

"Halt, there!" cried a hoarse voice in front. "You cannot pass this way—the Commander-in-Chief's quarters."

I looked up, and beheld a small but neat-looking cottage, which seemed to have suffered less than the others around. Lights were shining brightly from the windows, and I could even detect from time to time a figure muffled up in a cloak, passing to and fro across the window, while another, seated at a table, was occupied in writing. I turned into a narrow path which led into the little square of the village, and here, as I approached, the hum and murmur of voices announced a bivouac party. Stopping to ask what had been the result of the day, I learned that a tremendous attack had been made by the French in column upon the village, which was at first successful, but that afterwards the 71st and 79th, marching down from the heights, had repulsed the enemy, and driven them beyond the Dos Casas. Five hundred had fallen in that fierce encounter, which was continued through every street and alley of the little hamlet. The gallant Highlanders now occupied the battle-field; and hearing that the cavalry brigade was some miles distant, I willingly accepted their offer to share their bivouac, and passed the remainder of the night among them.

When day broke, our troops were under arms, but the enemy showed no disposition to renew the attack. We could perceive, however, from the road to the southward, by the long columns of dust, that reinforcements were still arriving, and learned during the morning, from a deserter, that Massena himself had come up, and Bessières also, with twelve hundred cavalry, and a battery of the Imperial Guard.

From the movements observable among the enemy, it was soon evident that the battle, though deferred, was not abandoned, and the march of a strong force towards the left of their position induced our Commander-in-Chief to despatch the seventh division, under Houston, to occupy the height of Naval d'Aver,—our extreme right,—in support of which our brigade of cavalry marched as a covering force. The British position was thus unavoidably extended to the enormous length of seven miles, occupying a succession of small eminences, from the division at Fort Conception to the height of Naval d'Aver, Fuentes d'Onoro forming nearly the centre of the line.

It was evident, from the thickening combinations of the French, that a more dreadful battle was still in reserve for us; and yet never did men look more anxiously for the morrow.

As for myself, I felt a species of exhilaration I had never before experienced. The events of the preceding day came dropping in upon me from every side, and at every new tale of gallantry or daring I felt my heart bounding with excited eagerness to win also my meed of honorable praise.

Craufurd, too, had recognized me in the kindest manner, and while saying that he did not wish to withdraw me from my regiment on a day of battle, added that he would make use of me for the present on his staff. Thus was I engaged from early morning till late in the evening bringing orders and despatches along the line. The troop-horse I rode—for I reserved my gray for the following day—was scarcely able to carry me along, as towards dusk I jogged along in the direction of Naval d'Aver. When I did reach our quarters, the fires were lighted, and around one of them I had the good fortune to find a party of the 14th occupied in discussing a very appetizing little supper. The clatter of plates and the popping of champagne corks were most agreeable sounds. Indeed, the latter appeared to me so much too flattering an illusion, that I hesitated to credit my senses in the matter, when Baker called out,—

"Come, Charley, sit down; you're just in the nick. Tom Marsden is giving us a benefit. You know Tom?"

And here he presented me in due form to that best of commissaries and most hospitable of horse-dealers.

"I can't introduce you to my friend on my right," continued Baker, "for my Spanish is only a skeleton battalion. But he's a trump—that I'll vouch for; never flinches his glass, and looks as though he enjoyed all our nonsense."

The Spaniard, who appeared to comprehend that he was alluded to, gravely saluted me with a low bow, and offered his glass to hob-nob with me. I returned the compliment with becoming ceremony, while Hampden whispered in my ear,—

"A fine-looking fellow. You know who he is? Julian, the Guerilla chief."

I had heard much of both the strangers. Tom Marsden was a household word in every cavalry brigade, equally celebrated for his contracts and his claret. He knew every one, from Lord Welling-ton to the last-joined cornet; and, while upon a march, there was no piece of better fortune than to be asked to dine with him. So, in the very thick of a battle, Tom's critical eye was scanning the squad-rons engaged, with an accuracy as to the number of fresh horses that would be required upon the morrow that nothing but long practice and infinite coolness could have conferred.

Of the Guerilla I need not speak. The bold feats he accom-plished, the aid he rendered to the cause of his country, have made his name historical. Yet still, with all this, fatigue, more powerful than my curiosity, prevailed, and I sank into a heavy sleep upon the grass, while my merry companions kept up their revels till near morning. The last piece of consciousness I am sensible of was see-ing Julian spreading his wide mantle over me as I lay, while I heard his deep voice whisper a kind wish for my repose.

CHAPTER XXV.

THE BATTLE OF FUENTES D'ONORO.

SO soundly did I sleep, that the tumult and confusion of the morning never awoke me; and the Guerilla, whose cavalry were stationed along the edge of the ravine near the heights of Echora, would not permit of my being roused before the last moment. Mike stood near me with my horses, and it was only when the squadrons were actually forming that I sprang to my feet and looked around me.

The day was just breaking. A thick mist lay upon the parched earth, and concealed everything a hundred yards from where we stood. From this dense vapor the cavalry defiled along the base of the hill, followed by the horse artillery and the Guards, disappear-ing as they passed us, but proving, by the mass of troops now assembled, that our position was regarded as the probable point of attack.

While the troops continued to take up their position, the sun shone out, and a light breeze blowing at the same moment, the heavy clouds moved past, and we beheld the magnificent panorama of the battle-field. Before us, at the distance of less than half a league, the French cavalry were drawn up in three strong columns. The Cuirassiers of the Guard, plainly distinguishable by their steel cuirasses, flanked by the Polish lancers and a strong hussar brigade; a powerful artillery train supported the left, and an infantry force occupied the entire space between the right and the rising ground opposite Poço Velho. Farther to the right again, the columns destined for the attack of Fuentes d'Onoro were forming, and we could see that, profiting by their past experience, they were bent upon attacking the village with an overwhelming force.

For above two hours the French continued to manœuvre, more than one alteration having taken place in their disposition. Fresh battalions were moved towards the front, and gradually the whole of their cavalry were assembled on the extreme left in front of our position. Our people were ordered to breakfast where we stood; and a little after seven o'clock a staff officer came riding down the line, followed in a few moments after by General Craufurd, when no sooner was his well-known brown cob recognized by the troops, than a hearty cheer greeted him along the whole division.

"Thank ye, boys; thank ye, boys, with all my heart! No man feels more sensibly what that cheer means than I do. Guards! Lord Wellington relies upon your maintaining this position, which is essential to the safety of the whole line. You will be supported by the light division. I need say no more. If such troops cannot keep their ground, none can. There's your place, 14th; the artillery and the 16th are with you. They've the odds of us in numbers, lads; but it will tell all the better in the *Gazette.* I see they're moving; so fall in, now, fall in; and, Merivale, move to the front. Ramsey, prepare at once to open your fire on the attacking squadrons."

As he spoke, the low murmuring sound of distantly-moving cavalry crept along the earth, growing louder and louder, till at length we could detect the heavy tramp of the squadrons as they came on in a trot, our pace being merely a walk. While we thus advanced into the plain, the artillery unlimbered behind us, and the Spanish cavalry, breaking into skirmishers, dashed boldly to the front.

It was an exciting moment. The ground dipped between the two armies, so as to conceal the head of the advancing column of the French, and as the Spanish skirmishers disappeared down the ridge, our beating hearts and straining eyes followed their last horseman.

"Halt! halt!" was passed from squadron to squadron, and the same instant the sharp ring of the pistol-shots and the clash of steel from the valley told us the battle had begun. We could hear the Guerilla war-cry mingle with the French shout, while the thickening crash of fire-arms implied a sharper conflict. Our fellows were already manifesting some impatience to press on, when a Spanish horseman appeared above the ridge; another followed, and another, and then pell-mell, broken and disordered, they fell back before the pursuing cavalry in flying masses; while the French, charging them hotly home, utterly routed and repulsed them.

The leading squadrons of the French now fell back upon their support; the column of attack thickened, and a thundering noise between their masses announced their brigade of light guns as they galloped to the front. It was then for the first time I felt dispirited; far as my eye could stretch, the dense mass of sabres extended, defiling from the distant hills and winding its slow length across the plain. I turned to look at our line, scarce one thousand strong, and could not help feeling that our hour was come. The feeling flashed vividly across my mind, but the next instant I felt my cheek redden with shame as I gazed upon the sparkling eyes and bold looks around me—the lips compressed, the hands knitted to their sabres; all were motionless, but burning to advance.

The French had halted on the brow of the hill to form, when Merivale came cantering up to us.

"Fourteenth, are you ready? Are you ready, lads?"

"Ready, sir! ready!" re-echoed along the line.

"Then push them home and charge! Charge!" cried he, raising his voice to a shout at the last word.

Heavens! what a crash was there! Our horses, in top condition, no sooner felt the spur than they bounded madly onwards. The pace—for the distance did not exceed four hundred yards—was like racing. To resist the impetus of our approach was impossible; and without a shot fired, scarcely a sabre-cut exchanged, we actually rode down their advanced squadrons—hurling them headlong upon their supporting division, and rolling men and horses beneath us on every side. The French fell back upon their artillery; but before they could succeed in opening their fire upon us, we had wheeled, and, carrying off about seventy prisoners, galloped back to our position with the loss of but two men in the affair. The whole thing was so sudden, so bold, and so successful, that I remember well, as we rode back, a hearty burst of laughter was ringing through the squadron at the ludicrous display of horsemanship the French presented as they tumbled headlong down the hill; and I cannot help treasuring the recollection, for, from that moment, all thought of anything short of victory completely quitted my mind, and many of my brother officers, who had participated in my feelings at the commencement of the day, confessed to me afterwards that it was then for the first time they felt assured of beating the enemy.

While we slowly fell back to our position, the French were seen advancing in great force from the village of Almeida, to the attack of Poço Velho; they came on at a rapid pace, their artillery upon their front and flank, large masses of cavalry hovering around them. The attack upon the village was now opened by the large guns; and amid the booming of the artillery and the crashing volleys of small fire-arms, rose the shout of the assailants, and the wild cry of the Guerilla cavalry, who had formed in front of the village. The French advanced firmly, driving back the pickets, and actually inundated the devoted village with a shower of grape; the blazing fires burst from the ignited roofs; and the black, dense smoke rising on high, seemed to rest like a pall over the little hamlet.

The conflict now was a tremendous one. Our seventh division held the village with the bayonet; but the French, continuing to pour in mass upon mass, drove them back with loss, and, at the end of an hour's hard fighting, took possession of the place.

The wood upon the left flank was now seen to swarm with light infantry, and the advancement of their whole left proved that they meditated to turn our flank. The space between the village and the hill of Naval d'Aver thus became the central position; and here the Guerilla force, led on by Julian Sanches, seemed to await the French with confidence. Soon, however, the cuirassiers came galloping to the spot, and, almost without exchanging a sabre-cut, the Guerillas fell back, and retired behind the Turones. This movement of Julian was more attributable to anger than to fear; for his favorite lieutenant, being mistaken for a French officer, was shot by a soldier of the Guards a few minutes before.

Montbrun pursued the Guerillas with some squadrons of horse, but they turned resolutely upon the French, and not till overwhelmed by numbers did they show any disposition to retreat.

The French, however, now threw forward their whole cavalry, and, driving back the English horse, succeeded in turning the right of the seventh division. The battle by this time was general. The staff officers who came up from the left informed us that Fuentes d'Onoro was attacked in force, Massena himself leading the assault in person; while thus for seven miles the fight was maintained hotly at intervals, it was evident that upon the maintenance of our position the fortune of the day depended. Hitherto we had been repulsed from the village and the wood; and the dark masses of infantry which were assembled upon our right seemed to threaten the hill of Naval d'Aver with as sad a catastrophe.

Craufurd now came galloping up amongst us, his eye flashing fire, and his uniform splashed and covered with foam.

"Steady, 16th, steady! Don't blow your horses! Have your fellows advanced, Malcolm?" said he, turning to an officer who stood beside him. "Ay, there they go!" pointing with his finger to the wood, where, as he spoke, the short ringing of the British rifle proclaimed the advance of that brigade. "Let the cavalry prepare to charge! And now, Ramsey, let us give it them home!"

Scarcely were the words spoken, when the squadrons were formed, and in an instant after the French light infantry were seen retreating from the wood, and flying in disorderly masses across the plain. Our squadrons, riding down amongst them, actually cut them to atoms, while the light artillery, unlimbering, threw in a deadly discharge of grape-shot.

"To the right, 14th, to the right!" cried General Stewart. "Have at their hussars!"

Whirling by them, we advanced at a gallop, and dashed towards the enemy, who, not less resolutely bent, came boldly forward to meet us. The shock was terrific! the leading squadrons on both sides went down almost to a man, and, all order being lost, the encounter became one of hand to hand.

The struggle was deadly; neither party would give way; and, while fortune now inclined hither and thither, Sir Charles Stewart singled out the French General Lamotte, and carried him off his prisoner. Meanwhile, Montbrun's cavalry and the cuirassiers came riding up, and, the retreat now sounding through our ranks, we were obliged to fall back upon the infantry. The French pursued us hotly; and so rapid was their movement, that, before Ramsey's brigade could limber up and away, their squadrons had surrounded him and captured his guns.

"Where is Ramsey?" cried Craufurd, as he galloped to the head of our division. "Cut off—cut off! Taken, by G—! There he goes!" said he, pointing with his finger, as a dense cloud of mingled smoke and dust moved darkly across the plain. "Form into column once more!"

As he spoke, the dense mass before us seemed agitated by some mighty commotion; the flashing of blades, and the rattling of small arms, mingled with shouts of triumph or defiance, burst forth, and the ominous cloud, lowering more darkly, seemed peopled by those in deadly strife. An English cheer pealed high above all other sounds; a second followed; the mass was rent asunder, and, like the forked lightning from a thunder-cloud, Ramsey rode forth at the head of his battery, the horses bounding madly, while the guns sprang behind them like things of no weight; the gunners leaped to their places, and fighting hand to hand with the French cavalry, they flew across the plain.

"Nobly done, gallant Ramsey!" said a voice behind me. I turned at the sound; it was Lord Wellington who spoke. My eye fixed upon his stern features, I forgot all else; when he suddenly recalled me to my recollection by saying,

"Follow your brigade, sir. Charge!"

In an instant I was with my people, who, intervening betwixt Ramsey and his pursuers, repulsed the enemy with loss, and carried off several prisoners. The French, however, came up in greater strength; overwhelming masses of cavalry came sweeping upon us, and we were obliged to retire behind the light division, which rapidly formed into squares to resist the cavalry. The seventh division, which was more advanced, were, however, too late for this movement, and, before they could effect their formation, the French were upon them. At this moment they owed their safety to the Chasseurs Britanniques, who poured in a flanking fire, so close, and with so deadly an aim, that their foes recoiled, beaten and bewildered.

Meanwhile, the French had become masters of Poço Velho; the formidable masses had nearly outflanked us on the right. The battle was lost, if we could not fall back upon our original position, and concentrate our force upon Fuentes d'Onoro. To effect this was a work of great difficulty; but no time was to be lost. The seventh division were ordered to cross the Turones, while Craufurd, forming the light division into squares, covered their retreat, and, supported by the cavalry, sustained the whole force of the enemy's attack.

Then was the moment to witness the cool and steady bravery of British infantry; the squares dotted across the enormous plain seemed as nothing amid that confused and flying multitude, composed of commissariat baggage, camp-followers, peasants, and, finally, broken pickets and videttes arriving from the wood. A cloud of cavalry hovered and darkened around them; the Polish lancers shook their long spears, impatient of delay, and the wild huzzas burst momentarily from their squadrons as they waited for the word to attack. But the British stood firm and undaunted; and although the enemy rode round their squares, Montbrun himself at their head, they never dared to charge them. Meanwhile, the seventh division fell back, as if on a parade, and crossing the river, took up their ground at Frenada, pivoting upon the first division; the remainder of the line also fell back, and assumed a position at right angles with their former one, the cavalry forming in front, and holding the French in check during the movement. This was a splendid manœuvre, and, when made in face of an overnumbering enemy, one unmatched during the whole war.

At sight of this new front the French stopped short, and opened a fire from their heavy guns. The British batteries replied with vigor, and silenced the enemy's cannon. The cavalry drew out of range, and the infantry gradually fell back to their former position. While this was going on, the attack upon Fuentes d'Onoro was continued with unabated vigor. The three British regiments in the lower town were pierced by the French tirailleurs, who poured upon them in overwhelming numbers; the 79th were broken, ten companies taken, and Cameron, their colonel, mortally wounded. Thus the lower village was in the hands of the enemy, while from the upper town the incessant roll of musketry proclaimed the obstinate resistance of the British.

At this period our reserves were called up from the right, in time to resist the additional troops which Drouet continued to bring on. The French, reinforced by the whole sixth corps, now came forward at a quick step. Dashing through the ruined streets of the lower town, they crossed the rivulet, fighting bravely, and charged against the height. Already their leading files had gained the crag beside the chapel. A French colonel, holding his cap upon his sword-point, waved on his men.

The grizzly features of the grenadiers soon appeared, and the dark column, half climbing, half running, were seen scaling the height. A rifle-bullet sent the French leader tumbling from the precipice; and a cheer—mad and reckless as the war-cry of an Indian—rent the sky, as the 71st and 79th Highlanders sprang upon the enemy.

Our part was a short one; advancing in half-squadrons, we were concealed from the observation of the enemy by the thick vineyards which skirted the lower town, waiting with impatience the moment when our gallant infantry should succeed in turning the tide of battle. We were ordered to dismount, and stood with our bridles on our arms, anxious and expectant. The charge of the French column was made close to where we were standing—the inspiriting cheers of the officers, the loud *vivas* of the men, were plainly heard by us as they rushed to the assault; but the space between us was intersected by walls and brushwood, which totally prevented the movements of cavalry.

Fearlessly their dark column moved up the heights, fixing the bayonets as they went. No tirailleurs preceded them, but the tall shako of the Grenadier of the Guard was seen in the first rank. Long before the end of the column had passed us, the leading files

34

were in action. A deafening peal of musketry—so loud, so dense, it seemed like artillery—burst forth. A volume of black smoke rolled heavily down from the heights and hid all from our view, except when the vivid lightning of the platoon firing rent the veil asunder, and showed us the troops almost in hand to hand conflict.

"It's Picton's division, I'm certain," cried Merivale; "I hear the bagpipes of the Highlanders."

"You are right, sir," said Hampden; "the 71st are in the same brigade, and I know their bugles well. There they go again!"

"Fourteenth! Fourteenth!" cried a voice from behind, and at the same moment a staff officer, without his hat, and his horse bleeding from a recent sabre-cut, came up. "You must move to the rear, Colonel Merivale; the French have gained the heights! Move round by the causeway—bring up your squadrons as quickly as you can, and support the infantry!"

In a moment we were in our saddles; but scarcely was the word to fall in given, when a loud cheer rent the very air; the musketry seemed suddenly to cease, and the dark mass which continued to struggle up the heights wavered, broke, and turned.

"What can that be?" said Merivale. "What can it mean?"

"I can tell you, sir," said I, proudly, while I felt my heart as though it would bound from my bosom.

"And what is it, boy? Speak!"

"There it goes again! That was an Irish shout! The 88th are at them!"

"By Jove! here they come!" said Hampden. "God help the Frenchmen now!"

The words were not well spoken, when the red coats of our gallant fellows were seen dashing through the vineyard.

"The steel, boys—nothing but the steel!" shouted a loud voice from the crag above our heads.

I looked up. It was the stern Picton himself who spoke.

The 88th now led the pursuit, and sprang from rock to rock in all the mad impetuosity of battle; and like some mighty billow rolling before the gale, the French went down the heights.

"Gallant 88th! Gloriously done!" cried Picton, as he waved his hat.

"Aren't we Connaught robbers, now?" shouted a rich brogue, as its owner, breathless and bleeding, pressed forward in the charge.

A hearty burst of laughter mingled with the din of the battle.

"Now for it, boys! Now for *our* work!" said old Merivale, drawing his sabre as he spoke. "Forward! and charge!"

We waited not a second bidding, but bursting from our concealment, galloped down into the broken column. It was no regular charge, but an indiscriminate rush. Scarcely offering resistance, the enemy fell beneath our sabres, or the still more deadly bayonets of the infantry, who were inextricably mixed up in the conflict.

The chase was followed up for above half a mile, when we fell back, fortunately in good time; for the French had opened a heavy fire from their artillery, and, regardless of their own retreating column, poured a shower of grape among our squadrons. As we retired, the struggling files of the Rangers joined us—their faces and accoutrements blackened and begrimed with powder; many of them, themselves wounded, had captured prisoners; and one huge fellow of the grenadier company was seen driving before him a no less powerful Frenchman, and to whom, as he turned from time to time reluctantly, and scowled upon his gaoler, the other vociferated some Irish imprecation, whose harsh intentions were made most palpably evident by a flourish of a drawn bayonet.

"Who is he?" said Mike; "who is he, ahagur?"

"Sorra one o' me knows," said the other; "but it's the chap that shot Lieutenant Mahony, and I never took my eye off him after; and if the Lieutenant's not dead, sure it'll be a satisfaction to him that I cotch him."

*   *   *   *   *   *   *   *

The lower town was now evacuated by the French, who retired beyond the range of our artillery; the upper continued in the occupation of our troops. Worn out and exhausted, surrounded by dead and dying, both parties abandoned the contest—and the battle was over.

Both sides laid claim to the victory; the French, because, having taken the village of Poço Velho, they had pierced the British line, and compelled them to fall back and assume a new position; the British, because the attack upon Fuentes d'Onoro had been successfully resisted, and the blockade of Almeida—the real object of the battle—maintained. The loss to each was tremendous: fifteen hundred men and officers, of whom three hundred were prisoners, were lost by the allies, and a far greater number fell among the forces of the enemy.

After the action, a brigade of the light division released the troops in the village, and the armies bivouacked once more in sight of each other.

CHAPTER XXVI.

A RENCONTRE.

THE day after the battle, as I awoke from a sound and heavy slumber, the result of thirteen hours on horseback, the first paragraph of a general order, dated Fuentes d'Onoro, arrested my attention. "Lieutenant O'Malley, 14th Light Dragoons, to serve as extra aide-de-camp to Major-General Craufurd, until the pleasure of his Royal Highness the Prince Regent is known."

A staff appointment was not exactly what I desired at the moment; but I knew that with Craufurd, my duties were more likely to be at the pickets and advanced posts of the army than in the mere details of note-writing or despatch-bearing; besides that, I felt, whenever anything of importance was to be done, I should always obtain his permission to do duty with my regiment.

Taking a hurried breakfast, therefore, I mounted my horse, and cantered over to Villa Formosa, where the General's quarters were, to return thanks for my promotion, and take the necessary steps for assuming my new functions.

Although the sun had risen about two hours, the fatigue of the previous day had impressed itself upon all around. The cavalry, men and horses, were still stretched upon the sward, sunk in sleep; the videttes, weary and tired, seemed anxiously watching for the relief, and the disordered and confused appearance of everything bespoke that discipline-had relaxed its stern features, in compassion for the bold exertions of the preceding day. The only contrast to this general air of exhaustion and weariness on every side was a corps of sappers, who were busily employed upon the high grounds above the village. Early as it was, they seemed to have been at work some hours—at least so their labors bespoke; for already a rampart of considerable extent had been thrown up, stockades implanted, and a breastwork was in a state of active preparation. The officer of the party, wrapped up in a loose cloak, and mounted upon a sharp-looking hackney, rode hither and thither, as the occasion warranted, and seemed, as well as from the distance I could guess, something of a tartar. At least I could not help remarking how at his approach the several inferior officers seemed suddenly so much more on the alert, and the men worked with an additional vigor and activity. I stopped for some minutes to watch him, and seeing an engineer captain of my acquaintance among the party, couldn't resist calling out:

"I say, Hachard, your friend on the chestnut mare must have had an easier day yesterday than some of us, or I'll be hanged if he'd be so active this morning." Hachard hung his head in some confusion, and did not reply; and, on my looking round, whom should I see before me but the identical individual I had been so coolly criticising, and who, to my utter horror and dismay, was no other than Lord Wellington himself. I did not wait for a second peep. Helter-skelter, through water, thickets, and brambles, away I went, clattering down the causeway like a madman. If a French squadron had been behind me, I should have had a stouter heart, although I did not fear pursuit. I felt his eye was upon me—his sharp and piercing glance, that shot like an arrow into me; and his firm look stared at me in every object around.

Onward I pressed, feeling in the very recklessness of my course some relief to my sense of shame, and ardently hoping that some accident—some smashed arm or broken collar-bone—might befall me, and rescue me from any notice my conduct might otherwise call for. I never drew rein till I reached the Villa Formosa, and pulled up short at a small cottage, where a double sentry apprised me of the General's quarters. As I came up, the low lattice sprang quickly open, and a figure, half dressed and more than half asleep, protruded his head.

"Well, what has happened? Anything wrong?" said he, whom I now recognized to be General Craufurd.

"No; nothing wrong, sir," stammered I, with evident confusion. "I'm merely come to thank you for your kindness in my behalf."

"You seemed in a devil of a hurry to do it, if I'm to judge by the pace you came at. Come in and take your breakfast with us; I shall be dressed presently, and you'll meet some of your brother aides-de-camp."

Having given my horse to an orderly, I walked into a little room, whose humble accommodations and unpretending appearance seemed in perfect keeping with the simple and unostentatious character of the General. The preparations for a good and substantial breakfast were, however, before me, and an English newspaper of a late date spread its most ample pages to welcome me. I had not been long absorbed in my reading, when the door opened, and the General, whose toilet was not yet completed, made his appearance.

"Egad, O'Malley, you startled me this morning. I thought we were in for it again."

I took this as the most seasonable opportunity to recount my mishap of the morning, and accordingly, without more ado, detailed the unlucky meeting with the Commander-in-Chief. When I came to the end, Craufurd threw himself into a chair and laughed till the very tears coursed down his bronzed features.

"You don't say so, boy? You don't really tell me you said that?

By Jove! I would rather have faced a whole platoon of musketry than have stood in your shoes! You did not wait for a reply, I think?"

"No, faith, sir, that I did not!"

"Do you suspect he knows you?"

"I trust not, sir; the whole thing passed so rapidly."

"Well, it's most unlucky in more ways than one!" He paused for a few moments as he said this, and then added, "Have you seen the general order?" pushing towards me a written paper as he spoke. It ran thus:

"G. O.　　　　　　　　　　　Adjutant-General's Office, Villa Formosa,
　　　　　　　　　　　　　　　　　"May 6, 1811.

"*Memorandum.*—Commanding officers are requested to send in to the Military Secretary, as soon as possible, the names of officers they may wish to have promoted in succession to those who have fallen in action."

"Now, look at this list. The Hon. Harvey Howard, Grenadier Guards, to be First Lieutenant, *vice* ——. No, not that. Henry Beauchamp—George Villiers. Ay, here it is! Captain Lyttleton, 14th Light Dragoons, to be Major in the 3d Dragoon Guards, *vice* Godwin, killed in action; Lieutenant O'Malley to be Captain, *vice* Lyttleton, promoted. You see, my boy, I did not forget you; you were to have had the vacant troop in your own regiment. Now, I almost doubt the prudence of bringing your name under Lord Wellington's notice. He may have recognized you, and if he did so,— why, I rather think—that is, I suspect—I mean, the quieter you keep the better."

While I poured forth my gratitude as warmly as I was able for the General's great kindness to me, I expressed my perfect concurrence in his views.

"Believe me, sir," said I, "I should much rather wait any number of years for my promotion than incur the risk of a reprimand!—the more so as it is not the first time I have blundered with his lordship." I here narrated my former meeting with Sir Arthur, at which Craufurd's mirth again burst forth, and he paced the room holding his sides in an ecstasy of merriment.

"Come, come, lad, we'll hope for the best; we'll give you the chance that he has not seen your face, and send the list forward as it is. But here come our fellows."

As he spoke, the door opened, and three officers of his staff entered, to whom, being severally introduced, we chatted away about the news of the morning until breakfast.

"I've frequently heard of you from my friend Hammersley," said

Captain Fitzroy, addressing me; "you were intimately acquainted, I believe?"

"Oh, yes! Pray, where is he now? We have not met for a long time."

"The poor fellow's invalided; that sabre-cut upon his head has turned out a sad affair, and he's gone back to England on a sick leave. Old Dashwood took him back with him as private secretary, or something of that sort."

"Ah!" said another; "Dashwood has daughters, hasn't he? No bad notion of his, for Hammersley will be a baronet some of these days, with a rent-roll of eight or nine thousand per annum."

"Sir George Dashwood," said I, "has but one daughter, and I am quite sure that in his kindness to Hammersley no intentions of the kind you mention were mixed up."

"Well, I don't know," said the third, a pale, sickly youth, with handsome but delicate features. "I was on Dashwood's staff until a few weeks ago, and certainly I thought there was something going on between Hammersley and Miss Lucy, who, be it spoken, is a devilish fine girl, though rather disposed to give herself airs."

I felt my cheek and my temples boiling like a furnace; my hand trembled as I lifted my coffee to my lips, and I would have given my expected promotion twice over to have had any reasonable ground of quarrel with the speaker.

"Egad, lads," said Craufurd, "that's the very best thing I know about a command. As a bishop is always sure to portion off his daughters with deaneries and rectories, so your knowing old general always marries his among his staff."

This sally was met with the ready laughter of the subordinates, in which, however little disposed, I was obliged to join.

"You are quite right, sir," rejoined the pale youth; "and Sir George has no fortune to give his daughter."

"How came it, Horace, that you got off safe?" said Fitzroy, with a certain air of affected seriousness in his voice and manner; "I wonder they let such a prize escape them."

"Well, it was not exactly their fault, I do confess. Old Dashwood did the civil towards me; and *la bella Lucie* herself was condescending enough to be less cruel than to the rest of the staff. Her father threw us a good deal together; and in fact I believe—I fear— that is—that I didn't behave quite well."

"You may rest perfectly assured of it, sir," said I; "whatever your previous conduct may have been, you have completely relieved your mind on this occasion, and behaved most shamefully!"

Had a shell fallen in the midst of us, the faces around me could not have been more horror-struck than when, in a cool, determined tone, I spoke those few words. Fitzroy pushed his chair slightly back from the table, and fixed his eyes full upon me. Craufurd grew dark purple over his whole face and forehead, and looked from one to the other of us, without speaking, while the honorable Horace Delawar, the individual addressed, never changed a muscle of his wan and sickly features, but, lifting his eyes slowly from his muffin, lisped softly out,

" You think so? How very good !"

" General Craufurd," said I, the moment I could collect myself sufficiently to speak, " I am deeply grieved that I should so far have forgotten myself as to disturb the harmony of your table ; but when I tell you that Sir George Dashwood is one of my warmest friends on earth; that from my intimate knowledge of him, I am certain that gentleman's statements are either the mere outpouring of folly, or worse ——"

" By Jove, O'Malley, you have a very singular mode of explaining away the matter. Delawar, sit down again. Gentlemen, I have only one word to say about this transaction—I'll have no squabbles or broils here ; from this room to the guard-house is a five minutes' walk. Promise me, upon your honors, that this altercation ends here, or, as sure as my name's Craufurd, you shall both be placed under arrest, and the man who refuses to obey me shall be sent back to England."

Before I well knew in what way to proceed, Mr. Delawar rose and bowed formally to the General, while I imitated his example. Silently we resumed our places, and after a pause of a few moments, the current of conversation was renewed, and other topics discussed, but with such evident awkwardness and constraint, that all parties felt relieved when the General rose from the table.

" I say, O'Malley, have you forwarded the returns to the Adjutant-General's office ?"

" Yes, sir ; I despatched them this morning before leaving my quarters."

" I am glad of it; the irregularities on this score have called forth a heavy reprimand at head-quarters."

I was also glad of it, and it chanced that by mere accident I remembered to charge Mike with the papers, which, had they not been lying unsealed upon the table before me, would in all likelihood have escaped my attention. The post started to Lisbon that same morning, to take advantage of which I had sat up writing for half the night. Little was I aware at the moment what a mass of trouble and annoyance was in store for me from the circumstance.

CHAPTER XXVII.

ALMEIDA.

ON the morning of the 7th we perceived, from a movement in the French camp, that the wounded were being sent to the rear, and shortly afterwards the main body of the army commenced its retreat. They moved with slow and, as it were, reluctant steps; and Bessières, who commanded the Imperial Guard, turned his eyes more than once to that position which all the bravery of his troops was unavailing to capture. Although our cavalry lay in force to the front of our line, no attempt was made to molest the retreating French; and Massena, having retired beyond the Aguada, left a strong force to watch the ford, while the remainder of the army fell back upon Ciudad Rodrigo.

During this time we had succeeded in fortifying our position at Fuentes d'Onoro so strongly as to resist any new attack, and Lord Wellington now turned his whole attention to the blockade of Almeida, which, by Massena's retreat, was now abandoned to its fate.

On the morning of the 10th, I accompanied General Craufurd in a reconnaissance of the fortress, which, from the intelligence we had lately received, could not much longer hold out against our blockade. The fire from the enemy's artillery was, however, hotly maintained, and, as night fell, some squadrons of the 14th, who were picketed near, were unable to light their watch-fires, being within reach of their shot. As the darkness increased, so did the cannonade, and the bright flashes from the walls and the deep booming of the artillery became incessant.

A hundred conjectures were afloat to account for the circumstance; some asserting that what we heard were mere signals to Massena's army; and others, that Brennier was destroying and mutilating the fortress before he evacuated it to the allies.

It was a little past midnight when, tired from the fatigues of the day, I had fallen asleep beneath a tree, an explosion, louder than any which preceded it, burst suddenly forth, and, as I awoke and looked about me, I perceived the whole heavens illuminated by one bright glare, while the crashing noise of falling stones and crumbling masonry told me that a mine had been sprung. The moment after all was calm, and still, and motionless; a thick black smoke increasing the sombre darkness of the night, shut out every star from view, and some drops of heavy rain began to fall.

The silence, ten times more appalling than the din which preceded it, weighed heavily upon my senses, and a dread of some unknown danger crept over me; the exhaustion, however, was greater than my fear, and again I sank into slumber.

Scarcely had I been half an hour asleep, when the blast of a trumpet again awoke me, and I found, amid the confusion and excitement about, that something of importance had occurred. Questions were eagerly asked on all sides, but no one could explain what had happened. Towards the town all was still as death, but a dropping irregular fire of musketry issued from the valley beside the Aguada. "What can this mean? what can it be?" we asked of each other. "A sortie from the garrison," said one; "A night attack by Massena's troops," cried another; and, while thus we disputed and argued, a horseman was heard advancing along the road at the top of his speed.

"Where are the cavalry?" cried a voice I recognized as one of my brother aides-de-camp. "Where are the 14th?"

A cheer from our party answered this question, and the next moment, breathless and agitated, he rode in amongst us.

"What is it? are we attacked?"

"Would to heaven that were all! But come along, lads, follow me."

"What can it be, then?" said I again, while my anxiety knew no bounds.

"Brennier has escaped; burst his way through Pack's division, and has already reached Valde Mula."

"The French have escaped!" was repeated from mouth to mouth; while, pressing spurs to our horses, we broke into a gallop, and dashed forward in the direction of the musketry. We soon came up with the 36th Infantry, who having thrown away their knapsacks, were rapidly pressing the pursuit. The maledictions which burst from every side proved how severely the misfortune was felt by all, while the eager advance of the men bespoke how ardently they longed to repair the mishap.

Dark as was the night, we passed them in a gallop. Suddenly the officer who commanded the leading squadron called out to halt.

"Take care there, lads!" cried he; "I hear the infantry before us; we shall be down upon our own people."

The words were hardly spoken, when a bright flash blazed out before us, and a smashing volley was poured into the squadron.

"The French! the French, by Jove!" said Hampden. "Forward, boys! charge them!"

Breaking into open order, to avoid our wounded comrades, several of whom had fallen by the fire, we rode down amongst them. In a moment their order was broken, their ranks pierced, and, fresh squadrons coming up at the instant, they were sabred to a man.

After this the French pursued their march in silence, and, even when assembling in force we rode down upon their squares, they never halted nor fired a shot. At Barba del Puerco, the ground being unfit for cavalry, the 36th took our place, and pressed them hotly home. Several of the French were killed, and above three hundred made prisoners, but our fellows following up the pursuit too rashly, came upon an advanced body of Massena's force, drawn up to await and cover Brennier's retreat; the result was the loss of above thirty men in killed and wounded.

Thus were the great efforts of the three preceding days rendered fruitless and nugatory. To maintain this blockade, Lord Wellington, with an inferior force, and a position by no means strong, had ventured to give the enemy battle; and now, by the unskilfulness of some and the negligence of others, were all his combinations thwarted, and the French General enabled to march his force through the midst of the blockading columns almost unmolested and uninjured.

Lord Wellington's indignation was great, as well it might be; the prize for which he had contested was torn from his grasp at the very moment he had won it, and although the gallantry of the troops in pursuit might, under other circumstances, have called forth eulogium, his only observation on the matter was a half-sarcastic allusion to the inconclusive effects of undisciplined bravery. "Notwithstanding," says the general order of the day, "what has been printed in gazettes and newspapers, we have never seen small bodies, unsupported, successfully opposed to large; nor has the experience of any officer realized the stories which all have read, of whole armies being driven by a handful of light infantry and dragoons."

CHAPTER XXVIII.

A NIGHT ON THE AZAVA.

MASSENA was now recalled, and Marmont having assumed the command of the French army, retired towards Salamanca, while our troops went into cantonments upon the Aguada. A period of inaction succeeded to our previous life of bustle and excitement, and the whole interest of the campaign was now centred in Beresford's army, exposed to Soult in Estremadura.

On the 15th, Lord Wellington set out for that province, having already directed a strong force to march upon Badajos.

"Well, O'Malley," said Craufurd, as he returned from bidding Lord Wellington good-bye, "your business is all right; the Commander-in-Chief has signed my recommendation, and you will get your troop."

While I continued to express my grateful acknowledgments for his kindness, the General, apparently inattentive to all I was saying, paced the room with hurried steps, stopping every now and then to glance at a large map of Spain which covered one wall of the apartment, while he muttered to himself some broken and disjointed sentences.

"Eight leagues—too weak in cavalry—with the left upon Fuenta Grenaldo—a strong position. O'Malley, you'll take a troop of dragoons and patrol the country towards Castro; you'll reconnoitre the position the sixth corps occupies, but avoid any collision with the enemy's pickets, keeping the Azava between you and them. Take rations for three days."

"When shall I set out, sir?"

"Now!" was the reply.

Knowing with what pleasure the hardy veteran recognized anything like alacrity and despatch, I resolved to gratify him; and, before half an hour had elapsed, was ready with my troop to receive his final orders.

"Well done, boy!" said he, as he came to the door of the hut, "you've lost no time. I don't believe I have any further instructions to give you; to ascertain as far as possible the probable movement of the enemy is my object, that's all." As he spoke this, he waved his hand, and wishing me "Good-bye," walked leisurely back into the house. I saw that his mind was occupied by other thoughts; and although I desired to obtain some more accurate information for my guidance, knowing his dislike to questions, I merely returned his salute, and set forth upon my journey.

The morning was beautiful; the sun had risen about an hour, and the earth, refreshed by the heavy dew of the night, was breathing forth all its luxuriant fragrance. The river, which flowed beside us, was clear as crystal, showing beneath its eddying current the shining, pebbly bed, while upon the surface the water-lilies floated or sank, as the motion of the stream inclined. The tall cork-trees spread their shadows about us, and the richly-plumed birds hopped from branch to branch, awaking the echoes with their notes.

It is but seldom that the heart of man is thoroughly attuned to the circumstances of the scenery around him. How often do we need a struggle with ourselves to enjoy the rich and beautiful landscape which lies smiling in its freshness before us! How frequently do the blue sky and the calm air look down upon the heart darkened and shadowed with affliction! And · how often have we felt the discrepancy between the louring look of winter and the glad sunshine of our hearts! The harmony of the world without with our thoughts within is one of the purest, as it is one of the greatest, sources of happiness. Our hopes and our ambitions lose their selfish character when feeling that fortune smiles upon us from all around; and the flattery which speaks to our hearts from the bright stars and the blue sky, the peaked mountain, or the humble flower, is greater in its mute eloquence than all the tongue of man can tell us.

This feeling did I experience in all its fulness, as I ruminated upon my bettered fortunes, and felt within myself that secret instinct that tells of happiness to come. In such moods of mind my thoughts strayed ever homeward, and I could not help confessing how little were my successes in my eyes, did I not hope for the day when I should pour forth my tale of war and battle-fields to the ears of those who loved me.

I resolved to write home at once to my uncle. I longed to tell him each incident of my career, and my heart glowed as I thought over the broken and disjointed sentences which every cottier around would whisper of my fortunes, far prouder as they would be in the humble deeds of one they knew, than in the proudest triumphs of a nation's glory.

Indeed, Mike himself gave the current to my thoughts. After riding beside me some time in silence, he remarked,

"And isn't it Father Rush will be proud when he sees your honor's a captain; to think of the little boy that he used to take before him on the ould gray mare for a ride down the avenue; to think of him being a real captain, six feet two without his boots, and galloping over the French as if they were lurchers! Peggy Mahon, that nursed you, will be the proud woman the day she hears it; and there won't be a soldier sober in his quarters that night in Portumna barracks! 'Pon my soul, there's not a thing with a red coat on it, if it was even a scarecrow to frighten the birds from the barley, that won't be treated with respect when they hear of the news."

The country through which we travelled was marked at every step by the traces of a retreating army; the fields of rich corn lay flattened beneath the tramp of cavalry, or the wheels of the baggage-wagons; the roads, cut up and nearly impassable, were studded here and there with marks which indicated a bivouac; at the same time, everything around bore a very different aspect from what we had observed in Portugal; there the vindictive cruelty of the French soldiery had been seen in full sway. The ruined château, the burned villages, the desecrated altars, the murdered peasantry,—all attested the revengeful spirit of a beaten and baffled enemy. No sooner, however, had they crossed the frontiers, than, as if by magic, their character became totally changed. Discipline and obedience succeeded to recklessness and pillage; and, instead of treating the natives with inhumanity and cruelty, in all their intercourse with the Spaniards the French behaved with moderation and even kindness. Paying for everything, obtaining their billets peaceably and quietly, marching with order and regularity, they advanced into the heart of the country, showing, by the most irrefragable proof, the astonishing evidences of a discipline which by a word could convert the lawless irregularities of a ruffian soldiery into the orderly habits and obedient conduct of a highly-organized army.

As we neared the Azava, the tracks of the retiring enemy became gradually less perceptible, and the country, uninjured by the march, extended for miles around us in all the richness and abundance of a favored climate. The tall corn, waving its yellow gold, reflected like a sea the clouds that moved slowly above it. The wild gentian and the laurel grew thickly around, and the cattle stood basking in the clear streams, while some listless peasant lounged upon the bank beside them. Strange as all these evidences of peace and tranquillity were, so near to the devastating track of a mighty army, yet I have more than once witnessed the fact, and remarked how but a short distance from the line of our hurried march, the country lay untouched and uninjured; and though the clank of arms and the dull roll of the artillery may have struck upon the ear of the far-off dweller in his native valley, he listened as he would have done to the passing thunder as it crashed above him; and when the bright sky and pure air succeeded to the louring atmosphere and darkening storm, he looked forth upon his smiling fields and happy home, while he muttered to his heart a prayer of thanksgiving that the scourge was passed.

We bivouacked upon the bank of the river—a truly Salvator Rosa scene; the rocks, towering high above us, were fissured by the channel of many a trickling stream, seeking, in its zigzag current, the bright river below. The dark pine-tree and the oak mingled their foliage with the graceful cedar, which spread its fan-like branches about us. Through the thick shade some occasional glimpses of a starry sky could yet be seen, and a faint yellow streak upon the silent river told that the queen of night was there.

When I had eaten my frugal supper, I wandered forth alone upon the bank of the stream, now standing to watch its bold sweeps as it traversed the lonely valley before me, now turning to catch a passing glance at our red watch-fires, and the hardy features which sat around. The hoarse and careless laugh, the deep-toned voice of some old campaigner holding forth his tale of flood and field, were the only sounds I heard ; and gradually I strolled beyond the reach of even these. The path beside the river, which seemed scarped from the rock, was barely sufficient for the passage of one man, a rude balustrade of wood being the only defence against the precipice, which, from a height of full thirty feet, looked down upon the stream. Here and there some broad gleam of moonlight would fall upon the opposite bank, which, unlike the one I occupied, stretched out into rich meadow and pasturage, broken by occasional clumps of ilex and beech. River scenery has been ever a passion with me. I can glory in the bold and broken outline of a mighty mountain ; I can gaze with delighted eyes upon the boundless sea, and know not whether to like it more in all the mighty outpouring of its wrath, when the white waves lift their heads to heaven, and break themselves in foam upon the rocky beach, or in the calm beauty of its broad and mirrored surface, in which the bright world of sun and sky are seen full many a fathom deep. But far before these, I love the happy and tranquil beauty of some bright river, tracing its winding current through valley and through plain, now spreading into some calm and waveless lake, now narrowing to an eddying stream, with mossy rocks and waving trees darkening over it. There's not a hut, however lowly, where the net of the fisherman is stretched upon the sward, around whose hearth I do not picture before me the faces of happy toil and humble contentment, while from the ruined tower upon the crag, methinks I hear the ancient sounds of wassail and of welcome ; and though the keep be fissured and the curtain fallen, and though for banner there "waves some tall wall-flower," I can people its crumbling walls with images of the past ; and the merry laugh of the warder and the clanking tread of the mailed warrior are as palpably before me as the tangled lichen that now trails from its battlements.

As I wandered on, I reached the little rustic stair which led downward from the path to the river side ; and, on examining further, perceived that in this place the stream was fordable ; a huge flat rock, filling up a great part of the river's bed, occupied the middle, on either side of which the current ran with increased force.

Bent upon exploring, I descended the cliff, and was preparing to cross, when my attention was attracted by the twinkle of a fire at some distance from me, on the opposite side ; the flame rose and fell in fitful flashes, as though some hand were ministering to it at the moment. As it was impossible, from the silence on every side, that it could proceed from a bivouac of the enemy, I resolved on approaching it and examining it for myself. I knew that the shepherds in remote districts were accustomed thus to pass the summer nights, with no other covering save the blue vault above them. It was not impossible, too, that it might prove a Guerilla party, who frequently, in small numbers, hang upon the rear of a retreating army. Thus conjecturing, I crossed the stream, and quickening my pace, walked forward in the direction of the blaze. For a moment a projecting rock obstructed my progress; while I was devising some means of proceeding farther, the sound of voices near me arrested my attention. I listened, and what was my astonishment to hear that they spoke in French. I now crept cautiously to the verge of the rock and looked over; the moon was streaming in its full brilliancy upon a little shelving strand beside the stream, and here I now beheld the figure of a French officer. He was habited in the undress uniform of a *chasseur à cheval,* but wore no arms; indeed, his occupation at the moment was anything but a warlike one, he being leisurely employed in collecting some flasks of champagne which apparently had been left to cool within the stream.

" *Eh bien, Alphonse,*" said a voice in the direction of the fire, "what are you delaying for ?"

" I'm coming, I'm coming," said the other ; " but, *par Dieu !* I can only find five of our bottles; one seems to have been carried away by the stream."

"No matter," replied the other, " we are but three of us, and one is, or should be, on the sick list."

The only answer to this was the muttered chorus of a French drinking-song, interrupted at intervals by an imprecation upon the missing flask. It chanced at this moment that a slight clinking noise attracted me, and on looking down I perceived at the foot of the rock the prize he sought for. It had been, as he conceived, carried away by an eddy of the stream, and was borne, as a true prisoner of war, within my grasp. I avow that from this moment my interest in the scene became considerably heightened; such a waif as a bottle of champagne was not to be despised in circumstances like mine, and I watched with anxious eyes every gesture of the impatient Frenchman, and alternately vibrated between hope and fear, as he neared or receded from the missing flask.

"Let it go to the devil," shouted his companion once more. " Jacques has lost all patience with you."

" Be it so, then," said the other as he prepared to take up his burden. At this instant I made a slight effort to change my position, so as to obtain a view of the rest of the party. The branch by which I supported myself, however, gave way beneath my grasp with a loud crash. I lost my footing, and slipping downward from the rock, came plump into the stream below. The noise, the splash, and, more than all, the sudden appearance of a man beside him, astounded the Frenchman, who almost let fall his pannier, and thus we stood confronting each other for at least a couple of minutes in silence. A hearty burst of laughter from both parties terminated this awkward moment, while the Frenchman, with the readiness of his country, was the first to open the negotiation.

"*Sacré Dieu!*" said he, "what can you be doing here? You're English, without doubt."

"Even so," said I; "but that is the very question I was about to ask you; what are you doing here?"

"*Eh bien,*" replied the other, gayly; "you shall be answered in all frankness. Our captain was wounded in the action of the 8th, and we heard had been carried up the country by some peasants. As the army fell back, we obtained permission to go in search of him. For two days all was fruitless; the peasantry fled at our approach; and although we captured some of our stolen property—among other things, the contents of this basket—yet we never came upon the track of our comrade till this evening. A good-hearted shepherd had taken him to his hut, and treated him with every kindness, but no sooner did he hear the gallop of our horses and the clank of our equipments, than, fearing himself to be made a prisoner, he fled up the mountains, leaving our friend behind him: *voilà notre histoire.* Here we are, three in all, one of us with a deep sabre-cut in his shoulder. If you are the stronger party, we are, I suppose, your prisoners; if not——"

What was to have followed, I know not, for at this moment his companion, who had finally lost all patience, came suddenly to the spot.

"A prisoner," cried he, placing a heavy hand upon my shoulder, while with the other he held his drawn sword pointed towards my breast.

To draw a pistol from my bosom was the work of a second; and while gently turning the point of his weapon away, I coolly said,—

"Not so fast, my friend,—not so fast! The game is in my hands, not yours. I have only to pull this trigger, and my dragoons are upon you; whatever fate befall me, yours is certain."

A half-scornful laugh betrayed the incredulity of him I addressed, while the other, apparently anxious to relieve the awkwardness of the moment, suddenly broke in with,—

"He is right, Auguste, and you are wrong; we are in his power; that is," added he, smiling, "if he believes there is any triumph in capturing such *pauvres diables* as ourselves."

The features of him he addressed suddenly lost their scornful expression, and sheathing his sword with an air of almost melodramatic solemnity, he gravely pulled up his moustaches, and after

35

a pause of a few seconds, solemnly ejaculated a malediction upon his fortune.

"*C'est toujours ainsi*," said he, with a bitterness that only a Frenchman can convey when cursing his destiny. "*Soyez bon enfant*, and see what will come of it. Only be good-natured, only be kind, and if you haven't bad luck at the end of it, it's only because fortune has a heavier stroke in reserve for you hereafter."

I could not help smiling at the Frenchman's philosophy, which, assuming as a good augury, he gayly said, "So, then, you'll not make us prisoners. Isn't it so?"

"Prisoners," said the other, "nothing of the kind. Come and sup with us; I'll venture to say our larder is as well stocked as your own; in any case an omelette, a cold chicken, and a glass of champagne, are not bad things in our circumstances."

I could not help laughing outright at the strangeness of the proposal. "I fear I must decline," said I; "you seem to forget that I am placed here to watch, not to join you."

"*A la bonne heure*," cried the younger of the two; "do both. Come along; *soyez bon camarade;* you are always near your own people; so don't refuse us."

In proportion as I declined, they both became more pressing in their entreaties, and at last I began to dread lest my refusal might seem to proceed from some fear as to the good faith of the invitation, and I never felt so awkwardly placed as when one plumply pressed me by saying,

"*Mais pourquoi pas, mon cher?*"

I stammered out something about duty and discipline, when they both interrupted me by a long burst of laughter.

"Come, come!" said they; "in an hour—in half an hour, if you will—you shall be back with your own people. We've had plenty of fighting latterly, and we are likely to have enough in future; we know something of each other by this time in the field; let us see how we get on in the bivouac!"

Resolving not to be outdone in generosity, I replied at once, "Here goes, then!"

Five minutes afterwards, I found myself seated at their bivouac fire. The captain, who was the oldest of the party, was a fine soldier-like fellow of some forty years old. He had served in the Imperial Guard, through all the campaigns of Italy and Austria, and abounded in anecdotes of the French army. From him I learned many of those characteristic traits which so eminently distinguish the imperial troops, and saw how completely their bravest and boldest feats of arms depended upon the personal valor of him who led them on. From the daring enterprise of Napoleon at Lodi to the conduct of the lowest corporal in the *grande armée*, the picture presents nothing but a series of the most brilliant chivalrous feats; while at the same time, the war-like character of the nation is displayed by that instinctive appreciation of courage and daring which teaches them to follow their officers to the very cannon's mouth.

"It was at Elchingen," said the captain, "you should have seen them. The regiment in which I was a lieutenant was ordered to form close column, and charge through a narrow ravine to carry a brigade of guns, which, by a flanking fire, were devastating our troops. Before we could reach the causeway, we were obliged to pass an open plain, in which the ground dipped for about a hundred yards; the column moved on, and, though it descended one hill, not a man ever mounted the opposite one. A very avalanche of balls swept the entire valley; and yet, amid the thunder and the smoke, the red glare of the artillery, and the carnage around them, our grenadiers marched firmly up. At last, Marshal Ney sent an aide-de-camp with orders to the troops to lie flat down, and in this position the artillery played over us for about half an hour. The Austrians gradually slackened, and finally discontinued their fire; this was the moment to resume the attack. I crept cautiously to my knees, and looked about. One word brought my men around me; but I found to my horror that of a battalion who came into action fourteen hundred strong, not five hundred remained, and that I myself, a mere lieutenant, was now the senior officer of the regiment. Our gallant colonel lay dead beside my feet. At this instant a thought struck me. I remembered a habit he possessed, in moments of difficulty and danger, of placing in his shako a small red plume which he commonly carried in his belt. I searched for it, and found it. As I held it aloft, a maddening cheer burst around me, while from out the line each officer sprang madly forward, and rushed to the head of the column. It was no longer a march. With a loud cry of vengeance, the mass rushed forward, the men trying to outstrip their officers, and come first in contact with the foe. Like tigers on the spring, they fell upon the enemy, who, crushed, overwhelmed, and massacred, lay in slaughtered heaps around the cannon. The cavalry of the Guard came thundering on behind us, a whole division followed, and three thousand five hundred prisoners and fourteen pieces of artillery were captured.

"I sat upon the carriage of a gun, my face begrimed with powder, and my uniform blackened and blood-stained. The whole thing appeared like some shocking dream. I felt a hand upon my shoulder, while a rough voice called in my ear, '*Capitaine du soixante-neuvième, tu es mon frère!*'

"It was Ney who spoke. This," added the brave captain, his eyes filling with tears as he said the words,—"this is the sabre he gave me."

I know not why I have narrated this anecdote; it has little in itself, but, somehow, to me it brings back in all its fulness the recollection of that night.

There was something so strongly characteristic of the Old Napoleonist in the tone of the narrative that I listened throughout with breathless attention. I began to feel, too, for the first time, what a powerful arm in war the Emperor had created by fostering the spirit of individual enterprise. The field thus opened to fame and distinction left no bounds to the ambition of any. The humble conscript, as he tore himself from the embraces of his mother, wiped his tearful eyes to see before him in the distance the bâton of a marshal. The bold soldier who stormed a battery, felt his heart beat more proudly and more securely beneath the cordon of the Legion than behind a cuirass of steel, and to a people in whom the sense of duty alone would seem cold, barren, and inglorious, he had substituted a highly-wrought chivalrous enthusiasm, and, by the prestige of his own name, the proud memory of his battles, and the glory of those mighty tournaments at which all Europe were the spectators, he had converted a nation into an army.

By a silent and instinctive compact we appeared to avoid those topics of the campaign in which the honor of our respective arms was interested; and once when, by mere accident, the youngest of the party adverted to Fuentes d'Onoro, the old captain adroitly turned the current of the conversation by saying, "Come, Alphonse, let's have a song."

"Yes," said the other, "*Le Pas de Charge.*"

"No, no," said the Captain; "if I am to have a choice, let it be that little Breton song you gave us on the Danube."

"So be it, then," said Alphonse. "Here goes!"

I have endeavored to convey, by a translation, the words he sang; but I feel conscious how totally their feeling and simplicity are lost when deprived of their own *patois*, and the wild but touching melody that accompanied them.

"THE BRETON HOME."

"When the battle is oe'r and the sounds of fight
  Have closed with the closing day,
How happy, around the watch-fire's light,
  To chat the long hours away;
To chat the long hours away, my boy,
  And talk of the days to come,
Or a better still, and a purer joy,
  To think of our far-off home.

> "How many a cheek will then grow pale,
>   That never felt a tear!
> And many a stalwart heart will quail,
>   That never quailed in fear!
> And the breast that, like some mighty rock,
>   Amid the foaming sea,
> Bore high against the battle's shock,
>   Now heaves like infancy.
>
> "And those who knew each other not
>   Their hands together steal,
> Each thinks of some long hallowed spot,
>   And all like brothers feel:
> Such holy thoughts to all are given;
>   The lowliest has his part;
> The love of home, like love of Heaven,
>   Is woven in our heart."

There was a pause as he concluded; each sunk in his own reflections. How long we should have thus remained, I know not; but we were speedily aroused from our reveries by the tramp of horses near us. We listened, and could plainly detect in their rude voices and coarse laughter the approach of a body of Guerillas. We looked from one to the other in silence and fear. Nothing could be more unfortunate should we be discovered. Upon this point we were left little time to deliberate; for, with a loud cheer, four Spanish horsemen galloped up to the spot, their carbines in the rest. The Frenchmen sprang to their feet, and seized their sabres, bent upon making a resolute resistance. As for me, my determination was at once taken. Remaining quietly seated upon the grass, I stirred not for a moment, but addressing him who appeared to be the chief of the Guerillas, said, in Spanish,

"These are my prisoners; I am a British officer of dragoons, and my party is yonder."

This evidently unexpected declaration seemed to surprise them, and they conferred for a few moments together. Meanwhile, they were joined by two others, in one of whom we could recognize, by his costume, the real leader of the party.

"I am captain in the light dragoons," said I, repeating my declaration.

"*Morte de Dios!*" replied he; "it is false; you are a spy!"

The word was repeated from lip to lip by his party, and I saw, in their louring looks and darkening features, that the moment was a critical one for me.

"Down with your arms!" cried he, turning to the Frenchmen. "Surrender yourselves our prisoners; I'll not bid you twice!"

The Frenchmen turned upon me an inquiring look, as though to say that upon me now their hopes entirely reposed.

"Do as he bids you," said I; while at the same moment I sprang to my legs, and gave a loud, shrill whistle, the last echo of which had not died away in the distance ere it was replied to.

"Make no resistance now," said I to the Frenchmen; "our safety depends on this."

While this was passing, two of the Spaniards had dismounted, and, detaching a coil of rope which hung from their saddle-peak, were proceeding to tie the prisoners wrist to wrist; the others, with their carbines to the shoulder, covered us man by man, the chief of the party having singled out me as his peculiar prey.

"The fate of Mascarenhas might have taught you better," said he, "than to play this game." And then added, with a grim smile, "But we'll see if an Englishman will not make as good a carbonado as a Portuguese!"

This cruel speech made my blood run cold, for I knew well to what he alluded. I was at Lisbon at the time it happened, but the melancholy fate of Julian Mascarenhas, the Portuguese spy, had reached me there. He was burned to death at Torres Vedras!

The Spaniard's triumph over my terror was short-lived, indeed, for scarcely had the words fallen from his lips, when a party of the 14th, dashing through the river at a gallop, came riding up. The attitude of the Guerillas, as they sat with presented arms, was sufficient for my fellows, who needed not the exhortation of him who rode foremost of the party.

"Ride them down, boys! Tumble them over! Flatten their broad beavers, the infernal thieves!"

"Whoop!" shouted Mike, as he rode at the chief, with the force of a catapult. Down went the Spaniard, horse and all; and before he could disentangle himself, Mike was upon him, his knee pressed upon his neck.

"Isn't it enough for ye to pillage the whole country, without robbing the king's throops?" cried he, as he held him fast to the earth with one hand, while he presented a loaded pistol to his face.

By this time the scene around me was sufficiently ludicrous. Such of the Guerillas as had not been thrown by force from their saddles, had slid peaceably down, and depositing their arms upon the ground, dropped upon their knees in a semicircle around us, and, amid the hoarse laughter of the troopers and the irrepressible merriment of the Frenchmen, rose up the muttered prayers of the miserable Spaniards, who believed that now their last hour was come.

"*Madre de Dios*, indeed!" cried Mike, imitating the tone of a repentant old sinner, in a patched mantle; "it's much the blessed Virgin thinks of the like o' ye, thieves and rogues as ye are; it a'most puts me beyond my senses to see ye there crossing yourselves like *rale* Christians."

If I could not help indulging myself in this retributive cruelty towards the chief, and leaving him to the tender mercies of Mike, I ordered the others to rise and form in line before me. Affecting to occupy myself entirely with them, I withdrew the attention of all from the French officers, who remained quiet spectators of the scene around them.

" *Point de façons*, gentlemen," said I, in a whisper. "Get to your horses and away! Now's your time. Good-bye!"

A warm grasp of the hand from each was the only reply, and I turned once more to my discomfited friends, the Guerillas.

"There, Mike, let the poor devil rise. I confess appearances were strong against me just now."

"Well, Captain, are you convinced by this time that I was not deceiving you?"

The Guerilla muttered some words of apology between his teeth, and, while he shook the dust from his cloak, and arranged the broken feather of his hat, cast a look of scowling and indignant meaning upon Mike, whose rough treatment he had evidently not forgiven.

"Don't be looking at me that way, you black thief! or I'll ——"

"Hold there!" said I; "no more of this. Come, gentlemen, we must be friends. If I mistake not, we've got something like refreshment at our bivouac. In any case you'll partake of our watch-fire till morning."

They gladly accepted our invitation, and ere half an hour had elapsed, Mike's performauce in the part of host had completely erased every unpleasant impression his first appearance gave rise to; and as for myself, when I did sleep at last, the confused mixture of Spanish and Irish airs which issued from the thicket beside me, proved that a most intimate alliance had grown up between the parties.

CHAPTER XXIX.

MIKE'S MISTAKE.

BEFORE daybreak the Guerillas were in motion. Having taken a most ceremonious leave of us, they mounted their horses and set out upon their journey. I saw their gaunt figures wind down the valley, and watched them till they disappeared in the distance. "Yes, brigands though they be," thought I, "there is something fine, something heroic, in the spirit of their unrelenting vengeance." The sleuth-hound never sought the lair of his victim with a more ravening appetite for blood than they track the retreating columns of the enemy. Hovering around the line of march, they sometimes swoop down in masses, and carry off part of the baggage, or the wounded. The wearied soldier, overcome by heat and exhaustion, who drops behind his ranks, is their certain victim; the sentry on an advanced post is scarcely less so. Whole pickets are sometimes attacked and carried off to a man; and when traversing the lonely passes of some mountain gorge, or defiling through the dense shadows of a wooded glen, the stoutest heart has felt a fear, lest from behind the rock that frowned above him, or from the leafy thicket whose branches stirred without a breeze, the sharp ring of a Guerilla carbine might sound his death knell.

It was thus in the retreat upon Corunna fell Colonel Lefebvre. Ever foremost in the attack upon our rearguard, this gallant youth (he was scarce six-and-twenty), a colonel of his regiment, and decorated with the Legion of Honor, led on every charge of his bold "*sabreurs*," riding up to the very bayonets of our squares, waving his hat above his head, and seeming actually to court his death-wound; but so struck were our brave fellows with his gallant bearing, that they cheered him as he came on.

It was in one of these moments as, rising high in his stirrups, he bore down upon the unflinching ranks of the British infantry, the shrill whistle of a ball strewed the leaves upon the roadside, the exulting shout of a Guerilla followed it, and the same instant Lefebvre fell forward upon his horse's mane, a deluge of blood bursting from his bosom. A broken cry escaped his lips—a last effort to cheer on his men; his noble charger galloped forward between our squares, bearing to us as our prisoner the corpse of his rider.

"Captain O'Malley," said a mounted dragoon to the advanced sentry at the bottom of the little hill upon which I was standing. "Despatches from head-quarters, sir," delivering into my hands a large sealed packet from the Adjutant-General's office. While he proceeded to search for another letter of which he was the bearer, I broke the seal and read as follows:

"Adjutant-General's Office, May 15.

"SIR,—On the receipt of this order you are directed, having previously resigned your command to the officer next in seniority, to repair to head-quarters at Fuentes d'Onoro, there to report yourself under arrest.

"I have the honor to be your obedient servant,

"GEORGE HOPETON, Military Secretary."

"What the devil can this mean?" said I to myself, as I read the lines over again and again. "What have I done lately, or what have I left undone, to involve me in this scrape? Ah!" thought I, "to be sure, it can be nothing else. Lord Wellington *did* recognize me that unlucky morning, and has determined not to let me pass unpunished. How unfortunate. Scarcely twenty-four hours have elapsed since fortune seemed to smile upon me from every side, and now the very destiny I most dreaded stares me fully in the face." A reprimand, or the sentence of a court-martial, I shrank from with a coward's fear. It mattered comparatively little from what source arising, the injury to my pride as a man and my spirit as a soldier would be almost the same.

"This is the letter, sir," said the orderly, presenting me with a packet, the address of which was in Power's handwriting. Eagerly tearing it open, I sought for something which might explain my unhappy position. It bore the same date as the official letter, and ran thus:

"My Dear Charley:—I joined yesterday, just in time to enjoy the heartiest laugh I have had since our meeting. If notoriety can gratify you, by Jove you have it; for Charles O'Malley and his man Mickey Free are by-words in every mess from Villa Formosa to the rear-guard. As it's only fair you should participate a little in the fun you've originated, let me explain the cause. Your inimitable man Mike, to whom it appears you entrusted the report of killed and wounded for the Adjutant-General, having just at that moment accomplished a letter to his friends at home, substituted his correspondence for your returns, and, doubtless, sent the list of the casualties as very interesting information to his sweetheart in Ireland. If such be the case, I hope and trust she has taken the blunder in better part than old Colbourn, who swears he'll bring you to a court-martial, under Heaven knows what charges. In fact, his passion has known no bounds since the event; and a fit of jaundice has given his face a kind of neutral tint between green and yellow, like nothing, I know of, except the facings of the 'dirty Half-hundred.'*

"As Mr. Free's letter may be as great a curiosity to you as it has been to us, I enclose you a copy of it, which Hopeton obtained for me. It certainly places the estimable Mike in a strong light as a despatch-writer. The occasional interruption to the current of the letter, you will perceive, arises from Mike having used the pen of a comrade, writing being doubtless an accomplishment forgotten in the haste of preparing Mr. Free for the world; and the amanuensis

* For the information of my unmilitary readers, I may remark that this *sobriquet* was applied to the 50th Regiment.

has, in more than one instance, committed to paper more than was meant by the author:

" ' Mrs. M'Gra:—Tear an ages, sure I need not be treating her that way. Now, just say Mrs. Mary—ay, that'll do—Mrs. Mary, it's maybe surprised you'll be to be reading a letter from your humble servant, sitting on the top of the Alps.—Arrah, maybe it's not the Alps; but sure she'll never know—fornent the whole French army, with Bony himself and all his jinnerals—God be between us and harm—ready to murther every mother's son of us, av they was able, Molly darlin'; but, with the blessing of Providence, and Lord Wellington, and Mister Charles, we'll bate them yet, as we bate them afore.

" ' My lips is wathering at the thought o' the plunder. I often think of Tim Riley that was hanged for sheep-stealing; he'd be worth his weight in gold here.

" ' Mr. Charles is now a captain—devil a less—and myself might be somethin' that same, but ye see I was always of a bashful nature, and recommended the master in my place. "He's mighty young, Mister Charles is," says my Lord Wellington to me,—" he's mighty young, Mr. Free." " He is, my lord," says I; " he's young, as you observe, but he's as much devilment in him as many that might be his father." "That's somethin', Mr. Free," says my lord; "ye say he comes from a good stock?" "The *rale* sort, my lord," says I; " an ould, ancient family, that's spent every sixpence they had in treating their neighbors. My father lived near him for years,"—you see, Molly, I said that to season the discoorse. "We'll make him a captain," says my lord; "but, Mr. Free, could we do nothing for you?" "Nothing at present, my lord. When my friends come into power," says I, "they'll think of me. There's many a little thing to give away in Ireland, and they often find it mighty hard to find a man for lord-lieutenant; and if that same, or a tide-waiter's place, was vacant——" "Just tell me," says my Lord. "It's what I'll do," says I. "And now, wishing you happy dreams, I'll take my lave." Just so, Molly, it's hand and glove we are. A pleasant face, agreeable manners, seasoned with natural modesty, and a good pair of legs,—them's the gifts to push a man's way in the world. And even with the ladies—but sure I am forgetting, my master was proposed for, and your humble servant too, by two illigant creatures in Lisbon; but it wouldn't do, Molly,—it's higher nor that we'll be looking—*rale* princesses, the devil a less. Tell Kitty Hannigan I hope she's well: she was a desarving young woman in her situation in life. Shusey Dogherty, at the cross-roads—if I don't forget the name—was a good-looking slip too; give her my affectionate salutations, as we say in the Portuguese. I hope I'll be able to bear the inclementuous nature of your climate when I go back; but I can't expect to stay long—for Lord Wellington can't do without me. We play duets on the guitar together every evening. The master is shouting for a blanket, so no more at present from

"'Your very affectionate friend,

"'MICKEY FREE.

"'P.S.—I don't write this myself, for the Spanish tongue puts me out o' the habit of English. Tell Father Rush, if he'd study the Portuguese, I'd use my interest for him with the Bishop of Toledo. It's a country he'd like—no regular stations, but promiscuous eating and drinking, and as pretty girls as ever confessed their sins.'

"My poor Charley, I think I am looking at you. I think I can see the struggle between indignation and laughter, which every line of this letter inflicts upon you. Get back as quickly as you can, and we'll try if Craufurd won't pull you through the business. In any case, expect no sympathy; and if you feel disposed to be angry with all who laugh at you, you had better publish a challenge in the next general order. George Scott, of the Grays, bids me say that if you're hard up for cash, he'll give you a couple of hundred for Mickey Free. I told him I thought you'd accept it, as your uncle has the breed of those fellows upon his estate, and might have no objection to weed his stud. Hammersley's gone back with the Dashwoods, but I don't think you need fear anything in that quarter. At the same time, if you wish for success, make a bold push for the peerage and half a dozen decorations, for Miss Lucy is most decidedly gone wild about military distinction. As for me, my affairs go on well; I've had half a dozen quarrels with Inez, but we parted good friends, and my bad Portuguese has got me out of all difficulties with papa, who pressed me tolerably close as to fortune. I shall want your assistance in this matter yet. If parchments will satisfy him, I think I could get up a qualification; but, somehow, the matter must be done, for I'm resolved to have his daughter.

"The orderly is starting, so no more till we meet.

"Yours ever,

"FRED POWER."

"Godwin," said I, as I closed the letter, "I find myself in a scrape at head-quarters; you are to take the command of the detachment, for I must set out at once."

"Nothing serious, I hope, O'Malley?"

"Oh, no! nothing of consequence. A most absurd blunder of my rascally servant."

"The Irish fellow yonder?"

"The same."

"He seems to take it easily, however."

"Oh, confound him! he does not know what trouble he has involved me in; not that he'll care much when he does."

"Why, he does not seem to be of a very desponding temperament. Listen to the fellow! I'll be hanged if he's not singing!"

"I'm devilishly disposed to spoil his mirth. They tell me, however, he always keeps the troop in good humor; and see, the fellows are actually cleaning his horses for him, while he is sitting on the bank!"

"Faith, O'Malley, that fellow knows the world. Just hear him."

Mr. Free was, as described, most leisurely reposing on a bank, a mug of something drinkable beside him, and a pipe of that curtailed proportion which an Irishman loves held daintily between his fingers. He appeared to be giving his directions to some soldiers of the troop, who were busily cleaning his horses and accoutrements for him.

"That's it, Jim! Rub 'em down along the hocks; he won't kick; it's only play. Scrub away, honey; that's the devil's own carbine to get clean."

"Well, I say, Mr. Free, are you going to give us that ere song?"

"Yes; I'll be hanged if I burnish your sabre if you don't sing."

"Tear an' ages! ain't I composin' it? Av I was Tommy Moore I couldn't be quicker."

"Well, come along, my hearty; let's hear it."

"Oh, murther," said Mike, draining the pot to its last few drops, which he poured pathetically upon the grass before him, and then having emptied the ashes from his pipe, he heaved a deep sigh, as though to say, life had no pleasures in store for him. A brief pause followed, after which, to the evident delight of his expectant audience, he began the following song, to the popular air of "Paddy O'Carroll:"

"BAD LUCK TO THIS MARCHING."

"Bad luck to this marching,
Pipeclaying and starching,
How neat one must be to be killed by the French!
I'm sick of parading,
Through wet and cowld wading,
Or standing all night to be shot in a trench.
To the tune of a fife
They dispose of your life,
You surrender your soul to some illigant lilt;
Now, I like Garryowen,
When I hear it at home,
But it's not half so sweet when you're going to be kilt.

> "Then though up late and early,
>   Our pay comes so rarely
> The devil a farthing we've ever to spare;
>   They say some disaster
>   Befell the paymaster;
> On my conscience I think that the money's not there!
>   And, just think, what a blunder,
>   They won't let us plunder,
> While the convents invite us to rob them, 'tis clear.
>   Though there isn't a village
>   But cries, 'Come and pillage,'
> Yet we leave all the mutton behind for Mounseer.
>
> "Like a sailor that's nigh land,
>   I long for that island
> Where even the kisses we steal if we please;
>   Where it is no disgrace
>   If you don't wash your face,
> And you've nothing to do but to stand at your ease.
>   With no sergeant t' abuse us,
>   We fight to amuse us,
> Sure it's better bate Christians than kick a baboon.
>   How I'd dance like a fairy,
>   To see ould Dunleary,
> And think twice ere I'd leave it to be a dragoon!"

"There's a sweet little bit for you," said Mike, as he concluded, "thrown off as aisy as a game at football."

"I say, Mr. Free, the Captain's looking for you; he's just received despatches from the camp, and wants his horses."

"In that case, gentlemen, I must take my leave of you, with the more regret, too, that I was thinking of treating you to a supper this evening. You needn't be laughing—it's in earnest I am. Coming, sir—coming!" shouted he, in a louder tone, answering some imaginary call, as an excuse for his exit.

When he appeared before me, an air of most business-like alacrity had succeeded to his late appearance, and having taken my orders to get the horses in readiness, he left me at once, and in less than half an hour we were upon the road.

CHAPTER XXX.

MAJOR MONSOON IN TROUBLE.

RIDING along towards Fuentes d'Onoro, I could not help feeling provoked at the absurd circumstances in which I was involved. To be made the subject of laughter for a whole army was by no means a pleasant consideration; but what I felt far worse was, the possibility that the mention of my name in connection with a reprimand might reach the ears of those who knew nothing of the cause.

Mr. Free himself seemed little under the influence of similar feelings, for when, after two hours' silence, I turned suddenly towards him with a half-angry look, and remarked, "You see, sir, what your confounded blundering has done," his cool reply was,—

"Ah! then, won't Mrs. M'Gra be frightened out of her life when she reads all about the killed and wounded in your honor's report? I wonder if they ever had the manners to send my own letter afterwards, when they found out their mistake!"

"*Their* mistake, do you say?—rather *yours!* You appear to have a happy knack of shifting blame from your own shoulders. Do you fancy that they've nothing else to do than to trouble their heads about your absurd letters?"

"Faith, it's easily seen you never saw my letter, or you wouldn't be saying that; and sure it's not much trouble it would give Colonel Fitzroy, or any o' the staff that write a good hand, just to put in a line to Mrs. M'Gra, to prevent her feeling alarmed about that murthering paper. Well, well, it's God's blessing! I don't think there's anybody of the name of Mickey Free high up in the army but myself, so that the family won't be going into mourning for me on a false alarm."

I had not patience to participate in this view of the case, so that I continued my journey without speaking. We had jogged along for some time after dark, when the distant twinkle of the watch-fires announced our approach to the camp. A detachment of the 14th formed the advanced post, and from the officer in command I learned that Power was quartered at a small mill about half a mile distant. Thither I accordingly turned my steps, but finding that the path which led abruptly down to it was broken and cut up in many places, I sent Mike back with the horses, and continued my way alone on foot.

The night was deliciously calm, and as I approached the little rustic mill, I could not help feeling struck with Power's taste in a billet.

A little vine-clad cottage, built close against a rock, nearly concealed by the dense foliage around it, stood beside a clear rivulet whose eddying current supplied water to the mill, and rose in a dew-like spray, which sparkled like gems in the pale moonlight. All was still within, but as I came nearer, I thought I could detect the chords of a guitar. "Can it be," thought I, "that Master Fred has given himself up to minstrelsy! or is it some little dress rehearsal for a serenade? But no," thought I, "that certainly is not Power's voice." I crept stealthily down the little path, and approached the window; the lattice lay open, and, as the curtain waved to and fro with the night air, I could see plainly all who were in the room.

Close beside the window sat a large, dark-featured Spaniard, his hands crossed upon his bosom, and his head inclined heavily forward, the attitude perfectly denoting deep sleep, even had not his cigar, which remained passively between his lips, ceased to give forth its blue smoke-wreath. At a little distance from him sat a young girl, who, by the uncertain light, I could perceive was possessed of all that delicacy of form and gracefulness of carriage which characterize her nation.

Her pale features—paler still from the contrast with her jet-black hair and dark costume—were lit up with an expression of animation and enthusiasm, as her fingers swept rapidly and boldly across the strings of a guitar.

"And you're not tired of it yet?" said she, bending her head downward towards one whom I now for the first time perceived.

Reclining carelessly at her feet, his arm leaning upon her chair, whilst his hand occasionally touched her taper fingers, lay my good friend, Master Fred Power. An undress jacket thrown loosely open, and a black neckcloth negligently knotted, bespoke the easy *nonchalance* with which he prosecuted his courtship.

"Do sing it again?" said he, pressing her fingers to his lips.

What she replied I could not catch; but Fred resumed: "No, no, he never wakes; the infernal clatter of that mill is his lullaby."

"But your friend will be here soon," said she. "Is it not so?"

"Oh, poor Charley! I'd almost forgotten him; by the bye, you musn't fall in love with him. There now, do not look angry. I only meant that, as I knew he'd be desperately smitten, you shouldn't let him fancy he got any encouragement."

"What would you have me do?" said she, artlessly.

"I have been thinking over that, too. In the first place, you'd better never let him hear you sing; scarcely ever smile; and, as far as possible, keep out of his sight."

"One would think, Senhor, that all these precautions were to be taken more on my account than his. Is he so very dangerous, then?"

"Not a bit of it! Good-looking enough he is, but—only a boy; at the same time a devilish bold one! and he'd think no more of springing through that window, and throwing his arms around your neck, the very first moment of his arrival, than I should of whispering how much I love you."

"How very odd he must be! I'm sure I should like him."

"Many thanks to both for your kind hints; and now to take advantage of them." So saying, I stepped lightly upon the window-sill, cleared the miller with one spring, and before Power could recover his legs, or Margeritta her astonishment, I clasped her in my arms, and kissed her on either cheek,

"Charley! Charley! that won't do!" cried Fred; while the young lady, evidently more amused at his discomfiture than affronted at the liberty, threw herself into a seat and laughed immoderately.

"Ha! Hilloa there! What is't?" shouted the miller, rousing himself from his nap, and looking eagerly around. "Are they coming? Are the French coming?"

A hearty renewal of his daughter's laughter was the only reply, while Power relieved his anxiety by saying,—

"No, no, Pedrillo, not the French; a mere marauding party— nothing more. I say, Charley," continued he, in a lower tone, "you had better lose no time in reporting yourself at head-quarters. We'll walk up together. Devilish awkward scrape yours."

"Never fear, Fred; time enough for all that. For the present, if you permit me, I'll follow up my acquaintance with our fair friend here."

"Gently, gently!" said he, with a look of most imposing serious-ness. "Don't mistake her; she's not a mere country girl: you understand?—been bred in a convent here—rather superior kind of thing."

"Come, come, Fred, I'm not the man to interfere with you for a moment."

"Good night, Senhor," said the old miller, who had been waiting patiently all this time to pay his respects before going.

"Yes, that's it," said Power, eagerly. "Good-night, Pedrillo."

"*Buonos noches*," lisped out Margeritta, with a slight curtsey.

I sprang forward to acknowledge her salutation, when Power coolly interposed between us, and closing the door after them, placed his back against it.

"Master Charley, I must read you a lesson——"

"You inveterate hypocrite, don't attempt this nonsense with *me*. But come, tell me how long you have been here?"

"Just twenty-four of the shortest hours I ever passed at an outpost. But listen—do you know that voice? Isn't it O'Shaughnessy?"

"To be sure it is. Hear the fellow's song?"

> "My father cared little for shot or shell,
> He laughed at death and dangers;
> And he'd storm the very gates of hell
> With a company of the 'Rangers.'
> So sing tow, row, row, row, row," &c.

"Ah then, Mister Power, it's twice I'd think of returning your visit, if I knew the state of your avenue. If there's a grand jury in Spain, they might give you a presentment for this bit of road. My knees are as bare as a commissary's conscience, and I've knocked as much flesh off my shin-bones as would make a cornet in the Hussars!"

A regular roar of laughter from both of us apprised Dennis of our vicinity.

"And it's laughing ye are? Wouldn't it be as polite just to hold a candle or lantern for me in this confounded watercourse?"

"How goes it, Major?" cried I, extending my hand to him through the window.

"Charley—Charley O'Malley, my son! I'm glad to see you. It's a hearty laugh you gave us this morning. My friend Mickey's a pleasant fellow for a secretary-at-war. But it's all settled now; Craufurd arranged it for you this afternoon."

"You don't say so! Pray tell me all about it."

"That's just what I won't; for, ye see, I don't know it; but I believe old Monsoon's affair has put everything out of their heads."

"Monsoon's affair! what is that? Out with it, Dennis."

"Faith, I'll be just as discreet about that as your own business. All I can tell you is, that they brought him up to head-quarters this evening with a sergeant's guard, and they say he's to be tried by court-martial; and Picton is in a blessed humor about it."

"What could it possibly have been? Some plundering affair, depend on it."

"Faith, you may swear it wasn't for his little charities, as Dr. Pangloss calls them, they've pulled him up," cried Power.

"Maurice is in high feather about it," said Dennis. "There are five of them up at Fuentes, making a list of the charges to send to Monsoon; for Bob Mahon, it seems, heard of the old fellow's doings up the mountains."

"What glorious fun!" said Power. "Let's haste and join them, boys."

"Agreed," said I. "Is it far from this?"

36

"Another stage. When we've got something to eat," said the Major, "if Power has any intentions that way——"

"Well, I really did begin to fear Fred's memory was lapsing; but somehow, poor fellow, smiles have been more in his way than sandwiches lately."

An admonishing look from Power was his only reply, as he walked towards the door. Bent upon teasing him, however, I continued,

"My only fear is, he may do something silly."

"Who? Monsoon, is it?"

"No, no. Not Monsoon; another friend of ours."

"Faith, I scarcely thought your fears of old Monsoon were called for. He's a fox—the devil a less."

"No, no, Dennis. I wasn't thinking of him. My anxieties were for a most soft-hearted young gentleman—one Fred Power."

"Charley, Charley!" said Fred, from the door where he had been giving directions to his servant about supper. "A man can scarce do a more silly thing than marry in the army; all the disagreeables of married life, with none of its better features."

"Marry—marry!" shouted O'Shaughnessy; "upon my conscience, it's incomprehensible to me how a man can be guilty of it. To be sure, I don't mean to say that there are not circumstances—such as half-pay, old age, infirmity, the loss of your limbs, and the like; but that, with good health and a small balance at your banker's, you should be led into such an embarrassment——"

"Men will flirt," said I, interrupting; "men will press taper fingers, look into bright eyes, and feel their witchery; and, although the fair owners be only quizzing them half the time, and amusing themselves the other, and though they be hackneyed coquettes——"

"Did you ever meet the Dalrymple girls, Dennis?" said Fred, with a look I shall never forget.

What the reply was I cannot tell. My shame and confusion were overwhelming, and Power's victory complete.

"Here comes the prog," cried Dennis, as Power's servant entered with a very plausible-looking tray, while Fred proceeded to place before us a strong army of decanters.

Our supper was excellent, and we were enjoying ourselves to the utmost, when an orderly sergeant suddenly opened the door, and raising his hand to his cap, asked if Major Power was there.

"A letter for you, sir."

"Monsoon's writing, by Jove! Come, boys, let us see what it means. What a hand the old fellow writes! The letters look all crazy, and are tumbling against each other on every side. Did you ever see anything half so tipsy as the crossing of that *t?*"

"Read it! Read it out, Fred!"

" ' Tuesday Evening.

" ' DEAR POWER,—I'm in such a scrape! Come up and see me at once; bring a little sherry with you, and we'll talk over what's to be done.

" ' Yours ever,

" ' B. MONSOON.

" ' Quarters-General.' "

We resolved to finish our evening with the Major; so that, each having armed himself with a bottle or two, and the remnants of our supper, we set out towards his quarters, under the guidance of the orderly. After a sharp walk of half an hour, we reached a small hut, where two sentries of the 88th were posted at the door.

O'Shaughnessy procured admittance for us, and in we went. At a small table, lighted by a thin tallow candle, sat old Monsoon, who, the weather being hot, had neither coat nor wig on; an old cracked china teapot, in which, as we found afterwards, he had mixed a little grog, stood before him, and a large mass of papers lay scattered around on every side; he himself being occupied in poring over their contents, and taking occasional draughts from his uncouth goblet.

As we entered noiselessly, he never perceived us, but continued to mumble over, in a low tone, from the documents before him :

"Upon my life, it's like a dream to me! What infernal stuff this brandy is!

" ' CHARGE No. 8.—For conduct highly unbecoming an officer and a gentleman, in forcing the cellar of the San Nicholas convent at Banos, taking large quantities of wine therefrom, and subsequently compelling the Prior to dance a bolero, thus creating a riot, and tending to destroy the harmony between the British and the Portuguese, so strongly inculcated to be preserved by the general orders.'

"Destroying the harmony! Bless their hearts ! How little they know of it ! I've never passed a jollier night in the Peninsula ! The Prior's a trump, and, as for the bolero, he *would* dance it. I hope they say nothing about my hornpipe.

" ' CHARGE No. 9.—For a gross violation of his duty as an officer, in sending a part of his brigade to attack and pillage the Alcalde of Banos, thereby endangering the public peace of the town, being a flagrant breach of discipline and direct violation of the articles of war.'

" ' Well, I'm afraid I was rather sharp on the Alcalde, but we did no harm except the fright. What sherry the old fellow had ! 'twould have been a sin to let it fall into the hands of the French.

" ' CHARGE No. 10.—For threatening, on or about the night of the 3d, to place the town of Banos under contribution, and subsequently forcing the authorities to walk in procession before him, in absurd and ridiculous costumes.'

"Lord, how good it was! I shall never forget the old Alcalde! One of my fellows fastened a dead lamb round his neck, and told him it was the golden fleece. The Commander-in-Chief would have laughed himself if he had been there. Picton is much too grave—never likes a joke.

"'CHARGE No. 11.—For insubordination and disobedience, in refusing to give up his sword, and rendering it necessary for the Portuguese guard to take it by force, thereby placing himself in a situation highly degrading to a British officer.'

"Didn't I lay about me before they got it'—Who's that?—Who's laughing there?—Ah, boys! I'm glad to see you.—How are you, Fred?—Well, Charley, I've heard of your scrape; very sad thing for so young a fellow as you are; I don't think you'll be broke; I'll do what I can—I'll see what I can do with Picton; we are very old friends—were at Eton together."

"Many thanks, Major; but I hear your own affairs are not flourishing. What's all this court-martial about?"

"A mere trifle; some little insubordination in the Legion. Those Portuguese are sad dogs. How very good of you, Fred, to think of that little supper."

While the Major was speaking, his servant, with a dexterity the fruit of long habit, had garnished the table with the contents of our baskets, and Monsoon, apologizing for not putting on his wig, sat down amongst us with a face as cheerful as though the floor was not covered with the charges of the court-martial to be held on him.

As we chatted away over the campaign and its chances, Monsoon seemed little disposed to recur to his own fortunes. In fact, he appeared to suffer much more from what he termed my unlucky predicament than from his own mishaps. At the same time, as the evening wore on, and the sherry began to tell upon him, his heart expanded into its habitual moral tendency, and by an easy transition he was led from the religious association of convents to the pleasures of pillaging them.

"What wine they have in their old cellars! It's such fun drinking it out of great silver vessels as old as Methuselah. 'There's much treasure in the house of the righteous,' as David says; and any one who has ever sacked a nunnery knows that."

"I should like to have seen that prior dancing the bolero," said Power.

"Wasn't it good, though! He grew jealous of me, for I performed

a hornpipe. Very good fellow the Prior; not like the Alcalde—
there was no fun in him. Lord bless him! he'll never forget me."

"What did you do with him, Major!"

"Well, I'll tell you; but you musn't let it be known, for I see
they have not put it in the court-martial. Is there no more sherry
there? There, that will do; I'm always contented. 'Better a dry
morsel with quietness,' as Moses says. Ay, Charley, never forget
that 'a merry heart is just like medicine.' Job found out that, you
know."

"Well, but the Alcalde, Major."

"Oh! the Alcalde, to be sure, these pious meditations make me
forget earthly matters."

"This old Alcalde at Banos, I found out was quite spoiled by Lord
Wellington. He used to read all the general orders, and got an
absurd notion in his head that, because we were his allies, we were
not allowed to plunder. Only think, he used to snap his fingers at
Beresford; didn't care twopence about the Legion; and laughed outright at Wilson. So, when I was ordered down there, I took another
way with him; I waited till nightfall, ordered two squadrons to turn
their jackets, and sent forward one of my aides-de-camp with a few
troopers to the Alcalde's house. They galloped into the courtyard,
blowing trumpets and making an infernal hubbub. Down came the
Alcalde in a passion.—'Prepare quarters quickly, and rations for
eight hundred men.'

"'Who dares to issue such an order?' said he.

"The aide-de-camp whispered one word in his ear, and the old
fellow grew pale as death. 'Is he here?—Is he coming?—Is he
coming?' said he, trembling from head to foot.

"I rode in myself at this moment, looking thus——

"'*Où est le malheureux?*' said I, in French; you know I speak
French like Portuguese."

"Devilish like, I've no doubt," muttered Power.

"'*Pardon, gracias eccellenza!*' said the Alcalde, on his knees."

"Who the deuce did he take you for, Major?"

"You shall hear: you'll never guess, though. Lord! I shall
never forget it. He thought I was Marmont: my aide-de-camp told
him so."

One loud burst of laughter interrupted the Major at this moment,
and it was some considerable time before he could continue his
narrative.

"And do you really mean," said I, "that you personated the Duke
de Raguse?"

"Did I not, though? If you had only seen me with a pair of
great moustaches, and a drawn sabre in my hand, pacing the room

up and down in the presence of the assembled authorities. Napoleon himself might have been deceived. My first order was to cut off all their heads; but I commuted the sentence to a heavy fine. Ah, boys! if they only understood at headquarters how to carry on a war in the Peninsula, they'd never have to grumble in England about increased taxation. How I'd mulct the nunneries! How I'd grind the corporate towns! How I'd inundate the country with exchequer bills; I'd sell the priors so much a head, and put the nuns up to auction by the dozen."

"You sacrilegious old villain! But continue the account of your exploits."

"Faith, I remember little more. After dinner I grew somewhat mellow, and a kind of moral bewilderment which usually steals over me about eleven o'clock induced me to invite the Alcalde and all the aldermen to come and sup. Apparently we had a merry night of it, and when morning broke, we were not quite clear in our intellects. Hence came that infernal procession; for when the Alcalde rode round the town with a paper cap, and all the aldermen after him, the inhabitants felt offended, it seems, and sent for a large Guerilla force, who captured me and my staff, after a very vigorous resistance. The Alcalde fought like a trump for us, for I promised to make him Prefect of the Seine; but we were overpowered, disarmed, and carried off. The remainder you can read in the court-martial, for you may think that, after sacking the town, drinking all night, and fighting in the morning, my memory was none of the clearest."

"Did you not explain that you were not the Marshal-General?"

"No, faith—I knew better than that; they'd have murdered me had they known their mistake. They brought me to head-quarters, in the hope of a great reward, and it was only when they reached this that they found out I was not the Duke de Raguse; so you see, boys, it's a very complicated business."

"'Gad, and so it is," said Power, "and an awkward one too."

"He'll be hanged, as sure as my name's Dennis!" vociferated O'Shaughnessy, with an energy that made the Major jump from his chair. "Picton will hang him!"

"I'm not afraid," said Monsoon; "they know me so well. Lord bless you, Beresford couldn't get on without me."

"Well, Major," said I, "in any case, you certainly take no gloomy nor desponding view of your case."

"Not I, boy. You know what Jeremiah says,—'A merry heart is a continual feast;' and so it is. I may die of repletion, but they'll never find me starved with sorrow."

"And, faith, it's a strange thing!" muttered O'Shaughnessy,

thinking aloud—"a most extraordinary thing! An honest fellow would be sure to be hanged; and there's that old rogue, that's been melting down more saints and blessed Virgins than the whole army together, he'll escape. Ye'll see he will!"

"There goes the patrol," said Fred; "we must start."

"Leave the sherry, boys; you'll be back again. I'll have it put up carefully."

We could scarcely resist a roar of laughter as we said "Good-night."

"Adieu, Major," said I; "we shall meet soon."

So saying, I followed Power and O'Shaughnessy towards their quarters.

"Maurice has done it beautifully!" said Power. "Pleasant revelations the old fellow will make on the court-martial, if he only remembers what we've heard to-night! But here we are, Charley; so good-night; and remember, you breakfast with me to-morrow."

CHAPTER XXXI.

THE CONFIDENCE.

I HAVE changed the venue, Charley," said Power, as he came into my room the following morning. "I've changed the venue, and come to breakfast with you."

I could not help smiling, as a certain suspicion crossed my mind, perceiving which, he quickly added,

"No, no, boy! I guess what you're thinking of. I'm not a bit jealous in that quarter. The fact is, you know one cannot be too guarded."

"Nor too suspicious of one's friends, apparently."

"A truce with quizzing. I say, have you reported yourself?"

"Yes; and received this moment a most kind note from the General. But it appears that I am not destined to have a long sojourn amongst you, for I'm desired to hold myself in readiness for a journey this very day."

"Where the deuce are they going to send you now?"

"I'm not certain of my destination. I rather suspect there are despatches for Badajos. Just tell Mike to get breakfast, and I'll join you immediately."

When I walked into the little room which served as my salon, I found Power pacing up and down, apparently rapt in meditation.

"I've been thinking, Charley," said he, after a pause of about ten minutes,—"I've been thinking over our adventures in Lisbon. Devilish strange girl that Senhora! When you resigned in my favor, I took it for granted that all difficulty was removed. Confound it! I no sooner began to profit by your absence, in pressing my suit, than she turned short round, treated me with marked coldness, exhibited a hundred wilful and capricious fancies, and concluded one day by quietly confessing to me—you were the only man she cared for."

"You are not serious in all this, Fred?" said I.

"Ain't I, though, by Jove! I wish to heaven I were not! My dear Charley, the girl is an inveterate flirt—a decided coquette. Whether she has a particle of heart or not, I can't say; but certainly her greatest pleasure is to trifle with that of another. Some absurd suspicion that you were in love with Lucy Dashwood piqued her vanity, and the anxiety to recover a lapsing allegiance led her to suppose herself attached to you, and made her treat all my advances with the most frigid indifference or wayward caprice—the more provoking," continued he, with a kind of bitterness in his tone, "as her father was disposed to take the thing favorably; and, if I must say it, I felt devilish spoony about her myself.

"It was only two days before I left, that, in a conversation with Don Emanuel, he consented to receive my addresses to his daughter on my becoming lieutenant-colonel. I hastened back with delight to bring her the intelligence, and found her with a lock of hair on the book before her, over which she was weeping. Confound me, if it was not yours! I don't know what I said, nor what she replied; but when we parted, it was with a perfect understanding that we were never to meet again. Strange girl! She came that evening, put her arm within mine as I was walking alone in the garden, and half in jest, half in earnest, talked me out of all my suspicions, and left me fifty times more in love with her than ever. Egad! I thought I used to know something about women, but here is a chapter I've yet to read. Come now, Charley, be frank with me; tell me all you know."

"My poor Fred! if you were not head and ears in love, you would see as plainly as I do that your affairs prosper. And after all, how invariable is it that the man who has been the veriest flirt with women—sighing, serenading, sonneteering, flinging himself at the feet of every pretty girl he meets with—should become the most thorough dupe to his own feelings when his heart is really touched. Your man of eight-and-thirty is always the greatest fool about women."

"Confound your impertinence! How the devil can a fellow with a moustache not stronger than a Circassian's eyebrow read such a lecture *to me ?*"

"Just for the very reason you've mentioned. You *glide* into an attachment at *my* time of life; you *fall* in love at *yours.*"

"Yes," said Power, musingly, "there is some truth in that. This flirting is sad work. It is just like sparring with a friend; you put on the gloves in perfect good humor, with the most friendly intentions of exchanging a few amicable blows; you find yourself insensibly warm with the enthusiasm of the conflict, and some unlucky hard knock decides the matter, and it ends in a downright fight.

"Few men, believe me, are regular seducers; and among those who behave 'vilely' (as they call it), three-fourths of the number have been more sinned against than sinning. You adventure upon love as upon a voyage to India. Leaving the cold northern latitudes of first acquaintance behind you, you gradually glide into the warmer and more genial climate of intimacy. Each day you travel southward shortens the miles and the hours of your existence: so tranquil is the passage, and so easy the transition, you suffer no shock by the change of temperature about you. Happy were it for us that in our courtship, as in our voyage, there were some certain Rubicon to remind us of the miles we have journeyed! Well were it if there were some meridian in love!"

"I'm not sure, Fred, that there is not that same shaving process they practice on the line occasionally performed for us by parents and guardians at home; and I'm not certain that the iron hoop of old Neptune is not a pleasanter acquaintance than the hair-trigger of some indignant and fire-eating brother. But come, Fred, you have not told me the most important point—how fare your fortunes now? or, in other words, what are your present prospects as regards the Senhora ?"

"What a question to ask me! Why not request me to tell you where Soult will fight us next, and when Marmont will cross the frontier? My dear boy, I have not seen her for a week, an entire week—seven full days and nights, each with their twenty-four hours of change and vacillation."

"Well, then, give me the last bulletin from the seat of war; that, at least, you can do. Tell me how you parted."

"Strangely enough. You must know we had a grand dinner at the villa the day before I left; and, when we adjourned for our coffee to the garden, my spirits were at the top of their bent. Inez never looked so beautiful—never was half so gracious; and as she leaned upon my arm, instead of following the others towards the little summer-house, I turned, as if inadvertently, into a narrow dark alley that skirts the lake."

"I know it well; continue."

Power reddened slightly, and went on:

"'Why are we taking this path?' said Donna Inez; 'this is surely not a short way?'

"'Oh! I—wished to make my adieux to my old friends the swans. You know I go to-morrow.'

"'Ah! that's true,' said she. 'I'd quite forgotten it.'

"This speech was not very encouraging; but as I felt myself in for the battle, I was not going to retreat at the skirmish. 'Now or never,' thought I. I'll not tell you what I said. I couldn't if I would. It is only with a pretty woman upon one's arm—it is only when stealing a glance at her bright eyes, as you bend beyond the border of her bonnet—that you know what it is to be eloquent. Watching the changeful color of her cheek with a more anxious heart than ever did mariner gaze upon the fitful sky above him, you pour out your whole soul in love. You leave no time for doubt,— no space for reply; the difficulties that shoot across her mind you reply to ere she is well conscious of them; and when you feel her hand tremble, or see her eyelid fall, like the leader of a storming party when the guns slacken in their fire, you spring boldly forward in the breach, and, blind to every danger around you, rush madly on, and plant your standard upon the walls."

"I hope you allow the vanquished the honors of war," said I, interrupting.

Without noticing my observation, he continued:

"I was on my knees before her, her hand passively resting in mine, her eyes bent upon me softly and tearfully ——"

"The game was your own, in fact."

"You shall hear.

"'Have we stood long enough thus, Senhor?' said she, bursting into a fit of laughter.

"I sprang to my legs in anger and indignation.

"'There, don't be passionate; it is so tiresome. What do you call that tree there?'

"'It is a tulip-tree,' said I, coldly.

"'Then, to put your gallantry to the test, do climb up there and pluck me that flower. No, the far one. If you fall into the lake and are drowned, why, it would put an end to this foolish interview.'

"'And if not?' said I.

"'Oh, then I shall take twelve hours to consider of it; and if my decision be in your favor, I'll give you the flower ere you leave to-morrow.'

"It's somewhat about thirty years since I went bird-nesting—and hang me if a tight jacket and spurs are the best equipment for climbing a tree!—but up I went, and, amid a running fire of laughter and quizzing, reached the branch, and brought it down safely.

"Inez took especial care to avoid me the rest of the evening. We did not meet until breakfast the following morning. I perceived then that she wore the flower in her belt; but, alas! I knew her too well to augur favorably from that; besides, instead of any trace of sorrow or depression at my approaching departure, she was in high spirits, and the life of the party. 'How can I manage to speak with her?' said I to myself; 'but one word—I already anticipate what it must be. But let the blow fall—anything is better than this uncertainty.'

"'The General and the staff have passed the gate, sir,' said my servant at this moment.

"'Are my horses ready?'

"'At the door, sir, and the baggage gone forward.'

"I gave Inez one look.

"'Did you say more coffee?' said she, smiling.

"I bowed coldly, and rose from the table. They all assembled upon the terrace to see me ride away.

"'You'll let us hear from you?' said Don Emanuel.

"'And pray don't forget the letter to my brother,' cried old Madame Forjas.

"Twenty similar injunctions burst from the party, but not a word said Inez.

"'Adieu, then!' said I. 'Farewell!'

"'Adios! Go with God!' chorused the party.

"'Good-bye, Senhora!' said I. 'Have *you* nothing to tell me ere we part?'

"'Not that I remember,' said she, carelessly. 'I hope you'll have good weather.'

"'There is a storm threatening,' said I, gloomily.

"'Well, a soldier cares little for a wet jacket.'

"'Adieu!' said I, sharply, darting at her a look that spoke my meaning.

"'Farewell!' repeated she, curtseying slightly, and giving one of her sweetest smiles.

"I drove the spurs into my horse's flanks, but holding him firmly on the curb at the same moment, instead of dashing forward, he bounded madly in the air.

"'What a pretty creature!' said she, as she turned towards the house; then, stopping carelessly, she looked round.

"'Should you like this bouquet?' she asked.

"Before I could reply, she disengaged it from her belt, and threw it towards me. The door closed behind her as she spoke. I galloped on to overtake the staff—*et voilà tout*. Now, Charley, read my fate for me, and tell me what this portends."

"I confess I only see one thing certain in the whole."

"And that is?" said Power.

"That Master Fred Power is more irretrievably in love than any gentleman on full pay I ever met with."

"By Jove! I half fear as much! Is that orderly waiting for you, Charley? Whom do you want, my man?"

"Captain O'Malley, sir. General Craufurd desires to see you at head-quarters immediately."

"Come, Charley, I'm going towards Fuentes. Take your cap; we'll walk down together."

So saying, we cantered towards the village, where we separated— Power to join some 14th men stationed there on duty, and I to the General's quarters to receive my orders.

CHAPTER XXXII.

THE CANTONMENT.

SOON after this the army broke up from Caja, and went into cantonments along the Tagus, the head-quarters being at Portalegre. We were here joined by four regiments of infantry lately arrived from England, and the 12th Light Dragoons. I shall not readily forget the first impression created among our reinforcements by the habits of our life at this period.

Brimful of expectation, they had landed at Lisbon, their minds filled with all the glorious expectancy of a brilliant campaign. Sieges, storming, and battle-fields floated before their excited imagination. Scarcely, however, had they reached the camp, when these illusions were dissipated. Breakfasts, dinners, private theatricals, pigeon matches, formed our daily occupation. Lord Wellington's hounds threw off regularly twice a week, and here might be seen every imaginable species of equipment, from that of the artillery officer, mounted on his heavy troop horse, to the infantry subaltern on a Spanish jennet. Never was anything more ludicrous than our turn-out. Every quadruped in the army was put into requisition; and even those who rolled not from their saddles from sheer necessity, were most likely to do so from laughing at their neighbors. The pace may not have equalled Melton, nor the fences have been as stubborn as in Leicestershire, but I'll be sworn there was more laughter, more fun, and more merriment, in one day with us than in a whole season with the best-organized pack in England. With a lively trust that the country was open and the leaps easy, every man took the field; indeed, the only anxiety evinced at all was to appear at the meeting in something like jockey fashion, and I must confess that this feeling was particularly conspicuous among the infantry. Happy the man whose kit boasted a pair of cords, or buckskins; thrice happy he who sported a pair of tops. I myself was in that enviable position, and well remember with what pride of heart I cantered up to cover in all the superior *éclat* of my costume, though, if truth were to be spoken, I doubt if I should have passed muster among my friends of the " Blazers." A round cavalry jacket, and a foraging cap with a hanging tassel, were the strange accompaniments of my more befitting nether garments. Whatever our costumes, the scene was a most animated one. Here, the shell-jacket of a heavy dragoon was seen storming the fence of a vineyard; there, the dark green of a rifleman was going the pace over the plain. The unsportsman-like figure of a staff officer might be observed emerging from a drain, while some neck-or-nothing Irishman, with light infantry wings, was flying at every fence before him, and overturning all in his way. The rules and regulations of the service prevailed not here; the starred and gartered general, the plumed and aiguilletted colonel, obtained but little deference, and less mercy, from his more humble subaltern. In fact, I am half disposed to think that many an old grudge of rigid discipline, or severe duty, met with its retribution here. More than once have I heard the muttered sentences around me which boded like this:

"Go the pace, Harry! never flinch it! There's old Colquhoun—take him in the haunches—roll him over!"

"See here, boys—watch how I'll scatter the staff—beg your pardon, General, hope I haven't hurt you. Turn about is fair play—I have taught *you* to take up a position now."

I need scarcely say there was one whose person was sacred from all such attacks; he was well mounted upon a strong half-bred horse; rode always foremost, following the hounds with the same steady pertinacity with which he would have followed the enemy; his compressed lip rarely opening for a laugh, when even the most ludicrous misadventure was enacting before him; and when, by chance, he would give way, the short ha! ha! was over in a moment, and the cold stern features were as fixed and impassive as before.

All the excitement, all the enthusiasm of a hunting-field, seemed powerless to turn his mind from the pre-occupation which the mighty interests he presided over exacted. I remember an incident which, however trivial in itself, is worth recording, as illustrative of what I mean. We were going along at a topping pace; the hounds, a few fields in advance, were hidden from our view by a small beech copse; the party consisted of not more than six persons, one of whom was Lord Wellington himself. Our run had been a splendid one, and as we were pursuing the fox to earth, every man of us pushed his horse to his full stride in the hot enthusiasm of such a moment.

"This way, my lord—this way," said Colonel Conyers, an old Melton man, who led the way. "The hounds are in the valley—keep to the left." As no reply was made, after a few moments' pause, Conyers repeated his admonition. "You are wrong, my lord; the hounds are hunting yonder."

"I know it!" was the brief answer, given with a shortness that almost savored of asperity; for a second or two not a word was spoken.

"How far is Niza, Gordon?" inquired Lord Wellington.

"About five leagues, my lord," replied the astonished aide-de-camp.

"That's the direction, is it not?"

"Yes, my lord."

"Let's go over and inspect the wounded."

No more was said, and before a second was given for consideration, away went his lordship, followed by his aide-de-camp, his pace the same stretching gallop, and apparently feeling as much excitement, as he dashed onward towards the hospital, as though following in all the headlong enthusiasm of a fox-chase.

Thus passed our summer; a life of happy ease and recreation succeeding to the harassing fatigues and severe privations of the preceding campaign. Such are the lights and shadows of a soldier's life—such the chequered surface of his fortune—constituting by their very change that buoyant temperament, that happy indifference, which enables him to derive its full enjoyment from each passing incident of his career.

While thus we indulged in all the fascinations of a life of pleasure, the rigid discipline of the army was never for a moment forgotten. Reviews, parades, and inspections, were of daily occurrence, and even a superficial observer could not fail to detect that under this apparent devotion to amusement and enjoyment our Commander-in-Chief concealed a deep stroke of his policy.

The spirits of both men and officers, broken in spite of their successes by the incessant privations they had endured, imperatively demanded this period of rest and repose. The infantry, many of whom had served in the ill-fated campaign of Walcheren, were still suffering from the effects of the intermittent fever. The cavalry, from deficient forage, severe marches, and unremitting service, were in great part unfit for duty. To take the field under circumstances like these was therefore impossible; and, with the double object of restoring their wonted spirit to his troops, and checking the ravages which sickness and the casualties of war had made with his ranks, Lord Wellington embraced the opportunity of the enemy's inaction to take up his present position on the Tagus.

Meanwhile that we enjoyed all the pleasures of a country life, enhanced tenfold by daily association with gay and cheerful companions, the master-mind, whose reach extended from the profoundest calculations of strategy to the minutest details of military organization, was never idle. Foreseeing that a period of inaction like the present must only be like the solemn calm that preludes the storm, he prepared for the future by those bold conceptions and unrivalled combinations which were to guide him through many a field of battle and of danger, to end his career of glory in the liberation of the Peninsula.

The failure of the attack upon Badajos had neither damped his ardor nor changed his views; and he proceeded to the investment of Ciudad Rodrigo with the same intense determination of uprooting the French occupation in Spain, by destroying their strongholds and cutting off their resources. Carrying aggressive war in one hand, he turned the other towards the maintenance of those defences which in the event of disaster or defeat must prove the refuge of the army.

To the lines of Torres Vedras he once more directed his attention. Engineer officers were despatched thither; the fortresses were put into repair; the bridges broken or injured during the French invasion were restored; the batteries upon the Tagus were rendered more effective, and furnaces for heating shot were added to them.

The inactivity and apathy of the Portuguese government but ill corresponded with his unwearied exertions; and, despite of continual remonstrances and unceasing representations, the bridges over the Leira and Alva were left unrepaired, and the roads leading to them so broken as to be almost impassable, might seriously have endangered the retreat of the army, should such a movement be deemed necessary.

It was in the first week of September I was sent with despatches for the engineer officer in command at the lines, and during the fortnight of my absence was enabled for the first time to examine those extraordinary defences which, for the space of thirty miles, extended over a country undulating in hill and valley, and presenting, by a succession of natural and artificial resources, the strongest and most impregnable barrier that has ever been presented against the advance of a conquering army.

CHAPTER XXXIII.

MICKEY FREE'S ADVÉNTURE.

WHEN I returned to the camp, I found the greatest excitement prevailing on all sides. Each day brought in fresh rumors that Marmont was advancing in force; that sixty thousand Frenchmen were in full march upon Ciudad Rodrigo, to raise the blockade, and renew the invasion of Portugal. Intercepted letters corroborated these reports; and the Guerillas who joined us spoke of large convoys which they had seen upon the roads from Salamanca and Tamanes.

Except the light division, which, under the command of Craufurd, were posted upon the right of the Aguada, the whole of our army occupied the country from El Bodon to Gallegos; the fourth division being stationed at Fuente Guenaldo, where some entrenchments had been hastily thrown up.

To this position Lord Wellington resolved upon retreating, as affording points of greater strength and more capability of defence than the other line of road, which led by Almeida upon the Coa. Of the enemy's intentions we were not long to remain in doubt; for on the morning of the 24th a strong body was seen descending from the pass above Ciudad Rodrigo, and cautiously reconnoitring the banks of the Aguada. Far in the distance a countless train of wagons, bullock-cars, and loaded mules were seen winding their slow length along, accompanied by several squadrons of dragoons.

Their progress was slow, but as evening fell they entered the gates of the fortress; and the cheering of the garrison mixing with the strains of martial music, faint from distance, reached us where we lay upon the far-off heights of El Bodon. So long as the light lasted, we could perceive fresh troops arriving; and even when the darkness came on, we could detect the position of the reinforcing columns by the bright watch-fires which gleamed along the plain.

By daybreak we were under arms, anxiously watching for the intentions of our enemy, which soon became no longer dubious.

Twenty-five squadrons of cavalry, supported by a whole division of infantry, were seen to defile along the great road from Ciudad Rodrigo to Guenaldo. Another column, equally numerous, marched straight upon Espeja. Nothing could be more beautiful, nothing more martial, than their appearance. Emerging from a close mountain gorge, they wound along the narrow road, and appeared upon the bridge of the Aguada just as the morning sun was bursting forth; his bright beams tipped the polished cuirassiers and their glittering equipments, they shone in their panoply like the gay troop of some ancient tournament. The lancers of Berg, distinguished by their scarlet dolmans and gorgeous trappings, were followed by the Cuirassiers of the Guard, who again were succeeded by the *chasseurs à cheval*, their bright steel helmets and light blue uniforms, their floating plumes and dappled chargers, looking the very *beau idéal* of light horsemen; behind, the dark masses of the infantry pressed forward, and deployed into the plain, while, bringing up the rear, the rolling din, like distant thunder, announced the " dread artillery."

On they came, the seemingly interminable line converging on to that one spot upon whose summit now we assembled a force of scarcely ten thousand bayonets.

While this brilliant panorama was passing before our eyes, we ourselves were not idle. Orders had been sent to Picton to come up from the left with his division. Alten's cavalry and a brigade of artillery were sent to the front, and every preparation which the nature of the ground admitted was made to resist the advance of the enemy. While these movements on either side occupied some hours, the scene was every moment increasing in interest. The large body of cavalry was now seen forming into columns of attack. Nine battalions of infantry moved up to their support, and, forming into columns, echelons, and squares, performed before us all the manœuvres of a review with the most admirable precision and rapidity; but from these our attention was soon taken by a brilliant display upon our left. Here, emerging from the wood which flanked the Aguada, were now to be seen the gorgeous staff of Marmont himself. Advancing at a walk, they came forward amid the *vivas* of the assembled thousands, burning with ardor and thirsting for victory. For a moment, as I looked, I could detect the Marshal himself, as, holding his plumed hat above his head, he returned the salute of a lancer regiment, who proudly waved their banners as he passed; but, hark! what are those clanging sounds, which, rising high above the rest, seem like the war-cry of a warrior?

"I can't mistake those tones," said a bronzed old veteran beside me; "those are the brass bands of the Imperial Guard. Can Napoleon be there? See! there they come." As he spoke, the head of a column emerged from the wood, and, deploying as they came, poured into the plain. For above an hour that mighty tide flowed on, and before noon, a force of sixty thousand men was collected in the space beneath us.

I was not long to remain an unoccupied spectator of this brilliant display, for I soon received orders to move down with my squadron to the support of the 11th Light Dragoons, who were posted at the base of the hill. The order at the moment was anything but agreeable, for I was mounted upon a hack pony, on which I had ridden over from Craufurd's division early in the morning, and suspecting that there might be some hot work during the day, had ordered Mike to follow with my horse. There was no time, however, for hesitation, and I moved my men down the slope in the direction of the skirmishers.

The position we occupied was singularly favorable. Our flanks being defended on either side by brushwood, we could only be assailed in front; and here, notwithstanding our vast inferiority of force, we steadily awaited the attack. As I rode from out the thick wood, I could not help feeling somewhat surprised at the sounds which greeted me. Instead of the usual low and murmuring tones—the muttered sentences which precede a cavalry advance—a roar of laughter shook the entire divison, while exclamations burst from every side around me: "Look at him now!" "They have him! —by Heavens, they have him!" "Well done!—well done!" "How the fellow rides!" "He's hit!—he's hit!" "No, no!" "Is he down!" "He's down!"

A loud cheer rent the air at this moment, and I reached the front in time to learn the reason of all this excitement. In the wide plain before me a horseman was seen, having passed the ford of the Aguada, to advance at the top of his speed towards the British lines. As he came nearer, it was perceived that he was accompanied by a led horse, and, apparently with total disregard of the presence of an enemy, rode boldly and carelessly forward. Behind him rode three lancers, their lances couched, their horses at speed. The pace was tremendous, and the excitement was intense; for sometimes, as the leading horseman of the pursuit neared the fugitive, he would bend suddenly upon the saddle, and, swerving to the right or the left, totally evade him, while again, at others, with a loud cry of bold defiance, rising in his stirrups, he would press on, and, with a shake of his bridle which bespoke the jockey, almost distance the enemy.

"That must be your fellow, O'Malley; that must be your Irish groom," cried a brother officer. There could be no doubt of it. It was Mike himself.

"I'll be hanged if he's not playing with them!" said Baker. "Look at the villain! He's holding in : that's more than the Frenchmen are doing. Look! look at the fellow on the gray horse! he has flung his trumpet to his back, and drawn his sabre."

A loud cheer burst from the French lines ; the trumpeter was gaining at every stride. Mike had got into deep ground, and the horses would not keep together. "Let the brown horse go; let him go, man!" shouted the dragoons, while I re-echoed the cry with my utmost might. But not so. Mike held firmly on, and, spurring madly, he lifted his horse at each stride, turning from time to time a glance at his pursuer. A shout of triumph rose from the French side ; the trumpeter was beside him ; his arm was uplifted ; the sabre above his head. A yell broke from the British, and with difficulty could the squadron be restrained. For above a minute the horses went side by side, but the Frenchman delayed his stroke until he could get a little in the front. My excitement had rendered me speechless ; if a word could have saved my poor fellow, I could not have spoken. A mist seemed to gather across my eyes, and the whole plain, and its peopled thousands, danced before my eyes.

"He's down!" "He's down, by Heavens!" "No! no! no!" "Look there—nobly done!" "Gallant fellow!" "He has him!—he has him, by ——!" A cheer that rent the very air above us broke from the squadrons, and Mike galloped in amongst us, holding the Frenchman by the throat with one hand ; the bridle of his horse he firmly grasped with his own in the other.

"How was it? how did he do it?" cried I.

"He broke his sword-arm with a blow, and the Frenchman's sabre fell to the earth."

"Here he is, Mister Charles ; and, musha, but it's trouble he gave me to catch him! And I hope your honor won't be displeased with me at losing the brown horse. I was obliged to let him go when the thief closed on me ; but, sure, there he is! May I never! if he's not galloping into the lines by himself." As he spoke, my brown charger came cantering up to the squadrons, and took his place in the line with the rest.

I had scarcely time to mount my horse, amid a buzz of congratulations, when our squadron was ordered to the front. Mixed up with detachments from the 11th and 16th, we continued to resist the enemy for above two hours.

Our charges were quick, sharp, and successive, pouring in our numbers whenever the enemy appeared for a moment to be broken, and then retreating under cover of our infantry when the opposing cavalry came down upon us in overwhelming numbers.

Nothing could be more perfect than the manner in which the

different troops relieved each other during this part of the day. When the French squadrons advanced, ours met them as boldly. When the ground became no longer tenable, we broke and fell back, and the bayonets of the infantry arrested their progress. If the cavalry pressed heavily upon the squares, ours came up to the relief, and as they were beaten back, the artillery opened upon them with an avalanche of grape shot.

I have seen many battles of greater duration, and more important in result,—many there have been in which more tactic was displayed, and greater combinations called forth; but never did I witness a more desperate hand-to-hand conflict than on the heights of El Bodon.

Baffled by our resistance, Montbrun advanced with the Cuirassiers of the Guard. Riding down our advanced squadrons, they poured upon us like some mighty river, overwhelming all before it, and charged, cheering, up the heights. Our brave troopers were thrown back upon the artillery, and many of them cut down beside the guns. The artillerymen and the drivers shared the same fate, and the cannon were captured. A cheer of exultation burst from the French, and their *vivas* rent the air. Their exultation was short-lived and that cheer their death-cry; for the 5th Foot, who had hitherto lain concealed in the grass, sprang madly to their feet, their gallant Major Ridge at their head. With a yell of vengeance they rushed upon the foe; the glistening bayonets glanced amid the cavalry of the French; the troops pressed hotly home; and while the cuirassiers were driven down the hill, the guns were recaptured, limbered up, and brought away. This brilliant charge was the first recorded instance of cavalry being assailed by infantry in line.

But the hill could no longer be held. The French were advancing on either flank; overwhelming numbers pressed upon the front, and retreat was unavoidable. The cavalry were ordered to the rear, and Picton's division, throwing themselves into squares, covered the retreating movement.

The French dragoons bore down upon every face of those devoted battalions; the shouts of triumph cheered them as the earth trembled beneath their charge; but the British infantry, reserving their fire until the sabres clanked with the bayonet, poured in a shattering volley, and the cry of the wounded and the groans of the dying rose from the smoke around them.

Again and again the French came on; and the same fate ever awaited them. The only movement in the British squares was closing up the spaces as their comrades fell or sank wounded to the earth.

At last reinforcements came up from the left: the whole retreated across the plain, until, as they approached Guenaldo, our cavalry, having re-formed, came to their aid with one crushing charge, which closed the day.

That same night Lord Wellington fell back, and, concentrating his troops within a narrow loop of land bounded on either flank by the Coa, awaited the arrival of the light division, which joined us at three in the morning.

The following day Marmont again made a demonstration of his force, but no attack followed. The position was too formidable to be easily assailed, and the experience of the preceding day had taught him that, however inferior in number, the troops he was opposed to were as valiant as they were ably commanded.

Soon after this, Marmont retired on the valley of the Tagus. Dorsenne also fell back, and, for the present, at least, no further effort was made to prosecute the invasion of Portugal.

CHAPTER XXXIV.

THE SAN PETRO.

NOT badly wounded, O'Malley, I hope?" said General Craufurd, as I waited upon him soon after the action.

I could not help starting at the question, while he repeated it, pointing at the same time to my left shoulder, from which a stream of blood was now flowing down my coat sleeve.

"I never noticed it, sir, till this moment; it can't be of much consequence, for I have been on horseback the entire day, and never felt it."

"Look to it at once boy; a man wants all his blood for this campaign. Go to your quarters; I shall not need you for the present, so pray see the Doctor at once."

As I left the General's quarters, I began to feel sensible of pain, and before a quarter of an hour had elapsed, had quite convinced myself that my wound was a severe one. The hand and arm were swollen, heavy and distended with hemorrhage beneath the skin; my thirst became great, and a cold shuddering sensation passed over me from time to time.

I sat down for a moment upon the grass, and was just reflecting within myself what course I should pursue, when I heard the tramp of feet approaching. I looked up, and perceived some soldiers in fatigue dresses, followed by a few others, who, from their noiseless gestures and sad countenances, I guessed were carrying some wounded comrade to the rear.

"Who is it, boys?" cried I.

"It's the Major, sir; the Lord be good to him!" said a hardy-looking 88th man, wiping his eye with the cuff of his coat as he spoke.

"Not your Major?—not Major O'Shaughnessy?" said I, jumping up and rushing forward towards the litter. Alas! too true—it was the gallant fellow himself; there he lay, pale and cold, his bloodless cheek and parted lips looking like death itself. . A thin blue rivulet trickled from his forehead, but his most serious wound appeared to be in his side; his coat was open, and showed a mass of congealed and clotted blood, from the midst of which with every motion of the way, a fresh stream kept welling upward. Whether from the shock or my loss of blood, or from both together, I know not, but I sank fainting to the ground.

*   *   *   *   *   *   *   *

It would have needed a clearer brain and a cooler judgment than I possessed to have conjectured where I was and what had occurred to me when I next recovered my senses. Weak, fevered, and with a burning thirst, I lay, unable to move, and could merely perceive the objects which lay within the reach of my vision. The place was cold, calm, and still as the grave. A lamp, which hung high above my head, threw a faint light around, and showed me within a niche of the opposite wall the figure of a gorgeously-dressed female. She appeared to be standing motionless, but as the pale light flickered upon her features, I thought I could detect the semblance of a smile. The splendor of her costume, and the glittering gems which shone upon her spotless robe, gleamed through the darkness with an almost supernatural brilliancy, and so beautiful did she look, so calm her pale features, that as I opened and shut my eyes and rubbed my lids, I scarcely dared to trust my erring senses, and believe it could be real. What could it mean? Whence this silence —this cold sense of awe and reverence? Was it a dream? was it the fitful vision of a disordered intellect? Could it be death? My eyes were riveted upon that beautiful figure. I essayed to speak, but could not. I would have beckoned her towards me, but my hands refused their office. I felt I knew not what charm she possessed to calm my throbbing brain and burning heart! but as I turned from the gloom and darkness around to gaze upon her fair brow and unmoved features, I felt like the prisoner who turns from the cheerless desolation of his cell, and looks upon the fair world and the smiling valleys lying sunlit and shadowed before him.

Sleep at length came over me. When I awoke, the day seemed

breaking, for a faint gray tint stole through a stained-glass window, and fell in many-colored patches upon the pavement. A low muttering sound attracted mé. I listened—it was Mike's voice. With difficulty raising myself upon one arm, I endeavored to see more around me. Scarcely had I assumed this position, when my eyes once more fell upon the white-clad figure of the preceding night. At her feet knelt Mike, his hands clasped, and his head bowed upon his bosom. Shall I confess my surprise—my disappointment! It was no other than an image of the blessed Virgin, decked out in all the gorgeous splendor which Catholic piety bestows upon her saints. The features, which the imperfect light and my more imperfect faculties had endowed with an expression of calm angelic beauty, were, to my waking senses, but the cold and barren mockery of loveliness. The eyes, which my excited brain gifted with looks of tenderness and pity, stared with no speculation in them; yet, contrasting my feelings of the night before, full as they were of their deceptions, with my now waking thoughts, I longed once more for that delusion which threw a dreamy pleasure over me, and subdued the stormy passions of my soul into rest and repose.

"Who knows," thought I, "but he who kneels yonder feels now as I did then? Who can tell how little the cold, unmeaning reality before him resembles the spiritualized creation the fervor of his love and the ardor of his devotion may have placed upon that altar? Who can limit or bound the depth of that adoration for an object whose attributes appeal not only to every sentiment of the heart, but also to every sense of the brain? I fancy that I can picture to myself how these tinselled relics, these tasteless wax-works, changed by the magic of devotion and of dread, became to the humble worshipper images of loveliness and beauty. The dim religious light; the reverberating footsteps echoed along those solemn aisles; the vaulted arches, into whose misty heights the sacred incense floats upward, while the deep organ is pealing its notes of praise or prayer,—these are no slight accessories to all the pomp and grandeur of a church whose forms and ceremonial, unchanged for ages, and hallowed by a thousand associations, appeal to the mind of the humblest peasant or the proudest noble, by all the weaknesses as by all the more favored features of our nature."

How long I might have continued to meditate in this strain I know not, but a muttered observation from Mike turned the whole current of my thoughts. His devotions over, he had seated himself upon the steps of the altar, and appeared to be resolving some doubts within himself concerning his late pious duties.

"Masses is dearer here than in Galway. Father Bush would be well pleased at two-and-sixpence for what I paid three doubloons for this morning. And sure it's droll enough. How expensive an amusement it is to kill the French. Here's half a dollar I gave for the soul of a cuirassier that I kilt yesterday, and nearly twice as much for an artilleryman I cut down at the guns ; and because the villain swore like a haythen, Father Pedro told me he'd cost more nor if he had died like a dacent man."

At these words he turned suddenly round towards the Virgin, and crossing himself devoutly, added,

"And sure it's yourself knows if it's fair to make me pay for devils that don't know their duties ; and, after all, if you don't understand English nor Irish, I've been wasting my time here this two hours."

"I say, Mike, how's the Major? How's Major O'Shaughnessy?"

"Charmingly, sir. It was only the loss of blood that ailed him. A thief with a pike—one of the chaps they call Poles, bekase of the long sticks they carry with them—stuck the Major in the ribs ; but Doctor Quill—God reward him !—he's a great doctor, and a funny divil too ; he cured him in no time."

"And where is he now, Mike?"

"Just convanient, in a small chapel off the sacristy ; and throuble enough we have to keep him quiet. He gave up the *confusion* of roses, and took to punch ; and faith, it isn't hymns nor paslams [psalms] he's singing all night. And they had me there, mixing materials and singing songs, till I heard the bell for matins ; and what between the punch and the prayers, I never closed my eyes."

"What do they call this convent?"

"It is a hard word, I misremember. It's something like saltpetre. But how's your honor? it's time to ask."

"Much better, Mike—much better. But, as I see that either your drink or your devotion seems to have affected your nerves, you'd better lie down for an hour or two. I shall not want you."

"That's just what I can't; for you see I'm making a song for this evening. The Rangers has a little supper, and I'm to be there ; and though I've made one, I'm not sure it'll do. Maybe your honor would give me your opinion about it?"

"With all my heart, Mike: let's hear it."

"Arrah ! is it here, before the Virgin and the two blessed saints that's up there in the glass cases? But, sure, when they make an hospital of the place, and after the Major's songs last night——"

"Exactly so, Mike: out with it."

"Well, ma'am," said he, turning towards the Virgin, "as I suspect you don't know English, maybe you'll think it's my offices I'm singing. So, saving your favor, here it is. It is to the air of 'Arrah, Catty, now can't you be aisy?'"

MR. FREE'S SONG.

"Oh what stories I'll tell when my sodgering's o'er,
  And the gallant Fourteenth is disbanded,
Not a drill nor parade will I hear of no more,
  When safely in Ireland landed.
With the blood that I spilt—the Frenchmen I kilt,
  I'll drive the young girls half crazy;
And some 'cute one will cry, with a wink of her eye,
  'Mister Free, now,—why can't you be aisy?'

"I'll tell how we routed the squadrons in fight,
  And destroyed them all at 'Talavera,'
And then I'll just add how we finished the night,
  In learning to dance the 'bolera;'
How by the moonshine we drank rale wine,
  And rose next day fresh as a daisy;
Then some one will cry, with a look mighty sly,
  'Arrah, Mickey,—now can't you be aisy?'

"I'll tell how the nights with Sir Arthur we spent,
  Around a big fire in the air too,
Or maybe enjoying ourselves in a tent,
  Exactly like Donnybrook fair too.
How he'd call out to me—'Pass the wine, Mr. Free,
  For you're a man never is lazy!'
Then some one will cry, with a wink of her eye,
  'Arrah, Mickey, dear,—can't you be aisy?'

"I'll tell, too, the long years in fighting we passed,
  Till Mounseer asked Bony to lead him;
And Sir Arthur, grown tired of glory at last,
  Begged of one Mickey Free to succeed him.
'But, acushla,' says I, 'the truth is I'm shy!
  There's a lady in Ballymacrazy!
And I swore on the book——' He gave me a look,
  And cried, 'Mickey,—now can't you be aisy?'"

"Arrah! Mickey, now can't you be *aisy?*" sang out a voice in chorus, and the next moment Dr. Quill himself made his appearance.

"Well, O'Malley, is it a penitential psalm you're singing, or is my friend Mike endeavoring to raise your spirits with a Galway sonata?"

"A little bit of his own muse, Doctor, nothing more. But, tell me, how goes it with the Major—is the poor fellow out of danger?"

"Except from the excess of his appetite, I know of no risk he runs. His servant is making gruel for him all day in a thing like the grog-tub of a frigate. But you've heard the news—Sparks has been exchanged; he came here last night; but the moment he caught sight of me, he took his departure. Begad! I'm sure he'd rather pass a month in Verdun than a week in my company."

"By the bye, Doctor, you never told me how this same antipathy of Sparks for you had its origin."

"Sure I drove him out of the 10th, before he was three weeks with the regiment."

"Ay, I remember; you began the story for me one night on the retreat from the Coa, but something happened to break it off in the middle."

"Just so; I was sent for to the rear to take off some gentlemen's legs that weren't in dancing condition; but as there's no fear of interruption now, I'll finish the story. But first let us have a peep at the wounded. What beautiful anatomists they are in the French artillery! Do you feel the thing I have now in my forceps?—there, don't jump—that's a bit of the brachial nerve, most beautifully displayed; faith, I think I'll give Mike a demonstration."

"Oh! Mister Quill, dear! Oh! Doctor darling!——"

"Arrah! Mickey, now can't you be aisy?" sang out Maurice, with a perfect imitation of Mike's voice and manner.

"A little lint here—bend your arm—that's it—don't move your fingers. Now, Mickey, make me a cup of coffee with a glass of brandy in it. And now, Charley, for Sparks. I believe I told you what kind of fellows the 10th were—regular out-and-outers; we hadn't three men in the regiment that were not from the south of Ireland—the *bocca Corkana* on their lips, fun and devilment in their eyes, and more drollery and humbug in their hearts than in all the messes in the service put together. No man had any chance among them if he wasn't a real droll one; every man wrote his own songs, and sang them too; it was no small promotion could tempt a fellow to exchange out of the corps. You may think, then, what a prize your friend Sparks proved to us; we held a court-martial upon him the week after he joined; it was proved in evidence that he had never said a good thing in his life, and had about as much notion of a joke as a Cherokee has of the Court of Chancery; and as to singing, Lord bless you! he had a tune with wooden turns to it, it was most cruel to hear; and then the look of him—those eyes, like dropsical oysters, and the hair standing every way, like a field of insane flax, and the mouth, with a curl in it like the slit in the side of a fiddle. A pleasant fellow that for a mess that always boasted the best-looking chaps in the service.

"'What's to be done with him?' said the Major; 'shall we tell him we are ordered to India, and terrify him about his liver?'

"'Or drill him into a hectic fever?'

"'Or drink him dry?'

"'Or get him into a fight, and wing him?'

"'Oh, no,' said I, 'leave him to me; we'll laugh him out of the corps.'

"'Yes, we'll leave him to you, Maurice,' said the rest.

"And that day week you might read in the *Gazette*, 'Pierce Flynn O'Haygerty, to be Ensign, 10th Foot, *vice* Sparks, exchanged.'"

"But how was it done, Maurice? You haven't told me that."

"Nothing easier. I affected great intimacy with Sparks; bemoaned our hard fate, mutually, in being attached to such a regiment. 'A d— corps this—low, vulgar fellows—practical jokes—not the kind of thing one expects in the army. But as for me, I've joined it partly from necessity. You, however, who might be in a crack regiment, I can't conceive your remaining in it.'

"'But why did you join, Doctor?' said he; 'what necessity could have induced you?'

"'Ah! my friend,' said I, 'that is the secret—that is the hidden grief that must lie buried in my own bosom.'

"I saw that his curiosity was excited, and took every means to increase it further. At length, as if yielding to a sudden impulse of friendship, and having sworn him to secrecy, I took him aside, and began thus:

"'I may trust you, Sparks,—I feel I may; and when I tell you that my honor, my reputation, my whole fortune is at stake, you will judge of the importance of the trust.'

"The goggle eyes rolled fearfully, and his features exhibited the most craving anxiety to hear my story.

"'You wish to know why I left the 56th. Now, I'll tell you; but mind, you're pledged, you're sworn, never to divulge it.'

"'Honor bright.'

"'There, that's enough; I'm satisfied. It was a slight infraction of the articles of war; a little breach of the rules and regulations of the service; a trifling misconception of the mess-code: they caught me one evening leaving the mess with—what do you think in my pocket? But you'll never tell! no, no, I know you'll not—eight forks and a gravy-spoon; silver forks every one of them. There now,' said I, grasping his hand, 'you have my secret; my fame and character are in your hands; for, you see, they made me quit the regiment—a man can't stay in a corps where he is laughed at.'

"Covering my face with my handkerchief, as if to conceal my shame, I turned away, and left Sparks to his meditations. That same evening we happened to have some strangers at mess; the bottle was passing freely round, and as usual, the good spirits of the party at the top of their bent, when suddenly, from the lower end of the table, a voice was heard demanding, in tones of the most pompous importance, permission to address the president upon a topic where the honor of the whole regiment was concerned.

"'I rise, gentlemen,' said Mr. Sparks, 'with feelings the most painful. Whatever may have been the laxity of habit and freedom of conversation habitual in this regiment, I never believed that so flagrant an instance as this morning came to my ears——'

"'Oh, murder!' said I. 'Oh, Sparks, darling! sure you're not going to tell?'

"'Doctor Quill,' replied he, in an austere tone, 'it is impossible for me to conceal it.'

"'Oh, Sparks, dear! will you betray me?'

"I gave him here a look of the most imploring entreaty, to which he replied by one of unflinching sternness.

"'I have made up my mind, sir,' continued he; 'it is possible the officers of this corps may look more leniently than I do upon this transaction; but know it they shall.'

"'Out with it, Sparks—tell it by all means!' cried a number of voices; for it was clear to every one by this time that he was involved in a hoax.

"Amid, therefore, a confused volley of entreaty on the one side, and my reiterated prayers for his silence on the other, Sparks thus began:

"'Are you aware, gentlemen, why Dr. Quill left the 56th?'

"'No, no, no!' rang from all sides; 'let's have it.'

"'No, sir!' said he, turning towards me, 'concealment is impossible; an officer detected with the mess-plate in his pocket——'

"They never let him finish, for a roar of laughter shook the table from one end to the other; while Sparks, horror-struck at the lack of feeling and propriety that could make men treat such a matter with ridicule, glared around him on every side.

"'Oh! Maurice, Maurice,' cried the Major, wiping his eyes, 'this is too bad—this is too bad!'

"'Gracious Heaven!' screamed Sparks, 'can you laugh at it?'

"'Laugh at it?' re-echoed the Paymaster, 'God grant I only don't burst a blood-vessel!' And once more the sounds of merriment rang out anew, and lasted for several minutes.

"'Oh! Maurice Quill,' cried an old captain, 'you've been too heavy on the lad. Why, Sparks, man, he's been humbugging you.'

"Scarcely were the words spoken when he sprang from the room; the whole truth flashed at once upon his mind; in an instant he saw that he had exposed himself to the merciless ridicule of a mess-table, and that all peace for him, in that regiment at least, was over.

"We got a glorious fellow in exchange for him; and Sparks descended into a cavalry regiment—I ask your pardon, Charley—where, as you are well aware, sharp wit and quick intellect are by no means indispensable. There, now, don't be angry, or you'll do yourself harm. So good-bye, for an hour or two."

CHAPTER XXXV.

THE COUNT'S LETTER.

O'SHAUGHNESSY'S wound, like my own, was happily only formidable from the loss of blood. The sabre or the lance is rarely, indeed, so death-dealing as the musket or the bayonet; and the murderous fire from a square of infantry is far more terrific in its consequences than the heaviest charge of a cavalry column. In a few weeks, therefore, we were once more about, and fit for duty; but, for the present, the campaign was ended. The rainy season, with attendant train of sickness and sorrow, set in; the troops were cantoned along the line of the frontier, the infantry occupying the villages, and the cavalry being stationed wherever forage could be obtained.

The 14th were posted at Avintas, but I saw little of them. I was continually employed upon the staff; and as General Craufurd's activity suffered no diminution from the interruption of the campaign, I rarely passed a day without eight or nine hours on horseback.

The preparations for the siege of Ciudad Rodrigo occupied our undivided attention. To the reduction of this fortress and of Badajos Lord Wellington looked as the most important objects, and prosecuted his plans with unremitting zeal. To my staff appointment I owed the opportunity of witnessing that stupendous feature of war—a siege; and as many of my friends formed part of the blockading force, I spent more than one night in the trenches. Indeed, except for this, the tiresome monotony of life was most irksome at this period. Day after day the incessant rain poured down; the supplies were bad, scanty, and irregular; the hospitals crowded with sick; field-sports impracticable; books there were none; and a dullness and spiritless depression prevailed on every side. Those who were actively engaged around Ciudad Rodrigo had, of course, the excitement and interest which the enterprise involved; but even there the works made slow progress; the breaching artillery was defective in every way; the rain undermined the faces of the bastions; the clayey soil sank beneath the weight of the heavy guns; and the storms of one night frequently destroyed more than a whole week's labor had effected.

Thus passed the dreary months along; the cheeriest and gayest amongst us were broken in spirits and subdued in heart by the tedium of our life. The very news which reached us partook of the gloomy features of our prospects; we heard only of strong reinforcements marching to the support of the French in Estramadura; we were told that the Emperor, whose successes in Germany enabled him to turn his active attention to the Spanish campaign, would himself be present in the coming spring, with overwhelming odds, and a firm determination to drive us from the Peninsula.

In that frame of mind which such gloomy and depressing prospects are well calculated to suggest, I was returning one night to my quarters at Mucia, when suddenly I beheld Mike galloping towards me with a large packet in his hand, which he held aloft to catch my attention. "Letters from England, sir," said he, "just arrived with the General's despatches." I broke the envelope at once, which bore the War-office seal, and as I did so, a perfect avalanche of letters fell at my feet. The first which caught my eye was an official intimation from the Horse Guards, that the Prince Regent had been graciously pleased to confirm my promotion to the troop, my commission to bear date from the appointment, &c., &c. I could not help feeling struck, as my eye ran rapidly across the lines, that although the letter came from Sir George Dashwood's office, it contained not a word of congratulation nor remembrance on his part, but was couched in the usual cold and formal language of an official document. Impatient, however, to look over my other letters, I thought but little of this; so, throwing them hurriedly into my sabretasche, I cantered on to my quarters without delay. Once more alone in silence, I sat down to commune with my far-off friends, and yet, with all my anxiety to hear of home, passed several minutes in turning over the letters, guessing from whom they might have come, and picturing to myself their probable contents. "Ah! Frank Webber, I recognize your slap-dash, bold hand without the aid of the initials in the corner; and this—what can this be?—this queer, misshapen thing, representing nothing but the forty-seventh proposition of Euclid, and the address seemingly put on with a cat's tail dipped in lampblack? Yes! true enough, it is from Mr. Free himself. And what have we here? This queer, quaint hand is no new acquaintance; how many a time have I looked upon it as the *ne plus ultra* of caligraphy! But here is one I'm not so sure of: who could have written this bolt-upright, old-fashioned superscription, not a letter of which seems on speaking terms with its neighbor?— the very O absolutely turns its back upon the M in O'Malley, and the final Y wags his tail with a kind of independent shake, as if he did not care a curse for his predecessors! And the seal, too—surely I know that griffin's head, and that stern motto, '*Non rogo sed capio.*' To be sure, it is Billy Considine's, the Count himself. The very paper, yellow and time-stained, looks coeval with his youth, and I could even venture to wager that his sturdy pen was nibbed half a century since. I'll not look further among the confused mass of three-cornered billets, and long, treacherous-looking epistles, the very folding of which denote the dun. Here goes for the Count!" So saying to myself, I drew closer to the fire, and began the following epistle:

"O'Malley Castle, Nov. 3.

"DEAR CHARLEY:—Here we sit in the little parlor, with your last letter, the *Times,* and a big map before us, drinking your health and wishing you a long career of the same glorious success you have hitherto enjoyed. Old as I am—eighty-two or eighty-three (I forget which) in June—I envy you with all my heart. Luck has stood to you, my boy; and if a French sabre or a bayonet finish you now, you've at least had a splendid burst of it. I was right in my own opinion of you, and Godfrey himself owns it now,—a lawyer, indeed! Bad luck to them! we've had enough of lawyers. There's old Hennesy—honest Jack, as they used to call him—that your uncle trusted for the last forty years, has raised eighteen thousand pounds on the title deeds, and gone off to America. The old scoundrel! But it's no use talking: the blow is a sore one to Godfrey, and the gout more troublesome than ever. Drumgold is making a motion in Chancery about it to break the sale, and the tenants are in open rebellion, and swear they'll murder a receiver, if one is sent down among them. Indeed, they came in such force into Galway during the assizes, and did so much mischief, that the cases for trial were adjourned, and the judges left, with a military escort to protect them. This, of course, is gratifying to our feelings; for, thank Providence, there is some good in the world yet. Kilmurry was sold last week for twelve thousand. Andy Blake would foreclose the mortgage, although we offered him every kind of satisfaction. This has done Godfrey a deal of harm; and some pitiful economy—taking only two bottles of claret after his dinner—has driven the gout to his head. They've been telling him he'd lengthen his days by this, and I tried it myself, and, faith, it was the longest day I ever spent in my life. I hope and trust you take your liquor like a gentleman—and an Irish gentleman.

"Kinshela, we hear, has issued an execution against the house and furniture; but the attempts to sell the demesne nearly killed your uncle. It was advertised in a London paper, and an offer made for it by an old general, whom you may remember when down here. Indeed, if I mistake not, he was rather kind to you in the beginning. It would appear he did not wish to have his name known, but we found him out, and such a letter as we sent him! It's little liking he'll have to buy a Galway gentleman's estate over his head, that same Sir George Dashwood! Godfrey offered to meet him anywhere he pleased, and if the doctor thought he could bear the sea-voyage, he'd even go over to Holyhead; but the sneaking fellow sent an apologetic kind of a letter, with some humbug excuse about very different motives, &c. But we've done with him, and I think he with us."

When I had read thus far, I laid down the letter, unable to go on; the accumulated misfortunes of one I loved best in the world, following so fast one upon another, the insult, unprovoked, gratuitous insult, to him upon whom my hopes of future happiness so much depended, completely overwhelmed me. I tried to continue. Alas! the catalogue of evils went on; each line bore testimony to some further wreck of fortune—some clearer evidence of a ruined house.

All that my gloomiest and darkest forebodings had pictured was come to pass; sickness, poverty, harassing, unfeeling creditors, treachery, and ingratitude, were goading to madness and despair a spirit whose kindliness of nature was unequalled. The shock of blasted fortunes was falling upon the dying heart; the convictions which a long life had never brought home, that men were false, and their words a lie, were stealing over the man, upon the brink of the grave; and he who had loved his neighbor like a brother was to be taught, at the eleventh hour, that the beings he trusted were perjured and forsworn.

A more unsuitable adviser than Considine, in difficulties like these, there could not be; his very contempt for all the forms of law and justice was sufficient to embroil my poor uncle still further, so that I resolved at once to apply for leave, and if refused, and no other alternative offered, to leave the service. It was not without a sense of sorrow bordering on despair that I came to this determination. My soldier's life had become a passion with me; I loved it for its bold and chivalrous enthusiasm; its hour of battle and strife; its days of endurance and hardship; its trials, its triumphs,—its very reverses were endeared by those they were shared with,—and the spirit of adventure, and the love of danger—that most exciting of all gambling—had now entwined themselves in my very nature. To surrender all these at once, and to exchange the daily, hourly enthusiasm of a campaign for the prospects now before me, was almost maddening. But still, a sustaining sense of duty, of what I owed to him who, in his love, had sacrificed all for me, overpowered every other consideration. My mind was made up.

Father Rush's letter was little more than a recapitulation of the Count's. Debts, distress, sickness, and the heart-burnings of altered fortunes, filled it, and when I closed it, I felt like one over all whose views in life a dark and ill-omened cloud was closing forever. Webber's I could not read: the light and cheerful raillery of a friend would have seemed, at such a time, like the cold, unfeeling sarcasm of an enemy. I sat down, at last, to write to the General, enclosing my application for leave, and begging of him to forward it, with a favorable recommendation, to head-quarters.

This done, I lay down upon my bed, and overcome by fatigue and fretting, fell asleep, to dream of my home and those I had left there, which, strangely, too, were presented to my mind with all the happy features that made them so dear to my infancy.

CHAPTER XXXVI.

THE TRENCHES.

I HAVE not had time, O'Malley, to think of your application," said Craufurd, "nor is it likely I can for a day or two. Read that." So saying, he pushed towards me a note, written in pencil, which ran thus:

"Ciudad Rodrigo, Dec. 18.

"DEAR C.:—Fletcher tells me that the breaches will be practicable by to-morrow evening, and I think so myself. Come over, then, at once, for we shall not lose any time.

"Yours, W."

"I have some despatches for your regiment, but if you prefer coming along with me——"

"My dear General, dare I ask for such a favor?"

"Well, come along; only remember that, although my division will be engaged, I cannot promise you anything to do; so now, get your horses ready; let's away."

It was in the afternoon of the following day that we rode into the large plain before Ciudad Rodrigo, and in which the allied armies were now assembled to the number of twelve thousand men. The loud booming of the siege artillery had been heard by me for some hours before; but notwithstanding this prelude and my own high-wrought expectations, I was far from anticipating the magnificent spectacle which burst upon my astonished view. The air was calm and still; a clear blue wintry sky stretched overhead. Below, the dense blue smoke of the deafening guns rolled in mighty volumes along the earth, and entirely concealed the lower part of the fortress; above this the tall towers and battlemented parapets rose into the thin transparent sky like fairy palaces. A bright flash of flame would now and then burst forth from the walls, and a clang-

38

ing crash of the brass metal be heard; but the unceasing roll of our artillery nearly drowned all other sounds, save when a loud cheer would burst from the trenches, while the clattering fall of masonry and the crumbling stones as they rolled down, bespoke the reason of the cry. The utmost activity prevailed on all sides; troops pressed forward to the reliefs in the parallels; ammunition wagons moved to the front; general and staff officers rode furiously about the plain, and all betokened that the hour of attack was no longer far distant.

While all parties were anxiously awaiting the decision of our chief, the general order was made known, which, after briefly detailing the necessary arrangements, concluded with the emphatic words, "Ciudad Rodrigo *must* be stormed to-night." All speculation as to the troops to be engaged in this daring enterprise was soon at an end. With his characteristic sense of duty, Lord Wellington made no invidious selection, but merely commanded that the attack should be made by whatever divisions might chance to be that day in the trenches. Upon the third and light divisions, therefore, this glorious task devolved. The former was to attack the main breach; to Craufurd's division was assigned the (if possible) more difficult enterprise of carrying the lesser one; while Pack's Portuguese brigade were to menace the convent of La Caridad by a feint attack, to be converted into a real one, if circumstances should permit.

The decision, however matured and comprehensive in all its details, was finally adopted so suddenly that every staff officer upon the ground was actively engaged during the entire evening in conveying the orders to the different regiments. As the day drew to a close, the cannonade slackened on either side; a solitary gun would be heard at intervals, and, in the calm stillness around, its booming thunder re-echoed along the valleys of the Sierra; but as the moon rose and night set in, these were no longer heard, and a perfect stillness and tranquillity prevailed around. Even in the trenches, crowded with armed and anxious soldiers, not a whisper was heard, and amid that mighty host which filled the plain, the tramp of a patrol could be distinctly noted, and the hoarse voice of a French sentry upon the walls, telling that all was well in Ciudad Rodrigo.

The massive fortress, looming larger as its dark shadow stood out from the sky, was still as the grave, while in the greater breach a faint light was seen to twinkle for a moment, and then suddenly to disappear, leaving all gloomy and dark as before.

Having been sent with orders to the third division, of which the 88th formed a part, I took the opportunity of finding out O'Shaughnessy, who was himself to lead an escalade party in

M'Kinnon's brigade. He sprang towards me as I came forward, and, grasping my hand with a more than usual earnestness, called out, "The very man I wanted! Charley, my boy, do us a service now!"

Before I could reply, he continued, in a lower tone, "A young fellow of ours, Harry Beauclerc, has been badly wounded in the trenches, but by some blunder his injury is reported a slight one, and although the poor fellow can scarcely stand, he insists upon going with the stormers."

"Come here, Major! come here!" cried a voice at a little distance.

"Follow me, O'Malley," cried O'Shaughnessy, moving in the direction of the speaker.

By the light of a lantern we could descry two officers leaning upon the ground; between them on the grass lay the figure of a third, upon whose features, as the pale light fell, the hand of death seemed rapidly stealing. A slight froth, tinged with blood, rested on his lip, and the florid blood, which stained the buff facing of his uniform, indicated that his wound was through the lungs.

"He has fainted," said one of the officers, in a low tone.

"Are you certain it is fainting?" said the other, in a still lower.

"You see how it is, Charley," said O'Shaughnessy; "this poor boy must be carried to the rear. Will you, then, like a kind fellow, hasten back to Colonel Campbell and mention the fact? It will kill Beauclerc should any doubt rest upon his conduct, if he ever recover this."

While he spoke, four soldiers of the regiment placed the wounded officer in a blanket. A long sigh escaped him, and he muttered a few broken words.

"Poor fellow! it's his mother he's talking of. He only joined a month since, and is a mere boy. Come, O'Malley, lose no time. By Jove! it is too late; there goes the first rocket for the columns to form. In ten minutes more the stormers must fall in."

"What's the matter, Giles?" said he to one of the officers who had stopped the soldiers as they were moving off with their burden; "what is it?"

"I have been cutting the white tape off his arm, for if he sees it on waking, he'll remember all about the storming."

"Quite right—thoughtfully done!" said the other; "but who is to lead his fellows? He was in the forlorn hope."

"I'll do it," cried I, with eagerness. "Come, O'Shaughnessy, you'll not refuse me."

"Refuse you, boy!" said he, grasping my hand within both of his, "never! But you must change your coat. The gallant 88th will never mistake their countryman's voice. But your uniform would be devilish likely to get you a bayonet through it; so come back with me, and we'll make you a Ranger in no time."

"I can give your friend a cap."

"And I," said the other, "a brandy flask, which, after all, is not the worst part of a storming equipage."

"I hope," said O'Shaughnessy, "they may find Maurice in the rear. Beauclerc's all safe in his hands."

"That they'll not," said Giles, "you may swear. Quill is at this moment in the trenches, and will not be the last man at the breach."

"Follow me now, lads," said O'Shaughnessy, in a low voice. "Our fellows are at the angle of this trench. Who the deuce can that be talking so loud?"

"It must be Maurice," said Giles.

The question was soon decided by the Doctor himself, who appeared giving directions to his hospital-sergeant.

"Yes, Peter, take the tools up to a convenient spot near the breach. There's many a snug corner there in the ruins; and although we mayn't have as good an operation-room as in old 'Stevens's,' yet we'll beat them hollow in cases."

"Listen to the fellow," said Giles, with a shudder. "The thought of his confounded thumbscrews and tourniquets is worse to me than a French howitzer."

"The devil a kinder-hearted fellow than Maurice," said O'Shaughnessy, "for all that; and if his heart was to be known this moment, he'd rather handle a sword than a saw."

"True for you, Dennis," said Quill, overhearing him; "but we are both useful in our way, as the hangman said to Lord Clare."

"But should you not be in the rear, Maurice?" said I.

"You are right, O'Malley," said he, in a whisper; "but, you see, I owe the Cork Insurance Company a spite for making me pay a gout premium, and that's the reason I'm here. I warned them at the time that their stinginess would come to no good."

"I say, Captain O'Malley," said Giles, "I find I can't be as good as my word with you; my servant has moved to the rear with all my traps."

"What is to be done?" said I.

"Is it shaving utensils you want?" said Maurice. "Would a scalpel serve your turn?"

"No, Doctor; I'm going to take a turn of duty with your fellows to-night."

"In the breach—with the stormers?"

"With the forlorn hope," said O'Shaughnessy. "Beauclerc is so badly wounded, that we've sent him back ; and Charley, like a good fellow, has taken his place."

"Martin told me," said Maurice, "that Beauclerc was only stunned; but, upon my conscience, the hospital mates nowadays are no better than the watchmakers ; they can't tell what's wrong with the instrument till they pick it to pieces. Whiz! there goes a blue light."

"Move on, move on," whispered O'Shaughnessy ; "they're telling off the stormers. That rocket is the order to fall in."

"But what am I to do for a coat?"

"Take mine, my boy," said Maurice, throwing off an upper garment of coarse gray frieze as he spoke.

"There's a neat bit of uniform," continued he, turning himself round for our admiration; "don't I look mighty like the pictures of George the First at the battle of Dettingen?"

A burst of approving laughter was our only answer to this speech, while Maurice proceeded to denude himself of his most extraordinary garment.

"What, in the name of Heaven, is it?" said I.

"Don't despise it, Charley; it knows the smell of gunpowder as well as any bit of scarlet in the service ;" while he added, in a whisper, "it's the ould Roscommon Yeomanry. My uncle commanded them in the year '42, and this was his coat. I don't mean to say that it was new then; for you see it's a kind of heirloom in the Quill family ; and it's not every one I'd be giving it to."

"A thousand thanks, Maurice," said I, as I buttoned it on, amid an ill-suppressed titter of laughter.

"It fits you like a sentry-box," said Maurice, as he surveyed me with a lantern. "The skirts separate behind in the most picturesque manner; and when you button the collar, it will keep your head up so high, that the devil a bit you'll see except the blessed moon. It's a thousand pities you haven't the three-cocked hat, with the feather trimming. If you wouldn't frighten the French, my name's not Maurice. Turn about here till I admire you. If you only saw yourself in a glass, you'd never join the dragoons again. And look now, don't be exposing yourself, for I wouldn't have those blue facings destroyed for a week's pay."

"Ah then, it's yourself is the darling, Doctor dear!" said a voice behind me. I turned round : it was Mickey Free, who was standing with a most profound admiration of Maurice beaming in every feature of his face. "It's yourself has a joke for every hour o' the day."

"Get to the rear, Mike—get to the rear with the cattle ; this is no place for you or them."

"Good-night, Mickey," said Maurice.

"Good-night, your honor," muttered Mike to himself; "may I never die till you set a leg for me."

"Are you dressed for the ball?" said Maurice, fastening the white tape upon my arm. "There now, my boy, move on, for I think I hear Picton's voice; not that it signifies now, for he's always in a heavenly temper when any one's going to be killed. I'm sure he'd behave like an angel if he only knew the ground was mined under his feet."

"Charley—Charley!" called out O'Shaughnessy, in a suppressed voice, "come up quickly."

"No. 24, John Forbes—here! Edward Gillespie—here!"

"Who leads this party, Major O'Shaughnessy?"

"Mr. Beauclerc, sir," replied O'Shaughnessy, pushing me forward by the arm while he spoke.

"Keep your people together, sir; spare the powder, and trust to your cold iron." He grasped my hand within his iron grip, and rode on.

"Who was it, Dennis?" said I.

"Don't you know him, Charley? That was Picton."

CHAPTER XXXVII.

THE STORMING OF CIUDAD RODRIGO.

WHATEVER the levity of the previous moment, the scene before us now repressed it effectually. The deep-toned bell of the cathedral tolled seven, and scarcely were its notes dying away in the distance, when the march of the columns was heard stealing along the ground. A low murmuring whisper ran along the advanced files of the forlorn hope; stocks were loosened, packs and knapsacks thrown to the ground; each man pressed his cap more firmly down upon his brow, and, with lip compressed and steadfast eye, waited for the word to move.

It came at last. The word "March!" passed in whispers from rank to rank, and the dark mass moved on. What a moment was that as we advanced to the foot of the breach! The consciousness that, at the same instant, from different points of that vast plain similar parties were moving on; the feeling that at a word the flame of the artillery and the flash of steel would spring from that dense cloud, and death and carnage, in every shape our imagination can conceive, be dealt on all sides; the hurried, fitful thought of home; the years long past, compressed into one minute's space; the last adieu of all we've loved, mingling with the muttered prayer to Heaven, with, high above all, the deep pervading sense that earth has no temptation strong enough to turn us from that path whose ending must be a sepulchre!

Each heart was too full for words. We followed noiselessly along the turf, the dark figure of our leader guiding us through the gloom. On arriving at the ditch, the party with the ladders moved to the front. Already some hay-packs were thrown in, and the forlorn hope sprang forward.

All was still and silent as the grave. " Quietly, my men—quietly!" said M'Kinnon; "don't press." Scarcely had he spoken when a musket, whose charge, contrary to orders, had not been drawn, went off. The whizzing bullet could not have struck the wall, when suddenly a bright flame burst forth from the ramparts, and shot upward towards the sky. For an instant the whole scene before us was as bright as noonday. On one side the dark ranks and glistening bayonets of the enemy; on the other, the red uniform of the British columns. Compressed like some solid wall, they stretched along the plain.

A deafening roll of musketry from the extreme right announced that the third division was already in action, while the loud cry of our leader, as he sprang into the trench, summoned us to the charge. The leading sections, not waiting for the ladders, jumped down, others pressing rapidly behind them, when a loud rumbling thunder crept along the earth, a hissing, crackling noise followed, and from the dark ditch a forked and livid lightning burst like the flame from a volcano, and a mine exploded. Hundreds of shells and grenades scattered along the ground were ignited at the same moment; the air sparkled with the whizzing fuses, the musketry plied incessantly from the walls, and every man of the leading company of the stormers was blown to pieces. While this dreadful catastrophe was enacting before our eyes, the different assaults were made on all sides; the whole fortress seemed girt around with fire. From every part arose the yells of triumph and the shouts of the assailants. As for us, we stood upon the verge of the ditch, breathless, hesitating, and horror-struck. A sudden darkness succeeded to the bright glare, but from the midst of the gloom the agonizing cries of the wounded and the dying rent our very hearts.

"Make way there! make way! here comes Mackie's party," cried an officer in the front, and as he spoke the forlorn hope of the 88th came forward at a run. Jumping recklessly into the ditch, they made towards the breach; the supporting division of stormers gave one inspiring cheer, and sprang after them. The rush was tremendous; for scarcely had we reached the crumbling ruins of the rampart, when the vast column, pressing on like some mighty torrent, bore down upon our rear. Now commenced a scene to which nothing I ever before conceived of war could in any degree compare. The whole ground, covered with combustibles of every deadly and destructive contrivance, was rent open with a crash; the huge masses of masonry bounded into the air like things of no weight; the ringing clangor of the iron howitzers, the crackling of the fuses, the blazing splinters, the shouts of defiance, the more than savage yells of those in whose ranks alone the dead and the dying were numbered, made up a mass of sights and sounds almost maddening with their excitement. On we struggled, the mutilated bodies of the leading files almost filling the way.

By this time the third division had joined us, and the crush of our thickening ranks was dreadful. Every moment some well-known leader fell dead or mortally wounded, and his place was supplied by some gallant fellow, who, springing from the leading files, would scarcely have uttered his cheer of encouragement ere he himself was laid low. Many a voice with whose notes I was familiar would break upon my ear in tones of heroic daring, and the next moment burst forth in a death-cry. For above an hour the frightful carnage continued, fresh troops continually advancing, but scarcely a foot of ground was made; the earth belched forth its volcanic fires, and that terrible barrier did no man pass. In turn the bravest and the boldest would leap into the whizzing flame, and the taunting cheers of the enemy triumphed in derision at the effort.

"Stormers, to the front! Only the bayonet! trust to nothing but the bayonet!" cried a voice whose almost cheerful accents contrasted strangely with the death-notes around, and Gurwood, who led the forlorn hope of the 52d, bounded into the chasm. All the officers sprang simultaneously after him; the men pressed madly on; a roll of withering musketry crashed upon them; a furious shout replied to it. The British, springing over the dead and dying, bounded like blood-hounds on their prey. Meanwhile, the ramparts trembled beneath the tramp of the light division, who, having forced the lesser breach, came down upon the flank of the French. The garrison, however, thickened their numbers, and bravely held their ground. Man to man now was the combat. No cry for quarter. No supplicating look for mercy; it was the death-struggle of vengeance and despair. At this instant, an explosion louder than the loudest thunder shook the air; the rent and torn-up ramparts sprang into the sky; the conquering and the conquered were alike the victims: for one of the greatest magazines had been ignited by a shell. The black smoke, streaked with a lurid flame, hung above the dead and the dying. The artillery and the murderous musketry were stilled, paralyzed, as it were, by the ruin and devastation before them. Both sides stood leaning upon their arms; the pause was but momentary; the cries of wounded comrades called upon their hearts. A fierce burst of vengeance rent the air. The British closed upon the foe. For an instant they were met; the next, the bayonets gleamed upon the ramparts, and Ciudad Rodrigo was won.

CHAPTER XXXVIII.

THE RAMPART.

WHILE such were the scenes passing around me, of my own part in them I absolutely knew nothing; for until the moment that the glancing bayonets of the light division came rushing on the foe, and the loud, long cheer of victory burst above us, I felt like one in a trance. Then I leaned against an angle of the rampart, overpowered and exhausted; a bayonet wound, which some soldier of our own ranks had given me when mounting the breach, pained me somewhat; my uniform was actually torn to rags; my head bare. Of my sword, the hilt and four inches of the blade alone remained, while my left hand firmly grasped the rammer of a cannon, but why or wherefore L could not even guess. As thus I stood, the unceasing tide of soldiery pressed on; fresh divisions came pouring in, eager for plunder, and thirsting for the spoil. The dead and the dying were alike trampled beneath the feet of that remorseless mass, who, actuated by vengeance and by rapine, sprang fiercely up the breach.

Weak and exhausted, faint from my wound, and overcome by my exertions, I sank among the crumbling ruins. The loud shouts which rose from the town, mingled with cries and screams, told the work of pillage was begun; while still a dropping musketry could be heard on the distant rampart, where even yet the French made resistance. At last even this was hushed; but to it succeeded the far more horrifying sounds of rapine and of murder. The forked flames of burning houses rose here and there amid the black darkness of the night; and through the crackling of the timbers, and the falling crash of roofs, the heart-rending shriek of women rent the very air. Officers pressed forward, but in vain were their efforts to restrain their men; the savage cruelty of the moment knew no bounds of restraint. More than one gallant fellow perished in his fruitless endeavor to enforce obedience; and the most awful denunciations were now uttered against those before whom at any other time they dared not mutter.

Thus passed the long night, far more terrible to me than all the dangers of the storm itself, with all its death and destruction dealing around it. I knew not if I slept; if so, the horrors on every side were pictured in my dreams; and when the gray dawn was breaking, the cries from the doomed city were still ringing in my ears. Close around me the scene was still and silent; the wounded had been removed during the night, but the thickly-packed dead lay side by side where they fell. It was a fearful sight to see them, as, blood-stained and naked (for already the camp-followers had stripped the bodies), they covered the entire breach. From the rampart to the ditch, the ranks lay where they had stood in life. A faint phosphoric flame flickered above their ghastly corpses, making even death still more horrible. I was gazing steadfastly, with all that stupid intensity which imperfect senses and exhausted faculties possess, when the sound of voices near aroused me.

"Bring him along—this way, Bob. Over the breach with the scoundrel, into the fosse."

"He shall die no soldier's death, by Heaven!" cried another and a deeper voice, "if I lay his skull open with my axe."

"Oh, mercy, mercy! as you hope for——"

"Traitor! don't dare to mutter here!" As the last words were spoken, four infantry soldiers, reeling from drunkenness, dragged forward a pale and haggard wretch, whose limbs trailed behind him like those of palsy; his uniform was that of a French chasseur, but his voice bespoke him English.

"Kneel down there, and die like a man! You were one once!"

"Not so, Bill; never. Fix bayonets, boys! That's right! Now take the word from me."

"Oh, forgive me! for the love of Heaven, forgive me!" screamed the voice of the victim; but his last accents ended in a death-cry, for, as he spoke, the bayonets flashed for an instant in the air, and the next were plunged into his body. Twice I had essayed to speak, but my voice, hoarse from shouting, came not, and I could but look upon this terrible murder with staring eyes and burning brain. At last speech came, as if wrested by the very excess of my agony, and I muttered aloud, "O God!" The words were not well spoken, when the muskets were brought to the shoulders, and, reeking with the blood of the murdered man, their savage faces scowled at me as I lay.

A short and heartfelt prayer burst from my lips, and I was still. The leader of the party called out, "Be steady! and together. One, two! Ground arms, boys! Ground arms!" roared he, in a voice like thunder; "it's the Captain himself!" Down went the muskets with a crash; while, springing towards me, the fellows caught me in their arms, and with one jerk mounted me upon their shoulders, the cheer that accompanied the sudden movement seeming like the yell of maniacs. "Ha, ha, ha! we have him now!" sang their wild voices, as, with blood-stained hands and infuriated features, they bore me down the rampart. My sensations of disgust and repugnance to the party seemed at once to have evidenced themselves, for the corporal, turning abruptly round, called out,

"Don't pity *him*, Captain; the scoundrel was a deserter; he escaped from the picket two nights ago, and gave information of all our plans to the enemy."

"Ay," cried another, "and, what's worse, he fired through an embrasure near the breach, for two hours, upon his own regiment. It was there we found him. This way, lads."

So saying, they turned short from the walls, and dashed down a dark and narrow lane into the town. My struggles to get free were perfectly ineffectual, and to my entreaties they were totally indifferent.

In this way, therefore, we made our entrance into the Plaza, where some hundred soldiers, of different regiments, were bivouacked. A shout of recognition welcomed the fellows as they came; while, suddenly, a party of 88th men, springing from the ground, rushed forward with drawn bayonets, calling out, "Give him up this minute, or, by the Father of Moses, we'll make short work of ye!"

The order was made by men who seemed well disposed to execute it; and I was accordingly grounded with a shock and a rapidity that savored much more of ready compliance than any respect for my individual comfort. A roar of laughter rang through the motley mass, and every powder-stained face around me seemed convulsed with merriment. As I sat passively upon the ground, looking ruefully about, whether my gestures or my words heightened the absurdity of my appearance, it is hard to say; but certainly the laughter increased at each moment, and the drunken wretches danced round me in ecstasy.

"Where is your Major? Major O'Shaughnessy, lads?" said I.

"He's in the church, with the General, your honor," said the sergeant of the regiment, upon whom the mention of his officer's name seemed at once to have a sobering influence. Assisting me to rise (for I was weak as a child), he led me through the dense crowd, who, such is the influence of example, now formed into line, and, as well as their state permitted, gave me a military salute as I passed. "Follow me, sir," said the sergeant; "this little dark street to the left will take us to the private door of the chapel."

"Wherefore are they there, sergeant?"

"There's a general of division mortally wounded."

"You did not hear his name?"

"No, sir. All I know is, he was one of the storming party at the lesser breach."

A cold, sickening shudder came over me; I durst not ask further, but pressed on with anxious steps towards the chapel.

"There, sir, yonder, where you see the light. That's the door."

So saying, the sergeant stopped suddenly, and placed his hand to his cap. I saw at once that he was sufficiently aware of his condition not to desire to appear before his officers; so, hurriedly thanking him, I walked forward.

"Halt, there! and give the countersign," cried a sentinel, who with fixed bayonet stood before the door.

"I am an officer," said I, endeavoring to pass in.

"Stand back, stand back!" said the harsh voice of the Highlander, for such he was.

"Is Major O'Shaughnessy in the church?"

"I dinna ken," was the short, rough answer.

"Who is the officer so badly wounded?"

"I dinna ken," replied he, as gruffly as before; while he added, in a louder key, "Stand back, I tell ye, man! Dinna ye see the staff coming?"

I turned round hastily, and at the same instant several officers, who, apparently from precaution, had dismounted at the end of the street, were seen approaching. They came hurriedly forward, but without speaking. He who was in advance of the party wore a short blue cape, over an undress uniform. The rest were in full regimentals. I had scarcely time to throw a passing glance upon him, when the officer I have mentioned as coming first, called out in a stern voice,

"Who are you, sir?"

I started at the sounds; it was not the first time those accents had been heard by me.

"Captain O'Malley, 14th Light Dragoons."

"What brings you here, sir? Your regiment is at Caya."

"I have been employed as acting aide-de-camp to General Craufurd," said I, hesitatingly.

"Is that your staff uniform?" said he, as with compressed brow and stern look he fixed his eyes upon my coat. Before I had time to reply, or, indeed, before I well knew how to do so, a gruff voice from behind called out,

"D— me! if that ain't the fellow that led the stormers through a broken embrasure! I say, my lord, that's the yeoman I was telling you of. Is it not so, sir?" continued he, turning towards me.

" Yes, sir. I led a party of the 88th at the breach."

"And devilish well you did it, too!" added Picton, for it was he who recognized me. "I saw him, my lord, spring down from the parapet upon a French gunner, and break his sword as he cleft his helmet in two. Yes, yes; I shall not forget in a hurry how you laid about you with the rammer of the gun! By Jove! that's it he has in his hand!"

While Picton ran hurriedly on, Lord Wellington's calm but stern features never changed their expression. The looks of those around were bent upon me with interest and even admiration; but his evinced nothing of either.

Reverting at once to my absence from my post, he asked me,

" Did you obtain leave for a particular service, sir?"

" No, my lord. It was simply from an accidental circumstance that——"

"Then report yourself at your quarters as under arrest."

" But, my lord," said Picton——. Lord Wellington waited not for the explanation, but walked firmly forward, and strode into the church. The staff followed in silence, Picton turning one look of kindness on me as he went, as though to say, " I'll not forget you."

" The devil take it," cried I, as I found myself once more alone, " but I'm unlucky. What would turn out with other men the very basis of their fortune, is ever with me the source of ill luck."

It was evident, from Picton's account, that I had distinguished myself at the breach; and yet, nothing was more clear than that my conduct had displeased the Commander-in-Chief. Picturing him ever to my mind's eye as the *beau idéal* of a military leader, by some fatality of fortune I was continually incurring his displeasure, for whose praise I would have risked my life. "And this confounded costume—what, in the name of every absurdity, could have ever persuaded me to put it on? What signifies it though a man should cover himself with glory, if in the end he is to be laughed at? Well, well, it matters not much; now my soldiering's over! And yet I could have wished that the last act of my campaigning had brought with it pleasanter recollections."

As thus I ruminated, the click of the soldier's musket near aroused me. Picton was passing out. A shade of gloom and depression was visible upon his features, and his lip trembled as he muttered some sentences to himself.

"Ha! Captain—I forget the name. Yes—Captain O'Malley; you are released from arrest. General Craufurd has spoken very well of you, and Lord Wellington has heard the circumstances of your case."

"Is it General Craufurd, then, that is wounded, sir?" said I, eagerly.

Picton paused for a moment, while with an effort he controlled his features into their stern and impassive expression, then added hurriedly, and almost harshly :—

"Yes, sir; badly wounded, through the arm and in the lung. He mentioned you to the notice of the Commander-in-Chief, and your application for leave is granted. In fact, you are to have the distinguished honor of carrying back despatches. There, now; you had better join your brigade."

"Could I not see my General once more? It may be for the last time."

"No, sir!" sternly replied Picton. "Lord Wellington believes you under arrest. It is as well he should suppose you obeyed his orders."

There was a tone of sarcasm in these words that prevented my reply; and muttering my gratitude for his well-timed and kindly interference in my behalf, I bowed deeply, and turned away.

"I say, sir," said Picton, as he turned towards the church, "should anything befall—that is, if, unfortunately, circumstances should make you in want, and desirous of a staff appointment, remember that you are known to General Picton."

Downcast and depressed by the news of my poor General, I wended my way, with slow and uncertain steps, towards the rampart. A clear, cold, wintry sky, and a sharp, bracing air, made my wound, slight as it was, more painful, and I endeavored to reach the reserves, where I knew the hospital staff had established for the present their quarters. I had not gone far when, from a marauding party, I learned that my man Mike was in search of me through the plain. A report of my death had reached him, and the poor fellow was half distracted.

Longing anxiously to allay his fears on my account, which I well knew might lead him into any act of folly or insanity, I pressed forward; besides—shall I confess it?—amid the manifold thoughts of sorrow and affliction which weighed me down, I could not divest myself of the feeling that so long as I wore my present absurd costume, I could be nothing but an object of laughter and ridicule to all who met me.

I had not long to look for my worthy follower, for I soon beheld him cantering about the plain. A loud shout brought him beside me; and truly the poor fellow's delight was great and sincere. With a thousand protestations of his satisfaction, and reiterated assurances of what he would have done to the French prisoners if anything had happened me, we took our way together towards the camp.

CHAPTER XXXIX.

THE DESPATCH.

I WAS preparing to visit the town on the following morning, when my attention was attracted by a dialogue which took place beneath my window.

"I say, my good friend," cried a mounted orderly to Mike, who was busily employed in brushing a jacket,—"I say, are you Captain O'Malley's man?"

"The least taste in life o' that same," replied he, with a half-jocular expression.

"Well, then," said the other, "take up these letters to your master. Be alive, my fine fellow, for they are despatches, and I must have a written return for them."

"Won't ye get off, and take a drop of somethin' refreshin'? the air is cowld this mornin'."

"I can't stay, my good friend, but thank you all the same; so be alive, will you?"

"Arrah, there's no hurry in life. Sure it's an invitation to dinner to Lord Wellington, or a tea-party at Sir Denny's; sure, my master's bothered with them every day o' the week; that's the misfortune of being an agreeable creature; and I'd be led into dissipation myself if I wasn't rear'd prudent."

"Well, come along; take these letters, for I must be off; my time is short."

"That's more nor your nose is, honey," said Mike, evidently somewhat piqued at the little effect his advances had made upon the Englishman. "Give them here," continued he, while he turned the various papers in every direction, affecting to read their addresses.

"There's nothing for me here, I see. Did none of the generals ask after me?"

"You *are* a queer one!" said the dragoon, not a little puzzled what to make of him.

Mike meanwhile thrust the papers carelessly into his pocket, and strode into the house, whistling a quickstep as he went, with the air of a man perfectly devoid of care or occupation. The next moment, however, he appeared at my door, wiping his forehead with the back of his hand, and apparently breathless with haste.

"Despatches, Mister Charles—despatches from Lord Wellington. The orderly is waiting below for a return."

"Tell him he shall have it in one moment," replied I. "And now bring me a light."

Before I had broken the seal of the envelope, Mike was once more at the porch.

"My master is writing a few lines to say he'll do it. Don't be talking of it," added he, dropping his voice, "but they want him to take another fortress."

What turn the dialogue subsequently took, I cannot say, for I was entirely occupied by a letter which accompanied the despatches. It ran as follows:—

"DEAR SIR:—The Commander-in-Chief has been kind enough to accord you the leave of absence you applied for, and takes the opportunity of your return to England to send you the accompanying letters to his Royal Highness the Duke of York. To his approval of your conduct in the assault of last night you owe this distinguished mark of Lord Wellington's favor, which I hope will be duly appreciated by you, and serve to increase your zeal for that service in which you have already distinguished yourself.

"Believe me that I am most happy in being made the medium of this communication, and have the honor to be,

"Very truly yours,

"T. PICTON."

"Quarter-General,
"Ciudad Rodrigo, Jan. 20, 1812."

I read and re-read this note again and again. Every line was conned over by me, and every phrase weighed and balanced in my mind. Nothing could be more gratifying, nothing more satisfactory to my feelings, and I would not have exchanged its possession for the brevet of a lieutenant-colonel.

"Halloo, orderly!" cried I from the window, as I hurriedly scaled my few words of acknowledgment; "take this note back to General Picton, and here's a guinea for yourself." So saying, I pitched into his ready hand one of the very few which remained to me in the world. "This is indeed good news!" said I to myself; "this is indeed a moment of unmixed happiness!"

As I closed the window, I could hear Mike pronouncing a glowing eulogium upon my liberality, from which he could not, however, help in some degree detracting, as he added,—

"But the devil thank him, after all! Sure it's himself has the illegant fortune and the fine place of it!"

Scarcely were the last sounds of the retiring horseman dying away in the distance, when Mike's meditations took another form, and he muttered between his teeth—"Oh! holy Agatha; a guinea, a raal gold guinea, to a thief of a dragoon that come with the letter, and here am I wearing a picture of the holy family for a back to my waistcoat, all out of economy; and sure, God knows, but maybe they'll take their dealing trick out of me in purgatory for this hereafter; and faith, it's a beautiful pair of breeches I'd have had, if I wasn't ashamed to put the twelve apostles on my legs."

While Mike ran on at this rate, my eyes fell upon a few lines of postscript in Picton's letter, which I had not previously noticed.

"The official despatches of the storming are of course entrusted to senior officers; but I need scarcely remind you that it will be a polite and proper attention to his Royal Highness to present your letters with as little delay as possible. Not a moment is to be lost on your landing in England."

"Mike!" cried I, "how look the cattle for a journey?"

"The chestnut is a little low in flesh, but in great wind, your honor; and the black horse is jumping like a filly."

"And Badger?" said I.

"Howld him, if you can, that's all; but it's murthering work this, carrying despatches day after day."

"This time, however, Mike, we must not grumble."

"Maybe it isn't far?"

"Why, as to that, I shall not promise much. I'm bound for England, Mickey."

"For England!"

"Yes, Mike, and for Ireland."

"For Ireland! whoop!" shouted he, as he shied his cap into one corner of the room, the jacket he was brushing into the other, and began dancing round the table with no bad imitation of an Indian war dance.

> "How I'll dance like a fairy,
> To see ould Dunleary,
> And think twice ere I leave it to be a dragoon."

"Oh! blessed hour! isn't it beautiful to think of the illuminations, and dinners, and speeches, and shaking of hands, huzzaing, and hip, hipping. Maybe there won't be pictures of us in all the shops— Mister Charles and his man Mister Free. Maybe they won't make plays out of us; myself dressed in the gray coat with the red cuffs, the cords, the tops, and the Caroline hat a little cocked, with a phiz in the side of it." Here he made a sign with his expanded fingers to represent a cockade, which he designated by this word. "I think I see myself dining with the Corporation, and the Lord Mayor of Dublin getting up to propose the health of the hero of El Boden, Mr. Free! and three times three, hurrah! hurrah! hurrah! Musha, but it's dry I am gettin' with the thoughts of the punch and the potteen negus."

"If you go on at this rate, we're not likely to be soon at our journey's end; so be alive now; pack up my kit; I shall start by twelve o'clock."

With one spring Mike cleared the stairs, and, overthrowing everything and everybody in his way, hurried towards the stable, chanting at the top of his voice the very poetical strain he had indulged me with a few minutes before.

My preparations were rapidly made. A few hurried lines of leave-taking to the good fellows I had lived so much with and felt so strongly attached to, with a firm assurance that I should join them again ere long, was all that my time permitted. To Power I wrote more at length, detailing the circumstances which my own letters informed me of, and also those which invited me to return home. This done, I lost not another moment, but set out upon my journey.

CHAPTER XL.

THE LEAVE.

AFTER an hour's sharp riding we reached the Aguada, where the river was yet fordable; crossing this, we mounted the Sierra by a narrow and winding pass which leads through the mountains towards Almeida. Here I turned once more to cast a last and farewell look at the scene of our late encounter. It was but a few hours that I had stood almost on the same spot, and yet how altered was all around. The wide plain, then bustling with all the life and animation of a large army, was now nearly deserted; some dismounted guns, some broken up, dismantled batteries, around which a few sentinels seemed to loiter rather than to keep guard; a strong detachment of infantry could be seen wending their way towards the fortress, and a confused mass of camp-followers, sutlers, and peasants, following their steps for protection against the pillagers and the still ruder assaults of their own Guerillas. The fortress, too, was changed indeed. Those mighty walls before whose steep sides the bravest fell back baffled and beaten, were now a mass of ruin and decay; the muleteer could be seen driving his mule along through the rugged ascent of that breach, to win whose top the best blood of Albion's chivalry was shed; and the peasant child looked timidly from those dark enclosures into the deep fosse below, where perished hundreds of our best and bravest. The air was calm, clear and unclouded; no smoke obscured the transparent atmosphere; the cannon had ceased; and the voices that rang so late in accents of triumphant victory were stilled in death. Everything, indeed, had undergone a mighty change; but nothing brought the altered fortunes of the scenes so vividly to my mind as when I remembered that when last I had seen those walls, the dark shako of the French grenadiers peered above their battlements, and now the gay tartan of the Highlander fluttered above them, and the red flag of England waved boldly in the breeze.

Up to that moment my sensations were those of unmixed pleasure. The thought of my home, my friends, my country, the feeling that I was returning with the bronze of battle upon my cheek, and the voice of praise still ringing in my heart,—these were proud thoughts, and my bosom heaved short and quickly as I revolved them; but as I turned my gaze for the last time towards the gallant army I was leaving, a pang of sorrow, of self-reproach, shot through me, and I could not help feeling how far less worthily was I acting in yielding to the impulse of my wishes, than had I remained to share the fortunes of the campaign.

So powerfully did these sensations possess me, that I sat motionless for some time, uncertain whether to proceed. Forgetting that I was the bearer of important information, I only remembered that by my own desire I was there; my reason but half convinced me that the part I had adopted was right and honorable, and more than once my resolution to proceed hung in the balance. It was just at this critical moment of my doubts that Mike, who had been hitherto behind, came up.

"Is it the upper road, sir?" said he, pointing to a steep and rugged path which led by a zigzag ascent towards the crest of the mountain.

I nodded in reply, when he added:

"Doesn't this remind your honor of Sleibh More, above the Shannon, where we used to be grouse-shooting? And there's the keeper's house in the valley : and that might be your uncle, the master himself, waving his hat to you."

Had he known the state of my conflicting feelings at the moment, he could not more readily have decided this doubt. I turned abruptly away, put spurs to my horse, and dashed up the steep pass at a pace which evidently surprised, and as evidently displeased, my follower.

How natural it is ever to experience a reaction of depression and lowness after the first burst of unexpected joy! The moment of happiness is scarce experienced ere come the doubts of its reality, the fears for its continuance, the higher state of pleasurable excitement, the more painful and the more pressing the anxieties that await on it; the tension of delighted feelings cannot last, and our overwrought faculties seek repose in regrets. Happy he who can so temper his enjoyments as to view them in their shadows as in their sunshine; he may not, it is true, behold the landscape in the blaze of its noonday brightness, but he need not fear the thunder-cloud nor the hurricane. The calm autumn of his bliss, if it dazzle not in its brilliancy, will not any more be shrouded in darkness and in gloom.

My first burst of pleasure over, the thought of my uncle's changed fortunes pressed deeply on my heart, and a hundred plans suggested themselves in turn to my mind to relieve his present embarrassments; but I knew how impracticable they would all prove when opposed by his prejudices. To sell the old home of his forefathers, to wander from the roof which had sheltered his name for generations, he would never consent to ; the law might by force expel him, and drive him a wanderer and an exile, but of his own free will the thing was hopeless. Considine, too, would encourage rather than repress such feelings; his feudalism would lead him to any lengths; and, in defence of what he would esteem a right, he would as soon shoot a sheriff as a snipe, and, old as he was, ask for no better amusement than to arm the whole tenantry and give battle to the king's troops on the wide plain of Scariff. Amid such conflicting thoughts I travelled on moodily and in silence, to the palpable astonishment of Mike, who could not help regarding me as one from whom fortune met the most ungrateful 'returns. At every new turn of the road he would endeavor to attract my attention by the objects around ; no white-turreted château, no tapered spire in the distance escaped him ; he kept up a constant ripple of half-muttered praise and censure upon all he saw, and instituted unceasing comparisons between the country and his own, in which, I am bound to say, Ireland rarely, if ever, had to complain of his patriotism.

When we arrived at Almeida, I learned that the *Medea* sloop of war was lying off Oporto, and expected to sail for England in a few days. The opportunity was not to be neglected; the official despatches, I was aware, would be sent through Lisbon, where the *Gorgon* frigate was in waiting to convey them; but should I be fortunate enough to reach Oporto in time, I had little doubt of arriving in England with the first intelligence of the fall of Ciudad Rodrigo. Reducing my luggage, therefore, to the smallest possible compass, and having provided myself with a juvenile guide for the pass of La Reyna, I threw myself, without undressing, upon the bed, and waited anxiously for the break of day to resume my journey.

As I ruminated over the prospect my return presented, I suddenly remembered Frank Webber's letter, which I had hastily thrust into a portfolio without reading, so occupied was I by Considine's epistle. With a little searching I discovered it, and, trimming my lamp, as I felt no inclination to sleep, I proceeded to the examination of what seemed a more than usually voluminous epistle. It contained four closely-written pages, accompanied by something like a plan in an engineering sketch. My curiosity becoming further stimulated by this, I sat down to peruse it. It began thus:

"Official Despatch of Lieutenant-General Francis Webber to Lord
. Castlereagh, detailing the assault and capture of the old pump in
Trinity College, Dublin, on the night of the second of December,
eighteen hundred and eleven, with returns of killed, wounded,
and missing, with other information from the seat of war.

"Head-quarters, No. 2, Old Square.

"My Lord,—In compliance with the instructions contained in your lordship's despatch of the twenty-first ultimo, I concentrated the force under my command, and, assembling the generals of division, made known my intentions in the following general order:

"A. G. O.
"The following troops will this evening assemble at head-quarters, and, having partaken of a sufficient dinner for the next two days, with punch for four, will hold themselves in readiness to march in the following order:

"Harry Nesbitt's brigade of Incorrigibles will form a blockading force, in the line extending from the Vice-Provost's house to the library. The light division, under Mark Waller, will skirmish from the gate towards the middle of the square, obstructing the march of the Cuirassiers of the Guard, which, under the command of old Duncan, the porter, are expected to move in that direction. Two columns of attack will be formed by the senior sophisters of the Old

Guard, and a forlorn hope of the 'cautioned' men at the last four examinations will form, under the orders of Timothy O'Rourke, beneath the shadow of the dining-hall.

"At the signal of the Dean's bell the stormers will move forward. A cheer from the united corps will then announce the moment of attack.

"The word for the night will be 'May the devil admire me!'

"The Commander of the Forces desires that the different corps should be as strong as possible, and expects that no man will remain, on any pretence whatever, in the rear, with the lush. During the main assault, Cecil Cavendish will make a feint upon the Provost's windows, to be converted into a real attack if the ladies scream.

"GENERAL ORDER.

"The Commissary-General Foley will supply the following articles for the use of the troops:—Two hams; eight pair of chickens, the same to be roasted; a devilled turkey; sixteen lobsters; eight hundred of oysters, with a proportionate quantity of cold sherry and hot punch.

"The army will get drunk by ten o'clock to-night.

"Having made these dispositions, my lord, I proceeded to mislead the enemy as to our intentions, in suffering my servant to be taken with an intercepted despatch. This, being a prescription by Doctor Colles, would convey to the Dean's mind the impression that I was still upon the sick list. This being done, and four canisters of Dartford gunpowder being procured on tick, our military chest being in a most deplorable condition, I waited for the moment of attack.

"A heavy rain, accompanied with a frightful hurricane, prevailed during the entire day, rendering the march of the troops, who came from the neighborhood of Merrion-square and Fitzwilliam street, a service of considerable fatigue. The outlying pickets in College-green, being induced, probably, by the inclemency of the season, were rather tipsy in joining, and having engaged in a skirmish with old M'Calister, tying his red uniform over his head, the moment of attack was precipitated, and we moved to the trenches by half-past nine o'clock.

"Nothing could be more orderly, nothing more perfect, than the march of the troops. As we approached the corner of the commons'-hall, a skirmish on the rear apprised us that our intentions had become known; and I soon learned from my aide-de-camp, Bob Moore, that the attack was made by a strong column of the enemy, under the command of old Fitzgerald.

" Perpendicular (as your lordship is aware he is styled by the army) came on in a determined manner, and before many minutes had elapsed had taken several prisoners, among others Tom Drummond—Long Tom—who, having fallen on all fours, was mistaken for a long eighteen. The success, however, was but momentary; Nesbitt's brigade attacked them in flank, rescued the prisoners, extinguished the Dean's lantern, and, having beaten back the heavy porters, took Perpendicular himself prisoner.

"An express from the left informed me that the attack upon the Provost's house had proved equally successful: there wasn't a whole pane of glass in the front, and from a footman who deserted, it was learned that Mrs. Hutchinson was in hysterics.

"While I was reading this despatch, a strong feeling of the line towards the right announced that something was taking place in that direction. Bob Moore, who rode by on Drummond's back, hurriedly informed me that Williams had put the lighted end of his cigar to one of the fuses, but the powder, being wet, did not explode, notwithstanding his efforts to effect it. Upon this, I hastened to the front, where I found the individual in question kneeling upon the ground, and endeavoring, as far as punch would permit him, to kindle a flame at the port-fire. Before I could interfere, the spark had caught; a loud, hissing noise followed; the different magazines successively became ignited, and the fire reached the great four-pound charge.

" I cannot convey to your lordship, by any words of mine, an idea of this terrible explosion; the blazing splinters were hurled into the air and fell in fiery masses on every side from the Park to King William; Ivey, the bell-ringer, was precipitated from the scaffold beside the bell, and fell headlong into the mud beneath; the surrounding buildings trembled at the shock; the windows were shattered, and, in fact, a scene of perfect devastation ensued on all sides.

"When the smoke cleared away, I rose from my recumbent position, and perceived with delight that not a vestige of the pump remained. The old iron handle was imbedded in the wall of the dining-hall, and its round knob stood out like the end of a queue.

"Our loss was, of course, considerable. Ordering the wounded to the rear, I proceeded to make an orderly and regular retreat. At this time, however, the enemy had assembled in force. Two battalions of porters, led on by Doctor Dobbin, charged us on the flank; a heavy brigade poured down upon us from the battery, and but for the exertions of Harry Nesbitt, our communication with our reserves must have been cut off. Cecil Cavendish also came up; for, although beaten in his great attack, the forces under his command had penetrated by the kitchen windows, and carried off a considerable quantity of cold meat.

"Concentrating the different corps, I made an echelon movement upon the chapel, to admit of the light division coming up. This they did in a few moments, informing me that they had left Perpendicular in the haha, which, as your lordship is aware, is a fosse of the very greenest and most stagnant nature. We now made good our retreat upon number '2,' carrying our wounded with us. The plunder we also secured, but we kicked the prisoners and suffered them to escape.

"Thus terminated, my lord, one of the brightest achievements of the under-graduate career. I enclose a list of the wounded, as also an account of the various articles returned in the Commissary-General's list.

"Harry Nesbitt: severely wounded; no coat nor hat; a black eye; left shoe missing.

"Cecil Cavendish: face severely scratched; supposed to have received his wound in the attack upon the kitchen.

"Tom Drummond: not recognizable by his friends; his features resembling a transparency disfigured by the smoke of the preceding night's illumination.

"Bob Moore: slightly wounded.

"I would beg particularly to recommend all these officers to your lordship's notice; indeed, the conduct of Moore, in kicking the Dean's lantern out of the porter's hand, was marked by great promptitude and decision. This officer will present to H. R. H. the following trophies, taken from the enemy: The Dean's cap and tassel; the key of his chambers; Dr. Dobbin's wig and bands; four porters' helmets, and a book on the cellar.

"I have the honor to remain, my lord, &c.,

"FRANCIS WEBBER.

"G. O.

"The Commander of the Forces returns his thanks to the various officers and soldiers employed in the late assault, for their persevering gallantry and courage. The splendor of the achievement can only be equalled by the humanity and good conduct of the troops. It only remains for him to add, that the less they say about the transaction, and the sooner they are severally confined to their beds with symptoms of contagious fever, the better.

"Meanwhile, to concert upon the future measures of the campaign, the army will sup to-night at Morrison's."

Here ended this precious epistle, rendering one fact sufficiently evident—that however my worthy friend had advanced in years, he had not grown in wisdom.

While ruminating upon the strange infatuation which could persuade a gifted and an able man to lavish upon dissipation and reckless absurdity the talents that might, if well directed, raise him to eminence and distinction, a few lines of a newspaper paragraph fell from the paper I was reading. It ran thus:

"LATE OUTRAGE IN TRINITY COLLEGE, DUBLIN.

"We have great pleasure in stating that the serious disturbance which took place within the walls of our University a few evenings since was in nowise attributable to the conduct of the students. A party of ill-disposed townspeople were, it would appear, the instigators and perpetrators of the outrage. That their object was the total destruction of our venerated University there can be but little doubt. Fortunately, however, they did not calculate upon the *esprit de corps* of the students, a body of whom, under the direction of Mr. Webber, successfully opposed the assailants, and finally drove them from the walls.

"It is, we understand, the intention of the board to confer some mark of approbation upon Mr. Webber, who, independently of this, has strong claims upon their notice, his collegiate success pointing him out as the most extraordinary man of his day."

"This, my dear Charley, will give you some faint conception of one of the most brilliant exploits of modern days. The bulletin, believe me, is not Napoleonized into any bombastic extravagance of success. The thing was splendid; from the brilliant firework of the old pump itself to the figure of Perpendicular dripping with duckweed, like an insane river-god, it was unequalled. Our fellows behaved like trumps; and, to do them justice, so did the enemy. But unfortunately, notwithstanding this, and the plausible paragraphs of the morning papers, I have been summoned before the board for Tuesday next.

"Meanwhile, I employ myself in throwing off a shower of small squibs for the journals, so that if the board deal not mercifully with me, I may meet with sympathy from the public. I have just despatched a little editorial bit for the *Times*, calling, in terms of parental tenderness, upon the University to say—

"'How long will the extraordinary excesses of a learned functionary be suffered to disgrace college? Is Doctor —— to be permitted to exhibit an example of more riotous insubordination than would be endured in an under-graduate? More on this subject hereafter.'

"'*Saunders' News Letter.*—Doctor Barret appeared at the head police-office, before Alderman Darley, to make oath that neither he nor Catty were concerned in the late outrage upon the pump,' &c., &c.

"Paragraphs like these are flying about in every provincial paper of the empire. People shake their heads when they speak of the University, and respectable females rather cross over by King William and the Bank than pass near its precincts.

"Tuesday Evening.

"Would you believe it, they've expelled me! Address your next letter as usual, for they haven't got rid of me yet. Yours,

"F. W."

"So I shall find him in his old quarters," thought I, "and evidently not much altered since we parted." It was not without a feeling of (I trust pardonable) pride that I thought over my own career in the interval. My three years of campaigning life had given me some insight into the world, and some knowledge of myself, and conferred upon me a boon of which I know not the equal —that, while yet young, and upon the very threshold of life, I should have tasted the enthusiastic pleasures of a soldier's fortune and braved the dangers and difficulties of a campaign at a time when, under other auspices, I might have wasted my years in unprofitable idleness or careless dissipation.

CHAPTER XLI.

LONDON.

TWELVE hours after my arrival in England I entered London. I cannot attempt to record the sensations which thronged my mind as the din and tumult of that mighty city awoke me from a sound sleep I had fallen into in the corner of the chaise. The seemingly interminable lines of lamplight, the crash of carriages, the glare of the shops, the buzz of voices, made up a chaotic mass of sights and sounds, leaving my efforts at thought vain and fruitless.

Obedient to my instructions, I lost not a moment in my preparations to deliver my despatches. Having dressed myself in the full uniform of my corps, I drove to the Horse Guards. It was now nine o'clock, and I learned that his Royal Highness had gone to dinner at Carlton House. In a few words which I spoke with the aide-de-camp, I discovered that no information of the fall of Ciudad Rodrigo had yet reached England. The greatest anxiety prevailed as to the events of the Peninsula, from which no despatches had been received for several weeks past.

To Carlton House I accordingly bent my steps, without any precise determination how I should proceed when there, nor knowing how far etiquette might be an obstacle to the accomplishment of my mission. The news of which I was the bearer was, however, of too important a character to permit me to hesitate, and I presented myself to the aide-de-camp in waiting, simply stating that I was entrusted with important letters to his Royal Highness, the purport of which did not admit of delay.

"They have not gone to dinner yet," lisped out the aide-de-camp, "and if you would permit me to deliver the letters——".

"Mine are despatches," said I, somewhat proudly, and in nowise disposed to cede to another the honor of personally delivering them into the hands of the Duke.

"Then you had better present yourself at the levée to-morrow morning," replied he, carelessly, while he turned into one of the window recesses, and resumed the conversation with one of the gentlemen in waiting.

I stood for some moments uncertain and undecided, reluctant on the one part to relinquish my claim as the bearer of despatches, and equally unwilling to defer their delivery till the following day.

Adopting the former alternative, I took my papers from my sabretasche, and was about to place them in the hands of the aide-de-camp, when the folding doors at the end of the apartment suddenly flew open, and a large and handsome man, with a high, bald forehead, entered hastily.

The different persons in waiting sprang from their lounging attitudes upon the sofas, and bowed respectfully as he passed on towards another door. His dress was a plain blue coat, buttoned to the collar, and his only decoration a brilliant star upon the breast. There was that air, however, of high birth and bearing about him that left no doubt upon my mind that he was of the blood royal.

As the aide-de-camp to whom I had been speaking opened the door for him to pass out, I could hear some words in a low voice, in which the phrases "letters of importance" and "your Royal Highness" occurred. The individual addressed turned suddenly about, and casting a rapid glance around the room, without deigning a word in reply, walked straight up to where I was standing.

"Despatches for me, sir?" said he, shortly, taking the packet from my hand as he spoke.

"For his Royal Highness the Commander-in-Chief," said I, bowing respectfully, and still uncertain in whose presence I was standing. He broke the seal without answering, and, as his eye caught the first lines of the despatch, broke out into an exclamation of—

"Ha! Peninsular news! When did you arrive, sir?"

"An hour since, sir."

"And these letters are from ——"

"General Picton, your Royal Highness."

"How glorious!—how splendidly done!" muttered he to himself, as he ran his eyes rapidly over the letter. "Are you Captain O'Malley, whose name is mentioned here so favorably?"

I bowed deeply in reply.

"You are most highly spoken of, and it will give me sincere pleasure to recommend you to the notice of the Prince Regent. But stay a moment." So saying, he hurriedly passed from the room, leaving me overwhelmed at the suddenness of the incident, and a mark of no small astonishment to the different persons in waiting, who had hitherto no other idea but that my despatches were from Hounslow or Knightsbridge.

"Captain O'Malley," said an officer covered with decorations, and whose slightly foreign accent bespoke the Hanoverian, "his Royal Highness requests you will accompany me." The door opened as he spoke, and I found myself in a most splendidly lit-up apartment, the walls covered with pictures, and the ceiling divided into panels, resplendent with the richest gilding. A group of persons, in court dresses, were conversing in a low tone as we entered, but suddenly ceased, and, saluting my conductor respectfully, made way for us to pass on. The folding-doors again opened as we approached, and we found ourselves in a long gallery, whose sumptuous furniture and costly decorations shone beneath the rich tints of a massive lustre of ruby glass, diffusing a glow resembling the most gorgeous sunset. Here also some persons in handsome uniform were conversing, one of whom accosted my companion by the title of "Baron." Nodding familiarly as he muttered a few words in German, he passed forward, and the next moment the doors were thrown suddenly wide, and we entered the drawing-room.

The buzz of voices and the sound of laughter reassured me as I came forward, and before I had time to think where and why I was there, the Duke of York advanced towards me with a smile of peculiar sweetness in its expression, and said, as he turned towards one side,—

"Your Royal Highness—Captain O'Malley."

As he spoke, the Prince moved forward, and bowed slightly.

"You've brought us capital news, Mr. O'Malley. May I beg, if you're not too much tired, you'll join us at dinner? I am most anxious to learn the particulars of the assault."

As I bowed my acknowledgments to the gracious invitation, he continued,—

"Are you acquainted with my friend here?—but of course you can scarcely be—you began too early as a soldier. So let me present you to my friend, Mr. Tierney,"—a middle-aged man, whose broad, white forehead and deep-set eyes gave a character to features that were otherwise not remarkable in expression, and who bowed rather stiffly.

Before he had concluded a somewhat labored compliment to me, we were joined by a third person, whose strikingly-handsome features were lit up with an expression of the most animated kind. He accosted the Prince with an air of easy familiarity, and while he led him from the group, appeared to be relating some anecdote, which actually convulsed his Royal Highness with laughter.

Before I had time or opportunity to inquire who the individual could be, dinner was announced, and the wide folding-doors being thrown open, displayed the magnificent dining-room of Carlton House, in all the blaze and splendor of its magnificence.

The sudden change from the rough vicissitudes of campaigning life to all the luxury and voluptuous elegance of a brilliant court, created too much confusion in my mind to permit of my impressions being the most accurate or most collected. The splendor of the scene, the rank, but even more the talent, of the individuals by whom I was surrounded, had all their full effect upon me; and although I found, from the tone of the conversation about, how immeasurably I was their inferior, yet by a delicate and courteous interest in the scene of which I had lately partaken, they took away the awkwardness which, in some degree, was inseparable from the novelty of my position among them.

Conversing about the Peninsula with a degree of knowledge which I could in nowise comprehend from those not engaged in the war, they appeared perfectly acquainted with all the details of the campaign; and I heard on every side of me anecdotes and stories which I scarcely believed known beyond the precincts of a regiment. The Prince himself—the grace and charm of whose narrative talents have seldom been excelled—was particularly conspicuous, and I could not help feeling struck with his admirable imitations of voice and manner. The most accomplished actor could not have personated the cannie, calculating spirit of the Scot, or the rollicking recklessness of the Irishman, with more tact and *finesse.*

But far above all this shone the person whom I have already alluded to as speaking to his Royal Highness in the drawing-room. Combining the happiest conversational eloquence with a quick, ready, and brilliant fancy, he threw from him, in all the careless profusion of boundless resource, a shower of pointed and epigrammatic witticisms—now illustrating a really difficult subject by one happy touch, as the blaze of the lightning will light up the whole surface of the dark landscape beneath it; now turning the force of an adversary's argument by some fallacious but unanswerable jest, accompanying the whole by those fascinations of voice, look, gesture, and manner, which have made those who once have seen never able to forget Brinsley Sheridan.

I am not able, were I even disposed, to record more particularly the details of that most brilliant evening of my life. On every side of me I heard the names of those whose fame as statesmen, or whose repute as men of letters, was ringing throughout Europe. They were then, too, not in the easy indolence of ordinary life, but displaying with their utmost effort those powers of wit, fancy, imagination, and eloquence which had won for them elsewhere their high and exalted position. The masculine understanding and powerful intellect of Tierney vied with the brilliant and dazzling conceptions of Sheridan. The easy *bonhomie* and English heartiness of Fox contrasted with the keen sarcasm and sharp raillery of O'Kelly. While contesting the palm with each, the Prince evinced powers of mind and eloquent facilities of expression that in any walk of life must have made their possessor a most distinguished man. Politics, war, women, literature, the turf, the navy, the opposition, architecture, and the drama, were all discussed with a degree of information and knowledge that proved to me how much of real acquirements can be obtained by those whose exalted station surrounds them with the collective intellect of a nation. As for myself, the time flew past unconsciously. So brilliant a display of all that was courtly and fascinating in manner, and all that was brightest in genius, was so new to me, that I really felt like one entranced. To this hour, my impression, however confused in details, is as though that evening were but yesternight; and although since that period I have enjoyed numerous opportunities of meeting with the great and the gifted, yet I treasure the memory of that evening as by far the most exciting of my whole life.

While I abstain from any mention of the many incidents of the evening, I cannot pass over one which, occurring to myself, is valuable but as showing, by one slight and passing trait, the amiable and kind feeling of one whose memory is hallowed in the service.

A little lower than myself, on the opposite side of the table, I perceived an old military acquaintance whom I had first met in Lisbon; he was then on Sir Charles Stewart's staff, and we met almost daily. Wishing to commend myself to his recollection, I endeavored for some time to catch his eye, but in vain; but at last, when I thought I had succeeded, I called to him,—

"I say, Fred, a glass of wine with you."

- When suddenly, the Duke of York, who was speaking to Lord Hertford, turned quickly round, and, taking the decanter in his hand, replied,—

"With pleasure, O'Malley; what shall it be, my boy?"

I shall never forget the manly good-humor of his look as he sat waiting for my answer. He had taken my speech as addressed to himself, and concluding that, from fatigue, the novelty of the scene, my youth, &c., I was not over collected, vouchsafed in this kind way to receive it.

"So," said he, as I stammered out my explanation, "I was deceived; however, don't cheat me out of my glass of wine. Let us have it now."

With this little anecdote, whose truth I vouch for, I shall conclude. More than one now living was a witness to it, and my only regret in the mention of it is my inability to convey the readiness with which he seized the moment of apparent difficulty to throw the protection of his kind and warm-hearted nature over the apparent folly of a boy.

It was late when the party broke up, and as I took my leave of the Prince, he once more expressed himself in gracious terms towards me, and gave me personally an invitation to a breakfast at Hounslow on the following Saturday.

CHAPTER XLII.

THE BELL AT BRISTOL.

ON the morning after my dinner at Carlton House, I found my breakfast-table covered with cards and invitations. The news of the storming of Ciudad Rodrigo was published in all the morning papers, and my own humble name in letters of three feet long, was exhibited in placards throughout the city. Less to this circumstance, however, than to the kind and gracious notice of the Prince, was I indebted for the attentions which were shown me by every one; and, indeed, so flattering was the reception I met

with, and so overwhelming the civility showered on me from all
sides, that it required no small effort on my part not to believe myself as much a hero as they would make me. An eternal round of
dinners, balls, breakfasts, and entertainments, filled up the entire
week. I was included in every invitation to Carlton House, and
never appeared without receiving from his Royal Highness the most
striking marks of attention. Captivating as all this undoubtedly
was, and fascinated as I felt at being the lion of London, the
courted and sought after by the high, the titled, and talented of the
great city of the universe, yet, amid all the splendor and seduction
of that new world, my heart instinctively turned from the glare and
brilliancy of gorgeous saloons—from the soft looks and softer voice
of beauty—from the words of praise, as they fell from the lips of
those whose notice was fame itself—to my humble home amid the
mountains of the west. Delighted and charmed as I felt by that
tribute of flattery which associated my name with one of the most
brilliant actions of my country, yet hitherto I had experienced no
touch of home or fatherland. England was to me as the high and
powerful head of my house whose greatness and whose glory shed a
halo far and near, from the proudest to the humblest of those that
call themselves Britons; but Ireland was the land of my birth—
the land of my earliest ties, my dearest associations—the kind
mother, whose breath had fanned my brow in infancy; and for
her in my manhood my heart beat with every throb of filial affection. Need I say, then, how ardently I longed to turn homeward;
for independent of all else, I could not avoid some self-reproach on
thinking what might be the condition of those I prized the most on
earth, at the very moment I was engaging in all the voluptuous
abandonment and all the fascinating excesses of a life of pleasure.
I wrote several letters home, but received no answer; nor did I, in
the whole round of London-society, meet with a single person who
could give me information of my family or my friends. The Easter
recess had sent the different members of Parliament to their homes;
and thus, within a comparatively short distance of all I cared for, I
could learn nothing of their fate.

The invitations of the Prince Regent, which were, of course, to be
regarded as commands, still detained me in London; and I knew
not in what manner to escape from the fresh engagements which
each day heaped upon me. In my anxiety upon the subject, I communicated my wishes to a friend on the Duke's staff, and the following morning, as I presented myself at his levee, he called me towards
him, and addressed me:—

"What leave have you got, Captain O'Malley?"

"Three months, your Royal Highness."

"Do you desire an unattached troop? for, if so, an opportunity occurs just at this moment."

"I thank you most sincerely, sir, for your condescension in thinking of me, but my wish is to join my regiment at the expiration of my leave."

"Why, I thought they told me you wanted to spend some time in Ireland?"

"Only sufficient to see my friends, your Royal Highness. That done, I'd rather join my regiment immediately."

"Ah! that alters the case. So then, probably, you'd like to leave us at once. I see how it is; you've been staying here against your will all this while. Then, don't say a word. I'll make your excuses at Carlton House; and the better to cover your retreat, I'll employ you on service. Here, Gordon, let Captain O'Malley have the despatches for Sir Henry Howard at Cork." As he said this, he turned towards me with an air of affected sternness in his manner, and continued: "I expect, Captain O'Malley, that you will deliver the despatches entrusted to your care without a moment's loss of time. You will leave London within an hour. The instructions for your journey will be sent to your hotel. And now," said he, again changing his voice to its natural tone of kindliness and courtesy— "and now, my boy, good-bye, and a safe journey to you. These letters will pay your expenses, and the occasion save you all the worry of leave-taking."

I stood confused and speechless, unable to utter a single word of gratitude for such unexpected kindness. The Duke saw at once my difficulty, and, as he shook me warmly by the hand, added, in a laughing tone,—

"Don't wait, now. You mustn't forget that your despatches are pressing."

I bowed deeply, attempted a few words of acknowledgment, hesitated, blundered, and broke down; and at last got out of the room, Heaven knows how! and found myself running towards Long's at the top of my speed. Within that same hour I was rattling along towards Bristol as fast as four posters could burn the pavement, thinking with ecstasy over the pleasures of my reception in England, but far more than all of the kindness evinced towards me by him who, in every feeling of his nature, and in every feature of his deportment, was "every inch a prince."

However astonished I had been at the warmth by which I was treated in London, I was still less prepared for the enthusiasm which greeted me in every town through which I passed. There was not a village where we stopped to change horses whose inhabitants did not simultaneously pour forth to welcome me with every demonstra-

40

tion of delight. That the fact of four horses and a yellow chaise should have elicited such testimonies of satisfaction, was somewhat difficult to conceive; even had the important news that I was the bearer of despatches been telegraphed from London by successive postboys, still the extraordinary excitement was unaccountable. It was only on reaching Bristol that I learned to what circumstance my popularity was owing. My friend Mike, in humble imitation of election practices, had posted a large placard on the back of the chaise, announcing, in letters of portentous length, something like the following :—

"Bloody news! Fall of Ciudad Rodrigo! Five thousand prisoners and two hundred pieces of cannon taken!"

This veracious and satisfactory statement, aided by Mike's personal exertions, and an unwearied performance on the trumpet he had taken from the French dragoon, had roused the population of every hamlet, and made our journey from London to Bristol one scene of uproar, noise and confusion. All my attempts to suppress Mike's oratory or music were perfectly unavailing. In fact, he had pledged my health so many times during the day—he had drunk so many toasts to the success of the British arms—so many to the English nation—so many in honor of Ireland—and so many in honor of Mickey Free himself, that all respect for my authority was lost in his enthusiasm for my greatness, and his shouts became wilder, and the blasts from the trumpet more fearful and incoherent; and finally, on the last stage of our journey, having exhausted, as it were, every tribute of his lungs, he seemed (if I were to judge by the evidence of my ears) to be performing something very like a hornpipe on the roof of the chaise.

Happily for me there is a limit to all human efforts, and even *his* powers at length succumbed; so that, when we arrived at Bristol, I persuaded him to go to bed, and I once more was left to the enjoyment of some quiet. To fill up the few hours which intervened before bedtime, I strolled into the coffee-room. The English look of every one, and everything around, had still its charm for me; and I was contemplating with no small admiration that air of neatness and propriety so observant from the bright-faced clock, that ticked unwearily upon the mantelpiece, to the trim waiter himself, with noiseless step, and that mixed look of vigilance and vacancy. The perfect stillness struck me, save when a deep voice called for "another brandy-and-water," and some more modestly-toned request would utter a desire for "more cream." The attention of each man, absorbed in the folds of his voluminous newspaper, scarcely deigning a glance at the new comer who entered, were all in keeping, giving, in their solemnity and gravity, a character of almost religious seriousness to what in any other land would be a scene of riotous noise and discordant tumult. I was watching all these with a more than common interest, when the door opened, and the waiter entered with a large placard. He was followed by another with a ladder, by whose assistance he succeeded in attaching the large square of paper to the wall, above the fireplace. Every one about rose up, curious to ascertain what was going forward; and I myself joined in the crowd around the fire. The first glance at the announcement showed me what it meant, and it was with a strange mixture of shame and confusion I read:

"'Fall of Ciudad Rodrigo; with a full and detailed account at the storming of the great breach—capture of the enemy's cannon, &c.—by Michael Free, 14th Light Dragoons.'"

Leaving the many around me busied in conjecturing who the aforesaid Mr. Free might be, and what peculiar opportunities he might have enjoyed for his report, I hurried from the room and called the waiter.

"What's the meaning of the announcement you've just put up in the coffee-room? Where did it come from?"

"Most important news, sir; exclusively in the columns of the *Bristol Telegraph;* the gentleman has just arrived——"

"Who, pray? What gentleman?"

"Mr. Free, sir, No. 13—large bedroom—blue damask—supper for two—oysters—a devil—brandy-and-water—mulled port."

"What the devil do you mean? Is the fellow at supper?"

Somewhat shocked by the tone I ventured to assume towards the illustrious narrator, the waiter merely bowed his reply.

"Show me to his room," said I; "I should like to see him."

"Follow me, if you please, sir—this way—what name shall I say, sir?"

"You need not mind announcing me—I'm an old acquaintance— just show me the room."

"I beg pardon, sir, but Mr. Meekins, the editor of the *Telegraph,* is engaged with him at present; and positive orders are given not to suffer any interruption."

"No matter: do as I bid you. Is that it? Oh! I hear his voice. There, that will do. You may go down stairs, I'll introduce myself."

So saying, and slipping a crown into the waiter's hand, I proceeded cautiously towards the door, and opened it stealthily. My caution was, however, needless; for a large screen was drawn across this part of the room, completely concealing the door. Closing this behind me, I took my place beneath the shelter of this ambuscade, determined on no account to be perceived by the parties.

Seated in a large arm-chair, a smoking tumbler of mulled port before him, sat my friend Mike, dressed in my full regimentals, even to the helmet, which, unfortunately, however, for the effect, he had put on back foremost; a short "dudeen" graced his lip, and the trumpet so frequently alluded to lay near him.

Opposite him sat a short, puny, round-faced little gentleman, with rolling eyes and turned-up nose. Numerous sheets of paper, pens, &c., lay scattered about; and he evinced, by his air and gesture, the most marked and eager attention to Mr. Free's narrative, whose frequent interruptions, caused by the drink and the oysters, were viewed with no small impatience by the anxious editor.

"You must remember, Captain, time's passing; the placards are all out; must be at press before one o'clock to-night; the morning edition is everything with us. You were at the first parallel, I think."

"Devil a one o' me knows. Just ring that bell near you. Them's elegant oysters; and you're not taking your drop of liquor. Here's a toast for you: 'May——' whoop—raal Carlingfords, upon my conscience. See, now, if I won't hit the little black chap up there, the first shot."

Scarcely were the words spoken, when a little painted bust of Shakspeare fell in fragments on the floor as an oyster-shell laid him low.

A faint effort at a laugh at the eccentricities of his friend was all the poor editor could accomplish, while Mike's triumph knew no bounds.

"Didn't I tell you? But come now, are you ready? Give the pen a drink, if you won't take one yourself."

"I'm ready, quite ready," responded the editor.

"Faith, and it's more nor I am. See now, here it is: The night was murthering dark; you could not see a stim."

"Not see a—a what?"

"A stim, bad luck to you; don't you know English? Hand me the hot water. Have you that down yet?"

"Yes. Pray proceed."

"The 5th division was orthered up, bekase they were fighting chaps; the 88th was among them; the Rangers——Oh! upon my soul, we must drink to the Rangers. Here, devil a one o' me will go on till we give them all the honors—hip—begin."

"Hip," sighed the luckless editor, as he rose from his chair, obedient to the command.

"Hurra—hurra—hurra! Well done! there's stuff in you yet, ould foolscap! The little bottle's empty—ring again, if ye plaze."

> "Oh, Father Magan
> Was a beautiful man,
> But a bit of a rogue, a bit of a rogue,
> He was just six feet high, .
> Had a cast in his eye,
> And an illigant brogue, an illigant brogue.

> "He was born in Killarney,
> And reared up in Blarney——"

"Arrah, don't be looking miserable and dissolute that way. Sure I'm only screwing myself up for you; besides, you can print the song av you like: it's a sweet tune—'Teddy, ye Gander.'"

"Really, Mr. Free, I see no prospect of our ever getting done."

"The saints in heaven forbid," interrupted Mike, piously; "the evening's young, and drink plenty. Here now, make ready!"

The editor once more made a gesture of preparation.

"Well, as I was saying," resumed Mike, "it was pitch dark when the columns moved up, and a cold, raw night, with a little thin rain falling. Have you that down?"

"Yes. Pray go on."

"Well, just as it might be here, at the corner of the trench I met Dr. Quill. 'They're waiting for you, Mr. Free,' says he, 'down there. Picton's asking for you.' 'Faith and he must wait,' says I, 'for I'm terrible dry.' With that, he pulled out his canteen and mixed me a little brandy-and-water. 'Are you taking it without a toast?' says Dr. Maurice. 'Never fear, Doctor,' says I; 'here's Mary Brady——'"

"But, my dear sir," interposed Mr. Meekins, "pray *do* remember this is somewhat irrelevant. In fifteen minutes it will be twelve o'clock."

"I know it, ould boy, I know it. I see what you're at. You were going to observe how much better we'd be for a broiled bone."

"Nothing of the kind, I assure you. For Heaven's sake, no more eating and drinking."

"No more eating nor drinking! Why not? You've a nice notion of a convivial evening. Faith, we'll have the broiled bone sure enough, and, what's more, a half-gallon of the strongest punch they can make us; an' I hope that, grave as you are, you'll favor the company with a song."

"Really, Mr. Free——"

"Arrah! none of your blarney. Don't be misthering me. Call me Mickey, or Mickey Free, if you like better."

"I protest," said the editor, with dismay, "that here we are two hours at work, and we haven't got to the foot of the great breach."

"And wasn't the army three months and a half in just getting that far, with a battering train, and mortars, and the finest troops ever were seen? and there you sit, a little fat creature, with your pen in your hand, grumbling that you can't do more than the whole British army.   Take care you don't provoke me to beat you; for I am quiet till I'm roused.   But, by the Rock o' Cashel——"

Here he grasped the brass trumpet with an energy that made the editor spring from his chair.

"For mercy's sake, Mr. Free——"

"Well, I won't; but sit down there, and don't be bothering me about sieges, and battles, and things you know nothing about."

"I protest," rejoined Mr. Meekins, "that, had you not sent to my office intimating your wish to communicate an account of the siege, I never should have thought of intruding myself upon you. And now, since you appear indisposed to afford the information in question, if you will permit me, I'll wish you a very good-night."

"Faith, and so you shall, and help me to pass one too; for not a step out o' that chair shall you take till morning. Do ye think I am going to be left here by myself, all alone?"

"I must observe——" said Mr. Meekins.

"To be sure, to be sure," said Mickey; "I see what you mean. You're not the best of company, it's true; but at a pinch like this ——There now, take your liquor."

"Once for all, sir," said the editor, "I would beg you to recollect that, on the faith of your message to me, I have announced an account of the storming of Ciudad Rodrigo for our morning edition. Are you prepared, may I ask, for the consequences of my disappointing ten thousand readers?"

"It's little I care for one of them.   I never knew much of reading myself."

"If you think to make a jest of me——" interposed Mr. Meekins, reddening with passion.

"A jest of you!   Troth it's little fun I can get out of you; you're as tiresome a crayture as ever I spent an evening with. See now, I told you before not to provoke me. We'll have a little more drink; ring the bell: who knows but you'll turn out better by-and-by?"

As Mike rose at these words to summon the waiter, Mr. Meekins seized the opportunity to make his escape. Scarcely had he reached the door, however, when he was perceived by Mickey, who hurled the trumpet at him with all his force, while he uttered a shout that nearly left the poor editor lifeless with terror. This time, happily, Mr. Free's aim failed him, and before he could arrest the progress of his victim, he had gained the corridor, and with one bound cleared the first flight of the staircase, his pace increasing every moment as Mike's denunciations grew louder and louder, till at last, as he reached the street, Mr. Free's delight overcame his indignation, and he threw himself upon a chair and laughed immoderately.

"Oh, may I never! if I didn't frighten the editor. The little spalpeen, couldn't eat his oysters and take his punch like a man. But sure if he didn't, there's more left for his betters." So saying, he filled himself a goblet and drank it off. "Mr. Free, we won't say much for your inclinations, for maybe they are not the best; but here's bad luck to the fellow that doesn't think you good company; and here," added he, again filling his glass—"and here's may the devil take editors, and authors, and compositors, that won't let us alone, but must be taking our lives, and our songs, and our little devilments, that belongs to one's own family, and tell them all over the world. A lazy set of thieves you are, every one of you; spending your time inventing lies—devil a more nor less; and here"—this time he filled again—"and here's a hot corner and Kilkenny coals, that's half sulphur, to the villain——"

For what particular class of offenders Mike's penal code was now devised, I was not destined to learn; for, overcome by punch and indignation, he gave one loud whoop, and measured his length upon the floor. Having committed him to the care of the waiters, from whom I learned more fully the particulars of his acquaintance with Mr. Meekins, I enjoined them strictly not to mention that I knew anything of the matter. I then betook myself to my bed, sincerely rejoicing that in a few hours more Mike would be again in that land where even his eccentricities and excesses would be viewed with a favorable and forgiving eye.

CHAPTER XLIII.

IRELAND.

ON the second evening after our departure from Bristol, the Skipper said to Mickey Free, "You'd better call your master up; he said he'd like to have a look at the coast."

The words were overheard by me, as I lay between sleeping and waking in the cabin of the packet, and without waiting for a second invitation, I rushed upon deck. The sun was setting, and one vast surface of yellow golden light played upon the water, as it rippled beneath a gentle gale. The white foam curled at our prow, and the rushing sound told the speed we were going at. The little craft was staggering under every sheet of her canvas, and her spars creaked as her white sails bent before the breeze. Before us, but to my landsman's eyes scarcely perceptible, were the ill-defined outlines of cloudy darkness they called land, at which I continued to gaze with a strange sense of interest, while I heard the names of certain well-known headlands assigned to apparently mere masses of fog-bank and vapor.

He who has never been separated in early years, while yet the budding affections of his heart are tender shoots, from the land of his birth and of his home, knows nothing of the throng of sensations that crowd upon him as he nears the shore of his country. The names, familiar as household words, come with a train of long-buried thoughts; the feeling of attachment to all we call our own —that patriotism of the heart—stirs strongly within him, as the mingled thrills of hope and fear alternately move him to joy or sadness.

Hard as are the worldly struggles between the daily cares of him who carves out his own career and fortune, yet he has never experienced the darkest poverty of fate who has not felt what it is to be a wanderer, without a country to lay claim to. Of all the desolations that visit us, this is the gloomiest and the worst. The outcast from the land of his fathers, whose voice must never be heard within the walls where his infancy was nurtured, nor his step be free upon the mountains where he gambolled in his youth,—this is indeed wretchedness. The instinct of country grows and strengthens with our years; the joys of early life are linked with it; the hopes of age point towards it; and he who knows not the thrill of ecstasy some well-remembered, long-lost-sight-of place can bring to his heart when returning after years of absence, is ignorant of one of the purest sources of happiness of our nature.

With what a yearning of the heart, then, did I look upon the dim and misty cliffs, that mighty framework of my island home, their stern sides lashed by the blue waters of the ocean, and their summits lost within the clouds! With what an easy and natural transition did my mind turn from the wild mountains and the green valleys to their hardy sons, who toiled beneath the burning sun of the Peninsula! and how, as some twinkling light of the distant shore would catch my eye, did I wonder within myself whether beside that hearth and board there might not sit some whose thoughts were wandering over the sea beside the bold steeps of El Bodon, or the death-strewn plain of Talavera! their memories calling up some trait of him who was the idol of his home; whose closing lids some fond mother had watched over; above whose peaceful slumber her prayers had fallen, but whose narrow bed was now beneath the breach of Badajos, and his sleep the sleep that knows no waking.

I knew not if in my sad and sorrowing spirit I did not envy him who thus had met a soldier's fate,—for what of promise had my own! My hope of being in any way instrumental to my poor uncle's happiness grew hourly less. His prejudices were deeply rooted and of long standing. To have asked him to surrender any of what he looked upon as the prerogatives of his house and name, would be to risk the loss of his esteem. What then remained for me? Was I to watch, day by day and hour by hour, the falling ruin of our fortunes? Was I to involve myself in the petty warfare of unavailing resistance to the law? And could I stand aloof from my best, my truest, my earliest friend, and see him, alone and unaided, oppose his weak and final struggle to the unrelenting career of persecution? Between these two alternatives, the former could be my only choice; and what a choice!

Oh, how I thought over the wild heroism of the battle-field, the reckless fury of the charge, the crash, the death-cry, and the sad picture of the morrow, when all was past, and a soldier's glory alone remained to shed its high halo over the faults and the follies of the dead.

As night fell, the twinkling of the distant lighthouses,—some throwing a column of light from the very verge of the horizon, others shining brightly, like stars, from some lofty promontory,—marked the different outlines of the coast, and conveyed to me the memory of that broken and wild mountain tract that forms the bulwark of the Green Isle against the waves of the Atlantic. Alone and silently I trod the deck, now turning to look towards the shore, where I thought I could detect the position of some well-known headland, now straining my eyes seaward to watch some bright and flitting star, as it rose from or merged beneath the foaming water, denoting the track of the swift pilot-boat, or the hardy lugger of the fisherman, while the shrill whistle of the floating sea-gull was the only sound, save the rushing waves that broke in spray upon our quarter.

What is it that so inevitably inspires sad and depressing thoughts as we walk the deck of some little craft in the silence of the night's dark hours? No sense of danger near, we hold on our course swiftly and steadily, cleaving the dark waves, and bending gracefully beneath the freshening breeze. Yet still the motion, which, in the bright sunshine of the noonday, tells of joy and gladness, brings now no touch of pleasure to our hearts. The dark and frowning sky, the boundless expanse of gloomy water, spread like some gigantic pall around us, and our thoughts either turn back upon the saddest features of the past, or look forward to the future with a sickly hope that all may not be as we fear it.

Mine were indeed of the gloomiest, and the selfishness alone of the thought prevented me from wishing that, like many another, I had fallen by a soldier's death on the plains of the Peninsula!

As the night wore on, I wrapped myself in my cloak and lay down beneath the bulwark. The whole of my past life came in review before me. I thought over my first meeting with Lucy Dashwood; the thrill of boyish admiration gliding into love—the hopes, the fears, that stirred my heart; the firm resolve to merit her affection, which made me a soldier. Alas! how little thought she of him to whose life she had been a guide-star and a beacon! As I thought over the hard-fought fields, the long, fatiguing marches, the nights around the watch-fires, and felt how, in the whirl and enthusiasm of a soldier's life, the cares and sorrows of every-day existence are forgotten, I shuddered to reflect upon the career that might now open before me,—to abandon, perhaps forever, the glorious path I had been pursuing for a life of indolence and weariness, while my name, that had already, by the chance of some fortunate circumstances, begun to be mentioned with a testimony of approval, should be lost in oblivion, or remembered but as that of one whose early promise was not borne out by the deeds of his manhood.

As day broke, overcome by watching, I slept, but was soon awoke by the stir and bustle around me. The breeze had freshened, and we were running under a reefed mainsail and foresail; and as the little craft bounded above the blue water, the white foam crested above her prow, and ran along in boiling rivulets towards the afterdeck. The tramp of the seamen, the hoarse voice of the captain, the shrill cry of the sea-birds, betokened, however, nothing of dread or danger; listlessly I leant upon my elbow, and asked what was going forward.

"Nothing, sir; only making ready to drop our anchor."

"Are we so near shore, then?" said I.

"You've only to round that point to windward, and have a clear run into Cork harbor."

I sprang at once to my legs; the land-fog prevented my seeing anything whatever, but I thought that in the breeze, fresh and balmy as it blew, I could feel the wind off shore.

"At last," said I—"at last!" as I stepped into the little wherry which shot alongside of us, and we glided into the still basin of Cove. How I remember every white-walled cottage, and the beetling cliffs, and that bold headland beside which the valley opens, with its dark green woods; and then Spike Island. And what a stir is yonder, early as it is. The men-of-war tenders seem alive with people, while still the little village is sunk in slumbers, not a smoke-wreath rising from its silent hearths. Every plash of the oars in the calm water, as I neared the land, every chance word of the bronzed and hardy fishermen, told upon my heart. I felt it was my home.

"Isn't it beautiful, sir?—isn't it illigant?" said a voice behind me, which there could be little doubt in my detecting, although I had not seen the individual since I left England.

"Is not what beautiful?" replied I, rather harshly, at the interruption of my own thoughts.

"Ireland, to be sure; and long life to her!" cried he with a cheer, that soon found its responsive echoes in the hearts of our sailors, who seconded the sentiment with all their energy.

"How am I to get up to Cork, lads?" said I. "I am pressed for time, and must get forward."

"We'll row your honor the whole way, av it's plazin' to you."

"Why, thank you; I'd rather find some quicker mode of proceeding."

"Maybe you'd have a chaise, sir; there's an illigant one at M'Cassidy's."

"Sure the blind mare's in foal," said the bow oar; "the divil a step she can go out of a walk; so, your honor, take Tim Riley's car, and you'll get up cheap. Not that you care for money; but he's going up at eight o'clock with two young ladies."

"Oh! be-gorra," said the other, "and so he is; and faix he might do worse—they're nice craytures."

"Well," said I, "your advice seems good; but perhaps they might object to my company."

"I've no fear; they're always with the officers. Sure the Miss Dalrymples ——"

"The Miss Dalrymples!—Push ahead, boys; it must be later than I thought; we must get the chaise; I can't wait."

Ten minutes more brought us to land.

*   *   *   *   *   *   *   *

My arrangements were soon made, and as my impatience to press forward became greater the nearer I drew to my destination, I lost not a moment.

The yellow chaise—sole glory of Cove—was brought forth at my request; and, by good fortune, four posters which had been down the preceding evening from Cork to some gentleman's seat near were about to return. These were also pressed into my service; and just as the first early riser of the little village was drawing his curtain to take a half-closed eye glance upon the breaking morning,

I rattled forth upon my journey at a pace which, could I only have secured its continuance, must soon have terminated my weary way.

Beautiful as the whole line of country is, I was totally unconscious of it; and even Mike's conversational powers, divided as they were between myself and the two postilions, were fruitless in arousing me from the deep preoccupation of my mind by thoughts of home.

It was, then, with some astonishment I heard the boy upon the wheeler ask whither he should drive me to.

"Tell his honor to wake up, we're in Cork now."

"In Cork! impossible already."

"Faith, maybe so—but it's Cork sure enough."

"Drive to the 'George;' it's not far from the Commander-in-Chief's quarters."

"'Tis five minutes' walk, sir; you'll be there before they're put to again."

"Horses for Fermoy!" shouted out the postilions, as we tore up to the door in a gallop. I sprang out, and, by the assistance of the waiter, discovered Sir Henry Howard's quarters, to whom my despatches were addressed. Having delivered them into the hands of an aide-de-camp, who sat bolt upright in his bed, rubbing his eyes to appear awake, I again hurried down stairs, and throwing myself into the chaise, continued my journey.

"Them's beautiful streets anyhow!" said Mike, "av they wasn't kept so dirty, and the houses so dark, and the pavement bad. That's Mr. Beamish's—that fine house there, with the brass rapper and the green lamp beside it: and there's the hospital; faix! and there's the place we beat the police, when I was here before; and the house with the sign of the Highlander is thrown down—and what's the big building with the stone posts at the door?"

"The bank, sir," said the postilion, with a most deferential air, as Mike addressed him.

"What bank, acushla?"

"Not a one of me knows, sir; but they call it the bank, though it's only an empty house."

"Cary' and Moore's Bank, perhaps?" said I, having heard that in days long past some such names had failed in Cork for a large amount.

"So it is; your honor's right," cried the postilion; while Mike, standing up on the box, and menacing the house with his clenched fist, shouted out at the very top of his voice,—

"Oh, bad luck to your cobwebbed windows and iron railings! sure it's my father's son ought to hate the sight of you."

"I hope your father never trusted his property in such hands?"

"I don't suspect he did, your honor; he never put much belief in the banks; but the house cost him dear enough without that."

As I could not help feeling some curiosity in this matter, I pressed Mickey for an explanation.

"But maybe it's not Cary and Moore's, after all; and I'm maybe cursing dacent people."

Having reassured his mind, by telling him that the reservation he made by the doubt would tell in their favor should he prove mistaken, he afforded me the following information:—

"When my father—the heavens be his bed!—was in the 'Cork,' they put him one night on guard at that same big house you just passed—av it was the same; but, if it wasn't that, it was another; and it was a beautiful fine night in August, and the moon up, and plenty of people walking about, and all kinds of fun and devilment going on—drinking and dancing, and everything.

"Well, my father was stuck up there, with his musket, to walk up and down, and not say, 'God save you kindly,' or the time of day, or anything, but just march as if he was in the barrack-yard; and by reason of his being the man he was, he didn't like it half, but kept cursing and swearing to himself like mad when he saw pleasant fellows and pretty girls going by, laughing and joking.

"'Good-evening, Mickey,' says one; 'fine sport ye have all to yourself, with your long feather in your cap.'

"'Arrah, look how proud he is,' says another, 'with his head up as if he didn't see a body.'

"'Shoulder hoo!' cried a drunken chap, with a shovel in his hand. They all began laughing away at my father.

"'Let the dacent man alone,' said an ould fellow in a wig; 'isn't he guarding the bank, wid all the money in it?'

"'Faix he isn't,' says another, 'for there's none left.'

"'What's that you're saying?' says my father.

"'Just that the bank's broke, devil a more,' says he.

"'And there's no goold in it?' says my father.

"'Divil a guinea.'

"'Nor silver?'

"'No, nor silver, nor as much as sixpence, either.'

"'Didn't ye hear that all day yesterday, when the people was coming in with their notes, the chaps there were heating the guineas in a frying-pan, pretending that they were making them as fast as they could; and sure, when they had a batch red-hot they spread them out to cool; and what between the heating and the cooling, and the burning the fingers counting them, they kept the bank open to three o'clock, and then they ran away.'

"'Is it truth yer telling?' says my father.

"'Sorra word o' lie in it! myself had two-and-fourpence of their notes.'

"'And so they're broke,' says my father, 'and nothing left?'

"'Not a brass farden.'

"'And what am I staying here for, I wonder, if there's nothing to guard?'

"'Faix, if it isn't for the pride of the thing——'

"'Oh, sorra taste.'

"'Well, maybe for divarsion.'

"'Nor that either.'

"'Faix! then, you're a droll man, to spend the evening that way,' says he; and all the crowd—for there was a crowd—said the same. So with that my father unscrewed his bayonet, and put his piece on his shoulder, and walked off to his bed in the barrack as peaceable as need be. But well, when they came to relieve him, wasn't there a raal commotion? and faith, you see, it went mighty hard with my father the next morning; for the bank was open just as usual, and my father was sintinced to fifty lashes, but got off with a week in prison, and three more rowling a big stone in the barrack-yard."

Thus chatting away, the time passed over, until we arrived at Fermoy. Here there was some little delay in procuring horses; and during the negotiation, Mike, who usually made himself master of the circumstances of every place through which he passed, discovered that the grocer's shop of the village was kept by a namesake, and possibly a relation of his own.

"I always had a notion, Mr. Charles, that I came from a good stock; and sure enough, here's 'Mary Free' over the door there, and a beautiful place inside; full of tay and sugar, and gingerbread, and glue, and coffee, and bran, pickled herrings, soap, and many other commodities."

"Perhaps you'd like to claim kindred, Mike," said I, interrupting; "I'm sure she'd feel flattered to discover a relative in a Peninsular hero."

"It's just what I'm thinking; av we were going to pass the evening here, I'd try if I couldn't make her out a second cousin at least."

Fortune upon this occasion seconded Mike's wishes, for when the horses made their appearance, I learned to my surprise that the near side one would not bear a saddle, and the off-sider could only run on his own side. In this conjuncture, the postilion was obliged to drive from what, *Hibernicè* speaking, is called the perch—no ill-applied denomination to a piece of wood which, about the thickness of one's arm, is hung between the two fore-springs, and serves as a resting-place, in which the luckless wight, weary of the saddle, is not sorry to repose himself.

"What's to be done?" cried I. "There's no room within; my traps barely leave space for myself amongst them."

"Sure, sir," said the postilion, "the other gentleman can follow in the morning coach; and if any accident happens to yourself on the road, by reason of a breakdown, he'll be there as soon as yourself."

This, at least, was an agreeable suggestion, and, as I saw it chimed with Mike's notions, I acceded at once; he came running up at the moment.

"I had a peep at her through the window, Mister Charles, and, faix, she has a great look of the family."

"Well, Mickey, I'll leave you twenty-four hours to cultivate the acquaintance; and to a man like you, I know the time is ample. Follow me by the morning's coach. Till then, good-bye."

Away we rattled once more, and soon left the town behind us. The wild mountain tract which stretched on either side of the road presented one bleak and brown surface, unrelieved by any trace of tillage or habitation; an apparently endless succession of fern-clad hills lay on every side; above, the gloomy sky of leaden, louring aspect frowned darkly; the sad and wailing cry of the pewit or the plover was the only sound that broke the stillness, and far as the eye could reach, a dreary waste extended. The air, too, was cold and chilly; it was one of those days which, in our springs, seemed to cast a retrospective glance towards the winter they have left behind them. The prospect was no cheering one; from heaven above or earth below there came no sight nor sound of gladness. The rich glow of the Peninsular landscape was still fresh in my memory— the luxurious verdure—the olive, the citron, and the vine—the fair valleys teeming with abundance—the mountains terraced with their vineyards—the blue transparent sky spreading o'er all—while the very air was rife with the cheering song of birds that peopled every grove. What a contrast was here! We travelled on for miles, but no village nor one human face did we see. Far in the distance a thin wreath of smoke curled upward; but it came from no hearth; it arose from one of those field-fires by which spendthrift husbandry cultivates the ground. It was indeed sad; and yet, I know not how, it spoke more home to my heart than all the brilliant display and all the voluptuous splendor I had witnessed in London. By degrees some traces of wood made their appearance, and, as we descended the mountain towards Cahir, the country assumed a more cultivated and cheerful look; patches of corn or of meadow-land stretched on either side, and the voice of children, and the lowing of oxen, mingled with the cawing of the rooks, as in dense clouds they followed the ploughman's track. The changed features of the prospect resembled the alternate phases of temperament of the dweller in the soil—the gloomy determination—the smiling carelessness—the dark spirit of boding—the reckless jollity—the almost savage ferocity of purpose, followed by a child-like docility and a womanly softness—the grave, the gay, the resolute, the fickle—the firm, the yielding, the unsparing, and the tender-hearted, blending their contrarieties into one nature, of whose capabilities one cannot predicate the bounds, but to whom, by some luckless fatality of fortune, the great rewards of life have been generally withheld, until one begins to feel that the curse of Swift was less the sarcasm wrung from indignant failures than the cold and stern prophecy of the moralist.

But how have I fallen into this strain? Let me rather turn my eyes forward towards my home. How shall I find all there? Have his altered fortunes damped the warm ardor of my poor uncle's heart? Is his smile sicklied over by sorrow? Or shall I hear his merry laugh, and his cheerful voice, as in days of yore? How I longed to take my place beside that hearth, and, in the same oak-chair where I have sat telling the bold adventures of a fox-chase or some long day upon the moors, speak of the scenes of my campaigning life, and make known to him those gallant fellows by whose side I have charged in battle or sat in the bivouac! How will he glory in the soldier-like spirit and daring energy of Fred Power! How will he chuckle over the blundering earnestness and Irish warmth of O'Shaughnessy! How will he laugh at the quaint stories and quainter jests of Maurice Quill! And how often will he wish once more to be young in hand as in heart to mingle with such gay fellows, with no other care, no other sorrow to depress him, save the passing fortune of a soldier's life!

CHAPTER XLIV.

THE RETURN.

WHILE lying asleep in the corner of the chaise, a rude shock awoke me; a shout followed, and the next moment the door was torn open, and I heard the postilion's voice crying:

"Spring out! jump out quickly, sir!"

A whole battery of kicks upon the front panel drowned the rest of his speech; but before I could obey his injunction, he was pitched upon the road, the chaise rolled over, and the pole snapped short in the middle, while the two horses belabored the carriage and each other with all their might. Managing as well as I was able to extricate myself, I leaped out upon the road, and by the aid of a knife, and at the cost of some bruises, succeeded in freeing the horses from their tackle. The postboy, who had escaped without any serious injury, labored manfully to aid me, blubbering the whole time upon the consequences his misfortune would bring down upon his head.

"Bad luck to ye!" cried he, apostrophizing the off-horse, a tall, raw-boned beast, with a Roman nose, a dipped back, and a tail ragged and jagged like a hand-saw. "Bad luck to ye! there never was a good one of your color!"

This, for the information of the "unjockeyed," I may add, was a species of brindled gray.

"How did it happen, Patsey—how did it happen, my lad?"

"It was the heap o' stones they left in the road since last autumn; and though I riz him at it fairly, he dragged the ould mare over it and broke the pole. Oh, wirra, wirra!" cried he, wringing his hands in an agony of grief, "sure there's neither luck nor grace to be had with ye since the day ye drew the judge down to the last assizes!"

"Well! what's to be done?"

"Sorra a bit o' me knows; the shay's ruined intirely, and the old devil there knows he's conquered us. Look at him there, listening to every word we're saying! You eternal thief! maybe its ploughing you'd like better."

"Come, come," said I, "this will never get us forward. What part of the country are we in?"

"We left Banagher about four miles behind us; that's Killimur you see with the smoke there in the hollow."

Now, although I did not see Killimur (for the gray mist of the morning prevented me recognizing any object a few hundred yards distant), yet, from the direction in which he pointed, and from the course of the Shannon, which I could trace indistinctly, I obtained a pretty accurate notion of where we were.

"Then, we are not very far from Portumna?"

"Just a pleasant walk before your breakfast."

"And is there not a short cut to O'Malley Castle over that mountain?"

"Faix and so there is; and ye can be no stranger to these parts if ye know that."

"I have travelled it before now. Just tell me, is the wooden bridge standing over the little stream? It used to be carried away every winter, in my time."

41

"It's just the same now. You'll have to pass by the upper ford; but it comes to the same, for that will bring you to the back gate of the demesne, and one way is just as short as the other."

"I know it, I know it; so now, do you follow me with my luggage to the castle, and I'll set out on foot."

So saying, I threw off my cloak, and prepared myself for a sharp walk of some eight miles over the mountain. As I reached the little knoll of land, which, overlooking the Shannon, affords a view of several miles in every direction, I stopped to gaze upon the scene, where every object around was familiar to me from infancy. The broad, majestic river, sweeping in bold curves between the wild mountains of Connaught and the wooded hills and cultivated slopes of the more fertile Munster—the tall chimneys of many a house rose above the dense woods, where in my boyhood I had spent hours and days of happiness. One last look I turned towards the scene of my late catastrophe, ere I began to descend the mountain. The postboy, with the happy fatalism of his country, and a firm trust in the future, had established himself in the interior of the chaise, from which a blue curl of smoke wreathed upward from his pipe; the horses grazed contentedly by the roadside, and were I to judge from the evidence before me, I should say that I was the only member of the party inconvenienced by the accident. A thin sleeting of rain began to fall, the wind blew sharply in my face, and the dark clouds, collecting in. masses above, seemed to threaten a storm. Without stopping for even a passing look at the many well-known spots about, I pressed rapidly on. My old experience upon the moors had taught me that sling trot in which, jumping from hillock to hillock, over the boggy surface, you succeed in accomplishing your journey not only with considerable speed, but perfectly dryshod.

By the lonely path which I travelled, it was unlikely I should meet any one; it was rarely traversed except by the foot of the sportsman, or some stray messenger from the castle to the town of Banagher. Its solitude, however, was in nowise distasteful to me; my heart was full to bursting. Each moment as I walked, some new feature of my home presented itself before me. Now, it was all happiness and comfort; the scene of its ancient hospitable board, its warm hearth, its happy faces, and its ready welcome, were all before me, and I increased my speed to the utmost, when suddenly a sense of sad and sorrowing foreboding would draw around me, and the image of my uncle's sick bed, his worn features, his pallid look, his broken voice, would strike upon my heart, and all the changes that poverty, desertion, and decay can bring to pass, would fall upon my heart, and, weak and trembling, I would stand for some moments unable to proceed.

Oh! how many a reproachful thought came home to me at what I scrupled not to call to myself the desertion of my home. Oh! how many a prayer I uttered, in all the fervor of devotion, that my selfish waywardness, and my yearning for ambition, might not bring upon me in after-life years of unavailing regret! As I thought thus, I reached the brow of a little mountain ridge, beneath which, at the distance of scarcely more than a mile, the dark woods of O'Malley Castle stretched before me. The house itself was not visible, for it was situated in a valley beside the river; but there lay the whole scene of my boyhood—there the little creek where my boat was kept, and where I landed on the morning after my duel with Bodkin; there stretched, for many a mile, the large, callow meadows, where I trained my horses, and schooled them for the coming season; and far in the distance, the brown and rugged peak of old Scariff was lost in the clouds. The rain by this time had ceased, the wind had fallen, and an almost unnatural stillness prevailed around. But yet the heavy masses of vapor frowned ominously, and the leaden hue of land and water wore a gloomy and depressing aspect. My impatience to get on increased every moment. Descending the mountain at the top of my speed, I at length reached the little oak paling that skirted the wood, opened the little wicket, and entered the path. It was the selfsame one I had trod in reverie and meditation the night before I left my home. I remember, too, sitting down beside the little well which, enclosed in a frame of rock, ran trickling across the path, to be lost among the gnarled roots and fallen leaves around. Yes, this was the very spot.

Overcome for the instant by my exertion and my emotion, I sat down upon the stone, and, taking off my cap, bathed my heated and throbbing temples in the cold spring. Refreshed at once, I was about to rise and press onward, when suddenly my attention was caught by a sound which, faint from the distance, scarce struck upon my ear. I listened again, but all was still and silent; the dull plash of the river, as it broke upon the reedy shore, was the only sound I heard. Thinking it probably some mere delusion of my heated imagination, I rose to push forward; but at the moment a slight breeze stirred in the leaves around me, the light branches rustled and bent beneath it, and a low, moaning sound swelled upward, increasing each instant as it came. Like the distant roar of some mighty torrent, it grew louder as the wind bore it towards me, and now falling, now swelling, it burst forth into one loud prolonged cry of agony and grief. Oh God! it was the death wail! I fell upon my knees, my hands clasped in agony; the sweat of misery dropped off my brow, and with a heart bleeding and breaking, I prayed—I know not what. Again the terrible cry smote upon my ear, and I could mark the horrible cadences of the death-song, as the voices of the mourners joined in chorus.

My suspense became too great to bear. I dashed madly forward, one sound still ringing in my ears, one horrid image before my eyes. I reached the garden-wall; I cleared the little rivulet beside the flower-garden. I traversed its beds (neglected and decayed), I gained the avenue, taking no heed of the crowds before me—some on foot, some on horseback, others mounted upon the low country car, many seated in groups upon the grass, their heads bowed upon their bosoms, silent and speechless. As I neared the house, the whole approach was crowded with carriages and horsemen; at the foot of the large flight of steps stood the black and mournful hearse, its plumes nodding in the breeze. With the speed of madness and the recklessness of despair, I tore my way through the thickly-standing groups upon the steps; I could not speak, I could not utter. Once more the frightful cry swelled upward, and its wild notes seemed to paralyze me; for, with my hands upon my temples, I stood motionless and still. A heavy footfall, as of persons marching in procession, came nearer and nearer, and, as the sounds without sank into sobs of bitterness and woe, the black pall of a coffin, borne on men's shoulders, appeared at the door, and an old man, whose gray hair floated in the breeze, and across whose stern features a struggle for self-mastery—a kind of spasmodic effort—was playing, held out his hand to enforce silence. His eye, lack-lustre and dimmed with age, roved over the assembled multitude, but there was no recognition in his look until at last he turned it on me. A slight hectic flush covered his pale cheek, his lip trembled, he essayed to speak, but could not. I sprang towards him, but, choked by agony, I could not utter; my look, however, spoke what my tongue could not. He threw his arms around me, and, muttering the words "Poor Godfrey!" pointed to the coffin.

CHAPTER XLV.

HOME.

MANY years have passed away since the time I am now about to speak of, and yet I cannot revert, even for a moment, to the period without a sad and depressing feeling at my heart. The wreck of fortune, the thwarting of ambition, the failure of enterprise, great though they be, are endurable evils. The never-dying hope that youth is blessed with will find its resting-place still within the breast, and the baffled and beaten will struggle on unconquered; but for the death of friends, for the loss of those in whom our dearest affections were centred, there is no solace; the terrible "never" of the grave knows no remorse, and even memory, that in our saddest hours can bring bright images and smiling faces before us, calls up here only the departed shade of happiness, a passing look at that Eden of our joys from which we are separated forever. And the desolation of the heart is never perfect till it has felt the echoes of a last farewell on earth reverberating within it.

Oh, with what tortures of self-reproach we think of all former intercourse with him that is gone! How would we wish to live our lives once more, correcting each passage of unkindness or neglect! How deeply do we blame ourselves for occasions of benefit lost, and opportunities unprofited by; and how unceasingly, through after-life, the memory of the departed recurs to us! In all the ties which affection and kindred weave around us, one vacant spot is there, unseen and unknown by others, which no blandishments of love, no caresses of friendship, can fill up. Although the rank grass and the tall weeds of the churchyard may close around the humble tomb, the cemetery of the heart is holy and sacred, pure from all the troubled thoughts and daily cares of the busy world. To that hallowed spot do we retire as into our chamber, and when unrewarded efforts bring discomfiture and misery to our minds, when our friends are false, and cherished hopes are blasted, we think on those who never ceased to love till they had ceased to live; and in the lonely solitude of our affliction we call upon those who hear not, and may never return.

*　　*　　*　　*　　*　　*　　*　　*

Mine was a desolate hearth. I sat moodily down in the old oak parlor, my heart bowed down with grief. The noiseless steps, the mourning garments of the old servants, the unnatural silence of those walls within which from my infancy the sounds of merriment and mirth had been familiar, the large old-fashioned chair where he was wont to sit, now placed against the wall,—all spoke of the sad past. Yet when some footsteps would draw near, and the door would open, I could not repress a thrill of hope that he was coming; more than once I rushed to the window and looked out; I could have sworn I heard his voice.

The old cob pony he used to ride was grazing peacefully before the door; poor Carlo, his favorite spaniel, lay stretched upon the terrace, turning ever and anon a look towards the window, and then, as if wearied of watching for him who came not, he would utter a long, low, wailing cry, and lie down again to sleep. The rich lawn, decked with field flowers of many a hue, stretched away towards the river, upon whose calm surface the white-sailed lugger scarce seemed to move; the sounds of a well-known Irish air came, softened by distance, as some poor fisherman sat mending his net upon the bank and the laugh of children floated on the breeze. Yes, they were happy!

Two months had elapsed since my return home; how passed by me I know not; a lethargic stupor had settled upon me. Whole days long I sat at the window, looking listlessly at the tranquil river and watching the white foam as, borne down from the rapids, it floated lazily along. The Count had left me soon, being called up to Dublin by some business, and I was utterly alone. The different families about called frequently to ask after me, and would, doubtless, have done all in their power to alleviate my sorrow and lighten the load of my affliction; but with a morbid fear, I avoided every one, and rarely left the house except at nightfall, and then only to stroll by some lonely and deserted path.

Life had lost its charm for me; my gratified ambition had ended in the blackest disappointment, and all for which I had labored and longed was only attained that I might feel it valueless.

Of my circumstances as to fortune I knew nothing, and cared not more; poverty and riches could matter little now; all my day-dreams were dissipated now, and I only waited for Considine's return to leave Ireland forever. I had made up my mind, if, by any unexpected turn of fate, the war should cease in the Peninsula, to exchange into an Indian regiment. The daily association with objects which recalled but one image to my brain, and that ever accompanied by remorse of conscience, gave me not a moment's peace. My every thought of happiness was mixed up with scenes which now presented nothing but the evidences of blighted hope. To remain, then, where I was, would be to sink into the heartless misanthropist, and I resolved that with my sword I would carve out a soldier's fortune and a soldier's grave.

Considine came at last. I was sitting alone, at my usual post beside the window, when the chaise rattled up to the door. For an instant I started to my legs; a vague something like hope shot through me; the whole might be a dream, and *he*—— The next moment I became cold and sick, a faintish giddiness obscured my sight, and though I felt his grasp as he took my hand, I saw him not.

An indistinct impression still dwells upon my mind of his chiding me for my weakness in thus giving way; of his calling upon me to assert my position, and discharge the duties of him whose successor I now was. I heard him in silence, and, when he concluded, faintly pledging myself to obey him, I hurried to my room, and throwing myself upon my bed, burst into an agony of tears. Hitherto my pent-up sorrow had wasted me day by day; but the rock was now smitten, and in that gush of misery my heart found relief.

When I appeared the following morning, the Count was struck with my altered looks. A settled sorrow could not conceal the changes which time and manhood had made upon me.; and as from a kind of fear of showing how deeply I grieved, I endeavored to conceal it, by degrees I was enabled to converse calmly and dispassionately upon my fortunes.

"Poor Godfrey," said he, "appointed me his sole executor a few days before it happened; he knew the time was drawing near, and, strange enough, Charley, though he heard of your return to England, he would not let us write. The papers spoke of you as being at Carlton House almost daily; your name appeared at every great festival; and, while his heart warmed at your brilliant success, he absolutely dreaded your coming home. 'Poor fellow!' he would say, 'what a change for him, to leave the splendor and magnificence of his Prince's board for our meagre fare and altered fortunes! And then,' he added, 'as for me—God forgive me! I can go now—but how should I bear to part with him if he comes back to me?' And now," said the Count, when he had concluded a detailed history of my dear uncle's last illness—"and now, Charley, what are your plans?"

Briefly, and in a few words, I stated to him my intentions. Without placing much stress upon the strongest of my reasons—my distaste to what had once been home—I avowed my wish to join my regiment at once.

He heard me with evident impatience, and, as I finished, seized my arm in his strong grasp. "No, no, boy,—none of this; your tone of assumed composure cannot impose on Bill Considine. You must not return to the Peninsula—at least, not yet awhile; the disgust of life may be strong at twenty, but it's not lasting; besides, Charley,"—here his voice faltered slightly—"*his* wishes you'll not treat lightly. Read this."

As he spoke, he took a blotted and ill-written letter from his breast-pocket, and handed it to me. It was in my poor uncle's hand, and dated the very morning of his death. It ran thus:

"DEAR BILL:—Charley must never part with the old house, come what will; I leave too many ties behind for a stranger's heritage; he must live among my old friends, and watch, protect, and comfort them. He has done enough for fame; let him now do something for affection. We have none of us been over good to these poor people; one of the name must try and save our credit. God bless you both! It is perhaps the last time I shall utter it.

"G. O'M."

I read these few and, to me, affecting lines over and over, forgetful of all save of him who penned them; when Considine, who supposed that my silence was attributable to doubt and hesitation, called out:

"Well, what now?"

"I remain," said I, briefly.

He seized me in his arms with transport, as he said:

"I know it, boy—I knew it. They told me you were spoiled by flattery, and your head turned by fortune; they said that home and country would weigh lightly in the balance against fame and glory; but I said no, I knew you better. I told them indignantly that I had nursed you on my knee; that I watched you from infancy to boyhood, from boy to man; that he of whose stock you came had one feeling paramount to all, his love of his own fatherland, and that you would not disgrace him. Besides, Charley, there's not an humble hearth for many a long mile around us where, amid the winter's blast—tempered, not excluded, by frail walls and poverty— there's not one such but where poor Godfrey's name rises each night in prayer, and blessings are invoked on him by those who never felt them themselves."

"I'll not desert them."

"I know you'll not, boy—I know you'll not. Now for the means."

Here he entered into a long and complicated account of my dear uncle's many difficulties, by which it appeared that, in order to leave the estate free of debt to me, he had for years past undergone severe privations. These, however—such is the misfortune of unguided effort—had but ill succeeded; and there was scarcely a farm on the property without its mortgage. Upon the house and demesne a bond for three thousand pounds still remained; and to pay off this, Considine advised my selling a portion of the property.

"It's old Blake lent the money; and only a week before your uncle died he served a notice for repayment. I never told Godfrey —it was no use; it could only embitter his last few hours; and, besides, we had six months to think of it. The half of that time has now elapsed, however; we must see to this."

"And did Blake really make this demand, knowing my poor uncle's difficulties?"

"Why, I half think he did not, for Godfrey was too fine a fellow ever to acknowledge anything of the sort. He had twelve sheep killed for the poor in Scariff, at a time when not a servant of the house tasted meat for months; ay, and our own table, too, none of the most abundant, I assure you."

What a picture was this! and how forcibly did it remind me of what I had witnessed in times past. Thus meditating, we returned to the house; and Considine, whose activity never slumbered, sat down to con over the rent-roll with old Maguire the steward.

When I joined the Count in the evening, I found him surrounded by maps, rent-rolls, surveys, and leases. He had been poring over those various documents, to ascertain from which portion of the property we could best recruit our falling finances. To judge from the embarrassed look and manner with which he met me, the matter was one of no small difficulty. The incumbrances upon the estate had been incurred with an unsparing hand; and except where some irreclaimable tract of bog or mountain rendered a loan impracticable, each portion of the property had its share of debt.

"You can't sell Killantry, for Basset has above six thousand pounds on it already; to be sure, there's the Priest's Meadows—fine land and in good heart; but Malony was an old tenant of the family, and I cannot recommend your turning him over to a stranger. The Widow M'Bride's farm is perhaps the best, after all, and it would certainly bring the sum we want; still, poor Mary was your nurse, Charley, and it would break her heart to do it."

Thus, wherever we turned, some obstacle presented itself, if not from moneyed causes, at least from those ties and associations which, in an attached and faithful tenantry, are sure to grow up between them and the owner of the soil.

Feeling how all-important these things were—endeavoring as I was to fulfil the will and work out the intentions of my uncle, I saw at once that to sell any portion of the property must separate me, to a certain extent, from those who had long looked up to our house, and who, in the feudalism of the west, could ill withdraw their allegiance from their own chief to swear fealty to a stranger. The richer tenants were those whose industry and habits rendered them objects of worth and attachment; to the poorer ones, to whose improvidence and whose follies (if you will) their poverty is owing, I was bound by those ties which the ancient habit of my house had contracted for centuries; the bond of benefit conferred can be stronger than the debt of gratitude itself. What was I then to do? My income would certainly permit of my paying the interest upon the several mortgages, and still retaining wherewithal to live; the payment of Blake's bond was my only difficulty, and, small as it was, it was still a difficulty.

"I have it, Charley!" said Considine; "I've found out the way of doing it. Blake will have no objection, I'm sure, to take the widow's farm in payment of his debt, giving you a power of redemption within five years. In that time, what with economy—some management—perhaps," added he, smiling slightly—"perhaps a wife with money, may relieve all your embarrassments at once. Well, well, I know you are not thinking of that just now; but come, what say you to my plan?"

"I know not well what to say. It seems to be the best; but still I have my misgivings."

"Of course you have, my boy; nor could I love you if you'd part with an old and faithful follower without them. But, after all, she is only a hostage to the enemy: we'll win her back, Charley."

"If you think so——"

"I do. I know it."

"Well, then, be it so; only one thing I bargain—she must herself consent to this change of masters. It will seem to her a harsh measure that the child she had nursed and fondled in her arms should live to disunite her from those her oldest attachments upon earth. We must take care, sir, that Blake cannot dispossess her; this would be too hard."

"No, no; that we'll guard against. And now, Charley, with prudence and caution, we'll clear off every encumbrance, and O'Malley Castle shall yet be what it was in days of yore. Ay, boy! with the descendant of the old house for its master, and not that general—how do you call him?—who came down here to contest the county, who, with his offer of thirty thousand pounds, thought to uproot the oldest family of the west. Did I ever show you the letter we wrote him?"

"No, sir," replied I, trembling with agitation as I spoke; "you merely alluded to it in one of yours."

"Look here, lad!" said he, drawing it from the recesses of a black leather pocket-book. "I took a copy of it. Read that."

The document was dated "O'Malley Castle, Dec. 9." It ran thus:

"Sir:—I have this moment learned from my agent that you, or some one empowered by you for the purpose, made an offer of several thousand pounds to buy up the different mortgages upon my property, with a subsequent intention of becoming its possessor. Now, sir, I beg to tell you that if your ungentlemanlike and underhand plot had succeeded, you dared not darken with your shadow the doorsill of the house you purchased. Neither your gold nor your flattery—and I hear you are rich in both—could wipe out from the minds and hearts of my poor tenantry the kindness of centuries. Be advised, then, sir; withdraw your offer. Let a Galway gentleman settle his own difficulties in his own way; his troubles and cares are quite sufficient, without your adding to them. There can be but one mode in which your interference with him could be deemed acceptable; need I tell you, sir, who are a soldier, how that is? As I know your official duties are important, and as my nephew—who feels with me perfectly in this business—is abroad, I can only say that failing health and a broken frame shall not prevent my undertaking a journey to England, should my doing so meet your wishes on that occasion.

<blockquote>"I am, sir, your obedient servant,
GODFREY O'MALLEY."</blockquote>

"This letter," continued Considine, "I enclosed in an envelope, with the following few lines of my own :—

"'Count Considine presents his compliments to ˌLieutenant-General Dashwood, and feeling that, as the friend of Mr. Godfrey O'Malley, the mild course pursued by that gentleman may possibly be attributed to his suggestion, he begs to assure General Dashwood that the reverse was the case, and that he strenuously counselled the propriety of laying a horsewhip upon the General's shoulders, as a preliminary step in the transaction.

"'Count Considine's address is No. 16 Kildare street.'"

"Great God!" said I, "is this possible?"

"Well may you say so, my boy; for—would you believe it?—after all that, he writes a long, blundering apology, protesting I know not what about motives of former friendship, and terminating with a civil hint that we have done with him forever. Of my paragraph he takes no notice; and thus ends the whole affair."

"And with it my last hope also!" muttered I to myself.

That Sir George Dashwood's intentions had been misconstrued and mistaken I knew perfectly well; that nothing but the accumulated evils of poverty and sickness could have induced my poor uncle to write such a letter I was well aware; but now, the mischief was accomplished, the evil was done, and nothing remained but to bear with patience and submission, and to endeavor to forget what thus became irremediable.

"Did Sir George Dashwood make no allusion to me, sir, in his reply?" inquired I, catching at anything like a hope.

"Your name never occurs in his letter. But you look pale, boy; all these discussions come too early upon you; besides, you stay too much at home, and take no exercise."

So saying, Considine bustled off towards the stables, to look after some young horses that had just been taken up; and I walked out alone, to ponder over what I had heard, and meditate on my plans for the future.

CHAPTER XLVI.

AN OLD ACQUAINTANCE.

THE irritation of my spirit gradually subsided as I wandered on. It was, to be sure, distressing to think over the light in which my uncle's letter had placed me before Sir George Dashwood, had even my reputation only with him been at stake; but with my attachment to his daughter, it was almost maddening. And yet there was nothing to be done; to disavow my participation would be to throw discredit upon my uncle. Thus were my hopes blighted; and thus, at that season when life was opening upon me, did I feel careless and indifferent to everything. Had my military career still remained to me, that, at least, would have suggested scenes sufficient to distract me from the past; but now my days must be spent where every spot teemed with memories of bygone happiness and joys never to come back again.

My mind was, however, made up, and I turned homeward. Without speaking a word to Considine, I sat down at my writing-table. In a few brief lines I informed my army agent of my intention of leaving the service, and desired that he would sell out for me at once. Fearing lest my resolution might not be proof against the advice and solicitation of my friends, I cautioned him against giving my address, or any clue by which letters might reach me.

This done, I addressed a short note to Mr. Blake, requesting to know the name of his solicitor in whose hands the bond was placed, and announcing my intention of immediate repayment.

Trifling as these details were in themselves, I cannot help recording how completely they changed the whole current of my thoughts. A new train of interests began to spring up within me; and where so lately the clang of the battle, the ardor of the march, the careless ease of the bivouac, had engrossed every feeling, now more humble and homely thoughts succeeded; and as my personal ambition had lost its stimulant, I turned with pleasure to those of whose fate and fortunes I was in some sort the guardian. There may be many a land where the verdure blooms more in fragrance and in richness,— where the clime breathes softer, and a brighter sky lights up the landscape; but there is none—I have travelled through many a one —where more touching and heart-bound associations are blended with the features of the soil than in Ireland, and cold must be the spirit and barren the affections of him who can dwell amid its mountains and its valleys, its tranquil lakes, its wooded fens, without feeling their humanizing influence upon him. Thus gradually new impressions and new duties succeeded; and ere four months elapsed, the quiet monotony of my daily life healed up' the wounds of my suffering. In the calm current of my present existence, a sense of content, if not of happiness, crept gently over me, and I ceased to long for the clash of arms and the loud blast of the trumpet.

Unlike all my former habits, I quickly abandoned the sports of the field. He who had participated in them with me was no longer there; and the very sight of the tackle itself suggested sad and depressing thoughts.

My horses I took but little pleasure in. To gratify the good and kind people about, I would walk through the stables, and make some passing remark, as if to show some interest; but I felt it not. No: it was only by the total change of all the ordinary channels of my ideas that I could bear up; and now my days were passed in the fields, either listlessly strolling along, or in watching the laborers as they worked. Of my neighbors I saw nothing; returning their calls, when they called upon me, was the extent of our intercourse; and I had no desire for any further. As Considine had left me to visit some friends in the south, I was quite alone; and, for the first time in my life, felt how soothing can be such-solitude. In each happy face, in every grateful look around me, I felt that I was fulfilling my uncle's last behest; and the sense of duty, so strong when it falls upon the heart accompanied by the sense of power, made my days pass rapidly away.

It was towards the close of autumn, when I one morning received a letter from London, informing me that my troop had been sold and the purchase-money—above four thousand pounds—lodged to my credit at my banker's.

As Mr. Blake had merely answered my former note by a civil message that the matter in question was by no means pressing, I lost not a moment, when this news reached me, to despatch Mike to Gurt-na-Morra with a few lines, expressing my anxious desire to finish the transaction, and begging of Mr. Blake to appoint a day for the purpose.

To this application Mr. Blake's reply was that he would do himself the honor of waiting upon me the following day, when the arrangements I desired could be agreed upon. Now this was exactly what I wished, if possible, to avoid. Of all my neighbors, he was the one I predetermined to have no intercourse with. I had not forgotten my last evening at his house, nor had I forgiven his conduct to my uncle. However, there was nothing for it but submission; the interview need not be long, and it should be a last one. Thus resolving, I waited in patience for the morrow.

I was seated at my breakfast the next morning, conning between whiles the columns of the last paper, and feeding my spaniel, who sat upon a large chair beside me, when the door opened, and the servant announced "Mr. Blake;" and the instant after that gentleman bustled in, holding out both his hands with all evidences of most friendly warmth, and calling out,

"Charley O'Malley, my lad! I'm delighted to see you at last!"

Now, although the distance from the door to the table at which I sat was not many paces, yet was it quite sufficient to chill down all my respectable relative's ardor before he approached; his rapid pace became gradually a shuffle, a slide, and finally a dead stop; his extended arms were reduced to one hand, barely advanced beyond his waistcoat; his voice, losing the easy confidence of its former tone, got husky and dry, and broke into a cough; and all these changes were indebted to the mere fact of my reception of him consisting in a cold and distant bow, as I told the servant to place a chair and leave the room.

Without any preliminary whatever, I opened the subject of our negotiation, expressed my regret that it should have waited so long, and my desire to complete it.

Whether it was that the firm and resolute tone I assumed had its effect at once, or that, disappointed at the mode in which I received his advances, he wished to conclude our interview as soon as need be, I know not; but he speedily withdrew from a capacious pocket a document in parchment, which having spread at large upon the table, and having leisurely put on his spectacles, he began to hum over its contents to himself in an undertone.

"Yes, sir, here it is," said he. "'Deed of conveyance between Godfrey O'Malley, of O'Malley Castle, Esq., on the one part'—perhaps you'd like your solicitor to examine it,—'and Blake, of Gurt'—because there is no hurry, Captain O'Malley,—'on the other.' In fact, after all, it is a mere matter of form between relatives," said he, as I declined the intervention of a lawyer. "I'm not in want of the money—'all the lands and tenements adjoining, in trust, for the payment of the said three thousand'—thank God, Captain, the sum is a trifle that does not inconvenience me. The boys are provided for; and the girls—the pickpockets, as I call them,—ha, ha, ha!—not ill off neither;—'with rights of turbary on the said premises'—who are most anxious to have the pleasure of seeing you. Indeed, I could scarcely keep Jane from coming over to-day. 'Sure he's my cousin,' says she; 'and what harm would it be if I went to see him?' Wild, good-natured girls, Captain! And your old friend Matthew—you haven't forgot Matthew?—has been keeping three coveys of partridge for you this fortnight. 'Charley,' says he—they call you Charley still, Captain—'shall have them, and no one else.' And poor Mary—she was a child when you were here—Mary is working a sash for you. But I'm forgetting—I know you have so much business on your hands——"

"Pray, Mr. Blake, be seated. I know nothing of any more importance than the matter before us. If you will permit me to give you a check for this money. The papers, I'm sure, are perfectly correct."

"If I only thought it did not inconvenience you——"

"Nothing of the kind, I assure you. Shall I say at sight, or in ten days hence?"

"Whenever you please, Captain. But it's sorry I am to come troubling you about such things, when I know you're thinking of other matters. And, as I said before, the money does not signify to me; the times, thank God, are good, and I've never been very improvident."

"I think you'll find that correct."

"Oh, to be sure it is! Well, well; I'm going away without saying half what I intended."

"Pray do not hurry yourself. I have not asked have you breakfasted, for I remember Galway habits too well for that. But if I might offer you a glass of sherry and water after your ride?"

"Will you think me a beast if I say yes, Captain? Time was when I didn't care for a canter of ten or fifteen miles in the morning no more than yourself; and that's no small boast. God forgive me, but I never see that clover-field where you pounded the Englishman, without swearing there never was a leap made before or since. Is this Mickey, Captain? Faith, and it's a fine, brown, hearty-looking chap you're grown, Mickey. That's mighty pleasant sherry! but where would there be good wine if it wasn't here? Oh! I remember now what it was I wanted. Peter—my son Peter, a slip of a boy—he's only sixteen—well, d'ye see, he's downright deranged about the army: he used to see your name in the papers every day, and that terrible business at—what's the name of the place?—where you rode on the chap's back up the breach."

"Ciudad Rodrigo, perhaps," said I, scarcely able to suppress a laugh.

"Well, sir, since that, he'll hear of nothing but going into the army; ay, and into the dragoons too. Now, Captain, isn't it mighty expensive in the dragoons?"

"Why, no, not particularly so—at least in the regiment I served with."

"I promised him I'd ask you; the boy's mad, that's the fact. I wish, Captain, you'd just reason with him a little; he'll mind what *you* say—there's no fear of that; and you see, though I'd like to do what's fair, I'm not going to cut off the girls for the sake of the boys;

with the blessing of Providence they'll never be able to reproach me
for that. What I say is this: treat *me* well, and I'll treat you the
same. Marry the man my choice would pick out for you, and it's
not a matter of a thousand or two I'll care for. There's Bodkin—
you remember him?" said he with a grin; "he proposed for Mary,
but since the quarrel with you, she could never bear the sight of him,
and Alley wouldn't come down to dinner if he was in the house.
Mary's greatly altered. I wish you heard her sing 'I'd mourn the
hopes that leave me;' queer girl she is; she was little more than a
child when you were here, and she remembers you just as if it was
yesterday."

While Mr. Blake ran on at this rate, now dilating upon my own
manifold virtues and accomplishments, now expatiating upon the
more congenial theme—the fascinations of his fair daughters, and
the various merits of his sons—I could not help feeling how changed
our relative position was since our last meeting; the tone of cool
and vulgar patronage he then assumed towards the unformed country lad was now converted into an air of fawning and deferential
submission, still more distasteful.

Young as I was, however, I had already seen a good deal of the
world; my soldiering had at least taught me something of men, and
I had far less difficulty in deciphering the intentions and objects of
my worthy relative than I should have had in the enigmatical mazes
of the parchment bond of which he was the bearer. After all, to
how very narrow an extent in life are we fashioned by our own estimate of ourselves! My changed condition affected me but little
until I saw how it affected others; that the position I occupied
should seem better, now that life had lost the great stimulus of ambition, was somewhat strange; and that flattery should pay its
homage to the mourning coat which it would have refused to my
soldier's garb, somewhat surprised me; still my bettered fortunes
shone only brightly by reflected light; for in my own heart I was
sad, spiritless, and oppressed.

Feeling somewhat ashamed at the coldness with which I treated a
man so much my elder, I gradually assumed towards Mr. Blake a
manner less reserved. He quickly availed himself of the change,
and launched out into an eloquent *exposé* of my advantages and
capabilities, the only immediate effect of which was to convince
me that my property and my prospects must have been very accurately conned over and considered by that worthy gentleman
before he could speak of the one or the other with such perfect
knowledge.

"When you get rid of these little encumbrances, your rent-roll
will be close on four thousand a year. There's Basset, sure, by only

reducing his interest from ten to five per cent., will give you a clear eight hundred per annum; let him refuse, and I'll advance the money. And, besides, look at Freney's farm; there's two hundred acres let for one-third of the value, and you must look to these things; for, you see, Captain, we'll want you to go into Parliament; you can't help coming forward at the next election, and by the great gun of Athlone, we'll return you."

Here Mr. Blake swallowed a full bumper of sherry, and, getting up a little false enthusiasm for the moment, grasped me by both hands and shook me violently; this done, like a skilful general, who, having fired the last shot of his artillery, takes care to secure his retreat, he retired towards the door, where his hat and coat were lying.

"I've a hundred apologies to make for encroaching upon your time; but, upon my soul, Captain, you are so agreeable, and the hours have passed away so pleasantly——May I never, if it is not one o'clock!—but you must forgive me."

My sense of justice, which showed me that the agreeability had been all on Mr. Blake's side, prevented me from acknowledging this compliment as it deserved; so I merely bowed stiffly without speaking. By this time he had succeeded in putting on his greatcoat, but still, by some mischance or other, the moment of his leave-taking was deferred; one time he buttoned it awry, and had to undo it all again; then, when it was properly adjusted, he discovered that his pocket-handkerchief was not available, being left in the inner coat pocket; to this succeeded a doubt as to the safety of the check, which instituted another search, and it was full ten minutes before he was completely caparisoned and ready for the road.

"Good-bye, Captain; good-bye!" said he, warmly, yet warily, not knowing at what precise temperature the metal of my heart was fusible. At a mild heat I had been evidently unsinged, and the white glow of his flattery seemed only to harden me. The interview was now over, and, as I thought sufficient had been done to convince my friend that the terms of distant acquaintance were to be the limits of our future intercourse, I assumed a little show of friendliness, and shook his hand warmly.

"Good-bye, Mr. Blake; pray present my respectful compliments to your friends. Allow me to ring for your horse; you are not going to have a shower, I hope."

"No, no, Captain, only a passing cloud," said he, warming up perceptibly under the influence of my advances, "nothing more. Why, what is it I'm forgetting now! Oh, I have it! Maybe I'm too bold; but sure an old friend and relation may take a liberty sometimes. It was just a little request of Mrs. Blake, as I was

42

leaving the house." He stopped here as if to take soundings, and perceiving no change in my countenance, continued, " It was just to beg that, in a kind and friendly way, you'd come over and eat your dinner with us on Sunday—nobody but the family, not a soul—Mrs. Blake and the girls—a boiled leg of mutton—Matthew—a fresh trout if we can catch one—plain and homely—but a hearty welcome, and a bottle of old claret, maybe, too—ah! ah! ah!"

Before the cadence of Mr. Blake's laugh had died away, I politely but resolutely declined the proffered invitation, and, by way of setting the question at rest forever, gave him to understand that, from impaired health and other causes, I had resolved upon strictly confining myself to the limits of my own house and grounds, at least for the present.

Mr. Blake then saluted me for the last time, and left the room. As he mounted his hackney, I could not help overhearing an abortive effort he made to draw Mike into something like conversation; but it proved an utter failure, and it was evident he deemed the man as incorrigible as the master.

"A very fine young man the Captain is—remarkable!—and it's proud I am to have him for a nephew!"

So saying, he cantered down the avenue, while Mickey, as he looked after him, muttered between his teeth, "And faix, it's prouder you'd be av he was your son-in-law!"

Mike's soliloquy seemed to show me, in a new light, the meaning of my relative's manner. It was for the first time in my life that such a thought had occurred to me, and it was not without a sense of shame that I now admitted it.

If there be something which elevates and exalts us in our esteem, tinging our hearts with heroism and our souls with pride, in the love and attachment of some fair and beautiful girl, there is something equally humiliating in being the object of cold and speculative calculation to a match-making family. Your character studied, your pursuits watched, your tastes conned over, your very temperament inquired into,—surrounded by snares, environed by practised attentions—one eye fixed upon· the registered testament of your relative, the other riveted upon your own caprices; and then those thousand little cares and kindnesses which come so pleasurably upon the heart when the offspring of true affection, perverted as they are by base views and sordid interest, are so many shocks to the feelings and understanding. Like the Eastern sirocco, which seems to breathe of freshness and of health, and yet bears but pestilence and death upon its breezes, so these calculated and well-considered traits of affection only render callous and harden the heart which has responded warmly, openly, and abundantly to the true outpourings of affection. At how many a previously happy hearth has the seed of this fatal passion planted its discord ! How many a fair and lovely girl, with beauty and attractions sufficient to win all that her heart could wish of fondness and devotion, has by this pernicious passion become a cold, heartless, worldly coquette, weighing men's characters by the adventitious circumstances of their birth and fortune, and scrutinizing the eligibility of a match with the practised acumen with which a notary investigates the solvency of a creditor. How do the traits of beauty, gesture, voice, and manner become converted into the commonplace and distasteful trickery of the world ! The very hospitality of the house becomes suspect— their friendship is but fictitious. Those rare and goodly gifts of fondness and sisterly affection which grow up in happier circumstances, are here but rivalry, envy, and ill-conceived hatred. The very accomplishments which cultivate and adorn life, that light but graceful frieze which gilds the temple of homely happiness, are here but the meditated and well-considered occasions of display. All the bright features of womanhood, all the freshness of youth, and all its fascinations, are but like those richly-colored and beautiful fruits, seductive to the eye and fair to look upon, but which within contain nothing but a core of rottenness and decay.

No, no ; unblessed by all which makes a hearth a home, I may travel on my weary way through life ; but such a one as this I will not make the partner of my sorrow and my joys, come what will of it !

CHAPTER XLVII.

A SURPRISE.

FROM the hour of Mr. Blake's departure, my life was no longer molested. My declaration, which had evidently, under his auspices, been made the subject of conversation through the country, was at least so far successful, as it permitted me to spend my time in the way I liked best, and without the necessity of maintaining a show of intercourse, when in reality I kept up none, with the neighborhood. While thus, therefore, my life passed on equably and tranquilly, many months glided over, and I found myself already a year at home, without it appearing more than a few weeks. Nothing seems so short in retrospect as monotony. The number, the variety, the interest of the events which occupy us, making our hours pass glibly and flowingly, will still suggest to the

mind the impressions of a longer period than when the daily routine of our occupations assumes a character of continued uni-
formity.   It seems to be the *amende* made by hours of weariness and
tedium, that, in looking back upon them, they appear to have passed
rapidly over.   Not that my life, at the period I speak of, was devoid
of interest; on the contrary, devoting myself with zeal and earnestness to the new duties of my station, I made myself thoroughly
acquainted with the condition of my property, the interests of my
tenantry, their prospects, their hopes, their objects.   Investigating
them as only he can who is the owner of the soil, I endeavored to
remedy the ancient vices of the land—the habits of careless, reckless waste, of indifference for the morrow; and, by instilling a feature of prudent foresight into that boundless confidence in the
future upon which every Irishman, of every rank, lives and trusts,
I succeeded at last in so far ameliorating their situation, that a walk
through my property, instead of presenting—as it at first did—a
crowd of eager and anxious suppliants, entreating for abatements in
rent, succor for their sick, and sometimes even food itself, showed
me now a happy and industrious people, confident in themselves,
and firmly relying on their own resources.

Another spring was now opening, and a feeling of calm and tranquil happiness, the result of my successful management of my
estate, made my days pass pleasantly along.   I was sitting at a late
breakfast in my little library ; the open window afforded a far and
wide prospect of the country, blooming in all the promise of the
season, while the drops of the passing shower still lingered upon the
grass, and were sparkling like jewels under the bright sunshine.
Masses of white and billowy cloud moved swiftly through the air,
coloring the broad river with many a shadow as they passed.   The
birds sang merrily, the trees shook their leaves in concert, and there
was that sense of movement in everything in earth and sky which
gives to spring its character of lightness and exhilaration.   The
youth of the year, like the youth of our own existence, is beautiful
in the restless activity which marks it.   The tender flower, that
seems to open as we look upon it; the grass, that springs before our
eyes,—all speak of promise.   The changing phases of the sky, like
the smiles and tears of infancy, excite without weariness, and while
they engage our sympathies, they fatigue not our compassion.

Partly lost in thought as I looked upon the fair and varied scene
before me, now turning to the pages of the book upon the breakfast-
table, the hours of the morning passed quickly over, and it was
already beyond noon.   I was startled from my reverie by sounds
which I could scarcely trust my ears to believe real.   I listened
again, and I thought I could detect them distinctly.   It seemed as

though some one were rapidly running over the keys of a piano-forte, essaying with the voice to follow the notes, and sometimes striking two or three bold and successive chords—then a merry laugh would follow, and drown all other sounds. "What can it be?" thought I. "There is, to be sure, a pianoforte in the large draw-ing-room; but then, who would venture upon such a liberty as this? Besides, who is capable of it? There! it can be no inexperienced performer gave that shake; my worthy housekeeper never accom-plished that." So saying, I jumped from the breakfast-table, and set off in the direction of the sound. A small drawing-room and billiard-room lay between me and the large drawing-room, and as I traversed them, the music grew gradually louder. Conjecturing that, whoever it might be, the performance would cease on my entrance, I listened for a few moments before opening the door. Nothing could be more singular, nothing more strange, than the effect of those unaccustomed sounds in that silent and deserted place. The character of the music, too, contributed not a little to this. Rapidly passing from grave to gay—from the melting soft-ness of some plaintive air to the reckless hurry and confusion of an Irish jig—the player seemed, as it were, to run wild through all the floating fancies of his memory. Now breaking suddenly off in the saddest cadence of a song, the notes would change into some quaint, old-fashioned crone, in which the singer seemed so much at home, and gave the queer drollery of the words that expression of arch-ness so eminently the character of certain Irish airs. "But what the deuce is this?" said I, as, rattling over the keys with a flowing but brilliant finger, she—for it was unquestionably a woman—with a clear and sweet voice, broken by laughter, began to sing the words of Mr. Bodkin's song, "The Man for Galway." When she had finished the last verse, her hand strayed, as it were, carelessly across the instrument, while she herself gave way to a free burst of merriment; and then, suddenly resuming the air, she chanted forth the following words, with a spirit and effect I can convey no idea of:—

> "To live at home,
>   And never roam;
> To pass his days in sighing,
>   To wear sad looks,
>   Read stupid books,
> And look half dead or dying:
>   Not show his face,
>   Nor join the chase,
> But dwell a hermit alway:
>   Oh! Charley dear!
>   To me 'tis clear,
> You're not the man for Galway!"

"You're not the man for Galway!" repeated she once more, while she closed the piano with a loud bang.

"And why not, my dear,—why not the man for Galway?" said I, as, bursting open the door, I sprang into the room.

"Oh! it's you, is it? at last! So I've unearthed you, have I?"

With these words she burst into an immoderate fit of laughter; leaving me, who intended to be the party giving the surprise, amazed, confused, and speechless, in the middle of the floor.

That my reader may sympathize a little in my distresses, let me present him with the *tableau* before me. Seated upon the piano stool was a young lady of at most eighteen years. Her face, had it not been for its expression of exuberant drollery and malicious fun, would have been downright beautiful; her eyes, of the deepest blue, and shaded by long lashes, instead of indulging the character of pensive and thoughtful beauty for which Nature destined them, sparkled with the most animated brightness; her nose, which, rather short, was still beautifully proportioned, gave, with a well-curled upper lip, a look of sauciness to the features quite bewitching; her hair—that brilliant auburn we see in a *Carlo Dolci*—fell in wild and massive curls upon her shoulders. Her costume was a dark-green riding-habit, not of the newest in its fashion, and displaying more than one rent in its careless folds; her hat, whip, and gloves lay on the floor beside her, and her whole attitude and bearing indicated the most perfect ease and carelessness.

"So you are caught—taken alive!" said she, as she pressed her hands upon her sides in a fresh burst of laughter.

"By Jove! this is a surprise indeed!" said I. "And, pray, into whose fair hands have I fallen a captive?" recovering myself a little, and assuming a half air of gallantry.

"So you don't know me, don't you?"

"Upon my life I do not."

"How good! Why, I'm Baby Blake."

"Baby Blake?" said I, thinking that a rather strange appellation for one whose well-developed proportions betokened nothing of infancy. "Baby Blake?"

"To be sure; your cousin Baby."

"Indeed!" said I, springing forward. "Let me embrace my relative."

Accepting my proffered salutation with the most exemplary coolness, she said:

"Get a chair, now, and let's have a talk together."

"Why the devil do they call you Baby?" said I, still puzzled by the palpable misnomer.

"Because I am the youngest, and I was always the baby," replied she, adjusting her ringlets with a most rural coquetry. "Now, tell me something. Why do you live shut up here like a madman, and not come near us at Gurt-na-Morra?"

"Oh! that's a long story, Baby. But, since we are asking questions, how did you get in here?"

"Just through the window, my dear; and I've torn my habit, as you see."

So saying, she exhibited a rent of about two feet long, thrusting through it a very pretty foot and ankle at the same time.

"As my inhospitable customs have cost you a habit, you must let me make you a present of one."

"No, will you though? That's a good fellow! Lord! I told them I knew you weren't a miser; that you were only odd, that's all."

"And how did you come over, Baby?"

"Just cantered over with little Paddy Byrne. I made him take all the walls and ditches we met, and they're scraping the mud off him ever since. I'm glad I made you laugh, Charley; they say you are so sad. Dear me, how thirsty I am! Have you any beer?"

"To be sure, Baby. But wouldn't you like some luncheon?"

"Of all things. Well, this is fun!" said she, as, taking my arm, I led her from the drawing-room. "They don't know where I'm gone—not one of them; and I've a great mind not to tell them, if you wouldn't blab."

"Would it be quite proper?"

"Proper!" cried she, imitating my voice; "I like that! as if I was going to run away with you. Dear me! what a pretty house! and what nice pictures! Who is the old fellow up there in the armor?"

"That's Sir Hildebrand O'Malley," said I, with some pride, in recognizing an ancestor of the thirteenth century.

"And the other old fright with the wig, and his hands stuck in his pockets?"

"My grandfather, Baby."

"Lord! how ugly he is! Why, Charley, he hasn't a look of you; one would think, too, he was angry at us. Ay, old gentleman! you don't like to see me leaning on cousin Charley's arm. That must be the luncheon; I'm sure I hear knives and forks rattling there."

The old butler's astonishment was not inferior to my own a few minutes before, when I entered the dining-room with my fair cousin upon my arm. As I drew a chair towards the table, a thought struck me that possibly it might only be a due attention to my fair guest if I invited the housekeeper, Mrs. Magra, to favor us with her presence; and accordingly, in an undertone, so as not to be overheard by old Simon, I said—

"Perhaps, Baby, you'd like to have Mrs. Magra to keep us company?"

"Who's she?" was the brief answer.

"The housekeeper; a very respectable old matron."

"Is she funny?"

"Funny! not a bit."

"Oh, then, never mind her. What made you think of her?"

"Why, I thought—perhaps you'd think—that is, people might say—in fact, I was doing a little bit proper on your account."

"Oh! that was it, was it? Thank you for nothing, my dear; Baby Blake can take care of herself. And now just help me to that wing there. Do you know, cousin Charley, I think you're an old quiz, and not half as good a fellow as you used to be."

"Come, come, Baby, don't be in such a hurry to pronounce upon me. Let us take a glass of wine. Fill Miss Blake's glass, Simon."

"Well, you may be better when one comes to know you. I detest sherry; no, never mind, I'll take it, as it's here. Charley, I'll not compliment you upon your ham; they don't know how to save them here. I'll give you such a receipt when you come over to see us. But will you come? that's the question."

"How can you ask me! Don't you think I'll return your visit?"

"Oh! hang your ceremony. Come and see us, like a good-natured fellow, that knew us since we played together, and quarrelled over our toys on the grass. Is that your sword up there? Did you hear that noise? that was thunder: there it comes. Look at that!"

As she spoke, a darkness like night overspread the landscape; the waves of the river became greatly agitated, and the rain, descending in torrents, beat with tremendous force against the windows; clap after clap of thunder followed; the lightning flashed fearfully through the gloom, and the wind, growing every moment stronger, drove the rain with redoubled violence against the glass. For a while we amused ourselves with watching the effects of the storm without; the poor laborers, flying from their work; the dripping figures seeking shelter beneath the trees; the barques; the very loaded carts themselves, all interested Miss Baby, whose eye roved from the shore to the Shannon, recognizing, with a practised eye, every house upon its banks, and every barque that rocked and pitched beneath the gale.

"Well, this is pleasant to look out at," said she, at length, and after the storm had lasted for above an hour, without evincing any show of abatement; "but what's to become of *me!*"

Now, that was the very question I had been asking myself for the last twenty minutes, without ever being able to find the answer.

"Eh, Charley, what's to become of me?"

"Oh, never fear: one thing's quite certain, you cannot leave this in such weather; the river is certainly impassable by this time at the ford, and to go by the road is out of the question; it is fully twelve miles. I have it, Baby; you, as I've said before, can't leave this, but I can. Now, I'll go over to Gurt-na-Morra, and return in the morning to bring you back; it will be fine by that time."

"Well, I like your notion; you'll leave me all alone here to drink tea, I suppose, with your friend Mrs. Magra; a pleasant evening I'd have of it: not a bit——"

"Well, Baby, don't be cross; I only meant this arrangement really for your sake. I needn't tell you how very much I'd prefer doing the honors of my poor house in person."

"Oh, I see what you mean—more propers. Well, well, I've a great deal to learn; but, look, I think it's growing lighter."

"No, far from it; it's only that gray mass along the horizon that always bodes continual rain."

As the prospect without had little cheering to look upon, we sat down beside the fire, and chatted away, forgetting very soon, in a hundred mutual recollections and inquiries, the rain and the wind, the thunder and the hurricane. Now and then, as some louder crash would resound above our heads, for a moment we would turn to the window, and comment upon the dreadful weather; but the next, we had forgotten all about it, and were deep in our confabulations.

As for my fair cousin, who at first was full of contrivances to pass the time—such as the piano, a game at backgammon, chicken hazard, battledore—she at last became mightily interested in some of my soldiering adventures, and it was six o'clock ere we again thought that some final measure must be adopted for restoring Baby to her friends, or, at least, guarding against the consequences her simple and guileless nature might have involved her in.

Mike was called into the conference, and at his suggestion it was decided that we should have out the phaeton, and that I should myself drive Miss Blake home—a plan which offered no other difficulties than this one, namely, that of about thirty horses in my stables, I had not a single pair which had ever been harnessed.

This, so far from proving the obstacle I deemed it, seemed, on the contrary, to overwhelm Baby with delight.

"Let's have them. Come, Charley; this will be rare fun; we couldn't have a team of four, could we?"

"Six, if you like it, my dear coz; only, who's to hold them?—

they're young thorough-breds; most of them never backed; some not bitted. In fact, I know nothing of my stable. I say, Mike, is there anything fit to take out?"

"Yes, sir; there's Miss Wildespin: she's in training, to be sure; but we can't help that; and the brown colt they call 'Billy the Bolter:' they're the likeliest we have; without your honor would take the two chestnuts we took up last week; they're rale devils to go; and if the tackle will hold them, they'll bring you to Mr. Blake's door in forty minutes."

"I vote for the chestnuts," said Baby, slapping her boot with her horse-whip.

"I move an amendment in favor of Miss Wildespin," said I, doubtfully.

"He'll never do for Galway," sang Baby, laying her whip on my shoulder with no tender hand; "yet you used to cross the country in good style when you were here before."

"And might do so again, Baby."

"Ah, no; that vile dragoon seat, with your long stirrup, and your heel dropped, and your elbow this way, and your head that! How could you ever screw your horse up to his fence, lifting him along as you came up through the heavy ground, and with a stroke of your hand sending him pop over, with his hind legs well under him?" Here she burst into a fit of laughter at my look of amazement, as with voice, gesture, and look, she actually dramatized the scene she described.

By the time that I had costumed my fair friend in my dragoon cloak and a foraging cap, with a gold band around it, which was the extent of muffling my establishment could muster, a distant noise without apprised us that the phaeton was approaching. Certainly the mode in which that equipage came up to the door might have ·inspired sentiments of fear in any heart less steeled against danger than my fair cousin's. The two blood chestnuts (for it was those that Mike harnessed, having a groom's dislike to take a racer out of training) were surrounded by about twenty people: some at their heads, some patting them on their flanks, some spoking the wheels, and a few, the more cautious of the party, standing at a respectable distance, and offering advice. The mode of progression was simply a spring, a plunge, a rear, a lunge, and a kick; and, considering it was the first time they ever performed together, nothing could be more uniform than their display; sometimes the pole would be seen to point straight upward, like a lightning conductor, while the infuriated animals appeared sparring with their fore legs at an imaginary enemy. Sometimes, like the picture in a school-book on mythology, they would seem in the act of diving,

while with their hind legs they dashed the splash-board into fragments behind them; their eyes flashing fire, their nostrils distended,
their flanks heaving, and every limb trembling with passion and
excitement.

"That's what I call a rare turn-out," said Baby, who enjoyed the
proceedings amazingly.

"Yes; but remember," said I, "we're not to have all these running footmen the whole way."

"I like that near sider with the white fetlock."

"You're right, Miss," said Mike, who entered at the moment, and
felt quite gratified at the criticism. "You're right, Miss; it's himself can do it."

"Come, Baby, are you ready?"

"All right, sir," said she, touching her cap knowingly with her
forefinger.

"Will the tackle hold, Mike?" said I.

"We'll take this with us, at any rate," pointing, as he spoke, to
a considerable coil of rope, a hammer, and a basket of nails, he
carried on his arm. "It's the break harness we have, and it ought
to be strong enough; but sure, if the thunder comes on again, they'd
smash a chain cable."

"Now, Charley," cried Baby, "keep their heads straight; for
when they go that way, they mean going."

"Well, Baby, let's start; but pray remember one thing. If I'm
not as agreeable on the journey as I ought to be; if I don't say as
many pretty things to my pretty coz, it's because these confounded
beasts will give me as much as I can do."

"Oh yes, look after the cattle, and take another time for squeezing
my hand. I say, Charley, you'd like to smoke, now, wouldn't you?
if so, don't mind me."

"A thousand thanks for thinking of it; but I'll not commit such
a trespass on good-breeding."

When we reached the door, the prospect looked dark and dismal
enough; the rain had almost ceased, but masses of black clouds
were hurrying across the sky, and the low rumbling noise of a
gathering storm crept along the ground. Our panting equipage,
with its two mounted grooms behind,—for, to provide against all
accidents, Mike ordered two such to follow us,—stood in waiting;
Miss Blake's horse, held by the smallest imaginable bit of boyhood,
bringing up the rear.

"Look at Paddy Byrne's face," said Baby, directing my attention
to the little individual in question.

Now, small as the aforesaid face was, it contrived, within its
limits, to exhibit an expression of unqualified fear. I had no time,

however, to give a second look, when I jumped into the phaeton and seized the reins. Mike sprang up behind at a look from me, and, without speaking a word, the stablemen and helpers flew right and left. The chestnuts, seeing all free before them, made one tremendous plunge, carrying the fore-carriage clear off the ground, and straining every nut, bolt, screw, and strap about us with the effort.

"They're off, now," cried Mickey.

"Yes, they are off, now," said Baby. "Keep them going."

Nothing could be easier to follow than this advice; and, in fact, so little merit had I in obeying it, that I never spoke a word. Down the avenue we went at the speed of lightning, the stones, and the water from the late rain, flying and splashing about us. In one series of plunges, agreeably diversified by a strong bang upon the splash-board, we reached the gate. Before I had time to utter a prayer for our safety, we were through, and fairly upon the high road.

"Musha, but the master's mad!" cried the old dame of the gate-lodge; "he wasn't out of this gate for a year and a half, and look now——"

The rest was lost in the clear ringing laugh of Baby, who clapped her hands in ecstasy and delight.

"What a spanking pair they are! I suppose you wouldn't let me get my hand on them?" said she, making a gesture as if to take the reins.

"Heaven forbid! my dear," said I; "they've nearly pulled my wrists off already."

Our road, like many in the west of Ireland, lay through a level tract of bog; deep ditches, half filled with water, on either side of us, but, fortunately, neither hill nor valley for several miles.

"There's the mail," said Baby, pointing to a dark speck at a long distance off.

Ere many minutes elapsed, our stretching gallop, for such had our pace sobered into, brought us up with it, and as we flew by, at top speed, Baby jumped to her feet, and turning a waggish look at our beaten rivals, burst out into a fit of triumphant laughter.

Mike was correct as to time; in some few seconds less than forty minutes we turned into the avenue of Gurt-na-Morra. Tearing along like the very moment of their starting, the hot and fiery animals galloped up the approach, and at length came to a stop in a deep ploughed field, into which, fortunately for us, Mr. Blake, animated less by the picturesque than the profitable, had converted his green lawn. This check, however, was less owing to my agency than to that of my servants; for, dismounting in haste, they flew to

the horses' heads, and with ready tact, and before I had helped my
cousin to the ground, succeeded in unharnessing them from the carriage, and led them, blown and panting, covered with foam and
splashed with mud, into the space before the door.

By this time we were joined by the whole Blake family, who
poured forth in astonishment at our strange and sudden appearance.
Explanation on my part was unnecessary, for Baby, with a volubil-
ity quite her own, gave the whole recital in less than three minutes.
From the moment of her advent to her departure, they had it all;
and while she mingled her ridicule at my surprise, her praise of my
luncheon, her jests at my prudence, the whole family joined heartily
in her mirth, while they welcomed, with most unequivocal warmth,
my first visit to Gurt-na-Morra.

I confess it was with no slight gratification I remarked that Baby's
visit was as much a matter of surprise to them as to me. Believing
her to have gone to visit at Portumna Castle, they felt no uneasiness
at her absence; so that, in her descent upon me, she was really only
guided by her own wilful fancy, and that total absence of all consciousness of wrong which makes a truly innocent girl the hardiest
of all God's creatures. I was reassured by this feeling, and satisfied
that, whatever the intentions of the elder members of the Blake
family, Baby was, at least, no participator in their plots, or sharer
in their intrigues.

CHAPTER XLVIII.

NEW VIEWS.

WHEN I found myself the next morning at home, I could
not help ruminating over the strange adventures of the preceding day, and felt a kind of self-reproach at the frigid
manner in which I had hitherto treated all the Blake advances, contrasting so ill for me with the unaffected warmth and kind good-
nature of their reception. Never alluding, even by accident, to my
late estrangement; never, by a chance speech, indicating that they
felt any soreness for the past, they talked away about the gossip of
the country,—its feuds, its dinners, its assizes, its balls, its garri-
sons,—all the varied subjects of country life were gayly and laugh-
ingly discussed; and when, as I entered my own silent and deserted
home, and contrasted its looks of melancholy and gloom with the
gay and merry scene I so lately departed from; when my echoing

steps reverberated along the flagged hall, I thought of the happy family picture I left behind me, and could not help avowing to myself that the goods of fortune I possessed were but ill dispensed, when, in the midst of every means and appliance for comfort and happiness, I lived a solitary man, companionless and alone.

I arose from breakfast a hundred times; now walking impatiently towards the window, now strolling into the drawing-room. Around, on every side, lay scattered the prints and drawings, as Baby had thrown them carelessly upon the floor; her handkerchief was also there. I took it up; I knew not why—some lurking leaven of old romance perhaps suggested it; but I hoped it might prove of delicate texture, and bespeaking that lady-like coquetry which so pleasantly associates with the sex in our minds. Alas! no. Nothing could be more palpably the opposite. Torn, and with a knot—some hint to memory—upon one corner, it was no aid to my careering fancy. And yet—and yet, what a handsome girl she is! how finely, how delicately formed that Greek outline of forehead and brow! how transparently soft that downy pink upon her cheek! with what varied expression those eyes can beam!—ay, that they can: but, confound it! there's this fault,—their very archness—their sly malice—will be interpreted by the ill-judging world to any but the real motive. "How like a flirt!" will one say; "how impertinent! how ill-bred!" The conventional stare of cold, patched and painted beauty, upon whose unblushing cheek no stray tinge of modesty has wandered, will be tolerated—even admired; while the artless beamings of the soul upon the face of rural loveliness will be condemned without appeal.

Such a girl may a man marry who destines his days to the wild west, but woe unto him!—woe unto him! should he migrate among the more civilized and less charitable *coteries* of our neighbors.

"Ah! here are the papers, and I was forgetting. Let me see— 'Bayonne'—ay, 'march of the troops—sixth corps.' What can that be without? I say, Mike, who is cantering along the avenue?"

"It's me, sir. I'm training the brown filly for Miss Mary, as your honor bid me last night."

"Ah, very true. Does she go quietly?"

"Like a lamb, sir; barrin' she does give a kick now and then at the sheet, when it bangs against her legs."

"Am I to go over with the books now, sir?" said a wild-looking shockhead appearing within the door.

"Yes, take them over, with my compliments; and say I hope Miss Mary Blake has caught no cold."

"You were speaking about a habit and hat, sir?" said Mrs. Magra, curtseying as she entered.

"Yes, Mrs. Magra; I want your advice. Oh, tell Barnes I really cannot be bored about those eternal turnips every day of my life. And, Mike, I wish you'd make them look over the four-horse harness. I want to try those grays; they tell me they'll run well together. Well, Freney, more complaints, I hope? nothing but trespasses; I don't care; so you'd not worry me, if they eat up every blade of clover in the grounds. I'm sick of being bored this way. Did you say that we'd eight couple of good dogs?—quite enough to begin with. Tell Jones to ride into Banagher and look after that box : Buckmaster sent it from London two months ago, and it has been lying there ever since. And, Mrs. Magra, pray let the windows be opened, and the house well aired. That drawing-room would be all the better for new papering."

These few and broken directions may serve to show my readers—what certainly they failed to convince myself of—that a new chapter of my life had opened before me; and that in proportion to the length of time my feelings had found neither vent nor outlet, they now rushed madly, tempestuously, into their new channels, suffering no impediment to arrest, no obstacle to oppose their current.

Nothing can be conceived more opposite to my late, than my present habits now became. The house, the grounds, the gardens, all seemed to participate in the new influence which beamed upon myself; the stir and bustle of active life was everywhere perceptible; and, amid numerous preparations for the moors and the hunting-field, for pleasure parties up the river, and fishing excursions up the mountains, my days were spent. The Blakes, without even for a moment pressing their attentions upon me, permitted me to go and come amongst them unquestioned and unasked. When, nearly every morning, I appeared in the breakfast-room, I felt exactly like a member of the family. The hundred little discrepancies of thought and habit which struck me forcibly at first looked daily less apparent; the careless inattentions of my fair cousins as to dress, their free-and-easy, boisterous manner, their very accents, which fell so harshly upon my ear, gradually made less and less impression, until at last, when a raw English ensign, just arrived in the neighborhood, remarked to me in confidence, " What devilish fine girls they were, if they were not so confoundedly Irish !" I could not help wondering what the fellow meant, and attributed the observation more to his ignorance than to its truth.

Papa and Mamma Blake, like prudent generals, so long as they saw the forces of the enemy daily wasting before them—so long as they could with impunity carry on the war at his expense—resolved to risk nothing by a pitched battle. Unlike the Dalrymples, they could leave all to time.

Oh! tell me not of dark eyes swimming in their own ethereal essence; tell me not of pouting lips, of glossy ringlets, of taper fingers, and well-rounded insteps; speak not to me of soft voices, whose seductive sounds ring sweetly in our hearts; preach not of those thousand womanly graces so dear to every man, and doubly so to him who lives apart from all their influences and fascinations; neither dwell upon congenial temperament, similarity of taste, of disposition, and of thought; these are not the great risks a man runs in life. Of all the temptations, strong as these may be, there is one greater than them all, and that is—propinquity !

Show me the man who has ever stood this test; show me the man, deserving the name of such, who has become daily and hourly exposed to the breaching artillery of flashing eyes, of soft voices, of winning smiles, and kind speeches, and who hasn't felt, and that too soon, a breach within the rampart of his heart. He may, it is true,— nay, he will, in many cases,—make a bold and vigorous defence; sometimes will he re-intrench himself within the stockades of his prudence, but, alas! it is only to defer the moment when he must lay down his arms. He may, like a wise man, who sees his fate inevitable, make a virtue of necessity, and surrender at discretion; or, like a crafty foe, seeing his doom before him, under the cover of the night he may make a sortie from the garrison, and run for his life. Ignominious as such a course must be, it is often the only one left.

But to come back. Love, like the small-pox, is most dangerous when you take it in the natural way. Those made matches, which Heaven is supposed to have a hand in, when placing an unmarried gentleman's property in the neighborhood of an unmarried lady's, which destine two people for each other in life, because their well-judging friends have agreed "they'll do very well; they were made for each other,"—these are the mild cases of the malady; this process of friendly vaccination takes out the poison of the disease, substituting a more harmless and less exciting affection. But the really dangerous instances are those from contact, that same propinquity, that confounded tendency every man yields to, to fall into a railroad of habit; that is the risk—that is the danger. What a bore it is to find that the absence of one person, with whom you are nowise in love, will spoil your morning's canter, or your rowing party upon the river! How much put out you are when she to whom you always gave your arm at dinner does not make her appearance in the drawing-room; and your tea too, some careless one, indifferent to your taste, puts a lump of sugar too little, or cream too much, while she—But no matter; habit has done for you what no direct influence of beauty could do, and, a slave to your own selfish indulgences, and the cultivation of that ease you prize so highly, you fall over head and ears in love.

Now, you are not, my good reader, by any means to suppose that this was my case. No, no; I was too much what the world terms the "old soldier" for that. To continue my illustration : like the fortress that has been often besieged, the sentry upon the walls keeps more vigilant watch ; his ear detects the far-off clank of the dread artillery ; he marks each parallel ; he notes down every breaching battery ; and if he be captured, at least it is in fair fight.

Such were some of my reflections as I rode slowly home one evening from Gurt-na-Morra. Many a time, latterly, had I contrasted my own lonely and deserted hearth with the smiling looks, the happy faces, and the merry voices I had left behind me ; and many a time did I ask myself, "Am I never to partake of a happiness like this ?" How many a man is seduced into matrimony from this very feeling ! How many a man whose hours have passed fleetingly at the pleasant tea-table, or by the warm hearth of some old country-house, going forth into the cold and cheerless night, reaches his far-off home only to find it dark and gloomy, joyless and companionless ? How often has the hard-visaged look of his old butler, as with sleepy eyes and yawning face he hands a bed-room candle, suggested thoughts of married happiness ? Of the perils of propinquity I have already spoken ; the risks of contrast are also great. Have you never, in strolling through some fragrant and rich conservatory, fixed your eye upon a fair and lovely flower, whose blossoming beauty seems to give all the lustre and all the incense of the scene around ? and how have you thought it would adorn and grace the precincts of your home, diffusing fragrance on every side. Alas ! the experiment is not always successful. Much of the charm and many of the fascinations which delight you are the result of association of time and of place. The lovely voice, whose tones have spoken to your heart, may, like some instrument, be delightful in the harmony of the orchestra, but, after all, prove a very middling performer in a duet.

I say not this to deter men from matrimony, but to warn them from a miscalculation which may mar their happiness. Flirtation is a very fine thing, but it's only a state of transition, after all. The tadpole existence of the lover would be great fun if one was never to become a frog under the hands of the parson. I say all this dispassionately and advisedly. Like the poet of my country, for many years of my life,

> "My only books were woman's looks,"

and certainly I subscribed to a circulating library.

43

All this long digression may perhaps bring the reader to where it brought me—the very palpable conviction that though not in love with my cousin Baby, I could not tell when I might eventually become so.

CHAPTER XLIX.

A RECOGNITION.

THE most pleasing part about retrospect is the memory of our bygone hopes. The past, however happy, however blissful, few would wish to live over again; but who is there that does not long for, does not pine after, the day-dream which gilded the future—which looked ever forward to the time to come as to a realization of all that was dear to us, lightening our present cares, soothing our passing sorrows, by that one thought?

Life is marked out in periods in which, like stages in a journey, we rest and repose ourselves, casting a look, now back upon the road we have been travelling, now throwing a keener glance towards the path left us. It is at such spots as these that remembrance comes full upon us, and that we feel how little our intentions have swayed our career or influenced our actions. The aspirations, the resolves of youth, are either looked upon as puerile follies, or a most distant day settled on for their realization. The principles we fondly looked to, like our guide-stars, are dimly visible—not seen; the friends we cherished are changed and gone; the scenes themselves seem no longer the sunshine and the shade we loved; and, in fact, we are living in a new world, where our own altered condition gives the type to all around us; the only link that binds us to the past being that same memory, that, like a sad curfew, tolls the twilight of our fairest dreams and most cherished wishes.

That these glimpses of the bygone season of our youth should be but fitful and passing—tinging, not coloring, the landscape of our life—we should be engaged in all the active bustle and turmoil of the world, surrounded by objects of hope, love, and ambition, stemming the strong tide in whose fountain is fortune.

He, however, who lives apart, a dreamy and passionless existence, will find that in the past more than in the future his thoughts have found their resting-place; memory usurps the place of hope, and he travels through life like one walking onward, his eyes still turning towards some loved forsaken spot, teeming with all the associations of his happiest hours, and preserving even in distance the outline that he loved.

Distance in time, as in space, smooths down all the inequalities of surface; and, as the cragged and rugged mountain, darkened by cliff and precipice, shows to the far-off traveller but some blue and misty mass, so the long-lost-sight-of hours lose all the cares and griefs that tinged them, and to our mental eye are but objects of uniform loveliness and beauty: and if we do not think of

> "The smiles—the tears
> Of boyhood's years,"

it is because, like April showers, they but chequer the spring of our existence.

For myself, baffled in hope at a period when most men but begin to feel it, I thought myself much older than I really was. The disappointments of the world, like the storms of the ocean, impart a false step of experience to the young heart, as he sails forth upon his voyage; and it is an easy error to mistake trials for time.

The goods of fortune by which I was surrounded took nothing from the bitterness of my retrospect; on the contrary, I could not help feeling that every luxury of my life was bought by my surrender of that career which had elated me in my own esteem, and which, setting a high and noble ambition before me, taught me to be a man.

To be happy, one must not only fulfil the duties and exactions of his station, but the station itself must answer to his views and aspirations in life. Now, mine did not sustain this condition. All that my life had of promise was connected with the memory of her who never could share my fortunes—of her for whom I had earned praise and honor; becoming ambitious as the road to her affection, only to learn after that my hopes were but a dream, and my paradise a wilderness.

While thus the inglorious current of my life ran on, I was not indifferent to the mighty events the great continent of Europe was witnessing. The success of the Peninsular campaign; the triumphant entry of the British into France; the downfall of Napoleon; the restoration of the Bourbons, followed each other with the rapidity of the most commonplace occurrences; and in the few short years in which I had sprung from boyhood to man's estate, the whole condition of the world was altered. Kings deposed; great armies disbanded; rightful sovereigns restored to their dominions; banished and exiled men returned to their country, invested with rank and riches; and peace, in the fullest tide of its blessings, poured down upon the devastated and blood-stained earth.

Years passed on; and between the careless abandonment to the mere amusement of the hour, and the darker meditation upon the past, time slipped away. From my own friends and brother officers I heard but rarely. Power, who at first wrote frequently, grew gradually less and less communicative. Webber, who had gone to Paris at the peace, had written but one letter; while from the rest a few straggling lines was all I received. In truth, be it told, my own negligence and inability to reply cost me this apparent neglect.

It was a fine evening in May, when, rigging up a sprit-sail, I jumped into my yawl, and dropped easily down the river. The light wind gently curled the crested water, the trees waved gently and shook their branches in the breeze, and my little bark, bending slightly beneath, rustled on her foamy track with that joyous bounding motion so inspiriting to one's heart. The clouds were flying swiftly past, tinging with their shadows the mountains beneath; the Munster shore, glowing with a rich sunlight, showed every sheep-cot and every hedge-row clearly out, while the deep shadow of tall Scariff darkened the silent river where Holy Island, with its ruined churches and melancholy tower, was reflected in the still water.

It was a thoroughly Irish landscape: the changeful sky; the fast flitting shadows; the brilliant sunlight; the plenteous fields; the broad and swelling stream; the dark mountain, from whose brown crest a wreath of thin blue smoke was rising, were all there smiling yet sadly, like her own sons, across whose louring brow some fitful flash of fancy, ever playing, dallies like sunbeams on the darkening stream, nor marks the depth that lies below.

I sat musing over the strange harmony of nature with the temperament of man, every phase of his passionate existence seeming to have its type in things inanimate, when a loud cheer from the land aroused me, and the words "Charley! Cousin Charley!" came wafted over the water to where I lay.

For some time I could but distinguish the faint outline of some figures on the shore, but as I came nearer I recognized my fair cousin Baby, who, with a younger brother of some eight or nine years old, was taking an evening walk.

"Do you know, Charley," said she, "the boys have gone over to the castle to look for you; we want you particularly this evening."

"Indeed, Baby! Well, I fear you must make my excuses."

"Then, once for all, I will not. I know this is one of your sulky moods, and I tell you frankly I'll not put up with them any more."

"No, no, Baby, not so; out of spirits if you will, but not out of temper."

"The distinction is much too fine for me, if there be any; but there, now, do be a good fellow; come up with us—come up with *me!*"

As she said this she placed her arm within mine. I thought, too—perhaps it was but a thought—she pressed me gently. I know she blushed, and turned away her head to hide it.

"I don't pretend to be proof against your entreaty, cousin Baby," said I, with half-affected gallantry, putting her fingers to my lips.

"There, how can you be so foolish; look at William, yonder; I am sure he must have seen you." But, William, God bless him! was bird's-nesting, or butterfly-hunting, or daisy-picking, or something of that kind.

Oh ye young brothers, who, sufficiently old to be deemed companions and *chaperons*, but yet young enough to be regarded as having neither eyes nor ears, what mischief have ye to answer for! what a long reckoning of tender speeches, of soft looks, of pressed hands, lies at your door! What an incentive to flirtation is the wily imp who turns ever and anon from his careless gambols to throw his laughter-loving eyes upon you, calling up the mantling blush to both your cheeks! He seems to chronicle the hours of your dalliance, making your secrets known unto each other. We have gone through our share of flirtation in this life. Match-making mothers, prying aunts, choleric uncles, benevolent and open-hearted fathers, we understand to the life, and care no more for such man-traps than a Melton man, well-mounted on his strong-boned thoroughbred, does for a four-barred ox-fence that lies before him. Like him, we take them flying; never relaxing the slapping stride of our loose gallop, we go straight ahead, never turning aside, except for a laugh at those who flounder in the swamps we sneer at. But we confess honestly we fear the little brother, the small urchin who, with nankeen trousers and three rows of buttons, performs the part of Cupid. He strikes real terror into our hearts; he it is who, with a cunning wink, or sly smile, seems to confirm the soft nonsense we are weaving; by some slight gesture he seems to check off the long reckoning of our attentions, bringing us every moment nearer to the time when the score must be settled and the debt paid. He it is who, by a memory delightfully oblivious of his task and his table-book, is tenacious to the life of what you said to Fanny; how you put your head under Lucy's bonnet; he can imitate to perfection the way you kneeled upon the grass; and the wretch has learned to smack his lips like a *gourmand*, that he may convey another stage of your proceeding.

Oh, for infant schools for everything under the age of ten! Oh, for factories for the children of the rich! The age of prying curiosity is from four-and-a-half to nine, and Fouché himself might get a lesson in *police* from an urchin in his alphabet.

I contrived soon, however, to forget the presence of even the little brother. The night was falling; Baby appeared getting fatigued with her walk, for she leaned somewhat more heavily upon my arm, and I—I cannot tell wherefore—fell into that train of thinking aloud which, somehow, upon a summer's eve, with a fair girl beside one, is the very nearest thing to love-making.

"There, Charley—don't now—ah, don't!—do let go my hand—they are coming down the avenue."

I had scarcely time to obey the injunction, when Mr. Blake called out:

"Well, indeed! Charley, this is really fortunate; we have got a friend to take tea with us, and wanted you to meet him."

Muttering an internal prayer for something not exactly the welfare of the aforesaid friend, whom I judged to be some Galway squire, I professed aloud the pleasure I felt in having come in so opportunely.

"He wishes particularly to make your acquaintance."

"So much the worse," thought I to myself; "it rarely happens that this feeling is mutual."

Evidently provoked at the little curiosity I exhibited, Blake added,

"He's on his way to Fermoy with a detachment."

"Indeed! what regiment, pray?"

"The 28th Foot."

"Ah! I don't know them."

By this time we reached the steps of the hall-door, and just as we did so, the door opened suddenly, and a tall figure in uniform presented himself. With one spring he seized my hand and nearly wrung it off.

"Why, what," said I, "can this be? Is it really——"

"Sparks," said he—"your old friend Sparks, my boy; I've changed into the infantry, and here I am. Heard by chance you were in the neighborhood—met Mr. Blake, your friend here, at the inn, and accepted his invitation to meet you."

Poor Sparks, albeit the difference of his costume, was the same as ever. Having left the 14th soon after I quitted them, he knew but little of their fortunes; and he himself had been on recruiting stations nearly the whole time since we had met before.

While we each continued to extol the good fortune of the other—he mine as being no longer in the service, and I his for still being so—we learned the various changes which had happened to each of us during our separation. Although his destination was ultimately

Fermoy, Portumna was ordered to be his present quarter; and I felt delighted to have once more an old companion within reach, to chat over former days of campaigning and nights of merriment in the Peninsula.

Sparks soon became a constant visitor and guest at Gurt-na-Morra; his good temper, his easy habits, his simplicity of character, rapidly enabled him to fall into all their ways; and, although evidently not what Baby would call "the man for Galway," he endeavored with all his might to please every one, and certainly succeeded to a considerable extent.

Baby alone seemed to take pleasure in tormenting the poor sub. Long before she met with him, having heard much from me of his exploits abroad, she was continually bringing up some anecdote of his unhappy loves or misplaced passions, which he evidently smarted under the more from the circumstance that he appeared rather inclined to like my fair cousin.

As she continued this for some time, I remarked that Sparks, who at first was all gayety and high spirits, grew gradually more depressed and dispirited. I became convinced that the poor fellow was in love; very little management on my part was necessary to obtain his confession; and, accordingly, the same evening the thought first struck me, as we were riding slowly home towards O'Malley Castle, I touched at first generally upon the merits of the Blakes, their hospitality, &c.; then diverged to the accomplishments and perfections of the girls; and, lastly, Baby herself, in all form, came up for sentence.

"Ah, yes!" said Sparks, with a deep sigh, "it is quite as you say; she is a lovely girl; and that liveliness in her character, that elasticity in her temperament, chastened down as it might be by the feeling of respect for the man she loved! I say, Charley, is it a very long attachment of yours?"

"A long attachment of mine! Why, my dear Sparks, you can't suppose that there is anything between us! I pledge you my word most faithfully."

"Oh no, don't tell me that; what good can there be in mystifying me?"

"I have no such intention, believe me. My cousin Baby, however I like and admire her, has no other place in my affection than a very charming girl, who has lightened a great many dreary and tiresome hours, and made my banishment from the world less irksome than I should have found it without her."

"And you are really not in love?"

"Not a bit of it!"

"Not going to marry her either?"

"Not the least notion of it!—a fact. Baby and I are excellent friends, for the very reason that we were never lovers; we have had no *petits jeux* of fallings out and makings up; no hide-and-seek trials of affected indifference and real disappointments; no secrets, no griefs nor grudges; neither quarrels nor keepsakes. In fact, we are capital cousins; quizzing every one for our own amusement; riding, walking, boating together; in fact, doing and thinking of everything save sighs and declarations; always happy to meet, and never broken-hearted when we part. And I can only add, as a proof of my sincerity, that if you feel as I suspect you do from your questions, I'll be your ambassador to the court of Gurt-na-Morra with sincere pleasure."

"Will you really?—Will you indeed, Charley, do this for me?—Will you strengthen my wishes by your aid, and give me all your influence with the family?"

I could scarcely help smiling at poor Sparks's eagerness or the unwarrantable value he put upon my alliance, in a case where his own unassisted efforts did not threaten much failure.

"I repeat it, Sparks, I'll make a proposal for you in all form, aided and abetted by everything recommendatory and laudatory I can think of; I'll talk of you as a Peninsular of no small note and promise; and observe rigid silence about your Welsh flirtation and your Spanish elopement."

"You'll not blab about the Dalrymples, I hope?"

"Trust me; I only hope you will always be as discreet. But now—when shall it be? Should you like to consider the matter more?"

"Oh no! nothing of the kind; let it be to-morrow; at once, if I am to fail; even that, anything's better than suspense."

"Well then, to-morrow be it," said I.

So I wished him a good-night, and a stout heart to bear his fortune withal.

CHAPTER L.

A MISTAKE.

I ORDERED my horses at an early hour; and long before Sparks —lover that he was—had opened his eyes to the light, was already on my way towards Gurt-na-Morra. Several miles slipped away before I well determined how I should open my negotiations: whether to papa Blake, in the first instance, or to madame, to whose peculiar province these secrets of the home department belonged; or why not at once to Baby? because, after all, with her it rested finally to accept or refuse. To address myself to the heads of the department seemed the more formal course; and, as I was acting entirely as an "Envoy Extraordinary," I deemed this the fitting mode of proceeding.

It was exactly eight o'clock as I drove up to the door. Mr. Blake was standing at the open window of the breakfast-room, sniffing the fresh air of the morning. The Blake mother was busily engaged with the economy of the tea-table; a very simple style of morning costume, and a nightcap with a flounce like a petticoat, marking her unaffected toilette. Above stairs, more than one head *en papillote* took a furtive peep between the curtains; and the butler of the family, in corduroys and a fur cap, was weeding turnips in the lawn before the door.

Mrs. Blake had barely time to take a hurried departure, when her husband came out upon the steps to bid me welcome. There is no physiognomist like your father of a family, or your mother with marriageable daughters. Lavater was nothing to them, in reading the secret springs of action—the hidden sources of all character. Had there been a good respectable bump allotted by Spurzheim to "honorable intentions," the matter had been all fair and easy,—the very first salute of the gentleman would have pronounced upon his views; but, alas! no such guide is forthcoming; and the science, as it now exists, is enveloped in doubt and difficulty. The gay, laughing temperament of some, the dark and serious composure of others; the cautious and reserved, the open and the candid, the witty, the sententious, the clever, the dull, the prudent, the reckless—in a word, every variety which the innumerable hues of character imprint upon the human face divine, are their study. Their convictions are the slow and patient fruits of intense observation and great logical accuracy. Carefully noting down every lineament and feature,—their change, their action, and their development,—they track a lurking motive with the scent of a bloodhound, and run down a growing passion with an unrelenting speed. I have been in the witness-box, exposed to the licensed badgering and privileged impertinence of a lawyer; winked, leered, frowned, and sneered at with all the long-practised tact of a *Nisi Prius* torturer; I have stood before the cold, fish-like, but searching eye of a prefect of police, as he compared my passport with my person, and thought he could detect a discrepancy in both; but I never felt the same sense of total exposure as when glanced at by the half-curious, half-prying look of a worthy father or mother in a family where there are daughters to marry, and "nobody coming to woo."

"You're early, Charley," said Mr. Blake, with an affected mixture of carelessness and warmth. "You have not had breakfast?"

"No, sir. I have come to claim a part of yours; and, if I mistake not, you seem a little later than usual."

"Not more than a few minutes. The girls will be down presently; they're early risers, Charley; good habits are just as easy as bad ones; and, the Lord be praised! my girls were never brought up with any other."

"I am well aware of it, sir; and, indeed, if I may be permitted to take advantage of the *à propos*, it was on the subject of one of your daughters that I wished to speak to you this morning, and which brought me over at this uncivilized hour, hoping to find you alone."

Mr. Blake's look for a moment was one of triumphant satisfaction; it was but a glance, however, and repressed the very instant after, as he said, with a well got-up indifference.

"Just step with me into the study, and we're sure not to be interrupted."

Now, although I have little time or space for such dallying, I cannot help dwelling for a moment upon the aspect of what Mr. Blake dignified with the name of his study. It was a small apartment with one window, the panes of which, independent of all aid from a curtain, tempered the daylight through the medium of cobwebs, dust, and the ill-trained branches of some wall-tree without.

Three oak chairs and a small table were the only articles of furniture; while round on all sides, lay the *disjecta membra* of Mr. Blake's hunting, fishing, shooting, and coursing equipments—old top boots, driving whips, odd spurs, a racing saddle, a blunderbuss, the helmet of the Galway Light Horse, a salmon net, a large map of the county with a marginal index to several mortgages marked with a cross, a stable lantern, the rudder of a boat, and several other articles representative of his daily associations; but not one book, save an odd volume of Watty Cox's Magazine, whose pages seemed as much the receptacle of brown hackles for trout-fishing as the resource of literary leisure.

"Here we'll be quite cosy, and to ourselves," said Mr. Blake, as, placing a chair for me, he sat down himself, with the air of a man resolved to assist, by advice and counsel, the dilemma of some dear friend.

After a few preliminary observations, which, like a breathing canter before a race, serve to get your courage up, and settle you well in your seat, I opened my negotiations by some very broad and sweeping truism about the misfortunes of a bachelor existence, the discomforts of his position, his want of home and happiness, the necessity for his one day thinking seriously about marriage; it being in a measure almost as inevitable a termination of the free-and-easy career of his single life as transportation for seven years is to that of a poacher. "You cannot go on, sir," said I, "trespassing forever upon your neighbor's preserves, you must be apprehended sooner or later; therefore, I think, the better way is to take out a license."

Never was a small sally of wit more thoroughly successful. Mr. Blake laughed till he cried, and, when he had done, wiped his eyes with a snuffy handkerchief, and cried till he laughed again. As, somehow, I could not conceal from myself a suspicion as to the sincerity of my friend's mirth, I merely consoled myself with the French adage, that "he laughs best who laughs last;" and went on.

"It will not be deemed surprising, sir, that a man should come to the discovery I have just mentioned much more rapidly by having enjoyed the pleasure or intimacy with your family; not only by the example of perfect domestic happiness presented to him, but by the prospect held out that a heritage of the fair gifts which adorn and grace a married life may reasonably be looked for among the daughters of those themselves the realization of conjugal felicity."

Here was a canter, with a vengeance; and as I felt blown, I slackened my pace, coughed, and resumed:

"Miss Mary Blake, sir, is, then, the object of my present communication; she it is who has made an existence that seemed fair and pleasurable before, appear blank and unprofitable without her. I have, therefore, to come at once to the point, visited you this morning, formally to ask her hand in marriage; her fortune, I may observe at once, is perfectly immaterial—a matter of no consequence (so Mr. Blake thought also); a competence fully equal to every reasonable notion of expenditure——"

"There—there; don't—don't," said Mr. Blake, wiping his eyes, with a sob like a hiccup; "don't speak of money, I know what you would say; a handsome settlement—a well-secured jointure, and all that. Yes, yes, I feel it all."

"Why yes, sir, I believe I may add, that everything in this respect will answer your expectations."

"Of course; to be sure. My poor dear Baby! How to do without her, that's the rub. You don't know, O'Malley, what that girl is to me—you can't know it; you'll feel it one day though—that you will."

"The devil I shall!" said I to myself. "The great point is, after all, to learn the young lady's disposition in the matter——"

"Ah, Charley! none of this with me, you sly dog! You think I don't know you. Why, I've been watching—that is, I have seen—no, I mean I've heard—they—they, people will talk, you know."

"Very true, sir. But, as I was going to remark——"

Just at this moment the door opened, and Miss Baby herself, looking most annoyingly handsome, put in her head.

"Papa, we're waiting breakfast. Ah, Charley, how d'ye do!"

"Come in, Baby," said Mr. Blake; "you haven't given me my kiss this morning."

The lovely girl threw her arms around his neck, while her bright and flowing locks fell richly upon his shoulder. I turned rather sulkily away; the thing always provokes me. There is as much cold, selfish cruelty in such *coram publico* endearments as in the luscious display of rich rounds and sirloins in a chop-house to the eyes of the starved and penniless wretch without, who, with dripping rags and watering lip, eats imaginary slices, while the pains of hunger are torturing him!

"There's Tim!" said Mr. Blake, suddenly. "Tim Cronin!—Tim!" shouted he to, as it seemed to me, an imaginary individual outside, while, in the eagerness of pursuit, he rushed out of the study, banging the door as he went, and leaving Baby and myself to our mutual edification.

I should have preferred it being otherwise; but, as the Fates willed it thus, I took Baby's hand, and led her to the window. Now, there is one feature of my countrymen which, having recognized strongly in myself, I would fain proclaim; and, writing as I do—however little people may suspect me—solely for the sake of a moral, would gladly warn the unsuspecting against. I mean a very decided tendency to become the consoler, the confidant of young ladies; seeking out opportunities of assuaging their sorrow, reconciling their afflictions, breaking eventful passages to their ears; not from any inherent pleasure in the tragic phases of the intercourse, but for the semi-tenderness of manner, that harmless hand-squeezing, that innocent waist-pressing, without which consolation is but like salmon without lobster—a thing maimed, wanting, and imperfect.

Now, whether this with me was a natural gift, or merely a " way we have in the army," as the song says, I shall not pretend to say; but I venture to affirm that few men could excel me in the practice I speak of some five-and twenty-years ago. Fair reader, do pray, if I have the happiness of being known to you, deduct them from my age before you subtract from my merits.

"Well, Baby dear, I have just been speaking about you to papa. Yes, dear,—don't look so incredulous—even of your own sweet self. Well, do you know I almost prefer your hair worn that way; those same silky masses look better falling thus heavily ——"

"There, now, Charley! ah, don't!"

"Well, Baby, as I was saying, before you stopped me, I have been asking your papa a very important question, and he has referred me to you for the answer. And now will you tell me, in all frankness and honesty, your mind on the matter?"

She grew deadly pale as I spoke these words, then suddenly flushed up again, but said not a word. I could perceive, however, from her heaving chest and restless manner, that no common agitation was stirring her bosom. It was cruelty to be silent, so I continued:

"One who loves you well, Baby dear, has asked his own heart the question, and learned that without you he has no chance of happiness; that your bright eyes are to him bluer than the deep sky above him; that your soft voice, your winning smile,—and what a smile it is!—have taught him that he loves, nay, adores you! Then, dearest,—what pretty fingers those are! Ah! what is this? Whence came that emerald? I never saw that ring before, Baby!"

"Oh, that," said she, blushing deeply,—"that is a ring the foolish creature Sparks gave me a couple of days ago; but I don't like it—I don't intend to keep it."

So saying, she endeavored to draw it from her finger, but in vain.

"But why, Baby, why take it off? Is it to give him the pleasure of putting it on again? There, don't look angry; we must not fall out, surely."

"No, Charley, if you are not vexed with me,—if you are not——"

"No, no, my dear Baby—nothing of the kind. Sparks was quite right in not trusting his entire fortune to my diplomacy; but at least he ought to have told me that he had opened the negotiation. Now, the question simply is—Do you love him? or, rather, because that shortens matters, will you accept him?"

"Love whom?"

"Love whom? Why, Sparks, to be sure!"

A flash of indignant surprise passed across her features, now pale as marble; her lips were slightly parted, her large full eyes were fixed upon me steadfastly, and her hand, which I had held in mine, she suddenly withdrew from my grasp.

"And so—and so it is of Mr. Sparks's cause you are so ardently the advocate?" said she, at length, after a pause of most awkward duration.

"Why, of course, my dear cousin. It was at his suit and solicitation I called on your father; it was he himself who entreated me to take this step; it was he——"

But before I could conclude, she burst into a torrent of tears, and rushed from the room.

Here was a situation ! What the deuce was the matter ? Did she or did she not care for him ? Was her pride or her delicacy hurt at my being made the means of the communication to her father ? What had Sparks done or said to put himself and me in such a devil of a predicament ? Could she care for any one else ?

"Well, Charley !" cried Mr. Blake, as he entered, rubbing his hands in a perfect paroxysm of good temper—"well, Charley, has love-making driven breakfast out of your head ?"

"Why, faith, sir, I greatly fear I have blundered my mission sadly. My cousin Mary does not appear so perfectly satisfied ; her manner ——"

"Don't tell me such nonsense. The girl's manner ! Why, man, I thought you were too old a soldier to be taken in that way."

"Well, then, sir, the best thing, under the circumstances, is to send over Sparks himself. Your consent, I may tell him, is already obtained."

"Yes, my boy; and my daughter's is equally sure. But I don't see what we want with Sparks at all. Among old friends and relatives, as we are, there is, I think, no need of a stranger."

"A stranger ! Very true, sir, he is a stranger ; but when that stranger is about to become your son-in-law ——"

"About to become what ?" said Mr. Blake, rubbing his spectacles, and placing them leisurely on his nose to regard me,—"to become what ?"

"Your son-in-law. I hope I have been sufficiently explicit, sir, in making known Mr. Sparks's wishes to you."

"Mr. Sparks ! Why, d— me, sir,—that is—I beg pardon for the warmth—you—you never mentioned his name to-day till now. You led me to suppose that—in fact you told me most clearly ——"

Here, from the united effects of rage and a struggle for concealment, Mr. Blake was unable to proceed, and walked the room with a melodramatic stamp perfectly awful.

"Really, sir," said I at last, "while I deeply regret any misconception or mistake I have been the cause of, I must, in justice to myself, say that I am perfectly unconscious of having misled you. I came here this morning with a proposition for the hand of your daughter in behalf of——"

"Yourself, sir. Yes, yourself. I'll be—no ! I'll not swear ; but— but just answer me if you ever mentioned one word of Mr. Sparks— if you ever alluded to him till the last few minutes ?"

I was perfectly astounded. It might be ; alas ! it was exactly as he stated. In my unlucky effort at extreme delicacy, I became only so very mysterious, that I left the matter open for them to suppose that it might be the Khan of Tartary who was in love with Baby.

There was but one course now open. I most humbly apologized for my blunder, repeated, by every expression I could summon up, my sorrow for what had happened, and was beginning a renewal of negotiation "*in re* Sparks," when, overcome by his passion, Mr. Blake could hear no more, but snatched up his hat and left the room.

Had it not been for Baby's share in the transaction, I should have laughed outright. As it was, I felt anything but mirthful; and the only clear and collected idea in my mind was, to hurry home with all speed, and fasten a quarrel on Sparks, the innocent cause of the whole mishap. Why this thought struck me, let physiologists decide.

A few moments' reflection satisfied me that, under present circumstances, it would be particularly awkward to meet with any others of the family. Ardently desiring to secure my retreat, I succeeded, after some little time, in opening the window-sash, consoling myself for any injury I was about to inflict upon Mr. Blake's young plantation in my descent, by the thought of the service I was rendering him, while also admitting a little fresh air into his sanctum.

For my patriotism's sake I will not record my sensations as I took my way through the shrubbery towards the stable. Men are ever so prone to revenge their faults and their follies upon such inoffensive agencies as time and place, wind or weather, that I was quite convinced that to any other but Galway ears my *exposé* would have been perfectly clear and intelligible,.and that in no other country under heaven would a man be expected to marry a young lady from a blunder in his grammar.

"Baby may be quite right," thought I; "but one thing is assuredly true—if I'll never do for Galway, Galway will never do for me. No, hang it! I have endured enough for above two years. I have lived in banishment, away from society, supposing that, at least, if I isolated myself from the pleasures of the world, I was exempt from its annoyances." But no; in the seclusion of my remote abode, troubles found their entrance as easily as elsewhere, so that I determined at once to leave home—where for, I knew not. If life had few charms, it had still fewer ties for me. If I was not bound by the bonds of kindred, I was untrammelled by their restraints.

The resolution once taken, I burned to put it into effect; and so impatiently did I press forward, as to call forth more than one remonstrance on the part of Mike at the pace we were proceeding at.

As I neared home, the shrill but stirring sounds of drum and fife met me, and shortly after a crowd of country people filled the road. Supposing it some mere recruiting party, I was endeavoring to press on, when the sounds of a full military band, in the exhilarating measure of a quickstep, convinced me of my error; and, as I drew to one side of the road, the advanced guard of an infantry regiment came forward. The men's faces were flushed, their uniforms dusty and travel-stained, their knapsacks strapped firmly on, and their gait the steady tramp of the march. Saluting the subaltern, I asked if anything of consequence had occurred in the south, that the troops were so suddenly under orders. The officer stared at me for a moment or two without speaking, and, while a slight smile curled his lip, then answered,—

"Apparently, sir, you seem very indifferent to military news, otherwise you can scarcely be ignorant of the cause of our route."

"On the contrary," said I, "I am, though a young man, an old soldier, and feel most anxious about everything connected with the service."

"Then it is very strange, sir, you should not have heard the news. Bonaparte has returned from Elba, has arrived at Paris, been received with the most overwhelming enthusiasm, and at this moment the preparations for war are resounding from Venice to the Vistula. All our disposable forces are on the march for embarkation. Lord Wellington has taken the command, and already, I may say, the campaign has begun."

The tone of enthusiasm in which the young officer spoke, the astounding intelligence itself, contrasting with the apathetic indolence of my own life, made me blush deeply, as I muttered some miserable apology for my ignorance.

"And you are now *en route?*"

"For Fermoy, from which we march to Cove for embarkation. The first battalion of our regiment sailed for the West Indies a week since, but a frigate has been sent after them to bring them back; and we hope all to meet in the Netherlands before the month is over. But I must beg your pardon for saying adieu. Good-bye, sir."

"Good-bye, sir; good-bye;" said I, as, still standing in the road, I was so overwhelmed with surprise that I could scarcely credit my senses.

A little further on I came up with the main body of the regiment, from whom I learned the corroboration of the news, and also the additional intelligence that Sparks had been ordered off with his detachment early in the morning, a veteran battalion being sent into garrison in the various towns of the south and west.

"Do you happen to know a Mr. O'Malley, sir?" said the Major, coming up with a note in his hand.

"I beg to present him to you," said I, bowing.

"Well, sir, Sparks gave me this note, which he wrote with a pencil as we crossed each other on the road this morning. He told me you were an old 14th man; but your regiment is in India, I believe; at least Power said they were under orders when we met him."

"Fred Power! are you acquainted with him? Where is he now, pray?"

"Fred is on the staff with General Vandeleur, and is now in Belgium."

"Indeed!" said I, every moment increasing my surprise at some new piece of intelligence. "And the 88th?" said I, recurring to my old friends in that regiment.

"Oh, the 88th are at Gibraltar or somewhere in the Mediterranean: at least, I know they are not near enough to open the present campaign with us. But if you'd like to hear any more news, you must come over to Borrisokane; we stop there to-night."

"Then I'll certainly do so."

"Come at six, then, and dine with us."

"Agreed," said I; "and now, good-morning."

So saying, I once more drove on; my head full of all that I had been hearing, and my heart bursting with eagerness to join the gallant fellows now bound for the campaign.

CHAPTER LI.

BRUSSELS.

I MUST not protract a tale already far too long by the recital of my acquaintance with the gallant 26th. It is sufficient that I should say that, having given Mike orders to follow me to Cove, I joined the regiment on their march, and accompanied them to Cork. Every hour of each day brought us in news of moment and importance; and, amid all the stirring preparations for the war, the account of the splendid spectacle of the *Champ de Mai* burst upon astonished Europe, and the intelligence spread far and near that the enthusiasm of France never rose higher in favor of the Emperor; and, while the whole world made preparations for the deadly

44

combat, Napoleon surpassed even himself, by the magnificent conceptions for the coming conflict, and the stupendous nature of those plans by which he resolved on resisting combined and united Europe.

While our admiration and wonder of the mighty spirit that ruled the destinies of the Continent rose high, so did our own ardent and burning desire for the day when the open field of fight should place us once more in front of each other.

Every hard-fought engagement of the Spanish war was thought of and talked over; from Talavera to Toulouse, all was remembered; and while among the old Peninsulars the military ardor was so universally displayed, among the regiments who had not shared the glories of Spain and Portugal, an equal, perhaps a greater, impulse was created for the approaching campaign.

When we arrived at Cork, the scene of bustle and excitement exceeded anything I ever witnessed. Troops were mustering in every quarter; regiments arriving and embarking; fresh bodies of men pouring in; drills, parades, and inspections going forward; arms, ammunition, and military stores distributing; and, amid all, a spirit of burning enthusiasm animated every rank for the approaching glory of the newly-arisen war.

While thus each was full of his own hopes and expectations, I alone felt depressed and downhearted. . My military caste was lost to me forever; my regiment many, many a mile from the scene of the coming strife; though young, I felt like one already old and bygone. The last-joined ensign seemed, in his glowing aspiration, a better soldier than I, as, sad and dispirited, I wandered through the busy crowds, surveying with curious eye each gallant horseman as he rode proudly past. What were wealth and fortune to me? What had they ever been, compared with all they cost me?—the abandonment of the career I loved—the path in life I sought and panted for? Day after day I lingered on, watching with beating heart each detachment as they left the shore; and when their parting cheer rang high above the breeze, I turned sadly back to mourn over a life that had failed in its promise, and an existence now shorn of its enjoyment.

It was on the evening of the 3d of June that I was slowly wending my way back towards my hotel; latterly I had refused all invitations to dine at the mess; and, by a strange spirit of contradiction, while I avoided society, could not yet tear myself away from the spot where every remembrance of my past life was daily embittered by the scenes around me. But so it was; the movement of the troops, their reviews, their arrivals and departures, possessed the most thrilling interest for me; while I could not endure to hear the mention of the high hopes and glorious vows each brave fellow muttered.

It was, as I remember, on the evening of the 3d of June, I entered my hotel, lower in spirits even than usual; the bugles of the gallant 71st, as they dropped down with the tide, played a well-known march I had heard the night before Talavera; all my bold and hardy days came rushing madly to my mind; and my present life seemed no longer endurable. The last Army List and the newspapers lay on my table, and I turned to read the latest promotions with that feeling of bitterness by which an unhappy man loves to tamper with his misery.

Almost the first paragraph I threw my eyes upon ran thus:—

"OSTEND, MAY 24.—The sloop-of-war *Vixen*, which arrived at our port this morning, brought, among several other officers of inferior note, Lieutenant-General Sir George Dashwood, appointed as Assistant-Adjutant-General on the staff of his Grace the Duke of Wellington. The gallant General was accompanied by his lovely and accomplished daughter, and his military secretary and aide-de-camp, Major Hammersley, of the 2d Life Guards. They partook of a hurried *déjeûné* with the Burgomaster, and left immediately after for Brussels."

Twice I read this over, while a burning, hot sensation settled upon my throat and temples. "So Hammersley still persists—he still hopes. And what then?—what can it be to me? My prospects have long since faded and vanished! doubtless, ere this, I am as much forgotten as though we had never met,—would that we never had!" I threw up the window-sash; a light breeze was gently stirring, and, as it fanned my hot and bursting head, I felt cool and relieved. Some soldiers were talking beneath the window, and among them I recognized Mike's voice.

"And so you sail at daybreak, sergeant?"

"Yes, Mr. Free; we have our orders to be on board before the flood-tide. The *Thunderer* drops down the harbor to-night, and we are merely here to collect our stragglers."

"Faix, it's little I thought I'd ever envy a sodger any more; but, some way, I wish I was going with you."

"Nothing easier, Mike," said another, laughing.

"Oh, true for you, but that's not the way I'd like to do it. If my master, now, would just get over his low spirits, and spake a word to the Duke of York, devil a doubt but he'd give him his commission back again, and then one might go in comfort."

"Your master likes his feather pillow better than a mossy stone under his head, I'm thinking; and he ain't far wrong, either."

"You're out there, neighbor. It's himself cares as little for hardships as any one of you; and sure it's not becoming me to say it, but the best blood and the best bred was always the last to give in for either cold or hunger, ay, or even complain of it."

Mike's few words shot upon me a new and a sudden conviction—what was to prevent my joining once more? Obvious as such a thought now was, yet never until this moment did it present itself so palpably. So habituated does the mind become to a certain train of reasoning, framing its convictions according to one preconceived plan, and making every fact and every circumstance concur in strengthening what may be but a prejudice, that the absence of the old 14th in India, the sale of my commission, the want of rank in the service, all seemed to present an insurmountable barrier to my re-entering the army. A few chance words now changed all this, and I saw that, as a volunteer, at least, the path of glory was still open, and the thought was no sooner conceived than the resolve to execute it. While, therefore, I walked hurriedly up and down, devising, planning, plotting, and contriving, each instant I would stop to ask myself how it happened I had not determined upon this before.

As I summoned Mike before me, I could not repress a feeling of false shame as I remembered how suddenly so natural a resolve must seem to have been adopted; and it was with somewhat of hesitation that I opened the conversation.

"And so, sir, you are going, after all?—long life to you! But I never doubted it. Sure, you wouldn't be your father's son, and not join divarsion when there was any going."   -

The poor fellow's eyes brightened up, his look gladdened, and before he reached the foot of the stairs I heard his loud cheer of delight, that once more we were off to the wars.

The packet sailed for Liverpool the next morning; by it we took our passage, and on the third morning I found myself in the waiting-room at the Horse Guards, expecting the moment of his Royal Highness's arrival; my determination being to serve as a volunteer in any regiment the Duke might suggest, until such time as a prospect presented itself of entering the service as a subaltern.

The room was crowded by officers of every rank and arm in the service. The old, gray-headed general of division; the tall, stout-looking captain of infantry; the thin and boyish figure of the newly-gazetted cornet, were all there. Every accent, every look that marked each trait of national distinction in the empire, had its representative,—the reserved, and distant Scotchman; the gay, laughing, exuberant Patlander; the dark-eyed and dark-browed North Briton, collected in groups, talking eagerly together; while every instant, as some new arrival would enter, all eyes would turn to the spot, in eager expectation of the Duke's coming. At last the clash of arms, as the guard turned out, apprised us of his approach, and we had scarcely time to stand up and stop the buzz of voices, when the door opened, and an aide-de-camp proclaimed, in a full tone,

"His Royal Highness the Commander-in-Chief!"

Bowing courteously on every side, he advanced through the crowd, turning his rapid and piercing look here and there through the room, while with that tact, the essential gift of his family, he recognized each person by his name, directing from one to the other some passing observation.

"Ah, Sir George Cockburn, how d'ye do?—your son's appointment is made out. · Major Conyers, that application shall be looked to. Forbes, you must explain that I cannot possibly put men in the regiment of their choice—the service is the first thing. Lord L——, your memorial is before the Prince Regent—the cavalry command will, I believe, however, include your name."

While he spoke thus, he approached the place where I was standing, when, suddenly checking himself, he looked at me for a moment somewhat sternly.

"Why not in uniform, sir?"

"Your Royal Highness, I am not in the army."

"Not in the army—not in the army? And why, may I beg to know, have you—but I'm speaking to *Captain* O'Malley, if I mistake not?"

"I held that rank, sir, once, but family necessities compelled me to sell out; I have no commission in the service, but am come to beseech your Royal Highness's permission to serve as a volunteer."

"As a volunteer, eh—a volunteer? Come, that's right, I like that; but still, we want such fellows as you—the man of Ciudad Rodrigo. Yes, my lord, this is one of the stormers; fought his way through the trench among the first; must not be neglected. Hold yourself in readiness, Captain—hang it, I was forgetting—Mr. O'Malley, I mean—hold yourself in readiness for a staff appointment. Smithson, take a note of this." So saying, he moved on; and I found myself in the street, with a heart bounding with delight, and a step proud as an emperor's.

With such rapidity did the events of my life now follow one upon the other, that I could take no note of time as it passed. On the fourth day after my conversation with the Duke I found myself in Brussels. As yet, I heard nothing of the appointment, nor was I gazetted to any regiment or any situation on the staff. It was strange enough, too, I met but few of my old associates, and not one of those with whom I had been most intimate in my Peninsular

career; but it so chanced that very many of the regiments who most
distinguished themselves in the Spanish campaigns, at the peace of
1814 were sent on foreign service. My old friend Power was, I
learned, quartered at Courtrai; and, as I was perfectly at liberty to
dispose of my movements at present, I resolved to visit him there.

It was a beautiful evening on the 12th of June. I had been in·
quiring concerning post-horses for my journey, and was returning
slowly through the park. The hour was late—near midnight—but
a pale moonlight, a calm, unruffled air, and stronger inducements
still, the song of the nightingales that abound in this place, prevailed on many of the loungers to prolong their stay; and so, from
many a shady walk and tangled arbor, the clank of a sabre would
strike upon the ear, or the low, soft voice of woman would mingle
its dulcet sound with the deep tones of her companion. I wandered
on, thoughtful and alone; my mind preoccupied so completely with
the mighty events passing before me, that I totally forgot my own
humble career, and the circumstances of my fortune. As I turned
into an alley which leads from the Great Walk towards the palace
of the Prince of Orange, I found my path obstructed by three persons who were walking slowly along in front of me. I was, as I
have mentioned, deeply absorbed in thought, so that I found myself
close behind them before I was aware of their presence. Two of the
party were in uniform, and by their plumes, upon which a passing
ray of moonlight flickered, I could detect they were general officers;
the third was a lady. Unable to pass them, and unwilling to turn
back, I was unavoidably compelled to follow, and, however unwilling, to overhear somewhat of their conversation.

"You mistake, George, you mistake. Depend upon it, this will
be no lengthened campaign; victory will soon decide for one side
or the other. If Napoleon beats the Prussians one day, and beats
us the next, the German states will rally to his standard, and the
old confederation of the Rhine will spring up once more, in all the
plenitude of its power. The *Champ de Mai* has shown the enthusiasm of France for their emperor. Louis Eighteenth fled from his
capital, with few to follow, and none to say, 'God bless him!' The
warlike spirit of the nation is roused again; the interval of peace,
too short to teach habits of patient and enduring industry, is yet
sufficient to whet the appetite for carnage, and nothing is wanting'
save the presence of Napoleon alone to restore all the brilliant delusions and intoxicating splendors of the empire."

"I confess," said the other, "I take a very different view from
yours in this matter. To me it seems that France is as tired of
battles as of the Bourbons——"

I heard no more, for, though the speaker continued, a misty confusion passed across my mind. The tones of his voice, well remembered as they were by me, left me unable to think, and as I stood motionless on the spot, I muttered, half aloud, "Sir George Dashwood." It was he, indeed; and she who leaned upon his arm could be no other than Lucy herself. I know not how it was; for many a long month I had schooled my heart, and taught myself to believe that time had dulled thê deep impression she had made upon me, and that were we to meet again, it would be with more sorrow on my part for my broken dream of happiness than of attachment and affection for her who inspired it; but now, scarcely was I near her— I had not gazed upon her looks, I had not even heard her voice— and yet, in all their ancient force came back the early passages of my love, and as her footfall sounded gently upon the ground, my heart beat scarce less audibly. Alas! I could no longer disguise from myself the avowal that she it was, and she only, who implanted in my heart the thirst for distinction, and the moment was ever present to my mind in which, as she threw her arms round her father's neck, she muttered, "Oh, why not a soldier?"

As I thus reflected, an officer in full dress passed me hurriedly, and taking off his hat as he came up with the party before me, bowed obsequiously.

"My Lord——, I believe, and Sir George Dashwood?" They replied by a bow. "Sir Thomas Picton wishes to speak with you both for a moment; he is standing beside the 'Basin.' If you will permit——" said he, looking toward Lucy.

"Thank you, sir," said Sir George; "if you will have the goodness to accompany us, my daughter will wait our coming here. Sit down, Lucy; we shall not be long away."

The next moment she was alone. The last echoes of their retiring footsteps had died away in the grassy walk, and in the calm and death-like stillness I could hear every rustle of her silk dress. The moonlight fell in fitful, straggling gleams between the leafy branches, and showed me her countenance, pale as marble. Her eyes were upturned slightly; her brown hair, divided upon her fair forehead, sparkled with a wreath of brilliants, which heightened the lustrous effect of her calm beauty; and now I could perceive her dress bespoke that she had been at some of the splendid entertainments which followed day after day in the busy capital.

Thus I stood within a few paces of *her* to be near whom, a few hours before, I would willingly have given all I possessed in the world; and yet now a barrier far more insurmountable than time and space intervened between us; still, it seemed as though fortune had presented this incident as a last farewell between us. Why should I not take advantage of it? Why should I not seize the only opportu-

nity that might ever occur of rescuing myself from the apparent load
of ingratitude which weighed on me ? I felt in the cold despair of
my heart that I could have no hold upon her affection; but a pride
scarce less strong than the attachment that gave rise to it urged me
to speak. By one violent effort I summoned up my courage; and
while I resolved to limit the few words I should say merely to my
vindication, I prepared to advance. Just at this instant, however,
a shadow crossed the path; a rustling sound was heard among the
branches, and the tall figure of a man in a dragoon cloak stood
before me. Lucy turned suddenly at the sound ; but scarcely had
her eyes been bent in the direction, when, throwing off his cloak, he
sprang forward, and dropped at her feet. All my feeling of shame
at the part I was performing was now succeeded by a sense of savage
and revengeful hatred. It was enough that I should be brought
to look upon her whom I had lost forever without the added
bitterness of witnessing her preference for a rival. The whirlwind
passion of my brain stunned and stupefied me. Unconsciously I
drew my sword from my scabbard, and it was only as the pale light
fell upon the keen blade that the thought flashed across me, " What
could I mean to do ?"

"No, Hammersley,"—it was he indeed,—said she, " it is unkind,
it is unfair, nay, it is unmanly to press me thus. I would not pain
you, were it not that in sparing you now I should entail deeper
injury upon you hereafter. Ask me to be your sister—your friend ;
ask me to feel proudly in your triumphs—to glory in your success ;
all this I do feel ; but oh ! I beseech you, as you value your happiness—as you prize mine—ask me no more than this."

There was a pause of some seconds, and at length the low tones
of a man's voice, broken and uncertain in their utterance, said,—

"I know it—I feel it. My heart never bade me hope—and now—
'tis over."

He stood up as he spoke, and while he threw the light folds of his
mantle round him, a gleam of light fell upon his features. They
were pale as death ; two dark circles surrounded his sunken eyes,
and his bloodless lip looked still more ghastly from the dark moustache that drooped above it.

"Farewell !" said he, slowly, as he crossed his arms sadly upon
his breast ; "I will not pain you more."

"Oh ! go not thus from me," said she, as her voice became
tremulous with emotion ; "do not add to the sorrow that weighs
upon my heart. I cannot, indeed I cannot, be other than I am ;
and I do but hate myself to think that I cannot give my love where
I have given all my esteem. If time——" But before she could
continue further, the noise of approaching footsteps was heard, and

the voice of Sir George, as he came near. Hammersley disappeared at once, and Lucy, with rapid steps, advanced to meet her father, while I remained riveted upon the spot. What a torrent of emotions then rushed upon my heart! What hopes, long dead or dying, sprang up to life again! What visions of long-abandoned happiness flitted before me! Could it be, then? dare I trust myself to think of it, that Lucy cared for me? The thought was maddening. With a bounding sense of ecstasy I dashed across the park, resolving at all hazards to risk everything upon the chance, and wait the next morning upon Sir George Dashwood. As I thought thus, I reached my hotel, where I found Mike in waiting with a letter. As I walked towards the lamp in the *porte cochère*, my eye fell upon the address. It was in General Dashwood's hand. I tore it open, and read as follows:

"DEAR SIR:—Circumstances, into which you will excuse me entering, having placed an insurmountable barrier to our former terms of intimacy, you will, I trust, excuse me declining the honor of any nearer acquaintance, and also forgive the liberty I take in informing you of it, which step, however unpleasant to my feelings, will save us both the great pain of meeting.

"I have only this moment heard of your arrival in Brussels, and take thus the earliest opportunity of communicating with you.

"With every assurance of my respect for you personally, and an earnest desire to serve you in your military career,

"I beg to remain,

"Very faithfully yours,

"GEORGE DASHWOOD."

"Another note, sir," said Mike, as he thrust into my hand a letter he had just received from an orderly.

Stunned, half stupefied, I broke the seal. The contents were but three lines.

"SIR:—I have the honor to inform you that Sir Thomas Picton has appointed you an extra aide-de-camp on his personal staff. You will therefore present yourself to-morrow morning at the Adjutant-General's office, to receive your appointment and instructions.

"I have the honor to be, &c.

"G. FITZROY."

Crushing the two letters in my fevered hand, I retired to my room, and threw myself, dressed as I was, upon my bed. Sleep, that seems to visit us in the saddest as in the happiest times of our existence, came over me, and I did not awake until the bugles of the 95th were sounding the *reveille* through the park, and the bright beams of the morning sun were peering through the window.

CHAPTER LII.

AN OLD ACQUAINTANCE.

MR. O'MALLEY," said a voice, as my door opened, and an officer in undress entered. "Mr. O'Malley, I believe you received your appointment last night on General Picton's staff?"

I bowed in reply, as he resumed:

"Sir Thomas desires that you will proceed to Courtrai with these despatches in all haste. I don't know if you are well mounted, but I recommend you, in any case, not to spare your cattle."

So saying, he wished me a good morning, and left me, in a state of no small doubt and difficulty, to my own reflections. What the deuce was I to do? I had no horse; I knew not where to find one. What uniform should I wear? For although appointed on the staff, I was not gazetted to any regiment that I knew of, and hitherto had been wearing an undress frock and a foraging cap, for I could not bear to appear as a civilian among so many military acquaintances. No time was, however, to be lost, so I proceeded to put on my old 14th uniform, wondering whether my costume might not cost me a reprimand in the very outset of my career. Meanwhile I despatched Mike to see after a horse, caring little for the time, the merits, or the price of the animal, provided he served my present purpose.

In less than twenty minutes my worthy follower appeared beneath my window, surrounded by a considerable mob, who seemed to take no small interest in the proceedings.

"What the deuce is the matter?" cried I, as I opened the sash and looked out.

"Mighty little's the matter, your honor; it's the savages here that's admiring my horsemanship," said Mike, as he belabored a tall, scraggy-looking mule with a stick which bore an uncommon resemblance to a broom-handle.

"What do you mean to do with that beast?" said I. "You surely don't expect me to ride a mule to Courtrai?"

" Faith, and if you don't, you are likely to walk the journey ; for there isn't a horse to be had for love or money in the town ; but I am told that Mr. Marsden is coming up to-morrow with plenty, so that you may as well take the journey out of the soft horns as spoil a better, and if he only makes as good use of his fore legs as he does of the hind ones, he'll think little of the road."

A vicious lash out behind served in a moment to corroborate Mike's assertion, and to scatter the crowd on every side.

However indisposed to exhibit myself with such a turnout, my time did not admit of any delay ; and so, arming myself with my despatches, and having procured the necessary information as to the road, I set out from the Belle Vue, amid an ill-suppressed titter of merriment from the mob, which nothing but fear of Mike and his broomstick prevented becoming a regular shout of laughter.

It was near nightfall as, tired and weary of the road, I entered the little village of Halle. All was silent and noiseless in the deserted streets ; not a lamp threw its glare upon the pavement, not even a solitary candle flickered through the casement. Unlike a town garrisoned by troops, neither sentry nor outpost was to be met with ; nothing gave evidence that the place was held by a large body of men ; and I could not help feeling struck, as the footsteps of my mule were echoed along the causeway, with the silence almost of desolation around me. By the creaking of a sign, as it swung mournfully to and fro, I was directed to the door of the village inn, where, dismounting, I knocked for some moments, but without success. At length, when I had made an uproar sufficient to alarm the entire village, the casement above the door slowly opened, and a head enveloped in a huge cotton nightcap—so, at least, it appeared to me from the size—protruded itself. After uttering a curse in about the most barbarous French I ever heard, he asked me what I wanted there; to which I replied, most nationally, by asking in return where the British dragoons were quartered.

"They left for Nivelle this morning, to join some regiments of your own country."

"Ah! ah!" thought I, "he mistakes me for a Brunswicker," to which, by the uncertain light, my uniform gave me some resemblance. As it was now impossible for me to proceed further, I begged to ask where I could procure accommodation for the night.

"At the Burgomaster's. Turn to your left at the end of this street, and you will soon find it. They have got some English officers there, who, I believe in my soul, never sleep."

This was, at least, pleasant intelligence, and promised a better termination to my journey than I had begun to hope for; so wishing

my friend a good-night, to which he willingly responded, I resumed
my way down the street. As he closed the window, once more leaving me to my reflections, I began to wonder within myself to what
arm of the service these officers belonged to whose convivial gifts he
bore testimony. As I turned the corner of the street, I soon discovered the correctness of his information. A broad glare of light
stretched across the entire pavement from a large house with a
clumsy stone portico before it. On coming nearer, the sound of
voices, the roar of laughter, the shouts of merriment that issued
forth, plainly bespoke that a jovial party were seated within. The
half-shutter which closed the lower part of the windows prevented
my obtaining a view of the proceedings; but having cautiously approached the casement, I managed to creep on the window-sill and
look into the room.

There the scene was certainly a curious one. Around a large table
sat a party of some twenty persons, the singularity of whose appearance may be conjectured when I mention that all those who appeared to be British officers were dressed in the robes of the *échevins*
(or aldermen) of the village; while some others, whose looks bespoke
them as sturdy Flemings, sported the cocked hats and cavalry helmets of their associates. He who appeared the ruler of the feast sat
with his back towards me, and wore, in addition to the dress of burgomaster, a herald's tabard, which gave him something the air of a
grotesque screen at its potations. A huge fire blazed upon the
ample hearth, before which were spread several staff uniforms, whose
drabbled and soaked appearance denoted the reason of the party's
change of habiliments. Every imaginable species of drinking-vessel
figured upon the board, from the rich flagon of chased silver to the
humble *cruche* we see in a Teniers picture. As well as I could hear,
the language of the company seemed to be French, or, at least, such
an imitation of that language as served as a species of neutral territory for both parties to meet in.

He of the tabard spoke louder than the others, and although, from
the execrable endeavors he made to express himself in French, his
natural voice was much altered, there was yet something in his accents which seemed perfectly familiar to me.

"*Mosheer l'Abbey,*" said he, placing his arm familiarly on the
shoulder of a portly personage, whose shaven crown strangely contrasted with a pair of corked moustaches—"*Mosheer l'Abbey, nous
sommes frères, et moi, savez-vous, suis évêque,*—'pon my life it's true; I
might have been Bishop of Saragossa, if I had only consented to
leave the 23d. *Jé suis bong Catholique.* Lord bless you, if you saw
how I loved the nunneries of Spain! *J'ai très* jolly *souvenirs* of
those nunneries—a goodly company of little silver saints; and this

waistcoat you see—*mong gilet*—was a satin petticoat of our Lady of Loretto."

Need I say that before this speech was concluded, I had recognized in the speaker nobody but that inveterate old villain, Monsoon himself?

"*Permettez, votre Excellence,*" said a hale, jolly-looking personage on his left, as he filled the Major's goblet with obsequious politeness.

"*Bong engfong,*" replied Monsoon, tapping him familiarly on the head. "Burgomaster, you are a trump; and when I get my promotion, I'll make you prefect in a wine district. Pass the lush, and don't look sleepy! 'Drowsiness,' says Solomon, 'clothes a man in rags;' and no man knew the world better than Solomon. Don't you be laughing, you raw boys. Never mind them, *Abbey; ils sont petits garçongs*—fags from Eton and Harrow; better judges of mutton broth than sherry negus."

"I say, Major, you are forgetting the song you promised us."

"Yes, yes," said several voices together; "the song, Major! the song!"

"Time enough for that; we're doing very well as it is. Upon my life, though, they hold a deal of wine. I thought we'd have had them fit to bargain with before ten; and see, it's near midnight; and I must have my forage accounts ready for the Commissary-General by to-morrow morning."

This speech having informed me the reason of the Major's presence there, I resolved to wait no longer a mere spectator of their proceedings; so, dismounting from my position, I commenced a vigorous attack upon the door.

It was some time before I was heard; but at length the door was opened, and I was accosted by an Englishman, who, in a strange compound of French and English, asked "what the devil I meant by all that uproar?" Determining to startle my old friend the major, I replied that "I was an aide-de-camp to General Picton, and had come down on very unpleasant business." By this time the noise of the party within had completely subsided, and, from a few whispered sentences, and their thickened breathing, I perceived that they were listening.

"May I ask, sir," continued I, "if Major Monsoon is here?"

"Yes," stammered the Ensign, for such he was.

"Sorry for it, for his sake," said I; "but my orders are peremptory."

A deep groan from within, and a muttered request to pass down the sherry, nearly overcame my gravity; but I resumed,—

"If you will permit me, I will make the affair as short as possible. The Major, I presume, is here?"

So saying, I pushed forward into the room, where now a slight scuffling noise and murmur of voices had succeeded silence. Brief as was the interval of our colloquy, the scene within had, notwithstanding, undergone considerable change. The English officers, hastily throwing off their aldermanic robes, were busily arraying themselves in their uniforms, while Monsoon himself, with a huge basin of water before him, was endeavoring to wash the cork from his countenance in the corner of his tabard.

"Very hard upon me, all this; upon my life, so it is. Picton is always at me, just as if we had not been school-fellows. The service is getting worse every day. *Regardez moi, Curey, mong* face *est propre?* Eh? There, thank you. Good fellow the Curey is, but takes a deal of fluid. Oh, Burgomaster! I fear it is all up with me! No more fun, no more jollification, no more plunder—and how I did do it! Nothing like watching one's little chances! 'The poor is hated even by his neighbor.' *Oui, Curey*, it is Solomon says that, and they must have had a heavy poor-rate in his day to make him say so. Another glass of sherry?"

By this time I approached the back of his chair, and, slapping him heartily on the shoulder, called out,—

"Major! old boy, how goes it?"

"Eh?—what?—how?—who is this? It can't be—egad, sure it is, though. Charley! Charley O'Malley, you scapegrace, where have you been? When did you join?"

"A week ago, Major. I could resist it no longer. I did my best to be a country gentleman, and behave respectably, but the old temptation was too strong for me. Fred Power and yourself, Major, had ruined my education; and here I am once more amongst you."

"And so Picton, and the arrest, and all that, was nothing but a joke?" said the old fellow, rolling his wicked eyes with a most cunning expression.

"Nothing more, Major; set your heart at rest."

"What a scamp you are," said he, with another grin. "*Il est mon fils—il est mon fils, Curey*," presenting me, as he spoke, while the Burgomaster, in whose eyes the Major seemed no inconsiderable personage, saluted me with profound respect.

Turning at once towards this functionary, I explained that I was the bearer of important despatches, and that my horse—I was ashamed to say my mule—having fallen lame, I was unable to proceed.

"Can you procure me a remount, monsieur?" said I, "for I must hasten on to Courtrai."

"In half an hour you shall be provided, as well as with a mounted guide for the road. *Le fils de son Excellence*," said he, with emphasis, bowing to the Major as he spoke, who, in his turn, repaid the courtesy with a still lower obeisance.

"Sit down, Charley; here is a clean glass. I am delighted to see you, my boy! They tell me you have got a capital estate, and plenty of ready. Lord! we so wanted you, as there's scarcely a fellow with sixpence among us. Give me the lad that can do a bit of paper at three months, and always be ready for a renewal! You haven't got a twenty-pound note?" This was said *sotto voce.* "Never mind, ten will do; you will give me the remainder at Brussels. Strange, is it not, I have not seen a bit of clean bank paper like this for above a twelvemonth!" This was said as he thrust his hand into his pocket, with one of those peculiar leers upon his countenance which, unfortunately, betrayed more satisfaction at his success than gratitude for the service. "You are looking fat—too fat, I think," said he, scrutinizing me from head to foot; "but the life we are leading just now will soon take that off. The slave-trade is luxurious indolence compared to it. Post haste to Nivelle one day; down to Ghent the next; forty miles over a paved road in a hand-gallop, and an aide-de-camp with a watch in his hand at the end of it, to report if you are ten minutes too late. And there is Wellington has his eye everywhere; there is not a truss of hay served to the cavalry, nor a pair of shoes half-soled in the regiment, that he don't know of. I've got it over the knuckles already."

"How so, Major?—how was that?"

"Why, he ordered me to picket two squadrons of the 7th, and a supper was waiting. I didn't like to leave my quarters, so I took up my telescope and pitched upon a sweet little spot of ground on a hill—rather difficult to get up, to be sure, but a beautiful view when you're on it. 'There is your ground, Captain,' said I, 'as I sent one of my people to mark the spot.' He did not like it much; however, he was obliged to go. And, would you believe it?—so much for bad luck!—there turned out to be no water within two miles of it—not a drop, Charley; and so, about eleven at night, the two squadrons moved down into Grammont to wet their lips, and, what is worse, to report me to the commanding officer. And, only think, they put me under arrest because Providence did not make a river run up a mountain!"

Just as the Major finished speaking, the distant clatter of horses' feet and the clank of cavalry was heard approaching. We all rushed eagerly to the door; and scarcely had we done so, when a squadron of dragoons came riding up the street at a fast trot.

"I say, good people," cried the officer, in French, "where does the Burgomaster live here?"

"Fred Power, 'pon my life!" shouted the Major.

"Eh, Monsoon! that you?　Give me a tumbler of wine, old boy; you are sure to have some, and I am desperately blown."

"Get down, Fred, get down; we have an old friend here."

"Who the deuce d'ye mean?" said he, as throwing himself from the saddle, he strode into the room.　"Charley O'Malley! by all that's glorious!"

"Fred, my gallant fellow!" said I.

"It was but this morning, Charley, that I so wished for you here. The French are advancing, my lad; they have crossed the frontier; Ziethen's corps have been attacked, and driven in; Blucher is falling back upon Ligny; and the campaign is opened.　But I must press forward; the regiment is close behind me, and we are ordered to push for Brussels in all haste."

"Then these despatches," said I, showing my packet, "'tis unnecessary to proceed with?"

"Quite so.　Get into the saddle, and come back with us."

The Burgomaster had kept his word with me; so, mounted upon a strong hackney, I set out with Power on the road to Brussels.　I have had occasion more than once to ask pardon of my reader for the prolixity of my narrative, so I shall not trespass on him here by the detail of our conversation as we jogged along.　Of me and my adventures he already knows enough—perhaps too much.　My friend Power's career, abounding as it did in striking incidents, and all the light and shadow of a soldier's life, yet not bearing upon any of the characters I have presented to your acquaintance, except in one instance, of that only shall I speak.

"And the Senhora, Fred, how goes your fortune in that quarter?"

"Gloriously, Charley!　I am every day expecting the promotion in my regiment which is to make her mine."

"You have heard from her lately, then?"

"Heard from her!　Why, man, she is in Brussels."

"In Brussels?"

"To be sure.　Don Emanuel is in high favor with the Duke, and is now Commissary-General with the army; and the Senhora is the *belle* of the Rue Royale, or, at least, it's a divided sovereignty between her and Lucy Dashwood.　And now, Charley, let me ask, what of her?　There—there, don't blush, man; there is quite enough moonlight to show how tender you are in that quarter."

"Once for all, Fred, pray spare me on that subject.　You have been far too fortunate in your *affaire de cœur*, and I too much the reverse, to permit much sympathy between us."

"Do you not visit, then? or is it a cut between you?"

"I have never met her since the night of the masquerade of the Villa—at least, to speak to——"

"Well, I must confess you seem to manage your own affairs much worse than your friends'; not but that in so doing you are exhibiting a very Irish feature of your character. In any case, you will come to the ball? Inez will be delighted to see you; and I have got over all my jealousy."

"What ball? I never heard of it."

"Never heard of it! Why, the Duchess of Richmond's, of course. Pooh, pooh! man; not invited?—of course you are invited; the staff are never left out on such occasions. You will find your card at your hotel when you return.

"In any case, Fred——"

"I shall insist upon your going. I have no *arrière pensée* about a reconciliation with the Dashwoods—no subtle scheme, on my honor; but simply I feel that you will never give yourself fair chances in the world by indulging your habit of shrinking from every embarrassment. Don't be offended, boy; I know you have pluck enough to storm a battery; I have seen you under fire before now. What avails your courage in the field if you have not presence of mind in the drawing-room? Besides, everything else out of the question, it is a breach of etiquette towards your chief to decline such an invitation."

"You think so?"

"Think so?—No; I am sure of it."

"Then, as to uniform, Fred?"

"Oh, as to that, easily managed. And, now I think of it, they have sent me an unattached uniform, which you can have; but remember, my boy, if I put you in my coat, I don't want you to stand in my shoes. Don't forget, also, that I am your debtor in horse-flesh, and fortunately able to repay you. I have got such a charger; your own favorite color, dark chestnut, and, except one white leg, not a spot about him; can carry sixteen stone over a five-foot fence, and as steady as a rock under fire."

"But, Fred, how are you——?"

"Oh, never mind me; I have six in my stable, and intend to share with you. The fact is, I have been transferred from one staff to another for the last six months, and four of my number are presents. Is Mike with you? Ah! glad to hear it: you will never get on without that fellow. Besides, it is a capital thing to have such a connecting link with one's nationality. No fear of your ever forgetting Ireland with Mr. Free in your company. You are not aware that we have been correspondents?—a fact, I assure you. Mike wrote me two letters; and such letters they were! The last was a Jeremiad over your decline and fall, with a very ominous picture of a certain Miss Baby Blake."

45

"Confound the rascal!"

"By Jove, though, Charley, you were coming it rather strong with Baby. Inez saw the letter, and as well as she could decipher Mike's hieroglyphics, saw there was something in it; but the name Baby puzzled her immensely, and she set the whole thing down to your great love of children. I don't think that Lucy quite agreed with her."

"Did she tell it to Miss Dashwood?" I inquired, with fear and trembling.

"Oh, that she did; in fact Inez never ceases talking of you to Lucy. But come, don't look so grave; let's have another brush with the enemy; capture a battery of their guns; carry off a French Marshal or two; get the Bath for your services, and be thanked in general orders, and I will wager all my *chatêaux en Espagne* that everything goes well."

Thus chatting away, sometimes over the past, of our former friends and gay companions, of our days of storm and sunshine; sometimes indulging in prospects for the future, we trotted along, and, as the day was breaking, mounted the ridge of low hills from whence, at the distance of a couple of leagues, the city of Brussels came into view.

CHAPTER LIII.

THE DUCHESS OF RICHMOND'S BALL.

WHETHER we regard the illustrious and distinguished personages who thronged around, or we think of the portentous moment in which it was given, the Duchess of Richmond's ball, on the night of the 15th of June, 1815, was not only one of the most memorable, but, in its interest, the most exciting entertainment that the memory of any one now living can compass,

There is always something of no common interest in seeing the bronzed and war-worn soldier mixing in the crowd of light-hearted and brilliant beauty. To watch the eye whose proud glance has flashed o'er the mail-clad squadrons, now bending meekly beneath the look of some timid girl; to-hear the voice that, high above the battle or the breeze, has shouted the hoarse word "Charge!" now subdued into the low, soft murmur of flattery or compliment,—this, at any time, is a picture full of its own charm; but when we see these heroes of a hundred fights; when we look upon these hardy veterans, upon whose brow the whitened locks of time are telling, indulging themselves in the careless gayety of a moment snatched, as it were, from the arduous career of their existence, while the tramp of the advancing enemy shakes the very soil they stand on, and where it may be doubted whether each aide-de-camp who enters comes a new votary of pleasure or the bearer of tidings that the troops of the foe are advancing, and already the work of death has begun,—this is, indeed, a scene to make the heart throb and the pulse beat high; this is a moment second in its proud excitement only to the very crash and din of battle itself; and into this entrancing whirlwind of passion and of pleasure, of brilliant beauty and ennobled greatness, of all that is lovely in woman and all that is chivalrous and heroic in man, I brought a heart which, young in years, was yet tempered by disappointment; still, such was the fascination, such the brilliancy of the spectacle, that scarcely had I entered, than I felt a change come over me. The old spirit of my boyish ardor—that high-wrought enthusiasm to do something—to be something which men may speak of—shot suddenly through me, and I felt my cheek tingle, and my temples throb, as name after name of starred and titled officers was announced, to think that to me, also, the path of glorious enterprise was opening.

"Come along, come along," said Power, catching me by the arm; "you've not been presented to the Duchess; I know her, I'll do it for you—or perhaps it is better Sir Thomas Picton should. In any case, '*filez*' after me, for the dark-eyed Senhora is surely expecting us. There, do you see that dark, intelligent-looking fellow leaning over the end of the sofa? that is Alava. And there, you know who that is—that *beau idéal* of a hussar? Look how jauntily he carries himself; see the careless but graceful sling with which he edges through the crowd; and look! mark his bow! Did you see that, Charley?—did you catch the quick glance he shot yonder, and the soft smile that showed his white teeth? Depend upon it, boy, some fair heart is not the better nor the easier for that look."

"Who is it?" said I.

"Lord Uxbridge, to be sure,—the handsomest fellow in the service. And there goes Vandeleur, talking with Vivian; the other, to the left, is Ponsonby."

"But stay, Fred, tell me who that is?" For a moment or two I had some difficulty in directing his attention to the quarter I desired. The individual I pointed out was somewhat above the middle size; his uniform, of blue and gold, though singularly plain, had a look of richness about it; besides that, among the orders which covered his breast, he wore one star of great brilliancy and

size. This, however, was his least distinction; for although surrounded on every side by those who might be deemed the very
types and pictures of their *caste*, there was something in the easy
but upright carriage of his head, the intrepid character of his features, the bold and vigorous flashing of his deep blue eye, that
marked him as no common man. He was talking with an old and
prosy-looking personage, in civilian dress; and while I could detect
an anxiety to get free from a tiresome companion, there was an air
of deferential and even kind attention in his manner absolutely
captivating.

"A thorough gentleman, Fred, whoever he be," said I.

"I should think so," replied Power, dryly; "and as our countrymen would say, 'The devil thank him for it!' That is the Prince
of Orange; but see, look at him now; his features have learned
another fashion." And true it was. With a smile of the most winning softness, and with a voice whose slightly foreign accent took
nothing from its interest, I heard him engaging a partner for a
waltz.

There was a flutter of excitement in the circle as the lady rose to
take his arm, and a muttered sound of "How very beautiful!
quelle est belle! c'est un ange!" on all sides. I leaned forward to
catch a glance as she passed—it was Lucy Dashwood. Beautiful
beyond anything I had ever seen her, her lovely features lit
up with pleasure and with pride, she looked in every way worthy
to lean upon the arm of royalty. The graceful majesty of her walk,
the placid loveliness of her gentle smile, struck every one as she
passed on. As for me, totally forgetting all else, not seeing or hearing aught around me, I followed her with my eye until she was lost
amongst the crowd, and then, with an impulse of which I was not
master, followed in her steps.

"This way, this way," said Power; "I see the Senhora." So saying, we entered a little boudoir, where a party was playing at cards.
Leaning on the back of a chair, Inez was endeavoring, with that
mixture of coquetry and half malice she possessed, to distract the
attention of the player. As Power came near, she scarcely turned
her head to give him a kind of saucy smile, while, seeing me, she
held out her hand with friendly warmth, and seemed quite happy
to meet me.

"Do, pray, take her away; get her to dance, to eat ice, or flirt
with you, for Heaven's sake!" said the half-laughing voice of her
victim. "I have revoked twice, and misdealt four times, since she
has been here. Believe me, I shall take it as the greatest favor if
if you'll ——"

As he got thus far, he turned round towards me, and I perceived it was Sir George Dashwood. The meeting was as awkward for him as for me, and while a deep blush covered my face, he muttered some unintelligible apology, and Inez burst into a fit of laughter at the ludicrous *contretemps* of our situation.

"I will dance with you now, if you like," said she, "and that will be punishing all three. Eh, Master Fred?"

So saying, she took my arm, as I led her towards the ball-room.

"And so you really are not friends with the Dashwoods? How very provoking, and how foolish too! But really, chevalier, I must say you treat ladies very ill. I don't forget your conduct to me. Dear me, I wish we could move forward; there is some one pushing me dreadfully!"

"Get on, ma'am, get on!" said a sharp, decided voice behind me. I turned, half smiling, to see the speaker. It was the Duke of Wellington himself, who, with his eye fixed upon some person at a distance, seemed to care very little for any intervening obstruction. As I made way for him to pass between us, he looked hardly at me, while he said, in a short, quick way,

"Know your face very well—how d'ye do?" With this brief recognition he passed on, leaving me to console Inez for her crushed sleeve, by informing her who had done it.

The ball was now at its height. The waltzers whirled past in the wild excitement of the dance. The inspiriting strains of the music, the sounds of laughter, the din, the tumult, all made up that strange medley which, reacting upon the minds of those who cause it, increases the feeling of pleasurable abandonment, making the old feel young, and the young intoxicated with delight.

As the Senhora leaned upon me, fatigued with waltzing, I was endeavoring to sustain a conversation with her, while my thoughts were wandering with my eyes to where I had last seen Lucy Dashwood.

"It must be something of importance; I'm sure it is," said she, at the conclusion of a speech of which I had not heard one word. "Look at General Picton's face!"

"Very pretty, indeed," said I; "but the air is unbecoming," replying to some previous observation she had made, and still lost in reverie. A hearty burst of laughter was her answer, and she gently took my arm, saying,

"You really are too bad! You never listen to one word I've been telling you, but keep continually staring with your eyes here and there, turning this way and looking that; and the dull and vacant, unmeaning smile, answering at random in the most provoking manner. There, now, pray pay attention, and tell me what that means." As she said this, she pointed with her fan to where a dragoon officer, in splashed and spattered uniform, was standing, talking to some three or four general officers. "But here comes the Duke; it can't be anything of consequence."

At the same instant the Duke of Wellington passed, with the Duchess of Richmond on his arm.

"No, Duchess; nothing to alarm you. Did you say ice?"

"There, you heard that, I hope?" said Inez; "there is nothing to alarm us."

"Go to General Picton, at once, but don't let it be remarked," said an officer, in a whisper, as he passed close by me.

"Inez, I have the greatest curiosity to know what that new arrival has to say for himself, and if you will permit me, I'll leave you with Lady Gordon for one moment——"

"Delighted, of all things. You are, without exception, the most tiresome—— Good-bye."

"Adieu!" said I, as I hurried through the crowd towards an open window, on the balcony outside of which Sir Thomas Picton was standing.

"Ah, Mr. O'Malley! have you a pencil? There, that'll do. Ride down to Etterbeck with this order for Godwin. You have heard the news, I suppose, that the French are in advance? The 79th will muster in the Grande Place. The 92d and the 28th along the Park and the Boulevard. Napoleon left Fresnes this morning. The Prussians have fallen back. Zeithen has been beaten. We march at once."

"To-morrow, sir?"

"No, sir; to-night. There, don't delay. But, above all, let everything be done quietly and noiselessly. The Duke will remain here for an hour longer, to prevent suspicion. When you've executed your orders, come back here."

I mounted the first horse I could find at the door, and galloped with top speed over the heavy causeway to Etterbeck. In two minutes the drum beat to arms, and the men were mustering as I left. Thence I hastened to the barracks of the Highland brigade and the 28th Regiment, and before half an hour was back in the ball-room, where, from the din and tumult, I guessed the scene of pleasure and dissipation continued unabated. As I hurried up the staircase, a throng of persons were coming down, and I was obliged to step aside to let them pass.

"Ah! come here, pray," said Picton, who, with a lady, cloaked and hooded, leaning upon his arm, was struggling to make way through the crowd. "The very man!"

"Will you excuse me, if I commit you to the care of my aide-de-camp, who will see you to your carriage? The Duke has just desired to see me." This he said in a hurried and excited tone; and the same moment beckoned to me to take the lady's arm.

It was with some difficulty I succeeded in reaching the spot, and had only time to ask whose carriage I should call for, ere we arrived in the hall.

"Sir George Dashwood's," said a low, soft voice, whose accents sank into my very heart. Heaven! it was Lucy herself; it was her arm that leaned on mine, her locks that fluttered beside me, her hand that hung so near, and yet I could not speak. I tried one word; but a choking feeling in my throat prevented utterance, and already we were upon the door-steps.

"Sir George Dashwood's carriage," shouted the footman, and the announcement was repeated by the porter. The steps were hurried down; the footman stood door in hand, and I led her forward, mute and trembling. Did she know me? I assisted her as she stepped in; her hand touched mine; it was the work of a second; to me it was the bliss of years. She leaned a little forward, and, as the servant put up the steps, said, in her soft, sweet tone, "Thank you, sir. Good-night."

I felt my shoulder touched by some one, who, it appeared, was standing close to me for some seconds; but so occupied was I in gazing at her, that I paid no attention to the circumstance. The carriage drove away, and disappeared in the thick darkness of a starless night. I turned to re-enter the house, and as I did so, the night lamp of the hall fell upon the features of the man beside me, and showed me the pale and corpse-like face of Hammersley. His eye was bent upon me with an expression of fierce and fiery passion, in which the sadness of long suffering also mingled. His bloodless lips parted, moved as though speaking, while yet no sound issued; and his nostrils, dilating and contracting by turns, seemed to denote some deep and hidden emotion that worked within him.

"Hammersley," said I, holding out my hand towards him. "Hammersley, do not always mistake me."

He shook his head mournfully as it fell forward upon his breast; and, covering his arm, moved slowly away without speaking.

General Picton's voice, as he descended the stairs, accompanied by Generals Vandeleur and Vivian, aroused me at once, and I hurried towards him.

"Now, sir; to horse. The troops will defile by the Namur gate; meet me there in an hour. Meanwhile tell Colonel Cameron that he must march with the light companies of his own and the 92d at once."

" I say, Picton, they'll say we were taken by surprise in England; won't they?" said a sharp strong voice, in a half-laughing tone, from behind.

"No, your Grace," said Sir Thomas, bowing slightly; "they'll scarcely do so when they hear the time we took to get under arms."

I heard no more; but, throwing myself into the saddle of my troop-horse, once more rode back to the Belle Vue, to make ready for the road.

The thin pale crescent of a new moon, across which masses of dark and inky clouds were hurrying, tipped with its faint and sickly light the tall minarets of the Hôtel de Ville, as I rode into the "Grande Place." Although midnight, the streets were as crowded as at noonday; horse, foot, and dragoons passing and hurrying hither; the wild pibroch of the Highlander; the mellow bugle of the 71st; the hoarse trumpet of the cavalry; the incessant roll of the drum, mingled their sounds with the tide of human voices, in which every accent was heard, from the reckless cheer of anticipated victory to the heart-piercing shriek of woman's agony. Lights gleamed from every window; from the doors of almost every house poured forth a crowd of soldiers and townsfolk. The sergeants on one side might be seen telling off their men, their cool and steady countenances evidencing no semblance of emotion; while near them, some young ensign, whose beardless cheek and vacant smile bespoke the mere boy, looked on with mingled pride and wonder at the wild scene before him. Every now and then some general officer, with his staff, came cantering past; and as the efforts to muster and form the troops grew more pressing, I could mark how soon we were destined to meet the enemy.

There are few finer monuments of the architecture of the middle ages than the Grande Place of Brussels. The rich façade of the Hôtel de Ville, with its long colonnade of graceful arches, upon every keystone of which some grim grotesque head is peering; the massive cornices; the heavy gorbels carved into ten thousand strange and uncouth fancies; but, finer than all, the taper and stately spire, fretted and perforated like some piece of silver filigree, stretches upward towards the sky, its airy pinnacle growing finer and more beautiful as it nears the stars it points to. How full of historic associations is every dark embrasure, every narrow casement around! Here may have stood the great Emperor Charles the Fifth, meditating upon that greatness he was about to forego forever; here, from this tall window, may have looked the sad and sickly features of Jeanne Laffolle, as, with wandering eye and idiot smile, she gazed upon the gorgeous procession beneath. There is not a stone that has not echoed to the tread of haughty prince or bold baron; yet never, in the palmiest days of ancient chivalry, did those proud dwellings of the great of old look out upon a braver and more valiant host than now thronged beneath their shadow. It was indeed a splendid sight, where the bright gleams of torch and lantern threw the red light around, to watch the measured tread and steady tramp of the Highland regiments as they defiled into the open space, each footstep, as it met the ground, seeming, in its proud and firm tread, to move in more than sympathy with the wild notes of their native mountains; silent and still they moved along; no voice spoke within their ranks, save that of some command to "Close up—take ground —to the right—rear rank—close order." Except such brief words as these, or the low muttered praise of some veteran general as he rode down the line, all was orderly and steady as on a parade. Meanwhile, from an angle of the square, the band of an approaching regiment was heard; and to the inspiriting quickstep of "The Young May Moon," the gallant 28th came forward, and took up their ground opposite to the Highlanders.

The deep bell of the Hôtel de Ville tolled one. The solemn sound rang out and died away in many an echo, leaving upon the heart a sense of some unknown depression; and there was something like a knell in the deep cadence of its bay; and over many a cheek a rapid trace of gloomy thought now passed, and true—too true, alas!—how many now listened for the last time!

"March! March!" passed from front to rear; and, as the bands burst forth again in strains of spirit-stirring harmony, the 79th moved on; the 28th followed; and as they debouched from the "Place," the 71st and the 92d succeeded them. Like wave after wave, the tide of armed men pressed on, and mounted the steep and narrow streets towards the upper town of Brussels. Here Pack's brigade was forming in the Place Royale; and a crowd of staff officers dictating orders, and writing hurriedly on the drum heads, were also seen. A troop of dragoons stood beside their horses at the door of the Belle Vue, and several grooms with led horses walked to and fro.

"Ride forward, sir, to the Bois de Cambre," said Picton, "and pivot the troops on the road to Mont St. Jean. You will then wait for my coming up, or further orders."

This command, which was given to me, I hastened to obey; with difficulty forcing my way through the opposing crowd, I at length reached the Namur gate. Here I found a detachment of the Guards, who as yet had got no orders to march, and were somewhat surprised to learn the forward movement. Ten minutes' ride brought me to the angle of the wood, whence I wrote a few lines to my host of the Belle Vue, desiring him to send Mike after me with my horses and my kit. The night was cold, dark, and threatening; the wind howled with a low and wailing cry through the dark pine trees; and as I stood alone in the solitude, I had time to think of the eventful hours before me, and of that field which ere long was to witness the triumph or the downfall of my country's arms. The road which led through the forest of Soignies caught an additional gloom from the dark, dense woods around. The faint moon only showed at intervals; and a louring sky, without a single star, stretched above us. It was an awful and a solemn thing to hear the deep and thundering roll of that mighty column, awakening the echoes of the silent forest as they went. So hurried was the movement, that we had scarcely any artillery, and that of the lightest calibre; but the clash and clank of cavalry, the heavy monotonous tramp of infantry was there; and as division followed after division, staff officers rode hurriedly to and fro, pressing on the eager troops.

"Move up there, 95th. Ah! 42d, we've work before us!" said Picton, as he rode up to the head of his brigade. The air of depression which usually sat upon his careworn features now changed for a light and laughing look, while his voice was softened and subdued into a low and pleasing tone. Although it was midsummer, the roads were heavy and deep with mud. For some weeks previously the weather had been rainy; and this, added to the haste and discomfort of the night march, considerably increased the fatigue of the troops. Notwithstanding these disadvantages, not a murmur nor complaint was heard on any side.

"I'm unco glad to get a blink o' them, onyhow," said a tall, raw-boned sergeant, who marched beside me.

"Faith, and maybe you won't be over pleased at the expression of their faces, when you see them," said Mike, whose satisfaction at the prospect before him was still as great as that of any other amid the thousands there.

The day was slowly breaking, as a Prussian officer, splashed and covered with foam, came galloping up at full speed past us. While I was yet conjecturing what might be the intelligence he brought, Power rode up to my side.

"We're in for it, Charley," said he. "The whole French army are on the march; and Blucher's aide-de-camp, who has arrived, gives the number at one hundred and fifty thousand men. The Prussians are drawn up between Saint Amand and Sombref, and the Nassau and Dutch troops are at Quatre Bras, both expecting to be attacked."

"Quatre Bras was the original rallying spot for our troops, was it not?" said I.

"Yes, yes. It is that we're now marching upon; but our Prussian friend seems to think we shall arrive too late. Strong French corps are already at Fresnes, under the command, it is said, of Marshal Ney."

The great object of the British Commander-in-Chief was to arrive at Quatre Bras in sufficient time to effect his junction with Blucher before a battle should be fought. To effect this no exertion was spared: efforts almost superhuman were made; for, however prepared for a forward movement, it was impossible to have anticipated anything until the intentions of Napoleon became clearly manifest. While Nivelle and Charleroi were exposed to him on one side, Namur lay open on the other; and he could either march upon Brussels, by Mons or Halle, or, as he subsequently attempted, by Quatre Bras and Waterloo. No sooner, however, were his intentions unmasked, and the line of his operations manifested, than Lord Wellington, with an energy equal to the mighty occasion that demanded it, poured down with the whole force under his command to meet him.

The march was a most distressing one—upwards of three-and-twenty miles, with deep and cut-up roads, in hot, oppressive weather, in a country almost destitute of water. Still the troops pressed forward, and by noon came within hearing of the heavy cannonade in front, which indicated the situation of the battle. From this time aide-de-camp followed aide-de-camp in quick succession, who, from their scared looks and hurried gestures, seemed to bode but ill fortune to the cause we cared for. What the precise situation of the rival armies might be we knew not; but we heard that the French were in overwhelming numbers; that the Dutch troops had abandoned their position; the Hanoverians being driven back, the Duke of Brunswick—the brave sovereign of a gallant people—fell charging at the head of his black hussars. From one phrase which constantly met our ears, it seemed that the Bois de Bossu was the key of the position. This had been won and lost repeatedly by both sides; and as we neared the battle-field, a despatch hurriedly announced to Picton the importance of at once recovering this contested point. The 95th were ordered up to the attack. Scarcely was the word given, when fatigue, thirst, and exhaustion were forgotten. With one cheer the gallant regiment formed into line, and advanced upon the wood. Meanwhile, the Highland brigade moved down towards the right; the Royals and the 28th debouched upon the left of the road; and in less than half an hour after our arrival our whole force was in action.

There is something appalling to the bravest army in coming up to battle at the time that an overwhelming and conquering foe are carrying victory triumphantly before them. Such was our position at Quatre Bras. Bravely and gloriously as the forces of the Prince of Orange fought, the day, however, was not theirs. The Bois de Bossu, which opened to the enemy the road to Brussels, was held by their tirailleurs; the valley to the right was ridden over by their mounted squadrons, who with lance and sabre carried all before them ; their dark columns pressed steadily on ; and a death-dealing artillery swept the allied ranks from flank to flank. Such was the field when the British arrived, and, throwing themselves into squares, opposed their unaided force to the dreadful charges of the enemy. The batteries showered down their storms of grape. Milhaud's heavy dragoons, assisted by crowds of lancers, rushed upon the squares, but they stood unbroken and undaunted, as sometimes upon three sides of their position the infuriated horsemen of the enemy came down. Once, and once only, were the French successful ; the 42d, who were stationed amid tall corn-fields, were surrounded with cavalry before they knew it. The word was given to form square ; the Lancers were already among them, and, fighting back to back, the gallant Highlanders met the foe. Fresh numbers poured down upon them, and already half the regiment was disabled and their colonel killed. These brave fellows were rescued by the 44th, who, throwing in a withering volley, fixed bayonets and charged. Meanwhile, the 95th had won and lost the wood, which, now in the possession of the French tirailleurs, threatened to turn the left of our position. It was at this time that a body of cavalry were seen standing to the left of the Enghien road, as if in observation. An officer, sent forward to reconnoitre, returned with the intelligence that they were British troops, for he had seen their red uniforms.

"I can't think it sir," said Picton. "It is hardly possible that any regiment from Enghien could have arrived already. Ride forward, O'Malley, and if they be our fellows let them carry that height yonder ; there are two guns there cutting the 92d to pieces."

I put spurs to my horse, cleared the road at once, and dashing across the open space to the left of the wood, rode on in the direction of the horsemen. When I came within the distance of three hundred yards I examined them with my glass, and could plainly detect the scarlet coats and bright helmets. "Ha," thought I, "the 1st Dragoon Guards, no doubt." Muttering to myself thus much, I galloped straight on ; and waving my hand as I came near, announced that I was the bearer of an order. Scarcely had I done so, when four horsemen, dashing spurs into their steeds, plunged hastily out from the line, and, before I could speak, surrounded me, while the foremost called out, as he flourished his sabre above his head, "*Rendezvous !*" At the same moment I was seized on each side, and led back a captive into the hands of the enemy.

"We guess your mistake, Capitaine," said the French officer before whom I was brought. "We are the regiment of Berg, and our scarlet uniform cost us dearly enough yesterday."

This allusion, I afterwards learned, was in reference to a charge by a cuirassier regiment, which, in mistaking them for English, poured a volley into them, and killed and wounded about twenty of their number.

CHAPTER LIV.

QUATRE BRAS.

THOSE who have visited the field of Quatre Bras will remember that on the left of the high road, and nearly at the extremity of the Bois de Bossu, stands a large Flemish farmhouse, whose high, pitched roof, pointed gables, and quaint, old-fashioned chimneys, remind one of the architecture so frequently seen in Teniers's pictures. The house, which, with its dependencies of stables, granaries, and out-houses, resembles a little village, is surrounded by a large, straggling orchard of aged fruit-trees, through which the approach from the high road leads. The interior of this quaint dwelling, like all those of its class, is only remarkable for a succession of small, dark, low-ceiled rooms, leading one into another; their gloomy aspect increased by the dark oak furniture, the heavy armories, and old-fashioned presses, carved in the grotesque taste of the sixteenth and seventeenth centuries. Those who visit it now may mark the trace of cannon-shot here and there through the building; more than one deep crack will attest the force of the dread artillery. Still the traveller will feel struck with the rural peace and quietude of the scene. The speckled oxen that stand lowing in the deep meadows; the splash of the silvery trout as he sports in the bright stream that ripples along over its gravelly bed; the cawing of the old rooks in the tall beech-trees; but, more than all, the happy laugh of children, speak of the spot as one of retired and tranquil beauty; yet, when my eyes opened upon it on the morning of the 17th of June, the scene presented features of a widely different interest. The day was breaking as the deep, full sound of the French bugles announced the *reveille*. Forgetful of where I was, I sprang from my bed and rushed to the window; the prospect before me at once recalled me to my recollection, and I remembered that I was a prisoner. The exciting events around left me but little time and as little inclination to think over my old misfortunes; and I watched, with all the interest of a soldier, the movement of the French troops in the orchard beneath. A squadron of dragoons, who seemed to have passed the night beside their horses, lay stretched or seated in all the picturesque groupings of a bivouac. Some were already up and stirring; others leaned half listlessly upon their elbows, and looked about as if unwilling to believe the night was over; and some, stretched in deep slumber, woke not with the noise and tumult around them. The room in which I was confined looked out upon the road to Charleroi; I could therefore see the British troops; and as the French army had fallen back during the night, only an advance guard maintaining the position, I was left to my unaided conjectures as to the fortune of the preceding day of battle. What a period of anxiety and agitation was that morning to me; what would I not have given to learn the result of the action since the moment of my capture! Stubborn as our resistance had been, we were evidently getting the worst of it; and if the Guards had not arrived in time, I knew we must have been beaten.

I walked up and down my narrow room, tortured and agonized by my doubts, now stopping to reason over the possibilities of success, now looking from the window to try if, in the gesture and bearing of those without, I could conjecture anything that passed. Too well I knew the vaunting character of the French soldier, in defeat as in victory, to put much confidence in their bearing. While, however, I watched them with an eager eye, I heard the tramp of horsemen coming along the paved causeway. From the moment my ear caught the sound to that of their arrival at the gate of the orchard, but few minutes had elapsed; their pace was indeed a severe one, and, as they galloped through the narrow path that led to the farm-house, they never drew rein till they reached the porch. The party consisted of about a dozen persons, whose plumed hats bespoke them staff officers; but their uniforms were concealed beneath their great-coats. As they came along the picket sprang to their feet, and the guard at the door beneath presented arms. This left no doubt upon my mind that some officer of rank was among them, and as I knew that Ney himself commanded on the preceding day, I thought it might be he. The sound of voices beneath informed me that the party occupied the room under that in which I was; and, although I listened attentively, I could hear nothing but the confused murmur of persons conversing together without detecting even a word. My thoughts now fell into another channel, and as I ruminated over my old position, I heard the noise of the sentry at my door as he brought his musket to the shoulder, and the next moment an officer in the uniform of the Chasseurs of the Guard entered. Bowing politely as he advanced to the middle of the room, he addressed me thus :

"You speak French, sir?" and, as I replied in the affirmative, continued:

"Will you then have the goodness to follow me this way?"

Although burning with anxiety to learn what had taken place, yet somehow I could not bring myself to ask the question. A secret pride mingled with my fear that all had not gone well with us, and I durst not expose myself to hear of our defeat from the lips of an enemy. I had barely time to ask into whose presence I was about to be ushered, when, with a slight smile of a strange meaning, he opened the door and introduced me into the saloon. Although I had seen at least twelve or fourteen horsemen arrive, there were but three persons in the room as I entered. One of these, who sat writing at a small table near the window, never lifted his head on my entrance, but continued assiduously his occupation. Another, a tall, fine-looking man of some sixty years or upwards, whose high, bald forehead and drooping moustache, white as snow, looked in every way the old soldier of the empire, stood leaning upon his sabre; while the third, whose stature, somewhat below the middle size, was yet cast in a strong and muscular mould, stood with his back to the fire, holding on his arms the skirts of a gray surtout which he wore over his uniform; his legs were cased in the tall boots worn by the *chasseur à cheval*, and on his head a low cocked-hat, without plume or feather, completed his costume. There was something which, at the very moment of my entrance, struck me as uncommon in his air and bearing, so much so that when my eyes had once rested on his pale but placid countenance, his regular, handsome, but somewhat stern features, I totally forgot the presence of the others and looked only at him.

"What's your rank, sir?" said he, hurriedly, and with a tone which bespoke command.

"I have none at present, save——"

"Why do you wear your epaulettes then, sir?" said he, harshly, while from his impatient look and hurried gesture I saw that he put no faith in my reply.

"I am an aide-de-camp to General Picton, but without regimental rank."

"What was the British force under arms yesterday?"

"I do not feel myself at liberty to give you any information as to the number or the movements of our army."

"*Diantre! Diantre!*" said he, slapping his boot with his horse-whip, "do you know what you've been saying there, eh? Cambronne, you heard him, did you?"

"Yes, sire, and if your Majesty would permit me to deal with him, I would before long have his information, if he possess any."

"Eh, *gaillard,*" said he, as he pinched the old general's ear in jest, "I believe you, with all my heart."

The truth flashed upon my mind. I was in the presence of the Emperor himself. As, however, up to this moment I was unconscious of his presence, I resolved now to affect ignorance of it throughout.

"Had you despatches, sir?" said he, turning towards me with a look of stern severity. "Were any despatches found upon him when he was taken?" This latter question was directed to the aide-de-camp who introduced me, and who still remained at the door.

"No, sire, nothing was found upon him except this locket."

As he said these words he placed in Napoleon's hands the keepsake which St. Croix had left with me years before in Spain, and which, as the reader may remember, was a miniature of the Empress Josephine.

The moment the Emperor threw his eyes upon it, the flush which excitement had called into his cheek disappeared at once: he became pale as death, his very lips as bloodless as his wan cheek.

"Leave me, Lefebvre; leave me, Cambronne, for a moment; I will speak with this gentleman alone."

As the door closed upon them, he leaned his arm upon the mantelpiece, and, with his head sunk upon his bosom, remained some moments without speaking.

"*Augure sinistre!*" muttered he within his teeth, as his piercing gaze was riveted upon the picture before him.

"*Violà la troisième fois; peut-être la dernière.*" Then suddenly rousing himself, he advanced close to me, and seizing me by the arm with a grasp like iron, inquired:

"How came you by that picture? The truth, sir; mark me, the truth."

Without showing any sign of feeling hurt at the insinuation of this question, I detailed, in as few words as I could, the circumstance by which the locket became mine. Long before I had concluded, however, I could mark that his attention flagged, and finally wandered far away from the matter before him.

"Why will you not give me the information I look for? I seek for no breach of faith. The campaign is all but over. The Prussians were beaten at Ligny, their army routed, their artillery captured, and ten thousand prisoners taken. Your troops and the Dutch were conquered yesterday, and they are in full retreat on Brussels. By to-morrow evening I shall date my bulletin from the palace of Laeken. Antwerp will be in my possession within twenty-four hours. Namur is already mine. Cambronne, Lefebvre," cried he, "*cet homme-là n'en sait rien,*" pointing to me as he spoke. "Let us see the other." With this he motioned slightly with his hand, as a sign for me to withdraw, and the next moment I was once more in the solitude of my prison-room, thinking over the singular interview I had just had with the great Emperor.

How anxiously pass the hours of one who, deprived of other means of information, is left to form his conjectures by some passing object or some chance murmur. The things which in the ordinary course of life are passed by unnoticed and unregarded, are now matters of moment. With what scrutiny he examines the features of those whom he dare not question! with what patient ear he listens to each passing word! Thus to me, a prisoner, the hours went by tardily yet anxiously. No sabre clanked; no war horse neighed; no heavy-booted cuirassier tramped in the court-yard beneath my window without setting a hundred conjectures afloat as to what was about to happen. For some time there had been a considerable noise and bustle in and about the dwelling. Horsemen came and went continually. The sounds of galloping could be heard along the paved causeway; then the challenge of the sentry at the gate; then the nearer tread of approaching steps, and many voices speaking together, would seem to indicate that some messenger had arrived with despatches. At length all these sounds became hushed and still; no longer were the voices heard, and except the measured tread of the heavy cuirassier, as he paced on the flags beneath, nothing was to be heard. My state of suspense, doubly greater now than when the noise and tumult suggested food for conjecture, continued till towards noon, when a soldier in undress brought me some breakfast, and told me to prepare speedily for the road.

Scarcely had he left the room, when the rumbling noise of wagons was heard below, and a train of artillery carts moved into the little court-yard, loaded with wounded men. It was a sad and frightful sight to see these poor fellows, as, crammed side by side in the straw of the *charrette*, they lay, their ghastly wounds opening with every motion of the wagon, while their wan, pale faces were convulsed with agony and suffering. Of every rank, from the sous-lieutenant to the humble soldier, from every arm of the service, from the heavy Cuirassier of the Guard to the light and intrepid tirailleur, they were there. I well remember one, an artilleryman of the Guard, who, as they lifted him forth from the cart, presented the horrifying spectacle of one both of whose legs had been carried away by a cannon-shot. Pale, cold, and corpse-like, he lay in their arms; his head lay heavily to one side, and his arms fell passively

46

as in death. It was at this moment that a troop of lancers, the advanced guard of D'Erlon's division, came trotting up the road. The cry of "*Vive l'Empereur!*" burst from them as they approached; its echo rang within the walls of the farm-house, when suddenly the dying man, as though some magic touch had called him back to life and vigor, sprang up erect between his bearers, his filmy eye flashing fire, a burning spot of red coloring his bloodless cheek; he cast one wild and hurried look around him, like one called back from death to look upon the living, and, as he raised his blood-stained hand above his head, shouted, in a heart-piercing cry, "*Vive l'Empereur!*" The effort was his last. It was the expiring tribute of allegiance to the chief he adored. The blood spouted in cataracts from his half-closed wounds, a convulsive spasm worked through his frame, his eyes rolled fearfully, as his outstretched hands seemed striving to clutch some object before them—and he was dead. Fresh arrivals of wounded continued to pour in; and now I thought I could detect at intervals the distant noise of the cannonade; the wind, however, was from the southward, and the sounds were too indistinct to be relied on.

"*Allons! allons! mon cher*," said a rough but good-natured-looking fellow, as he strode into my room. He was the quartermaster of Milhaud's dragoons, under whose care I was now placed, and came to inform me that we were to set out immediately.

Monsieur Bonnard was a character in his way; and if it were not so near the conclusion of my history, I should like to present him to my readers. As it is, I shall merely say that he was a thorough specimen of one class of his countrymen—a loud talker, a loud swearer, a vaporing, boasting, overbearing, good-natured, and even soft-hearted fellow, who firmly believed that Frenchmen were the climax of the species, and Napoleon the climax of Frenchmen. Being a great *bavard*, he speedily told me all that had taken place during the last two days. From him I learned that the Prussians had really been beaten at Ligny, and had fallen back, he knew not where; they were, however, he said, hotly pursued by Grouchy, with thirty-five thousand men, while the Emperor himself was now following the British and Dutch armies with seventy thousand men.

"You see," continued he, "*l'affaire est faite!*—who can resist the Emperor?"

These were sad tidings for me; and although I did not place implicit confidence in my informant, I had still my fears that much of what he said was true.

"And the British, now," said I; "what direction have they taken?"

"Bah! they're in retreat on Brussels, and will probably capitulate to-morrow."

"Capitulate!"

"*Oui, oui: ne vous fâchez pas, camarade,*" said he, laughing. "What could you do against Napoleon? You did not expect to beat him, surely? But come, we must move on; I have my orders to bring you to Planchenoit this evening, and our horses are tired enough already."

"Mine, methinks, should be fresh," said I.

"*Parbleu non,*" replied he; "he has twice made the journey to Fresnes this morning with despatches for Marshal Ney. The Emperor is enraged with the Marshal for having retreated last night, having the wood in his possession. He says he should have waited till daybreak, and then fallen upon your retreating columns. As it is, you are getting away without much loss. *Sacriste,* that was a fine charge!" These last words he muttered to himself, adding, between his teeth, "sixty-four killed and wounded."

"What was that? who were they?" said I.

"Our fellows," replied he, frankly. "The Emperor ordered up two twelve-pounders and eight squadrons of lancers; they fell upon your light dragoons in a narrow part of the high road. But suddenly we heard a noise in front; your hussars fell back, and a column of your heavy dragoons came thundering down upon us. *Parbleu!* they swept over us as if we were broken infantry; and there! there!" said he, pointing to the court-yard, from whence the groans of the wounded still rose, "there are the fruits of that terrible charge."

I could not restrain an outbreak of triumphant pleasure at this gallant feat of my countrymen.

"Yes, yes," said the honest Quartermaster, "it was a fine thing; but a heavy reckoning is at hand. But come, let us take the road."

In a few moments more I found myself seated upon a heavy Norman horse, whose lumbering demi-peak saddle was nearly cleft in two by a sabre-cut.

"Ay, ay," said Monsieur Bonnard, as he saw my eye fixed upon the spot, "it was one of your fellows did that; and the same cut clove poor Pierre from the neck to the seat."

"I hope," said I, laughing, "the saddle may not prove an unlucky one."

"No, no," said the Frenchman, seriously; "it has paid its debt to fate."

As we pressed on our road, which, broken by the heavy guns, and ploughed up in many places by the artillery, was nearly impassable, we could distinctly hear from time to time the distant boom of the large guns, as the retiring and pursuing armies replied to each other; while behind us, but still a long way off, a dark mass· appeared on the horizon : they were the advancing columns of Ney's division.

"Have the troops come in contact more than once this morning?"

"Not closely," said the Quartermaster. "The armies have kept a respectful distance; they were like nothing I can think of," said the figurative Frenchman, "except two hideous serpents wallowing in mire, and vomiting at each other whole rivers of fire and flame."

As we approached Planchenoit, we came up to the rear-guard of the French army; from them we learned that Ney's division, consisting of the eighth corps, had joined the Emperor; that the British were still in retreat, but that nothing of any importance had occurred between the rival armies, the French merely firing their heavy guns from time to time, to ascertain by the reply the position of the retreating forces. The rain poured down in torrents; gusts of cold and stormy wind swept across the wide plains, or moaned sorrowfully through the dense forest. As I rode on by the side of my companion, I could not help remarking how little the effects of a fatiguing march and unfavorable weather were apparent on those around me. The spirit of excited gayety pervaded every rank; and, unlike the stern features which the discipline of our service enforces, the French soldiers were talking, laughing, and even singing, as they marched; the canteens passed freely from hand to hand, and jests and toasts flew from front to rear along the dark columns; many carried their loaves of dark rye-bread on the tops of their bayonets; and to look upon that noisy and tumultuous mass as they poured along, it would have needed a practised eye to believe them the most disciplined of European armies.

The sun was just setting as, mounting a ridge of high land beside the high road, my companion pointed with his finger to a small farm-house, which, standing alone in the plain, commanded an extensive view on every side of it.

"There," said he, "there is the *quartier général;* the Emperor sleeps there to-night. The King of Holland will afford him a bed to-morrow night."

The dark shadows of the coming night were rapidly falling as I strained my eyes to trace the British position. A hollow, rumbling sound announced the movement of artillery in our front.

"What is it, Arnotte?" said the Quartermaster to a dragoon officer who rode past.

"It is nothing," replied the other, laughing, "but a *ruse* of the Emperor. He wishes to ascertain if the enemy are in force, or if we have only a strong rear-guard before us."

As he spoke, fifteen heavy guns opened their fire, and the still air reverberated with a loud thunder. The sound had not died away—the very smoke lay yet heavily upon the moist earth—when forty pieces of British cannon rang out their answer, and the very plain trembled beneath the shock.

"Ha! they are there, then," exclaimed the dragoon, as his eyes flashed with ecstasy. "Look! see! the artillery are limbering up already. The Emperor is satisfied."

And so it was. A dark column of twelve hundred horse that accompanied the guns into the plain, now wheeled slowly round, and wound their long track far away to the right. The rain fell in torrents; the wind was hushed; and, as the night fell in darkness, the columns moved severally to their destinations. The bivouacs were formed, the watch-fires were lighted, and seventy thousand men and two hundred pieces of cannon occupied the heights of Planchenoit.

"My orders are to bring you to La Caillon," said the Quartermaster; "and if you only can spur your jaded horse into a trot, we shall soon reach it."

About a hundred yards from the little farm-house stood a small cottage of a peasant. Here some officers of Marshal Soult's staff had taken up their quarters, and thither my guide now bent his steps.

"*Comment! Bonnard,*" said an aide-de-camp, as we rode up, "another prisoner? *Sacrebleu!* we shall have the whole British staff among us. You are in better luck than your countryman, the General, I hope," said the aide-de-camp; "his is a sad affair; and I'm sorry for it, too; he's a fine, soldier-like looking fellow."

"Pray, what has happened?" said I. "To what do you allude?"

"Merely to one of your people who has just been taken with some letters and papers of Bourmont's in his possession. The Emperor is in no very amicable humor towards that traitor, and resolves to pay off some part of his debt on his British correspondent."

"How cruel! how unjust!"

"Why, yes, it is hard, I confess, to be shot for the fault of another. *Mais que voulez-vous?*"

"And when is this atrocious act to take place?"

"By daybreak to-morrow," said he, bowing as he turned towards the hut. "Meanwhile, let me counsel you, if you would not make another in the party, to reserve your indignation for your return to England."

"Come along," said the Quartermaster; "I find they have got quarters for you in the granary of the farm. I'll not forget you at supper time."

So saying, he gave his horse to an orderly, and led me by a little path to a back entrance of the dwelling. Had I time or inclination for such a scene, I might have lingered long to gaze at the spectacle before me. The guard held their bivouac around the quarters of the Emperor; and here, beside the watch-fires, sat the bronzed and scarred veterans who had braved every death and danger from the Pyramids to the Kremlin. On every side I heard the names of those whom history has already consigned to immortality; and, as the fitful blaze of a wood-fire flashed from within the house, I could mark the figure of one who, with his hands behind his back, walked leisurely to and fro, his head leaned a little forward, as though in deep thought; but as the light fell upon his pale and placid features, there was nothing there to indicate the stormy strife of hope and fear that raged beneath. From the rapid survey I took around, I was roused by an officer, who, saluting me, politely desired me to follow him. We mounted a flight of stone steps, which, outside the wall of the building, led to the upper story of a large but ruined granary. Here a sentry was posted, who permitting us to pass forward, I found myself in a small, mean-looking apartment, whose few articles of coarse furniture were dimly lighted by the feeble glimmer of a lamp. At the further end of the room sat a man, wrapped in a large blue cavalry cloak, whose face, covered with his hands as he bent downwards, was completely concealed from view. The noise of the opening door did not appear to arouse him, nor did he notice my approach. As I entered, a faint sigh broke from him, as he turned his back upon the light; but he spoke not a word.

I sat for some time in silence, unwilling to obtrude myself upon the sorrows of one to whom I was unknown; and, as I walked up and down the gloomy chamber, my thoughts became riveted so completely upon my own fortunes that I ceased to remember my fellow-prisoner. The hours passed thus lazily along, when the door suddenly opened, and an officer in the dress of a lancer of the Guard stood for an instant before me, and then springing forward, clasped me with both hands, and called out:

"Charles, *mon ami, c'est bien toi ?*"

The voice recalled to my recollection what his features, altered by time and years, had failed to do. It was Jules St. Croix, my former prisoner in the Peninsula. I cannot paint the delight with which I saw him again; his presence now, while it brought back the memory of some of my happiest days, also assured me that I was not friendless.

His visit was a brief one, for he was in attendance on Marshal Lobau's staff. In the few minutes, however, of his stay, he said:

"I have a debt to pay, Charles; and have come to discharge it.

In an hour hence I shall leave this with despatches for the left of our line. Before I go, I'll come here with two or three others, as it were, to wish you a good night. I'll take care to carry a second cloak and a foraging cap; I'll provide a fast horse; you shall accompany us for some distance. I'll see you safe across our pickets: for the rest you must trust to yourself. *C'est arrangé, n'est-ce pas?"*

One firm grasp of his hand, to which I responded by another, followed, and he was gone.

Everything concurred to show me that a tremendous battle must ensue on the morrow, if the British forces but held their position. It was then with a feeling of excitement approaching to madness that I saw my liberty before me; that once more I should join in the bold charge and the rude shock of arms, hear the wild cry of my gallant countrymen, and either live to triumph with them in victory, or wait not to witness our defeat. Thus flew my hopes, as with increasing impatience I waited St. Croix's coming, and with anxious heart listened to every sound upon the stairs which might indicate his approach. At length he came. I heard the gay and laughing voices of his companions as they came along; the door opened, and affecting the familiarity of old acquaintance, to deceive the sentry, they all shook me by the hand, and spoke in terms of intimacy.

"Labedoyère is below," said St. Croix, in a whisper; "you must wait here a few moments longer, and I'll return for you; put on the cloak and cap, and speak not a word as you pass out... The sentry will suppose that one of our party has remained behind; for I shall call out as if speaking to him, as I leave the room."

The voice of an officer calling in tones of impatience for the party to come down, cut short the interview, and again assuring me of their determination to stand by me, they left the chamber, and descended into the court. Scarcely had the door closed behind them, when my fellow-prisoner, whom I had totally forgotten, sprang on his legs, and came towards me. His figure screening the lamplight as he stood, prevented my recognizing his features; but the first tones of his voice told me who he was.

"Stay, sir," cried he, as he placed his hand upon my arm; "I have overheard your project. In an hour hence you will be free. Can you—will you perform a service for one who will esteem it not the less that it will be the last that man can render him? The few lines which I have written here with my pencil are for my daughter."

I could bear no more, and called out in a voice broken as his own,

"Oh, be not deceived, sir. Will you, even in an hour like this, accept a service from one whom you have banished from your house?"

The old man started as I spoke; his hand trembled till it shook my very arm, and, after a pause and with an effort to seem calm and collected, he added:

"My hours are few. Some despatches of General Bourmont with which the Duke entrusted me were found in my possession. My sentence is a hurried one—and it is death! By to-morrow's sun-rise——"

"Stay, stay!" said I. "You shall escape; my life is in no danger. I have, as you see, even friends among the staff; besides, I have done nothing to compromise or endanger my position."

"No, sir," said he, sternly, "I will not act such a part as this. The tears you have seen in these old eyes are not for myself. I fear not death. Better it were it should have come upon the field of glorious battle; but as it is, my soldier's honor remains intact, untainted."

"You refuse the service on account of him who proffers it," said I, as I fell heavily upon a seat, my head bowed upon my bosom.

"Not so, not so, my boy," replied he, kindly. "The near approach of death, like the fading light of day, gives us a longer and a clearer view before us. I feel that I have wronged you; that I have imputed to you the errors of others; but, believe me, if I have wronged you, I have punished my own heart; for, Charles, I have loved you like a son."

"Then prove it," said I, "and let me act towards you as towards a father. You will not? You refuse me still? Then, by Heaven, I remain to share your fate! I well know the temper of him who has sentenced you, and that by one word of mine my destiny is sealed forever."

"No, no, boy! This is but rash and insane folly. Another year or two, nay, perhaps a few months more, and in the common course of nature I had ceased to be; but you, with youth, with fortune, and with hope——"

"Oh, not with hope!" said I, in a voice of agony.

"Nay, say not so," replied he, calmly, while a sickly smile played sadly over his face; "you will give this letter to my daughter, you will tell her that we parted as friends should part; and if, after that, when time shall have smoothed down her grief, and sorrow be rather a dark dream of the past than a present suffering; if, then, you love her, and if——"

"Oh, tempt me not thus!" said I, as the warm tears gushed from my eyes; "lead me not thus astray from what my honor tells me I should do. Hark! they are coming already. I hear the clank of their sabres; they are mounting the steps; not a moment is to be lost!   Do you refuse me still?"

"I do," replied he, firmly; "I am resolved to abide the course of fate."

"Then so do I," cried I, as, folding my arms, I sat down beside the window, determined on my course.

"Charley, Charley," said.he, stooping over me, "my friend, my last hope, the protector of my child——"

"I will not go," said I, in a hollow whisper.

Already they were at the door; I heard their voices as they challenged the sentry; I heard his musket as he raised it to his shoulder. The thought flashed across me—I jumped up, and, throwing the loose mantle of the French dragoon around him, and replacing his own with the foraging cap of St. Croix, I sprang into a corner of the room, and, seating myself so as to conceal my face, waited the result.   The door opened, the party entered, laughing and talking together.

"Come, Eugène," said one, taking Sir George by the arm, "you have spent long enough time here to learn the English language. We shall be late at the outpost. *Messieurs les Anglais*, good-night, good-night!"

This was repeated by the others as they passed out with Sir George Dashwood among them, who, seeing that my determination was not to be shaken, and that any demur on his part must necessarily compromise both, yielded to a *coup de main* that he never would have consented to from an appeal to his reason.   The door closed; their steps died away in the distance.   Again a faint sound struck my ear; it was the challenge of the sentry beneath, and I heard the tramp of horses' feet.   All was still, and in a burst of heartfelt gratitude I sank upon my knees, and thanked God that he was safe.

So soundly did I sleep, that not before I was shaken several times by the shoulder could I awake on the following morning.

"I thought there were two prisoners here," said a gruff voice, as an old moustached-looking veteran cast a searching look about the room.   "However, we shall have enough of them before sunset. Get—get up; *Monsieur le Duc de Dalmatie* desires some information you can give him."

As he said this, he led me from the room, and, descending the flight of stone steps, we entered the court-yard.   It was but four o'clock, the rain still falling in torrents, yet every one was up and stirring.

"Mount this horse," said my gruff friend, "and come with me towards the left; the Marshal has already gone forward."

The heavy mist of the morning, darkened by the louring clouds which almost rested on the earth, prevented our seeing above a hundred yards before us; but the hazy light of the watch-fires showed me the extent of the French position, as it stretched away along the ridge towards the Halle road. We rode forward at a trot, but in the deep clayey soil we sank at each moment to our horses' fetlocks. I turned my head as I heard the tramp and splash of horsemen behind, and perceived that I was followed by two dragoons, who, with their carbines on the rest, kept their eyes steadily upon me to prevent any chance of escape. In a slight hollow of the ground before us stood a number of horsemen, who conversed together in a low tone as we came up.

"There! that is the Marshal," said my companion, in a whisper, as we joined the party.

"Yes, Monsieur le Duc," said an engineer colonel, who stood beside Soult's horse, with a colored plan in his hand—"Yes, that is the *Château de Goumont,* yonder. It is, as you perceive, completely covered by the rising ground marked here; they will, doubtless, place a strong artillery force in this quarter."

"Ah! who is this?" said the Marshal, turning his eyes suddenly upon me, and then casting a look of displeasure around him, lest I should have overheard any portion of their conversation. "You are deficient in cavalry, it would appear, sir?" said he to me.

"You must feel, Monsieur le Duc," said I, calmly, "how impossible it is for me, as a man of honor and a soldier, to afford you any information as to the army I belong to."

"I do not see that, sir. You are a prisoner in our hands; your treatment, your fortune, your very life depends on us. Besides, sir, when French officers fall into the power of your people, I have heard they meet not very ceremonious treatment."

"Those who say so, say falsely," said I, "and wrong both your countrymen and mine. In any case——"

"The Guards are an untried force in your service," said he, with a mixture of inquiry and assertion.

I replied not a word.

"You must see, sir," continued he, "that all the chances are against you. The Prussians beaten, the Dutch discouraged, the Belgians only waiting for victory to incline to our standard, to desert your ranks, and pass over to ours; while your troops, scarcely forty thousand, nay, I might say, not more than thirty-five thousand. Is it not so?"

Here was another question, so insidiously conveyed that even a change of feature on my part might have given the answer. A half smile, however, and a slight bow was all my reply; while Soult muttered something between his teeth, which called forth a laugh from those around him.

"You may retire, sir, a little," said he, dryly, to me.

Not sorry to be freed from the awkwardness of my position, I fell back to the little rising ground behind. Although the rain poured down without ceasing, the rising sun dispelled, in part, the heavy vapor, and by degrees different portions of the wide plain presented themselves to view; and as the dense masses of fog moved slowly along, I could detect, but still faintly, the outline of the large, irregular building which I had heard them call the *Château de Goumont*, and from whence I could hear the clank of masonry, as at intervals the wind bore the sounds towards me. These were the sappers piercing the walls for musketry; and this I could now perceive was looked upon as a position of no small importance. Surrounded by a straggling orchard of aged fruit trees, the château lay some hundred yards in advance of the British line, commanded by two eminences, one of which, in the possession of the French, was already occupied by a park of eleven guns; of the other I knew nothing, except the passing glance I had obtained of its position on the map. The second corps, under Jerome Bonaparte, with Foy and Kellerman's brigade of light artillery, stretched behind us. On the right of these came D'Erlon's corps, extending to a small wood, which my companion told me was Frischermont; while Lobau's division was stationed to the extreme right towards St. Lambert, to maintain the communication with Grouchy at Wavre, or, if need be, to repel the advance of the Prussians, and prevent their junction with the Anglo-Dutch army. The Imperial Guard with the cavalry formed the reserve. Such was, in substance, the information given me by my guide, who seemed to expatiate with pleasure over the magnificent array of battle, while he felt a pride in displaying his knowledge of the various divisions and their leaders.

"I see the Marshal moving towards the right," said he; "we had better follow him."

It was now about eight o'clock, as from the extremity of the line I could see a party of horsemen advancing at a sharp canter.

"That must be Ney," said my companion. "See how rashly he approaches the English lines!"

And so it was. The party in question rode fearlessly down the slope, and did not halt until they reached within about three hundred yards of what appeared a ruined church.

"What is that building yonder?"

"That—that," replied he, after a moment's thought, "that must be La Haye Sainte; and yonder, to the right of it, is the road to Brussels. There, look now! your people are in motion. See! a column is moving towards the right, and the cavalry are defiling on the other side of the road. I was mistaken—that cannot be Ney. Heavens! it was the Emperor himself, and here he comes."

As he spoke, the party galloped forward, and pulled up short within a few yards of where we stood.

"Ha!" cried he, as his sharp glance fell upon me, "there is my taciturn friend of Quatre Bras. You see, sir, I can dispense with your assistance now; the chess-board is before me;" and then added in a tone he intended not to be overheard, "Everything depends on Grouchy."

"Well, Haxo," he called out to an officer who galloped up, *chapeau* in hand, "what say you? are they entrenched in that position?"

"No, sire, the ground is open, and in two hours more will be firm enough for the guns to manœuvre."

"Now, then, for breakfast," said Napoleon, as with an easy and tranquil smile he turned his horse's head, and cantered gently up the heights towards La Belle Alliance. As he approached the lines the cry of "*Vive l'Empereur!*" burst forth. Regiment after regiment took it up; and from the distant wood of Frischermont to the far left beside Merke-braine, the shout resounded. So sudden, so simultaneous was the outbreak, that he himself, accustomed as he well was to the enthusiasm of his army, seemed, as he reined in his horse, and looked with proud and elated eye upon the countless thousands, astounded and amazed. He lifted with slow and graceful action his unplumed hat above his head, and while he bowed that proud front before which kings have trembled, the acclamation burst forth anew, and rent the very air.

At this moment the sun shone brilliantly out from the dark clouds, and flashed upon the shining blades and glistening bayonets along the line. A dark and louring shadow hung gloomily over the British position, while the French sparkled and glittered in the sunbeams. His quick glance passed with lightning speed from one to the other; and I thought that, in his look, upturned to heaven, I could detect the flitting thought which bade him hope it was an augury. The bands of the Imperial Guard burst forth in joyous and triumphant strains, and amid the still repeated cries of "*l'Empereur! l'Empereur!*" he rode slowly along towards La Belle Alliance.

CHAPTER LV.

WATERLOO.

NAPOLEON'S first intention was to open the battle by an attack upon the extreme right; but Ney, who returned from an observation of the ground, informed him that a rivulet, swollen by the late rains, had now become a foaming torrent, perfectly impassable to infantry. To avoid this difficulty, he abandoned his favorite manœuvre of a flank movement, and resolved to attack the enemy by the centre. Launching his cavalry and artillery by the road to Brussels, he hoped thus to cut off the communication of the British with their own left, as well as with the Prussians, for whom he trusted that Grouchy would be more than a match.

The reserves were in consequence all brought up to the centre. Seven thousand cavalry and a massive artillery assembled upon the heights of La Belle Alliance, and waited but the order to march. It was eleven o'clock, and Napoleon mounted his horse and rode slowly along the line; again the cry of "*Vive l'Empereur!*" resounded, and the bands of the various regiments struck up their spirit-stirring strains as the gorgeous staff moved along. On the British side all was tranquil; and still the different divisions appeared to have taken up their ground, and the long ridge from Terla-Haye to Merke-braine bristled with bayonets. Nothing could possibly be more equal than the circumstances of the field. Each army possessed an eminence whence their artillery might play. A broad and slightly undulating valley lay between both. The ground permitted in all places both cavalry and infantry movements, and except the crumbling walls of the Château of Hougoumont, or the farm-house of La Haye Sainte, both of which were occupied by the British, no advantage, either by nature or art, inclined to either side. It was a fair stand-up fight. It was the mighty tournament, not only of the two greatest nations, but the two deadliest rivals and bitterest enemies, led on by the two greatest military geniuses that the world has ever seen—it might not be too much to say or ever will see. As for me, condemned to be an inactive spectator of the mighty struggle, doomed to witness all the deep-laid schemes and well-devised plans of attack which were destined for the overthrow of my country's arms, my state was one of torture and suspense. I sat upon the little rising ground of Rossomme. Before me, in the valley, where yet the tall corn waved in ripe luxuriance, stood the quiet and peaceful-looking old Château of Hougoumont, and the blossoming branches of the orchard; the birds were gayly singing their songs, the shrill whistle of the fatal musketry was to be heard, and through my glass I could detect the uniform of the soldiers who held the position, and my heart beat anxiously and proudly as I recognized the Guards. In the orchard and the garden were stationed some riflemen—at least their dress and the scattered order they assumed bespoke them such. While I looked, the tirailleurs of Jerome's division advanced from the front of the line, and, descending the hill in a sling trot, broke into scattered parties, keeping up, as they went, a desultory and irregular fire. The English skirmishers, less expert in this peculiar service, soon. fell back, and the head of Reille's brigade began their march towards the château. The English artillery is unmasked and opens its fire. Kellermann advances at a gallop his twelve pieces of artillery; the château is concealed from view by the dense smoke, and as the attack thickens, fresh troops pour forward, the artillery thundering on either side; the entire lines of both armies stand motionless spectators of the terrific combat, while every eye is turned towards that devoted spot from whose dense mass of cloud and smoke the bright glare of artillery is flashing, as the crashing masonry, the burning rafters, and the loud yell of battle add to the frightful interest of the scene. For above an hour the tremendous attack continues without cessation; the artillery stationed upon the height has now found its range, and every ringing shot tells upon the tottering walls; some wounded soldiers return faint and bleeding from the conflict, but there are few who escape. A crashing volley of firearms is now heard from the side where the orchard stands; a second and a third succeed, one after the other, as rapid as lightning itself. A silence follows, when, after a few moments, a deafening cheer bursts forth, and an aide-de-camp gallops up to say that the orchard has been carried at the point of the bayonet, the Nassau sharpshooters who held it having, after a desperate resistance, retired before the irresistible onset of the French infantry. "*A moi! maintenant!*" said General Foy, as he drew his sabre, and rode down to the head of his splendid division, which, anxious for the word to advance, were standing in the valley. "*En avant! mes braves,*" cried he, while, pointing to the château with his sword, he dashed boldly forward. Scarcely had he advanced a hundred yards, when a cannon-shot, "ricocheting" as it went, struck his horse in the counter, and rolled him dead on the plain. Disengaging himself from the lifeless animal, he at once sprang to his feet, and hurried forward. The column was soon hid from my view, and I was left to mourn over the seemingly inevitable fate that impended over my gallant countrymen.

In the intense interest which chained me to this part of the field, I had not noticed till this moment that the Emperor and his staff were standing scarcely thirty yards from where I was. Napoleon, seated upon a gray, almost white, Arabian, had suffered the reins to fall loosely on the neck, as he held with both hands his telescope to his eye; his dress, the usual green coat with white facings, the uniform of the *chasseurs à cheval*, was distinguished merely by the cross of the Legion; his high boots were splashed and mud-stained, from riding through the deep and clayey soil; his compact and clean-bred charger looked also slightly blown and heated; but he himself, and I watched his features well, looked calm, composed, and tranquil. How anxiously did I scrutinize that face; with what a throbbing heart did I canvass every gesture, hoping to find some passing trait of doubt, of difficulty, or of hesitation; but none was there: unlike one who looked upon the harrowing spectacle of a battle-field, whose all was depending on the game before him; gambling with one throw his last, his only stake, and that the empire of the world. Yet, could I picture to myself one who felt at peace within himself—naught of reproach—naught of regret to move or stir his spirit, whose tranquil barque had glided over the calm sea of life, unruffled by the breath of passion—I should have fancied such was he.

Beside him sat one whose flashing eye and changing features looked in every way his opposite. Watching with intense anxiety the scene of the deadly struggle round the château, every look, every gesture, told the changing fortune of the moment; his broad and brawny chest glittered with orders and decorations, but his heavy brow and louring look, flushed almost black with excitement, could not easily be forgotten. It was Soult, who, in his quality of Major-General, accompanied the Emperor throughout the day.

"They have lost it again, sire," said the Marshal, passionately; "and see, they are forming beneath the cross-fire of the artillery; the head of the column keeps not its formation two minutes together. Why does he not move up?"

"Domont, you know the British; what troops are those in the orchard? They use the bayonet well."

The officer addressed pointed his glass for a moment to the spot. Then turning to the Emperor, replied, as he touched his hat, "They are the Guards, sire."

During this time Napoleon spoke not a word; his eye ever bent upon the battle, he seemed to pay little if any attention to the conversation about him. As he looked, an aide-de-camp, breathless and heated, galloped up.

"The columns of attack are formed, sire; everything is ready, and the Marshal only waits the order."

Napoleon turned upon his saddle, and, directing his glass towards Ney's division, looked fixedly for some moments at them. His eye moved from front to rear slowly, and at last carrying his telescope along the line, he fixed it steadily upon the far left. Here, towards St. Lambert, a slight cloud seems to rest on the horizon, as the Emperor continued to gaze steadfastly at it. Every glass of the staff was speedily turned in that direction.

"It is nothing but a cloud; some exhalation from the low grounds in that quarter," whispered one.

"To me," said another, "they look like trees, part of the Bois de Wavre."

"They are men," said the Emperor, speaking for the first time. "*Est-ce Grouchy! Est-ce Blucher?*"

Soult inclines to believe it to be the former, and proceeds to give his reasons, but the Emperor, without listening, turns towards Domont, and orders him, with his division of light cavalry and Subervic's brigade, to proceed thither at once. If it be Grouchy, to establish a junction with him; to resist, should it prove to be the advanced guard of Marshal Blucher. Scarcely is the order given when a column of cavalry, wheeling "fours about," unravels itself from the immense mass, and seems to serpentine like an enormous snake between the squares of the mighty army. The pace increases at every moment, and at length we see them merge from the extreme right and draw up, as if on parade, above half a mile from the wood. This movement, by its great precision and beauty, had attracted our entire attention, not only from the attack on Hougoumont, but also an incident which had taken place close beside us. This was the appearance of a Prussian hussar who had been taken prisoner between Wavre and Planchenoit: he was the bearer of a letter from Bulow to Wellington, announcing his arrival at St. Lambert, and asking for orders.

This at once explains the appearance on the right; but the prisoner also adds that the three Prussian corps were at Wavre, having pushed their patrols two leagues from the town without ever encountering any portion of the force under the command of Grouchy. For a moment not a word is spoken. A silence like a panic pervades the staff; the Emperor himself was the first to break it.

"This morning," said he, turning towards Soult, "the chances were ninety to one in our favor; Bulow's arrival has already lost us thirty of the number; but the odds are still sufficient, if Grouchy but repair the *horrible fault* he has committed."

He paused for a moment, and, as he lifted up his own hand, and turned a look of indignant passion towards the staff, added, in a voice the sarcasm of whose tone there is no forgetting:

"*Il s'amuse à Gembloux!* Still," said he, speaking rapidly and with more energy than I had hitherto noticed, "Bulow may be entirely cut off. Let an officer approach. Take this letter, sir,"—giving, as he spoke, Bulow's letter to Lord Wellington—give this letter to Marshal Grouchy; tell him that at this moment he should be before Wavre; tell him that already, had he obeyed orders——but no, tell him to march at once, to press forward his cavalry, to come up in two hours, in three at furthest. You have but five leagues to ride; see, sir, that you reach him within an hour."

As the officer hurries away at the top of his speed, an aide-de-camp from General Domont confirms the news; they are the Prussians whom he has before him. As yet, however, they are debouching from the wood, and have attempted no forward movement.

"What's Bulow's force, Marshal?"

"Thirty thousand, sire."

"Let Lobau take ten thousand, with the Cuirassiers of the Young Guard, and hold the Prussians in check."

"*Maintenant, pour les autres.*" This he said with a smile, as he turned his eye once more towards the field of battle. The aide-de-camp of Marshal Ney, who, bareheaded and expectant, sat waiting for orders, presented himself to view. The Emperor turned towards him as he said, with a clear and firm voice:

"Tell the Marshal to open the fire of his batteries; to carry La Haye Sainte with the bayonet, and leaving an infantry division for its protection, to march against La Papelotte and La Haye. They must be carried by the bayonet."

The aide-de-camp was gone; Napoleon's eye followed him as he crossed the open plain, and was lost in the dense ranks of the dark columns. Scarcely five minutes elapsed when eighty guns thundered out together, and, as the earth shook and trembled beneath, the mighty movement of the day began its execution. From Hougoumont, where the slaughter and the carnage continued unslackened and unstayed, every eye was now turned towards the right. I knew not what troops occupied La Haye Sainte, or whether they were British who crowned the heights above it; but in my heart how fervently did I pray that they might be so. Oh! in that moment of suspense and agonizing doubt, what would I not have given to know that Picton himself and the fighting 5th were there; that behind the ridge the Greys, the Royals, and the Enniskilleners sat motionless, but burning to advance; and the breath of battle waved among the tartans of the Highlanders, and blew upon the flashing features of my own island countrymen. Had I known this, I could have marked the onset with a less failing spirit.

"There goes Marcognet's division," said my companion, springing to his legs; "they're moving to the right of the road. I should like to see the troops that will stand before them."

So saying, he mounted his horse, and, desiring me to accompany him, rode to the height beside La Belle Alliance. The battle was now raging from the Château de Hougoumont to St. Lambert, where the Prussian tirailleurs, as they issued from the wood, were skirmishing with the advance posts of Lobau's brigade. The attack upon the centre, however, engrossed all my attention, and I watched the dark columns as they descended into the plain, while the incessant roll of the artillery played about them. To the right of Ney's attack, D'Erlon advanced with three divisions, and the artillery of the Guard. Towards this part of the field my companions moved. General Le Vasseur desired to know if the division on the Brussels road were English or Hanoverian troops, and I was sent for to answer the question. We passed from square to square until at length we found ourselves upon the flank of D'Erlon's division. Le Vasseur, who at the head of his cuirassiers waited but the order to charge, waved impatiently with his sword for us to approach. We were now to the right of the high road, and about four hundred yards from the crest of the hill where, protected by a slight edge, Picton with Kempt's brigade waited the attack of the enemy.

Just at this moment an incident took place which, while in itself one of the most brilliant achievements of the day, changed in a signal manner my own fortunes. The head of D'Erlon's column pressed with fixed bayonets up the gentle slope. Already the Belgian infantry give way before them. The brave Brunswickers, overwhelmed by the heavy cavalry of France, at first began to waver; then are broken; and at last retreat in disorder up the road, a whirlwind of pursuing squadrons thundering behind them. *"En avant! en avant! la victoire est à nous,"* is shouted madly through the impatient ranks; and the artillery is called up to play upon the British squares, upon which, fixed and immovable, the cuirassiers have charged without success. Like a thunderbolt, the flying artillery dashes to the front; but scarcely has it reached the bottom of the ascent, when, from the deep ground, the guns become embedded in the soil: the wheels refuse to move. In vain the artillery drivers whip and spur their laboring cattle. Impatiently the leading files of the column prick with their bayonets the struggling horses. The hesitation is fatal; for Wellington, who, with eagle glance, watches from an eminence beside the high road the advancing column, sees the accident. An order is given; and, with one fell swoop, the heavy cavalry brigade pour down. Picton's division deploys into line; the bayonets glance above the ridge; and with a shout that tells above the battle, on they come, the fighting 5th. One volley is exchanged; but the bayonet is now brought to the charge, and the French division retreat in close column, pursued by their gallant enemy. Scarcely had the leading divisions fallen back, and the rear been pressed down upon, or thrown into disorder, than the cavalry trumpets sound a charge. The bright helmets of the Enniskilleners come flashing in the sunbeams, and the Scotch Greys, like a white-crested wave, are rolling upon the foe. Marcognet's division is surrounded; the dragoons ride them down on every side; the guns are captured; the drivers cut down, and two thousand prisoners are carried off. A sudden panic seems to seize upon the French, as cavalry, infantry, and artillery are hurried back on each other. Vainly the French attempt to rally: the untiring enemy press madly on; the household brigade, led on by Lord Uxbridge, came thundering down the road, riding down with their gigantic force the mailed cuirassiers of France. Borne along with the retreating torrents, I was carried on amidst the densely commingled mass. The British cavalry, which, like the lightnings that sever the thunder-cloud, pierce through in every direction, plunge madly upon us. The roar of battle grew louder, as hand to hand they fought. Milhaud's heavy dragoons, with the 4th Lancers, came up at a gallop. Picton pressed forward, waving his plumed hat above his head; his proud eye flashes with the fire of victory. That moment is his last. Struck in the forehead by a musket-ball, he falls dead from the saddle; and the wild yell of the Irish regiments, as they ring his death-cry, are the last sounds which he hears. Meanwhile, the Life Guards are among us; prisoners of rank are captured on every side; and I, seizing the moment, throw myself among the ranks of my countrymen, and am borne to the rear with the retiring squadrons.

As we reached the crest of the hill above the road, a loud cheer in the valley beneath us burst forth, and from the midst of the dense smoke a bright and pointed flame shot up towards the sky. It was the farm-house La Haye Sainte, which the French had succeeded in setting fire to with hot shot. For some time past the ammunition of the corps that held it had failed, and a dropping, irregular musketry was the only reply to the incessant rattle of the enemy. As the smoke cleared away, we discovered that the French had carried the position; and as no quarter was given in that deadly hand-to-hand conflict, not one returned to our ranks to tell the tale of their defeat.

"This is the officer that I spoke of," said an aide-de-camp, as he rode up to where I was standing, bare-headed and without a sword. "He has just made his escape from the French lines, and will be able to give your lordship some information."

The handsome features and gorgeous costume of Lord Uxbridge were known to me; but I was not aware, till afterwards, that a soldier-like, resolute-looking officer beside him was General Graham. It was the latter who first addressed me.

"Are you aware, sir," said he, "if Grouchy's force is arrived?"

"They had not; on the contrary, shortly before I escaped, an aide-de-camp was despatched to Gembloux to hasten his coming. And the troops, for they must be troops, were debouching from the wood yonder. They seem to form a junction with the corps to the right; they are the Prussians. They arrived there before noon from St. Lambert, and are part of Bulow's corps. Count Lobau and his division of ten thousand men were despatched, about an hour since, to hold them in check."

"This is great news," said Lord Uxbridge. "Fitzroy must know it at once."

So saying, he dashed spurs into his horse, and soon disappeared amid the crowd on the hilltop.

"You had better see the Duke immediately, sir," said Graham. "Your information is too important to be delayed. Captain Calvert, let this officer have a horse; his own is too tired to go much further."

"And a cap, I beg of you," added I, in an undertone, "for I have already found a sabre."

By a slightly circuitous route we reached the road, upon which a mass of dismounted artillery-carts, baggage-wagons and tumbrils were heaped together as a barricade against the attack of the French dragoons, who more than once had penetrated to the very crest of our position. Close to this, and on a little rising ground, from which a view of the entire field extended, from Hougoumont to the far left, the Duke of Wellington stood, surrounded by his staff. His eye was bent upon the valley before him, where the advancing columns of Ney's attack still pressed onwards, while the fire of sixty great guns poured death and carnage into his lines. The second Belgian division, routed and broken, had fallen back upon the 27th regiment, who had merely time to throw themselves into square, when Milhaud's cuirassiers, armed with their terrible long, straight swords, came sweeping down upon them. A line of impassable bayonets, a living *chevaux-de-frise*, of the best blood of Britain, stood firm and motionless before the shock. The French *mitraille* played mercilessly on the ranks, but the chasms were filled up like magic, and in vain the bold horsemen of Gaul galloped round the bristling files. At length the word "Fire!" was heard within the square, and as the bullets at pistol-range rattled upon them, the cuirass afforded them no defence against the deadly volley. Men and horses rolled indiscriminately upon the earth. Then would come a charge of our dashing squadrons, who, riding recklessly upon the foe, were in their turn to be repulsed by numbers, and fresh attacks poured down upon our unshaken infantry.

"That column yonder is wavering. Why does he not bring up his supporting squadrons?" inquired the Duke, pointing to a Belgian regiment of light dragoons, who were formed in the same brigade with the 7th Hussars.

"He refuses to oppose his light cavalry to cuirassiers, my lord," said an aide-de-camp, who had just returned from the division in question.

"Tell him to march his men off the ground," said the Duke, with a quiet and impassive tone.

In less than ten minutes the "Belgian regiment" was seen to defile from the mass, and take the road to Brussels, to increase the panic of that city, by circulating and strengthening the report that the English were beaten, and Napoleon in full march upon the capital.

"What's Ney's force? can you guess, sir?" said the Duke of Wellington, turning to me.

"About twelve thousand men, my lord."

"Are the Guard among them?"

"No, sir; the Guard are in reserve above La Belle Alliance."

"In what part of the field is Bonaparte?"

"Nearly opposite to where we stand."

"I told you, gentlemen, Hougoumont never was the great attack. The battle must be decided here," pointing, as he spoke, to the plain beneath us, where Ney still poured in his devoted columns, where yet the French cavalry rode down upon our firm squares.

As he spoke, an aide-de-camp rode up from the valley.

"The 92d requires support, my lord. They cannot maintain their position half an hour longer without it."

"Have they given way, sir?"

"No——"

"Well, then, they must stand where they are. I hear cannon towards the left—yonder, near Frischermont."

At this moment the light cavalry swept past the base of the hill on which we stood, hotly followed by the French heavy cuirassier brigade. Three of our guns were taken; and the cheering of the French infantry, as they advanced to the charge, presaged their hope of victory.

"Do it, then," said the Duke, in reply to some whispered question of Lord Uxbridge, and shortly after the heavy trot of advancing squadrons was heard behind.

They were the Life Guards and the Blues, who, with the 1st Dragoon Guards and the Enniskilleners, were formed into close column.

"I know the ground, my lord," said I to Lord Uxbridge.

"Come along, sir, come along," said he, and he threw his hussar jacket loosely behind him, to give freedom to his sword-arm. "Forward, my men, forward! but steady; hold your horses in hand. Threes about, and together—charge!"

"Charge!" he shouted. As the word flew from squadron to squadron, each horseman bent upon his saddle, and that mighty mass, as though instinct with one spirit, dashed like a thunderbolt upon the column beneath them. The French, blown and exhausted, inferior besides in weight, both of man and horse, offered but a short resistance. As the tall corn bends beneath the sweeping hurricane, wave succeeding wave, so did the steel-clad squadrons of France fall before the nervous arm of Britain's cavalry. Onward they went, carrying death and ruin before them, and never stayed their course until the guns were recaptured, and the cuirassiers, repulsed, disordered, and broken, had retired beneath the protection of their artillery.

There was, as a brilliant and eloquent writer on the subject mentions, a terrible sameness in the whole of this battle,—incessant charges of cavalry upon the squares of our infantry, whose sole manœuvre consisted in either deploying into line to resist the attack of infantry, or falling back into square when the cavalry advanced: performing those two evolutions under the devastating fire of artillery, before the unflinching heroism of that veteran infantry whose glories had been reaped upon the blood-stained fields of Austerlitz, Marengo, and Wagram, or opposing an unbroken front to the whirlwind swoop of infuriated cavalry. Such were the enduring and devoted services demanded from the English troops, and such they failed not to render. Once or twice had temper nearly failed them, and the cry ran through the ranks, "Are we never to move forward? Only let us at them!" But the word was not yet spoken which was to undam the pent-up torrent, and bear down with unrelenting vengeance upon the now exulting columns of the enemy.

It was six o'clock. The battle had continued with unchanged fortune for three hours. The French, masters of La Haye Sainte, could never advance farther into our position. They had gained the orchard of Hougoumont, but the château was still held by the British Guards, although its blazing roof and crumbling walls made its occupation rather the desperate stand of unflinching valor than the maintenance of an important position. The smoke which hung upon the field rolled in slow and heavy masses back upon the French lines, and gradually discovered to our view the entire of the army. We quickly perceived that a change was taking place in their position. The troops, which on their left stretched far beyond Hougoumont, were now moved nearer to the centre. The attack upon the château seemed less vigorously supported, while the oblique direction of their right wing, which, pivoting upon Planchenoit, opposed a face to the Prussians, all denoted a change in their order of battle. It was now the hour when Napoleon was at last convinced that nothing but the carnage he could no longer support could destroy the unyielding ranks of British infantry; that although Hougoumont had been partially, La Haye Sainte completely won; that upon the right of the road the farm-houses Papelotte and La Haye were nearly surrounded by his troops, which with any other army must prove the forerunner of defeat, yet still the victory was beyond his grasp. The bold stratagems whose success the experience of a life had proved were here found to be powerless. The decisive manœuvre of carrying one important point of the enemy's lines, of turning him upon the flank, or piercing him through the centre, were here found impracticable. He might launch his avalanche of grape-shot, he might pour down his crashing columns of cavalry, he might send forth the iron storm of his brave infantry; but, though death in every shape heralded their approach, still were others found to fill the fallen ranks, and feed with their heart's blood the unslaked thirst for slaughter. Well might the gallant leader of this gallant host, as he watched the reckless onslaught of the untiring enemy, and looked upon the unflinching few who, bearing the proud badge of Britain, alone sustained the fight,—well might he exclaim, "Night or Blucher!"

It was now seven o'clock, when a dark mass was seen to form upon the heights above the French centre, and divide into three gigantic columns, of which the right occupied the Brussels road. These were the reserves, consisting of the Old and Young Guards, and amounting to twelve thousand—the *élite* of the French army—reserved by the Emperor for a great *coup de main*. These veterans of a hundred battles had been stationed from the beginning of the day, inactive spectators of the fight; their hour was now come, and with a shout of "*Vive l'Empereur!*" which rose triumphantly over the din and crash of battle, they began their march. Meanwhile, aides-de-camp galloped along the lines, announcing the arrival of Grouchy, to reanimate the drooping spirits of the men; for, at last, a doubt of victory was breaking upon the minds of those who never before, in the most adverse hour of fortune, deemed *his* star could be set that led them on to glory.

"They are coming; the attack will be made on the centre, my lord," said Lord Fitzroy Somerset, as he directed his glass upon the column. Scarcely had he spoken, when the telescope fell from his hand, as his arm, shattered by a French bullet, fell motionless to his side.

"I see it," was the cool reply of the Duke, as he ordered the Guards to deploy into line, and lie down behind the ridge, which now the French artillery had found the range of, and were laboring at their guns. In front of them the 52d, 71st, and 95th were formed; the artillery stationed above and partly upon the road, loaded with grape, and waited but the word to open.

It was an awful, a dreadful moment. The Prussian cannon thundered on our left, but so desperate was the French resistance, they made but little progress. The dark columns of the Guard had now commenced the ascent, and the artillery ceased their fire as the bayonets of the grenadiers showed themselves upon the slope. Then began that tremendous cheer from right to left of our line which those who heard never can forget. It was the impatient, long-restrained burst of unslaked vengeance. With the instinct which valor teaches, they knew the hour of trial was come; and that wild cry flew from rank to rank, echoing from the blood-stained walls of Hougoumont to the far-off valley of La Papelotte. "They come! they come!" was the cry; and the shout of "*Vive l'Empereur!*" mingled with the outburst of the British line.

Under an overwhelming shower of grape, to which succeeded a charge of cavalry of the Imperial Guard, the head of Ney's column fired its volley and advanced with the bayonet. The British artillery now opened at half range, and although the plunging fire scathed and devastated the dark ranks of the Guard, on they came, Ney himself, on foot, at their head. Twice the leading division of that gallant column turned completely round, as the withering fire wasted and consumed them; but they were resolved to win.

Already they gained the crest of the hill, and the first line of the British were falling back before them. The artillery closes up; the flanking fire from the guns upon the road opens upon them; the head of their column breaks like a shell; the Duke seizes the moment, and advances on foot towards the ridge.

"Up, Guards, and at them!" he cried.

The hour of triumph and vengeance had arrived. In a moment the Guards were on their feet; one volley was poured in; the bayonets were brought to the charge; they closed upon the enemy. Then was seen the most dreadful struggle that the history of all war can present. Furious with long-restrained passion, the Guards rushed upon the leading divisions; the 71st, the 95th, and 26th overlapped them on the flanks. Their generals fell thickly on every side; Michel, Jamier, and Mallet are killed; Friant lies wounded upon the ground; Ney, his dress pierced and ragged with balls, shouts still to advance; but the leading files waver; they fall back; the supporting divisions thicken; confusion, panic succeeds; the British press down; the cavalry come galloping up to their assistance; and at last pell-mell, overwhelmed and beaten, the French fall back upon the Old Guard. This was the decisive moment of the day—the Duke closed his glass, as he said,

"The field is won.   Order the whole line to advance."

On they came, four deep, and poured like a torrent from the height.

"Let the Life Guards charge them," said the Duke; but every aide-de-camp on his staff was wounded, and I myself brought the order to Lord Uxbridge.

Lord Uxbridge had already anticipated his orders, and bore down with four regiments of heavy cavalry upon the French centre. The Prussian artillery thundered upon their flank, and at their rear. The British bayonet was in their front; while a panic fear spread through their ranks, and the cry of *"Sauve qui peut!"* resounded on all sides.   In vain Ney, the bravest of the brave; in vain Soult, Bertrand, Gourgaud, and Labedoyère, burst from the broken, disorganized mass, and called on them to stand fast.   A battalion of the Old Guard, with Cambronne at their head, alone obeyed the summons. Forming into square, they stood between the pursuers and their prey, offering themselves a sacrifice to the tarnished honor of their arms.   To the order to surrender they answered with a cry of defiance; and as our cavalry, flushed and elated with victory, rode round their bristling ranks, no quailing look, no craven spirit was there.   The Emperor himself endeavored to repair the disaster; he rode with lightning speed hither and thither, commanding, ordering, nay imploring too; but already the night was falling, the confusion became each moment more inextricable, and the effort was a fruitless one.   A regiment of the Guards and two batteries were in reserve behind Planchenoit; he threw them rapidly into position; but the overwhelming impulse of flight drove the mass upon them, and they were carried away upon the torrent of the beaten army.   No sooner did the Emperor see this, his last hope, desert him, than he dismounted from his horse, and drawing his sword, threw himself into a square, which the first regiment of Chasseurs of the Old Guard had formed with a remnant of the battalion.   Jerome followed him, as he called out,—

"You are right, brother; here should perish all who bear the name of Bonaparte."

The same moment the Prussian light artillery rend the ranks asunder, and the cavalry charge down upon the scattered fragments. A few of his staff, who never left him, place the Emperor upon a horse and fly through the death-dealing artillery and musketry. A squadron of the Life Guards, to which I had attached myself, came up at the moment, and as Blucher's hussars rode madly here and there, where so lately the crowd of staff officers had denoted the presence of Napoleon, expressed their rage and disappointment in curses and cries of vengeance.

Cambronne's battalion stood yet unbroken, and seemed to defy every attack that was brought against them. To the second summons to surrender they replied as indignantly as at the first; and Vivan's brigade was ordered to charge them. A crowd of British horse bore down on every face of the devoted square; but firm as in their hour of victory, the heroes of Marengo never quailed; and twice the bravest blood of Britain recoiled, baffled and dismayed. There was a pause for some minutes, and even then as we surveyed our broken and blood-stained squadrons, a cry of admiration burst from our ranks at the gallant bearing of that glorious infantry. Suddenly the tramp of approaching cavalry was heard; I turned my head, and saw two squadrons of the Second Life Guards. The officer who led them on was bare-headed, his long dark hair streaming wildly behind him and upon his pale features, to which not even the headlong enthusiasm of battle had lent one touch of color. He rode straight to where I was standing, his dark eyes fixed upon me with a look so fierce, so penetrating, that I could not look away. The features, save in this respect, had almost a look of idiocy. It was Hammersley.

"Ha!" he cried at last, "I have sought you out the entire day, but in vain. It is not yet too late. Give me your hand, boy. You once called on me to follow *you*, and I did not refuse; I trust you'll do the like by me. Is it not so?"

A terrible perception of his meaning shot through my mind as I clasped his clay-cold hand in mine, and for a moment I did not speak.

"I had hoped for better than this," said he, bitterly, and a glance of withering scorn flashed from his eye. "I did trust that he who was preferred before me was at least not a coward."

As the word fell from his lips I nearly leaped from my saddle, and mechanically raised my sabre to cleave him on the spot.

"Then follow me!" shouted he, pointing with his sword to the glistening ranks before us.

"Come on!" said I, with a voice hoarse with passion, while, burying my spurs in my horse's flanks, I sprang on a full length before him, and bore down upon the enemy. A loud shout, a deafening volley, the agonizing cry of the wounded and the dying, were all I heard, as my horse, rearing madly upwards, plunged twice into the air, and then fell dead upon the earth, crushing me beneath his cumbrous weight, lifeless and insensible.

   *   *   *   *   *   *   *   *

The day was breaking; the cold, gray light of the morning was struggling through the misty darkness, when I once more recovered my consciousness. There are moments in life when memory can so suddenly conjure up the whole past before us, that there is scarcely time for a doubt ere 'the disputed reality is palpable to our senses. Such was this to me. One hurried glance upon the wide, bleak plain before me, and every circumstance of the battle-field was present to my recollection. The dismounted guns, the broken wagons, the heaps of dead or dying, the straggling parties who on foot or horseback traversed the field, and the dark litters which carried the wounded, all betokened the sad evidences of the preceding day's battle.

Close around me where I lay, the ground was marked with the bodies of our cavalry, intermixed with the soldiers of the Old Guard. The broad brow and the stalwart chest of the Saxon lay bleaching beside the bronzed and bearded warrior of Gaul, while the torn-up ground attested the desperation of that struggle which closed the day.

As my eye ranged over this harrowing spectacle, a dreadful anxiety shot through me as I asked myself whose had been the victory. A certain confused impression of flight and pursuit remained in my mind; but, at the moment, the circumstances of my own position in the early part of the day increased the difficulty of reflection, and left me in a state of intense and agonizing uncertainty. Although not wounded, I had been so crushed by my fall that it was not without pain I got upon my legs. I soon perceived that the spot around me had not yet been visited by those vultures of the battle-field who strip alike the dead and dying. The distance of the place from where the great conflict of the battle had occurred was probably the reason; and now, as the straggling sunbeams fell upon the earth, I could trace the helmet of the Enniskilleners, or the tall bearskin of the Scotch Greys, lying in thick confusion where the steel cuirass and long sword of the French dragoons showed the fight had been hottest. As I turned my eyes hither and thither, I could see no living thing near me. In every attitude of struggling agony they lay around; some buried beneath their horses, some bathed in blood, some, with clenched hands and darting eye-balls, seemed struggling even in death. But all was still—not a word, not a sigh, not a groan was there. I was turning to leave the spot, and, uncertain which way to direct my steps, looked once more around, when my glance rested upon the pale and marble features of one who, even in that moment of doubt and difficulty, there was no mistaking. His coat, torn widely open, was grasped in either hand, while his breast was shattered with balls, and bathed in gore. Gashed and mutilated as he lay, still the features bore no trace of suffering; cold, pale, motionless, but with the tranquil look of sleep, his eyelids were closed, and his half-parted lips seemed to quiver in life. I knelt down beside him; I took his hand in mine; I bent over and whispered his name; I placed my hand upon his heart, where even still the life-blood was warm—but he was dead. Poor Hammersley! His was a gallant soul; and, as I looked upon his blood-stained corpse, my tears fell fast and hot upon his brow to think how far I had myself been the cause of a life blighted in its hope, and a death like his.

CHAPTER LVI.

BRUSSELS.

ONCE more I would entreat my reader's indulgence for the prolixity of a narrative which has grown beneath my hands to a length I had never ·intended. This shall, however, be the last time for either the offence or the apology. My story is now soon concluded.

After wandering about for some time, uncertain which way to take, I at length reached the Charleroi road, now blocked by carriages and wagons conveying the wounded towards Brussels. Here I learned for the first time that we had gained the battle, and heard of the total annihilation of the French army, and the downfall of the Emperor. On arriving at the farm-house of Mont St. Jean, I found a number of officers, whose wounds prevented their accompanying the army in its forward movement. One of them, with whom I was slightly acquainted, informed me that General Dashwood had spent the greater part of the night upon the field in search of me, and that my servant Mike was in a state of distraction at my absence that bordered on insanity. While he was speaking, a burst of laughter and the tones of a well-remembered voice behind attracted my attention.

"Made a very good thing of it, upon my life. A dressing-case—not gold, you know, but silver-gilt—a dozen knives, with blood-stone handles, and a little coffee-pot, with the imperial arms—not to speak of three hundred naps in a green silk purse—Lord! it reminds me of the Peninsula. Do you know, those Prussians are mere barbarians—haven't a notion of civilized war. Bless your heart, my fellows in the Legion would have ransacked the whole coach, from the boot to the sword-case, in half the time they took to cut down the coachman."

"The Major! as I live," said I. "How goes it, Major?"

"Eh, Charley! when did you turn up? Delighted to see you. They told me you were badly wounded, or killed, or something of that kind; but I should have paid the little debt to your executors all the same."

"All the same, no doubt, Major; but where, in Heaven's name, did you fall upon that mine of pillage you have just been talking of?"

"In the Emperor's carriage, to be sure, boy. While the Duke was watching all day the advance of Ney's columns, and keeping an anxious look-out for the Prussians, I sat in a window in this old farm-house, and never took my eye off the garden at Planchenoit. I saw the imperial carriage there in the morning—it was there also at noon—and they never put the horses to it till past seven in the evening. The roads were very heavy, and the crowd was great. I judged the pace couldn't be a fast one; and with four of the Enniskilleners I charged it like a man. The Prussians, however, had the start of us; and if they hadn't thought, from my seat on horseback and my general appearance, that I was Lord Uxbridge, I should have got but a younger son's portion. However, I got in first, filled my pockets with a few little *souvenirs* of the Emperor, and then, laying my hands upon what was readiest, got out in time to escape being shot; for two of Blucher's hussars, thinking I must be the Emperor, fired at me through the window."

"What an escape you had!"

"Hadn't I, though? Fortunate, too, my Enniskilleners saw the whole thing; for I intend to make the circumstance the ground of an application for a pension. Harkye, Charley, don't say anything about the coffee-pot and the knives. The Duke, you know, has strange notions of his own on these matters. But isn't that your fellow fighting his way yonder?"

"Tear an' ages! don't howld me—that's himself—devil a one else!"

This exclamation came from Mickey Free, who, with his dress torn and dishevelled, his eyes bloodshot and strained, was upsetting and elbowing all before him, as he made his way towards me through the crowd.

"Take that fellow to the guard-house! Lay hold of him, sergeant. Knock him down! Who is the scoundrel?"

Such were the greetings he met with on every side. Regardless of everything and everybody, he burst his way through the dense mass.

"Oh, murther! oh, Mary! oh, Moses! Is he safe here after all?"

The poor fellow could say no more, but burst into a torrent of tears. A roar of laughter around him soon, however, turned the current of his emotions; when, dashing the scalding drops from his eyelids, he glared fiercely like a tiger on every side.

"You're laughing at me, are ye?" cried he, "bekase I love the hand that fed me, and the master that stood to me. But let us see now which of us two has the stoutest heart; you with your grin on you, or myself with the salt tears on my face."

As he spoke, he sprang upon them like a madman, striking right and left at everything before him. Down they went beneath his blows, levelled with the united strength of energy and passion, till at length, rushing upon him in numbers, he was overpowered and thrown to the ground. It was with some difficulty I accomplished his rescue; for his enemies felt by no means assured how far his amicable propensities for the future could be relied upon; and, indeed, Mike himself had a most constitutional antipathy to binding himself by any pledge. With some persuasion, however, I reconciled all parties; and having, by the kindness of a brother officer, provided myself with a couple of troop horses, I mounted, and set out for Brussels, followed by Mickey, who had effectually cured his auditory of any tendency to laughter at his cost.

As I rode up to the Belle Vue, I saw Sir George Dashwood in the window. He was speaking to the Ambassador, Lord Clancarty; but the moment he caught my eye, hurried down to meet me.

"Charley, safe—safe, my boy! Now am I really happy. The glorious day had been one of sorrow to me for the rest of my life had anything happened to you. Come up with me at once; I have more than one friend here who longs to thank you."

So saying, he hurried me along; and, before I could well remember where I was, introduced me to a number of persons in the saloon.

"Ah! very happy to know you, sir," said Lord Clancarty; "perhaps we had better walk this way. My friend Dashwood has explained to me the very pressing reasons there are for this step; and I, for my part, see no objection."

"What, in Heaven's name, can he mean!" thought I, as he stopped short, expecting me to say something, while, in utter confusion, I smiled, simpered, and muttered some commonplaces.

"Love and war, sir," resumed the Ambassador, "very admirable associates, and you certainly have contrived to couple them most closely together. A long attachment, I believe?"

"Yes, sir, a very long attachment," stammered I, not knowing which of us was about to become insane.

"A very charming person, indeed; I have seen the lady," replied his lordship, as he opened the door of a small room, and beckoned me to follow. The table was covered with paper and materials for writing; but, before I had time to ask for any explanation of this unaccountable mystery, he added, "Oh, I was forgetting; this must be witnessed: wait one moment."

With these words he left the room, while I, amazed and thunder-struck, vacillating between fear and hope, trembling lest the delusive glimmering of happiness should give way at every moment, and yet totally unable to explain by any possible supposition how fortune could so far have favored me.

While yet I stood hesitating and uncertain, the door opened, and the Senhora entered. She looked a little pale, though not less beautiful than ever; and her features wore a slight trace of serious-ness, which rather heightened than took from the character of her loveliness.

"I heard you had come, Chevalier," said she, "and so I ran down to shake hands with you. We may not meet again for some time."

"How so, Senhora? You are not going to leave us, I trust?"

"Then you have not seen Fred? Oh, I forgot, you know nothing of our plans."

"Here we are at last," said the Ambassador, as he came in, fol-lowed by Sir George, Power, and two other officers. "Ah, *ma belle*, how fortunate to find you here! I assure you it is a matter of no small difficulty to get people together at such a time as this."

"Charley, my dear friend," cried Power, "I scarcely hoped to have had a shake hands with you ere I left."

"Do, Fred, tell me what all this means? I am in a maze of doubt and difficulty, and cannot comprehend a word I hear about me."

"Faith, my boy, I have little time for explanation. The man who was at Waterloo yesterday, is to be married to-morrow, and to sail for India in a week, has quite enough upon his hands."

"Colonel Power, will you please to put your signature here," said Lord Clancarty, addressing himself to me.

"If you will allow me," said Fred, "I had rather represent my-self."

"Is not this the Colonel, then? Why, confound it, I have been wishing him joy the last quarter of an hour."

A burst of laughter from the whole party, in which it was pretty evident I took no part, followed this announcement.

"And so you are not Colonel Power? Nor going to be married either?"

I stammered out something, while, overwhelmed with confusion, I stooped down to sign the paper. Scarcely had I done so, when a renewed burst of laughter broke from the party.

"Nothing but blunders, upon my soul," said the Ambassador, as he handed the paper from one to another.

What was my confusion to discover that, instead of Charles O'Malley, I had written the name of Lucy Dashwood. I could bear no more. The laughing and raillery of my friends came upon my wounded and irritated feelings like the most poignant sarcasm. I seized my cap, and rushed from the room. Desirous of escaping from all that knew me, anxious to bury my agitated and distracted thoughts in solitude and quiet, I opened the first door before me, and, seeing it an empty and unoccupied room, threw myself upon a sofa, and buried my head within my hands. Oh, how often had the phantom of happiness passed within my reach, but still glided from my grasp! How often had I beheld the goal I aimed at, as it were before me, and the next moment all the bleak reality of my evil fortune was louring around me!

"Oh Lucy, Lucy!" I exclaimed aloud, "but for you and a few words carelessly spoken, I had never trod that path of ambition whose end has been the wreck of all my happiness. But for you, I had never loved so fondly; I had never filled my mind with one image which, excluding every other thought, leaves no pleasure but in it alone. Yes, Lucy, but for you I should have gone tranquilly down the stream of life with naught of grief or care, save such as are inseparable from the passing chances of mortality; loved, perhaps, and cared for by some one who would have deemed it no disgrace to have linked her fortune to my own. But for you, and I had never been——"

"A soldier, you would say," whispered a soft voice, as a light hand gently touched my shoulder. "I had come," continued she, "to thank you for a gift no gratitude can repay,—my father's life; but, truly, I did not think to hear the words you have spoken; nor, having heard them, can I feel their justice. No, Mr. O'Malley, deeply grateful as I am to you for the service you once rendered myself, bound as I am, by every tie of thankfulness, by the greater one to my father, yet do I feel that in the impulse I have given to your life, if so be that to me you owe it, I have done more to repay my debt to you than by all the friendship, all the esteem, I owe you; if, indeed, by my means, you became a soldier, if my few and random words raised within your breast that fire of ambition which has been your beacon-light to honor and to glory, then am I indeed proud."

"Alas! alas! Lucy—Miss Dashwood, I would say—forgive me if

I know not the very words I utter. How has my career fulfilled the promise that gave it birth? For you, and you only, to gain your affection, to win your heart, I became a soldier; hardship, danger, even death itself were courted by me, supported by the one thought that you had cared for or had pitied me; and now, and now——"

"And now," said she, while her eyes beamed upon me with a very flood of tenderness, "is it nothing that in my woman's heart I have glowed with pride at triumphs I could read of but dared not share in? Is it nothing that you have lent to my hours of solitude and of musing the fervor of that career, the maddening enthusiasms of that glorious path my sex denied me? I have followed you in my thoughts across the burning plains of the Peninsula, through the long hours of the march in the dreary nights even to the battle-field. I have thought of you; I have dreamed of you; I have prayed for you."

"Alas! Lucy, but not loved me."

The very words, as I spoke them, sank with a despairing cadence upon my heart. Her hand, which had fallen upon mine, trembled violently. I pressed my lips upon it, but she moved it not. I dared to look up. Her head was turned away, but her heaving bosom betrayed her emotion.

"No, no, Lucy," cried I passionately, "I will not deceive myself; I ask for more than you can give me. Farewell!"

Now, and for the last time, I pressed her hand once more to my lips; my hot tears fell fast upon it. I turned to go, and threw one last look upon her. Our eyes met. I cannot say what it was, but in a moment the whole current of my thoughts was changed; her look was bent upon me, beaming with softness and affection; her hand gently pressed my own, and her lips murmured my name.

The door burst open at this moment, and Sir George Dashwood appeared. Lucy turned one fleeting look upon her father, and fell fainting into my arms.

"God bless you, my boy!" said the old General, as he hurriedly wiped a tear from his eye; "I am now, indeed, a happy father."

CHAPTER LVII.

CONCLUSION.

* * * * * * * *

THE sun had set about half an hour. Already were the dusky shadows blending with the faint twilight, as on a lovely June evening we entered the little village of Portumna,—we, I say, for Lucy was beside me. For the last few miles of the way I had spoken little. Thoughts of the many times I had travelled that same road, in how many moods, occupied my mind; and although, as we flew rapidly along, some well-known face would every now and then present itself, I had but time for the recognition ere we were past. Arousing myself from my reverie, I was pointing out to Lucy certain well-known spots in the landscape, and directing her attention to places with the names of which she had been for some time familiar, when suddenly a loud shout rent the air, and the next moment the carriage was surrounded by hundreds of country people, some of whom brandished blazing pine torches; others carried rude banners in their hands; but all testified the most fervent joy as they bade us welcome. The horses were speedily unharnessed, and their places occupied by a crowd of every age and sex, who hurried us along through the straggling street of the village, now a perfect blaze of bonfires.

Mounds of turf, bog-fir, and tar-barrels sent up their ruddy blaze, while hundreds of wild but happy faces flitted around and through them,—now dancing merrily in chorus, now plunging madly into the midst of the fire, and scattering the red embers on every side. Pipers were there, too, mounted upon cars or turf-kishes; even the very roof-tops rang out their merry notes; the ensigns of the little fishing-craft waved in the breeze, and seemed to feel the general joy around them; while over the door of the village inn stood a brilliantly-lighted transparency, representing the head of the O'Malleys holding a very scantily-robed young lady by the tips of the fingers; but whether this damsel was intended to represent the genius of the west or my wife, I did not venture to inquire.

If the welcome were rude, assuredly it was a hearty one. Kind wishes and blessings poured in on every side, and even our own happiness took a brighter coloring from the beaming looks around us. The scene was wild. The lurid glare of the red torchlight, the frantic gestures, the maddening shouts, the forked flames rising amidst the dark shadows of the little hamlet, had something strange and almost unearthly in their effect; but Lucy showed no touch of fear. It is true she grasped my hand a little closer, but her fair cheek glowed with pleasure, and her eye brightened as she looked ; and as the rich light fell upon her beauteous features, how many a blessing, heartfelt and deep, how many a word of fervent praise, was spoken.

'Ah ! then, the Lord be good to you ; it's yourself has the darlin' blue eyes. Look at them, Mary ; ain't they like the blossoms on a peacock's tail ? Musha, may sorrow never put a crease on that beautiful cheek ! The saints watch over you ! for your mouth is like a moss-rose. Be good to her, yer honor, for she's a raal gem. Devil fear you, Mr. Charles, but you'd have a beauty.''

We wended our way slowly, the crowd ever thickening around us, until we reached the market-place. Here the procession came to a stand, and I could perceive, by certain efforts around me, that some endeavor was making to enforce silence.

" Whist there ! howld your prate ; be still, Paddy. Tear an' ages, Molly Blake, don't be howldin' me that way ; let us hear his riverence. Put him up on the barrel. Haven't you got a chair for the priest? Run and bring a table out of Mat Haley's. Here, father,— here, your riverence ; take care, will you ?—you'll have the holy man in the blaze !''

By this time I could perceive that my worthy old friend Father Rush was in the midst of the mob, with what appeared to be a written oration, as long as the tail of a kite, between his hands.

" Be aisy, there, ye savages ; who's tearin' the back of my neck ? Howld me up straight—steady, now—hem !''

"Take the laste taste in life of this to wet your lips, your riverence," said a friendly voice, while at the same moment a smoking tumbler of what seemed to be punch appeared on the heads of the crowd.

"Thank you, Judy," said the father, as he drained the cup. "Howld the light up higher ; I can't read my speech. There, now ; be quiet, will ye ? Here goes. Peter, stand to me now, and give me the word.''

This admonition was addressed to a figure on a barrel behind the priest, who, as well as the imperfect light would permit me to descry, was the coadjutor of the parish, Peter Nolan. Silence being perfectly established, Father Rush began :—

> "When Mars, the god of war on high,
>   Of battles first did think,
>   He girt his sword upon his thigh,
>   And ——

And—what is't, Peter ?''

> "And mixed a drop of drink."

"And mixed a drop of drink," quoth Father Rush, with great emphasis. Scarcely were the words spoken, than a loud shout of laughter showed him his mistake, and he overturned upon the luckless curate the full vial of his wrath.

"What is it that you mean, Father Peter? I'm ashamed of ye; faith, it's maybe yourself, not Mars, you are speaking of."

The roar of merriment around prevented my hearing what passed; but I could see by Peter's gestures—for it was too dark to see his face—that he was expressing deep sorrow for the mistake. After a little time, order was again established, and Father Rush resumed:

> "But love drove battles from his head,
>   And sick of wounds and scars,
>   To Venus bright he knelt, and said ——

And said—and said; what the blazes did he say?"

> "I'll make you Mrs. Mars,"

shouted Peter, loud enough to be heard.

"Bad luck to you, Peter Nolan, it's yourself's the ruin of me this blessed night. Here have I come four miles with my speech in my pocket, '*per imbres et ignes.*'" Here the crowd crossed themselves devoutly. "Ay, just so; and he spoilt it for me entirely." At the earnest entreaty, however, of the crowd, Father Rush, with renewed caution to his unhappy prompter, again returned to the charge:

> "Thus love compelled the god to yield,
>   And seek for purer joys;
>   He laid aside his helm and shield,
>   And took——

Took—took——"

> "And took to corduroys,"

cried Father Nolan.

This time, however, the good priest's patience could endure no more, and he levelled a blow at his luckless colleague, which missing his aim, lost him his own balance, and brought him down from his eminence upon the heads of the mob.

Scarcely had I recovered the perfect convulsion of laughter into which the scene had thrown me, when the broad brim of Father Nolan's hat appeared at the window of the carriage. Before I had time to address him, he took it reverently from his head, disclosing in the act the ever-memorable features of Master Frank Webber!

"What! Eh!—can it be?" said I.

"It is surely not——" said Lucy, hesitating at the name.

"Your aunt, Miss Judy Macan, no more than the Rev. Peter No, lan, I assure you; though, I confess, it has cost me much more to personate the latter character than the former, and the reward by no means so tempting."

Here poor Lucy blushed deeply at the remembrance of the scene alluded to; and, anxious to turn the conversation, I asked by what stratagem he had succeeded to the functions of the worthy Peter.

"At the cost of twelve tumblers of the strongest punch ever brewed at the O'Malley Arms. The good father gave in only ten minutes before the oration began, and I had barely time to change my dress and mount the barrel, without a moment's preparation."

The procession once more resumed its march, and hurried along through the town, we soon reached the avenue. Here fresh preparations for welcoming us had also been made; but, regardless of blazing tar barrels and burning logs, the reckless crowd pressed madly on, their wild cheers waking the echoes as they went. We soon reached the house, and with a courtesy which even the humblest and poorest native of this country is never devoid of, the preparations of noise and festivity had not extended to the precincts of the dwelling. With a tact which those of higher birth and older blood might be proud of, they limited the excesses of their reckless and careless merriment to their own village, so that, as we approached the terrace, all was peaceful, still, and quiet.

I lifted Lucy from the carriage, and, passing my arm around her, was assisting her to mount the steps, when a bright gleam of moonlight burst forth, and lit up the whole scene. It was, indeed, an impressive one. Among the assembled hundreds there who stood bare-headed, beneath the cold moonlight, not a word was now spoken—not a whisper heard. I turned from the lawn, where the tall beech-trees were throwing their gigantic shadows, to where the river, peering at intervals through the foliage, was flowing on its silvery track, plashing amid the tall flaggers that lined its banks—all were familiar, all were dear to me from childhood. How doubly were they so now! I lifted up my eyes towards the door, and what was my surprise at the object before them! Seated in a large chair was an old man, whose white hair, flowing in straggling masses upon his neck and shoulders, stirred with the night air; his hands rested upon his knees, and his eyes, turned slightly upward, seemed to seek for some one he found it difficult to recognize. Changed as he was by time, heavily as years had done their work upon him, the stern features were not to be mistaken. As I looked, he called out, in a voice whose unshaken firmness seemed to defy the touch of time:

"Charley O'Malley! come here, my boy. Bring her to me, till I bless you both. Come here, Lucy: I may call you so. Come here, my children. I have tried to live on to see this day, when the head of an old house comes back with honor, with fame, and with fortune, to dwell amidst his own people in the old home of his fathers."

The old man bent above us, his white hair falling upon the fair locks of her who knelt beside him, and pressed his cold and quivering hand within her own.

"Yes, Lucy," said I, as I led her within the house, "this is home."

Here now ends my story. The patient reader who has followed me so far, deserves at my hands that I should not trespass upon his kindness one moment beyond the necessity; if, however, any lurking interest may remain for some of those who have accompanied me through this my history, it may be as well that I should say a few words further, ere they disappear forever.

Power went to India immediately after his marriage, distinguished himself repeatedly in the Burmese war, and finally rose to a high command, that he at this moment holds, with honor to himself and advantage to his country.

O'Shaughnessy, on half-pay, wanders about the Continent; passing his summers on the Rhine, his winters at Florence or Geneva. Known to and by everybody, his interest in the service keeps him *au courant* to every change and regulation, rendering him an invaluable companion to all to whom an army list is inaccessible. He is the same good fellow he ever was, and adds to his many excellent qualities the additional one of being the only man who can make a bull in French!

Monsoon, the Major, when last I saw him, was standing on the pier at Calais, endeavoring, with a cheap telescope, to make out the Dover cliffs, from a nearer prospect of which certain little family circumstances might possibly debar him. He recognized me in a moment, and held out his hand, while his eye twinkled with its ancient drollery.

"Charley, my son, how goes it? Delighted to see you. What a pity I did not meet you yesterday! Had a little dinner at Crillon's. Harding, Vivian, and a few others. They all wished for you; 'pon my life they did."

"Civil, certainly," thought I, "as I have not the honor of being known to them."

"You are at Maurice's," resumed he; "a very good house, but give you bad wine, if they don't know you. They know me," added he, in a whisper: "never try any tricks upon me. I'll just drop in upon you at six."

"It is most unfortunate, Major; I can't have the pleasure you speak of; we start in half an hour."

"Never mind, Charley, never mind; another time. By the bye, now I think of it, don't you remember something of a ten-pound note you owe me?"

"As well as I remember, Major, the circumstance was reversed: you are the debtor."

"Upon my life you are right; how droll. No matter, let me have the ten, and I'll give you a check for the whole."

The Major thrust his tongue into his cheek as he spoke, gave another leer, pocketed the note, and sauntered down the pier muttering something to himself about King David and greenhorns; but how they were connected I could not precisely overhear.

Baby Blake, or Mrs. Sparks, to call her by her more fitting appellation, is as handsome as ever, and not less good-natured and light-hearted, her severest trials being her ineffectual efforts to convert Sparks into something like a man for Galway.

Last of all, Mickey Free. Mike remains attached to our fortune firmly, as at first he opened his career; the same gay, rollicksome Irishman, making songs, making love, and occasionally making punch, he spends his days and his nights pretty much as he was wont to do some thirty years ago. He obtains an occasional leave of absence for a week or so, but for what precise purpose, or with what exact object, I have never been completely able to ascertain. I have heard it as true, that a very fascinating companion and a most agreeable gentleman frequents a certain oyster-house in Dublin, called Burton Bindon's. I have also been told of a distinguished foreigner, whose black moustache and broken English were the admiration of Cheltenham for the last two winters. I greatly fear, from the high tone of the conversation in the former, and for the taste in continental characters in the latter resort, that I could fix upon the individual whose convivial and social gifts have won so much of their esteem and admiration; but were I to run on thus, I should recur to every character of my story, with each and all of whom you have doubtless grown well wearied. So here, for the last time, and with every kind wish, I say—adieu!

STANDARD AND POPULAR BOOKS

PUBLISHED BY

PORTER & COATES, PHILADELPHIA, PA.

WAVERLEY NOVELS. By Sir Walter Scott.

*Waverley.
*Guy Mannering.
The Antiquary.
Rob Roy.
Black Dwarf; and Old Mortality.
The Heart of Mid-Lothian.
The Bride of Lammermoor; and A
    Legend of Montrose.
*Ivanhoe.
The Monastery.
The Abbott.
Kenilworth.
The Pirate.

The Fortunes of Nigel.
Peveril of the Peak.
Quentin Durward.
St. Ronan's Well.
Redgauntlet.
The Betrothed; and The Talisman.
Woodstock.
The Fair Maid of Perth.
Anne of Geierstein.
Count Robert of Paris; and Castle
    Dangerous.
Chronicles of the Canongate.

Household Edition. 23 vols. Illustrated. 12mo. Cloth, extra, black and gold, per vol., $1.00; sheep, marbled edges, per vol., $1.50; half calf, gilt, marbled edges, per vol., $3.00. Sold separately in cloth binding only.

Universe Edition. 25 vols. Printed on thin paper, and containing one illustration to the volume. 12mo. Cloth, extra, black and gold, per vol., 75 cts.

World Edition. 12 vols. Thick 12mo. (Sold in sets only.) Cloth, extra, black and gold, $18.00; half imt. Russia, marbled edges, $24.00.

This is the best edition for the library or for general use published. Its convenient size, the extreme legibility of the type, which is larger than is used in any other 12mo edition, either English or American.

TALES OF A GRANDFATHER. By Sir Walter Scott, Bart. 4 vols. Uniform with the Waverley Novels.

Household Edition. Illustrated. 12mo. Cloth, extra, black and gold, per vol, $1.00; sheep, marbled edges, per vol., $1.50; half calf, gilt, marbled edges, per vol., $3.00.

This edition contains the Fourth Series—Tales from French history—and is the only complete edition published in this country.

(1)

CHARLES DICKENS' COMPLETE WORKS. Author's Edition. 14 vols., with a portrait of the author on steel, and eight illustrations by F. O. C. Darley, Cruikshank, Fildes, Eytinge, and others, in each volume. 12mo. Cloth, extra, black and gold, per vol., $1.00; sheep, marbled edges, per vol., $1.50; half imt. Russia, marbled edges, per vol., $1.50: half calf, gilt, marbled edges, per vol., $2.75.

*Pickwick Papers.
*Oliver Twist, Pictures of Italy, and American Notes.
*Nicholas Nickleby.
Old Curiosity Shop, and Reprinted Pieces.
Barnaby Rudge, and Hard Times.
*Martin Chuzzlewit.
Dombey and Son.
*David Copperfield.

Christmas Books, Uncommercial Traveller, and Additional Christmas Stories.
Bleak House.
Little Dorrit.
Tale of Two Cities, and Great Expectations.
Our Mutual Friend.
Edwin Drood, Sketches, Master Humphrey's Clock, etc., etc.

Sold separately in cloth binding only.
*Also in Alta Edition, one illustration, 75 cents.
The same. Universe Edition. Printed on thin paper and containing one illustration to the volume. 14 vols., 12mo. Cloth, extra, black and gold, per vol., 75 cents.
The same. World Edition. 7 vols., thick 12mo., $12.25. (Sold in sets only.)

CHILD'S HISTORY OF ENGLAND. By CHARLES DICKENS. Popular 12mo. edition; from new electrotype plates. Large clear type. Beautifully illustrated with 8 engravings on wood. 12mo. Cloth, extra, black and gold, $1.00.
Alta Edition. One illustration, 75 cents.

"Dickens as a novelist and prose poet is to be classed in the front rank of the noble company to which he belongs. He has revived the novel of genuine practical life, as it existed in the works of Fielding, Smollett, and Goldsmith; but at the same time has given to his material an individual coloring and expression peculiarly his own. His characters, like those of his great exemplars, constitute a world of their own, whose truth to nature every reader instinctively recognizes in connection with their truth to darkness."
—*E. P. Whipple.*

MACAULAY'S HISTORY OF ENGLAND. From the accession of James II. By THOMAS BABINGTON MACAULAY. With a steel portrait of the author. Printed from new electrotype plates from the last English Edition. Being by far the most correct edition in the American market. 5 volumes, 12mo. Cloth, extra, black and gold, per set, $5.00; sheep, marbled edges, per set, $7.50; half imitation Russia, $7.50; half calf, gilt, marbled edges, per set, $15.00.
Popular Edition. 5 vols., cloth, plain, $5.00.
8vo. Edition. 5 volumes in one, with portrait. Cloth, extra, black and gold, $3.00; sheep, marbled edges, $3.50.

MARTINEAU'S HISTORY OF ENGLAND. From the beginning of the 19th Century to the Crimean War. By HARRIET MARTINEAU. Complete in 4 vols., with full Index. Cloth, extra, black and gold, per set, $4.00; sheep, marbled edges, $6.00; half calf, gilt, marbled edges, $12.00.

HUME'S HISTORY OF ENGLAND. From the invasion of Julius Cæsar to the abdication of James II, 1688. By DAVID HUME. Standard Edition. With the author's last corrections and improvements; to which is prefixed a short account of his life, written by himself. With a portrait on steel. A new edition from entirely new stereotype plates. 5 vols., 12mo. Cloth, extra, black and gold, per set, $5.00; sheep, marbled edges, per set, $7.50; half imitation Russia, $7.50; half calf, gilt, marbled edges, per set, $15.00.

Popular Edition. 5 vols. Cloth, plain, $5.00.

GIBBON'S DECLINE AND FALL OF THE ROMAN EMPIRE. By EDWARD GIBBON. With Notes, by Rev. H. H. MILMAN. Standard Edition. To which is added a complete Index of the work. A new edition from entirely new stereotype plates. With portrait on steel. 5 vols., 12mo. Cloth, extra, black and gold, per set, $5.00; sheep, marbled edges, per set, $7.50; half imitation Russia, $7.50; half calf, gilt, marbled edges, per set, $15.00.

Popular Edition. 5 vols. Cloth, plain, $5.00.

ENGLAND, PICTURESQUE AND DESCRIPTIVE. By JOEL COOK, author of "A Holiday Tour in Europe," etc. With 487 finely engraved illustrations, descriptive of the most famous and attractive places, as well as of the historic scenes and rural life of England and Wales. With Mr. Cook's admirable descriptions of the places and the country, and the splendid illustrations, this is the most valuable and attractive book of the season, and the sale will doubtless be very large. 4to. Cloth, extra, gilt side and edges, $7.50; half calf, gilt, marbled edges, $10.00; half morocco, full gilt edges, $10.00; full Turkey morocco, gilt edges, $15.00; tree calf, gilt edges, $18.00.

This work, which is prepared in elegant style, and profusely illustrated, is a comprehensive description of England and Wales, arranged in convenient form for the tourist, and at the same time providing an illustrated guide-book to a country which Americans always view with interest. There are few satisfactory works about this land which is so generously gifted by Nature and so full of memorials of the past. Such books as there are, either cover a few counties or are devoted to special localities, or are merely guide-books. The present work is believed to be the first attempt to give in attractive form a description of the stately homes, renowned castles, ivy-clad ruins of abbeys, churches, and ancient fortresses, delicious scenery, rock-bound coasts, and celebrated places of England and Wales. It is written by an author fully competent from travel and reading, and in position to properly describe his very interesting subject; and the artist's pencil has been called into requisition to graphically illustrate its well-written pages. There are 487 illustrations, prepared in the highest style of the engraver's art, while the book itself is one of the most attractive ever presented to the American public.

Its method of construction is systematic, following the most convenient routes taken by tourists, and the letter-press includes enough of the history and legend of each of the places described to make the story highly interesting. Its pages fairly overflow with picture and description, telling of everything attractive that is presented by England and Wales. Executed in the highest style of the printer's and engraver's art, "England, Picturesque and Descriptive," is one of the best American books of the year.

HISTORY OF THE CIVIL WAR IN AMERICA. By the Comte De Paris. With Maps faithfully Engraved from the Originals, and Printed in Three Colors. 8vo. Cloth, per volume, $3.50; red cloth, extra, Roxburgh style, uncut edges, $3.50; sheep, library style, $4.50; half Turkey morocco, $6.00. Vols. I, II, and III now ready.

The third volume embraces, without abridgment, the fifth and sixth volumes of the French edition, and covers one of the most interesting as well as the most anxious periods of the war, describing the operations of the Army of the Potomac in the East, and the Army of the Cumberland and Tennessee in the West.

It contains full accounts of the battle of Chancellorsville, the attack of the monitors on Fort Sumter, the sieges and fall of Vicksburg and Port Hudson; the battles of Port Gibson and Champion's Hill, and the fullest and most authentic account of the battle of Gettysburg ever written.

"The head of the Orleans family has put pen to paper with excellent result. . . . . Our present impression is that it will form by far the best history of the American war."—*Athenæum, London.*

"We advise all Americans to read it carefully, and judge for themselves if 'the future historian of our war,' of whom we have heard so much, be not already arrived in the Comte de Paris."—*Nation, New York.*

"This is incomparably the best account of our great second revolution that has yet been even attempted. It is so calm, so dispassionate, so accurate in detail, and at the same time so philosophical in general, that its reader counts confidently on finding the complete work thoroughly satisfactory."—*Evening Bulletin, Philadelphia.*

"The work expresses the calm, deliberate judgment of an experienced military observer and a highly intelligent man. Many of its statements will excite discussion, but we much mistake if it does not take high and permanent rank among the standard histories of the civil war. Indeed that place has been assigned it by the most competent critics both of this country and abroad."—*Times, Cincinnati.*

"Messrs. Porter & Coates, of Philadelphia, will publish in a few days the authorized translation of the new volume of the Comte de Paris' History of Our Civil War. The two volumes in French—the fifth and sixth—are bound together in the translation in one volume. Our readers already know, through a table of contents of these volumes, published in the cable columns of the *Herald*, the period covered by this new installment of a work remarkable in several ways. It includes the most important and decisive period of the war, and the two great campaigns of Gettysburg and Vicksburg.

"The great civil war has had no better, no abler historian than the French prince who, emulating the example of Lafayette, took part in this new struggle for freedom, and who now writes of events, in many of which he participated, as an accomplished officer, and one who, by his independent position, his high character and eminent talents, was placed in circumstances and relations which gave him almost unequalled opportunities to gain correct information and form impartial judgments.

"The new installment of a work which has already become a classic will be read with increased interest by Americans because of the importance of the period it covers and the stirring events it describes. In advance of a careful review we present to-day some extracts from the advance sheets sent us by Messrs. Porter & Coates, which will give our readers a foretaste of chapters which bring back to memory so many half-forgotten and not a few hitherto unvalued details of a time which Americans of this generation at least cannot read of without a fresh thrill of excitement."

HALF-HOURS WITH THE BEST AUTHORS. With short Biographical and Critical Notes. By CHARLES KNIGHT.

New Household Edition. With six portraits on steel. 3 vols., thick 12mo. Cloth, extra, black and gold, per set, $4.50; half imt. Russia, marbled edges, $6.00; half calf, gilt, marbled edges, $12.00.

Library Edition. Printed on fine laid and tinted paper. With twenty-four portraits on steel. 6 vols., 12mo. Cloth, extra, per set, $7.50; half calf, gilt, marbled edges, per set, $18.00; half Russia, gilt top, $21.00; full French morocco, limp, per set, $12.00; full smooth Russia, limp, round corners, in Russia case, per set, $25.00; full seal grained Russia, limp, round corners, in Russia case to match, $25.00.

The excellent idea of the editor of these choice volumes has been most admirably carried out, as will be seen by the list of authors upon all subjects. Selecting some choice passages of the best standard authors, each of sufficient length to occupy half an hour in its perusal, there is here food for thought for every day in the year: so that if the purchaser will devote but one-half hour each day to its appropriate selection he will read through these six volumes in one year, and in such a leisurely manner that the noblest thoughts of many of the greatest minds will be firmly in his mind forever. For every Sunday there is a suitable selection from some of the most eminent writers in sacred literature. We venture to say if the editor's idea is carried out the reader will possess more and better knowledge of the English classics at the end of the year than he would by five years of desultory reading.

They can be commenced at any day in the year. The variety of reading is so great that no one will ever tire of these volumes. It is a library in itself.

THE POETRY OF OTHER LANDS. A Collection of Translations into English Verse of the Poetry of Other Languages, Ancient and Modern. Compiled by N. CLEMMONS HUNT. Containing translations from the Greek, Latin, Persian, Arabian, Japanese, Turkish, Servian, Russian, Bohemian, Polish, Dutch, German, Italian, French, Spanish, and Portuguese languages. 12mo. Cloth, extra, gilt edges, $2.50; half calf, gilt, marbled edges, $4.00; Turkey morocco, gilt edges, $6.00.

" Another of the publications of Porter & Coates, called 'The Poetry of Other Lands,' compiled by N. Clemmons Hunt, we most warmly commend. It is one of the best collections we have seen, containing many exquisite poems and fragments of verse which have not before been put into book form in English words. We find many of the old favorites, which appear in every well-selected collection of sonnets and songs, and we miss others, which seem a necessity to complete the bouquet of grasses and flowers, some of which, from time to time, we hope to republish in the 'Courier.'"— *Cincinnati Courier.*

" A book of rare excellence, because it gives a collection of choice gems in many languages not available to the general lover of poetry. It contains translations from the Greek, Latin, Persian, Arabian, Japanese, Turkish, Servian, Russian, Bohemian, Polish, Dutch, German, Italian, French, Spanish, and Portuguese languages. The book will be an admirable companion volume to any one of the collections of English poetry that are now published. With the full index of authors immediately preceding the collection, and the arrangement of the poems under headings, the reader will find it convenient for reference. It is a gift that will be more valued by very many than some of the transitory ones at these holiday times."— *Philadelphia Methodist.*

THE FIRESIDE ENCYCLOPÆDIA OF POETRY.   Edited by HENRY T. COATES.   This is the latest, and beyond doubt the best collection of poetry published.   Printed on fine paper and illustrated with thirteen steel engravings and fifteen title pages, containing portraits of prominent American poets and fac-similes of their handwriting, made expressly for this book. 8vo.   Cloth, extra, black and gold, gilt edges, $5.00; half calf, gilt, marbled edges, $7.50; half morocco, full gilt edges, $7.50; full Turkey morocco, gilt edges, $10.00; tree calf, gilt edges, $12.00; plush, padded side, nickel lettering, $14.00.

"The editor shows a wide acquaintance with the most precious treasures of English verse, and has gathered the most admirable specimens of their ample wealth. Many pieces which have been passed by in previous collections hold a place of honor in the present volume, and will be heartily welcomed by the lovers of poetry as a delightful addition to their sources of enjoyment. It is a volume rich in solace, in entertainment, in inspiration, of which the possession may well be coveted by every lover of poetry. The pictorial illustrations of the work are in keeping with its poetical contents, and the beauty of the typographical execution entitles it to a place among the choicest ornaments of the library."—*New York Tribune.*

"Lovers of good poetry will find this one of the richest collections ever made. All the best singers in our language are represented, and the selections are generally those which reveal their highest qualities. . . . . The lights and shades, the finer play of thought and imagination belonging to individual authors, are brought out in this way (by the arrangement of poems under subject-headings) as they would not be under any other system. . . . . We are deeply impressed with the keen appreciation of poetical worth, and also with the good taste manifested by the compiler."—*Churchman.*

"Cyclopædias of poetry are numerous, but for sterling value of its contents for the library, or as a book of reference, no work of the kind will compare with this admirable volume of Mr. Coates It takes the gems from many volumes, culling with rare skill and judgment."—*Chicago Inter-Ocean.*

THE CHILDREN'S BOOK OF POETRY.   Compiled by HENRY T. COATES.   Containing over 500 poems carefully selected from the works of the best and most popular writers for children; with nearly 200 illustrations.   The most complete collection of poetry for children ever published. 4to.   Cloth, extra, black and gold, gilt side and edges, $3.00; full Turkey morocco, gilt edges, $7.50.

"This seems to us the best book of poetry for children in existence. We have examined many other collections, but we cannot name another that deserves to be compared with this admirable compilation."—*Worcester Spy.*

"The special value of the book lies in the fact that it nearly or quite covers the entire field. There is not a great deal of good poetry which has been written for children that cannot be found in this book. The collection is particularly strong in ballads and tales, which are apt to interest children more than poems of other kinds; and Mr. Coates has shown good judgment in supplementing this department with some of the best poems of that class that have been written for grown people. A surer method of forming the taste of children for good and pure literature than by reading to them from any portion of this book can hardly be imagined. The volume is richly illustrated and beautifully bound."—*Philadelphia Evening Bulletin.*

" A more excellent volume cannot be found. We have found within the covers of this handsome volume, and upon its fair pages, many of the most exquisite poems which our language contains. It must become a standard volume, and can never grow old or obsolete."—*Episcopal Recorder.*

THE COMPLETE WORKS OF THOS. HOOD. With engravings
on steel. 4 vols., 12mo., tinted paper. Poetical Works; Up
the Rhine; Miscellanies and Hood's Own; Whimsicalities,
Whims, and Oddities. Cloth, extra, black and gold, $6.00;
red cloth, paper label, gilt top, uncut edges, $6.00; half calf,
gilt, marbled edges, $14.00; half Russia, gilt top, $18.00.

Hood's verse, whether serious or comic—whether serene like a cloudless
autumn evening or sparkling with puns like a frosty January midnight
with stars—was ever pregnant with materials for the thought. Like every
author distinguished for true comic humor, there was a deep vein of melancholy pathos running through his mirth, and even when his sun shone
brightly its light seemed often reflected as if only over the rim of a cloud.

Well may we say, in the words of Tennyson, "Would he could have
stayed with us." for never could it be more truly recorded of any one—in
the words of Hamlet characterizing Yorick—that "he was a fellow of infinite jest, of most excellent fancy."　　D. M. MOIR.

THE ILIAD OF HOMER RENDERED INTO ENGLISH
BLANK VERSE. By EDWARD, EARL OF DERBY. From
the latest London edition, with all the author's last revisions
and corrections, and with a Biographical Sketch of Lord
Derby, by R. SHELTON MACKENZIE, D.C.L. With twelve
steel engravings from Flaxman's celebrated designs. 2 vols..
12mo. Cloth, extra, bev. boards, gilt top, $3.50; half calf, gilt,
marbled edges, $7.00; half Turkey morocco, gilt top, $7.00.

The same. Popular edition. Two vols. in one. 12mo. Cloth,
extra, $1.50.

"It must equally be considered a splendid performance; and for the present we have no hesitation in saying that it is by far the best representation
of Homer's Iliad in the English language."—London Times.

"The merits of Lord Derby's translation may be summed up in one word,
it is eminently attractive; it is instinct with life; it may be read with fervent
interest; it is immeasurably nearer than Pope to the text of the original. .
. . . Lord Derby has given a version far more closely allied to the original,
and superior to any that has yet been attempted in the blank verse of our
language."—Edinburg Review.

THE WORKS OF FLAVIUS JOSEPHUS. Comprising the Anti-
quities of the Jews; a History of the Jewish Wars, and a Life
of Flavius Josephus, written by himself. Translated from the
original Greek, by WILLIAM WHISTON, A.M. Together with
numerous explanatory Notes and seven Dissertations concerning Jesus Christ, John the Baptist, James the Just, God's command to Abraham, etc., with an Introductory Essay by Rev.
H. STEBBING, D.D. 8vo. Cloth,. extra, black and gold, plain
edges, $3.00; cloth, red, black and gold, gilt edges, $4.50; sheep,
marbled edges, $3.50; Turkey morocco, gilt edges, $8.00.
This is the largest type one volume edition published.

THE ANCIENT HISTORY OF THE EGYPTIANS, CARTHA-
GINIANS, ASSYRIANS, BABYLONIANS, MEDES AND
PERSIANS, GRECIANS AND MACEDONIANS. Including
a History of the Arts and Sciences of the Ancients. By
CHARLES ROLLIN. With a Life of the Author, by JAMES
BELL. 2 vols., royal 8vo. Sheep, marbled edges, per set, $6.00.

COOKERY FROM EXPERIENCE. A Practical Guide for House-
keepers in the Preparation of Every-day Meals, containing
more than One Thousand Domestic Recipes, mostly tested by
Personal Experience, with Suggestions for Meals, Lists of
Meats and Vegetables in Season, etc. By Mrs. SARA T. PAUL.
12mo. Cloth, extra, black and gold, $1.50.
Interleaved Edition. Cloth, extra, black and gold, $1.75.

THE COMPARATIVE EDITION OF THE NEW TESTAMENT.
Both Versions in One Book.

The proof readings of our Comparative Edition have been gone
over by so many competent proof readers, that we believe the text
is absolutely correct.

Large 12mo., 700 pp. Cloth, extra, plain edges, $1.50; cloth,
extra, bevelled boards and carmine edges, $1.75; imitation panelled
calf, yellow edges, $2.00; arabesque, gilt edges, $2.50; French morocco, limp, gilt edges, $4.00; Turkey morocco, limp, gilt edges,
$6.00.

The Comparative New Testament has been published by Porter & Coates.
In parallel columns on each page are given the old and new versions of the
Testament; divided also as far as practicable into comparative verses, so that
it is almost impossible for the slightest new word to escape the notice of
either the ordinary reader or the analytical student. It is decidedly the
best edition yet published of the most interest-exciting literary production
of the day. No more convenient form for comparison could be devised
either for economizing time or labor. Another feature is the foot-notes,
and there is also given in an appendix the various words and expressions
preferred by the American members of the Revising Commission. The
work is handsomely printed on excellent paper with clear, legible type. It
contains nearly 700 pages.

THE COUNT OF MONTE CRISTO. By ALEXANDRE DUMAS.
Complete in one volume, with two illustrations by George G.
White. 12mo. Cloth, extra, black and gold, $1.25.

THE THREE GUARDSMEN. By ALEXANDRE DUMAS. Complete in one volume, with two illustrations by George G.
White. 12mo. Cloth, extra, black and gold, $1.25.

There is a magic influence in his pen, a magnetic attraction in his descriptions, a fertility in his literary resources which are characteristic of Dumas
alone, and the seal of the master of light literature is set upon all his works.
Even when not strictly historical, his romances give an insight into the
habits and modes of thought and action of the people of the time described,
which are not offered in any other author's productions.

THE LAST DAYS OF POMPEII. By Sir EDWARD BULWER
LYTTON, Bart. Illustrated. 12mo. Cloth, extra, black and
gold, $1.00. Alta edition, one illustration, 75 cts.

JANE EYRE. By CHARLOTTE BRONTÉ (Currer Bell). New Library Edition. With five illustrations by E. M. WIMPERIS.
12mo. Cloth, extra, black and gold, $1.00.

SHIRLEY. By CHARLOTTE BRONTÉ (Currer Bell). New Library
Edition. With five illustrations by E. M. WIMPERIS. 12mo.
Cloth, extra, black and gold, $1.00.